EVERYMAN'S LIBRARY

EVERYMAN,
I WILL GO WITH THEE,
AND BE THY GUIDE,
IN THY MOST NEED
TO GO BY THY SIDE

EVELYN WAUGH

Black Mischief, Scoop,
The Loved One,
The Ordeal of Gilbert Pinfold

with an Introduction by
Ann Pasternak Slater

EVERYMAN'S LIBRARY

265

First included in Everyman's Library, 2003
Black Mischief first published by Chapman & Hall, 1932
Scoop first published by Chapman & Hall, 1938
The Loved One first published by Chapman & Hall, 1948
The Ordeal of Gilbert Pinfold first published by Chapman & Hall, 1957
© Evelyn Waugh. Published by arrangement with PFD on behalf of
the Evelyn Waugh Trust.
Introduction, Bibliography and Chronology © Everyman's Library,
2003
Typography by Peter B. Willberg

ISBN 1-85715-265-4

A CIP catalogue record for this book is available from the
British Library

Published by Everyman's Library,
Gloucester Mansions, 140A Shaftesbury Avenue,
London WC2H 8HD

Distributed by Random House (UK) Ltd.,
20 Vauxhall Bridge Road, London SW1V 2SA

Printed and bound in Germany
by GGP Media, Pössneck

E V E L Y N   W A U G H

CONTENTS

———

INTRODUCTION

Evelyn Waugh's attention was first drawn to Abyssinia at a house-party in September 1930, when a friend described entertaining two of the Abyssinian crown princes at the British embassy in Cairo. The princes arrived in silk capes and bowler hats, which they retained throughout lunch. Neither spoke any language familiar to the embassy interpreters. Electrified, Waugh sent a peremptory note to his agent – 'I want very much to go to Abyssinia for the coronation of the Emperor. Could you get a paper to send me ... I think I am going anyway.' A meeting was arranged with Jack Driberg, a respectable member of the Colonial service reputed to speak eleven African languages and to have eaten human flesh twice – a clear if distant progenitor of Basil Seal, *Black Mischief*'s polyglot, anthropophagous anti-hero. Further research in the country-house library revealed a history rich in absurdity and incalculable antiquity. This is Waugh's summary: 'The Abyssinian Church had canonized Pontius Pilate, and consecrated their bishops by spitting on their heads; the real heir to the throne was hidden in the mountains, fettered with chains of solid gold ... we looked up the royal family in the *Almanack de Gotha* and traced their descent from Solomon and the Queen of Sheba; we found a history which began: "the first certain knowledge we have of Ethiopian history is when Cush ascended the throne immediately after the Deluge".' A chance encounter on a train a fortnight later brought Waugh the commission he required, and in November he left for Addis Ababa as special correspondent to *The Times*.

In the Preface to *Black Mischief* Waugh denies any resemblance between Haile Selassie and Seth, Emperor of Azania. The disclaimer is palpably disingenuous. SETH IMPERATOR IMMORTALIS, *Chief of the Chiefs of Sakuyu, Lord of Wanda and Tyrant of the Seas, Bachelor of the Arts of Oxford University* clearly mirrors the Conquering Lion of the Tribe of Judah, Elect of God and Emperor of Ethiopia. Selassie's little book, *My Life and Ethiopia's Progress, 1892–1937*, dictated by the illiterate

Emperor during his wartime exile in Bath, innocently corrobo-
rates the parallel in retrospect. Its style is interesting. The
translator speaks with relish of 'the full resources of Amharic
stylistics which are apt to aid and abet a desire for almost
total opacity' – an enigmatic archaism beautifully evoked in
the ambiguously treacherous manoeuverings of *Black Mischief*'s
first and penultimate chapters ('*I fear for Seth's health and await
word from your Lordship as to how best he may be relieved of what
troubles him*'.) More often, however, Selassie's text is more
notable for naivety than opacity of tone. Chapter 12, *About the
improvements by ordinance and proclamation, of internal administration
and about efforts to allow foreign civilization to enter Ethiopia*, details
the programme of modernization just before his coronation,
the very stuff of Waugh's novel. Among 'some of the major
works We now remember', the Emperor lists 'Our causing to
stop the cutting off of hands and feet, which had ... been
customary for a very long time ... Our whole people were
very pleased.' In his rag-bag of contemporary fads Selassie
proudly enumerates the purchase of two printing presses; the
invitation of foreign kings and princes; the import of cars and
bicycles; the abolition of chain-gangs; the creation of new
orders, a new flag, a new national anthem, a military march;
the erasure of slavery from parts of the penal code; the
imperial purchase of the Bank of Abyssinia.

Many of these earnest improvements were observed with
amusement by Selassie's western guests. At the coronation,
Waugh noted in his diary, 'Great upset Europeans distribution
honours. Barton [the British Minister Plenipotentiary] Star
Ethiopia first class. Everyone else something better.' Another
witness recalled, 'Officials moved among the distinguished
foreign guests with trays of Coronation medallions and asked
them to take one each as a memento ... The wife of one of
the foreign delegates took a handful and then, seeing that she
was observed, murmured weakly, "*Pour les enfants!*"' In *Black
Mischief*, honours and reforms (like the newly introduced
contraceptive device) are equally without substance – they are
'the Emperor's juju', bonbon novelties, nothing more. When
Seth's army grows restless, his grand promise, 'They shall be
paid. I have said it', is fulfilled – by printing a lavish run of

his own, valueless currency. This triggers revolution, downfall and death for the immortal emperor. The similarities to Selassie are compelling.

The response of the western press to Selassie's coronation was predictable. In *Black Mischief* Waugh catches it in a single malicious pastiche:

Mr Randall typed: *His Majesty B.A. . . . ex undergrad among the cannibals . . . scholar emperor's desperate bid for throne . . . barbaric spendour . . . conquering hordes . . . ivory . . . elephants . . . east meets west.*

Waugh's own perception was more discriminating. He disdained the cliché of barbaric splendour. Instead, 'a unique stage of the interpenetration of two cultures' caught his eye. 'It seemed to me that here, at least, truth was stranger than the newspaper reports. For instance, one newspaper stated that the Emperor's banqueting-hall was decorated with inlaid marble, ivory, and malachite. That,' he adds dryly, 'is not very strange to anyone who has been into any of the cheaper London hotels.' It is typical of Waugh that at the coronation ceremony he alone should have noticed the royal crown lying on a silk-covered table 'neatly concealed in a cardboard hat-box'. Or that the Emperor provided a dozen new footballs for the recreation of his ambassadorial guests. Or that the Tomb of Menelik was decorated with enlarged coloured photographs of the imperial family and 'a fumed oak grandfather clock'. (Compare *Black Mischief*: 'Upstairs, Seth was deep in a catalogue of wireless apparatus. "Oh, Ali, I have decided on the Tudor model in fumed oak." ') Other journalists sent home shots of Abyssinian nobles in top hats and flowing robes. Waugh's derisive eye turned instead to the incongruities of western couture at the imperial luncheon-table – 'American cinema men in green suits. French journalists in dinner jackets.' In his diary, western indecorum and journalistic mendacity both arouse his scorn. Sir Percival Phillips, his highly-paid rival on the *Daily Mail*, described the Abyssinian landscape as 'nothing but a vast wilderness, no sign of life save vultures wheeling watchfully against the blue sky and surprised baboons darting to cover in the undergrowth'. In his own dispatches, Waugh painted a pointedly dull landscape of dust, anthills, brown mimosa trees, and miles of featureless bush.

If one turns from Waugh's diaries, his *Times* articles, and the related travel book *Remote People*, directly to *Black Mischief*, one is struck – perversely but compellingly – by the pedestrian realism on which it is securely founded. This is certainly not the common response to a novel which is (literally) incredibly funny and heartless. We are fortunate that its presumed sacrilegious immorality was originally attacked in a hostile notice which appeared in *The Tablet*. Among other details offensive to his Catholic sensibilities, Oldmeadow, the Editor of *The Tablet*, objected above all to the sordid presentation of Prudence's afternoon assignation with Basil and to her shocking end – consumed by her lover and the big chiefs in a cannibal banquet. The notice was so obtuse that Waugh was goaded to a uniquely revealing reply:

The story deals with the conflict of civilization, with all its attendant and deplorable ills, and barbarism. The plan of my book throughout was to keep the darker aspects of barbarism continually and unobtrusively present, a black and mischievous background against which the civilized and semi-civilized characters performed their parts: I wished it to be like the continuous, remote throbbing of those hand-drums, constantly audible, never visible, which every traveller in Africa will remember as one of his most haunting impressions.

So much for Waugh's subject. His method followed:

I introduced the cannibal theme in the first chapter *and repeated it in another key in the incident of the soldiers eating their boots*, thus hoping to prepare the reader for the sudden tragedy when barbarism at last emerges from the shadows and usurps the stage. [my italics]

It is an unprecedented betrayal of his covert, favoured fictional technique, of theme and virtuoso variation – what in *Pinfold* he later termed mere 'elegance and variety of contrivance'. He never analysed his methods so openly again.

It is easy for any reader, once alerted, to register *Black Mischief*'s bourdon bass of beating drums, and to note the carefully plotted, unobtrusive references to cannibalism from 'the native Sakuyu, black, naked, anthropophagous' and 'the painful case of the human sacrifices at the Bishop of Popo's consecration', to the cannibal banquet at the end. Other imperceptibly significant trails consolidate the degenerative sequence.

INTRODUCTION

Take, for instance, the word 'grunt'. It suggests bestiality, a primitive inarticulacy whose semantic penumbra gradually modulates from the relatively innocuous to the grotesque. We first hear the word – twice – when Youkoumian ignores his wife, who is trussed like a chicken on the floor, and snuggles into bed with little grunts of contentment. It recurs as the atheist French minister, M. Ballon, also settles down to sleep. We hear it again when the Azanian traditionalists object to birth control. And yet again, when Dame Mildred Porch squeezes into the Legation car with a grunt. Poor senile Achon grunts when the imperial sword of Azania is laid on his lap. Finally the motif emerges for what it is. In the closing cannibal feast, 'black figures sprawled and grunted, alone and in couples'. And the headman, who has plied Basil with stewed Prudence, answers his question, 'Where is the white woman?' with another grunt, rubbing his stomach: 'The white woman? Why, here . . . You and I and the big chiefs – we have just eaten her.' To adapt one of Eliot's notes to *The Waste Land*, 'The collocation of these representatives of eastern and western asceticism is not an accident.' In Waugh's case, it is barbarism, not asceticism, that unites east and west. Their shared linguistic motif, the grunt they use in common, is no accident either.

The Azanians treat their women as beasts of burden. On Azania's only train they are herded with the children into the single cattle-truck. Azanian kine have 'rickety shanks and elaborately branded hide'. At the imperial banquet, the native Baroness Batulle appears in deshabille, displaying 'shoulders and back magnificently tattooed and cicatrized with arabesques'. There is little distinction between animals, men and women, particularly in men's bestial treatment of women. The worst exemplars are Youkoumian, grossly indifferent to his wife's predicament, and Basil, arch-parasite, who breezily tells Prudence, 'You're a grand girl, Prudence, and I'd like to eat you' – and does. When he glimpses Basil for the first time, Seth is yearning for 'a representative of Progress and the New Age'. It is one of the novel's many ironies that Basil is, on the contrary, the final embodiment of extreme barbarism, just as Seth, in his childish pursuit of the new, is the avatar and acolyte of Progress in its most fatuous forms.

EVELYN WAUGH

Waugh was by nature a traditionalist. It is not surprising that, for him, Progress is regressive. Basil convinces Seth that he can continue to feed his chieftains the raw meat of their traditional *gebbur*, if he calls it steak tartare. Likewise, he reassures him that primitive nakedness is now sanitized as *Nacktkultur*. Seth proclaims: 'At my stirrups run woman's suffrage, vaccination and vivisection. I am the New Age. I am the Future...' Ectogenesis and autogyros are the stuff of his dreams. But in Basil's eyes it is fortunate that Seth has taken on his country's modernization at a time when bi-cameral legislature, proportional representation, independent judiciary and the freedom of the press are 'just a few ideas that have ceased to be modern'. Seth falls instead for the attendant ills of civilization – the passing fads whose value is neatly summarized by the trampled banner abandoned by Seth's ill-starred Birth-Control Gala, which testifies STERILITY from the gutter.

Ultimately, as in *A Handful of Dust*, there is no distinction between primitive and civilized barbarism. Seth attempts to recast native banquets in up-to-date nutritional terms ('Vitamin C: Small Roasted Sucking Porks; Vitamin D: Hot Sheep and Onions ... Vitamin G: Coffee; Vitamin H: Jam'). In England, Lord Monomark imposes equally batty fads on his weary workforce ('Two raw onions and a plate of oatmeal porridge. That's all I've taken for luncheon in the last eight months.'). Prudence and Basil's sordid coupling, so vehemently reproved by *The Tablet*, is matched in London by the squalor of Sonia and Alastair's ménage – duns at the door and copulating lapdogs fouling the bed.

The main *difference* is the incalculable antiquity, and occasional dignity of the African culture, and the mindless infantilism of the Europeans. Seth's reign causes a brief ripple, but, with his passing, Azania returns to its old ways. A new road skirts the abandoned lorry blocking the imperial highway. Native Sakuyu, who have made it their home, repair it painstakingly with mud, grass and flattened tins. Life in the British Legation continues as it always has done. Bretherton and Reppington drain their sundowners to the strains of Gilbert and Sullivan:

INTRODUCTION

Three little maids from school are we,
Pert as a schoolgirl well can be

An unpalatable truth lurks in its complacent proprieties:

'Is it weakness of intellect, birdie,' I cried,
'Or a rather tough worm in your little inside?'

When *The Tablet*'s Editor protested at Prudence's end, stewed to a pulp with peppers and aromatic roots, Waugh retorted coldly that his criticism betrayed a defective digestion. 'It cannot matter whether she was roasted, grilled, braised or pickled, cut into sandwiches or devoured hot on toast as a savoury.' Civilized barbarism is a hard truth to swallow at the best of times. Conrad had already served it up in *Heart of Darkness*. Later, Golding would do so again in *Lord of the Flies*.

*

In August 1935 Waugh returned to Abyssinia, with a hundred or so other journalists, to await its invasion by Italy once the rainy season was over. This time he was sent by the *Daily Mail*, one of only two papers taking a pro-Italian stance.

Waugh's personal life had changed radically. The annulment of his first marriage was working its way through the Vatican. He was courting Laura Herbert and serenely happy. On the long sea-journey to Djibouti he learned to type.

there is no news and if there wrew wr were funny how hard that work is to get right wr were gotvit were were were were were if there were we should not be allowed to send it by the censor whom i have tild tou about

His inexpertise is happily transferred to William Boot:

The keys rose together like bristles on a porcupine, jammed and were extricated; curious anagrams appeared on the paper before him...

The assignment was not a success. Five months' close proximity deepened Waugh's previous loathing of the press. He found journalists 'lousy competitive hysterical lying'. He missed the one great scoop and his own scoops were dogged with failure. The major story was the involvement of an American-backed entrepreneur, Rickett – one of several prototypes for

Scoop's Mr Baldwin – who aroused Waugh's suspicions on the boat to Djibouti. Rickett's airy name-dropping of the pack he hunted with in the Midlands sounded fishy. And whenever he received telegrams in code, which he often did, he pocketed them saying, 'From my huntsman. He says the prospects for cubbin' are excellent.' (This is transferred directly to *Scoop*, when William meets Mr Baldwin for the second time on the train to Marseille. ' "I have so much on my hands – naturally – and in winter I am much occupied with sport. I have a little pack of hounds in the Midlands." "Oh? Which?" "You might not have heard of us. We march with the Fernie..." ') Waugh's engagingly amateurish response was to write a letter (not a cable) to Penelope Betjeman to enquire whether anything was known of Rickett among her hunting friends. In fact, Rickett negotiated a vast concession of mineral rights from Haile Selassie – in the terrain to be covered by the Italian advance. It was an ingenious act of self-defence on the Emperor's part. When the story broke, however, Waugh was out of Addis Ababa on a different trail. A resident Frenchman, improbably named Count Maurice de Roquefeuil de Bousquet, had been working a mica concession in Jijiga. He had been imprisoned with his wife for spying, after a Somali woman was caught leaving his house with a film hidden in her left armpit. Within hours, Waugh stumbled on secret information about the Abyssinian line of defence. Neither story was of the least interest to the *Daily Mail*, whose attention was solely on Rickett. A similar reversal occurred later. As a fellow-Catholic and, at that time, political sympathizer, Waugh was friendly with the Italians. He obtained advance details of the Italian Minister's departure from Addis, which he knew signalled the beginning of the Italian invasion. To outmanoeuvre his rivals, Waugh cabled the news in Latin. The *Daily Mail* thought it gibberish, and binned it.

Waugh in Abyssinia, the travel book describing this period, is marked by a pattern of reversal. The journalists' predictions were constantly mistaken, and the book employs an ironic refrain: 'How wrong we were!' Everyone, including the Abyssinians, believed the main campaign would be fought in the south. The Italians attacked from the north. Many colourful fates were predicted for Haile Selassie – suicide, assassination, death in battle, rescue by British aeroplane. In the event, he went to the station and quietly took a train down to the coast. 'How wrong we were!' Similar reversals recur in the press bulletins. A story was floated that an American nurse had been blown up in Adowa. Waugh and his colleagues wired back, 'Nurse unupblown'. It becomes a feature of *Scoop*: 'ADEN UNWARWISE', 'UNPROCEED LAKUWARD', 'NEWS EXYOU UNRECEIVED'.

The *Daily Mail* sacked Waugh. In a letter to Lady Diana Cooper (the original of Mrs Stitch), he reported, 'The Mail now takes all its war news from a chap in Jibouti; he doesnt speak French, has never set foot in Abyssinia ... He sits in his hotel describing an entirely imaginary campaign – 18,000 abyssinians and 500,000 sheep killed by poison gas ... in a place he found on the map which in point of fact consists of one brackish well.' A bitter observation, lightly transferred to *Scoop*:

In his room in the annexe Sir Jocelyn Hitchcock covered his keyhole with stamp-paper ... he went to the map on the wall and took out his flag ... hovering uncertainly over the unscaled peaks and uncharted rivers of that dark terrain, finally decided, and pinned it firmly in the spot marked as the city of Laku.

... 'Hitchcock's story has broken. He's at the Fascist headquarters scooping the world.'
　'Where?'
　'Town called Laku.'
　'But he can't be. Bannister told me there was no such place.'

Sir Jocelyn Hitchcock was based on Sir Percival Phillips, whom Waugh had first encountered reporting Haile Selassie's coronation. He died in 1937, before the publication of *Scoop*.

In December 1935 Waugh left Abyssinia with relief. On his way home he decided to call on an acquaintance he had met in London. She was the wife of the Counsellor at the British Legation in Tehran. Unfortunately he misremembered her posting. He sent a telegram to the British Ambassador in Baghdad, enquiring, 'Would I be welcome if I came to you for weekend Evelyn Waugh'. The reply was oddly unenthusiastic:

'Fairly. Ambassador.' 'I did a thing at Bagdad [*sic*] that only happens in nightmares,' he told Lady Diana Cooper. It was the first of several episodes of mistaken identity fuelling *Scoop*.

In the summer of 1936, Waugh returned to Abyssinia to observe it under Italian rule. By now, he had lost all his pro-Italian fervour. Only the Fascist road-building programme fired him. He flew to Asmara, in the north, where a town originally built for a population of 2,000 now accommodated 60,000 Italian navvies – and what Waugh tactfully describes as 'seven unattached white women' provided by the Italian authorities. A telegram, announcing the arrival of the ambiguously gendered Evelyn Waugh, aroused the Italian Press Officer to a fever of romantic anticipation. He met every possible plane and train. 'His friends declared that he had, with great difficulty, procured a bouquet of crimson roses. The trousered and unshaven figure which finally greeted him must have been a hideous blow.'

These trivial, miscellaneous experiences shape *Scoop*, which is elaborately built on a playful pattern of mistaken identities, anagram, metathesis, reversal, transposition and transfiguration.

The pattern is introduced by an arresting cameo on the first page:

Algernon Stitch was standing in the hall; his bowler hat was on his head; his right hand, grasping a crimson, royally emblazoned dispatch case, emerged from the left sleeve of his overcoat; his other hand burrowed petulantly in the breast pocket ... He spoke indistinctly, for he was holding a folded copy of the morning paper between his teeth.

'Can't get it on,' he seemed to say.

This is a funny muddle of a specific kind. It turns on cross-over: the Minister has his hand down the wrong coat-sleeve. Transposition and cross-over recur throughout the novel. In the Megalopolitan offices 'on a hundred lines reporters talked at cross purposes'. In Ishmaelia, the lost luggage-van finally reappears intact – because 'mysteriously it had become attached to the special train; had in fact been transposed'. The plot turns on two major transpositions. William Boot is mistakenly sent to Ishmaelia instead of John Boot. And on William's triumphal return, Uncle Theodore Boot is persuaded to take William's place at Lord Copper's ghastly celebratory banquet.

Linguistic reversals sustain the pattern in miniature. The novel opens on 'a biting-cold mid-June morning'. Newsboys are selling 'the lunch-time editions of the evening papers'. At Boot Magna, a telegram is delivered by 'Troutbeck, the aged boy'. At the railway-station, a cretin is picking at paint-bubbles on the fence with 'a toe-like thumb nail'.

Misunderstandings and metatheses sustain the mode. Mr Salter, at the Megalopolitan offices, has been told to regale William with heavy hospitality and light conversation about country matters – mangel-wurzels, and root crops generally:

> There was a pause, during which Mr Salter planned a frank and disarming opening. 'How are your roots, Boot?' It came out wrong.
> 'How are your boots, root?' he asked.
> William, glumly awaiting some fulminating rebuke, started and said, 'I beg your pardon?'
> 'I mean brute,' said Mr Salter.

The novel's interchangeable press magnates, Lord Copper and Lord Zinc – of the *Beast* and the *Brute*, respectively – are paralleled by Pip and Pop, the Bedtime Pets, in the *Beast*'s Children's Corner. There is a recipe, on the same page, for 'Waffle Scramble'. There is further calculated confusion in the cat's cradle of Latin young Josephine Stitch fails to construe. Not to mention the crossword anagram Mrs Stitch mistakenly identifies as 'Hottentot' or 'Terracotta' (it is 'detonated'). Later, Pip and Pop are transmogrified into the Popotakis Ping-Pong Parlour at Jacksonburg. The game of ping-pong's instant reversibility – its high-speed ricochet, a to-and-fro getting nowhere – epitomizes the novel's elaborately inconclusive narrative structure. In the same ping-pong mode, Ishmaelia has two political parties, the Marxists and the Fascists. They are diametrically identical, indistinguishably opposed.

> 'I gather it's between the Reds and the Blacks.'
> 'Yes, but it's not quite as easy as that. You see, they are all Negroes. And the Fascists won't be called black because of their racial pride,

EVELYN WAUGH

so they are called White after the White Russians. And the Bolshevists *want* to be called black because of *their* racial pride. So when you *say* black you mean red, and when you *mean* red you say white...'

Even Mr Salter is confused here. The Reds are black, so 'when you *say* black you mean red'. But the Fascists are White Shirts, so the next phrase should run, 'and when you *mean* black [not 'red'] you say white'. The point is not just that they are indistinguishable, but that propaganda makes black seem white – a simplifying gloss implied but withheld by Waugh when William hears the orators of both sides. At Hyde Park, the Ishmaelian Marxist claims that all whites are really black ('Who built the Pyramids? A Negro. Who invented the circulation of the blood? A Negro.') At his makeshift embassy, the Fascist maintains that all blacks are really white ('As you will see for yourself, we are pure Aryans. In fact we were the first white colonizers of Central Africa.')

Checkerboard reversals of this kind are also maintained in linguistic miniature. For instance, the venerable Ishmaelian Minister is described 'like ... a Victorian worthy in negative, black face, white whiskers, black hands'. And when the Reds take over Jacksonburg, 'a red flag hung black against the night sky'.

At his return to Abyssinia in 1936, Waugh confessed that 'it was fun being pro-Italian when it was an unpopular and (I thought) losing cause. I have little sympathy with these exultant Fascists now.' *Scoop* is not a political novel. Rather, it is, as Waugh noted in his diary, 'light and excellent'. Its lightheartedness is epitomized by its two major literary sources. One structural cross-binding delicately securing the novel's three-part structure is Beatrix Potter's *Tale of Johnny Town-Mouse*, which begins:

Johnny Town-Mouse was born in a cupboard. Timmie Willie was born in a garden. Timmie Willie was a little country-mouse who went to town by mistake in a hamper.

Book I revolves around William Boot's apprehensive journey up to town, away from his secure country nest. At this point, John Boot, his sophisticated metropolitan cousin, is a self-evident Johnny Town-Mouse. In Book III, his role passes to Mr Salter, reluctantly forced out of frenetic, familiar London into the bucolic terrors of Boot Magna. When it was being considered for a film, Waugh stressed the importance of the novel's tripartite structure: 'The central section is not the climax of the story. The climax is the reception of Boot in London.' He was anxious not to have the story cropped of its final conclusion, which is partly explained by Waugh's other major source.

That source is, of course, the fairy tale, *Beauty and the Beast*. It haunts the text in the premonitory pairing of the rival papers, the *Brute* and the *Beast*. It recurs in various waffle scrambles, for example Salter's confusion of boots/roots/brute and William's schoolboy nickname of 'Beastly'. It emerges into full daylight – like cannibalism from the shadows in *Black Mischief* – at William's triumphal return to London as BOOT OF THE *BEAST*. William is the Beast – transfigured from dud cub reporter to the cynosure of Fleet Street (the very reverse of what happened to poor, sacked Evelyn). Yet Waugh specifically did not want to end the novel on this high note. He was insistent in his instructions to *Scoop*'s would-be film-makers: 'Boot should return home without ambition ever to leave again.' Like Timmie Willie, William returns happily to the total obscurity from which he came.

The whole novel is thus a long hiding to nowhere. It ends where it began. The maze of its narrative is characterized by U-turns, detours, and red herrings that (intentionally) confuse the reader as much as its cast. In the last pages, a vinous optimism descends. Happy endings abound, as befit a fairy tale – a happy ending for Uncle Theodore, with his shady London chambers and feline prowlings after dark; a happily dull ending for Mr Salter as art editor of *Home Knitting*; a happy anticlimactic ending for William, safe at home in Boot Magna, composing *Lush Places* once more. '...*the waggons lumber in the lane under their golden glory of harvested sheaves*, he wrote; *maternal rodents pilot their furry brood through the stubble* ...'

Waugh, however, was a realist. The novel ends on a chillier note: 'Outside the owls hunted maternal rodents and their furry brood.' It was 1938. War was on its way.

*

xxi

EVELYN WAUGH

After the war ended, Waugh took Laura on a brief jaunt to California, ostensibly to discuss the filming of *Brideshead Revisited*. His diary for the six-week visit was lacklustre, until he found 'a deep mine of literary gold in the cemetery of Forest Lawn'. 'Wonderful literary raw material,' he told his agent. 'I go there two or three times a week, am on easy terms with the chief embalmer & next week am to lunch with Dr HUBERT EATON himself.' His excitement is matched by that of Dennis Barlow, the protagonist of *The Loved One*, who ends the novel carrying back to England 'the artist's load, a great, shapeless chunk of experience ... to work on it hard and long, for God knew how long'. That was a private joke. Waugh finished *The Loved One* in ten weeks. *Scoop* had taken him three years.

As usual, Waugh's fiction is closely modelled on fact. In what his diary epigrammatically calls 'an essay for *Life* about death', he mimics the Forest Lawn brochure's enamoured detail: 'the largest wrought-iron gates in the world ... 300 acres of park land, judiciously planted with evergreen (for no plant which sheds its leaf has a place there) ... lawns, watered and drained by 80 miles of pipe ... countless radios concealed about the vegetation, which ceaselessly discourse the "Hindu Love-song" ... The Tudor-style Administration Building, the Mortuary (Tudor exterior, Georgian Interior) all designed to defy the operations of time in "Class A steel and concrete" ... foundations penetrating 33 feet into solid rock.'

The novel recasts the details with due satiric heightening:

This perfect replica of an old English Manor, a notice said, *like all the buildings of Whispering Glades, is constructed throughout of Grade A steel and concrete with foundations extending into solid rock. It is certified proof against fire earthquake and   Their name liveth for evermore who record it in Whispering Glades.*

At the blank patch a signwriter was even then at work and Dennis, pausing to study it, discerned the ghost of the words 'high explosive' freshly obliterated and the outlines of 'nuclear fission' about to be filled in as a substitute.

The similarities were so close that Waugh's publishers feared a libel suit. Two ploys were devised to protect them. In the dust-jacket's blurb, Waugh's pithy ironies can be clearly heard:

This is a nightmare induced by the unfamiliar diet of Southern California. That region, where all men are displaced persons, is unique only in the splendid elaboration of its graveyards, and to these Mr Evelyn Waugh turned for solace and inspiration during a brief visit...

In addition, Waugh persuaded a young friend, Lord Stanley of Alderley, to write to his lawyers instructing them to add a codicil to his will. At his death, his body should be shipped to Forest Lawn for burial, since he understood that cemetery bore some resemblance to the beautiful one so movingly described by his friend, Mr Evelyn Waugh. This was to form the basis of the defence in case of prosecution. It was ten years before Lord Stanley thought it safe to cancel the codicil.

There is a Jamesian quality to this cynically aristocratic Old World exploitation of naive American snobbery. The novel itself is self-consciously subtitled 'An Anglo-American Tragedy'. Dennis identifies himself as 'the protagonist of a Jamesian problem' of 'American innocence and European experience'. Yet were one to epitomize the novel's theme, one would turn from Henry James to two four-letter words, the Cult of the Sham. This is neatly symbolized, as often in Waugh, by an item of clothing. Aimée shows the curious Dennis an article of 'casket-wear'. It is a suit complete with shirt-front, cuffs, collar and bow-tie, buttoned down the front – at the back, slit from neck to toe. It was, Waugh concludes, 'the apotheosis of the "dickey"'. The dickey is a sham shirt front. 'Apotheosis' resonates with all the connotations of the cult.

Whispering Glades is a necropolis devoted to sham. Its music is canned, its art is phoney. Its architectural simulacra are specious – from St Peter-without-the-Walls to the horribly uneuphonious Wee Kirk o'Auld Lang Syne. Above all, its painted stiffs are cosmetic – dandified in death, pipes placed in rigor mortis mouths, telephones in lifeless hands, a monocle fixed in the unseeing eye.

The indictment extends beyond the graveyard. Whether living or dead, Hollywood is peopled by shams. There is 'false and fruity' Sir Ambrose Abercrombie. His parody of English dress is almost as absurd as Waugh's own loud checks – Eton Rambler tie and I Zingari ribbon on his boater; deer-stalker cap and Inverness cape for the rain. There is the impressively named Lorenzo Medici, only '... he says it "Medissy," like that; how you said it [i.e. correctly] kinda sounds like a wop and Mr Medici is a very fine young man with a very, very fine and wonderful record...' Consider, too, Baby Aaronson, the Hollywood starlet, who 'set a new note in personal publicity'. Initially transformed by the studios to Juanita del Pablo, a scowling, black-haired Spanish anti-Fascist refugee, she becomes radically reconfigured as a roguish, red-headed Irish colleen called anything from Dierdre to Oonagh – with only the loss of half her nose and all her teeth en route. Guru Brahmin, Aimée's agony aunt and ethical adviser, in the magazine photo is a bearded, almost naked sage. In reality, he is Mr Slump, a drunken, chain-smoking journalist.

The linguistic equivalent to Sham is euphemism, a stylistic trope that recurs throughout the novel, often casually understated. Aimée lives in 'the concrete cell which she called her apartment'. When she and Dennis swear undying love at the Heart of Bruce, she asks 'What is a "canty day," Dennis?' and is answered, 'Something like hogmanay, I expect ... People being sick on the pavement in Glasgow.' The language of the funerary profession is conducted entirely in euphemism. Dennis himself, in his down-market animal mortuary, is adept, offering the owner of a dead Sealyham 'interment or incineration' ('Pardon me?' 'Buried or burned?'). At Whispering Glades, the complexion of the Loved One is recorded as 'rural, athletic, and scholarly – that is to say red, brown or white'.

Whispering Glades is discreetly termed 'a restricted park', because its clientele won't mix with Orientals, Asians and Blacks: 'the Waiting Ones ... prefer to be with their own people'. Making arrangements for Sir Francis Hinsley, a 'strangulated Loved One' (who hanged himself – or 'passed over with his suspenders'), Dennis assures the Mortuary Hostess he fulfils the racial requirements. As often, the euphemism is robustly rebutted by reality:

'... Let me assure you Sir Francis was quite white.'

As he said this there came vividly into Dennis's mind that image which lurked there, seldom out of sight for long; the sack of body suspended and the face above it with eyes red and horribly starting from their sockets, the cheeks mottled in indigo like the marbled end-papers of a ledger and the tongue swollen and protruding like an end of black sausage.

Euphemism, like the capable hands of Mr Joyboy, can massage away any 'special little difficulties' of this kind. It is a national characteristic. The New World systematically eradicates the little difficulties that give life its sharpness – just as Kaiser's Stoneless Peaches lose all savour with the stone, leaving a ball of damp, sweet cotton wool. In the Old World, Waugh observes, funerary architecture dwells on the decay of the body: 'often you find, gruesomely portrayed, the corpse half decayed with marble worms writhing in the marble adipocere'. Yet in Whispering Glades there is no place for deciduous trees, let alone corrupting flesh. And in the replica Lake Island [sic] of Innisfree there are ever-blooming bean-rows but no bees, only a piped murmur in the bee-loud glade. 'No sore fannies and plenty of poetry', as the ferryman says. The mock-up of Yeats's Lake Isle nirvana conceals a further barbed allusion. In the happier hunting-ground of Whispering Glades, death is robbed of its sting: the biblical exclamation, 'O death where is thy sting, O grave thy victory?' acquires an absurd literalism.

At the entrance gates to Whispering Glades, the testament of Wilbur Kenworthy, the Dreamer, emends the Revelation of St John, 'And behold I saw a new Heaven and a new Earth', to the exclusively profane 'Behold I dreamed a dream and I saw a New Earth sacred to *Happiness*.' Death is 'the biggest success story of all time', as Dr Eaton, Wilbur Kenworthy's original, urges his visitors. 'Be happy,' his inscription runs, 'because Forest Lawn has eradicated the old customs of Death and depicts Life not Death.'

In the non-sectarian cults of this land, the sacred is secular-ized and sanctification bestowed on the profane. For instance, at Whispering Glades, there is 'a cult' of Joyboy, the senior embalmer. Aimée sees the Guru Brahmin as 'a spiritual director'. Similarly, she goes to meet Dennis as her 'manifest destiny'. Their oath of love at the Heart of Bruce, uttered in Burns's incomprehensible dialect, has 'all the sanctity of mumbo-jumbo' – but, for her, it holds 'a sacred force'. Dennis overhears a Mortuary Hostess informing Mrs Bogolov (a name, via the Russian word for God, *Bog*, implying lover of God) that 'the Dreamer does not approve of wreaths or crosses. We just arrange the flowers in their natural beauty'. Here, 'natural' arrangement is a de-natured paradox – comparable to Kaiser's stoneless peach. It is paralleled by the Slumber Room attendant who sprays the flowers with scent. Yet, even though wreaths and crosses are forbidden, the Dreamer allows Sir Francis to be commemorated by the Cricket Club's floral tribute of cross bats and wickets. 'Dr Kenworthy had himself given judgment; the trophy was essentially a reminder of life, not of death; that was the *crux*' [my italics]. Neither crux nor cross carry Christian connotations. The new religion is entirely secularized. It is a celebration of life alone.

In a letter to Cyril Connolly, who first published *The Loved One* in *Horizon* in 1948, Waugh identified five ideas he had in mind. Third: 'there is no such thing as an American. They are all exiles, uprooted, transplanted and doomed to sterility. The ancestral gods they have abjured get them in the end. I tried to indicate this in Aimée's last hours.' Aimée, the loved one, is the 'vestal virgin' of Whispering Glades – what she calls her ' true home'. She acquires classic status, because she alone invests the simulacra, the fake objects of worship, with absolute faith. Twice her faith is shattered, when Joyboy and Dennis court her. In their different ways, both use the language of death – Joyboy puts smiles on the corpses sent down for her to paint, Dennis plagiarizes the vows of dead poets. Twice betrayed, Aimée turns to her guru. The drunken Slump advises her to take a jump from a nice high window. Defending himself to a colleague, he demands impenitently, 'Well, for Christ's sake, with a name like that?'

Aimée's surname is Thanatogenos. Thanatism was a Greek belief that the soul died with the body. At her death, Aimée is pointedly compared to Iphigenia, Alcestis and Antigone – all of them sacrificial victims of classic legend. Like them, in the end, she is a victim of her ancestral gods. Her job in Whispering Glades has made her the handmaid of a cult that worships the indestructibility of the flesh. In this sense, she is her mother's daughter. Her mother 'took to New Thought and wouldn't have it that there was such a thing as death'. Denying the mortality of the flesh, however, means that the American cult of life has jettisoned the immortality of the soul. And without a soul, man is no more than a beast. As Cassius laments in *Othello*: 'I have lost the immortal part of myself, and what remains is bestial.'

This is why, in the Happier Hunting Ground, pets are given human rites. The words of the Burial of the Dead are impiously emended ('Dog that is born of bitch hath but a short time to live, and is full of misery. He cometh up, and is cut down like a flower...'). It is also why, in a final cruel twist, Dennis arranges for Joyboy to be sent an annual memorial card for 'his little pet': *Your little Aimée is wagging her tail in heaven tonight, thinking of you.* Forest Lawn and Whispering Glades have eradicated the old customs of Death. Their cult celebrates a sham, the eternal life of the flesh. For a Catholic like Waugh, they have forfeited the soul.

*

In 1954, at the age of fifty, Waugh set out on a winter cruise to Ceylon. He was suffering from insomnia and had been taking a cocktail of various narcotics generously laced with whisky. The combination of phenobarbitone and alcohol triggered an extended episode of hallucinatory psychosis. The persistence of his hallucinations on board, after his medication ran out, can be attributed to bromide poisoning, which takes some weeks to clear. Though there is no diary covering this period, the events leading up to it are well documented, and tally with those in *Pinfold* – from the Bruiser's Box and the BBC interview to Betjeman's gift of a fine Pre-Raphaelite wash-stand. Waugh's single surviving letter from shipboard to Lady Diana Cooper describes his hallucinations. His odd behaviour is even remembered by a sympathetic fellow-passenger: 'People were saying there's something funny about that man, he's talking to the toast-rack. There were little lamps on the tables with pink shades and he'd have a long conversation with those...' This woman, whose name was Gwen, had a cabin not far from Waugh's. He used to knock on her door at all times of day and night, asking – as we can see from the novel, with some pathos – for 'Margaret'. We might even guess that Waugh saw in Gwen something of the gentle Margaret of his own – and Pinfold's – delusions, for her reminiscences are kindly:

One afternoon I started doing a crossword in the small bar lounge, and he was sitting at the other side – it wasn't a very big place, and he looked a bit lost. So I looked across at him and said, 'Mr Waugh, you ought to know this. How do you spell Naiad? Is it NIAID or NAIAD?' And he looked up and smiled, and said, 'That's always a word that puzzles me. What are you doing?' So I went over to him and he was perfectly alright. We had quite a long talk about children's books, *The Wind in the Willows*, and *Alice*. He was absolutely lucid then...

The Ordeal of Gilbert Pinfold ends, as *The Loved One* had done, with a recognition of its first-hand origins: 'a hamper to be unpacked of fresh, rich experience – perishable goods'. The work's subtitle, *A Conversation Piece*, goes further. It suggests that this is not, in fact, a work of fiction. Certainly, there is a radical difference between *Pinfold* and Waugh's other novels. All derive from his own experiences. But the rest are *worked* into narratives of apparent phantasmagoric anarchy – an impression that belies their beautifully executed, exquisitely co-ordinated covert satirical structure. Waugh was justifiably proud of his craftsmanship, which he modestly describes in the self-portrait that opens *Pinfold*.

A decade earlier, he stated that

I have come to the conclusion that there is no such thing as normality. That is what makes story-telling such an absorbing task, the attempt to reduce to order the anarchic raw materials of life ... The artist's only service to the disintegrated society of today is to create little independent systems of order of his own.

Pinfold, however, reverses this pattern. Pinfold, like Waugh, is an artist. He too tries to make sense of the anarchic raw materials of life, to reduce his experiences on the *Caliban* to a little independent order-system of his own. Throughout the 'Conversation Piece', one rationale is added to another to create a tottering hypothetical superstructure on the shaky foundations of delusion. But there *is* no order to these events. They are pure hallucination, the unredeemed and malevolent anarchy of the aberrant mind.

Like many writers, Pinfold believes that most artists have only one or two ideas. 'A novelist is condemned to produce a succession of novelties, new names for characters, new incidents for his plots, new scenery' (as Waugh had done in his two versions of Abyssinia). 'But, Mr Pinfold maintained, most men harbour the germs of one or two books only; all else is professional trickery of which the most daemonic of masters ... were flagrantly guilty.' In *Pinfold*, for once, there was no need for Waugh to resort to professional trickery – to invent novelties, exaggerate events, to embellish and unify. The novelty lies in the absence of trickery. The story is exactly as it was.

There is also a prophetic irony to Pinfold's delusions. They voice the adverse criticism Waugh was himself to receive, particularly after his death, when he was widely reviled for his snobbery, greed, irascibility, homophobia, homosexuality, anti-Semitism, bigotry and bad manners. Pinfold's bewildered rationality, the pathos and courage with which he undergoes the nightmare absurdity of his tribulations, are observed with the dispassionate objectivity of the supreme artist, who found his own follies fair game.

Ann Pasternak Slater

ANN PASTERNAK SLATER is a Fellow of St Anne's College, Oxford. She has written on Shakespeare (*Shakespeare the Director*) and has translated Tolstoy's 'The Death of Ivan Ilyich' and 'Master and Man' as well as the memoirs of Alexander Pasternak (*A Vanished Present*). She has edited and introduced *The Complete Short Stories* of Evelyn Waugh and *The Complete English Works* of George Herbert for Everyman's Library.

SELECT BIBLIOGRAPHY

MAJOR PRIMARY TEXTS

1. FICTION

Decline and Fall, An Illustrated Novelette, Chapman & Hall, 1928; Doubleday, Doran, New York, 1929.

Vile Bodies, Chapman & Hall, 1930; Cape, Smith, New York, 1930.

Black Mischief, Chapman & Hall, 1932; Farrar & Rinehart, New York, 1932.

A Handful of Dust, Chapman & Hall, 1934; Farrar & Rinehart, New York, 1934.

Mr. Loveday's Little Outing and Other Sad Stories, Chapman & Hall, 1936; Little, Brown, Boston, 1936.

Scoop: A Novel About Journalists, Chapman & Hall, 1938; Little, Brown, Boston, 1938.

Put Out More Flags, Chapman & Hall, 1942; Little, Brown, Boston, 1942.

Work Suspended, Chapman & Hall, 1942.

Brideshead Revisited: The Sacred and Profane Memories of Captain Charles Ryder, Chapman & Hall, 1945; Little, Brown, Boston, 1945.

Scott-King's Modern Europe, Chapman & Hall, 1947; Little, Brown, Boston, 1949.

The Loved One, Chapman & Hall, 1948; Little, Brown, Boston, 1948.

Work Suspended and Other Stories Written Before the Second World War, Chapman & Hall, 1949.

Helena, Chapman & Hall, 1950; Little, Brown, Boston, 1950.

Men At Arms, Chapman & Hall, 1952; Little, Brown, 1952.

Love Among the Ruins: A Romance of the Near Future, Chapman & Hall, 1953.

Tactical Exercise (US edition of short stories), Little, Brown, Boston, 1954.

Officers and Gentlemen, Chapman & Hall, 1955; Little, Brown, Boston, 1955.

The Ordeal of Gilbert Pinfold, Chapman & Hall, 1957; Little, Brown, Boston, 1957.

Unconditional Surrender, Chapman & Hall, 1961; US edition: *The End of the Battle*, Little, Brown, Boston, 1961.

Basil Seal Rides Again or The Rake's Regress, Chapman & Hall, 1963; Little, Brown, Boston, 1963.

Sword of Honour. A Final Version of the Novels: Men at Arms (1952),

Officers and Gentlemen (1955), and *Unconditional Surrender* (1961), Chapman & Hall, 1965; Little, Brown, Boston, 1966.

DAVIS, ROBERT MURRAY, ed., *Evelyn Waugh, Apprentice: The Early Writings, 1910–1927*, Pilgrim Books, Oklahoma, 1985.

2. TRAVEL

Labels, A Mediterranean Journal, Duckworth, 1930; US edition: *A Bachelor Abroad, A Mediterranean Journal*, Cape, Smith, New York, 1930.

Remote People, Duckworth, 1931; US edition: *They Were Still Dancing*, Farrar & Rinehart, New York, 1932.

Ninety-Two Days, The Account of a Tropical Journey Through British Guiana and Part of Brazil, Duckworth, 1934; Farrar & Rinehart, New York, 1934.

Waugh in Abyssinia, Longman, Green & Co., 1936; Longman, Green & Co., New York, 1936.

Robbery Under Law: The Mexican Object-Lesson, Chapman & Hall, 1939; US edition: *Mexico: An Object Lesson* Little, Brown, Boston, 1939.

The Holy Places, The Queen Anne Press, 1952; Queen Anne Press and British Book Center, New York, 1953.

A Tourist in Africa, Chapman & Hall, 1960; Little, Brown, Boston, 1960.

3. BIOGRAPHY, AUTOBIOGRAPHY, AND OTHER

Rossetti, His Life and Works, Duckworth, 1928; Dodd, Mead & Co., New York, 1928.

Edmund Campion: Jesuit and Martyr, Longman's, 1935; Sheed & Ward, New York, 1935.

The Life of the Right Reverend Ronald Knox, Chapman & Hall, 1959; US edition: *Monsignor Ronald Knox*, Little, Brown, Boston, 1959.

A Little Learning. The First Volume of an Autobiography, Chapman & Hall, 1964; Little, Brown, Boston, 1964.

AMORY, MARK, ed., *The Letters of Evelyn Waugh*, Weidenfeld & Nicolson, 1980.

DAVIE, MICHAEL, ed., *The Diaries of Evelyn Waugh*, Weidenfeld & Nicolson, 1976.

GALLAGHER, DONAT, ed., *The Essays, Articles and Reviews of Evelyn Waugh*, Methuen, 1983.

COOPER, ARTEMIS, ed., *Mr. Wu and Mrs. Stitch: The Letters of Evelyn Waugh and Diana Cooper*, Hodder & Stoughton, 1991.

MOSLEY, CHARLOTTE, ed., *The Letters of Nancy Mitford and Evelyn Waugh*, Hodder & Stoughton, 1996.

Waugh is one of the great letter-writers.

EVELYN WAUGH

SECONDARY TEXTS

1. BIOGRAPHY AND PERSONAL REMINISCENCE

DONALDSON, FRANCES, *Evelyn Waugh. Portrait of a Country Neighbour*, Weidenfeld & Nicolson, 1967. A well-written, warm and honest portrait of Waugh from the late forties.

HASTINGS, SELINA, *Evelyn Waugh: A Biography*, Sinclair-Stevenson, 1994. Lively and sympathetic.

PATEY, DOUGLAS LANE, *The Life of Evelyn Waugh: A Critical Biography*, Blackwell, 1998. An intelligent intellectual biography.

PRYCE-JONES, DAVID, ed., *Evelyn Waugh and His World*, Weidenfeld & Nicolson, 1973. Essays and photographs by friends on different aspects of Waugh.

ST JOHN, JOHN, *To the War With Waugh*, Leo Cooper, 1973. Written by a fellow-member of the Royal Marines.

STANNARD, MARTIN, *Evelyn Waugh: The Early Years 1903–1939*, Dent, 1986, and *Evelyn Waugh: No Abiding City 1939–1966* Dent, 1992. Admirably industrious and full documentation, marred by a lack of sympathy.

SYKES, CHRISTOPHER, *Evelyn Waugh: A Biography*, Collins, 1975. Factually inaccurate, but with the vitality and insight of critical friendship.

WAUGH, ALEC, *My Brother Evelyn & Other Profiles*, Cassell, 1967.

2. BIBLIOGRAPHY

Necessary tools for the Waugh scholar:

DAVIS, ROBERT MURRAY, Paul A. Doyle, Donat Gallagher, Charles E. Linck and Winnifred M. Boggards, *A Bibliography of Evelyn Waugh*, Whitston Publishing Co., New York, 1986.

DAVIS, ROBERT MURRAY, *A Catalogue of the Evelyn Waugh Collection at the Humanities Research Center, The University of Texas at Austin*, Whitston Publishing Co., New York, 1981.

DAVIS, ROBERT MURRAY, Paul A. Doyle, Heinz Kosok, Charles E. Linck Jr., *Evelyn Waugh: A Checklist of Primary and Secondary Material*, Whitston Publishing Co., New York, 1972.

3. CRITICISM

BEATY, FREDRICK L., *The Ironic World of Evelyn Waugh: A Study of Eight Novels*, Northern Illinois University Press, 1994.

DAVIS, ROBERT MURRAY, *Evelyn Waugh, Writer*, Pilgrim Books, Oklahoma, 1981. Full-length study using fascinating unpublished manuscript variants.

SELECT BIBLIOGRAPHY

GARNETT, ROBERT R., *From Grimes to Brideshead, The Early Novels of Evelyn Waugh*, Associated University Presses, 1990.

HEATH, JEFFREY, *The Picturesque Prison: Evelyn Waugh and His Writing*, Weidenfeld & Nicolson, 1982.

HOLLIS, CHRISTOPHER, 'Evelyn Waugh', British Council 'Writers and their Work' series, Longman's, 1966. Brief and pithy.

LITTLEWOOD, IAN, *The Writings of Evelyn Waugh*, Basil Blackwell, 1983.

LODGE, DAVID, 'Evelyn Waugh', Columbia University Press, 1971. Broad, fast-moving and suggestive essay by a fellow-Catholic novelist.

MYERS, WILLIAM, *Evelyn Waugh and the Problem of Evil*, Faber and Faber, 1991.

PAGE, NORMAN, *An Evelyn Waugh Chronology*, Macmillian, 1997.

PASTERNAK SLATER, ANN, 'Waugh's Handful of Dust: Right Things in Wrong Places', *Essays in Criticism*, January 1982, pp. 48-68. Establishes some essential Waugh techniques.

STANNARD, MARTIN, ed., *Evelyn Waugh: The Critical Heritage*, Routledge & Kegan Paul, 1984. All the contemporary reviews.

STOPP, FREDERICK J., *Evelyn Waugh, Portrait of an Artist*, Chapman & Hall, 1958. The first and best critical study of Waugh.

WILSON, EDMUND, ' "Never Apologise, Never Explain": The Art of Evelyn Waugh', *Classics and Commercials. A Literary Chronicle of the Forties*, W. H. Allen, 1951, pp. 140-6. A judicious eulogy, followed by post-*Brideshead* disillusion in 'Splendors and Miseries of Evelyn Waugh', ibid., pp. 298-305.

WILSON, JOHN HOWARD, *Evelyn Waugh, A Literary Biography, 1903-1924*, Associated University Presses, 1996.

CHRONOLOGY

DATE	AUTHOR'S LIFE	LITERARY CONTEXT
1898	Birth of Alec Waugh, Evelyn's brother.	
1903	28 October: birth of Evelyn Waugh to Arthur and Catherine Waugh in Hampstead.	James: *The Ambassadors.* Shaw: *Man and Superman.*
1904		Conrad: *Nostromo.*
1905		James: *The Golden Bowl.* Forster: *Where Angels Fear to Tread.*
1908		Forster: *A Room with a View.* Bennett: *The Old Wives' Tale.* Grahame: *The Wind in the Willows.*
1910	Attends Heath Mount Preparatory School.	Forster: *Howards End.*
1911	Begins keeping a diary.	Lawrence: *The White Peacock.* Beerbohm: *Zuleika Dobson.*
1912		Beerbohm: *A Christmas Garland.* Brooke: *Collected Poems.* Shaw: *Pygmalion.*
1913		Lawrence: *Sons and Lovers.* Proust: *A la Recherche du temps perdu* (to 1927). Conrad: *Chance.*
1914		Joyce: *Dubliners.*
1915		Ford: *The Good Soldier.* Conrad: *Victory.* Buchan: *The Thirty-nine Steps.* Woolf: *The Voyage Out.*
1916		Joyce: *A Portrait of the Artist as a Young Man.*
1917	Alec Waugh's *Loom of Youth* published. Evelyn attends Lancing College, Sussex.	Yeats: *The Wild Swans at Coole.* Eliot: *Prufrock and Other Observations.*
1918		Brooke: *Collected Poems.*
1919		Shaw: *Heartbreak House.* Beerbohm: *Seven Men.* Firbank: *Valmouth.*
1920		Pound: *Hugh Selwyn Mauberley.*

Emmeline Pankhurst founds the Women's Social and Political Union.

Russo-Japanese war. Franco-British *entente cordiale.*
Liberal government in Britain: Campbell-Bannerman Prime Minister. First Russian revolution.

Asquith becomes Prime Minister.

Death of Edward VII.

Coronation of George V. Agadir crisis. Industrial unrest in Britain.

Outbreak of World War I.
Asquith forms coalition government with Balfour.

Easter Rising in Dublin. Lloyd George becomes Prime Minister.

Bolshevik revolution in Russia. US joins war.

Armistice. Women over 30 gain vote.
Versailles peace conference.

League of Nations formed. Prohibition in the US.

DATE	AUTHOR'S LIFE	LITERARY CONTEXT
1921		Huxley: *Crome Yellow*. Pirandello: *Six Characters in Search of an Author*.
1922	January: attends Hertford College, Oxford, as a Scholar reading History. Begins contributing graphics, and later pieces to undergraduate magazines.	Joyce: *Ulysses*. Eliot: *The Waste Land*. Housman: *Last Poems*. Fitzgerald: *The Beautiful and the Damned*.
1923		Cummings: *The Enormous Room*. Firbank: *The Flower Beneath the Foot*. Huxley: *Antic Hay*.
1924	Leaves Oxford with a third-class degree. Begins novel, *The Temple at Thatch*. Makes film, *The Scarlet Woman*. Attends Heatherley's Art School, London.	Forster: *A Passage to India*. Shaw: *Saint Joan*. Ford: *Parade's End* (to 1928).
1925	Schoolmaster at Arnold House, Llanddulas, Denbighshire (January–July). Destroys *The Temple at Thatch* on Harold Acton's criticism. Attempts suicide. Writes 'The Balance'. Begins as schoolmaster in Aston Clinton, Berkshire (September).	Fitzgerald: *The Great Gatsby*. Kafka: *The Trial*.
1926	*P.R.B.: An Essay on the Pre-Raphaelite Brotherhood 1847–1854* privately printed. 'The Balance' published.	Faulkner: *Soldier's Pay*. Nabokov: *Mary*. Henry Green: *Blindness*. Firbank: *Concerning the Eccentricities of Cardinal Pirelli*.
1927	Sacked from Aston Clinton (February). Story for *The New Decameron* commissioned; writes 'The Tutor's Tale: A House of Gentlefolks'. Temporary schoolmaster in London, also contributing to *The Daily Express*. Meets Evelyn Gardner (April). Writes *Rossetti, His Life and Works*. Takes carpentry lessons. Proposes to Evelyn Gardner (December).	Woolf: *To the Lighthouse*. Hemingway: *Men Without Women*. Dunne: *An Experiment with Time*.
1928	Begins writing *Decline and Fall*. *Rossetti* published (April). Marries Evelyn Gardner (June). *Decline and Fall* published (September).	Lawrence: *Lady Chatterley's Lover*. Woolf: *Orlando*. Yeats: *The Tower*. Lewis: *The Childermass*. Nabokov: *King, Queen, Knave*.

CHRONOLOGY

Establishment of USSR. Stalin becomes General Secretary of the Communist party Central Committee. Mussolini marches on Rome. Coalition falls and Bonar Law forms Conservative ministry.

Baldwin becomes Prime Minister. Women gain legal equality in divorce suits. Hitler's coup in Munich fails. German hyper-inflation.

First Labour government formed by Ramsay MacDonald. Hitler in prison. Death of Lenin. Baldwin becomes Prime Minister again after a Conservative election victory.

Locarno conference.

British general strike. First television demonstrated.

Lindbergh makes first solo flight over Atlantic.

Hoover becomes US President. Stalin de facto dictator in USSR: first Five Year Plan. Women's suffrage in Britain reduced from age 30 to age 21.

DATE	AUTHOR'S LIFE	LITERARY CONTEXT
1929	Mediterranean cruise with his wife (February–March). *Vile Bodies* begun. Marriage breaks down (July). Divorce (September).	Faulkner: *The Sound and the Fury*. Cocteau: *Les Enfants terribles*. Hemingway: *A Farewell to Arms*. Henry Green: *Living*. Priestley: *The Good Companions*. Remarque: *All Quiet on the Western Front*.
1930	*Vile Bodies* published (January). Received into the Catholic Church; *Labels, A Mediterranean Journal* published (September). Travels to Abyssinia to report coronation of Haile Selassie for *The Times* (October–November); travels in East and Central Africa.	Eliot: *Ash Wednesday*. Faulkner: *As I Lay Dying*. Nabokov: *The Defence*.
1931	Returns to England (March). *Remote People* completed (August) and published (November). *Black Mischief* begun (September).	Faulkner: *Sanctuary*. Woolf: *The Waves*.
1932	Working on film scenario for Ealing Studios (January–February). Writes 'Excursion in Reality' (March). *Black Mischief* completed (June) and published (October). Sails for British Guiana (December).	Huxley: *Brave New World*. Faulkner: *Light in August*. Betjeman: *Mount Zion*. Nabokov: *Glory*.
1933	Travels in British Guiana and Brazil (January–May). Writes 'The Man Who Liked Dickens' (February). Meets 'white mouse named Laura' Herbert at Herbert family home in Italy (September). 'Out of Depth' and *Ninety-Two Days* written (October–November).	Malraux: *La Condition humaine*. Stein: *The Autobiography of Alice B. Toklas*.
1934	In Fez, Morocco, begins *A Handful of Dust* (January–February). *Ninety-Two Days* published (March) and *A Handful of Dust* completed (April). Expedition to Spitzbergen in the Arctic (July–August). *A Handful of Dust* published (September). Begins *Edmund Campion: Jesuit and Martyr* (September); writes 'Mr Crutwell's Little Outing' and 'On Guard'.	

CHRONOLOGY

HISTORICAL EVENTS

Wall Street crash. First year of the Depression.

Gandhi begins civil disobedience campaign in India. Nazis win seats from the moderates in German election.

Britain abandons Gold Standard.

Unemployment in Britain reaches 2.8 million. F. D. Roosevelt's landslide victory in US presidential election.

Hitler becomes Chancellor of Germany. Roosevelt's 'New Deal' in US.

Riots in Paris; Doumergue forms National Union ministry to avert civil war. Dollfuss murdered in attempted Nazi coup in Austria.

DATE	AUTHOR'S LIFE	LITERARY CONTEXT
1935	Completes *Campion* (May); writes 'Winner Takes All' (July). Travels to Abyssinia to report on imminent Italian invasion for *The Daily Mail* (August–December).	Isherwood: *Mr. Norris Changes Trains*. Eliot: *Murder in the Cathedral*. Odets: *Waiting for Lefty*. Graham Greene: *England Made Me*.
1936	Writes *Waugh in Abyssinia* (April–October). Annulment to first marriage agreed by Rome (July); engagement to Laura Herbert. Returns to Abyssinia to report on Italian occupation (July–September). *Waugh in Abyssinia* published. *Scoop* begun (October).	Faulkner: *Absalom, Absalom!* Nabokov: *Despair*.
1937	Marriage to Laura Herbert (17 April); honeymoon in Italy. Decides to rewrite *Scoop* (July). Moves into Piers Court, Stinchcombe, Gloucestershire (August).	Hemingway: *To Have and Have Not*. Orwell: *The Road to Wigan Pier*. Sartre: *La Nausée*. Betjeman: *Continual Dew*. Steinbeck: *Of Mice and Men*.
1938	Birth of daughter, Teresa Waugh (March). *Scoop* published (May). Two trips, both with Laura: to Hungary (May) and Mexico (August–October). Writes 'An Englishman's Home' and begins *Robbery Under Law: The Mexican Object-Lesson*.	Graham Greene: *Brighton Rock*. Beckett: *Murphy*. Orwell: *Homage to Catalonia*.
1939	Completes *Robbery Under Law*; writes 'The Sympathetic Passenger' (May). Begins *Work Suspended*. *Robbery Under Law* published (June). Birth of son, Auberon Waugh (November). Joins Royal Marines (December) and abandons *Work Suspended*.	Joyce: *Finnegans Wake*. Eliot: *The Family Reunion*. Steinbeck: *The Grapes of Wrath*. Henry Green: *Party Going*. Auden: *Journey to a War*. Isherwood: *Goodbye to Berlin*.
1940	Expedition to Dakar, West Africa (August–September). Transfers to Commandos in Scotland (November). Birth and death of daughter, Mary Waugh (December).	Hemingway: *For Whom the Bell Tolls*. Graham Greene: *The Power and the Glory*. Dylan Thomas: *Portrait of the Artist as a Young Dog*. Faulkner: *The Hamlet*. Henry Green: *Pack my Bag: A Self-Portrait*. Betjeman: *Old Lights for New Chancels*.

CHRONOLOGY

DATE	AUTHOR'S LIFE	LITERARY CONTEXT
1941	Sails for service in Egypt (February); raid on Bardia (April). At Battle of Crete (May). Disillusioned with war. July–August, on circuitous route home, writes *Put Out More Flags*. Rejoins Royal Marines (September).	Acton: *Peonies and Ponies*. Fitzgerald: *The Last Tycoon*.
1942	*Put Out More Flags* published. Transfers to Blues, Special Service Brigade; birth of daughter, Margaret Waugh (June). *Work Suspended* published (December).	Anouilh: *Eurydice*. Sartre: *Les Mouches*. Camus: *L'Etranger*, *Le Mythe de Sisyphe*.
1943	Transferred to London (March). Father dies (June).	Davies: *Collected Poems*. Henry Green: *Caught*.
1944	Given leave to write (January); begins *Brideshead Revisited* (January–June). Birth of daughter, Harriet Waugh (May). On British Military Mission to the Partisans in Yugoslavia (from July).	Eliot: *Four Quartets*. Anouilh: *Antigone*. Camus: *Caligula*. Sartre: *Huis Clos*.
1945	Returns to London (March). *Brideshead Revisited* published and *Helena* begun (May). Demobbed; returns to Piers Court.	Broch: *The Death of Virgil*. Betjeman: *New Bats in Old Belfries*. Orwell: *Animal Farm*. Henry Green: *Loving*. Mitford: *The Pursuit of Love*.
1946	*When the Going was Good* published (selection from previous travel books). Travels to Nuremberg (March) and Spain (June). Writes 'Scott-King's Modern Europe' and *Wine in Peace and War*.	Rattigan: *The Winslow Boy*. Cocteau: *L'Aigle à deux têtes*. Henry Green: *Back*. Dylan Thomas: *Deaths and Entrances*.
1947	Visits New York and Los Angeles for projected film of *Brideshead Revisited* (January–March). Writes 'Tactical Exercise'. Writes first draft of *The Loved One* (May–July). Birth of son, James Waugh (June). Visits Scandinavia (August–September).	Mann: *Doctor Faustus*. Camus: *La Peste*. Diary of Anne Frank is published. Henry Green: *Concluding*.

CHRONOLOGY

HISTORICAL EVENTS

USSR is invaded. Japanese attack Pearl Harbor. US joins war.

Fall of Singapore. Germans reach Stalingrad. Battle of El Alamein.

Germans retreat in Russia, Africa and Italy.

Allied landings in Normandy. Red Army reaches Belgrade and Budapest. Butler's Education Act.

Hitler commits suicide. Germany surrenders. World War II ends after atom bombs are dropped on Hiroshima and Nagasaki. United Nations founded. Attlee forms Labour government.

Nuremberg trials. 'Iron Curtain' speech by Churchill. Beginning of Cold War.

Independence of India and Pakistan. Warsaw Communist conference.

DATE	AUTHOR'S LIFE	LITERARY CONTEXT
1948	*The Loved One* published (February). Begins lecture tour in USA (October).	Eliot: *Notes Towards the Definition of Culture*. Graham Greene: *The Heart of the Matter*. Faulkner: *Intruder in the Dust*. Henry Green: *Nothing*. Acton: *Memoirs of an Aesthete*.
1949	Returns from America (March). 'Compassion' published.	Orwell: *Nineteen Eighty-Four*. De Beauvoir: *The Second Sex*. Graham Greene: *The Third Man*. Mitford: *Love in a Cold Climate*. Miller: *Death of a Salesman*.
1950	Birth of son, Septimus Waugh (July). *Helena* published. Last visit to America.	Hemingway: *Across the River and into the Trees*. Eliot: *The Cocktail Party*. Henry Green: *Doting*.
1951	Middle East tour for *Life Magazine* (January–March). Writes *Men at Arms* (June–December).	Salinger: *The Catcher in the Rye*. Powell: *A Question of Upbringing* (the first of the 12 novels comprising *A Dance to the Music of Time* (1952–75). Mitford: *The Blessing*.
1952	Writes *The Holy Places* and 'Love Among the Ruins'. *Men at Arms* published (September). Christmas in Goa.	Beckett: *Waiting for Godot*. Miller: *The Crucible*.
1953	Begins *Officers and Gentlemen* (March).	Hartley: *The Go-Between*.
1954	Voyage to Ceylon and mental breakdown (February). Contributes to "U" and "non U" debate. Death of his mother (December).	
1955	*Officers and Gentlemen* published (May). Trip to Jamaica, writing *The Ordeal of Gilbert Pinfold* (from December).	Nabokov: *Lolita*. Miller: *A View from the Bridge*. Graham Greene: *Loser Takes All*, *The Quiet American*. Murdoch: *Under the Net*.
1956	Moves to Combe Florey, Taunton, Somerset.	Beckett: *Molloy*. Camus: *La Chute*. Faulkner: *Requiem for a Nun*. Mitford, Waugh, Betjeman et al: *Noblesse Oblige*.

CHRONOLOGY

HISTORICAL EVENTS

Marshall Aid: US contributes $5.3 billion for European recovery. Soviet blockade of West Berlin: Allied airlifts begin (to 1949). State of Israel founded. Apartheid introduced in South Africa. Yugoslavia under Tito expelled from Comintern. National Health Service inaugurated in Britain.

Federal and Democratic Republics established in Germany. People's Republic of China proclaimed. Korean war begins (to 1953). NATO founded.

McCarthy witch hunts – persecution of Communists throughout US.

Conservatives return to power in Britain. Burgess and Maclean defect to USSR.

Death of George VI: accession of Elizabeth II.

Stalin dies and is succeeded by Khrushchev.

Vietnam war begins. Nasser gains power in Egypt.

West Germany joins NATO.

Suez crisis. Invasion of Hungary by USSR.

DATE	AUTHOR'S LIFE	LITERARY CONTEXT
1957	*Pinfold* completed (January) and published (July). First plans for *Unconditional Surrender* (July).	Camus: *L'Exil et le Royaume*. Pasternak: *Doctor Zhivago*. Pinter: *The Birthday Party*. Nabokov: *Pnin*. Spark: *The Comforters*.
1958	Travels to Rhodesia (February–March), collecting material for—	Betjeman: *Collected Poems*.
1959	*The Life of the Right Reverend Ronald Knox* published (October).	Spark: *Memento Mori*. Eliot: *The Elder Statesman*. Graham Greene: *The Complaisant Lover*. Beckett: *Endgame*.
1960	*A Tourist in Africa* published.	Spark: *The Ballad of Peckham Rye*. Updike: *Rabbit, Run*. Pinter: *The Caretaker*. Betjeman: *Summoned by Bells*.
1961	*Unconditional Surrender* published (September). Trip to West Indies with his daughter Margaret (November–February).	Graham Greene: *A Burnt-Out Case*. Albee: *The American Dream*. Huxley: *Religion without Revelation*. Mitford: *Don't Tell Alfred*. Spark: *The Prime of Miss Jean Brodie*.
1962	Working on *A Little Learning*. Begins 'Basil Seal Rides Again' (August).	Albee: *Who's Afraid of Virginia Woolf?* Isherwood: *Down There on a Visit*.
1963	Publication of 'Basil Seal Rides Again'.	Stoppard: *A Walk on Water*. Pinter: *The Lover*. Spark: *The Girls of Slender Means*.
1964	Serial publication of *A Little Learning* (June–July).	Sartre: *Les Mots*. Ayme: *The Minotaur*. Isherwood: *A Single Man*.
1965	War trilogy revised and published as *Sword of Honour* (September).	Pinter: *The Homecoming*. Albee: *Tiny Alice*.
1966	Evelyn Waugh dies on Easter Sunday, 10 April, at Combe Florey.	Albee: *A Delicate Balance*.

CHRONOLOGY

BLACK MISCHIEF

WITH NINE DRAWINGS BY THE AUTHOR

H.I.M. Seth of Azania
from the painting by a native artist

Preface

BLACK MISCHIEF WAS written after a winter spent in East and Central Africa, an account of which appeared in *Remote People* and now survives, abridged, in *When the Going was Good.*

The scene of the novel was a fanciful confusion of many territories. It was natural for people to suppose that it derived from Abyssinia, at that time the sole independent native monarchy. There are certain resemblances between Debra Dowa and the Addis Ababa of 1930. There was never the smallest resemblance between Seth and the Emperor Haile Selassie. The Arabs of Matodi never existed on the Ethiopian coast. Their model, so far as they had one, was in Zanzibar.

Thirty years ago it seemed an anachronism that any part of Africa should be independent of European administration. History has not followed what then seemed its natural course.

E. W.

Combe Florey 1962

With love to Mary and Dorothy Lygon

CHAPTER 1

'*WE, SETH, EMPEROR of Azania, Chief of the Chiefs of Sakuyu, Lord of Wanda and Tyrant of the Seas, Bachelor of the Arts of Oxford University, being in this the twenty-fourth year of our life, summoned by the wisdom of Almighty God and the unanimous voice of our people to the throne of our ancestors, do hereby proclaim...*' Seth paused in his dictation and gazed out across the harbour where in the fresh breeze of early morning the last dhow was setting sail for the open sea. 'Rats,' he said; 'stinking curs. They are all running away.'

The Indian secretary sat attentive, his fountain pen poised over the pad of writing paper, his eyes blinking gravely behind rimless pince-nez.

'Is there still no news from the hills?'

'None of unquestionable veracity, your majesty.'

'I gave orders that the wireless was to be mended. Where is Marx? I told him to see to it.'

'He evacuated the town late yesterday evening.'

'He evacuated the town?'

'In your majesty's motor-boat. There was a large company of them – the stationmaster, the chief of police, the Armenian Archbishop, the Editor of the *Azanian Courier*, the American vice-consul. All the most distinguished gentlemen in Matodi.'

'I wonder you weren't with them yourself, Ali.'

'There was not room. I supposed that with so many distinguished gentlemen there was danger of submersion.'

'Your loyalty shall be rewarded. Where had I got to?'

'The last eight words in reproof of the fugitives were an interpolation?'

'Yes, yes, of course.'

5

'I will make the erasure. Your majesty's last words were "*do hereby proclaim*".'

'*Do hereby proclaim amnesty and free pardon to all those of our subjects recently seduced from their loyalty, who shall during the eight days subsequent to this date return to their lawful allegiance. Furthermore . . .*'

*

They were in the upper story of the old fort at Matodi. Here, three hundred years before, a Portuguese garrison had withstood eight months' siege from the Omani Arabs; at this window they had watched for the sails of the relieving fleet, which came ten days too late.

Over the main door traces of an effaced escutcheon were still discernible, an idolatrous work repugnant to the prejudice of the conquerors.

For two centuries the Arabs remained masters of the coast. Behind them in the hills the native Sakuyu, black, naked, anthropophagous, had lived their own tribal life among their herds – emaciated, puny cattle with rickety shanks and elaborately branded hide. Farther away still lay the territory of the Wanda – Galla immigrants from the mainland who, long before the coming of the Arabs, had settled in the north of the island and cultivated it in irregular communal holdings. The Arabs held aloof from the affairs of both these people; war drums could often be heard inland and sometimes the whole hillside would be aflame with burning villages. On the coast a prosperous town arose: great houses of Arab merchants with intricate latticed windows and brass-studded doors, courtyards planted with dense mango trees, streets heavy with the reek of cloves and pineapple, so narrow that two mules could not pass without altercation between their drivers; a bazaar where the money changers, squatting over their scales, weighed out the coinage of a world-wide trade, Austrian thalers, rough stamped Mahratta gold, Spanish and Portuguese guineas. From Matodi the dhows sailed to the mainland, to Tanga, Dar-es-Salaam, Malindi and Kismayu, to meet the caravans coming down from the great lakes with ivory and slaves. Splendidly dressed Arab gentlemen paraded the water-front hand in hand and gossiped in the coffee houses. In early spring when the monsoon was blowing from the north-east, fleets came down from the Persian Gulf bringing to market a people of fairer skin who spoke a pure Arabic barely intelligible to the islanders, for with the passage of years their language had become full of alien words – Bantu from the mainland, Sakuyu and Galla from the interior – and the slave markets had infused a richer and darker strain into their Semitic blood; instincts of swamp and forest mingled with the austere tradition of the desert.

In one of these Muscat trading fleets came Seth's grandfather, Amurath, a man wholly unlike his companions, a slave's son, sturdy, bow-legged, three-quarters Negro. He had received education of a kind from Nestorian monks near Basra. At Matodi he sold his dhow and entered the Sultan's service.

It was a critical time in local history. The white men were returning. From Bombay they had fastened on Aden. They were in Zanzibar and the Sudan. They were pushing up round the Cape and down through the Canal. Their warships were cruising the Red Sea and the Indian Ocean intercepting slavers; the caravans from Tabora were finding difficulty in getting through to the coast. Trade in Matodi was almost at a standstill and a new listlessness became apparent in the leisured life of the merchants; they spent their days in the town moodily chewing khat. They could no longer afford to keep up their villas round the bay. Gardens ran wild and roofs fell into disrepair. The grass huts of the Sakuyu began to appear on the more remote estates. Groups of Wanda and Sakuyu came into town and swaggered insolently about the bazaars; an Arab party returning from one of the country villas was ambushed and murdered within a mile of the walls. There were rumours of a general massacre, planned in the hills. The European powers watched their opportunity to proclaim a Protectorate.

In this uncertain decade there suddenly appeared the figure of Amurath; first as commander-in-chief of the Sultan's forces, then as general of an independent army; finally as Emperor Amurath the Great. He armed the Wanda and at their head inflicted defeat after defeat on the Sakuyu, driving off their cattle, devastating their villages and hunting them down in the remote valleys of the island. Then he turned his conquering army against his old allies on the coast. In three years he proclaimed the island a single territory and himself its ruler. He changed its name. Until now it had been scored on the maps as Sakuyu Island; Amurath renamed it the Empire of Azania. He founded a new capital at Debra Dowa, two hundred miles inland on the borders of the Wanda and Sakuyu territories. It was the site of his last camp, a small village, partially burnt out. There was no road to the coast, only a faltering bush path which an experienced scout could follow. Here he set up his standard.

Presently there was a railway from Matodi to Debra Dowa. Three European companies held the concession in turn and failed; at the side of the line were the graves of two French engineers who went down with blackwater, and of numerous Indian coolies. The Sakuyu would wrench up the steel sleepers to forge spear heads and pull down lengths of copper telegraph wire to adorn their women. Lions came into the labour lines at night and carried off workmen; there were mosquitoes, snakes, tsetse fly, spirillum ticks; there were deep water courses to be bridged which for a few days in the year bore a great torrent down from the hills, bundling with it timber and boulders and an occasional corpse; there was a lava field to be crossed, a great waste of pumice five miles broad; in the hot season the metal blistered the hands of workmen; during the rains landslides and washouts would obliterate the work of months. Reluctantly, step by step, barbarism retreated; the seeds of progress took root and, after years of slow growth, burst finally into flower in the single, narrow-gauge track of the Grand Chemin de Fer Impérial d'Azanie. In the sixteenth year of his reign Amurath travelled in the first train from Matodi to Debra Dowa. With him sat delegates from France, Great Britain, Italy and the United States, his daughter and heir, her husband, while, in a cattle truck behind, rode a dozen or so illegitimate children; in another coach sat the hierarchies of the various Churches of Azania; in another the Arab sheiks from the coast, the paramount chief of the Wanda, and a shrivelled, scared old Negro, with one eye, who represented the Sakuyu. The train was decked with bunting, feathers and flowers; it whistled continuously from coast to capital; levies of irregular troops lined the way; a Jewish nihilist from Berlin threw a bomb which failed to explode; sparks from the engine started several serious bush fires; at Debra Dowa Amurath received the congratulations of the civilized world and created the French contractor a Marquess in the Azanian peerage.

The first few trains caused numerous deaths among the inhabitants, who for some time did not appreciate the speed or strength of this new thing that had come to their country. Presently they became more cautious and the service less frequent. Amurath had drawn up an elaborate time-table of express trains, local trains, goods trains, boat trains, schemes for cheap return tickets and excursions; he had printed a map showing the future developments of the line in a close mesh all over the island. But the railway was the last great achievement of his life; soon after its opening he lapsed into a coma from which he never recovered consciousness; he had a wide reputation for immortality; it was three years before his ministers, in response to insistent rumours, ventured to announce his death to the people. In the succeeding years the Grand Chemin de Fer Impérial d'Azanie failed to develop on the lines adumbrated by its founder. When Seth came down from Oxford there was a weekly service; a goods train at the back of which was hitched a single shabby saloon car, upholstered in threadbare plush. It took two days to accomplish the journey, resting the night at Lumo, where a Greek hotel proprietor had proposed a contract profitable to the president of the line; the delay was officially attributed to the erratic efficacy of the engine lights and the persistence of the Sakuyu in their depredations of the permanent way.

Amurath instituted other changes, less sensational than the railway, but nevertheless noteworthy. He proclaimed the abolition of slavery and was warmly applauded in the European Press; the law was posted up prominently in the capital in English, French and Italian where every foreigner might read it; it was never promulgated in the provinces nor translated into any of the native languages; the ancient system continued unhampered but European intervention had been anticipated. His Nestorian upbringing had strengthened his hand throughout in his dealings with the white men. Now he declared Christianity the official religion of the Empire, reserving complete freedom of conscience to his Mohammedan and pagan subjects. He allowed and encouraged an influx of

missionaries. There were soon three Bishops in Debra Dowa –
Anglican, Catholic and Nestorian – and three substantial cath-
edrals. There were also Quaker, Moravian, American-Baptist,
Mormon and Swedish-Lutheran missions handsomely supported
by foreign subscribers. All this brought money into the new capital
and enhanced his reputation abroad. But his chief safeguard against
European intrusion was a force of ten thousand soldiers, maintained
under arms. These he had trained by Prussian officers. Their brass
bands, goosestep and elaborate uniforms were at first the object
of mild amusement. Then there was an international incident.
A foreign commercial agent was knifed in a disorderly house on
the coast. Amurath hanged the culprits publicly in the square before
the Anglican Cathedral – and with them two or three witnesses
whose evidence was held to be unsatisfactory – but there was a talk
of indemnities. A punitive force was landed, composed half of
European, half of mainland native troops. Amurath marched out
against them with his new army and drove them in hopeless rout to
the seashore where they were massacred under the guns of their own
fleet. Six European officers of field rank surrendered and were
hanged on the battlefield. On his triumphal return to the capital
Amurath offered the White Fathers a silver altar to Our Lady of
Victories.

Throughout the highlands his prestige became super-human.
'I swear by Amurath' was a bond of inviolable sanctity. Only the
Arabs remained unimpressed. He ennobled them, creating the
heads of the chief families Earls, Viscounts and Marquesses, but
these grave, impoverished men whose genealogies extended to the
time of the Prophet preferred their original names. He married his
daughter into the house of the old Sultan – but the young man
accepted the elevation and his compulsory baptism into the
National Church without enthusiasm. The marriage was considered
a great disgrace by the Arabs. Their fathers would not have ridden
a horse with so obscure a pedigree. Indians came in great numbers
and slowly absorbed the business of the country. The large houses of
Matodi were turned into tenements, hotels or offices. Soon the maze
of mean streets behind the bazaar became designated as the 'Arab
quarter'.

Very few of them migrated to the new capital, which was spreading out round the palace in a haphazard jumble of shops, missions, barracks, legations, bungalows and native huts. The palace itself, which occupied many acres enclosed by an irregular fortified stockade, was far from orderly or harmonious. Its nucleus was a large stucco villa of French design; all round this were scattered sheds of various sizes which served as kitchens, servants' quarters and stables; there was a wooden guard-house and a great thatched barn which was used for state banquets; a domed, octagonal chapel and the large rubble and timber residence of the Princess and her consort. The ground between and about the buildings was uneven and untidy; stacks of fuel, kitchen refuse, derelict carriages, cannon and ammunition lay in prominent places; sometimes there would be a flyblown carcase of a donkey or camel, and after the rains pools of stagnant water; gangs of prisoners, chained neck to neck, could often be seen shovelling as though some project were on hand of levelling or draining, but except for the planting of a circle of eucalyptus trees, nothing was done in the old Emperor's time to dignify his surroundings.

Many of Amurath's soldiers settled round him in the new capital; in the first few years they were reinforced by a trickle of detribalized natives, drawn from their traditional grounds by the glamour of city life; the main population, however, was always cosmopolitan, and as the country's reputation as a land of opportunity spread through the less successful classes of the outside world Debra Dowa gradually lost all evidence of national character. Indians and Armenians came first and continued to come in yearly increasing numbers. Goans, Jews and Greeks followed, and later a race of partially respectable immigrants from the greater powers, mining engineers, prospectors, planters and contractors, on their world-wide pilgrimage in quest of cheap concessions. A few were lucky and got out of the country with modest fortunes; most were disappointed and became permanent residents, hanging round the bars and bemoaning over their cups the futility of expecting justice in a land run by a pack of niggers.

When Amurath died, and the courtiers at last could devise no further explanation of his prolonged seclusion, his daughter reigned as Empress. The funeral was a great occasion in East African history.

A Nestorian patriarch came from Iraq to say the Mass; delegates from the European powers rode in the procession and as the bugles of the Imperial guard sounded the last post over the empty sarcophagus, vast crowds of Wanda and Sakuyu burst into wailing and lamentation, daubed their bodies with chalk and charcoal, stamped their feet, swayed and clapped in frantic, personal grief at the loss of their master.

Now the Empress was dead and Seth had returned from Europe to claim his Empire.

*

Noon in Matodi. The harbour lay still as a photograph, empty save for a few fishing boats moored motionless against the sea wall. No breeze stirred the royal standard that hung over the old fort. No traffic moved on the water-front. The offices were locked and shuttered. The tables had been cleared from the hotel terrace. In the shade of a mango the two sentries lay curled asleep, their rifles in the dust beside them.

'*From Seth, Emperor of Azania, Chief of the Chiefs of Sakuyu, Lord of Wanda and Tyrant of the Seas, Bachelor of the Arts of Oxford University, to His Majesty of the King of England, Greeting. May this reach you. Peace be to your house . . .*'

He had been dictating since dawn. Letters of greeting, Patents of Nobility, Pardons, Decrees of Attainder, Army Ordinances, police regulations, orders to European firms for motor-cars, uniforms, furniture, electric plant, invitations to the Coronation, proclamations of a public holiday in honour of his victory, lay neatly clipped together on the secretary's table.

'Still no news from the hills. We should have heard of the victory by now.' The secretary recorded these words, considered them with his head cocked slightly to one side and then drew a line through them. 'We should have heard, shouldn't we, Ali?'

'We should have heard.'

'What has happened? Why don't you answer me? Why have we heard nothing?'

'Who am I? I know nothing. I only hear what the ignorant people are saying in the bazaar, since the public men evacuated the city.

The ignorant people say that your majesty's army has not gained the victory you predict.'

'Fools, what do they know? What can they understand? I am Seth, grandson of Amurath. Defeat is impossible. I have been to Europe. I know. We have the Tank. This is not a war of Seth against Seyid but of Progress against Barbarism. And Progress must prevail. I have seen the great tattoo of Aldershot, the Paris Exhibition, the Oxford Union. I have read modern books – Shaw, Arlen, Priestley. What do the gossips in the bazaars know of all this? The whole might of Evolution rides behind him; at my stirrups run woman's suffrage, vaccination and vivisection. I am the New Age. I am the Future.'

'I know nothing of these things,' said Ali. 'But the ignorant men in the bazaars say that your majesty's guards have joined Prince Seyid. You will remember my pointing out that they had received no wages for several months?'

'They shall be paid. I have said it. As soon as the war is over they shall be paid. Besides I raised them in rank. Every man in the brigade is now a full corporal. I issued the edict myself. Ungrateful curs. Old-fashioned fools. Soon we will have no more soldiers. Tanks and aeroplanes. That is modern. I have seen it. That reminds me. Have you sent off instructions for the medals?'

Ali turned over the file of correspondence.

'Your majesty has ordered five hundred Grand Cross of Azania, first class; five hundred second; and seven hundred third; also designs for the Star of Seth, silver gilt and enamel with parti-coloured ribbon...'

'No, no. I mean the Victory Medal.'

'I have received no instructions concerning the Victory Medal.'

'Then take this down.'

'The invitation to the King of England?'

'The King of England can wait. Take down the instructions for the Victory Medal. Obverse, the head of Seth – that is to be copied from the photograph taken in Oxford. You understand – it is to be modern, European – top hat, spectacles, evening dress collar and tie. Inscription SETH IMPERATOR IMMORTALIS. The whole to be simple and in good taste. Many of my grandfather's medals were florid. Reverse. The figure of Progress. She holds in one hand an aeroplane, in the other some small object symbolic of improved education. I will give you the detail of that later. The idea will come to me . . . a telephone might do . . . I will see. Meanwhile begin the letter:

'*From Seth, Emperor of Azania, Chief of the Chiefs of Sakuyu, Lord of Wanda and Tyrant of the Seas, Bachelor of the Arts of Oxford University, to Messrs Mappin and Webb of London, Greeting. May this reach you. Peace be to your house . . .*'

*

Evening and a small stir of life. Muezzin in the minaret. Allah is great. There is no Allah but Allah and Mohammed is his prophet. Angelus from the mission church. *Ecce ancilla Domini: fiat mihi secundum verbum tuum.* Mr Youkoumian behind the bar of the Amurath Café and Universal Stores mixed himself a sundowner of mastika and water.

'What I want to know is do I get paid for the petrol?'

'You know I am doing all I can for you, Mr Youkoumian. I'm your friend. You know that. But the Emperor's busy today. I've only just got off. Been on all day. I'll try and get your money for you.'

'I've done a lot for you, Ali.'

'I know you have, Mr Youkoumian, and I hope I am not ungrateful. If I could get you your money just by asking for it you should have it this evening.'

'But I must have it this evening. I'm going.'

'Going?'

'I've made my arrangements. Well, I don't mind telling you, Ali, since you're a friend.' Mr Youkoumian glanced furtively round the empty bar – they were speaking in Sakuyu – 'I've got a launch beached outside the harbour, behind the trees near the old sugar mill in the bay. What's more, there's room in it for another passenger. I wouldn't tell this to anyone but you. Matodi's not going to be a healthy place for the next week or two. Seth's beaten. We know that. I'm going to my brother on the mainland. Only I want my money for the petrol before I go.'

'Yes, Mr Youkoumian, I appreciate your offer. But you know it's very difficult. You can hardly expect the Emperor to pay for having his own motor-boat stolen.'

'I don't know anything about that. All I know is that yesterday evening Mr Marx came into my store and said he wanted the Emperor's motor-boat filled up with petrol. Eighty rupees' worth. I've served Mr Marx with petrol before for the Emperor. How was I to know he wanted to steal the Emperor's motor-boat? Should I have given it to him if I did?'

Mr Youkoumian spread his hands in the traditional gesture of his race. 'I am a poor man. Is it right that I should suffer in this way? Is it fair? Now, Ali, I know you. You're a just man. I've done a lot for you in the past. Get me my eighty rupees and I will take you to stay with my brother in Malindi. Then when the troubles are over, we can come back or stay or go somewhere else, just as we like. You don't want your throat cut by the Arabs. I'll look after you.'

'Well, I appreciate your offer, Mr Youkoumian, and I'll do what I can. I can't say more than that.'

'I know you, Ali. I trust you as I'd trust my own father. Not a word to anyone about the launch, eh?'

'Not a word, Mr Youkoumian, and I'll see you later this evening.'

'That's a good fellow. Au revoir and remember, not a word to anyone about the launch.'

When Ali had left the Amurath Café, Youkoumian's wife emerged from the curtain behind which she had been listening to the conversation.

'What's all this you've been arranging? We can't take that Indian to Malindi.'

'I want my eighty rupees. My dear, you must leave these business matters to me.'

'But there isn't room for anyone else in the launch. We're overloaded already. You know that.'

'I know that.'

'Are you mad, Krikor? Do you want to drown us all?'

'You must leave these things to me, my flower. There is no need to worry. Ali is not coming with us. All I want is my eighty rupees for

Mr Marx's petrol. Have you finished your packing? We start as soon
as Ali returns with the money.'

'Krikor, you wouldn't . . . you aren't going to leave me behind,
are you?'

'I should not hesitate to do so if I thought it necessary. Finish your
packing, girl. Don't cry. Finish your packing. You are coming to
Malindi. I have said it. Finish your packing. I am a just man and
a peaceful man. You know that. But in time of war one must look
after oneself and one's own family. Yes, one's family, do you hear
me? Ali will bring us the money. We shall not take him to Malindi.
Do you understand? If he is a trouble I shall hit him with my stick.
Don't stand there like a fool. Finish your packing.'

The sun had now set. As Ali walked back to the fort through
the dark lane he was aware of new excitement in the people around
him. Groups were hurrying to the water-front, others stood in their
doorways chattering eagerly. He heard the words 'Seyid', 'Victory'
and 'Army'. In the open space before the harbour he found
a large crowd collected with their backs to the water, gazing inland
over the town. He joined them and in the brief twilight saw
the whole dark face of the hills alight with little points of fire. Then
he left the crowd and went to the old fort. Major Joab, the officer
of the guard, stood in the court studying the hills through
field-glasses.

'You have seen the fires inland, secretary?'

'I have seen them.'

'I think there is an army encamped there.'

'It is the victorious army, major.'

'Praise God. It is what we have waited to see.'

'Certainly. We should praise God whether in prosperity or adver-
sity,' said Ali, piously; he had accepted Christianity on entering
Seth's service. 'But I bring orders from the Emperor. You are to
take a picket and go with them to the Amurath Bar. There you will
find the Armenian Youkoumian, a little fat man wearing a black
skull cap. You know him? Very well. He is to be put under arrest and
taken a little outside the town. It does not matter where, but take him
some distance from the people. There you are to hang him. Those
are the Emperor's orders. When it is done, report to me personally.

There is no need to mention the matter directly to His Majesty. You understand?'

'I understand, secretary.'

Upstairs, Seth was deep in a catalogue of wireless apparatus.

'Oh, Ali, I have decided on the Tudor model in fumed oak. Remind me tomorrow to write for it. Is there still no news?'

Ali busied himself in arranging the papers on the table and fitting the typewriter into its case.

'Is there no news?'

'There is news of a kind, Majesty. I opine that there is an army bivouacked in the hills. Their fires are visible. If your majesty will come outside, you will see them. No doubt they will march into the city tomorrow.'

Seth sprang gaily from his chair and ran to the window.

'But this is magnificent news. The best you could have brought. Ali, I will make you a Viscount tomorrow. The army back again. It is what we have been longing for the last six weeks, eh, Viscount?'

'Your majesty is very kind. I said *an* army. There is no means of knowing which one it may be. If, as you surmise, it is General Connolly, is it not curious that no runner has come to salute your majesty with news of the victory?'

'Yes, he should have sent word.'

'Majesty, you are defeated and betrayed. Everyone in Matodi knows it except yourself.'

For the first time since the beginning of the campaign, Ali saw that there was uncertainty in his master's mind. 'If I am defeated,' said Seth, 'the barbarians will know where to find me.'

'Majesty, it is not too late to escape. Only this evening I heard of a man in the town who has a launch hidden outside the harbour. He means to leave in it himself, for the mainland, but he would sell it at a price. There are ways for a small man to escape where a great man like your majesty would be trapped. For two thousand rupees he will sell this boat. He told me so, in so many words. He named the price. It is not much for the life of an Emperor. Give me the money, Majesty, and the boat shall be here before midnight. And in the morning Seyid's troops will march into the town and find it empty.'

Ali looked hopefully across the table, but before he had finished speaking he realized that Seth's mood of uncertainty was past.

'Seyid's troops will not march into the town. You forget that I have the Tank. Ali, you are talking treasonable nonsense. Tomorrow I shall be here to receive my victorious general.'

'Tomorrow will show, Majesty.'

'Tomorrow will show.'

'Listen,' said Ali, 'my friend is very loyal to your majesty and a most devoted man. Perhaps if I were to use my influence he might reduce his price.'

'I shall be here in the morning to receive my army.'

'Suppose he would accept eighteen hundred rupees?'

'I have spoken.'

Without further discussion Ali picked up his typewriter and left the room. As he opened the doors his ears caught the inevitable shuffle of bare feet, as a spy slipped away down the dark passage. It was a sound to which they had grown accustomed during the past months.

In his own quarters Ali poured out a glass of whisky and lit a cheroot. Then he drew out a fibre trunk from beneath the bed and began a methodical arrangement of his possessions preparatory to packing them. Presently there was a knock at the door and Major Joab came in.

'Good evening, secretary.'

'Good evening, major. The Armenian is dead?'

'He is dead. Heavens, how he squealed. You have whisky there.'

'Will you help yourself?'

'Thank you, secretary . . . you seem to be preparing for a journey.'

'It is well to be prepared – to have one's things in good order.'

'I think there is an army in the hills.'

'It is what they are saying.'

'I think it is the army of Seyid.'

'That, too, is being said.'

'As you say, secretary, it is well to be prepared.'

'Will you take a cheroot, major? I expect that there are many people in Matodi who would be glad to leave. The army will be here tomorrow.'

'It is not far away. And yet there is no way of leaving the town. The boats are all gone. The railway is broken. The road leads straight to the encampment.'

Ali folded a white drill suit and bent over the trunk, carefully arranging the sleeves. He did not look up as he said: 'I heard of a man who had a boat. It was spoken of in the bazaar, I forget by whom. An ignorant fellow no doubt. But this man, whoever it was, spoke of a boat concealed outside the harbour. He was going to the mainland tonight. There was room for two others, so they said. Do you think a man would find passengers to the mainland at five hundred rupees each? That is what he asked.'

'It is a great price for a journey to the mainland.'

'It is not much for a man's life. Do you think such a man, supposing there is any truth in the tale, would find passengers?'

'Perhaps. Who can tell? A man of affairs who can take his wisdom with him – a foreigner with no stock but a typewriter and his clothes. I do not think a soldier would go.'

'A soldier might pay three hundred?'

'It is not likely. What life would there be for him in a foreign country? And among his own people he would be dishonoured.'

'But he would not hinder others from going. A man who would pay five hundred rupees for his passage money, would not grudge another hundred to the guard who allowed him to pass?'

'Who can say? Some soldiers might hold that a small price for their honour.'

'But two hundred.'

'I think soldiers are for the most part poor men. It is seldom they earn two hundred rupees . . . Well, I must bid you good night, secretary. I must return to my men.'

'How late do you stay on guard, major?'

'Till after midnight. Perhaps I shall see you again.'

'Who can say? . . . Oh, major, you have forgotten your papers.'

'So I have. Thank you, secretary. And good night.'

The major counted the little pile of notes which Ali had placed on the dressing-table. Two hundred exactly. He buttoned them into his tunic pocket and returned to the guard-house.

Here, in the inner room, sat Mr Youkoumian talking to the captain. Half an hour before the little Armenian had been very near death, and awe of the experience still overcast his normally open and loquacious manner. It was not until the rope was actually round his neck that he had been inspired to mention the existence of his launch. His face was damp and his voice jerky and subdued.

'What did the Indian dog say?'

'He wanted to sell me a place in the boat for five hundred rupees. Does he know where it is hidden?'

'Fool that I was, I told him.'

'It is of little consequence. He gave me two hundred rupees to let him past the guard, also some whisky and a cheroot. There is no need for us to worry about Ali. When do we start?'

'There is one point, officers . . . my wife. There is not room for her in the boat. She must not know of our departure. Where was she when you – when we left the café together?'

'She was making a noise. One of the corporals locked her in the loft.'

'She will get out of there.'

'You leave all that to us.'

'Very well, major. I am a just man and a peaceable man. You know that. I only want to be sure that everything will be agreeable for everyone.'

Ali finished his packing and sat down to wait. 'What's Major Joab up to?' he wondered. 'It is curious his refusing to leave the town. I suppose he thinks he will get a price for Seth in the morning.'

*

Night and the fear of darkness. In his room at the top of the old fort Seth lay awake and alone, his eyes wild with the inherited terror of the jungle, desperate with the acquired loneliness of civilization. Night was alive with beasts and devils and the spirits of dead enemies; before its power Seth's ancestors had receded, slid away from its attack, abandoning in retreat all the baggage of Individuality; they had lain six or seven in a hut; between them and night only a wall of mud and a ceiling of thatched grass; warm, naked bodies breathing in the darkness an arm's reach apart, indivisibly unified so that they ceased to be six or seven scared blacks and became one person of more than human stature, less vulnerable to the peril that walked near them. Seth could not expand to meet the onset of fear. He was alone, dwarfed by the magnitude of the darkness, insulated from his fellows, strapped down to mean dimensions.

The darkness pulsed with the drumming of the unknown conquerors. In the narrow streets of the city the people were awake – active and apprehensive. Dark figures sped to and fro on furtive errands, hiding from each other in doorways till the way was empty. In the houses they were packing away bundles in secret places, little hoards of coins and jewellery, pictures and books, ancestral sword hilts of fine workmanship, shoddy trinkets from Birmingham and Bombay, silk shawls, scent bottles, anything that might attract attention next morning when the city was given over to loot. Huddled groups of women and children were being herded to refuge in the cellars of the old houses or into the open country beyond the walls; goats, sheep, donkeys, livestock and poultry of all kinds jostled with them for precedence in the city gates. Mme Youkoumian, trussed like a chicken on the floor of her own bedroom, dribbled through her gag and helplessly writhed her bruised limbs.

Ali, marching back to the fort under arrest between two soldiers, protested angrily to the captain of the guard.

'You are making a great mistake, captain. I have made all arrangements with the major for my departure.'

'It is the Emperor's orders that no one leaves the city.'

'When we see the major he will explain everything.'

The captain made no reply. The little party marched on; in front between two other soldiers shambled Ali's servant, bearing his master's trunk on his head.

When they reached the guard-room, the captain reported. 'Two prisoners, major, arrested at the South Gate attempting to leave the city.'

'You know me, major; the captain has made a mistake. Tell him it is all right for me to go.'

'I know you, secretary; captain, report the arrests to His Majesty.'

'But, major, only this evening I gave you two hundred rupees. Do you hear, captain, I gave him two hundred rupees. You can't treat me like this. I shall tell His Majesty everything.'

'We had better search his luggage.'

The trunk was opened and the contents spread over the floor. The two officers turned them over with interest and appropriated the few articles of value it contained. The minor possessions were tossed to the corporals. At the bottom, wrapped in a grubby night-shirt, were two heavy objects which, on investigation, proved to be the massive gold crown of the Azanian Empire and an elegant ivory sceptre presented to Amurath by the President of the French Republic. Major Joab and the captain considered this discovery for some time in silence. Then the major answered the question that was in both their minds. 'No,' he said, 'I think we had better show these to Seth.'

'Both of them?'

'Well, at any rate, the sceptre. It would not be so easy to dispose of. Two hundred rupees,' said the major bitterly, turning on Ali, 'two hundred rupees and you proposed to walk off with the Imperial regalia.'

From the inner room Mr Youkoumian listened to this conversation in a mood of sublime contentment; the sergeant had given him a cigarette out of a box lifted from the shop at the time of his arrest; the captain had given him brandy – similarly acquired – of his own distillation; a fiery, comforting spirit. The terrors of the gallows were far behind him. And now Ali had been caught red-handed with the crown jewels. Nothing was required to complete Mr Youkoumian's happiness, except a calm sea for their crossing to the mainland; and the gentle night air gave promise that this, too, would be vouch-safed him.

It was only a matter of a few words for Major Joab to report the circumstances of Ali's arrest. The damning evidence of the sceptre and the soiled nightshirt was laid before Seth on the table. The prisoner stood between his captors without visible interest or emotion. When the charge had been made, Seth said, 'Well, Ali.'

Until now they had spoken in Sakuyu. Ali answered, as he always spoke to his master, in English. 'It is regrettable that this should have

happened. These ignorant men have greatly disturbed the preparations for your majesty's departure.'

'For *my* departure?'

'For whom else would I prepare a boat? What other reason could
I have for supervising the safe conduct of your majesty's sceptre, and
of the crown which the officers have omitted to bring from the
guard-room?'

'I don't believe you, Ali.'

'Your majesty wrongs himself. You are a distinguished man,
educated in Europe – not like these low soldiers. Would you have
trusted me had I been unworthy? Could I, a poor Indian, hope to
deceive a distinguished gentleman educated in Europe? Send these
low men out and I will explain everything to you.'

The officers of the guard had listened uneasily to these alien
sentences; now at Seth's command they withdrew their men. 'Shall
I make preparations for the execution, Majesty?'

'Yes ... no ... I will tell you when. Stand by for further orders
below, major.'

The two officers saluted and left the room. When they had gone
Ali sat down opposite his master and proceeded at his ease. There
was no accusation or reproach in the Emperor's countenance, no
justice or decision, trust or forgiveness; one emotion only was apparent in the dark young face before him, blank terror. Ali saw this
and knew that his case was won. 'Majesty, I will tell you why the
officers have arrested me. It is to prevent your escape. They are
plotting to sell you to the enemy. I know it. I have heard it all from
one of the corporals who is loyal to us. It was for this reason that
I prepared the boat. When all was ready I would have come to you,
told you of their treachery and brought you away safely.'

'But, Ali, you say they would hand me over to the enemy. Am
I then really beaten?'

'Majesty, all the world knows. The British General Connolly has
joined Prince Seyid. They are there on the hills together now.
Tomorrow they will be in Matodi.'

'But the Tank?'

'Majesty, Mr Marx, the distinguished mechanic who made the
tank, fled last night, as you well know.'

'Connolly too. Why should he betray me? I trusted him. Why does everyone betray me? Connolly was my friend.'

'Majesty, consider the distinguished general's position. What would he do? He might conquer Seyid and your majesty would reward him, or he might be defeated. If he joins Seyid, Seyid will reward him, and no one can defeat him. How would you expect a distinguished gentleman, educated in Europe, should choose?'

'They are all against me. All traitors. There is no one I can trust.'

'Except me, Majesty.'

'I do not trust you. You, least of all.'

'But you must trust me. Don't you understand? If you do not trust me there will be no one. You will be alone, quite alone.'

'I am alone. There is no one.'

'Then since all are traitors, trust a traitor. Trust me. You must trust me. Listen. It is not too late to escape. No one but I knows of the boat. The Armenian Youkoumian is dead. Do you understand, Majesty? Give the order to the guards to let me pass. I will go to where the boat is hidden. In an hour I will have it here, under the sea wall. Then when the guard is changed you will join me. Don't you understand? It is the only chance. You must trust me. Otherwise you will be alone.'

The Emperor stood up. 'I do not know if I can trust you. I do not think there is anyone I can trust. I am alone. But you shall go. Why should I hang you? What is one life more or less when all are traitors. Go in peace.'

'Your majesty's faithful servant.'

Seth opened the door; again the scamper of the retreating spy.

'Major.'

'Majesty.'

'Ali is to go free. He may leave the fort.'

'The execution is cancelled?'

'Ali may leave the fort.'

'As your majesty commands.' Major Joab saluted. As Ali left the lighted room he turned back and addressed the Emperor.

'Your majesty does well to trust me.'

'I trust no one . . . I am alone.'

The Emperor was alone. Faintly on the night air he heard the throbbing of drums from the encamped army. Quarter-past two. Darkness for nearly four hours more.

Suddenly the calm was splintered by a single, shrill cry – a jet of sound, spurting up from below, breaking in spray over the fort, then ceasing. Expressive of nothing, followed by nothing; no footsteps; no voices; silence and the distant beat of the tomtoms.

Seth ran to the door. 'Hullo! Who is there? What is that? Major! Officer of the guard!' No answer. Only the inevitable scuffle of the retreating spy. He went to the window. 'Who is there? What has happened? Is there no one on guard?'

A long silence.

Then a quiet voice from below. 'Majesty?'

'Who is that?'

'Major Joab of the Imperial Infantry at your majesty's service.'

'What was that?'

'Majesty?'

'What was that cry?'

'It was a mistake, your majesty. There is no cause for alarm.'

'What has happened?'

'The sentry made a mistake. That is all.'

'What has he done?'

'It is only the Indian, Majesty. The sentry did not understand his orders. I will see to it that he is punished.'

'What has happened to Ali? Is he hurt?'

'He is dead, your majesty. It is a mistake of the sentry's. I am sorry your majesty was disturbed.'

Presently Major Joab, the captain of the guard, and Mr Youkoumian, accompanied by three heavily burdened corporals, left the fort by a side door and made their way out of the town along the coast path towards the disused sugar mills.

And Seth was alone.

*

Another dawn. With slow feet Mr Youkoumian trudged into Matodi. There was no one about in the streets. All who could had left the city during the darkness; those who remained lurked behind barred doors and barricaded windows; from the cracks of shutters and through keyholes a few curious eyes observed the weary little figure dragging down the lane to the Amurath Café and Universal Stores.

Mme Youkoumian lay across the bedroom doorstep. During the night she had bitten through her gag and rolled some yards across the floor; that far her strength had taken her. Then, too exhausted to cry out or wrestle any further with the ropes that bound her, she had lapsed into intermittent coma, disturbed by nightmares, acute spasms of cramp and the scampering of rats on the earthen floor. In the green and silver light of dawn this bruised, swollen and dusty figure presented a spectacle radically repugnant to Mr Youkoumian's most sensitive feelings.

'Krikor, Krikor. Oh praise God you've come...I thought I should never see you again.... Blessed Mary and Joseph.... Where have you been?...What has happened to you?...Oh, Krikor, my own husband, praise God and his angels who have brought you back to me.'

Mr Youkoumian sat down heavily on the bed and pulled off his elastic-sided button boots. 'I'm tired,' he said. 'God, how tired I am. I could sleep for a week.' He took a bottle from the shelf and poured out a drink. 'I have had one of the most disagreeable nights of my life. First I am nearly hanged. Will you believe it? The noose was actually round my neck. Then I am made to walk out as far as the sugar mills, then the next thing I know I am alone, lying on the beach. My luggage is gone, my boat is gone, the damned soldiers are gone and I have a lump on the back of my head the size of an egg. Just you feel it.'

'I'm tied up, Krikor. Cut the string and let me help you. Oh, my poor husband.'

'How it aches. What a walk back. And my boat gone. I could have got fifteen hundred rupees for that boat yesterday. Oh my head. Fifteen hundred rupees. My feet ache too. I must go to bed.'

'Let me loose, Krikor, and I will attend to you, my poor husband.'

'No, it doesn't matter, my flower. I'll go to bed. I could sleep for a week.'

'Krikor, let me loose.'

'Don't worry. I shall be all right when I have had a sleep. Why, I ache all over.' He tossed off the drink and with a little grunt of relief drew his feet up on to the bed and rolled over with his face to the wall.

'Krikor, please . . . you must let me loose . . . don't you see? I've been like this all night. I'm in such pain . . .'

'You stay where you are. I can't attend to you now. You're always thinking of yourself. What about me? I'm tired. Don't you hear me?'

'But, Krikor —'

'Be quiet, you slut.'

And in less than a minute Mr Youkoumian found consolation for the diverse fortunes of the night in profound and prolonged sleep.

He was awakened some hours later by the entry into Matodi of the victorious army. Drums banging, pipes whistling, the soldiers of Progress and the New Age passed under his window. Mr Youkoumian rolled off the bed, rubbing his eyes, and peeped through the chink of the shutters.

'God save my soul,' he remarked. 'Seth's won after all.' Then with a chuckle, 'What a pair of fools Major Joab and the captain turn out to be.'

Mme Youkoumian looked up from the floor with piteous appeal in her dark eyes. He gave her a friendly little prod in the middle with his stockinged foot. 'Stay there, that's a good girl, and don't make a noise. I'll come and see to you in a minute or two.' Then he lay down on the bed, nuzzled into the bolster, and after a few preliminary grunts and wriggles, relapsed into slumber.

It was a remarkable procession. First in tattered, field grey uniforms came the brass band of the Imperial Guard, playing *John Brown's Body*.

> *Mine eyes have seen the glory of the coming of the Lord;*
> *He is trampling out the vintage where the grapes of wrath are stored;*
> *He has loosed the mighty lightning of his terrible swift sword;*
> *His truth is marching on.*

Behind them came the infantry; hard, bare feet rhythmically kicking up the dust, threadbare uniforms, puttees wound up anyhow, caps at all angles, Lee-Enfield rifles with fixed bayonets slung on their shoulders; fuzzy heads, jolly nigger-minstrel faces, black chests shining through buttonless tunics, pockets bulging with loot. Dividing these guardsmen from the irregular troops rode General Connolly on a tall, grey mule, with his staff officers beside him. He was a stocky Irishman in early middle age who had seen varied service in the Black and Tans, the South African Police and the Kenya Game Reserves before enlisting under the Emperor's colours. But on this morning his appearance was rather that of a lost explorer than a conquering commander-in-chief. He had a week's growth of reddish beard below his cavalry moustaches; irregular slashes had converted his breeches into shorts; open shirt and weather-worn white topee took the place of tunic and cap. Field-glasses, map case, sword and revolver holster hung incongruously round him. He was smoking a pipe of rank local tobacco.

On their heels came the hordes of Wanda and Sakuyu warriors. In the hills these had followed in a diffuse rabble. Little units of six or a dozen trotted round the stirrups of the headmen; before them they drove geese and goats pillaged from surrounding farms. Sometimes they squatted down to rest; sometimes they ran to catch up. The big chiefs had bands of their own – mounted drummers thumping great bowls of cowhide and wood, pipers blowing down six-foot chanters of bamboo. Here and there a camel swayed above the heads of the mob. They were armed with weapons of every kind: antiquated rifles, furnished with bandoliers of brass cartridges and empty cartridge cases; short hunting spears, swords and knives; the great, seven-foot broad-bladed spear of the Wanda; behind one chief a slave carried a machine-gun under a velvet veil; a few had short bows and iron-wood maces of immemorial design.

The Sakuyu wore their hair in a dense fuzz; their chests and arms were embossed with ornamental scars; the Wanda had their teeth filed into sharp points, their hair braided into dozens of mud-caked pigtails. In accordance with their unseemly usage, any who could wore strung round his neck the members of a slain enemy.

As this great host swept down on the city and surged through the gates, it broke into a dozen divergent streams, spurting and trickling on all sides like water from a rotten hose-pipe, forcing out jets of men, mounts and livestock into the by-ways and back streets, eddying down the blind alleys and into enclosed courts. Solitary musicians, separated from their bands, drummed and piped among the straggling crowds; groups split away from the mêlée and began dancing in the alleys; the doors of the liquor shops were broken in and a new and nastier element appeared in the carnival, as drink-crazed warriors began to re-enact their deeds of heroism, bloodily laying about their former comrades-in-arms with knives and clubs.

'God,' said Connolly, 'I shall be glad when I've got this menagerie off my hands. I wonder if his nibs has really bolted. Anything is possible in this abandoned country.'

No one appeared in the streets. Only rows of furtive eyes behind the shuttered windows watched the victors' slow progress through the city. In the main square the General halted the guards and such of the irregular troops as were still amenable to discipline; they squatted on the ground, chewing at bits of sugar cane, crunching nuts and polishing their teeth with little lengths of stick, while above the drone of confused revelling which rose from the side streets, Connolly from the saddle of his mule in classical form exhorted his legions.

'Guards,' he said loudly, 'Chiefs and tribesmen of the Azanian Empire. Hear me. You are good men. You have fought valiantly for your Emperor. The slaughter was very splendid. It is a thing for which your children and your children's children will hold you in honour. It was said in the camp that the Emperor had gone over the sea. I do not know if that is true. If he has, it is to prepare a reward for you in the great lands. But it is sufficient reward to a soldier to have slain his enemy.

'Guards, Chiefs and tribesmen of the Azanian Empire. The war is over. It is fitting that you should rest and rejoice. Two things only I charge you are forbidden. The white men, their houses, cattle, goods or women you must not take. Nor must you burn anything or any of the houses nor pour out the petrol in the streets. If any man do this he shall be killed. I have spoken. Long live the Emperor.

'Go on, you lucky bastards,' he added in English. 'Go and make whoopee. I must get a brush up and some food before I do anything else.'

He rode across to the Grand Azanian Hotel. It was shut and barred. His two servants forced the door and he went in. At the best of times, even when the fortnightly Messageries liner was in and gay European sightseers paraded every corner of the city, the Grand Azanian Hotel had a gloomy and unwelcoming air. On this morning a chill of utter desolation struck through General Connolly as he passed through its empty and darkened rooms. Every movable object had been stripped from walls and floor and stowed away subterraneously during the preceding night. But the single bath at least was a fixture. Connolly set his servants to work pumping water and unpacking his uniform cases. Eventually an hour later he emerged, profoundly low in spirits, but clean, shaved and very fairly dressed. Then he rode towards the fort where the Emperor's colours hung limp in the sultry air. No sign of life came from the houses; no welcome; no resistance. Marauding bands of his own people skulked from corner to corner; once a terrified Indian rocketed up from the gutter and shot across his path like a rabbit. It was not until he reached the White Fathers' mission that he heard news of the Emperor. Here he encountered a vast Canadian priest with white habit and sun-hat and spreading crimson beard, who was at that moment occupied in shaking almost to death the brigade sergeant-major of the Imperial Guard. At the General's approach the reverend father released his victim with one hand – keeping a firm grip in his woollen hair with the other – removed the cheroot from his mouth and waved it cordially.

'Hullo, General, back from the wars, eh? They've been very anxious about you in the city. Is this creature part of the victorious army?'

'Looks like one of my chaps. What's he been up to?'

'Up to? I came in from Mass and found him eating my breakfast.' A tremendous buffet on the side of his head sent the sergeant-major dizzily across the road. 'Don't you let me find any more of your fellows hanging round the mission today or there'll be trouble. It's always the same when you have troops in a town. I remember in

Duke Japheth's rebellion, the wretched creatures were all over the place. They frightened the sisters terribly over at the fever hospital.'

'Father, is it true that the Emperor's cut and run?'

'If he hasn't he's about the only person. I had that old fraud of an American Archbishop in here the other night, trying to make me join him in a motor-boat. I told him I'd sooner have my throat cut on dry land than face that crossing in an open boat. I'll bet he was sick.'

'But you don't know where the Emperor is?'

'He might be over in the fort. He was the other day. Silly young ass, pasting up proclamations all over the town. I've got other things to bother about than young Seth. And mind you keep your miserable savages from my mission or they'll know the reason why. I've got a lot of our people camped in here so as to be out of harm's way, and I am not going to have them disturbed. Good morning to you, General.'

General Connolly rode on. At the fort he found no sentry on guard. The courtyard was empty save for the body of Ali, which lay on its face in the dust, the cord which had strangled him still tightly twined round his neck. Connolly turned it over with his boot but failed to recognize the swollen and darkened face.

'So His Imperial Majesty *has* shot the moon.'

He looked into the deserted guard-house and the lower rooms of the fort; then he climbed the spiral stone staircase which led to Seth's room, and here, lying across the camp bed in spotted silk pyjamas recently purchased in the Place Vendôme, utterly exhausted by the horror and insecurity of the preceding night, lay the Emperor of Azania fast asleep.

From his bed Seth would only hear the first, rudimentary statement of his victory. Then he dismissed his commander-in-chief and with remarkable self-restraint insisted on performing a complete and fairly elaborate toilet before giving his mind to the details of the situation. When, eventually, he came downstairs dressed in the full and untarnished uniform of the Imperial Horse Guards, he was in a state of some elation. 'You see, Connolly,' he cried, clasping his general's hand with warm emotion, 'I was right. I knew that it was impossible for us to fail.'

'We came damn near it once or twice,' said Connolly.

'Nonsense, my dear fellow. We are Progress and the New Age. Nothing can stand in our way. *Don't you see?* The world is already ours; it is our world now, because we are of the Present. Seyid and his ramshackle band of brigands were the Past. Dark barbarism. A cobweb in a garret; dead wood; a whisper echoing in a sunless cave. We are Light and Speed and Strength, Steel and Steam, Youth, Today and Tomorrow. Don't you see? Our little war was won on other fields five centuries back.' The young darky stood there transfigured; his eyes shining; his head thrown back; tipsy with words. The white man knocked out his pipe on the heel of his riding boot and felt for a pouch in his tunic pocket.

'All right, Seth, say it your way. All I know is that *my* little war was won the day before yesterday and by two very ancient weapons – lies and the long spear.'

'But my tank? Was it not that which gave us the victory?'

'Marx's tin can? A fat lot of use that was. I told you you were wasting money, but you would have the thing. The best thing you can do is to present it to Debra Dowa as a war memorial, only you couldn't get it so far. My dear boy, you can't take a machine like that over this country under this sun. The whole thing was red hot after five miles. The two poor devils of Greeks who had to drive it nearly went off their heads. It came in handy in the end though. We used it as a punishment cell. It was the one thing these black bastards would really take notice of. It's all right getting on a high horse about progress now that everything's over. It doesn't hurt anyone. But if you want to know, you were as near as nothing to losing the whole bag of tricks at the end of last week. Do you know what that clever devil Seyid had done? Got hold of a photograph of you taken at Oxford in cap and gown. He had several thousand printed and circulated among the guards. Told them you'd deserted the Church in England and that there you were in the robes of an English Mohammedan. All the mission boys fell for it. It was no good telling them. They were going over to the enemy in hundreds every night. I was all in. There didn't seem a damned thing to do. Then I got an idea. You know what the name of Amurath means among the tribesmen. Well, I called

General Connolly at Ukaka
from the painting by a native artist

a shari of all the Wanda and Sakuyu chiefs and spun them the
yarn. Told them that Amurath never died – which they believed
already most of them – but that he had crossed the sea to com-
mune with the spirits of his ancestors; that you were Amurath,
himself, come back in another form. It went down from the word
go. I wish you could have seen their faces. The moment they'd
heard the news they were mad to be at Seyid there and then. It was
all I could do to keep them back until I had him where I wanted
him. What's more, the story got through to the other side and in
two days we had a couple of thousand of Seyid's boys coming over
to us. Double what we'd lost on the Mohammedan story and real
fighters – not dressed-up mission boys. Well, I kept them back as
best I could for three days. We were on the crest of the hills all the
time and Seyid was down in the valley, kicking up the devil burning
villages, trying to make us come down to him. He was getting
worried about the desertions. Well, on the third day I sent half
a company of guards down with a band and a whole lot of mules
and told them to make themselves as conspicuous as they could
straight in front of him in the Ukaka pass. Trust the guards to do
that. He did just what I expected; thought it was the whole army
and spread out on both sides trying to surround them. Then I let
the tribesmen in on his rear. My word, I've never seen such
a massacre. Didn't they enjoy themselves, bless them. Half of
them haven't come back yet; they're still chasing the poor devils
all over the hills.'

'And the usurper Seyid, did he surrender?'

'Yes, he surrendered all right. But, look here, Seth, I hope you
aren't going to mind about this, but you see how it was, well, you see,
Seyid surrendered and . . .'

'You don't mean you've let him escape?'

'Oh no, nothing like that, but the fact is, he surrendered to a party
of Wanda . . . and, well, you know what the Wanda are.'

'You mean . . .'

'Yes, I'm afraid so. I wouldn't have had it happen for anything.
I didn't hear about it until afterwards.'

'They should not have eaten him – after all, he was my
father . . . It is so . . . so barbarous.'

'I knew you'd feel that way about it, Seth, and I'm sorry. I gave the headmen twelve hours in the tank for it.'

'I am afraid that as yet the Wanda are totally out of touch with modern thought. They need education. We must start some schools and a university for them when we get things straight.'

'That's it, Seth, you can't blame them. It's want of education. That's all it is.'

'We might start them on Montessori methods,' said Seth dreamily. 'You can't blame them.' Then rousing himself: 'Connolly, I shall make you a Duke.'

'That's nice of you, Seth. I don't mind so much for myself, but Black Bitch will be pleased as Punch about it.'

'And, Connolly.'

'Yes.'

'Don't you think that when she is a Duchess, it might be more suitable if you were to try and call your wife by another name? You see, there will probably be a great influx of distinguished Europeans for my coronation. We wish to break down colour barriers as far as possible. Your name for Mrs Connolly, though suitable as a term of endearment in the home, seems to emphasize the racial distinction between you in a way which might prove disconcerting.'

'I dare say you're right, Seth. I'll try and remember when we're in company. But I shall always think of her as Black Bitch, somehow. By the way, what has become of Ali?'

'Ali? Yes, I had forgotten. He was murdered by Major Joab yesterday evening. And that reminds me of something else. I must order a new crown.'

CHAPTER 2

'LOVEY DOVEY, CAT'S eyes.'

'You got that out of a book.'

'Well, yes. How did you know?'

'I read it too, It's been all round the compound.'

'Anyway, I said it as a quotation. We have to find new things to say somehow sometimes, don't we?'

William and Prudence rolled apart and lay on their backs, sun hats tilted over their noses, shading their eyes from the brilliant equatorial sun. They were on the crest of the little hills above Debra Dowa; it was cool there, eight thousand feet up. Behind them in a stockade of euphorbia trees stood a thatched Nestorian shrine. At its door the priest's youngest child lay sunning his naked belly, gazing serenely into the heavens, indifferent to the flies which settled on the corners of his mouth and sauntered across his eyeballs. Below them the tin roofs of Debra Dowa and a few thin columns of smoke were visible among the blue gums. At a distance the Legation syce sat in charge of the ponies.

'William, darling, there's something so extraordinary on your neck. I believe it's two of them.'

'Well, I think you might knock it off.'

'I believe it's that kind which sting worst.'

'Beast.'

'Oh, it's gone now. It *was* two.'

'I can feel it walking about.'

'No, darling, that's me. I think you might *look* sometimes when I'm being sweet to you. I've invented a new way of kissing. You do it with your eyelashes.'

'I've known that for years. It's called a butterfly kiss.'

36

'Well you needn't be so high up about it. I only do these things for your benefit.'

'It was very nice, darling. I only said it wasn't very new.'

'I don't believe you liked it at all.'

'It was so like the stinging thing.'

'Oh, how maddening it is to have no one to make love with except you.'

'Sophisticated voice.'

'That's not sophisticated. It's my gramophone record voice. My sophisticated voice is quite different. It's like this.'

'I call that American.'

'Shall I do my vibrant-with-passion voice?'

'No.'

'Oh dear, men are hard to keep amused.' Prudence sat up and lit a cigarette. 'I think you're effeminate and under-sexed,' she said, 'and I hate you.'

'That's because you're too young to arouse serious emotion. You might give me a cigarette.'

'I hoped you'd say that. It happens to be the last. Not only the last in my pocket but the last in Debra Dowa. I got it out of the Envoy Extraordinary's bedroom this morning.'

'Oh Lord, when will this idiotic war be over? We haven't had a bag for six weeks. I've run out of hair-wash and detective stories and now no cigarettes. I think you might give me some of that.'

'I hope you go bald. Still, I'll let you have the cigarette.'

'Pru, how sweet of you. I never thought you would.'

'I'm that kind of girl.'

'I think I'll give you a kiss.'

'No, try the new way with eyelashes.'

'Is that right?'

'Delicious. Do it some more.'

Presently they remounted and rode back to the Legation. On the way William said:

'I hope it doesn't give one a twitch.'

'What doesn't, darling?'

'That way with the eyelashes. I've seen people with twitches. I dare say that's how they got it. There was once a man who got run in for winking at girls in the street. So he said it was a permanent affliction and he winked all through his trial and got off. But the sad thing is that now he can't stop and he's been winking ever since.'

'I will say one thing for you,' said Prudence. 'You do know a lovely lot of stories. I dare say that's why I like you.'

*

Three Powers – Great Britain, France and the United States – maintained permanent diplomatic representatives at Debra Dowa. It was not an important appointment. Mr Schonbaum, the doyen, had adopted diplomacy late in life. Indeed the more formative years of his career had already passed before he made up his mind, in view of the uncertainty of Central European exchanges, to become a citizen of the republic he represented. From the age of ten until the age of forty he had lived an active life variously engaged in journalism, electrical engineering, real estate, cotton broking, hotel management, shipping and theatrical promotion. At the outbreak of the European war he had retired first to the United States, and then, on its entry into the war, to Mexico. Soon after the declaration of peace he became an American citizen and amused himself in politics. Having subscribed largely to a successful Presidential campaign, he was offered his choice of several public preferments, of which the ministry at Debra Dowa was by far the least prominent or lucrative. His European upbringing, however, had invested diplomacy with a glamour which his later acquaintance with the great world had never completely dimmed; he had made all the money he needed; the climate at Debra Dowa was reputed to be healthy and the environment romantic. Accordingly he had chosen that post and had not regretted it, enjoying during the last eight years a popularity and prestige which he would hardly have attained among his own people.

The French Minister, M. Ballon, was a Freemason.

His Britannic Majesty's minister, Sir Samson Courteney, was a man of singular personal charm and wide culture whose comparative ill-success in diplomatic life was attributable rather to inattention than to incapacity. As a very young man he had great things predicted of him. He had passed his examinations with a series of

papers of outstanding brilliance; he had powerful family connec-
tions in the Foreign Office; but almost from the outset of his career it
became apparent that he would disappoint expectations. As third
secretary at Peking he devoted himself, to the exclusion of all other
interests, to the construction of a cardboard model of the Summer
Palace; transferred to Washington he conceived a sudden enthusiasm for bicycling and would disappear for days at a time to return
dusty but triumphant with reports of some broken record for speed
or endurance; the scandal caused by this hobby culminated in the
discovery that he had entered his name for an international
long-distance championship. His uncles at the Foreign Office hastily
shifted him to Copenhagen, marrying him, on his way through
London, to the highly suitable daughter of a Liberal cabinet minister. It was in Sweden that his career was finally doomed. For some
time past he had been noticeably silent at the dinner table when
foreign languages were being spoken; now the shocking truth
became apparent that he was losing his mastery even of French;
many ageing diplomats, at loss for a word, could twist the conversation and suit their opinions to their vocabulary; Sir Samson recklessly improvised or lapsed into a kind of pidgin English. The
uncles were loyal. He was recalled to London and established in
a department of the Foreign Office. Finally, at the age of fifty, when
his daughter Prudence was thirteen years old, he was created
a Knight of St Michael and St George and relegated to Azania.
The appointment caused him the keenest delight. It would have
astonished him to learn that anyone considered him unsuccessful
or that he was known throughout the service as the 'Envoy Extraordinary'.

The Legation lay seven miles out of the capital; a miniature
garden city in a stockaded compound, garrisoned by a troop of
Indian cavalry. There was wireless communication with Aden and
a telephone service, of capricious activity, to the town. The road,
however, was outrageous. For a great part of the year it was
furrowed by water-courses, encumbered with boulders, landslides
and fallen trees, and ambushed by cut-throats. On this matter Sir
Samson's predecessor had addressed numerous remonstrances to
the Azanian government with the result that several wayfarers were

hanged under suspicion of brigandage; nothing, however, was done about the track; the correspondence continued and its conclusion was the most nearly successful achievement of Sir Samson's career. Stirred by his appointment and zealous for his personal comfort, the Envoy Extraordinary had, for the first time in his life, thrown himself wholeheartedly into a question of public policy. He had read through the entire file bearing on the subject and within a week of presenting his papers, reopened the question in a personal interview with the Prince Consort. Month after month he pressed forward the interchange of memoranda between Palace, Legation, Foreign Office and Office of Works (the posts of Lord Chamberlain, Foreign Secretary and Minister of Works were all, as it happened at that time, occupied by the Nestorian Metropolitan), until one memorable day Prudence returned from her ride to say that a caravan of oxen, a load of stones and three chain-gangs of convicts had appeared on the road. Here, however, Sir Samson suffered a setback. The American commercial attaché acted, in his simple spare time, as agent for a manufacturer of tractors, agricultural machinery and steam-rollers. At his representation the convicts were withdrawn and the Empress and her circle settled down to the choice of a steam-roller. She had always had a weakness for illustrated catalogues and after several weeks' discussion had ordered a threshing machine, a lawn mower and a mechanical saw. About the steamroller she could not make up her mind. The Metropolitan Archbishop (who was working with the American attaché on a halfcommission basis) supported a very magnificent engine named Pennsylvania Monarch; the Prince Consort, whose personal allowance was compromised by any public extravagance, headed a party in favour of the more modest Kentucky Midget. Meanwhile guests to the British Legation were still in most seasons of the year obliged to ride out to dinner on mule-back, preceded by armed Askaris and a boy with a lantern. It was widely believed that a decision was imminent, when the Empress's death and the subsequent civil war postponed all immediate hope of improvement. The Envoy Extraordinary bore the reverse with composure but real pain. He had taken the matter to heart and he felt hurt and disillusioned. The heap of stones at the roadside remained for him as a continual reproach, the monument to his single ineffective excursion into statesmanship.

In its isolation, life in the compound was placid and domestic. Lady Courteney devoted herself to gardening. The bags came out from London laden with bulbs and cuttings and soon there sprang up round the Legation a luxuriant English garden; lilac and lavender, privet and box, grass walks and croquet lawn, rockeries and wildernesses, herbaceous borders, bowers of rambler roses, puddles of water-lilies and an immature maze.

William Bland, the honorary attaché, lived with the Courteneys. The rest of the staff were married. The Second Secretary had clock golf and the Consul two tennis courts. They called each other by their Christian names, pottered in and out of each other's bungalows and knew the details of each other's housekeeping. The Oriental Secretary, Captain Walsh, alone maintained certain reserves. He suffered from recurrent malaria and was known to ill-treat his wife. But since he was the only member of the Legation who understood Sakuyu, he was a man of importance, being in frequent demand as arbiter in disputes between the domestic servants.

The unofficial British population of Debra Dowa was small and rather shady. There was the manager of the bank and his wife (who was popularly believed to have an injection of Indian blood); two subordinate bank clerks; a shipper of hides who described himself as President of the Azanian Trading Association; a mechanic on the railway who was openly married to two Azanians; the Anglican Bishop of Debra Dowa and a shifting community of canons and curates; the manager of the Eastern Exchange Telegraph Company; and General Connolly. Intercourse between them and the Legation was now limited to luncheon on Christmas Day, to which all the more respectable were invited, and an annual garden party on the King's Birthday which was attended by everyone in the town, from the Georgian Prince who managed the Perroquet Night Club to the Mormon Missionary. This aloofness from the affairs of the town was traditional to the Legation, being dictated partly by the difficulties of the road and partly by their inherent disinclination to mix with social inferiors. On Lady Courteney's first arrival in Debra

Dowa she had attempted to break down these distinctions, saying that they were absurd in so small a community. General Connolly had dined twice at the Legation and a friendship seemed to be in bud when its flowering was abruptly averted by an informal call paid on him by Lady Courteney in his own quarters. She had been lunching with the Empress and turned aside on her way home to deliver an invitation to croquet. Sentries presented arms in the courtyard, a finely uniformed servant opened the door, but this dignified passage was interrupted by a resolute little Negress in a magenta tea-gown who darted across the hall and barred her way to the drawing-room.

'I am Black Bitch,' she had explained simply. 'What do you want in my house?'

'I am Lady Courteney. I came to see General Connolly.'

'The General is drunk today and he doesn't want any more ladies.'

After that Connolly was not asked even to Christmas luncheon.

Other less dramatic incidents occurred with most of the English community until now, after six years, the Bishop was the only resident who ever came to play croquet on the Legation lawn. Even his Lordship's visits had become less welcome lately. His strength did not enable him to accomplish both journeys in the same day, so that an invitation to luncheon involved also an invitation for the night and, usually, to luncheon next day as well. More than this, the Envoy Extraordinary found these incursions from the outside world increasingly disturbing and exhausting as his momentary interest in Azania began to subside. The Bishop would insist on talking about Problems and Policy, Welfare, Education and Finance. He knew all about native law and customs and the relative importance of the various factions at court. He had what Sir Samson considered an ostentatious habit of referring by name to members of the royal household and to provincial governors, whom Sir Samson was content to remember as 'the old black fellow who drank so much Kummel' or 'that what-do-you-call-him Prudence said was like Aunt Sarah' or 'the one with glasses and gold teeth'.

Besides, the Bishop's croquet was not nearly up to Legation standards.

As it happened, however, they found him at table when, twenty minutes late for luncheon, Prudence and William returned from their ride.

'Do you know,' said Lady Courteney, 'I thought for once you *had* been massacred. It would have pleased Monsieur Ballon so much. He is always warning me of the danger of allowing you to go out alone during the crisis. He was on the telephone this morning asking what steps we had taken to fortify the Legation. Madame Ballon had made sandbags and put them all round the windows. He told me he was keeping his last cartridge for Madame Ballon.'

'Everyone is in a great state of alarm in the town,' said the Bishop. 'There are so many rumours. Tell me, Sir Samson, you do not think really, seriously, there is any danger of a massacre?'

The Envoy Extraordinary said: 'We seem to have tinned asparagus for luncheon every day...I can't think why...I'm so sorry – you were talking about the massacre. Well, I hardly know. I haven't really thought about it... Yes, I suppose there might be one. I don't see what's to stop them, if the fellows take it into their heads. Still I dare say it'll all blow over, you know. Doesn't do to get worried...I should have thought we could have grown it ourselves. Much better than spending so much time on that Dutch garden. So like being on board ship, eating tinned asparagus.'

For some minutes Lady Courteney and Sir Samson discussed the relative advantages of tulips and asparagus. Presently the Bishop said: 'One of the things which brought me here this morning was to find out if there was any News. If I could take back something certain to the town...You cannot imagine the distress everyone is in...It is the silence for so many weeks and the rumours. Up here you must at least know what is going on.'

'News,' said the Envoy Extraordinary. 'News. Well, we've generally got quite a lot going on. Let's see, when were you here last? You knew that the Anstruthers have decided to enter David for Uppingham? Very sensible of them, I think. And Percy Legge's sister in England is going to be married – the one who was out here staying with them last year – you remember her? Betty Anstruther got run away with and had a nasty fall the other morning. I thought that pony was too strong for the child. What else is there to tell the Bishop, my dear?'

'The Legges' Frigidaire is broken and they can't get it mended until after the war. Poor Captain Walsh has been laid up with fever again. Prudence began another novel the other day . . . or wasn't I to tell about that, darling?'

'You certainly were not to. And anyway it isn't a novel. It's a Panorama of Life. Oh, I've got some news for all of you. Percy scored twelve-hundred-and-eighty at bagatelle this morning.'

'No, I say,' said Sir Samson, 'did he really?'

'Oh, but that was on the chancery table,' said William. 'I don't count that. We've all made colossal scores there. The pins are bent. I still call my eleven-hundred-and-sixty-five at the Anstruthers' a record.'

For some minutes they discussed the demerits of the chancery bagatelle table. Presently the Bishop said:

'But is there no news about the war?'

'No, I don't think so. Can't remember anything particularly. I leave all that to Walsh, you know, and he's down with fever at the moment. I dare say when he comes back we shall hear something. He keeps in touch with all these local affairs . . . There were some cables the other day, now I come to think of it. Was there anything about the war in them, William, d'you know?'

'I can't really say, sir. The truth is we've lost the cipher book again.'

'Awful fellow, William, he's always losing things. What would you say if you had a chaplain like that, Bishop? Well, as soon as it turns up, get them deciphered, will you? There might be something wanting an answer.'

'Yes, sir.'

'Oh, and William – I think you ought to get those pins put straight on the chancery bagatelle board. It's an awful waste of time playing if it doesn't run true.'

*

'Golly,' said William to Prudence when they were alone. 'Wasn't the Envoy on a high horse at luncheon. Telling me off right and left.

First about the cipher book and then about the bagatelle. Too
humiliating.'

'Poor sweet, he was only showing off to the Bishop. He's probably
frightfully ashamed of himself already.'

'That's all very well, but why should I be made to look a fool just
so as he can impress the Bishop?'

'Sweet, sweet William, please don't be in a rage. It isn't my fault if
I have a martinet for a father, is it, darling? Listen, I've got a whole
lot of new ideas for us to try.'

*

The Legges and the Anstruthers came across to tea: cucumber
sandwiches, gentleman's relish, hot scones and seed-cake.

'How's Betty after her fall?'

'Rather shaken, poor mite. Arthur wants her to start riding
again as soon as she can. He's afraid she may lose her nerve permanently.'

'But not on Majesty.'

'No, we hope Percy will lend her Jumbo for a bit. She can't really
manage Majesty yet, you know.'

'More tea, Bishop? How is everyone at the Mission?'

'Oh dear, how bare the garden is looking. It really is heart-
breaking. This is just the time it should be at its best. But all the
antirrhinums are in the bag, heaven knows where.'

'This war is too exasperating. I've been expecting the wool for
baby's jacket for six weeks. I can't get on with it at all and there are
only the sleeves to finish. Do you think it would look too absurd if
I put in the sleeves in another colour?'

'It might look rather sweet.'

'More tea, Bishop? I want to hear *all* about the infant school
some time.'

'I've found the cipher book, sir.'

'Good boy, where was it?'

'In my collar drawer. I'd been decoding some telegrams in bed
last week.'

'Splendid. It doesn't matter as long as it's safe, but you know how
particular the F.O. are about things like that.'

'Poor Monsieur Ballon. He's been trying to get an aeroplane from Algiers.'

'Mrs Schonbaum told me that the reason we're all so short of supplies is that the French Legation have been buying up everything and storing it in their cellars.'

'I wonder if they'd like to buy my marmalade. It's been rather a failure this year.'

'More tea, Bishop? I want to talk to you some time about David's confirmation. He's getting such an independent mind, I'm sometimes quite frightened what he'll say next.'

'I wonder if you know anything about this cable. I can't make head or tail of it. It isn't in any of the usual codes. *Kt to QR3, CH.*'

'Yes, they're all right. It's a move in the chess game Percy's playing with Babbit at the F.O. He was wondering what had become of it.'

'Poor Mrs Walsh. Looking quite done up. I'm sure the altitude isn't good for her.'

'I'm sure Uppingham is just the place for David.'

'More tea, Bishop? I'm sure you must be tired after your ride.'

*

Sixty miles southward in the Ukaka pass bloody bands of Sakuyu warriors played hide-and-seek among the rocks, chivvying the last fugitives of the army of Seyid, while behind them down the gorge, from cave villages of incalculable antiquity, the women crept out to rob the dead.

*

After tea the Consul looked in and invited Prudence and William over to play tennis.

'I'm afraid the balls are pretty well worn out. We've had some on order for two months. Confound this war.'

When it was too dark to play, they dropped in on the Legges for cocktails, overstayed their time and ran back to the Legation to change for dinner. They tossed for first bath. Prudence won but William took it. He finished her bath salts and they were both very late for dinner. The Bishop, as had been feared, stayed the night. After dinner a log fire was lit in the hall; the evenings were cold in the hills. Sir Samson settled down to his knitting. Anstruther and Legge came in to make up the bridge table with Lady Courteney and the Bishop.

Legation bridge was played in a friendly way.

'I'll go one small heart.'

'One no-trump, and I hope you remember what that means, partner.'

'How you two do cheat.'

'No.'

'I say, can't you do better than that?'

'What did you call?'

'A heart.'

'Oh, well, I'll go two hearts.'

'That's better.'

'Damn, I've forgotten what a no-trump call means. I shall have to pass.'

'No. I'm thinking of riding Vizier with a gag. He's getting heavy in the mouth.'

'No. Then it's you to play, Bishop. It's hopeless using a steel bit out here.'

'I say, what a rotten dummy; is that the best you can do, partner?'

'Well, you wanted me to put you up. If you can make the syces water the bit before bridling it's all right.'

Prudence played the gramophone to William, who lay on his back in front of the hearth smoking one of the very few remaining cigars. 'Oh dear,' he said, 'when will the new records come?'

'I say, Prudence, do come and look at the jumper. I'm starting on the sleeves.'

'Envoy, you *are* clever.'

'Well, it's very exciting . . .'

'Pretty tune that. I say, is it my turn?'

'Percy, *do* attend to the game.'

'Sorry, anyway I've taken the trick.'

'It was ours already.'

'No, I say, was it? Put on the other side, Prudence – the one about Sex Appeal Sarah.'

'*Percy*, it's you to play again. Now trump it this time.'

'Sorry, no trumps left. Good that about "*start off with cocktails and end up with Eno's*".'

*

A few miles away at the French Legation the minister and the first secretary were discussing the report of the British movements which was brought to them every evening by Sir Samson's butler.

'Bishop Goodchild is there again.'

'*Clericalism.*'

'That is how they keep in touch with the town. He is an old fox, Sir Courteney.'

'It is quite true that they have made no attempt to fortify the Legation. I have confirmed it.'

'No doubt they have made their preparations in another quarter. Sir Courteney has been financing Seth.'

'Without doubt.'

'I think he is behind the fluctuations of the currency.'

'They are using a new code. Here is a copy of today's telegram. It means nothing to me. Yesterday there was one the same.'

'*Kt to QR3 CH*. No, that is not one of the ordinary codes. You must work on that all night. Pierre will help.'

'I should not be surprised if Sir Samson were in the pay of the Italians.'

'It is more than likely. The guard has been set?'

'They have orders to shoot at sight.'

'Have the alarms been tested?'

'All are in order.'

'Excellent. Then I will wish you good night.'

M. Ballon ascended the stairs to bed. In his room he first tested the steel shutters, then the lock of the door. Then he went across to the bed where his wife was already asleep and examined the mosquito curtains. He squirted a little Flit round the windows and door, sprayed his throat with antiseptic and rapidly divested

Prudence and William

himself of all except his woollen cummerbund. He slipped on his pyjamas, examined the magazine of his revolver and laid it on the chair at his bedside; next to it he placed his watch, electric torch and a bottle of Vittel. He slipped another revolver under his pillow. He tiptoed to the window and called down softly: 'Sergeant.'

There was a click of heels in the darkness. 'Excellence.'

'Is all well?'

'All well, Excellence.'

M. Ballon moved softly across to the electric switches, and before extinguishing the main lamp switched on a small electric night-light which shed a faint blue radiance throughout the room. Then he cautiously lifted the mosquito curtain, flashed his torch round to make sure that there were no insects there, and finally, with a little grunt, lay down to sleep. Before losing consciousness his hand felt, found and grasped a small curved nut which he kept under his bolster in the belief that it would bring him good luck.

*

Next morning by eleven o'clock the Bishop had been seen off the premises and the British Legation had settled down to its normal routine. Lady Courteney was in the potting-shed; Sir Samson was in the bath; William, Legge and Anstruther were throwing poker dice in the chancery; Prudence was at work on the third chapter of the *Panorama of Life*. *Sex*, she wrote in round, irregular characters, *is the crying out of the Soul for Completion*. Presently she crossed out '*Soul*' and substituted '*Spirit*'; then she inserted '*of man*', changed it to '*manhood*' and substituted '*humanity*'. Then she took a new sheet of paper and copied out the whole sentence. Then she wrote a letter. *Sweet William. You looked so lovely at breakfast you know all half awake and I wanted to pinch you only didn't. Why did you go away at once? Saying 'decode'. You know you hadn't got to. I suppose it was the Bishop. Darling, he's gone now so come back and I will show you something lovely. The Panorama of Life is rather a trial today. Very literary and abstruse but it won't get any* LONGER. *Oh dear. Prudence. XXXX.* She folded this letter very carefully into a three-cornered hat, addressed it *The Honble William Bland, Attaché Honoraire, près La Legation de Grande Bretagne*, and sent it down to the chancery, with instructions to the boy to wait for an answer. William scribbled, *So sorry darling desperately busy today see you at luncheon. Longing to read Panorama. W.*, and threw four kings in two.

Prudence disconsolately abandoned her fountain pen and went out to watch her mother thinning the michaelmas daisies.

Prudence and William had left an inflated india-rubber sea-serpent behind them in the bathroom. Sir Samson sat in the warm water engrossed with it. He swished it down the water and caught it in his toes; he made waves for it; he blew it along; he sat on it and let it shoot up suddenly to the surface between his thighs; he squeezed some of the air out of it and made bubbles. Chance treats of this kind made or marred the happiness of the Envoy's day. Soon he was rapt in daydream about the pleistocene age, where among mists and vast, unpeopled crags schools of deep-sea monsters splashed and sported; oh happy fifth day of creation, thought the Envoy Extraordinary, oh radiant infant sun, newly weaned from the breasts of darkness, oh rich steam of the soggy continents, oh jolly whales and sea-serpents frisking in new brine . . . Knocks at the door. William's voice outside.

'Walker's just ridden over, sir. Can you see him?'

Crude disillusionment.

Sir Samson returned abruptly to the twentieth century, to a stale and crowded world; to a bath grown tepid and an india-rubber toy. 'Walker? Never heard of him.'

'Yes, sir, you know him. The American secretary.'

'Oh, yes, to be sure. Extraordinary time to call. What on earth does the fellow want? If he tries to borrow the tennis marker again, tell him it's broken.'

'He's just got information about the war. Apparently there's been a decisive battle at last.'

'Oh, well, I'm glad to hear that. Which side won, do you know?'

'He did tell me, but I've forgotten.'

'Doesn't matter. I'll hear all about it from him. Tell him I'll be down directly. Give him a putter and let him play clock golf. And you'd better let them know he'll be staying to luncheon.'

Half an hour later Sir Samson came downstairs and greeted Mr Walker.

'My dear fellow, how good of you to come. I couldn't get out before; the morning is always rather busy here. I hope they've been looking after you properly. I think it's about time for a cocktail, William.'

'The Minister thought that you'd like to have news of the battle. We got it on the wireless from Matodi. We tried to ring you up yesterday evening but couldn't get through.'

'No, I always have the telephone disconnected after dinner. Must keep some part of the day for oneself, you know.'

'Of course, we haven't got any full details yet.'

'Of course not. Still, the war's over, William tells me, and I, for one, am glad. It's been on too long. Very upsetting to everything. Let me see, which of them won it?'

'Seth.'

'Ah yes, to be sure. Seth. I'm very glad. He was . . . now let me see . . . which was he?'

'He's the old Empress's son.'

'Yes, yes, now I've got him. And the Empress, what's become of her?'

'She died last year.'

'I'm glad. It's very disagreeable for an old lady of her age to get involved in all these disturbances. And What's-his-name, you know the chap she was married to? He dead, too?'

'Seyid? There's no news of him. I think we may take it that we've seen the last of him.'

'Pity. Nice fellow. Always liked him. By the by, hadn't one of the fellows been to school in England?'

'Yes, that's Seth.'

'Is it, by Jove. Then he speaks English?'

'Perfectly.'

'That'll be one in the eye for Ballon, after all the trouble he took to learn Sakuyu. Here's William with the cocktails.'

'I'm afraid they won't be up to much this morning, sir. We've run out of Peach Brandy.'

'Well, never mind. It won't be long now before we get everything straight again. You must tell us all your news at luncheon. I hear Mrs Schonbaum's mare is in foal. I'll be interested to see how she does. We've never had any luck breeding. I don't believe the native syces understand bloodstock.'

*

At the French Legation, also, news of Seth's victory had arrived. 'Ah,' said M. Ballon, 'so the English and the Italians have triumphed. But the game is not over yet. Old Ballon is not outwitted yet. There is a trick or two still to be won. Sir Samson must look to his laurels.'

While at that moment the Envoy was saying: 'Of course, it's all a question of the altitude. I've not heard of anyone growing asparagus up here but I can't see why it shouldn't do. We get the most delicious green peas.'

CHAPTER 3

TWO DAYS LATER news of the battle of Ukaka was published in Europe. It made very little impression on the million or so Londoners who glanced down the columns of their papers that evening.

'Any news in the paper tonight, dear?'

'No, dear, nothing of interest.'

*

'Azania? That's part of Africa, ain't it?'

'Ask Lil, she was at school last.'

'Lil, where's Azania?'

'I don't know, father.'

'What do they teach you at school, I'd like to know.'

*

'Only niggers.'

*

'It came in a crossword quite lately. *Independent native principality.* You would have it it was Turkey.'

*

'Azania? It sounds like a Cunarder to me.'

'But, my dear, surely you remember that *madly* attractive black-amoor at Balliol.'

*

'Run up and see if you can find the atlas, deary... Yes, where it always is, behind the stand in father's study.'

*

'Things look quieter in East Africa. That Azanian business cleared up at last.'

*

'Care to see the evening paper? There's nothing in it.'

*

In Fleet Street, in the offices of the daily papers: 'Randall, there might be a story in the Azanian cable. The new bloke was at Oxford. See what there is to it.'

Mr Randall typed: *His Majesty B.A. . . . ex-undergrad among the cannibals . . . scholar emperor's desperate bid for throne . . . barbaric splendour . . . conquering hordes . . . ivory . . . elephants . . . east meets west . . .*

*

'Sanders. Kill that Azanian story in the London edition.'

*

'Anything in the paper this morning?'
'No, dear, nothing of interest.'

*

Late in the afternoon Basil Seal read the news on the Imperial and Foreign page of *The Times* as he stopped at his club on the way to Lady Metroland's to cash a bad cheque.

For the last four days Basil had been on a racket. He had woken up an hour ago on the sofa of a totally strange flat. There was a gramophone playing. A lady in a dressing jacket sat in an armchair by the gas-fire, eating sardines from the tin with a shoe-horn. An unknown man in shirtsleeves was shaving, the glass propped on the chimneypiece.

The man had said: 'Now you're awake you'd better go.'
The woman: 'Quite thought you were dead.'
Basil: 'I can't think why I'm here.'
'I can't think why you don't go.'
'Isn't London hell?'
'Did I have a hat?'
'That's what caused half the trouble.'
'What trouble?'

'Oh, why don't you go?'

So Basil had gone down the stairs, which were covered in worn linoleum, and emerged through the side door of a shop into a busy street which proved to be King's Road, Chelsea.

Incidents of this kind constantly occurred when Basil was on a racket.

At the club he found a very old member sitting before the fire with tea and hot muffins. He opened *The Times* and sat on the leather-topped fender.

'You see the news from Azania?'

The elderly member was startled by the suddenness of his address. 'No ... no ... I am afraid I can't really say that I have.'

'Seth has won the war.'

'Indeed ... well, to tell you the truth I haven't been following the affair very closely.'

'Very interesting.'

'No doubt.'

'I never thought things would turn out quite in this way, did you?'

'I can't say I've given the matter any thought.'

'Well, fundamentally it is an issue between the Arabs and the christianized Sakuyu.'

'I see.'

'I think the mistake we made was to underestimate the prestige of the dynasty.'

'Oh.'

'As a matter of fact, I've never been satisfied in my mind about the legitimacy of the old Empress.'

'My dear young man, no doubt you have some particular interest in the affairs of this place. Pray understand that I know nothing at all about it and that I feel it is too late in the day for me to start improving my knowledge.'

The old man shifted himself in his chair away from Basil's scrutiny and began reading his book. A page came in with the message: 'No reply from either of those numbers, sir.'

'Don't you hate London?'

'Eh?'

'Don't you hate London?'

'No, I do not. Lived here all my life. Never get tired of it. Fellow who's tired of London is tired of life.'

'Don't you believe it,' said Basil.

'I'm going away for some time,' he told the hall-porter as he left the club.

'Very good, sir. What shall I do about correspondence?'

'Destroy it.'

'Very good, sir.' Mr Seal was a puzzle to him. He never could forget Mr Seal's father. He had been a member of the club. Such a different gentleman. So spick and span, never without silk hat and an orchid in his buttonhole. Chief Conservative Whip for twenty-five years. Who would have thought of him having a son like Mr Seal? *Out of town until further notice. No letters forwarded* he entered against Basil's name in his ledger. Presently the old gentleman emerged from the smoking-room.

'Arthur, is that young man a member here?'

'Mr Seal, sir? Oh yes, sir.'

'What d'you say his name is?'

'Mr Basil Seal.'

'Basil Seal, eh? Basil Seal. Not Christopher Seal's son?'

'Yes, sir.'

'Is he now? Poor old Seal. 'Pon my soul, what a sad thing. Who'd have thought of that? Seal of all people . . . ' and he shuffled back into the smoking-room, to the fire and his muffins, full of the comfort that glows in the hearts of old men when they contemplate the misfortunes of their contemporaries.

Basil walked across Piccadilly and up to Curzon Street. Lady Metroland was giving a cocktail party.

'Basil,' she said, 'you had no business to come. I particularly didn't ask you.'

'I know. I only heard you had a party quite indirectly. What I've really come for is to see if my sister is here.'

'Barbara? She may be. She said she was coming. How horrible you look.'

'Dirty?'

'Yes.'

'Not shaven?'

'No.'

'Well, I've only just woken up. I haven't been home yet.' He looked round the room. 'All the same people. You don't make many new friends, Margot.'

'I hear you've given up your constituency?'

'Yes, in a way. It wasn't worth while. I told the P.M. I wasn't prepared to fight on the tariff issue. He had a chance to hold over the bill but the Outrage section were too strong so I threw in my hand. Besides, I want to go abroad. I've been in England too long.'

'Cocktail, sir.'

'No, bring me a Pernod and water will you? . . . there isn't any? Oh well, whisky. Bring it into the study. I want to go and telephone. I'll be back soon, Margot.'

'God, what I feel about that young man,' said Lady Metroland.

Two girls were talking about him.

'Such a lovely person.'

'Where?'

'Just gone out.'

'You don't mean Basil Seal?'

'Do I?'

'Horrible clothes, black hair over his face.'

'Yes, tell me about him.'

'My dear, he's enchanting . . . Barbara Sothill's brother, you know. He's been in hot water lately. He'd been adopted as candidate somewhere in the West. Father says he was bound to get in at the next election. Angela Lyne was paying his expenses. But they had trouble over something. You know how careful Angela is. I never thought Basil was really her tea. They never quite made sense, I mean, did they? So that's all over.'

'It's nice his being so dirty.'

Other people discussed him.

'No, the truth about Basil is just that he's a *bore*. No one minds him being rude, but he's so *teaching*. I had him next to me at dinner once and he would talk all the time about Indian dialects. Well, what *was* one to say? And I asked afterwards and apparently he doesn't know anything about them either.'

'He's done all kinds of odd things.'

'Well, yes, and I think that's so boring too. Always in revolutions and murders and things, I mean, what is one to say? Poor Angela is *literally* off her head with him. I was there yesterday and she could talk of nothing else but the row he's had with his committee in his constituency. He does seem to have behaved rather oddly at the Conservative ball and then he and Alastair Trumpington and Peter Pastmaster and some others had a five-day party up there and left a lot of bad cheques behind and had a motor accident and one of them got run in – you know what Basil's parties are. I mean, that sort of thing is all right in London, but you know what provincial towns are. So what with one thing and another they've asked him to stand down. The trouble is that poor Angela still fancies him rather.'

'What's going to happen to him?'

'I *know*. That's the *point*. Barbara says she won't do another thing for him.'

Someone else was saying, 'I've given up trying to be nice to Basil. He either cuts me or corners me with an interminable lecture about Asiatic politics. It's odd Margot having him here – particularly after the way he's always getting Peter involved.'

Presently Basil came back from telephoning. He stood in the doorway, a glass of whisky in one hand, looking insolently round the room, his head back, chin forward, shoulders rounded, dark hair over his forehead, contemptuous grey eyes over grey pouches, a proud, rather childish mouth, a scar on one cheek.

'My word, he is a corker,' remarked one of the girls.

His glance travelled round the room. 'I'll tell you who I want to see, Margot. Is Rex Monomark here?'

'He's over there somewhere, but, Basil, I absolutely forbid you to tease him.'

'I won't tease him.'

Lord Monomark, owner of many newspapers, stood at the far end of the drawing-room discussing diet. Round him in a haze of cigar smoke were ranged his ladies and gentlemen in attendance: three almost freakish beauties, austerely smart, their exquisite, irregular features eloquent of respect; two gross men of the world, wheezing appreciation; a dapper elderly secretary, with pink, bald pate and in his eyes that glazed, gin-fogged look that is common to sailors and the secretaries of the great, and comes from too short sleep.

'Two raw onions and a plate of oatmeal porridge,' said Lord Monomark. 'That's all I've taken for luncheon in the last eight months. And I feel two hundred per cent better – physically, intellectually and ethically.'

The group was slightly isolated from the rest of the party. It was very rarely that Lord Monomark consented to leave his own house and appear as a guest. The few close friends whom he honoured in this way observed certain strict conventions in the matter: new people were not to be introduced to him except at his own command; politicians were to be kept at a distance; his cronies of the moment were to be invited with him; provision had to be made for whatever health system he happened to be following. In these conditions he liked now and then to appear in society – an undisguised Haroun al-Rashid among his townspeople – to survey the shadow-play of fashion, and occasionally to indulge the caprice of singling out one of these bodiless phantoms and translating her or him into the robust reality of his own world. His fellow guests, meanwhile, flitted in and out as though unconscious of his presence, avoiding any appearance of impinging on the integrity of this glittering circle.

'If I had my way,' said Lord Monomark, 'I'd make it compulsory throughout the country. I've had a notice drafted and sent round the office recommending the system. Half the fellows think nothing of spending one and six or two shillings on lunch every day – that's out of eight or nine pounds a week.'

'Rex, you're wonderful.'

'Read it out to Lady Everyman, Sanders.'

'*Lord Monomark wishes forcibly to bring to the attention of his staff the advantages to be derived from a carefully chosen diet . . .*' Basil genially intruded himself into the party.

'Well, Rex, I thought I'd find you here. It's all stuff about that onion and porridge diet, you know. Griffenbach exploded that when I was in Vienna three years ago. But that's not really what I came to talk about.'

'Oh, Seal, isn't it? I've not seen you for a long time. I remember now you wrote to me some time ago. What was it about, Sanders?'

'Afghanistan.'

'Yes, of course. I turned it over to one of my editors to answer. I hope he explained.'

Once, when Basil had been a young man of promise, Lord Monomark had considered taking him up and invited him for a cruise in the Mediterranean. Basil at first refused and then, after they had sailed, announced by wireless his intention of joining the yacht at Barcelona; Lord Monomark's party had waited there for two sultry days without hearing news and then sailed without him. When they next met in London Basil explained rather inadequately that he had found at the last minute he couldn't manage it after all. Countless incidents of this kind had contributed to Basil's present depreciated popularity.

'Look here, Rex,' he said, 'what I want to know is what you're going to do about Seth.'

'Seth?' Lord Monomark turned an inquiring glance on Sanders. 'What am I doing about Seth?'

'Seth?'

'It seems to me there's an extremely tricky political situation developing there. You've seen the news from Ukaka. It doesn't tell one a thing. I want to get some first-hand information. I'm probably sailing almost at once. It occurred to me that I might cover it for you in the *Excess*.'

Towards the end of this speech, Lord Monomark's bewilderment was suddenly illuminated. This was nothing unusual after all. It was simply someone after a job. 'Oh,' he said, 'I'm afraid I don't interfere with the minor personnel of the paper. You'd better go and see one of the editors about it. But I don't think you'll find him anxious to take on new staff at the moment.'

'I'll tell them you sent me.'

'No, no, I never interfere. You must just approach them through the normal channels.'

'All right. I'll come up and see you after I've fixed it up. Oh, and I'll send you Griffenbach's report on the onion and porridge diet if

I can find it. There's my sister. I've got to go and talk to her now, I'm afraid. See you before I sail.'

Barbara Sothill no longer regarded her brother with the hero-worship which had coloured the first twenty years of her life.

'Basil,' she said. 'What on earth have you been doing? I was lunching at mother's today and she was wild about you. She's got one of her dinner parties and you promised to be in. She said you hadn't been home all night and she didn't know whether to get another man or not.'

'I was on a racket. We began at Lottie Crump's. I rather forget what happened except that Allan got beaten up by some chaps.'

'And she's just heard about the committee.'

'Oh *that*. I meant to give up the constituency anyhow. It's no catch being in the Commons now. I'm thinking of going to Azania.'

'Oh, were you? – and what'll you do there?'

'Well, Rex Monomark wants me to represent the *Excess*, but I think as a matter of fact I shall be better off if I keep a perfectly free hand. The only thing is I shall need some money. D'you think our mother will fork out five hundred pounds?'

'I'm sure she won't.'

'Well, someone'll have to. To tell you the truth I can't very well stay on in England at the moment. Things have got into rather a crisis. I suppose you wouldn't like to give me some money.'

'Oh, Basil, what's the good? You know I can't do it except by getting it from Freddy and he was furious last time.'

'I can't think why. He's got packets.'

'Yes, but you might try and be a little polite to him sometimes – just in public I mean.'

'Oh, of course if he thinks that by lending me a few pounds he's setting himself up for life as a good fellow...'

*

In the days when Sir Christopher was Chief Whip, Lady Seal had entertained frequently and with relish. Now, in her widowhood, with Barbara successfully married and her sons dispersed, she limited herself to four or five dinner parties every year. There was nothing elastic or informal about these occasions. Lady Metroland was a comparatively rich woman and it was her habit when she was tired to say casually to her butler at cocktail time, 'I am not going out tonight. There will be about twenty to dinner,' and then to sit down to the telephone and invite her guests, saying to each, 'Oh, but you *must* chuck them tonight. I'm all alone and feeling like death.' Not so Lady Seal, who dispatched engraved cards of invitation a month in advance, supplied defections from a secondary list one week later, fidgeted with place cards and a leather board as soon as the acceptances began to arrive, borrowed her sister's chef and her daughter's footmen and on the morning of the party exhausted herself utterly by trotting all over her house in Lowndes Square arranging flowers. Then at half-past five when she was satisfied that all was ready she would retire to bed and doze for two hours in her darkened room; her maid would call her with cachet Faivre and clear China tea; a touch of ammonia in the bath; a touch of rouge on the cheeks; lavender water behind the ears; half an hour before the glass, fiddling with her jewel case while her hair was being done; final conference with the butler; then a happy smile in the drawing-room for all who were less than twenty minutes late. The menu always included lobster cream, saddle of mutton and brown-bread ice, and there were silver-gilt dishes ranged down the table holding a special kind of bonbon supplied to Lady Seal for twenty years by a little French shop whose name she would sometimes coyly disclose.

Basil arrived among the first guests. There was carpet on the steps; the doors opened with unusual promptness; the hall seemed full of chrysanthemums and footmen.

'Hullo, her ladyship got a party? I forgot all about it. I'd better change.'

'Frank couldn't find your evening clothes, Mr Basil. I don't think you can have brought them back last time you went away. I don't think her Ladyship is expecting you to dinner.'

'Anyone asked for me?'

'There *were* two persons, sir.'

'Duns?'

'I couldn't say, sir. I told them that we had no information about your whereabouts.'

'Quite right.'

'Mrs Lyne rang up fifteen times, sir. She left no message.'

'If anyone else wants me, tell them I've gone to Azania.'

'Sir?'

'Azania.'

'Abroad?'

'Yes, if you like.'

'Excuse me, Mr Basil. . . .'

The Duke and Duchess of Stayle had arrived. The Duchess said, 'So you are not dining with us tonight. You young men are all so busy nowadays. No time for going out. I hear things are going very well up in your constituency.' She was often behindhand with her news. As they went up the Duke said, 'Clever young fellow that. Wonder if he'll ever come to anything though.'

Basil went into the dark little study next to the front door and rang up the Trumpingtons.

'Sonia, are you and Alastair doing anything tonight?'

'We're at home. Basil, what have you been doing to Alastair? I'm furious with you. I think he's going to die.'

'We had rather a racket. Shall I come to dinner?'

'Yes, do. We're in bed.'

He drove to Montagu Square and was shown up to their room. They lay in a vast, low bed, with a backgammon board between them. Each had a separate telephone, on the tables at the side, and by the telephone a goblet of 'black velvet'. A bull terrier and chow flirted on their feet. There were other people in the room: one playing the gramophone, one reading, one trying Sonia's face things at the dressing-table. Sonia said, 'It's such a waste not going out after dark. We have to stay in all day because of duns.'

Alastair said, 'We can't have dinner with these infernal dogs all over the place.'

Sonia: 'You're a cheerful chap to be in bed with, aren't you?' and to the dog, 'Was oo called infernal woggie by owid man? Oh God, he's made a mess again.'

Alastair: 'Are those chaps staying to dinner?'

'We asked one.'

'Which?'

'Basil.'

'Don't mind him, but all those others.'

'I do hope not.'

They said: 'Afraid we'll have to. It's so late to go anywhere else.'

Basil: 'How dirty the bed is, Sonia.'

'I know. It's Alastair's dog. Anyway, you're a nice one to talk about dirt.'

'Isn't London hell?'

Alastair: 'I don't, anyway, see why those chaps shouldn't have dinner downstairs.'

They said: 'It *would* be more comfortable.'

'What are their names?'

'One we picked up last night. The other has been staying here for days.'

'It's not only the expense I mind. They're boring.'

They said: 'We wouldn't stay a moment if we had anywhere else to go.'

'Ring for dinner, sweet. I forget what there is, but I know it's rather good. I ordered it myself.'

There was whitebait, grilled kidneys and toasted cheese. Basil sat between them on the bed and they ate from their knees. Sonia threw a kidney to the dogs and they began a fight.

Alastair: 'It's no good. I can't eat anything.'

Sonia's maid brought in the trays. She asked her: 'How are the gentlemen getting on downstairs?'

'They asked for champagne.'

'I suppose they'd better have it. It's very bad.'

Alastair: 'It's very good.'

'Well it tasted awful to me. Basil, sweety, what's your news?'

'I'm going to Azania.'

'Can't say I know much about that. Is it far?'

'Yes.'

'Fun?'

'Yes.'

'Oh, Alastair, why not us too?'

'Hell, now those dogs have upset everything again.'

'How pompous you're being.'

After dinner they all played happy families. 'Have you got Miss Chips the Carpenter's daughter?'

'*Not at home* but have *you* got Mr Chips the Carpenter? *Thank you and* Mrs Chips the Carpenter's wife? *Thank you* and Basil have *you* got Miss Chips? *Thank you*. That's the Chips family.'

Basil left early so as to see his mother before she went to bed.

Sonia said, 'Good-bye, darling. Write to me from wherever it is. Only I don't expect we'll be living here much longer.'

One of the young men said: 'Could you lend me a fiver? I've a date at the Café de Paris.'

'No, you'd better ask Sonia.'

'But it's so boring. I'm *always* borrowing money from *her*.'

*

In the course of the evening Lady Seal had found time to touch her old friend Sir Joseph Mannering on the sleeve and say, 'Don't go at once, Jo. I'd like to talk to you afterwards.' As the last guests left he came across to the fireplace, hands behind his coat-tails and on his face an expression of wisdom, discretion, sympathy, experience and contentment. He was a self-assured old booby who in the easy and dignified role of family friend was invoked to aggravate most of the awkward situations that occurred in the lives of his circle.

'A delightful evening, Cynthia, typically delightful. I sometimes think that yours is the only house in London nowadays where I can be sure both of the claret and the company. But you wanted to consult me. Not, I hope, that little trouble of Barbara's.'

'No, it's nothing about Barbara. What's the child been doing?'

'Nothing, nothing. It was just some idle bit of gossip I heard. I'm glad it isn't worrying you. I suppose Basil's been up to some mischief again.'

'Exactly, Jo. I'm at my wits' end with the boy. But what was it about Barbara?'

'Come, come, we can't fuss about too many things. I *did* hear Basil had been up to something. Of course there's plenty of good in the boy. It only wants bringing out.'

'I sometimes doubt it.'

'Now, Cynthia, you're overwrought. Tell me exactly what has been happening.'

It took Lady Seal some time to deliver herself of the tale of Basil's misdemeanours. '... if his father were alive ... spent all the money his Aunt left him on that idiotic expedition to Afghanistan ... give him a very handsome allowance ... all and more than all that I can afford ... paid his debts again and again ... no gratitude ... no self-control ... no longer a child, twenty-eight this year ... his father ... the post kind Sir William secured him in the bank in Brazil ... great opening and such interesting work ... never went to the office once ... never know where or whom he is with ... most undesirable friends, Sonia Trumpington, Peter Pastmaster, all sorts of people whose names I've never even heard ... of course I couldn't really *approve* of his going about so much with Mrs Lyne – though I dare say there was nothing *wrong* in it – but at least I hoped she might steady him a little ... stand for Parliament ... his father ... be-haved in the most irresponsible way in the heart of his constituency ... Prime Minister ... Central Office ... Sonia Trumpington threw it at the mayor ... Conservative ball ... one of them actually arrested ... come to the end, Jo ... I've made up my mind. I won't do another thing for him – it's not fair on Tony that I should spend all the money on Basil that should go to them equally ... marry and settle down ... if his father were alive ... it isn't even as though he were the kind of man who would do in Kenya,' she concluded hopelessly.

Throughout the narration Sir Joseph maintained his air of wisdom, discretion, sympathy, experience and contentment; at suitable moments he nodded and uttered little grunts of comprehension. At length he said: 'My dear Cynthia. I had no idea it was as bad as that. What a terrible time you have had and how brave you have been. But you mustn't let yourself worry. I dare say even this disagreeable incident may turn to good. It may very likely be the turning-point in the boy's life ... Learned his lesson.

I shouldn't wonder if the reason he hasn't come home is that he's ashamed to face you. I tell you what, I think I'd better have a talk to him. Send him round as soon as you get into touch with him. I'll take him to lunch at the club. He'll probably take advice from a man he might resent from a woman. Didn't he begin reading for the Bar once? Well, let's set him going at that. Keep him at home. Don't give him enough money to go about. Let him bring his friends here. Then he'll only be able to have friends he's willing to introduce to you. We'll try and get him into a different set. He didn't go to any dances all last summer, I remember you telling me. Heaps of jolly girls coming out he hasn't had the chance of meeting yet. Keep him to his work. The boy's got brains, bound to find it interesting. Then when you're convinced he's steadied up a bit, let him have chambers of his own in one of the Inns of Court. Let him feel you trust him. I'm sure he'll respond . . . '

For nearly half an hour they planned Basil's future, punctually rewarding each stage of his moral recuperation. Presently Lady Seal said: 'Oh Jo, what a help you are. I don't know what I should do without you.'

'Dear Cynthia, it is one of the privileges of maturity to bring new strength and beauty to old friendships.'

'I shan't forget how wonderful you've been tonight, Jo.'

The old boy bounced back in his taxi-cab to St James's and Lady Seal slowly ascended the stairs to her room; both warm at heart and aglow from their fire-lit, nursery game of 'let's pretend'. She sat before her bedroom fire, slipped off her dress and rang the bell beside the chimney-piece.

'I'll have my milk now, Bradshawe, and then go straight to bed.'

The maid lifted the jug from the fender where it had been keeping warm and deftly held back the skin with a silver apostle-spoon as she poured the hot milk into a glass. Then she brought the jewel case and held it while wearily, one by one, the rings, bracelet, necklace and earrings were slipped off and tumbled in. Then she began taking the pins from her mistress's hair. Lady Seal held the glass in both hands and sipped.

'Don't trouble to brush it very long tonight, I'm tired.'

'I hope the party was a success, my lady.'

'I suppose so. Yes, I'm sure it was. Captain Cruttwell is very silly, but it was kind of him to come at all at such short notice.'

'It's the first time Her Grace's youngest daughter has been to dinner?'

'Yes, I think it is. The child looked very well, I thought, and talked all the time.'

Lady Seal sipped the hot milk, her thoughts still wandering innocently in the soft places where Sir Joseph had set them. She saw Basil hurrying to work in the morning, by bus at first, later – when he had proved his sincerity – he should have a two-seater car; he would be soberly but smartly dressed and carry some kind of business-like attaché-case or leather satchel with him. He would generally have papers to go through before changing for dinner. They would dine together and afterwards often go out to the theatre or cinema. He would eat with good appetite, having lunched quickly and economically at some place near his work. Quite often she would entertain for him, small young people's parties of six or eight – intelligent, presentable men of his own age, pretty, well-bred girls. During the season he would go to two dances a week, and leave them early... 'Bradshawe, where is the spoon? It's forming a skin again.'... Later she went to tea with him in his rooms in Lincoln's Inn. He lifted a pile of books from the arm-chair before she sat down. 'I've brought you a looking-glass.' 'Oh, Mother, how sweet of you.' 'I saw it in Helena's shop this morning and thought it just the thing to go over your fire. It will lighten the room. It's got a piece chipped off in one place but it is a good one.' 'I *must* try it at once.' 'It's down in the car, dear. Tell Andrews to bring it up...'

A knock at the door.

'What can they want at this time? See who it is, Bradshawe.'

'Mr Basil, my lady.'

'Oh, dear.'

Basil came in, so unlike the barrister of her dream that it required an effort to recognize him.

'I'll ring for you in a few minutes, Bradshawe... Basil, I really can't talk to you now. I have a great deal to say and I am very tired. Where have you been?'

'Different places.'

'You might have let me know. I expected you at dinner.'

'Had to go and dine with Alastair and Sonia. Was the party a success?'

'Yes, I think so, so far as can be expected. I had to ask poor Toby Cruttwell. Who else *was* there I *could* ask at the last moment? I do wish you wouldn't fiddle with things. Shut the jewel case like a good boy.'

'By the way, I've given up politics; did you know?'

'Yes, I am most distressed about the whole business – vexed and distressed, but I can't discuss it now. I'm so tired. It's all arranged. You are to lunch with Sir Joseph Mannering at his club and he will explain everything. You are to meet some new girls and later have tea – I mean rooms – in Lincoln's Inn. You'll like that, won't you, dear? Only you mustn't ask about it now.'

'What I came to say is that I'm just off to Azania.'

'No, no, dear boy. You are to lunch with Jo at The Travellers'.'

'And I shall need some money.'

'It's all decided.'

'You see I'm fed up with London and English politics. I want to get away. Azania is the obvious place. I had the Emperor to lunch once at Oxford. Amusing chap. The thing is this,' said Basil, scratching in his pipe with a delicate pair of gold manicure scissors from the dressing-table. 'Every year or so there's *one* place in the globe worth going to where things are happening. The secret is to find out where and be on the spot in time.'

'Basil dear, *not* with the scissors.'

'History doesn't happen everywhere at once. Azania is going to be terrific. Anyway, I'm off there tomorrow. Flying to Marseilles and catching the Messageries ship. Only I must raise at least five hundred before I start. Barbara wanted to give it to me but I thought the simplest thing was to compound for my year's allowance. There may be a few debts that'll want settling while I'm away. I thought of giving you a power of attorney...'

'Dear boy, you are talking nonsense. When you've had luncheon with Sir Joseph you'll understand. We'll get into touch with him first thing in the morning. Meanwhile run along and get a good night's sleep. You aren't looking at all well, you know.'

'I must have at least three hundred.'

'There. I've rung for Bradshawe. You'll forget all about this place in the morning. Good night, darling boy. The servants have gone up. Don't leave the lights burning downstairs, will you?'

So Lady Seal undressed and sank at last luxuriously into bed. Bradshawe softly paddled round the room performing the last offices; she picked up the evening gown, the underclothes, and the stockings, and carried them outside to her workroom; she straightened the things on the dressing-table, shut the drawers, wiped the points of the nail scissors with a wad of cotton; she opened the windows four inches at the top, banked up the fire with a shovelful of small coal, hitched on the wire guard, set a bottle of Vichy water and a glass on the chamber cupboard beside the bed and stood at the door, one hand holding the milk tray, the other on the electric switch.

'Is that everything for the night, my lady?'

'That's all, Bradshawe. I'll ring in the morning. Good night.'

'Good night, my lady.'

*

Basil went back to the telephone and called Mrs Lyne. A soft, slightly impatient voice answered him. 'Yes, who is it?'

'Basil.'

A pause.

'Hullo, are you there, Angela? Basil speaking.'

'Yes, darling, I heard. Only I didn't quite know what to say…I've just got in…Such a dull evening…I rang you up today…couldn't get on to you.'

'How odd you sound.'

'Well, yes…why did you ring up? It's late.'

'I'm coming round to see you.'

'My dear, you can't possibly.'

'I was going to say good-bye – I'm going away for some time.'

'Yes, I suppose that's a good thing.'

'Well, don't you want me to come?'

'You'll have to be sweet to me. You see I've been in rather a muddle lately. You will be sweet, darling, won't you? I don't think I could bear it if you weren't.'

And later, as they lay on their backs smoking, her foot just touching his under the sheets, Angela interrupted him to say: 'How would it be if, just for a little, we didn't talk about this island? . . . I'm going to find things different when you've gone.'

'I'm mad for it.'

'I know,' said Angela. 'I'm not kidding myself.'

'You're a grand girl.'

'It's time you went away . . . shall I tell you something?'

'What?'

'I'm going to give you some money.'

'Well, that is nice.'

'You see, when you rang up I knew that was what you wanted. And you've been sweet tonight really, though you were boring about that island. So I thought that just for tonight I'd like to have you not asking for money. Before, I've enjoyed making it awkward for you. Did you know? Well I had to have *some* fun, hadn't I? – and I think I used to embarrass even you sometimes. And I used to watch you steering the conversation round. I knew that anxious look in your eye so well . . . I had to have something to cheer me up all these weeks, hadn't I? You don't do much for a girl. But tonight I thought it would be a treat just to let you be nice and no bother and I've enjoyed myself. I made out a cheque before you came . . . on the dressing-table. It's for rather a lot.'

'You're a grand girl.'

'When d'you start?'

'Tomorrow.'

'I'll miss you. Have a good time.'

Next morning at twenty to ten Lady Seal rang her bell. Bradshawe drew the curtains and shut the windows, brought in the orange juice, the letters and the daily papers.

'Thank you, Bradshawe. I had a very good night. I only woke up once and then was asleep again almost directly. Is it raining?'

'I'm afraid so, my lady.'

'I shall want to see Mr Basil before he goes out.'

'Mr Basil has gone already.'

'So early. Did he say where?'

'He did say, my lady, but I am not sure of the name. Somewhere in Africa.'

'How very provoking. I know there was something I wanted him to do today.'

At eleven o'clock a box of flowers arrived from Sir Joseph Mannering and at twelve Lady Seal attended a committee meeting; it was four days before she discovered the loss of her emerald bracelet and by that time Basil was on the sea.

*

Croydon, Le Bourget, Lyons, Marseilles; colourless, gusty weather, cloud-spray dripping and trickling on the windows; late in the afternoon, stillness from the roar of the propellers; sodden turf; the road from the aerodrome to the harbour heavily scented with damp shrub; wind-swept sheds on the quay; an Annamite boy swabbing the decks; a surly steward, the ship does not sail until tomorrow, the commissaire knows of the allotment of the cabins, he is on shore, it is not known when he will return, there is nowhere to leave the baggage, the baggage-room is shut and the commissaire has the key, anyone might take it if it were left on deck – twenty francs – the luggage could go in one of the cabins, it will be safe there, the steward has the key, he will see to it. Dinner at the restaurant de Verdun. Basil alone with a bottle of fine burgundy.

Next afternoon they sailed. She was an ugly old ship snatched from Germany after the war as part of the reparations; at most hours of the day two little men in alpaca coats played a fiddle and piano in the deck bar; luncheon at twelve, dinner at seven; red Algerian wine; shrivelled, blotchy dessert; a small saloon full of children; a smoking-room full of French officials and planters playing cards. The big ships do not stop at Matodi. Basil at table talking excellent French ceaselessly, in the evenings paying attention to a woman of mixed blood from Madagascar, getting bored with her and with the ship, sitting sulkily at meals with a book, complaining to the captain about the inadequacy of the wireless bulletins, lying alone in his bunk for hours at a time, smoking cheroots and gazing blankly at the pipes on the ceiling.

At Port Said he sent lewd postcards to Sonia, disposed of his mother's bracelet at a fifth of its value to an Indian jeweller, made friends with a Welsh engineer in the bar of the Eastern Exchange, got drunk with him, fought him, to the embarrassment of the Egyptian policeman, and returned to the ship next morning a few minutes before the companion-way was raised, much refreshed by his racket.

A breathless day in the canal; the woman from Madagascar exhausted with invitation. The Red Sea, the third-class passengers limp as corpses on the lower deck; fiddle and piano indefatigable; dirty ice swimming in the dregs of lemon juice; Basil in his bunk sullenly consuming cheroots, undeterred by the distress of his cabin-companion. Jibuti; portholes closed to keep out the dust, coolies jogging up the planks with baskets of coal; contemptuous savages in the streets scraping their teeth with twigs; an Abyssinian noble-woman in a green veil shopping at the French Emporium; an ill-intentioned black monkey in an acacia tree near the post office. Basil took up with a Dutch South African; they dined on the pavement of the hotel and drove later in a horse-cab to the Somali quarter where in a lamplit mud hut Basil began to talk of the monetary systems of the world until the Boer fell asleep on a couch of plaited hide and the four dancing girls huddled together in the corner like chimpanzees and chattered resentfully among themselves.

The ship was sailing for Azania at midnight. She lay far out in the bay, three lines of lights reflected in the still water; the sound of fiddle and piano was borne through the darkness, harshly broken by her siren intermittently warning passengers to embark. Basil sat in the stern of the little boat, one hand trailing in the sea; half-way to the ship the boatmen shipped their oars and tried to sell him a basket of limes; they argued for a little in broken French, then splashed on irregularly towards the liner; an oil lantern bobbed in the bows. Basil climbed up the companion-way and went below; his companion was asleep and turned over angrily as the light went up; the porthole had been shut all day and the air was gross; Basil lit a cheroot and lay for some time reading. Presently the old ship began to vibrate and later, as she drew clear of the bay, to pitch very slightly in the Indian Ocean. Basil turned out the light and lay happily smoking in the darkness.

*

In London Lady Metroland was giving a party. Sonia said: 'No one asks us to parties now except Margot. Perhaps there aren't any others.'

'The boring thing about parties is that it's far too much effort to meet new people, and if it's just all the ordinary people one knows already one might just as well stay at home and ring them up instead of having all the business of remembering the right day.'

'I wonder why Basil isn't here. I thought he was bound to be.'

'Didn't he go abroad?'

'I don't think so. Don't you remember, he had dinner with us the other evening?'

'Did he? When?'

'Darling, how *can* I remember that?...there's Angela – she'll know.'

'Angela, has Basil gone away?'

'Yes, somewhere quite extraordinary.'

'My dear, is that rather heaven for you?'

'Well, in a way...'

*

Basil was awakened by the clank and rattle of steel cable as the anchor was lowered. He went up on deck in pyjamas. The whole sky was aflame with green and silver dawn. Half-covered figures of other passengers sprawled asleep on benches and chairs. The sailors paddled between them on bare feet, clearing the hatches; a junior officer on the bridge shouting orders to the men at the winch. Two lighters were already alongside preparing to take off cargo. A dozen small boats clustered round them, loaded with fruit.

Quarter of a mile distant lay the low sea-front of Matodi; the minaret, the Portuguese ramparts, the mission church, a few ware-houses taller than the rest, the Grand Hotel de l'Empereur Amurath stood out from the white-and-dun cluster of roofs; behind and on

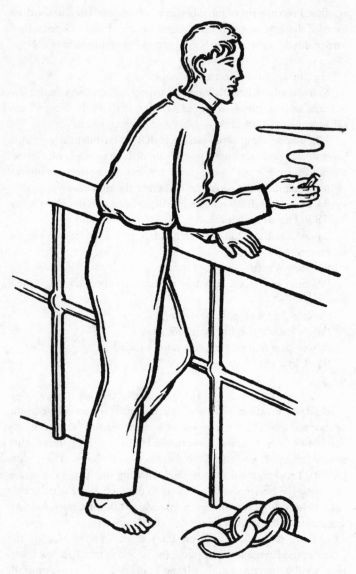

Basil

either side stretched the meadowland and green plantations of the Azanian coast-line, groves of tufted palm at the water's edge. Beyond and still obscured by mist rose the great crests of the Sakuyu mountains, the Ukaka pass and the road to Debra Dowa.

The purser joined Basil at the rail.

'You disembark here, Mr Seal, do you not?'

'Yes.'

'You are the only passenger. We sail again at noon.'

'I shall be ready to go ashore as soon as I am dressed.'

'You are making a long stay in Azania?'

'Possibly.'

'On business? I have heard it is an interesting country.'

But for once Basil was disinclined to be instructive. 'Purely for pleasure,' he said. Then he went below, dressed and fastened his bags. His cabin companion looked at his watch, scowled and turned his face to the wall; later he missed his shaving soap, bedroom slippers and the fine topee he had bought a few days earlier at Port Said.

CHAPTER 4

THE MATODI TERMINUS of the Grand Chemin de Fer d'Azanie
lay half a mile inland from the town. A broad avenue led to it,
red earth scarred by deep ruts and potholes; on either side grew
irregular lines of acacia trees. Between the trees were strings of
different-coloured flags. A gang of convicts, chained neck to neck,
were struggling to shift a rusty motor-car which lay on its side
blocking the road. It had come to grief there six months previously,
having been driven recklessly into some cattle by an Arab driver.
He was now doing time in prison in default of damages. White
ants had devoured the tyres; various pieces of mechanism had been
removed from time to time to repair other engines. A Sakuyu
family had set up house in the back, enclosing the space between
the wheels with an intricate structure of rags, tin, mud and grass.

That was in the good times when the Emperor was in the hills.
Now he was back again and the town was overrun with soldiers and
government officials. It was by his orders that this motor-car was
being removed. Everything had been like that for three weeks, bustle
everywhere, proclamations posted up on every wall, troops drilling,
buglings, hangings, the whole town kept awake all day; in the Arab
Club feeling ran high against the new régime.

Mahmud el Khali bin Sai-ud, frail descendant of the oldest
family in Matodi, sat among his kinsmen, moodily browsing over
his lapful of khat. The sunlight streamed in through the lattice
shutters, throwing a diaper of light over the worn carpets and
divan; two of the amber mouthpieces of the hubble-bubble
were missing; the rocking-chair in the corner was no longer safe,
the veneer was splitting and peeling off the rosewood table. These
poor remnants were all that remained of the decent people of

78

Matodi; the fine cavaliers had been scattered and cut down in battle. Here were six old men and two dissipated youngsters, one of whom was liable to fits of epilepsy. There was no room for a gentleman in Matodi nowadays, they remarked. You could not recount an anecdote in the streets or pause on the water-front to discuss with full propriety the sale of land or the pedigree of a stallion, but you were jostled against the wall by black men or Indians, dirty fellows with foreskins; unbelievers, descendants of slaves; judges from up-country, upstarts, jacks-in-office, giving decisions against you in the courts...Jews foreclosing on mortgages...taxation...vulgar display...no respect of leisure, hanging up wretched little flags everywhere, clearing up the streets, moving derelict motor-cars while their owners were not in a position to defend them. Today there was an ordinance forbidding the use of Arab dress. Were they, at their time of life, to start decking themselves out in coat and trousers and topee like a lot of half-caste bank clerks?...besides, the prices tailors charged...it was a put-up job...you might as well be in a British colony.

Meanwhile, with much overseeing and shouting and banging of behinds, preparations were in progress on the route to the railway station; the first train since the troubles was due to leave that afternoon.

It had taken a long time to get a train together. On the eve of the battle of Ukaka the stationmaster and all the more responsible members of his staff had left for the mainland. In the week that followed Seth's victory they had returned one by one with various explanations of their absence. Then there had been the tedious business of repairing the line which both armies had ruined at several places; they had had to collect wood fuel for the engine and wire for the telegraph lines. This had been the longest delay, for no sooner was it procured from the mainland than it was stolen by General Connolly's disbanded soldiers to decorate the arms and legs of their women. Finally, when everything had been prepared, it was decided to delay the train a few days until the arrival of the mail ship from Europe. It thus happened that Basil Seal's arrival in Matodi coincided with the date fixed for Seth's triumphal return to Debra Dowa.

Arrangements for his departure had been made with great care
by the Emperor himself, and the chief features embodied in
a proclamation in Sakuyu, Arabic and French, which was posted
prominently among the many pronouncements which heralded the
advent of Progress and the New Age.

ORDER FOR THE DAY OF THE EMPEROR'S DEPARTURE

(1) *The Emperor will proceed to Matodi railway station at 14.30 hours (8.30
Mohammedan time). He will be attended by his personal suite, the Commander-
in-Chief and the General Staff. The guard of honour will be composed of the first
battalion of the Imperial Life Guards. Full dress uniform (boots for officers), will
be worn by all ranks. Civilian gentlemen will wear jacket and orders. Ball
ammunition will not be issued to the troops.*

(2) *The Emperor will be received at the foot of the station steps by the
stationmaster who will conduct him to his carriage. The public will not be admitted
to the platforms, or to any of the station buildings with the exception of the following,
in the following order of precedence. Consular representatives of foreign powers, the
Nestorian Metropolitan of Matodi, the Vicar Apostolic, the Mormon elder, officers
of H.I.M. forces, directors of the Grand Chemin de Fer d'Azanie, peers of the
Azanian Empire, representatives of the Press. No person, irrespective of rank, will
be admitted to the platform improperly dressed or under the influence of alcohol.*

(3) *The public will be permitted to line the route to the station. The police will
prevent the discharge of firearms by the public.*

(4) *The sale of alcoholic liquor is forbidden from midnight until the departure
of the Imperial train.*

(5) *One coach will be available for the use of the unofficial travellers to Debra
Dowa. Applications should be made to the stationmaster. No passenger will be
admitted to the platform after 14.00.*

(6) *Any infringement of the following regulations renders the offender liable to
a penalty not exceeding ten years' imprisonment, or confiscation of property and
loss of rights, or both.*

*

Basil read this at the railway station, where he drove in a horse-
cab as soon as he landed. He went to the booking-office and bought
a first-class ticket to Debra Dowa. It cost two hundred rupees.

'Will you please reserve me a seat on this afternoon's train?'

'That is impossible. There is only one carriage. The places have been booked many days.'

'When is the next train?'

'Who can say? Perhaps next week. The engine must come back from Debra Dowa. The others are broken and the mechanic is busy on the tank.'

'I must speak to the stationmaster.'

'I am the stationmaster.'

'Well, listen, it is very urgent that I go to Debra Dowa today.'

'You should have made your arrangements sooner. You must understand, monsieur, that you are no longer in Europe.'

As Basil turned to go, a small man who had been sitting fanning himself on a heap of packing-cases, scrambled down and came across the booking-hall towards him. He was dressed in alpaca and skull cap; he had a cheerful, round, greasy, yellowish face and 'Charlie Chaplin' moustache.

''Ullo Englishmans, you want something.'

'I want to go to Debra Dowa.'

'O.K. I fix it.'

'That's very nice of you.'

'Honour to fix it. You know who I am. Look here.' He handed Basil a card on which was printed: *M. Krikor Youkoumian, Grand Hotel et Bar Amurath Matodi, Grand Hotel Café Epicerie, et Bibliothèque Empereur Seyid Debra Dowa. Tous les renseignements.* The name Seyid had been obliterated in purple ink and *Seth* substituted for it.

'You keep that,' said Mr Youkoumian. 'You come to Debra Dowa. You come to me. I fix everything. What's your name, sir?'

'Seal.'

'Well look, Mr Seal. You want to come to Debra Dowa. I got two seats. You pay me two hundred rupees, I put Mme Youkoumian in the mule truck. 'Ow's that, eh?'

'I'm not going to pay anything like that, I'm afraid.'

'Now listen, Mr Seal. I fix it for you. You don't know this country. Stinking place. You miss this train, you stay in Matodi one, two, three, perhaps six weeks. How much you pay then? I like Englishmens. They are my favourite gentlemen. Look, you give me hundred and fifty rupees I put Mme Youkoumian with the mules. You don't understand what that will be like. They are the General's mules. Very savage stinking animals. All day they will stamp at her. No air in the truck. 'Orrible, unhealthy place. Very like she die or is kicked. She is good wife, work 'ard, very loving. If you are not Englishmans I would not put Mme Youkoumian with the mules for less than five hundred. I fix it for you, O.K.?'

'O.K.,' said Basil. 'You know, you seem to me a good chap.'

'Look, 'ow about you give me money now. Then I take you to my café. Dirty little place, not like London. But you see. I got fine brandy. Very fresh, I made him myself Sunday.'

Basil and Mr Youkoumian took their seats in the train at two o'clock and settled down to wait for the arrival of the Imperial party. There were six other occupants of the carriage – a Greek who offered them oranges and soon fell asleep, four Indians who discussed their racial grievances in an eager undertone, and an Azanian nobleman with his wife who shared a large pie of spiced mutton, lifting the slices between pieces of newspaper and eating silently and almost continuously throughout the afternoon. Mr Youkoumian's personal luggage was very small, but he had several crates of merchandise for his Debra Dowa establishment: by a distribution of minute tips he had managed to get these into the mail van. Mme Youkoumian squatted disconsolately in a corner of the van clutching a little jar of preserved cherries which her husband had given her to compensate for the change of accommodation; a few feet from her in the darkness came occasional nervous brays and whinnies and a continuous fretful stamping of the straw.

In spite of Seth's proclamation the police were at some difficulty in keeping the platform clear of the public; twenty or thirty of them prosecuted a vigorous defence with long bamboo staves, whacking the woolly heads as they appeared above the corrugated iron fence. Even so, large numbers of unauthorized spectators were established out of reach on the station roof. The Indian who supplied pictures of local colour to an International Press Agency was busily taking snapshots of the notables. These had not observed the Emperor's instructions to the letter. The Nestorian Metropolitan swayed on the arm of his chaplain, unquestionably drunk; the representative of the *Courier d'Azanie* wore an open shirt, a battered topee, crumpled white trousers and canvas shoes; the Levantine shipping agent who acted as vice-consul for Great Britain, the Netherlands, Sweden, Portugal and Latvia had put on a light water-proof over his pyjamas and come to the function straight from bed; the Eurasian bank manager who acted as vice-consul for Soviet Russia, France and Italy was still asleep; the general merchant of inscrutable ancestry who represented the other great powers was at the moment employed on the mainland making final arrangements for the trans-shipment from Alexandria of a long-awaited consignment of hashish. Some Azanian dignitaries in national costume sat in a row on the carpets their slaves had spread for them, placidly scratching the soles of their bare feet and conversing intermittently on questions of sex. The stationmaster's livestock – two goats and a few small turkeys – had been expelled in honour of the occasion from their normal quarters in the ladies' waiting-room, and wandered at will about the platform gobbling at fragments of refuse.

It was more than an hour after the appointed time when the drums and fifes of the Imperial guard announced the Emperor's arrival. They had been held up by the derelict motor-car which had all the morning resisted the efforts of the convicts to move it. The Civil Governor, on whom rested the ultimate responsibility for this mishap, was soundly thrashed and degraded from the rank of Viscount to that of Baronet before the procession could be resumed. It was necessary for the Emperor to leave his car and complete the journey on mule back, his luggage bobbing behind him on the heads of a dozen suddenly conscripted spectators.

He arrived in a bad temper, scowled at the stationmaster and the two vice-consuls, ignored the native nobility and the tipsy Bishop, and bestowed only the most sour of smiles on the press photographers. The guard presented arms, the interlopers on the roof set up an uncertain cheer and he strode across to the carriage prepared for him. General Connolly and the rest of the royal entourage bundled into their places. The stationmaster stood hat in hand waiting for orders.

'His Majesty is now ready to start.'

The stationmaster waved his hat to the engine-driver; the guard once more presented their arms. The drums and fifes struck up the national anthem. The two daughters of the director of the line scattered rose petals round the steps of the carriage. The engine whistled, Seth continued to smile . . . nothing happened. At the end of the verse the band music died away; the soldiers stood irresolutely at the present; the Nestorian Metropolitan continued to beat the time of some interior melody; the goats and turkeys wandered in and out among the embarrassed spectators. Then, when all seemed frozen in silence, the engine gave a great wrench, shaking the train coach by coach from the tender to the mule boxes, and suddenly, to the immense delight of the darkies on the roof, shot off by itself into the country.

'The Emperor has given no orders for a delay.'

'It is a thing I did not foresee,' said the stationmaster. 'Our only engine has gone away alone. I think I shall be disgraced for this affair.'

But Seth made no comment. The other passengers came out on to the platform, smoking and making jokes. He did not look out at them. This gross incident had bruised his most vulnerable feelings. He had been made ridiculous at a moment of dignity and triumph; he had been disappointed in plans he had made eagerly; his own superiority was compromised by contact with such service. Basil passed his window and caught a glimpse of a gloomy but very purposeful black face under a white sun helmet. And at that moment the Emperor was resolving. 'My people are a worthless people. I give orders; there is none to obey me. I am like a great musician without an instrument. A wrecked car broadside across the line of my procession . . . a royal train without an engine . . . goats on the plat-form . . . I can do nothing with these people. The Metropolitan is drunk. Those old landowners giggled when the engine broke away; I must find a man of culture, a modern man . . . a representative of Progress and the New Age.' And Basil again passed the window; this time in conversation with General Connolly.

Presently, amid cheers, the runaway engine puffed backwards into the station.

Mechanics ran out to repair the coupling.

At last they started.

Basil began the journey in a cheerful temper. He had got on very well with the General and had accepted an invitation to 'Pop in for a spot any time' when they reached the capital.

*

The train which brought the Emperor to Debra Dowa also brought the mail. It was a great day at the British Legation. The bags were brought into the dining-room and they all sat round dealing out the letters and parcels, identifying the handwritings and reading over each other's shoulders... 'Peter's heard from Flora.' 'Do let me read Anthony's letter after you, Mabel.' 'Here's a page to go on with.' 'Does anyone want Jack's letter from Sybil?' 'Yes, I do, but I haven't finished Mabel's from Agnes yet.' 'What a lot of money William owes. Here's a bill for eighty-two pounds from his tailor.' 'And twelve from his book-shop.' 'Who's this from, Prudence? I don't know the writing...'

'Awful lot of official stuff,' complained Sir Samson. 'Can't bother about that now. You might take charge of it, Peter, and have a look through it when you get time.'

'It won't be for a day or two, I'm afraid, sir. We're simply snowed under with work in the chancery over this gymkhana.'

'Yes, yes, my boy, of course, all in good time. Always stick to the job in hand. I dare say there's nothing that needs an answer, and anyway there's no knowing when the next mail will go... I say, though, here's something interesting, my word it is. Can't make head or tail of the thing. It says, "*Good luck. Copy this letter out nine times and send it to nine different friends*" ... What an extraordinary idea.'

'Envoy dear, do be quiet. I want to try the new records.'

'No, but Prudence, do listen. It was started by an American officer in France. If one breaks the chain one gets bad luck, and if one sends it on, good luck. There was one woman lost her husband and another one who made a fortune at roulette – all through doing it and not doing it ... you know I should never have believed that possible ...'

Prudence played the new records. It was a solemn thought to the circle that they would hear these eight tunes daily, week after week, without release, until that unpredictable day when another mail should arrive from Europe. In their bungalows, in their compound, in their rare, brief excursions into the outer world, these words would run in their heads... Meanwhile they opened their letters and unrolled their newspapers.

'Envoy, what *have* you got there?'

'My dear, another most extraordinary thing. Look here. It's all about the Great Pyramid. You see it's all a "cosmic allegory". It depends on the "Displacement factor". Listen, "*The combined length of the two tribulation passages is precisely* 153 *Pyramid inches* – 153 *being the number symbolic of the Elect in Our Lord's mystical enactment of the draught of* 153 *great fishes.*" I say, I must go into this. It sounds frightfully interesting! I can't think who sends me these things. Jolly decent of them whoever it is.'

Eleven *Punch*es, eleven *Graphic*s; fifty-nine copies of *The Times*, two *Vogue*s and a mixed collection of *New Yorker*s, *Week End Review*s, *St James's Gazette*s, *Horses and Hounds, Journals of Oriental Studies*, were unrolled and distributed. Then came novels from Mudie's, cigars, soda-water sparklets.

'We ought to have a Christmas tree next time the bag comes in.'

Several Foreign Office dispatches were swept up and incinerated among the litter of envelopes and wrappings.

'Apparently inside the Pyramid there is a chamber of the Triple Veil of Ancient Egyptian Prophecy... the east wall of the Ante-chamber symbolizes Truce in Chaos...'

'There is a card announcing a gala night at the Perroquet tomorrow, Envoy. Don't you think we might go?'

'... *Four limestone blocks representing the Final Tribulation in* 1936 ...'

'*Envoy.*'

'Eh... I'm so sorry. Yes, we'll certainly go. Haven't been out for weeks.'

'By the way,' said William, 'we had a caller in today.'

'Not the Bishop?'

'No, someone new. He wrote his name in the book. Basil Seal.'

'What does *he* want, I wonder? Know anything about him?'

'I seem to have heard his name. I don't quite know where.'

'Ought we to ask him to stay? He didn't bring any letters?'

'No.'

'Thank God. Well, we'll ask him to luncheon one day. I expect he'll find it too hot to come out often.'

'Oh,' said Prudence, 'somebody *new*. That's more than one could have hoped for. Perhaps he'll be able to teach us backgammon.'

That evening M. Ballon received a disquieting report.

'*Mr Basil Seal, British politician travelling under private title, has arrived in Debra Dowa, and is staying in M. Youkoumian's house. He is avoiding all open association with the Legation. This evening he called, but presented no credentials. He is obviously expected. He has been seen in conversation with General Connolly, the new Duke of Ukaka.*'

'I do not like the look of this Mr Seal. The old fox, Sir Courteney, is playing a deep game – but old Ballon will outwit him yet.'

*

The Victory Ball at the Perroquet exceeded all its promoter's highest expectations in splendour and gaiety. Every side of Azanian life was liberally represented. The court circle and diplomatic corps, the army and government services, the Church, commerce, the native nobility and the cosmopolitan set.

A gross of assorted novelties – false noses, paper caps, trumpets and dolls – had arrived by the mail from Europe, but demands exceeded the supply. Turbans and tarbooshes bobbed round the dancing floor; there were men in Azanian state robes, white jackets, uniforms, and reach-me-down tail coats; women of all complexions in recently fashionable gowns, immense imitation jewels and lumpy ornaments of solid gold. There was Mme 'Fifi' Fatim Bey, the town courtesan, and her present protector Viscount Boaz, the Minister of the Interior; there was the Nestorian Patriarch and his favourite deacon; there was the Duke and Duchess of Ukaka; there was the manager, Prince Fyodor Krononin, elegant and saturnine, reviewing the late arrivals at the door; there was Basil Seal and Mr Youkoumian, who had been hard at work all that day, making champagne for the party. At a long table near the back were the British Legation in full force.

'Envoy, you *can't* wear a false nose.'

'I don't at all see why not. I think it's very amusing.'

'I don't think that you ought really to be here at all.'

Viscount Boaz and Mme Fifi Fatim Bey at
the Victory Ball at the Perroquet

'Why? M. Ballon is.'

'Yes, but *he* doesn't look as if he were enjoying himself.'

'I say, shall I send him one of those chain letters?'

'Yes, I don't see why you shouldn't do that.'

'It will puzzle him terribly.'

'Envoy, who's that young man? I'm sure he's English.'

Basil had gone across to Connolly's table.

'Hullo, old boy. Take a pew. This is Black Bitch.'

'How do you do.' The little Negress put down her trumpet, bowed with grave dignity and held out her hand. 'Not Black Bitch any more. Duchess of Ukaka now.'

'My word, hasn't she got an ugly mug?' said the Duke. 'But she's a good little thing.'

Black Bitch flashed a great, white grin of pleasure at the compliment. It was a glorious night for her; it would have been rapture enough to have her man back from the wars; but to be made a Duchess and taken to supper among all the white ladies . . . all in the same day . . .

*

'You see,' said M. Ballon to his first secretary. '*That is* the man, over there with Connolly. You are having him watched?'

'Ceaselessly.'

'You have instructed the waiter to attend carefully to the conversation at the English table?'

'He reported to me just now in the cloakroom. It is impossible to understand. Sir Samson speaks all the time of the dimensions of the Great Pyramid.'

'A trap, doubtless.'

*

The Emperor had signified his intention of making an appearance some time during the evening. At the end of the ballroom a box had been improvised for him with bunting, pots of palm, and gilt cardboard. Soon after midnight he came. At a sign from Prince Fyodor the band stopped in the middle of the tune and struck up the national anthem. The dancing couples scuttled to the side

of the ballroom; the guests at supper rose awkwardly to their
feet, pushing their tables forward with a rattle of knives and glass;
there was a furtive self-conscious straightening of ties and removing
of paper caps. Sir Samson Courteney alone absent-mindedly
retained his false nose. The royal entourage in frogged uniforms
advanced down the polished floor; in their centre, half a pace ahead,
looking neither to right nor left, strode the Emperor in evening
dress, white kid gloves, heavily starched linen, neat pearl studs and
jet black face.

'Got up just as though he were going to sing Spirituals at a party,'
said Lady Courteney.

Prince Fyodor glided in front and ushered him to his table. He sat
down alone. The suite ranged themselves behind his chair. He gave
a slight nod to Prince Fyodor. The band resumed the dance music.
The Emperor watched impassively as the company began to settle
down to a state of enjoyment.

Presently, by means of an agency, he invited the wife of the
American minister to dance with him. The other couples fell back.
With gravity and grace he led Mrs Schonbaum into the centre,
danced with her twice round the room, led her back to her table,
bowed and returned to his box.

'Why, he dances beautifully,' reported Mrs Schonbaum. 'I often
wonder what they would say back home to see me dancing with
a man of colour.'

'I do pray he comes and dances with Mum,' said Prudence. 'Do
you think it's any use me trying to vamp him, or does he only go for
wives?'

The evening went on.

The *maître d'hôtel* approached Prince Fyodor in some distress.

'Highness, they are complaining about the champagne.'

'Who are?'

'The French Legation.'

'Tell them we will make a special price for them.'

*

'. . . Highness, more complaints of the champagne.'

'Who this time?'

'The Duke of Ukaka.'

'Take away the bottle, pour in a tumbler of brandy and bring it back.'

'... Highness, is it proper to serve the Minister of the Interior with more wine? He is pouring it in his lady's lap.'

'It is proper. You ask questions like an idiot.'

*

The English party began to play consequences on the menu cards. They were of the simplest sort: *The amorous Duke of Ukaka met the intoxicated Mme Ballon in the Palace w.c. He said to her 'Floreat Azania'*...

'Envoy, if you laugh so much we'll have to stop playing.'

'Upon my soul, though, that's funny.'

'Mum, do you think that young man with the Connollys is the one who called?'

'I dare say. We must ask him to something some time. Perhaps he'll be here for the Christmas luncheon ... but he seems to have plenty of friends already.'

'Mum, don't be snobbish – particularly now Connolly's a Duke. Do let's have him to everything always ...'

*

Basil said, 'I've been trying to catch the Emperor's eye. I don't believe he remembers me.'

'The old boy's on rather a high horse now the war's over. He'll come down a peg when the bills start coming in. They've brought us a better bottle of fizz this time. Like Fyodor's impudence trying to palm off that other stuff on us.'

'I wonder if it would be possible to arrange an audience.'

'Look here, old boy, have you come here to enjoy yourself or have you not? I've been in camp with that Emperor off and on for the last six months and I want to forget him. Give Black Bitch some bubbly and help yourself and for the love of Mike talk smut.'

*

'Monsieur Jean, something terrible has come to my knowledge,' said the French second secretary.

'Tell me,' said the first secretary.

'I can scarcely bring myself to do so. It affects the honour of the Minister's wife.'

'Incredible. Tell me at once. It is your duty to France.'

'For France then . . . when affected by wine she made an assignation with the Duke of Ukaka. He loves her.'

'Who would have thought it possible? Where?'

'In the toilette at the Palace.'

'But there is no toilette at the Palace.'

'Sir Samson Courteney has written evidence to that effect. The paper has been folded into a narrow strip. No doubt it was conveyed to him by one of his spies. Perhaps in a roll of bread.'

'Extraordinary. We will keep this from the Minister. We will watch, ourselves. It is a secret between us. No good can come of it. Alas, poor Monsieur Ballon. He trusted her. We must prevent this thing.'

'For France.'

'For France and Monsieur Ballon.'

'. . . I have never observed Madame Ballon the worse for drink . . . '

*

Paper caps were resumed: bonnets of liberty, conical dunce's hats, jockey caps, Napoleonic casques, hats for pierrots and harlequins, postmen, highlanders, old Mothers Hubbard and little Misses Muffet over faces of every complexion, brown as boots, chalk white, dun and the fresh boiled pink of Northern Europe. False noses again: brilliant sheaths of pigmented cardboard attached to noses of every anthropological type, the high arch of the Semite, freckled Nordic snouts, broad black nostrils from swamp villages of the mainland, the pulpy inflamed flesh of the alcoholic, and unlovely syphilitic voids. Ribbons of coloured papers tangled and snapped about the dancers' feet; coloured balls volleyed from table to table. One, erratically thrown by Madame Fifi, bounced close to the royal box; the Minister of the Interior facetiously applauded her aim.

Prince Fyodor glanced anxiously about him. His patrons were beginning to enjoy themselves. If only the Emperor would soon leave; an *incident* might occur at any moment.

But Seth sat alone among the palms and garlands, apparently deep in thought; his fingers fidgeted with the stem of his wine glass; sometimes, without raising his head, he half furtively surveyed the room. The equerries behind his chair despaired of permission to dance. If only His Majesty would go home, they could slip back before the fun was all over...

*

'Old boy, your pal the Great Panjandrum is something of a damper on this happy throng. Why can't the silly mutt go off home and leave us to have a jolly up?'

*

'Can't conceive why young Seth doesn't move. Can't be enjoying himself.'

*

But the Emperor sat tight. This was the celebration of his Victory. This was the society of Debra Dowa. There was the British Minister happy as a parent at a children's party. There was the Minister of the Interior, behaving hideously. There was the Commander-in-Chief of the Azanian army. And with him was Basil Seal. Seth recognized him in his first grave survey of the restaurant and suddenly, on this triumphal night in his own capital, he was overcome by shyness. It was nearly three years since they last met and Seth recalled the light drizzle of rain in the Oxford quadrangle, a scout carrying a tray of dirty plates, a group of undergraduates in tweeds lounging about among bicycles in the porch. He had been an undergraduate of no account in his College, amiably classed among Bengali babus, Siamese, and grammar school scholars as one of the remote and praiseworthy people who had come a long way to the University. Basil had enjoyed a reputation of peculiar brilliance among his contemporaries. On the rare occasions when evangelically minded undergraduates asked Seth to tea or coffee, his name occurred in the conversation with awed disapproval. He played poker for high stakes. His luncheon parties lasted until dusk, his dinner parties dispersed in riot. Lovely young women visited him from London in high-powered cars. He went away for week-ends without leave and climbed into College over the tiles at night. He had travelled all over Europe, spoke six languages, called dons by their Christian names and discussed their books with them.

Seth had met him at breakfast with the Master of the College. Basil had talked to him about Azanian topography, the Nestorian Church, Sakuyu dialects, the idiosyncrasies of the chief diplomats in Debra Dowa. Two days later he invited him to luncheon. There had been two peers present and the President of the Union, the editor of a new undergraduate paper and a young don. Seth had sat silent and entranced throughout the afternoon. Later, after long consultation with his scout, he had returned the invitation. Basil accepted and at the last moment made his excuses for not coming. There the acquaintance had ended. Three years had intervened, during which Seth had become Emperor, but Basil still stood for him as the personification of all that glittering, intangible Western culture to which he aspired. And there he was, unaccountably, at the Connollys' table. What must he be thinking? If only the Minister for the Interior were more sober...

The *maître d'hôtel* again approached Prince Fyodor.

'Highness, there is someone at the door who I do not think should be admitted.'

'I will see him.'

But as he turned to the door, the newcomer appeared. He was a towering Negro in full gala dress: on his head a lion's-mane busby; on his shoulders a shapeless fur mantle; a red satin skirt; brass bangles and a necklace of lion's teeth; a long, ornamental sword hung at his side; two bandoliers of brass cartridges circled his great girth; he had small blood-shot eyes and a tousle of black wool over his cheeks and chin. Behind him stood six unsteady slaves carrying antiquated rifles.

It was one of the backwoods peers, the Earl of Ngumo, feudal overlord of some five hundred square miles of impenetrable highland territory. He had occupied himself throughout the civil war in an attempt to mobilize his tribesmen. The battle of Ukaka occurring before the levy was complete, saved him the embarrassment of declaring himself for either combatant. He had therefore left his men in the hills and marched down with a few hundred personal attendants to pay his respects to the victorious side. His celebrations had lasted for some days already and had left some mark upon even his rugged constitution.

Prince Fyodor hurried forward. 'The tables are all engaged. I regret very much that there is no room. We are full up.'

The Earl blinked dully and said, 'I will have a table, some gin and some women and some raw camel's meat for my men outside.'

'But there is no table free.'

'Do not be put out. That is a simple matter. I have some soldiers with me who will quickly find room.'

The band had stopped playing and a hush fell on the crowded restaurant; scared faces under the paper hats and false noses.

'Under the table, Black Bitch,' said Connolly. 'There's going to be a rough house.'

Mr Youkoumian's plump back disappeared through the service door.

'*Now* what's happening?' said the British Minister. 'Someone's up to something, I'll be bound.'

But at that moment the Earl's bovine gaze, moving up the rows of scared faces to its natural focus among the palms and bunting, reached the Emperor. His hand fell to the jewelled hilt of his sword – and twenty hands in various parts of the room felt for pistols and bottle necks – a yard of tarnished damascene flashed into the light and with a roar of homage he sank to his knees in the centre of the polished floor.

Seth rose and folded his hands in the traditional gesture of welcome.

'Peace be upon your house, Earl.'

The vassal rose and Prince Fyodor's perplexities were solved by the departure of the royal party.

'I will have that table,' said the Earl, pointing to the vacated box.

And soon, quite unconscious of the alarm he had caused, with a bottle of M. Youkoumian's gin before him, and a vast black cheroot between his teeth, the magnate was pacifically winking at the ladies as they danced past him.

Outside the royal chauffeur was asleep and only with difficulty could be awakened. The sky was ablaze with stars; dust hung in the cool air, fragrant as crushed herbs; from the Ngumo camp, out of sight below the eucalyptus trees, came the thin smoke of burning dung and the pulse and throb of the hand drummers. Seth drove back alone to the black litter of palace buildings.

'Insupportable barbarians,' he thought. 'I am sure that the English lords do not behave in that way before their King. Even my loyalest officers are ruffians and buffoons. If I had *one* man by me whom I could trust . . . a man of progress and culture . . .'

*

Six weeks passed. The victorious army slowly demobilized and dispersed over the hills in a hundred ragged companies; livestock and women in front, warriors behind laden with alarm clocks and nondescript hardware looted in the bazaars; soldiers of progress and the new age homeward bound to the villages.

The bustle subsided and the streets of Matodi resumed their accustomed calm: copra, cloves, mangoes and khat; azan and angelus; old women with obdurate donkeys; trays of pastry black with flies; shrill voices in the mission school reciting the catechism; lepers and pedlars, and Arab gentlemen with shabby gamps decently parading the water-front at the close of day. In the derelict van outside the railway station, a patient black family repaired the ravages of invasion with a careful architecture of mud, twigs, rag and flattened petrol tins.

Two mail ships outward bound from Marseilles, three on the home journey from Madagascar and Indo-China paused for their normal six hours in the little bay. Four times the train puffed up from Matodi and Debra Dowa; palm belt, lava fields, bush and upland; thin cattle scattered over the sparse fields; shallow furrows in the brittle earth; white-gowned Azanian ploughboys scratching up furrows with wooden ploughs; conical grass roofs in stockades

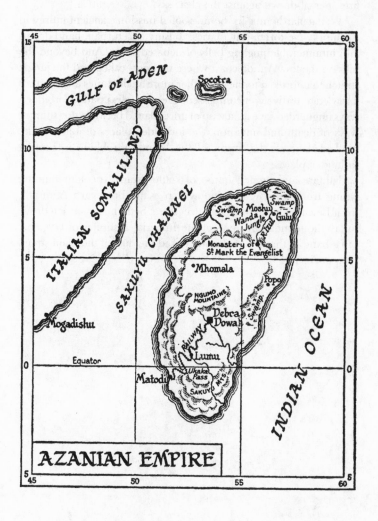

Map of the Azanian Empire

of euphorbia and cactus; columns of smoke from the tukal fires, pencil-drawn against the clear sky.

Vernacular hymns in the tin-roofed missions, ancient liturgy in the murky Nestorian sanctuaries; tonsure and turban, hand drums and innumerable jingling bells of debased silver. And beyond the hills on the low Wanda coast where no liners called and the jungle stretched unbroken to the sea, other more ancient rites and another knowledge furtively encompassed; green, sunless paths; forbidden ways unguarded save for a wisp of grass plaited between two stumps, ways of death and initiation, the forbidden places of juju and the masked dancers; the drums of the Wanda throbbing in sunless, forbidden places.

Fanfare and sennet; tattoo of kettle drums; tricolour bunting strung from window to window across the Boulevard Amurath, from Levantine café to Hindu drugstore; Seth in his Citroën drove to lay the foundation stone of the Imperial Institutes of Hygiene; brass band of the Imperial army raised the dust of the main street. Floreat Azania.

CHAPTER 5

ON THE SOUTH side of the Palace Compound, between the kitchen and the stockade, lay a large irregular space where the oxen were slaughtered for the public banquets. A minor gallows stood there which was used for such trivial, domestic executions as now and then became necessary within the royal household. The place was deserted now except for the small cluster of puzzled blacks who were usually congregated round the headquarters of the One Year Plan and a single dog who gnawed her hindquarters in the patch of shadow cast by two corpses, which rotated slowly face to face, half circle East, half circle West, ten foot high in the limpid morning sunlight.

The Ministry of Modernization occupied what had formerly been the old Empress' oratory; a circular building of concrete and corrugated iron, its outer wall enriched with posters from all parts of Europe and the United States advertising machinery, fashion and foreign travel. The display was rarely without attendance and today the customary loafers were reinforced by five or six gentlemen in the blue cotton cloaks which the official class of Debra Dowa assumed in times of bereavement. These were mourners for the two criminals – peculators and perjurers both – who had come to give a dutiful tug at their relatives' heels in case life might not yet be extinct, and had stayed to gape, entranced by the manifestations of Progress and the New Age.

On the door was a board painted in Arabic, Sakuyu and French with the inscription:

MINISTRY OF MODERNIZATION
HIGH COMMISSIONER & COMPTROLLER GENERAL:
MR BASIL SEAL
FINANCIAL SECRETARY: MR KRIKOR YOUKOUMIAN

A vague smell of incense and candle-grease still possessed the
interior; in all other ways it had been completely transformed.
Two partitions divided it into unequal portions. The largest was
Basil's office, which contained nothing except some chairs, a table
littered with maps and memoranda, and a telephone. Next door
Mr Youkoumian had induced a more homely note: his work was
economically confined to two or three penny exercise-books filled
with figures and indecipherable jottings, but his personality
extended itself and pervaded the room, finding concrete expression
in the seedy red plush sofa that he had scavenged from one of the
state apartments, the scraps of clothing hitched negligently about
the furniture, the Parisian photographs pinned to the walls, the
vestiges of food on enamelled tin plates, the scent spray, cigarette
ends, spittoon and the little spirit-stove over which perpetually
simmered a brass pan of coffee. It was his idiosyncrasy to prefer
working in stockinged feet, so that when he was at his post a pair of
patent leather, elastic-sided boots proclaimed his presence from the
window-ledge.

In the vestibule sat a row of native runners with whose services
the modernizing party were as yet unable to dispense.

At nine in the morning both Basil and Mr Youkoumian were at
their desks. Instituted a month previously by royal proclamation, the
Ministry of Modernization was already a going concern. Just how
far it was going, indeed, was appreciated by very few outside its
circular placarded walls. Its function as defined in Seth's decree was
'*to promote the adoption of modern organization and habits of life throughout the
Azanian Empire*' which, liberally interpreted, comprised the right of
interference in most of the public and private affairs of the nation. As
Basil glanced through the correspondence that awaited him and the
rough agenda for the day, he felt ready to admit that anyone but
himself and Mr Youkoumian would have bitten off more than he
could chew. Reports from eight provincial viceroys on a question-

naire concerning the economic resources and population of their territory – documents full of ponderous expressions of politeness and the minimum of trustworthy information; detailed recommendations from the railway authorities at Matodi; applications for concessions from European prospectors; inquiries from tourist bureaux about the possibilities of big-game hunting, surf bathing and mountaineering; applications for public appointments; protests from missions and legations; estimates for building; details of court etiquette and precedence – everything seemed to find its way to Basil's table. The other ministers of the crown had not yet begun to feel uneasy about their own positions. They regarded Basil's arrival as a direct intervention of heaven on their behalf. Here was an Englishman who was willing to leave them their titles and emoluments and take all the work off their hands. Each was issued with the rubber stamp REFER TO BUREAU OF MODERNIZATION, and in a very few days the Minister of the Interior, the Lord Chamberlain, the Justiciar, the City Governor, and even Seth himself, acquired the habit of relegating all decisions to Basil with one firm stab of indelible ink. Two officials alone, the Nestorian patriarch and the Commander-in-Chief of the army, failed to avail themselves of the convenient new institution, but continued to muddle through the routine of their departments in the same capricious, dilatory but independent manner as before the establishment of the new régime.

Basil had been up very late the night before working with the Emperor on a codification of the criminal law, but the volume of business before him left him undismayed.

'Youkoumian.'

''Ullo. Mr Seal?'

The financial secretary padded in from the next room.

'Connolly won't have boots.'

'Won't 'ave boots? But, Mr Seal, he got to 'ave boots. I bought them from Cape Town. They come next ship. I bought them, you understand, as a personal enterprise, out of my own pocket. What in 'ell can I do with a thousand pair of boots if Connolly won't take them?'

'You ought to have waited.'

'Waited? And then when the order is out and everyone knows Guards to 'ave boots, what'll 'appen then? Some pig wanting to make money will go to the Emperor and say I get you boots damned cheaper than Youkoumian. Where am I then? They might as well go barefoot all same as they do now like the dirty niggers they are. No, Mr Seal, that is not business. I fix it so that one morning the Army Order says Guards must have boots. Everyone say, but where are boots? No one got enough boots in this stinking hole. Someone say, I get you boots in three weeks, month, five weeks, so long. I come up and say, *I* got boots. How many pairs you want? Thousand? O.K. I fix it. That is business. What does the General say?'

Basil handed him the letter. It was emphatic and almost ungenerously terse, coming as it did in answer to a carefully drafted recommendation beginning, '*The Minister of Modernization presents his compliments to the Commander-in-Chief of the Imperial Army and in pursuance of the powers granted him by royal decree begs to advise . . .*'

It consisted of a single scrap of lined paper torn from a note-book across which Connolly had scrawled in pencil: *The Minister of Damn All can go to blazes. My men couldn't move a yard in boots. Try and sell Seth top hats next time. Ukaka C. in C.*

'Well,' said Mr Youkoumian doubtfully, 'I *could* get top 'ats.'

'That is one of Connolly's jokes, I'm afraid.'

'Jokes, is it? And 'ere am I with a thousand pair black boots on my 'ands. Ha. Ha. Like 'ell it's a joke. There isn't a thousand people in the whole country that wears boots. Besides these aren't the kind of boots people buys for themselves. Government stuff. Damn rotten. See what I mean?'

'Don't you worry,' Basil said. 'We'll find a use for them. We might have them served out to the clergy.' He took back the General's note, glanced through it frowning and clipped it into the file of correspondence; when he raised his head his eyes were clouded in an expression characteristic to him, insolent, sulky and curiously childish. 'But as a matter of fact,' he added, 'I shouldn't mind a showdown with Connolly. It's nearly time for one.'

'They are saying that the General is in love with Madame Ballon.'

'I don't believe it.'

'I am convinced,' said Mr Youkoumian. 'It was told me on very 'igh authority by the barber who visits the French Legation. Every-one in the town is speaking of it. Even Madame Youkoumian has heard. I tell you 'ow it is,' he added complacently. 'Madame Ballon drinks. That is 'ow Connolly first 'ad 'er.'

*

Quarter of an hour later both Basil and Mr Youkoumian were engaged in what seemed more important business.

A morning's routine at the Ministry of Modernization.

'Now, look, Mister, I tell you exactly how we are fixed. We have His Majesty's interests to safeguard. See what I mean? You think there is tin in the Ngumo mountains in workable quantities. So do we. So do other companies. They want concession too. Only today two gentlemen come to ask me to fix it for them. What do I do? I say, we can only give concession to company we have confidence in. Look. How about if on your board of directors you had a man of financial status in the country; someone who His Majesty trusts ... see what I mean? ... someone with a fair little block of share allo-cated to him. He would protect His Majesty's interests and interests of company too ... see?'

'That's all very well, Mr Youkoumian, but it isn't so easy to find anyone like that. I can't think of anyone at the moment.'

'No, can't you? Can't you think?'

'Unless, of course, you yourself? But I can hardly suggest that. You are far too busy.'

'Mister, I have learned how to be busy and still have time for things that please me ...'

*

Next door: Basil and the American commercial attaché: 'The situation is this, Walker. I'm – the Emperor is spending a quarter of a million sterling on road construction this year. It can't come out of the ordinary revenue. I'm floating a loan to raise the money. You're acting over here for Cosmopolitan Oil Trust and for Stetson cars. Every mile of road we make is worth five hundred cars a year and

God knows how many gallons of oil. If your companies like to take up the loan I'm prepared to give them a ten-years' monopoly...'

Later, the editor of the *Courier d'Azanie*.

M. Bertrand did not look a man of any importance – nor, in fact, was he. The *Courier* consisted of a single sheet, folded quarto, which was issued weekly to rather less than a thousand subscribers in Debra Dowa and Matodi. It retailed in French the chief local events of the week – the diplomatic entertainments, official appointments, court circular, the programmes of the cinemas and such few items of foreign news as came through on the wireless. It occupied one day a week of M. Bertrand's time, the remainder of which was employed in printing menus, invitation cards, funeral and wedding announce-ments, in acting as local correspondent for a European news-agency and in selling stationery over the counter of his little office. It was in the hope of a fat order for crested note-paper that he presented himself in answer to Basil's invitation at the offices of the new Ministry.

'Good morning, Monsieur Bertrand. It's good of you to come. We may as well get to business at once. I want to buy your paper.'

'Why, certainly, Monsieur Seal. I have a very nice cream-laid line suitable for office use or a slightly more expensive quality azure-tinted with a linen surface. I suppose you would want the name of the Ministry embossed at the head?'

'I don't think you understand me. I mean the *Courier d'Azanie*.'

M. Bertrand's face showed disappointment and some vexation. It was really unpardonably high-handed of this young man to demand a personal call from the proprietor and editor-in-chief whenever he bought a copy of his journal.

'I will tell my clerk. You wish to subscribe regularly?'

'No, no, you don't understand. I wish to become the proprietor – to own the entire concern. What is your price?'

Slowly the idea took root, budded and blossomed; then M. Bertrand said: 'Oh no, that would be quite impossible. I don't want to sell.'

'Come, come. It can't be worth much to you and I am willing to pay a generous price.'

'It is not that, sir; it is a question of prestige, you understand,' he spoke very earnestly. 'You see, as the proprietor and editor of the *Courier* I am *someone*. Twice a year Madame Bertrand and I dine at the French Legation; once we go to the garden party, we go to the Court and the polo club. That is something. But if I become Bertrand, job-printer, who will regard me then? Madame Bertrand would not forgive it.'

'I see,' said Basil. To be someone in Debra Dowa . . . it seemed a modest ambition; it would be a shame to deprive M. Bertrand. 'I see. Well, suppose that you retained the position of editor and were nominally proprietor. That would fulfil my purpose. You see I am anxious to enlarge the scope of your paper. I wish it to publish leading articles explaining the political changes. Listen . . . ' and for a quarter of an hour Basil outlined his intentions for the *Courier*'s development . . . three sheets, advertisements of European firms and government services to meet increased cost of production; enlarged circulation; features in Sakuyu and Arabic; intelligent support of government policy . . . At the end of the interview M. Bertrand left, slightly bewildered, carrying with him a fair-sized cheque and the notes for a leading article forecasting possible changes in the penal code . . . convict settlements to replace local prisons . . . What extraordinary subjects to mention in the *Courier*!

At eleven the Anglican Bishop came to protest against the introduction of State Lotteries.

At a quarter past William came from Sir Samson Courteney to discuss the possibility of making a road out to the Legation. William and Basil did not like each other.

At half-past the Lord Chamberlain came to consult about cookery. A banquet was due to some Wanda notables next week. Seth had forbidden raw beef. What was he to give them? 'Raw beef,' said Basil. 'Call it steak tartare.'

'That is in accordance with modern thought?'

'Perfectly.'

At noon Basil went to see the Emperor.

The heat, rarely intolerable in the hills, was at this time of day penetrating and devitalizing. The palace roofs glared and shimmered. A hot breeze lifted the dust and powdered the bodies of the dangling courtiers and carried across the yard a few waste shreds of paper, baked crisp and brittle as dead leaves. Basil sauntered with half-shut eyes to the main entrance.

Soldiers stood up and saluted clumsily; the captain of the guard trotted after him and plucked at his sleeve.

'Good morning, captain.'

'Good morning, Excellency. You are on your way to the Emperor?'

'As usual.'

'There is a small matter. If I could interest your excellency... It is about the two gentlemen who were hanged. One was my cousin.'

'Yes?'

'His post has not yet been filled. It has always been held by my family. My uncle has made a petition to His Majesty...'

'Yes, yes. I will speak on his behalf.'

'But that is exactly what you must not do. My uncle is a wicked man, Excellency. It was he who poisoned my father. I am sure of it. He wanted my mother. It would be most unjust for him to have the post. There is my little brother – a man of supreme ability and devotion...'

'Very well, captain, I'll do what I can.'

'The angels preserve your excellency.'

The Emperor's study was strewn with European papers and catalogues; his immediate concern was a large plan of Debra Dowa on which he was working with ruler and pencil.

'Come in, Seal, I'm just rebuilding the city. The Anglican Cathedral will have to go, I think, and all the South quarter. Look, here is Seth Square with the avenues radiating from it. I'm calling this, Boulevard Basil Seal.'

'Good of you, Seth.'

'And this, Avenue Connolly.'

'Ah, I wanted to talk about him.' Basil sat down and approached his subject discreetly. 'I wouldn't say anything against him. I know you like him and in his rough-and-tumble way he's a decent soldier. But d'you ever feel that he's *not quite modern*?'

'He never made full use of our tank.'

'Exactly. He's opposed to progress throughout. He wants to keep the army under *his* control. Now there's the question of boots. I don't think we told you, but the matter came before the Ministry and we sent in a recommendation that the Guards should be issued with boots. It would increase their efficiency a hundred per cent. Half the sick list is due to hook-worm which as you know comes from going about barefooted. Besides, you know, there's the question of prestige. There's not a single Guards regiment in Europe without boots. You've seen them for yourself at Buckingham Palace. You'll never get the full respect of the powers until you give your troops boots.'

'Yes, yes, by all means. They shall have boots at once.'

'I was sure you'd see it that way. But the trouble is that Connolly's standing out against it. Now we've no power at present to issue an army ordinance. That has to come through him – or through you as commander-in-chief of the army.'

'I'll make out an order today. Of course they must have boots. I'll hang any man I see barefooted.'

'Fine. I thought you'd stand by us, Seth. You know,' he added reflectively, 'we've got a much easier job now than we should have had fifty years ago. If we'd had to modernize a country then it would have meant constitutional monarchy, bi-cameral legislature, proportional representation, women's suffrage, independent judicature, freedom of the Press, referendums ... '

'What is all that?' asked the Emperor.

'Just a few ideas that have ceased to be modern.'

Then they settled down to the business of the day.

'The British Legation are complaining again about their road.'

'That is an old question. I am tired of it. Besides, you will see from the plan I have orientated all the roads leading out of the capital; they go by the points of the compass. I cannot upset my arrangements.'

'The Minister feels very strongly about it.'

'Well, another time ... no, I tell you what I will do. Look, we will name this street after him. Then he will be satisfied.'

The Emperor took up his indiarubber and erased Connolly's name from the new metropolis. *Avenue Sir Samson Courteney* he wrote in its place.

'I wish we had a tube railway,' he said. 'Do you think it would pay?'

'No.'

'So I feared. But one day we will have one. Listen. You can tell Sir Samson that. When there is a tube railway he shall have a private station in the Legation compound. Now listen; I have had a letter from the Society for the Prevention of Cruelty to Animals. They want to send out a Commission to investigate Wanda methods of hunting. Is it cruel to spear lions, do you think?'

'No.'

'No. However, here is the letter. From Dame Mildred Porch. Do you know her?'

'I've heard of her. An intolerable old gas-bag.'

'What is gas-bag? An orator?'

'Yes, in a way.'

'Well, she is returning from South Africa and wishes to spend a week here. I will say yes?'

'I shouldn't.'

'I will say yes . . . And another thing. I have been reading in my papers about something very modern called Birth Control. What is it?'

Basil explained.

'I must have a lot of that. You will see to it. Perhaps it is not a matter for an ordinance, what do you think? We must popularize it by propaganda – educate the people in sterility. We might have a little pageant in its honour . . .'

*

Sir Samson accepted the rebuff to his plans with characteristic calm. 'Well, well, I don't suppose young Seth will keep his job long. There's bound to be another revolution soon. The boy's head over heels in debt, they tell me. I dare say the next government, whoever they are, will be able to afford something. And anyway, you may laugh at me, Prudence, but I think it's uncommonly decent of the young fellow to name that avenue after me. I've always liked him. You never know. Debra Dowa may become a big city one day. I like to think of all the black johnnies in a hundred years' time driving up and down in their motor-cars and going to the shops and saying "Number a hundred Samson Courteney" and wondering who I was. Like, like . . . '

'Like the Avenue Victor Hugo, Envoy.'

'*Exactly, or St James's Square.*'

But the question of the boots was less easily settled.

On the afternoon of the day when the new ordinance was issued, Basil and Mr Youkoumian were in conference. A major difficulty had arisen with regard to the plans for the new guest house at the Palace. The Emperor had been captivated by some photographs he had discovered in a German architectural magazine and had decided to have the new building constructed of steel and vita-glass. Basil had spent half the morning in a vain attempt to persuade the royal mind that this was not a style at all suitable to his tropical climate and he was now at work with his financial secretary on a memorandum of the prohibitive extravagance of the new plans, when the door was pushed noisily open and the Duke of Ukaka strode into the room.

'Clear out, Youkoumian,' he said. 'I want to talk to your boss.'

'O.K., General. I'll 'op off. No offence.'

'Nonsense. Mr Youkoumian is financial secretary of the Ministry. I should like him to be present at our interview.'

'What, me, Mr Seal? I got nothing to say to the General.'

'I wish you to stay.'

'Quick,' said the Duke, making a menacing motion towards him.

'Very sorry, gentlemen,' said Mr Youkoumian and shot through the door into his own office.

First trick to Connolly.

'I notice even that little dago has the sense to take off his boots.'

Second trick to Connolly.

But in the subsequent interview Basil held his own. The General began: 'Sorry to have to sling that fellow out. Can't stand his smell. Now let's talk. What's all this infernal nonsense about boots?'

'His Majesty's ordinance seemed perfectly explicit to me.'

'*His Majesty's trousers.* For the Lord's sake come off the high horse, old boy, and listen to me. I don't give a hoot in hell about your modernization. It's none of my business. You can set every damn coon in the place doing crossword puzzles for all I care. But I'm not going to have any monkeying about with my men. You'll lame the whole army in a day if you try to make 'em wear boots. Now look here, there's no reason why we should scrap over this. I've been in the country long enough to see through Youkoumian's game. Selling junk to government has been the staple industry of Debra Dowa as long as I can remember it. I'd as soon you got the boodle as anyone else. Listen. If I tip the wink to the people on the line I can have the whole consignment of boots carried off by Sakuyu. You'll get compensation, the ordinance will be forgotten and no one will be any the worse off. What do you say? Is it a deal?'

For an appreciable time Basil hesitated in a decision of greater importance than either of them realized. The General sat jauntily on the edge of the table bending his riding-cane over his knee; his expression was one of cordiality and of persuasive good sense. Basil hesitated. Was it some atavistic sense of a caste, an instinct of superiority, that held him aloof? Or was it vexed megalomania because Mr Youkoumian had trotted so obediently from the room in his stockinged feet?

'You should have made your representations before,' he said. 'The tone of your first note made discussion impossible. The boots will be issued to the war department next week.'

'Blood young fool,' said Connolly and took his leave.

As the door opened Mr Youkoumian hastily stepped back from the keyhole. The General pushed past him and left the Ministry.

'Oh, Mr Seal, why the 'ell do you want a bust-up with 'im for? Look, how about I go after 'im and fix it, eh, Mr Seal?'

'You won't do anything of the sort. We'll carry right on with the plans for the pageant of contraception.'

'Oh dear, oh dear, Mr Seal, there ain't no sense at all in 'aving bust-ups.'

*

News of the rupture spread like plague through the town. It was first-class gossip. The twenty or so spies permanently maintained by various interests in the Imperial Household carried tidings of the split through the Legations and commercial houses; runners informed the Earl of Ngumo; Black Bitch told her hairdresser; a Eurasian bank clerk told his manager and the bank manager told the Bishop; Mr Youkoumian recounted the whole incident in graphic gesture over the bar of the Empereur Seth; Connolly swore hideously about it at the Perroquet to Prince Fyodor; the Minister of the Interior roared out a fantastically distorted version to the assembled young ladies of the leading *maison de société*. That evening there was no dinner table of any importance in Debra Dowa where the subject was not discussed in detail.

'Pity,' remarked Sir Samson Courteney. 'I suppose this'll mean that young Seal will be coming up here more than ever. Sorry, Prudence, I dare say he's all right, but the truth is I can never find much to say to the chap . . . interested in different things . . . always going on about local politics . . . Damn fool thing to quarrel about, anyway. Why shouldn't he wear boots if he wants to?'

'That wasn't quite the point, Envoy.'

'Well, it was something of the kind, I know.'

*

'Ha! Ha!' said Monsieur Ballon. 'Here is a thing Sir Samson did *not* foresee. Where is his fine web now, eh? Gossamer in the wind. Connolly is our man.'

'Alas, blind, trusting husband, if he only knew,' murmured the first to the second secretary.

'The Seal–Courteney faction and their puppet emperor have lost the allegiance of the army. We must consolidate our party.'

It was in this way it happened that next morning there occurred an event unique in Black Bitch's experience. She was in the yard in front of her house laundering some of the General's socks (for she could not bear another woman to touch her man's clothes), chewing nut and meditatively spitting the dark juice into the soap-suds, when a lancer dismounted before her in the crimson and green uniform of the French Legation.

'Her Grace the Duchess of Ukaka.'

She lifted her dress, so as not to soil it, and wiped her hands on her knickers. 'Me,' she said.

The man saluted, handed her a large envelope, saluted again, mounted and rode away.

The Duchess was left alone with her large envelope; she squatted on her heels and examined it, turning it this way and that, holding it up to her ear and shaking it, her head sagely cocked on one side. Then she rose, padded into the house and across the hall to her bedroom; there, after circumspection, she raised a loose corner of the fibre matting and slipped the letter beneath it.

Two or three times during the next hour she left her wash-tub to see if her treasure was safe. At noon the General returned to luncheon and she handed it over to him, to await his verdict.

'Hullo, Black Bitch, what do you suppose this is? Madame Ballon wants us to dine at the French Legation tomorrow.'

'You go?'

'But it's for both of us, old girl. The invitation is addressed to you. What d'you think of that?'

'Oh, my! Me dine with Madame Ballon! Oh my, that's good!'

The Duchess could not contain her excitement; she threw back her head, rolled her eyes, and emitting deep gurgles of pleasure began spinning about the room like a teetotum.

'Good for the old geeser,' said the Duke, and later when the acceptance was written and dispatched by the hand of the Imperial Guard's most inspiring sergeant-major, and Connolly had answered numerous questions about the proper conduct of knife, fork, glass and gloves, and the Duchess had gone bustling off to Mr Youkoumian's store for ribbon and gold braid and artificial peonies to embellish her party frock, he went back to barracks with unusual warmth at heart towards the French Legation, remarking again, 'Good for the old geeser. He's the first person who's troubled to ask Black Bitch to anything in eight years. And wasn't she pleased as Punch about it too, bless her black heart?'

As the time approached Black Bitch's excitement became almost alarming and her questions on etiquette so searching that the General was obliged to thump her soundly on the head and lock her in a cupboard for some hours before she could be reduced to a condition sufficiently subdued for diplomatic society. The dinner party, however, was a great success. The French Legation were there in full force, the director of the railway with his wife and daughters, and Lord Boaz, the Minister for the Interior. Black Bitch as Duchess of Ukaka took precedence and sat beside M. Ballon, who spoke to her in English in praise of her husband's military skill, influence and discretion. Any small errors in deportment which she may have committed were completely eclipsed by the Minister for the Interior who complained of the food, drank far too much, pinched the ladies on either side of him, pocketed a dozen cigars and a silver pepper mill which happened to take his fancy and later in the drawing-room insisted on dancing by himself to the gramophone until his slaves appeared to hoist him into his car and carry him back to Mme 'Fifi', of whose charms he had been loudly boasting throughout the evening with a splendour of anatomical detail which was, fortunately, unintelligible to many of the people present.

In the dining-room when the succession of wines finally ended with the few ceremonial spoonfuls of sweet champagne and the men were left alone – the Minister for the Interior being restrained with difficulty from too precipitately following the ladies – M. Ballon signalled for a bottle of eau de vie and, moving round to the General's side, filled his glass and prompted him to some frank criticism of the Emperor and the present régime.

In the drawing-room the French ladies crowded about their new friend, and before the evening was out several of them, including Madame Ballon, had dropped the 'Duchess' and were on terms of calling her 'Black Bitch'. They asked her to come and see their gardens and children, they offered to teach her tennis and piquet, they advised her about an Armenian dressmaker in the town and a Hindu fortune-teller; they were eager to lend her the patterns of their pyjamas; they spoke seriously of pills; best of all they invited her to sit on the committee which was being organized in the French colony to decorate a car for the forthcoming Birth-Control Gala. There was no doubt about it; the Connollys had made the French set.

Ten days later the boots arrived at Debra Dowa; there were some formalities to be observed, but these were rendered simple by the fact that the departments involved were now under the

control of the Ministry of Modernization. Mr Youkoumian drew up
an application to himself from the Ministry of War for the delivery of
the boots; he made out a chit from the War Office to the Ministry of
Supplies; passed it on to the Treasury, examined and countersigned
it, drew himself a cheque and in the name of the Customs and Excise
Department allowed his own claim to rebate of duty on the import-
ation of articles of 'national necessity'. The whole thing took ten
minutes. A few hours later a thousand pairs of black boots had been
dumped in the square of the Guards barracks, where a crowd of
soldiers rapidly collected and studied them throughout the entire
afternoon with vivid but nervous interest.

That evening there was a special feast in honour of the boots.
Cook-pots steaming over the wood fires; hand drums beating; bare
feet shuffling unforgotten tribal rhythms; a thousand darkies
crooning and swaying on their haunches, white teeth flashing in
the fire-light.

They were still at it when Connolly returned from dinner at the
French consulate.

'What in hell are the boys making whoopee for tonight? It's not
one of their days, is it?'

'Yes, General, very big day,' said the sentry. 'Boots day.'

The singing reached Basil as he sat at his writing-table at the
Ministry, working long after midnight at the penal code.

'What's going on at the barracks?' he asked the servant.

'Boots.'

'They like 'em, eh?'

'They like 'em fine.'

'That's one in the eye for Connolly,' he said, and next day,
meeting the General in the Palace yard, he could not forbear to
mention it. 'So the boots went down all right with your men after all,
Connolly.'

'They went down.'

'No cases of lameness yet, I hope?'

The General leant over in his saddle and smiled pleasantly. 'No
cases of lameness,' he replied. 'One or two of bellyache, though. I'm
just writing a report on the matter to the Commissioner of Supplies –
that's our friend Youkoumian, isn't it? You see, my adjutant made

rather a silly mistake. He hadn't had much truck with boots before
and the silly fellow thought they were extra rations. My men ate the
whole bag of tricks last night.'

*

Dust in the air; a light wind rattling the leaves in the eucalyptus
trees. Prudence sat over the Panorama of Life gazing through the
window across the arid Legation croquet lawn; dun grass rubbed
bare between the hoops, a few sapless stalks in the beds beyond. She
drew little arabesques in the corners of the page and thought about
love.

It was the dry season before the rains, when the cattle on the
hills strayed miles from their accustomed pastures and herdsmen
came to blows over the brackish dregs of the drinking holes; when,
preceded by a scutter of children, lions would sometimes appear,
parading the streets of the town in search of water; when Lady
Courteney remarked that her herbaceous borders were a positive
eye-sore.

How out of tune with Nature is the spirit of man! wrote Prudence in her
sprawling, schoolroom characters. *When the earth proclaims its fertility,
in running brooks, bursting seed, mating of birds and frisking of lambs, then the
thoughts of man turn to athletics and horticulture, water-colour painting and
amateur theatricals. Now in the arid season when Nature seems all dead under the
cold earth, there is nothing to think about except sex.* She bit her pen and read
it through, substituting *hot soil* for *cold earth*. 'I am sure I've got
something wrong in the first part,' she thought, and called to Lady
Courteney who, watering-can in hand, was gloomily surveying
a withered rose tree. 'Mum, how soon after the birds mate are the
lambs born?'

'Eggs, dear, not lambs,' said her mother and pottered off towards
some azalea roots which were desperately in need of water.

'Damn the panorama of life,' said Prudence, and she began
drawing a series of highly stylized profiles which by an emphasis of
the chin and disordering of the hair had ceased during the last six
weeks to be portraits of William and had come to represent Basil
Seal. 'To think that I wanted to be in love so much,' she thought,
'that I even practised on William.'

'Luncheon,' said her mother, repassing the window. 'And I shall be late again. Do go in and be bright to your father.'

But when Lady Courteney joined them in the dining-room she found father, daughter and William sitting in moody silence.

'Tinned asparagus,' said Sir Samson. 'And a letter from the Bishop.'

'He's not coming out to dinner again?'

'No, no, it isn't as bad as that. But apparently Seth wants to pull down his Cathedral for some reason. What does he expect *me* to do about it I should like to know? Shocking ugly building, anyhow. I wish, Prudence and William, you'd take the ponies out this after-noon. They haven't had any proper exercise for days.'

'Too hot,' said Prudence.

'Too busy,' said William.

'Oh, well,' said Sir Samson Courteney. And later he remarked to his wife: 'I say, there isn't any trouble between those two, is there? They used to be such pals.'

'I've been meaning to mention it for some time, Sam, only I was so worried about the antirrhinums. I don't think Prudence is at all herself. D'you think it's good for a girl of her age living at this height all the year round? It might be an idea to send her back to England for a few months. Harriet could put her up in Belgrave Place. I'm not sure it wouldn't be a good thing for her to go out in London for a season and meet some people of her own age. What d'you think?'

'I dare say you're right. All that What-d'you-call-it of Life she keeps working away at . . . Only you must write to Harriet. I'm far too busy at the moment. Got to think of something to say to the Bishop.'

But next day Prudence and William went out with the ponies. She had an assignation with Basil.

'Listen, William, you're to go out of the city by the lane behind the Baptist school and the Jewish abattoirs, then past the Parsee death-house and the fever hospital.'

'Not exactly the prettiest ride.'

'Darling, don't be troublesome. You might get seen the other way. Once you're clear of the Arab cemetery you can go where you like. And you're to fetch me at Youkoumian's at five.'

'Jolly afternoon for me leading Mischief all the time.'

'Now, William, you know you manage him perfectly. You're the only person I'd trust to take him. I can't leave him outside Youkoumian's can I, because of *discretion*.'

'What you don't seem to see is that it's pretty dim for me, floundering about half the day, I mean, in a dust heap with two ponies while you neck with the chap who's cut me out.'

'*William*, don't be *coarse*. And anyway, "cut you out" nothing. You had me all to yourself for six months and weren't you just bored blue with it?'

'Well, I dare say he'll be bored soon.'

'Cad.'

Basil still lived in the large room over Mr Youkoumian's store. There was a verandah, facing on to a yard littered with scrap iron and general junk, accessible by an outside staircase. Prudence passed through the shop, out and up. The atmosphere of the room was rank with tobacco smoke. Basil, in shirtsleeves, rose from the deck-chair to greet her. He threw the butt of his Burma cheroot into the tin hip-bath which stood unemptied at the side of the bed; it sizzled and went out and floated throughout the afternoon, slowly unfurling in the soapy water. He bolted the door. It was half dark in the room. Dusty parallels of light struck through the shutters on to the floor-boards and the few shabby mats. Prudence stood isolated, waiting for him, her hat in her hand. At first neither spoke. Presently she said, 'You might have shaved,' and then 'Please help with my boots.'

Below, in the yard, Madame Youkoumian upbraided a goat. Strips of sunlight traversed the floor as an hour passed. In the bath water, the soggy stub of tobacco emanated a brown blot of juice.

Banging on the door.

'Heavens,' said Prudence, 'that can't be William already.'

'Mr Seal, Mr Seal.'

'Well, what is it? I'm resting.'

'Well, you got to stop,' said Mr Youkoumian. 'They're looking for you all over the town. Damn fine rest I've had this afternoon, like 'ell I 'aven't.'

'What is it?'

'Emperor must see you at once. 'E's got a new idea. Very modern and important. Some damn fool nonsense about Swedish drill.'

Basil hurried to the Palace to find his master in a state of high excitement.

'I have been reading a German book. We must draft a decree at once ... Communal physical exercises. The whole population, every morning, you understand. And we must get instructors from Europe. Cable for them. Quarter of an hour's exercise a morning. And community singing. That is very important. The health of the nation depends on it. I have been thinking it over. Why is there no cholera in Europe? Because of community singing and physical jerks ... and bubonic plague ... and leprosy.'

Back in her room Prudence reopened the Panorama of Life and began writing: *a woman in love* ...

*

'A woman,' said Mr Youkoumian. 'That's what Seth needs to keep 'im quiet. Always sticking 'is nose in too much everywhere. You listen to me, Mr Seal – if we can fix Seth with a woman our modernization will get along damn fine.'

'There's always Fifi.'

'Oh Mr Seal, 'e 'ad 'er when 'e was a little boy. Don't you worry. I'll fix it O.K.'

Royal interruptions of the routine of the Ministry were becoming distressingly frequent in the last few days as the Emperor assimilated the various books that had arrived for him by the last mail. Worst of all, the pageant of birth control was proving altogether more trouble than it was worth; in spite of repeated remonstrances, however, it continued to occupy the mind of the Emperor in precedence of all other interests. He had already renamed the site of the Anglican Cathedral, Place Marie Stopes.

'Heaven knows what will happen if he ever discovers psycho-analysis,' remarked Basil, gloomily foreseeing a Boulevard Krafft-Ebing, an Avenue Oedipus and a pageant of coprophagists.

'He'll discover every damn modern thing,' said Mr Youkoumian, 'if we don't find him a woman damn quick ... 'ere's another letter from the Vicar Apostolic. If I 'adn't ordered all that stuff from Cairo

I'd drop the whole pageant. But you can't use it for nothing else but what it's for – so far as I can see, not like boots what they can eat.'

The opposition to the pageant was firm and widespread. The Conservative Party rallied under the leadership of the Earl of Ngumo. This nobleman, himself one of a family of forty-eight (most of whom he had been obliged to assassinate on his succession to the title), was the father of over sixty sons and uncounted daughters. This progeny was a favourite boast of his; in fact, he maintained a concert party of seven minstrels for no other purpose than to sing at table about this topic when he entertained friends. Now in ripe age, with his triumphs behind him, he found himself like some scarred war veteran surrounded by pacifists, his prestige assailed and his proudest achievements held up to vile detraction. The new proposals struck at the very roots of sport and decency and he expressed the general feeling of the landed gentry when he threatened amid loud grunts of approval to dismember any man on his estates whom he found using the new-fangled and impious appliances.

The smart set, composed (under the leadership of Lord Boaz) of cosmopolitan blacks, courtiers, younger sons and a few of the decayed Arab intelligentsia, though not actively antagonistic, were tepid in their support; they discussed the question languidly in Fifi's salon and, for the most part, adopted a sophisticated attitude maintaining that of course *they* had always known about these things, but why invite trouble by all this publicity; at best it would only make contraception middle-class. In any case this circle was always suspect to the popular mind and their allegiance was unlikely to influence public opinion in the Emperor's favour.

The Churches came out strong on the subject. No one could reasonably accuse the Nestorian Patriarch of fanatical moral inflexibility – indeed there had been incidents in his Beatitude's career when all but grave scandal had been caused to the faithful – but whatever his personal indulgence, his theology had always been unimpeachable. Whenever a firm lead was wanted on a question of opinion, the Patriarch had been willing to forsake his pleasures and pronounce freely and intransigently for the tradition he had inherited. There had been the ugly affair of the Metropolitan of

Matodi who had proclaimed himself fourth member of the Trinity;
there was the parish priest who was unsound about the Dual
Will; there was the ridiculous heresy that sprang up in the province
of Mhomala that the prophet Esaias had wings and lived in a tree;
there was the painful case of the human sacrifices at the Bishop of
Popo's consecration – on all these and other uncertain topics the
Patriarch had given proof of a sturdy orthodoxy.

Now, on the question of Birth Control, his Beatitude left the
faithful in no doubt as to where their duty lay. As head of
the Established Church he called a conference which was attended
by the Chief Rabbi, the Mormon Elder and the chief representatives
of all the creeds of the Empire; only the Anglican Bishop excused
himself, remarking in a courteous letter of refusal, that his work
lay exclusively among the British community who, since they were
already fully informed and equipped in the matter, could scarcely
be injured in any way by the Emperor's new policy; he wished
his Beatitude every success in the gallant stand he was making for
the decencies of family life, solicited his prayers and remarked
that he was himself too deeply embroiled with the progressive
party, who were threatening the demolition of his Cathedral, to
confuse the issue with any other cause, however laudable it might
be in itself.

As a result of the conference, the Patriarch composed an encyc-
lical in rich, oratorical style and dispatched copies of it by runners to
all parts of the island. Had the influence of the Established Church
on the popular mind been more weighty, the gala should have been
doomed, but, as has already been mentioned, the Christianizing of
the country was still so far incomplete that the greater part of the
Empire retained with a minimum of disguise their older and grosser
beliefs, and it was, in fact, from the least expected quarter, the
tribesmen and villagers, that the real support of Seth's policy suddenly appeared.

This development was due directly and solely to the power of
advertisement. In the dark days when the prejudice of his people
compassed him on every side and even Basil spoke unsympathetic-
ally of the wisdom of postponing the gala, the Emperor found
among the books that were mailed to him monthly from Europe

a collection of highly inspiring Soviet posters. At first the difficulties of imitation appeared to be insuperable. The *Courier* office had no machinery for reproducing pictures. Seth was contemplating the wild expedient of employing slave labour to copy his design when Mr Youkoumian discovered that some years ago an enterprising philanthropist had by bequest introduced lithography into the curriculum of the American Baptist school. The apparatus survived the failure of the attempt. Mr Youkoumian purchased it from the pastor and resold it at a fine profit to the Department of Fine Arts in the Ministry of Modernization. An artist was next found in the Armenian colony who, on Mr Youkoumian's introduction, was willing to elaborate Seth's sketches. Finally there resulted a large, highly coloured poster well calculated to convey to the illiterate the benefits of birth control. It was in many ways the highest triumph of the new Ministry and Mr Youkoumian was the hero. Copies were placarded all over Debra Dowa; they were sent down the line to every station latrine, capital and coast; they were sent into the interior to vice-regal lodges and headmen's huts, hung up at prisons, barracks, gallows and juju trees, and wherever the poster was hung there assembled a cluster of inquisitive, entranced Azanians.

It portrayed two contrasted scenes. On one side a native hut of hideous squalor, overrun with children of every age, suffering from every physical incapacity – crippled, deformed, blind, spotted and insane; the father prematurely aged with paternity squatted by an empty cook-pot; through the door could be seen his wife, withered and bowed with child-bearing, desperately hoeing at their inadequate crop. On the other side a bright parlour furnished with chairs and table; the mother, young and beautiful, sat at her ease eating a huge slice of raw meat; her husband smoked a long Arab hubble-bubble (still a caste mark of leisure throughout the land), while a single healthy child sat between them reading a newspaper. Inset between the two pictures was a detailed drawing of some up-to-date contraceptive apparatus and the words in Sakuyu: WHICH HOME DO YOU CHOOSE?

Interest in the pictures was unbounded; all over the island woolly heads were nodding, black hands pointing, tongues clicking against filed teeth in unsyntactical dialects. Nowhere was there any doubt about the meaning of the beautiful new pictures.

See: on right hand: there is rich man: smoke pipe like big chief: but his wife she no good; sit eating meat: and rich man no good: he only one son.

See: on left hand: poor man: not much to eat: but his wife she very good, work hard in field: man he good too: eleven children: one very mad, very holy. And in the middle: Emperor's juju. Make you like that good man with eleven children.

And as a result, despite admonitions from squire and vicar, the peasantry began pouring into town for the gala, eagerly awaiting initiation to the fine new magic of virility and fecundity.

Once more, wrote Basil Seal, in a leading article in the *Courier, the people of the Empire have overridden the opposition of a prejudiced and interested minority, and with no uncertain voice have followed the Emperor's lead in the cause of Progress and the New Age.*

So brisk was the demand for the Emperor's juju that some time before the day of the carnival Mr Youkoumian was frantically cabling to Cairo for fresh supplies.

Meanwhile the Nestorian Patriarch became a very frequent guest at the French Legation.

'We have the army, we have the Church,' said M. Ballon. 'All we need now is a new candidate for the throne.'

*

'If you ask me,' said Basil, one morning soon after the distribution of the poster, 'loyalty to the throne is one of the hardest parts of our job.'

'Oh, gosh, Mr Seal, don't you ever say a thing like that. I seen gentlemen poisoned dead for less. What's 'e done now?'

'Only this.' He handed Mr Youkoumian a chit which had just arrived from the Palace: *For your information and necessary action, I have decided to abolish the following*:

Death penalty.

Marriage.

The Sakuyu language and all native dialects.

Infant mortality.

Totemism.

Inhuman butchery.

Mortgages.

Emigration.

Please see to this. Also organize system of reservoirs for city's water supply and draft syllabus for competitive examination for public services. Suggest compulsory Esperanto. Seth.

"E's been reading books again, Mr Seal, that's what it is. You won't get no peace from 'im not till you fix 'im with a woman. Why can't 'e drink or something?"

In fact, the Ministry's triumph in the matter of Birth Control was having highly embarrassing consequences. If before, Basil and Mr Youkoumian had cause to lament their master's tenacity and singleness of purpose, they were now harassed from the opposite extreme of temperament. It was as though Seth's imagination like a volcanic lake had in the moment of success become suddenly swollen by the irruption of unsuspected subterranean streams until it darkened and seethed and overflowed its margins in a thousand turbulent cascades. The earnest and rather puzzled young man became suddenly capricious and volatile; ideas bubbled up within him, bearing to the surface a confused sediment of phrase and theory, scraps of learning half understood and fantastically translated.

'It's going to be awkward for us if the Emperor goes off his rocker.'

'Oh my, Mr Seal, you do say the most damned dangerous things.'

That afternoon Basil called at the Palace to discuss the new proposals, only to find that since his luncheon the Emperor's interests had veered suddenly towards archaeology.

'Yes, yes, the abolitions. I sent you a list this morning, I think. It is a mere matter of routine. I leave the details to the Ministry. Only you must be quick, please ... it is not that which I want to discuss with you now. It is our Museum.'

'Museum?'

'Yes, of course we must have a Museum. I have made a few notes to guide you. The only serious difficulty is accommodation. You see, it must be inaugurated before the arrival of the Cruelty to Animals

Commission at the beginning of next month. There is hardly time to build a house for it. The best thing will be to confiscate one of the town palaces. Ngumo's or Boaz's would do after some slight adjustments. But that is a matter for the Ministry to decide. On the ground floor will be the natural history section. You will collect examples of all the flora and fauna of the Empire – lions, butterflies, birds' eggs, specimens of woods, everything. That should easily fill the ground floor. I have been reading,' he added earnestly, 'about ventilation. That is very important. The air in the cases must be continually renewed – a cubic metre an hour is about the right draught – otherwise the specimens suffer. You will make a careful note of that. Then on the first floor will be the anthropological and historical section – examples of native craft, Portuguese and Arab work, a small library. Then in the Central Hall, the relics of the Royal House. I have some of the medals of Amurath upstairs under one of the beds in a box – photographs of myself, some of my uniforms, the cap and gown I wore at Oxford, the model of the Eiffel Tower which I brought back from Paris. I will lend some pages of manuscript in my own hand to be exhibited. It will be most interesting.'

For some days Mr Youkoumian busied himself with the collection of specimens. Word went round that there was a market for objects of interest at the Ministry of Modernization and the work of the office was completely paralysed by the hawkers of all races who assembled in and around it, peddling brass pots and necklaces of carved nut, snakes in baskets and monkeys in cages, cloths of beaten bark and Japanese cotton, sacramental vessels pouched by Nestorian deacons, iron-wood clubs, homely household deities, tanned human scalps, cauls and navel strings and wonder-working fragments of meteorite, amulets to ward off the evil eye from camels, M. Ballon's masonic apron purloined by the Legation butler, and a vast, monolithic phallus borne by three oxen from a shrine in the interior. Mr Youkoumian bargained briskly and bought almost everything he was offered, reselling them later to the Ministry of Fine Arts of which Basil had created him the director. But when, at a subsequent interview, Basil mentioned their progress to the Emperor he merely nodded a listless approval, and even while he unscrewed the cap of his fountain pen to sign the order evicting the Earl of Ngumo from his town house, began to speak of the wonders of astronomy.

'Do you realize the magnitude of the fixed stars? They are immense. I have read a book which says that the mind boggles at their distances. I did not know that word, boggles. I am immediately founding an Institute for Astronomical Research. I must have Professors. Cable for them to Europe. Get me tiptop professors, the best procurable.'

But next day he was absorbed in ectogenesis. 'I have read here,' he said, tapping a volume of speculative biology, 'that there is to be no more birth. The ovum is fertilized in the laboratory and then the foetus is matured in bottles. It is a splendid idea. Get me some of those bottles . . . and no boggling.'

Even while discussing the topic that immediately interested him, he would often break off in the middle of a sentence, with an irrelevant question. 'How much are autogyros?' or 'Tell me exactly, please, what is Surrealism?' or 'Are you convinced of Dreyfus' innocence?' and then, without pausing for the reply, would resume his adumbrations of the New Age.

The days passed rapturously for Mr Youkoumian who had found, in the stocking of the Museum, work for which early training and all his natural instincts richly equipped him; he negotiated endlessly between the Earl of Ngumo and Viscount Boaz, armed with orders for the dispossession of the lowest bidder; he bought and resold, haggled, flattered and depreciated, and ate and slept in a clutter of dubious antiques. But on Basil the strain of modernity began to leave its traces. Brief rides with Prudence through the tinder-dry countryside, assignations furtively kept and interrupted at a moment's notice by some peremptory, crazy summons to the Palace, alone broke the unquiet routine of his day.

'I believe that odious Emperor is slowly poisoning you. It's a thing he does do,' said Prudence. 'And I never saw anyone look so ill.'

'You know it sounds absurd, but I miss Connolly. It's rather a business living all the time between Seth and Youkoumian.'

'Of course, you wouldn't remember that there's me too, would you?' said Prudence. 'Not just to cheer me up, you wouldn't.'

'You're a grand girl, Prudence. What Seth calls tiptop. But I'm so tired I could die.'

And a short distance away the Legation syce moodily flicked with his whip at a train of ants while the ponies shifted restlessly among the stones and shelving earth of a dry watercourse.

*

Two mornings later the Ministry of Modernization received its sharpest blow. Work was going on as usual. Mr Youkoumian was interviewing a coast Arab who claimed to possess some 'very old, very genuine' Portuguese manuscripts; Basil, pipe in his mouth, was considering how best to deal with the Emperor's latest memorandum, *Kindly insist straw hats and gloves compulsory peerage*, when he received an unexpected and disturbing call from Mr Jagger, the contractor in charge of the demolition of the Anglican Cathedral; a stocky, good-hearted little Britisher who after a succession of quite honourable bankruptcies in Cape Town, Mombasa, Dar-es-Salaam and Aden had found his way to Debra Dowa where he had remained ever since, occupied with minor operations in the harbour and along the railway line. He threaded his way through the antiquities which had lately begun to encroach on Basil's office, removed a seedy-looking caged vulture from the chair and sat down; his manner was uncertain and defiant.

'It's not playing the game, Mr Seal,' he said. 'I tell you that fair and square and I don't mind who knows it, not if it's the Emperor himself.'

'Mr Jagger,' said Basil impressively, 'you should have been long enough in this country to know that that is a very rash thing to say. Men have been poisoned for less. What is your trouble?'

'This here's my trouble,' said Mr Jagger, producing a piece of paper from a pocket full of pencils and foot rules and laying it on the table next to the mosaic portrait of the late Empress recently acquired by the Director of Fine Arts. 'What is it, eh, that's what I want to know?'

'What indeed?' said Basil. He picked it up and examined it closely.

In size, shape and texture it resembled an English five-pound note and was printed on both sides with intricate engraved devices of green and red. There was an Azanian eagle, a map of the Empire, a soldier in the uniform of the Imperial Guard, an aeroplane and a classical figure bearing a cornucopia, but the most prominent place was taken by a large medallion portrait of Seth in top hat and European tail coat. The words *Five Pounds* lay in flourished script across the middle; above them THE IMPERIAL BANK OF AZANIA and below them a facsimile of Seth's signature.

The normal currency of the capital and the railway was in Indian rupees, although East African shillings, French and Belgian colonial francs and Maria Theresa thalers circulated with equal freedom; in the interior the mediums of exchange were rock-salt and cartridges.

'This is a new one on me,' said Basil. 'I wonder if the Treasury know anything about it. Mr Youkoumian, come in here a minute, will you?'

The Director of Fine Arts and First Lord of the Treasury trotted through the partition door in his black cotton socks; he carried a model dhow he had just acquired.

'No, Mr Seal,' he pronounced, 'I ain't never seen a thing like that before. Where did the gentleman get it?'

'The Emperor's just given me a whole packet of them for the week's wages bill. What is the Imperial Bank of Azania, anyway? I never see such a thing all the time I been in the country. There's something here that's not on the square. You must understand, Mr Seal, that it's not anyone's job breaking up that Cathedral. Solid granite shipped all the way from Aberdeen. Why, Lord love you, the pulpit alone weighs seven and a half ton. I had two boys hurt only this morning through the font swinging loose as they were hoisting it into a lorry. Smashed up double one of them was. The Emperor ain't got no right to try putting that phoney stuff across me.'

'You may be quite confident,' said Basil with dignity, 'that in all your dealings with His Majesty you will encounter nothing but the highest generosity and integrity. However, I will institute inquiries on your behalf.'

'No offence meant, I'm sure,' said Mr Jagger.

Basil watched him across the yard and then snatched up his topee from a fossilized tree-fern. 'What's that black lunatic been up to this time?' he asked, starting off towards the Palace.

'Oh, Mr Seal, you'll get into trouble one day with the things you say.'

The Emperor rose to greet him with the utmost cordiality.

'Come in, come in. I'm very glad you've come. I'm in some perplexity about Nacktkultur. Here have I spent four weeks trying to enforce the edict prescribing trousers for the official classes, and now I read that it is more modern not to wear any at all.'

'Seth, what's the Imperial Bank of Azania?'

The Emperor looked embarrassed.

'I thought you might ask . . . Well, actually it is not quite a bank at all. It is a little thing I did myself. I will show you.'

He led Basil to a high cupboard which occupied half the wall on one side of the library, and opening it showed him a dozen or so shelves stacked with what might have been packets of writing paper.

'What is that?'

'Just under three million pounds,' said the Emperor proudly. 'A little surprise. I had them done in Europe.'

'But you can't possibly do this.'

'Oh, yes, I assure you. It was easy. All these on this shelf are for a thousand pounds each, and now that the plates have been made, it is quite inexpensive to print as many more as we require. You see there were a great many things which needed doing and I had not a great many rupees. Don't look angry, Seal. Look, I'll give you some.' He pressed a bundle of fivers into Basil's hand. 'And take some for Mr Youkoumian, too. Pretty fine picture of me, eh? I wondered about the hat. You will see that in the fifty-pound notes I wear a crown.'

For some minutes Basil attempted to remonstrate; then quite suddenly he abandoned the argument.

'I knew you would understand,' said the Emperor. 'It is so simple. As soon as these are used up we will send for some more. And tomorrow you will explain to me about Nacktkultur, eh?'

Basil returned to his office very tired.

'There's only one thing to hope for now. That's a fire in the Palace to get rid of the whole lot.'

'We must change these quick,' said Mr Youkoumian. 'I know a damn fool Chinaman might do it. Anyway, the Ministry of Fine Arts can take one at par for the historical section.'

It was on that afternoon that Basil at last lost his confidence in the permanence of the One Year Plan.

CHAPTER 6

FROM DAME MILDRED PORCH TO HER HUSBAND

S.S. Le Président Carnot Matodi
March 8th

My Dear Stanley,

I am writing this before disembarking. It will be posted at Marseilles and should reach you as nearly as I can calculate on 17th of the month. As I wrote to you from Durban, Sarah and I decided to break our return journey in Azania. The English boat did not stop here. So we had to change at Aden into this outward-bound French ship. Very dirty and unseamanlike. I have heard very disagreeable accounts of the hunting here. Apparently the natives dig deep pits into which the poor animals fall; they are often left in these traps for several days without food or water (imagine what that means in the heat of the jungle) and are then mercilessly butchered in cold blood. Of course the poor ignorant people know no better. But the young Emperor is by all accounts a comparatively enlightened and well-educated person and I am sure he will do all he can to introduce more humane methods if it is really necessary to kill these fine beasts at all – as I very much doubt. I expect to resume our journey in about a fortnight. I enclose cheque for another month's household expenses. The coal bill seemed surprisingly heavy in your last accounts. I hope that you are not letting the servants become extravagant in my absence. There is no need for the dining-room fire to be lit before luncheon at this time of year.

Yours affec.
Mildred

March 8th

Disembarked Matodi 12.45. Quaint and smelly. Condition of mules and dogs appalling, also children. In spite of radio message British consul was not there to meet us. Quite civil native led us to his office. Tip five annas. Seemed *satisfied. Consul not English at all. Some sort of Greek. Very unhelpful (probably drinks). Unable or unwilling to say when train starts for Debra Dowa, whether possible engage sleeper. Wired Legation. Went to Amurath Hotel. Positive pot-house. Men sitting about drinking all over terrace. Complained. Large bedroom overlooking harbour apparently clean. Sarah one of her headaches. Complained of her room over street. Told her very decent little room.*

March 9th
No news of train. Sarah disagreeable about her room. Saw Roman Missionary. Unhelpful. Typical dago attitude towards animals. Later saw American Baptists. Middle-class and unhelpful because unable talk native languages. No answer Legation. Wired again.

March 10th
No news train. Wired Legation again. Unhelpful answer. Fed doggies in market-place. Children tried to take food from doggies. Greedy little wretches. Sarah still headache.

March 11th
Hotel manager suddenly announced train due to leave at noon. Apparently has been here all the time. Sarah very slow packing. Outrageous bill. Road to station blocked brown motor lorry. Natives living in it. Also two goats. Seemed well but cannot be healthy for them so near natives. Had to walk last quarter-mile. Afraid would miss train. Arrived with five minutes to spare. Got tickets, no sleepers. Just in time. V. hot and exhausted. Train did not start until three o'clock. Arrived dinnertime Lumo station where apparently we have to spend night. Shower bath and changed underclothes. Bed v. doubtful. Luckily remembered Keatings Durban. Interesting French hotel manager about local conditions. Apparently there was quite civil war last summer. How little the papers tell us. New Emperor v. go-ahead. English adviser named Seal. Any relation Cynthia Seal? Hotel man seemed to doubt government's financial stability. Says natives are complete savages *but no white slave traffic – or so he says.*

March 12th
Awful night. Bitten all over. Bill outrageous. Thought manager decent person too. Explained provisions hard to get. Humbug. Train left at seven in morning. Sarah nearly missed it. Two natives in carriage. I must say quite civil but v.

uncomfortable as no corridor and had left so early. Tiring journey. Country seemed dry. Due in Debra Dowa some time this afternoon. Must say shall be thankful.

Dame Mildred Porch and Miss Sarah Tin were in no way related to each other, but constant companionship and a similarity of interests had so characterized them that a stranger might easily have taken them to be sisters as they stepped from the train on to the platform at Debra Dowa. Dame Mildred was rather stout and Miss Tin rather spare. Each wore a khaki sun-hat in an oilcloth cover, each wore a serviceable washable frock, and thick shoes and stockings, each had smoked spectacles and a firm mouth. Each carried an attaché-case containing her most inalienable possessions – washing things and writing things, disinfectant and insecticide, books, passport, letters of credit – and held firmly to her burden in defiance of an eager succession of porters who attempted in turn to wrest it from her.

William pushed his way forward and greeted them amiably. 'Dame Mildred Porch? Miss Tin? How are you? So glad you got here all right. I'm from the Legation. The Minister couldn't come himself. He's very busy just now, but he asked me to come along and see if you were all right. Any luggage? I've got a car outside and can run you up to the Hotel.'

'Hotel? But I thought we should be expected at the Legation. I wired from Durban.'

'Yes, the Minister asked me to explain. You see, we're some way out of the town. No proper road. Awful business getting in and out. The Minister thought you'd be much more comfortable in the town itself. Nearer the animals and everything. But he particularly said he hoped you'd come over to tea one day if you ever have the time.'

Dame Mildred and Miss Tin exchanged that look of slighted citizenship which William had seen in the eyes of every visitor he had ever greeted at Debra Dowa. 'I'll tell you what,' he said. 'I'll go and look for the luggage. I dare say it's got stolen on the way. Often is, you know. And I'll get our mail out at the same time. No King's Messengers or anything here. If there's no European travelling it's put in charge of the guard. We thought of wiring to you to look after it and then we thought probably you had the devil of a lot of luggage yourselves.'

By the time that the two-seater car had been loaded with the Legation bags and the two ladies there was very little room left for their luggage. 'I say, d'you mind awfully,' said William. 'I'm afraid we'll have to leave this trunk behind. The hotel'll fetch it up for you in no time.'

'Young man, did you come to meet us or your own mail?'

'Now, you know,' said William, 'that simply isn't a fair question. Off we go.' And the overladen little car began jolting up the broad avenue into the town.

'Is *this* where we are to stay?' asked Miss Tin as they drew up opposite the *Grand Café et Hotel Restaurant de l'Empereur Seth.*

'It doesn't look terribly smart,' admitted William, 'but you'll find it a mine of solid comfort.'

He led them into the murky interior, dispersing a turkey and her brood from the Reception Hall. 'Anyone in?' There was a bell on the counter which he rang.

''Ullo,' said a voice from upstairs. 'One minute,' and presently Mr Youkoumian descended, buttoning up his trousers. 'Why, it's Mr Bland. 'Ullo, sir, 'ow are you? I 'ad the Minister's letter about the road this afternoon and the answer I am afraid is nothing doing. Very occupied, the Emperor . . . '

'I've brought you two guests. They are English ladies of great importance. You are to make them comfortable.'

'I fix them O.K.' said Mr Youkoumian.

'I'm sure you'll find everything comfortable here,' said William. 'And I hope we shall see you soon at the Legation.'

'One minute, young man, there are a number of things I want to know.'

'I fix you O.K.,' said Mr Youkoumian again.

'Yes, you ask Mr Youkoumian here. He'll tell you everything far better than I could. Can't keep them waiting for the mail, you know.'

'Impudent young puppy,' said Dame Mildred as the car drove away. 'I'll report him to the Foreign Office as soon as I get home. Stanley shall ask a question about him in the House.'

Mail day at the British Legation. Sir Samson and Lady Courteney, Prudence and William, Mr Legge and Mrs Legge, Mr and Mrs Anstruther, sitting round the fireplace opening the bags. Bills, provisions, family news, official dispatches, gramophone records, newspapers scattered on the carpet. Presently William said, 'I say, d'you know who I ran into on the platform? Those two cruelty-to-animals women who kept telegraphing.'

'How very annoying. What *have* you done with them?'

'I shot them into Youkoumian's. They wanted to come and stay here.'

'Heaven forbid. I do hope they won't stay long. Ought we to ask them to tea or anything?'

'Well, I *did* say that perhaps you'd like to see them some time.'

'Hang it, William, that's a bit thick.'

'Oh, I don't suppose they thought I meant it.'

'I sincerely hope not.'

March 12th (continued)

Arrived Debra Dowa late in afternoon. Discourteous cub from Legation met us and left Sarah's trunk at station. Brought us to frightful *hotel. But Armenian proprietor v. obliging. Saved me visit to bank by changing money for us into local currency. Quaint bank-notes with portrait of Emperor in European evening dress. Mr Seal came in after dinner. He is Cynthia's son. V. young and ill-looking. Off-hand manner. V. tired, going to bed early.*

That evening M. Ballon's report included the entry: *Two British ladies arrived, suspects. Met at station by Mr Bland. Proceeded Youkoumian's.*

*

'They are being watched?'

'Without respite.'

'Their luggage?'

'A trunk was left at the station. It has been searched but nothing incriminating was found. Their papers are in two small bags which never leave their hands.'

'Ah, they are old stagers. Sir Samson is calling out his last reserves.'

'*Frightful* hotel. But Armenian proprietor v. obliging.'

March 13th Sunday

No news Sarah's trunk. Went to Anglican Cathedral but found it was being pulled down. Service in Bishop's drawing-room. Poor congregation. V. silly sermon. Spoke to Bishop later about cruelty to animals. Unhelpful. Old humbug. Later went to write name in book at Palace. Sarah in bed. Town very crowded, apparently preparing for some local feast or carnival. Asked Bishop about it but he could not tell me. Seemed unaccountably embarrassed. Asked Mr Youkoumian. Either he cannot have understood my question or I cannot have understood what I thought him to say. Did not press point. He did not speak English at all well but is an obliging man.

March 14th

Hideous night. Mosquito in net and v. large brown bugs in bed. Up and dressed at dawn and went for long walk in hills. Met quaint caravan — drums, spears, etc. No news Sarah's trunk.

Other people besides Dame Mildred were interested in the little cavalcade which had slipped unobtrusively out of the city at dawn that day. Unobtrusively, in this connection, is a relative term. A dozen running slaves had preceded the procession, followed by a train of pack mules; then ten couples of mounted spearmen, a platoon of uniformed Imperial Guardsmen and a mounted band, blowing down reed flutes eight feet long and beating hand drums of hide and wood. In the centre on a mule loaded with silver and velvet trappings, had ridden a stout figure, heavily muffled in silk shawls. It was the Earl of Ngumo travelling incognito on a mission of great delicacy.

'Ngumo left town today. I wonder what he's after.'

'I think the Earl's pretty fed up, Mr Seal. I take his 'ouse Saturday for the Museum. 'E's gone back to 'is estates, I expect.'

'Estates, nothing. He's left five hundred men in camp behind him. Besides, he left on the Popo road. That's not his way home.'

'Oh gosh, Mr Seal, I 'ope there ain't going to be no bust-up.'

Only three people in Debra Dowa knew the reason for the Earl's departure. They were M. Ballon, General Connolly and the Nestorian Patriarch. They had dined together on Saturday night at the French Legation, and after dinner, when Mme Ballon and Black

Bitch had withdrawn to the salon to discuss their hats and physical disorders, and the sweet champagne frothed in the shallow glasses, the Patriarch had with considerable solemnity revealed his carefully guarded secret of State.

'It happened in the time of Gorgias, my predecessor, of evil memory,' said his Beatitude, 'and the intelligence was delivered to me on my assumption of office, under a seal so holy that only extreme personal vexation induces me to break it. It concerns poor little Achon. I say "poor little" although he must now, if he survives at all, be a man at least ninety years of age, greatly my own senior. He, as you know, was the son of the Great Amurath and it is popularly supposed that a lioness devoured him while hunting with his sister's husband, Seyid, in the Ngumo mountains. My Lords, nothing of the kind happened. By order of his sister and the Patriarch Gorgias the wretched boy was taken while under the influence of liquor to the monastery of St Mark the Evangelist and incarcerated there.'

'But this is a matter of vital importance,' cried M. Ballon. 'Is the man still alive?'

'Who can say? To tell you the truth I have not visited the Monastery of St Mark the Evangelist. The Abbot is inclined to the lamentable heresy that the souls in hell marry and beget hobgoblins. He is pertinacious in error. I sent the Bishop of Popo there to reason with him and they drove the good man out with stones.'

*

'Would they accept an order of release over your signature?'

'It is painful to me to admit it, but I am afraid they would not. It will be a question of hard cash or nothing.'

'The Abbot may name his own price. I must have Achon here in the capital. Then we shall be ready to strike.'

The bottle circulated and before they left for the drawing-room M. Ballon reminded them of the gravity of the occasion. 'Gentlemen. This is an important evening in the history of East Africa. The future of the country and perhaps our own lives depend on the maintenance of absolute secrecy in regard to the Earl of Ngumo's expedition on Monday. All inside this room are sworn to inviolable silence.'

As soon as his guests were gone he assembled his subordinates and explained the latest developments; before dawn the news was in Paris. On the way home in the car Connolly told Black Bitch about it. 'But it's supposed to be secret for a little, so keep your silly mouth shut, see.'

March 14th (continued)

As Keatings obviously deteriorated, went to store attached hotel to buy some more. Met native Duchess who spoke English. V. helpful re bugs. Went with her to her home where she gave me insecticide of her own preparation. Gave me tea and biscuits. V. interesting conversation. She told me that it has just been discovered that Emperor is not real heir to the throne. Elderly uncle in prison. They have gone to get him out. Most romantic, but hope new Emperor equally enlightened re animals.

March 15th

Better night. Native Duchess's insecticide v. helpful though nasty smell. Received invitation dine Palace tonight. Short notice but thought it best accept for us both. Sarah says nothing to wear unless trunk turns up.

It was the first time since Seth's accession that European visitors had been entertained at the Palace. The Ministry of Modernization was called in early that morning to supervise the invitations and the menu.

'It shall be an entirely Azanian party. I want the English ladies to see how refined we are. I was doubtful about asking Viscount Boaz. What do you think? Will he be sober? ... and there is the question of food. I have been reading that now it is called Vitamins. I am having the menu printed like this. It is good, modern, European dinner, eh?'

Basil looked at the card. A month ago he might have suggested emendations. Today he was tired.

'That's fine, Seth, go ahead like that.'

'You see,' said the Emperor proudly, 'already we Azanians can do much for ourselves. Soon we shall not need a Minister of

Modernization. No, I do not mean that, Basil. Always you are my friend and adviser.'

So the menu for Seth's first dinner party went to the *Courier* office to be printed and came back a packet of handsome gilt-edged cards, laced with silk ribbons in the Azanian colours and embossed with a gold crown.

'It is so English,' explained Seth. 'From courtesy to your great Empire.'

MARCH 15TH

Imperial Banquet for Welcoming the English Cruelty to Animals

MENU OF FOODS

VITAMIN A	VITAMIN E
Tin Sardines	*Spiced Turkey*
VITAMIN B	VITAMIN F
Roasted Beef	*Sweet Puddings*
VITAMIN C	VITAMIN G
Small Roasted Sucking Porks	*Coffee*
VITAMIN D	VITAMIN H
Hot Sheep and Onions	*Jam*

At eight o'clock that evening Dame Mildred and Miss Tin arrived at the Palace for the banquet. The electric-light plant was working that evening and a string of coloured bulbs shone with Christmas welcome over the main doorway. A strip of bright lino-leum had been spread on the steps and as the taxi drew up a dozen or so servants ran down to conduct the guests into the hall. They were in mixed attire; some in uniforms of a kind, tunic frogged with gold braid discarded or purloined in the past from the wardrobes of visiting diplomats; some in native costume of striped silk. As the two ladies stepped from the car a platoon of Guards lounging on the Terrace alarmed them with a ragged volley of welcome.

There was a slight delay as the driver of the taxi refused to accept the new pound note which Dame Mildred tendered him in payment, but the captain of the Guard, hurrying up with a jingle of spurs, curtailed further discussion by putting the man under arrest and signified in a few graphic gestures his sorrow for the interruption and his intention of hanging the troublesome fellow without delay.

The chief saloon was brilliantly lighted and already well filled with the flower of Azanian native society. One of the first acts of the new reign had been an ordinance commanding the use of European evening dress. This evening was the first occasion for it to be worn and all round the room stood sombre but important figures completely fitted up by Mr Youkoumian with tail coats, white gloves, starched linen and enamelled studs; only in a few cases were shoes and socks lacking; the unaccustomed attire lent a certain dignified rigidity to their deportment. The ladies had for the most part allowed their choice to fix upon frocks of rather startling colour; aniline greens and violets with elaborations of ostrich feather and sequin. Viscountess Boaz wore a backless frock newly arrived from Cairo combined with the full weight of her ancestral jewellery; the Duchess of Mhomala carried on her woolly head a three-pound tiara of gold and garnets; Baroness Batulle exposed shoulders and back magnificently tattooed and cicatrized with arabesques.

Beside all this finery the guests of honour looked definitely dowdy as the Lord Chamberlain conducted them round the room and performed the introductions in French scarcely more comfortable than Dame Mildred's own.

Two slaves circulated among them carrying trays of brandy. The English ladies refused. The Lord Chamberlain expressed his concern. Would they have preferred whisky; no doubt some could be produced? Or beer?

'*Mon bon homme,*' said Dame Mildred severely, '*il vous faut comprendre que nous ne buvons rien de tout, jamais*'; an announcement which considerably raised their prestige among the company; they were not much to look at, certainly, but at least they knew a thing or two which the Azanians did not. A useful sort of woman to take on a journey, reflected the Lord Chamberlain, and inquired with polite interest whether the horses and camels in their country were as conveniently endowed.

Further conversation was silenced by the arrival of the Emperor, who at this moment entered the hall from the far end and took his seat on the raised throne which had stood conspicuously on the dais throughout the preliminary presentations. Court etiquette was still in a formative stage. There was a moment of indecision during which the company stood in embarrassed silence waiting for a lead. Seth said something to his equerry, who now advanced down the room and led forward the guests of honour. They curt-seyed and stood on one side, while the other guests filed past in strict precedence. Most of them bowed low in the Oriental manner, raising the hand to forehead and breast. The curtsey, however, had been closely observed and found several imitators among both sexes. One elderly peer, a stickler for old-world manners, prostrated himself fully and went through the mimic action of covering his head with dust. When all had saluted him in their various ways, Seth led the party in to dinner, fresh confusion over the places and some ill-natured elbowing; Dame Mildred and Miss Tin sat on either side of the Emperor; soon everyone was eating and drinking at a great pace.

March 15th (continued)
Dinner at Palace. Food v. nasty. Course after course different kinds of meat, overseasoned and swimming in grease. Tried to manage some of it from politeness. Sarah ate nothing. Emperor asked great number of questions, some of which I was unable to answer. How many suits of clothes had the King of England? Did he take his bath before or after his breakfast? Which was the more civilized? What was the best shop to buy an artesian well? etc. Sarah v. silent. Told Emperor about co-education and 'free-discipline'. Showed great interest.

Dame Mildred's neighbour on her other side was the punctilious man who had prostrated himself in the drawing-room; he seemed engrossed in his eating. In point of fact he was rehearsing in his mind and steeling his nerve to enunciate some English conversation in which he had painfully schooled himself during that day; at last it came up suddenly.

"'Ow many ox 'ave you?' he demanded, lifting up sideways from his plate a great bearded face, "ow many sons? 'ow many daughters? 'ow many brothers? 'ow many sisters? My father is dead fighting.'

Dame Mildred turned to him a somewhat startled scrutiny. There were crumbs and scraps of food in various parts of his beard. 'I beg your pardon?' she said.

But the old gentleman had shot his bolt; he felt that he had said all and more than all that good breeding required, and to tell the truth was more than a little taken aback by his own fluency. He gave her a nervous smile and resumed his dinner without again venturing to address her.

*

'Which of the white ladies would you like to have?'

'The fat one. But both are ugly.'

'Yes. It must be very sad for the English gentleman to marry English ladies.'

*

Presently, when the last vitamin had been guzzled, Viscount Boaz rose to propose the health of the guests of honour. His speech was greeted by loud applause and was then done into English by the Court Interpreter.

'Your Majesty, Lords and Ladies. It is my privilege and delight this evening to welcome with open arms of brotherly love to our city Dame Mildred Porch and Miss Tin, two ladies renowned throughout the famous country of Europe for their great cruelty to animals. We Azanians are a proud and ancient nation but we have much to learn from the white people of the West and North. We too, in our small way, are cruel to our animals' – and here the Minister for the Interior digressed at some length to recount with hideous detail what he had himself once done with a woodman's axe to a wild boar – 'but it is to the great nations of the West and North, especially to their worthy representatives that are with us tonight, that we look as our natural leaders on the road of progress. Ladies and gentlemen, we must be Modern, we must be refined in our Cruelty to Animals. That is the message of the New Age brought to us by our guests this evening. May I, in conclusion, raise my glass and ask you to join with me in wishing them old age and prolonged fecundity.'

The toast was drunk and the company sat down. Boaz's neighbours congratulated him on his speech. There seemed no need for a reply and, indeed, Dame Mildred, rarely at a loss for telling phrases, would on this occasion have been hard put to it to acknowledge the welcome in suitable terms. Seth appeared not to have heard either version of the speech. He sat inattentive, his mind occupied with remote speculation. Dame Mildred attempted two or three conversations.

'A very kindly meant speech, but he seems to misunderstand our mission . . . It is so interesting to see your people in their own milieu. Do tell me who is who . . . Have they entirely abandoned native costume? . . . '

But she received only abstracted answers.

Finally she said, 'I was so interested to learn about your Uncle Achon.' The Emperor nodded. 'I do hope they get him out of the monastery. Such a useless life, I always think, and so selfish. It makes people introspective to think all the time about their own souls, don't you think? So sensible of that Earl of wherever it is to go and look for him.'

But Seth had not heard a word.

March 16th
Could not sleep late after party. Attempted to telephone legation. No reply. Attempted to see Mr Seal. Said he was too busy. No sign of Sarah's trunk. She keeps borrowing my things. Tried to pin *down Emperor last night, no result. Went for walk in town. V. crowded, no one working. Apparently some trouble about currency. Saw man strike camel, would have reported him but no policeman about. Begin to feel I am wasting my time here.*

The Monastery of St Mark the Evangelist, though infected of late with the taint of heresy, was the centre of Azanian spiritual life. Here in remote times Nestorian missionaries from Mesopotamia had set up a church, and here, when the great Amurath proclaimed Christianity the official creed of the Empire, the old foundations had been

unearthed and a native community installed. A well-substantiated
tradition affirmed that the little river watering the estate was, in fact,
the brook Kedron conveyed there subterraneously; its waters were
in continual requisition for the relief of skin diseases and stubborn
boils. Here too were preserved, among other relics of less certain
authenticity, David's stone prised out of the forehead of Goliath
(a boulder of astonishing dimensions), a leaf from the Barren Fig
Tree, the rib from which Eve had been created and a wooden cross
which had fallen from heaven quite unexpectedly during Good
Friday luncheon some years back. Architecturally, however, there
was nothing very remarkable: no cloister or ambulatory, library,
gallery, chapter house or groined refectory. A cluster of mud huts
around a larger hut; a single stone building, the Church dedicated to
St Mark by Amurath the Great. It could be descried from miles
around, perched on a site of supreme beauty, a shelf of the great
escarpment that overlooked the Wanda lowlands, and through it the
brook Kedron, narrowed at this season to a single thread of silver,
broke into innumerable iridescent cascades as it fell to join the
sluggish Izol five thousand feet below. Great rocks of volcanic origin
littered the fields. The hillside was full of unexplored caverns
whence hyenas sallied out at night to exhume the corpses which it
was a pious practice to transport from all over the empire to await
the last trump on that holy ground.

The Earl of Ngumo had made good time. The road lay through
the Sakuyu cattle country, high plains covered with brown slippery
grass. At first the way led along the caravan route to the royal cities
of the north; a clearly defined track well frequented. They
exchanged greetings with mule trains coming into market and
unusual bands of travellers, loping along on foot, drawn to the
capital by the name of the great Gala and the magnetic excitement
which all the last weeks had travelled on the ether, radiating in
thrilling waves to bazaar, farm and jungle, gossiped about over
camp fires, tapped out on hollow tree trunks in the swamplands,
sniffed, as it were, on the breeze, sensed by subhuman faculties that
something was afoot.

Later they diverged into open country; only the heaps of stones
bridging the watercourses and an occasional wooden culvert told

them they were still on the right road. On the first night they camped among shepherds. The simple men recognized a great nobleman and brought him their children to touch.

'We hear of changes in the great city.'

'There are changes.'

On the second night they reached a little town. The headman had been forewarned of their approach. He came out to meet them, prostrating himself and covering his head with dust.

'Peace be upon your house.'

'You come from the great city of changes. What is your purpose among my people?'

'I wish well to your people. It is not suitable for the low to babble of what the high ones do.'

They slept in and around the headman's hut; in the morning he brought them honey and eggs, a trussed chicken, dark beer in a jug and a basket of flat bread: they gave him salt in bars, and continued their journey.

The third night they slept in the open; there was a picket of royal Guards somewhere in that country. Late on the fourth day they reached the Monastery of St Mark the Evangelist.

A monk watching on the hilltop sighted them and fired a single musket shot into the still air; a troop of baboons scattered frightened into the rocks. In the church below the great bell was rung to summon the community. The Abbot under his yellow sunshade stood in the enclosure to greet them; he wore steel-rimmed spectacles. A little deacon beside him plied a horsehair fly whisk.

Obeisance and benediction. The Earl presented the Patriarch's letter of commendation, which was slipped unopened into the folds of the Abbot's bosom, for it is not etiquette to show any immediate curiosity about such documents. Official reception in the twilit hut; the Earl seated on a chair hastily covered with carpet. The chief men of the monastery stood round the wall with folded hands. The Abbot opened the letter of introduction, spat and read it aloud amid grunts of approval; it was all preamble and titles of honour; no word of business. A visit to the shrine of the Barren Fig Tree; the Earl kissed the lintel of the door three times, laid his forehead against the steps of the sanctuary and made a present of a small bag of silver. Dinner in the Abbot's lodging; it was one of the numerous fast days of the Nestorian Church; vegetable mashes in wooden bowls, one of bananas, one of beans; earthenware jugs and brown vessels of rough beer. Ponderous leave-takings for the night. The Earl's tent meanwhile had been pitched in the open space within the enclosure; his men squatted on guard; they had made a fire; two or three monks joined them; soon they began singing, wholly secular words in monotonous cadence. Inside the tent a single small lamp with floating wick. The Earl squatted among his rugs waiting for the Abbot who, he knew, would come that night. Presently through the flap of the tent appeared the bulky white turban and straggling beard of the prelate. The two great men squatted opposite each other, on either side of the little lamp; outside the guards singing at the camp fire; beyond the stockade the hyenas and a hundred hunting sounds among the rocks. Grave courtesies: 'Our little convent resounds with the fame of the great Earl ... his prowess in battle and in bed ... the thousand enemies slain by his hand ... the lions he has speared ... his countless progeny ... '

'All my life I have counted the days wasted until I saluted the Abbot ... his learning and sanctity ... his dauntless fidelity to the faith, his chastity ... the austerities of his spiritual practices ... '

Slowly by a multitude of delicately graded steps the conversation was led to a more practical level. Was there any particular object in the Earl's visit, other than the infinite joy afforded to all by his presence?

What object could be more compelling than the universal ambition to pay respect to the Abbot and the glorious shrine of the Barren Fig Tree? But there was, as it so happened, a little matter, a thing scarcely worth a thought, which since he were here, the Earl might mention if it would not be tedious to his host.

Every word of the Earl's was a jewel, valued beyond human computation; what was this little matter?

It was an old story ... in the days of His Beatitude Gorgias of evil memory ... a prisoner, brought to the convent; now an old man ... One of whom only high ones might speak ... supposing that this man were alive ...

'Oh, Earl, you speak of that towards which my lips and ears are sealed. There are things which are not suitable.'

'Abbot, once there comes a time for everything when it must be spoken of.'

'What should a simple monk know of these high affairs? But I have indeed heard it said that in the times of His Beatitude Gorgias of evil memory, there was such a prisoner.'

'Does he still live?'

'The monks of St Mark the Evangelist guard their treasures well.'

After this all-important admission they sat for some time in silence; then the Abbot rose and with ample formalities left his guest to sleep. Both parties felt that the discussion had progressed almost too quickly. There were decencies to be observed.

Negotiations were resumed after Mass next morning and occupied most of the day; before they parted for the night Earl and Abbot had reduced their differences to a monetary basis. Next morning the price was decided and Achon, son of Amurath, legitimate Emperor of Azania, Chief of the Chiefs of Sakuyu, Lord of Wanda and Tyrant of the Seas, was set at liberty.

The event took place without ceremony. After a heavy breakfast of boiled goat's-meat, cheese, olives, smoked mutton, goose and mead – it was one of the numerous feast days of the Nestorian Church – the Earl and the Abbot set out for the hillside unaccompanied except by a handful of slaves. A short climb from the compound brought them to the mouth of a small cave.

'We will wait here. The air is not good.'

Instead they sent in a boy with lantern and hammer. From the depths they heard a few muffled words and then a series of blows as a staple was splintered from the rock. Within five minutes the slave had returned leading Achon by a chain attached to his ankle. The prince was completely naked, bowed and shrivelled, stained white hair hung down his shoulders, a stained white beard over his chest; he was blind, toothless and able to walk only with the utmost uncertainty.

The Earl had considered a few words of homage and congratulation. Instead he turned to the Abbot. 'He won't be able to ride.'

'That was hardly to be expected.'

Another night's delay while a litter was constructed; then on the fifth morning the caravan set out again for Debra Dowa. Achon swung between the shoulders of four slaves, heavily curtained from curious eyes. Part of the time he slept; at others he crooned quietly to himself, now and then breaking into little moans of alarm at the sudden jolts and lurches in his passage. On the eighth day, under cover of darkness, the little procession slipped by side roads and unfrequented lanes into the city, and, having delivered his charge to the Patriarch, the Earl hurried out to the French Legation to report to M. Ballon the successful performance of his mission.

*

Meanwhile Dame Mildred was not enjoying herself at all. Everyone seemed to conspire to be unhelpful and disobliging. First there was the intolerable impudence of that wretched boy at the Legation. She had attempted to ring them up every morning and afternoon; at last when she had almost despaired of effecting connection Mme Youkoumian had announced that she was through. But it had been a most unsatisfactory conversation. After some minutes with an obtuse native butler ('probably drinks' Dame Mildred had decided) the voice had changed to a pleasant, slightly languid English tone.

'I am Dame Mildred Porch. I wish to speak to the Minister.'

'Oh, I don't suppose you can do that, you know. Can *I* do anything for you?'

'Who are you?'

'I'm William.'

'Well, I wish to speak to you in particular . . . it's about Miss Tin's trunk.'

'Drunk?'

'Miss Sarah Tin, the organizing secretary of the overseas department of the League of Dumb Chums. She has lost her trunk.'

'Ah.'

There was a long pause. Dame Mildred could hear a gramophone being played at the other end of the line.

'Hullo . . . Hullo . . . Are you there?'

Then William's gentle drawl said: 'You know the trouble about the local telephone is that one's always getting cut off.'

There had been a click and the dance music suddenly ceased. 'Hullo . . . Hullo.' She rattled the machine but there was no answer. 'I'm convinced he did it on purpose,' she told Miss Tin. 'If we could only prove it.'

Then there was trouble about her money. The twenty or so pounds which she had changed into Bank of Azania currency on her first afternoon seemed to be quite worthless. Even Mr Youkoumian, from whom she had first received them, was unable to help, remarking that it was a question of politics; he could not accept the notes himself in settlement of the weekly hotel bill or in payment for the numerous articles of clothing which Miss Tin was obliged to purchase from day to day at his store.

Then there was the Emperor's prolonged neglect of the cause of animals. The banquet, so far from being the prelude to more practical association, seemed to be regarded as the end of her visit. Her daily attempts to obtain an audience were met with consistent refusal. At times she fell into a fever of frustration; there, all over the country, were dumb chums being mercilessly snared and speared, and here was she, impotent to help them; throughout those restless Azanian nights Dame Mildred was continually haunted by the appealing reproachful eyes, limpid as spaniel puppies', of murdered lions and the pathetic patient whinnying of trapped baboons. Consciousness of guilt subdued her usually confident manner. Who was she to complain – betrayer that she was of mandril, hyena and wild pig, wart hog and porcupine – if Mr Youkoumian overcharged her bill or mislaid her laundry?

'Mildred, I don't think you're looking at all well. I don't believe this place agrees with you.'

'No, Sarah, I'm not sure that it does. Oh, do let's go away. I don't like the people or the way they look or anything and we aren't doing any good.'

*

'Basil, Mum wants me to go home – back to England, I mean.'
'I shan't like that.'

'Do you mean it? Oh, lovely Basil, I don't want to go a bit.'

'We may all have to go soon. Things seem breaking up here . . . only I'm not so sure about going to England . . . Can't we go somewhere else?'

'Darling, what's the good of talking . . . we'll see each other again, whatever happens. You do promise that, don't you?'

'You're a grand girl, Prudence, and I'd like to eat you.'

'So you shall, my sweet . . . anything you want.'

*

Strips of sunlight through the shutters; below in the yard a native boy hammering at the engine of a broken motor-car.

*

'I am sending Mme Ballon and the other ladies of the Legation down to the coast. I do not anticipate serious trouble. The whole thing will pass off without a shot being fired. Still it is safer so. Monsieur Floreau will accompany them. He will have the delicate work of destroying the Lumo bridge. That is necessary because Seth has three regiments at Matodi who might prove loyal. The train leaves on the day before the Gala. I suggest that we advise Mr and Mrs Schonbaum a few hours before it starts. It would compromise the *coup d'état* if there were an international incident. The British must fend for themselves.'

'What is the feeling in the army, General?'

'I called a meeting of the Staff today and told them of Prince Achon's arrival in Debra Dowa. They know what is expected of them. Yesterday their salaries were paid in the new notes.'

'And the Prince, your Beatitude?'

'He is no worse.'

'But content?'

'Who can say? He has been sleeping most of the day. He does not speak. He is all the time searching for something on the floor, near his foot. I think he misses his chain. He eats well.'

*

'Mr Seal, I think I go down to Matodi day after tomorrow. Got things to fix there, see? How about you come too?'

'No good this week, Youkoumian. I shall have to wait and see poor Seth's gala.'

'Mr Seal, you take my tip and come to Matodi. I hear things. You don't want to get into no bust-up.'

'I've been hearing things too. I want to stay and see the racket.'

'Damn foolishness.'

*

It was not often that the Oriental Secretary called on the Minister. He came that evening after dinner. They were playing animal snap.

'Come in, Walsh. Nice to see you. You can settle a dispute for us. Prudence insists that a giraffe neighs like a horse. Now, does it?'

Later he got the Minister alone.

'Look here, sir. I don't know how closely you've followed local affairs, but I thought I ought to come and tell you. There's likely to be trouble on Tuesday on the day of this Birth-Control Gala.'

'Trouble? I should think so. I think the whole thing perfectly disgusting. None of us are going.'

'Well, I don't exactly know what sort of trouble. But there's *something* up. I've just heard this evening that the French and Americans are going down to the coast *en bloc* by the Monday train. I thought you ought to know.'

'Pooh, another of these native disturbances. I remember that last civil war was just the same. Ballon thought he was going to be attacked the whole time. I'd sooner risk being bombed up here than bitten by mosquitoes at the coast. Still, jolly nice of you to tell me.'

'You wouldn't mind, sir, if my wife and myself went down on the train.'

'Not a bit, not a bit. Jolly glad. You can take charge of the bags. Can't say I envy you, but I hope you have a jolly trip.'

*

On the morning preceding the Gala, Basil went as usual to his office. He found Mr Youkoumian busily packing a canvas grip with the few portable objects of value that had been collected for the museum. 'I better take care of these in case anything 'appens,' he explained. 'Catching train eleven o'clock. Very much crowded train. I think many wise men will be aboard. You better come too, Mr Seal. I fix it O.K.'

'What *is* going to happen?'

'I don't know nothing, Mr Seal. I don't ask no questions. All I think that if there is a bust-up I will better be at the coast. They were preaching in all the churches Sunday against the Emperor's Birth Control. Madame Youkoumian told me which is a very pious and church-going woman. But I think there is more than that going to happen. I think General Connolly knows something. You better come to the coast, Mr Seal. No?'

There was nothing to do that morning; no letters to answer; no chits from the Palace; the work of the Ministry seemed suddenly over. Basil locked his office door, pocketed the key and strode across the yard to see Seth. Two officers at the gate-house hushed their conversation as Basil passed them.

He found Seth, in an elegant grey suit and pale-coloured shoes, moodily poring over the map of the new city.

'They have stopped work on the Boulevard Seth. Jagger has dismissed his men. Why is this?'

'He hadn't been paid for three weeks. He didn't like the new bank-notes.'

'Traitor. I will have him shot. I sent for Connolly an hour ago. Where is he?'

'A great number of Europeans left for the coast by this morning's train – but I don't think Connolly was with them.'

'Europeans leaving? What do I care? The city is full of my people. I have watched them from the tower with my field-glasses. All day they come streaming in by the four roads . . . But the work must go on. The Anglican Cathedral for example; it should be down by now. I'll have it down if I have to work with my own hands. You see, it is right in the way of the great northern thoroughfare. Look at it on the plan – so straight . . . '

'Seth, there's a lot of talk going about. They say there may be trouble tomorrow.'

'God, have I not had trouble today and yesterday? Why should I worry about tomorrow?'

*

That evening Dame Mildred and Miss Tin saw a very curious sight. They had been to tea with the Bishop and, leaving him, made a slight detour, in order to take advantage of the singular sweetness of the evening air. As they passed the Anglican Cathedral they noticed a young man working alone. He wore light grey and parti-coloured shoes and he was engaged in battering at the granite archway at the West End with an energy very rare among Azanian navvies.

'How like the Emperor.'

'Don't be absurd, Sarah.'

They left the grey figure chipping diligently in the twilight, and returned to their hotel where the Youkoumians' departure had utterly disorganized the service.

'Just when we had begun to make them understand how we liked things . . . ' complained Dame Mildred.

*

Next morning the ladies were up early. They had been awakened before dawn by the traffic under their windows, mules and ponies, chatter and scuffling, cars hooting for passage. Dame Mildred opened the shutters and looked down into the crowded street. Miss Tin joined her.

'I've been ringing for twenty minutes. There doesn't seem to be a soul in the hotel.'

Nor was there; the servants had gone out last night after dinner and had not returned. Fortunately Dame Mildred had the spirit stove, without which she never ventured abroad, some biscuits and cubes of bouillon. They breakfasted in this way upstairs while the crowd outside grew every moment in volume and variety, as the sun, brilliant and piercing as on other less notable mornings, mounted over the city. Dust rose from the crowded street and hung sparkling in the air.

'So nice for the Emperor to have a good day for his Pageant. Not at all like any of the pageants I can remember in England. Do you remember the Girl Guides' rally when there was that terrible hail storm – in August too? *How* the Brownies cried.'

The route of the procession lay past the Hotel de l'Empereur Seth. Shop fronts had been boarded up and several of the house-holders had erected stands and temporary balconies outside their windows. Some weeks earlier, when the Pageant had first been announced, Mr Youkoumian had advertised accommodation of this kind and sold a number of tickets to prospective sightseers. In the subsequent uncertainty he had abandoned this among other of his projects. Now, however, two or three Indians, a Greek and four or five Azanians in gala clothes presented themselves at the hotel to claim their seats in the stand. They explored the deserted vestibule and dining-room, climbed the stairs and finally reached the bed-rooms of the English ladies. Hardened by long exposure to rebuffs and injustice, the Indians paid no attention to Dame Mildred's protests. Instead, they pulled up the bed across the window, seated themselves in positions of excellent advantage and then, producing small bags of betel nuts from their pockets, settled down to wait, patiently chewing and spitting. Encouraged by this example the other intruders took possession of the other windows. The Greek politely offered Miss Tin a place in their midst and accepted her refusal with somewhat puzzled concern. The two ladies of the Azanian party wandered round the room, picking up and examin-ing the articles on the washstand and dressing-table, and chattering with simple pleasure over the contents of the chest-of-drawers.

'This is an intolerable outrage. But I don't see what we can do about it at the moment. Sir Samson will have to lodge a complaint.'

'We can't possibly remain here. We can't possibly go out into the street. There is only one place for us – the roof.'

This position was easily accessible by means of a ladder and trap-door. Hastily equipping themselves with rugs, pillows, sunshades, two light novels, cameras and the remains of the biscuits, the resolute ladies climbed up into the blazing sunlight. Dame Mildred handed up their provisions to Miss Tin, then followed her. The trap-door could not be bolted from above, but fortunately the tin roof was weighted in many places by rock boulders, placed there to strengthen it in times of high wind. One of these they rolled into place, then, sliding down the hot corrugations to the low cement parapet, they made their nest in a mood of temporary tranquillity.

'We shall see very well from here, Sarah. There will be plenty of time to have those natives punished tomorrow.'

Indeed, from where they sat the whole city lay very conveniently exposed to their view. They could see the irregular roofs of the palace buildings in their grove of sapling blue gums and before them the still unfinished royal box from which the Emperor proposed to review the procession; small black figures could be observed working on it, tacking up coloured flags, spreading carpets and bobbing up the path with pots of palm and fern. They could see the main street of the city diverge, to the barracks on one side and the Christian quarter on the other. They could see the several domes and spires of the Catholic, Orthodox, Armenian, Anglican, Nestorian, American Baptist and Mormon places of worship; the minaret of the mosque, the Synagogue and the flat white roof of the Hindu snake temple. Miss Tin took a series of snapshots.

'Don't use all the films, there are bound to be some interesting things later.'

The sun rose high in the heavens; the corrugated iron radiated a fierce heat. Propped on their pillows under green parasols the two ladies became drowsy and inattentive to the passage of time.

The procession was due to start at eleven, but it must have been past noon before Dame Mildred, coming to with a jerk and snort, said, 'Sarah, I think something is beginning to happen.'

A little dizzily, for the heat was now scarcely bearable, the ladies leant over the parapet. The crowd was halloing loudly and the women gave out their peculiar throbbing whistle; there seemed to be a general stir towards the royal box, a quarter of a mile down the road.

'That must be the Emperor arriving.'

A dozen lancers were cantering down the street, forcing the crowds back into the side alleys and courtyards, only to surge out again behind them.

'The procession will come up from the direction of the railway station. Look, here they are.'

Fresh swelling and tumult in the crowded street. But it was only the lancers returning towards the Palace.

Presently Miss Tin said, 'You know, this may take all day. How hungry we shall be.'

'I've been thinking of that for some time. I am going to go down and forage.'

'Mildred, you can't. *Anything* might happen to you.'

'Nonsense, we can't live on this roof all day with four petit-beurre biscuits.'

She rolled back the stone and carefully, rung by rung, descended the ladder. The bedroom doors were open, and as she passed she saw that quite a large party was now assembled at the windows. She reached the ground floor, crossed the dining-room and opened the door at the far end where, she had been informed by many penetrating smells during the past weeks, lay the kitchen quarters. Countless flies rose with humming alarm as she opened the larder door. Uncovered plates of horrible substances lay on the shelves; she drew back instinctively; then faced them again. There were some black olives in an earthenware basin and half a yard of brick-dry bread. Armed with these and breathing heavily she again climbed to the trap-door.

'Sarah, open it at once.' The rock was withdrawn. 'How could you be so selfish as to shut it? Supposing I had been pursued.'

'I'm sorry, Mildred. Indeed I am, but you were so long and I grew nervous. And, my dear, you have been missing such a lot. All kinds of things have been happening.'

'What things?'

'Well, I don't know exactly, but look.'

Indeed, below, the crowds seemed to be in a state of extreme agitation, jostling and swaying without apparent direction around a wedge-shaped phalanx of police who were forcing a way with long bamboo staves; in their centre was an elderly man under arrest.

'Surely, those are clothes of the native priests? What can the old man have been up to?'

'Almost anything. I have never had any belief in the clergy after that curate we liked so much who was Chaplain of the Dumb Chums and spoke so feelingly and then . . .'

'Look, here *is* the procession.'

Rising strains of the Azanian anthem; the brass band of the Imperial Guards swung into sight, drowning the sounds of conflict. The Azanians loved a band and their Patriarch's arrest was immediately forgotten. Behind the soldiers drove Viscount and Viscountess Boaz, who had eventually consented to act as patrons. Then, marching four abreast in brand-new pinafores, came the girls of the Amurath Memorial High School, an institution founded by the old Empress to care for the orphans of murdered officials. They bore, somewhat unsteadily, a banner whose construction had occupied the embroidery and dressmaking class for several weeks. It was emblazoned in letters of appliquéd silk with the motto: WOMEN OF TOMORROW DEMAND AN EMPTY CRADLE. Slowly the mites filed by, singing sturdily.

'Very sensible and pretty,' said Miss Tin. 'Dear Mildred, what very stale bread you have brought.'

'The olives are excellent.'

'I never liked olives. Good gracious, look at this.'

The first of the triumphal cars had come into sight. At first an attempt had been made to induce ladies of rank to take part in the tableaux; a few had wavered, but Azanian society still retained certain standards; the peerage were not going to have their wives and daughters exhibiting themselves in aid of charity; the idea had to be dropped and the actresses recruited less ambitiously from the demi-monde. This first car, drawn by oxen, represented the place of women in the modern world. Enthroned under a canopy of coloured cotton sat Mlle 'Fifi' Fatim Bey; in one hand a hunting-crop to symbolize sport, in the other a newspaper to symbolize learning; round her were grouped a court of Azanian beauties with typewriters, tennis rackets, motor-bicycling goggles, telephones, hitch-hiking outfits and other patents of modernity inspired by the European illustrated papers. An orange-and-green appliquéd standard bore the challenging motto: THROUGH STERILITY TO CULTURE.

Enthusiastic applause greeted this pretty invention. Another car came into sight down the road, bobbing decoratively above the black pates; other banners.

Suddenly there was a check in the progress and a new note in the voice of the crowd.

'Has there been an accident? I do hope none of the poor oxen are hurt.'

The trouble seemed to be coming from the front of the procession, where bodies of men had pushed through from the side streets and were endeavouring to head the procession back. The brass band stopped, faltered and broke off, scattering before the assault and feebly defending their heads with trombones and kettle drums.

'Quick, Sarah, your camera. I don't know what in the world is happening, but I must get a snap of it. Of course the sun *would* be in the wrong place.'

'Try with the very small stop.'

'I do pray they come out; I had such bad luck with those very interesting films of Cape Town that the wretched man ruined on the boat. You know it looks like quite a serious riot. Where are the police?'

The attackers, having swept the band out of the road and underfoot, were making easy work of the High School Orphans; they were serious young men armed with clubs, the athletic group, as the ladies learned later, of Nestorian Catholic Action, muscular Christians who for many weeks now had been impatiently biding their time to have a whack at the modernists and Jews who were behind the new movement.

Down went the embroidered banner as the girls in their pinafores ran for safety between the legs of the onlookers.

The main focus of the assault was now the triumphal car immediately in front of the Hotel de l'Empereur Seth. At the first sign of disturbance the members of the tableau had abandoned their poses and huddled together in alarm; now without hesitation they forsook their properties and bundled out of the wagon into the street. The Christian party swarmed on to it and one of them began addressing the crowd. Dame Mildred snapped him happily as he turned in their direction, arms spread, mouth wide open, in all the fervour of democratic leadership.

Hitherto, except for a few jabs with trumpets and drumsticks, the attackers had met with no opposition. Now, however, the crowd began to take sides, individual scuffles broke out among them and a party of tribesmen from up-country, happily welcoming this new diversion in a crowded day, began a concerted charge to the triumphal car, round which there was soon raging a contest of I'm-king-of-the-castle game. The Nestorian orator was thrown overboard and a fine savage in lion skins began doing a jig in his place. The patient oxen stood unmoved by the tumult.

'Quick, Sarah, another roll of films. What *can* the police be thinking of?'

Then authority asserted itself.

From the direction of the royal box flashed out a ragged volley of rifle shots. A bullet struck the parapet with a burst of splintered concrete and ricocheted, droning, over the ladies' heads. Another volley and something slapped on to the iron roof a few yards from where they sat. Half comprehending, Dame Mildred picked up and examined the irregular disc of hot lead. Shrill wails of terror rose from the street below and then a clattering of horses and oxen. Without a word spoken Dame Mildred and Miss Tin rolled to cover.

The parapet was a low one and the ladies were obliged to lie full length in positions of extreme discomfort. Dame Mildred slid out her arm for a cushion and hastily withdrew it as a third burst of firing broke out as though on purpose to frustrate her action. Presently silence fell, more frightening than the tumult. Dame Mildred spoke in an awed whisper.

'Sarah, that was a *bullet*.'

'I know. Do be quiet or they'll start again.'

For twenty minutes by Miss Tin's wrist-watch the two ladies lay in the gutter, their faces almost touching the hot, tarnished iron of the roof. Dame Mildred shifted on to her side.

'Oh, *what is it*, Mildred?'

'Pins and needles in my left leg. I don't care if I am shot.'

Dim recollections of some scouting game played peaceably in somewhat different circumstances among Girl Guides in the bracken of Epping prompted Dame Mildred to remove her topee and, holding it at arm's length, expose it over the edge of their rampart. The silence of the stricken field was unbroken. Slowly, with infinite caution, she raised her head.

'For heaven's sake, take care, Mildred. *Snipers*.'

But everything was quiet. At length she sat up and looked over. From end to end the street was silent and utterly deserted. The strings of flags hung limp in the afternoon heat. The banner of the Amurath High School lay spread across the way, dishevelled and dusty from a thousand footsteps but still flaunting its message bravely to the heavens, WOMEN OF TOMORROW DEMAND AN EMPTY CRADLE. The other banner lay crumpled in the gutter. Only one word was visible in the empty street. STERILITY pleaded in orange-and-green silk to an unseeing people.

'I think it is all over.'

The ladies sat up and stretched their cramped legs, dusted themselves a little, straightened their hats and breathed deeply of the fresh air. Dame Mildred retrieved her camera and wound on the film. Miss Tin shook out the pillows and looked for food. The olives were dry and dull-skinned, the bread crisp as biscuit and gritted with dust.

'*Now* what are we going to do? I'm thirsty and I think one of my headaches is coming on.'

Regular steps of marching troops in the street below.

'Look out. They're coming again.'

The two ladies slid back under cover. They heard the grounding of rifle butts, some unintelligible orders, marching steps proceeding down the street. Inch by inch they emerged again.

'Some of them are still there. But I think it's all right.'

A picket of Guards squatted round a machine-gun on the pavement opposite.

'I'm going down to find something to drink.'

They rolled back the stone from the trap-door and descended into the silent hotel. The sightseers had left their bedrooms. There was no one about on either floor.

'I wonder where they keep the Evian.'

They went into the bar. Alcohol everywhere, but no water. In a corner of the kitchen they found a dozen or so bottles bearing the labels of various mineral waters – Evian, St Galmiet, Vichy, Malvern – all empty. It was Mr Youkoumian's practice to replenish them, when required, from the foetid well at the back of the house.

'I must get something to drink or I shall die. I'm going out.'

'*Mildred.*'

'I don't care, I am.'

She strode through the twilit vestibule into the street. The officer in charge of the machine-gun section waved her back. She walked on, making pacific gestures. He spoke to her rapidly and loudly, first in Sakuyu, then in Arabic. Dame Mildred replied in English and French.

'*Taisez-vous, officer. Je désire de l'eau. Où peut-on trouver ça, s'il vous plait?*'

The soldier showed her the hotel, then the machine-gun.

'British subject. Me. British subject. No savvy? Oh, don't any of you speak a word of English?'

The soldiers grinned and nodded, pointing her back to the hotel.

'It's no good. They won't let us out. We must wait.'

'Mildred, I'm going to drink wine.'

'Well, let's take it up to the roof – it seems the only safe place.'

Armed with a bottle of Mr Youkoumian's Koniak they strode back up the ladder.

'Oh dear, it's very strong.'

'I think it may help my headache.'

The afternoon wore on. The burning sun dipped towards the edge of the mountains. The ladies sipped raw brandy on the iron roof.

At length there was a fresh movement in the street. An officer on mule-back galloped up, shouting an order to the picket. They dismantled their machine-gun, hoisted it on to their shoulders, fell in, and marched away towards the Palace. Other patrols tramped past the hotel. From their eminence they could see bodies of troops converging from all sides on the Palace square.

'They're calling in the guard. It must be all right now. But I feel too sleepy to move.'

Presently, as the soldiers withdrew, little bodies of civilians emerged from hiding. A marauding band of Christians swung confidently into view.

'I believe they're coming here.'

Splintering of glass and drunken, boastful laughter came from the bar below. Another party broke in the shutters of the drapers opposite and decked themselves with lengths of bright stuff. But oblivious of the excursions below them, worn out by the heat and anxiety of the day, and slightly drugged by Mr Youkoumian's spirit, the two ladies slept.

It was after seven when they awoke. The sun had set and there was a sharp chill in the air. Miss Tin shivered and sneezed.

'My head's splitting. I'm very hungry again,' she said, 'and thirstier than ever.'

The windows were all dark. Blackness encircled them save for a line of light which streamed across the street from the door of the bar and a dull red glow along the rooftops of the South quarter, in which the Indian and Armenian merchants had their warehouses.

'That can't be sunset at this time. Sarah, I believe the town is on fire.'

'*What* are we to do? We can't stay here all night.'

A sound of tipsy singing rose from below and a small knot of Azanians came into sight, swaying together with arms across each other's shoulders; two or three of them carried torches and lanterns. A party sallied out from the bar below; there was a confused scuffling. One of the lamps was dropped in a burst of yellow flame. The tussle broke up, leaving a little pool of burning oil in the centre of the road.

'We can't possibly go down.'

Two hours dragged by; the red glow behind the rooftops died, revived and died again; once there was a short outbreak of firing some distance away. The beleaguered ladies sat and shuddered in the darkness. Then the lights of a car appeared and stopped outside the hotel. A few topers emerged from the bar and clustered round it. There were some words spoken in Sakuyu and then a clear English drawl rose to them.

'Well, the old girls don't seem to be here. These chaps say they haven't seen anyone.'

And another answered: 'I dare say they've been raped.'

'I hope so. Let's try the Mission.'

'Stop,' shrieked Dame Mildred. 'Hi! Stop.'

The motor-car door clicked to; the engine started up.

'Stop,' cried Miss Tin. 'We're up here.'

Then, in a moment of inspiration, untaught in the Girl Guides, Dame Mildred threw down the half-empty bottle of brandy. William's head popped out of the car window and shouted a few words of easily acquired abuse in Sakuyu; then a pillow followed the bottle on to the roadway.

'I believe there's someone up there. Be an angel and go and see, Percy. I'll stick in here if there's going to be any bottle-throwing.'

The second secretary advanced with caution and had reached only the foot of the stairs when the two ladies greeted him.

'Thank God you've come,' said Miss Tin.

'Well,' he said, a little confused by this sudden cordiality; 'jolly nice of you to put it like that. All I mean is, we just dropped in to see that you were all right. Minister said we'd better. Not scared or anything, I mean.'

'*All right?* We've had the most terrible day of our lives.'

'Oh I say, not as bad as that, I hope. We heard at the Legation that there'd been some kind of a disturbance. Well, you'll be right as rain now, you know. Everything pretty quiet except for a few drunks. If there's anything we can do, just let us know.'

'Young man, do you intend leaving us here all night?'

'Well . . . I suppose it sounds inhospitable, but there's nothing else for it. Full up at the Legation, you know. The Bishop arrived unexpectedly and two or three of the commercial fellows took fright and came over for some reason. Jolly awkward . . . You see how it is, don't you?'

'Do you realize that the town is on fire?'

'Yes, rare old blaze. We passed quite near it. It looks awfully jolly from the Legation.'

'Young man, Miss Tin and myself are coming with you now.'

'Oh, look here, I say, you know . . .'

'Sarah, get in the car. I will bring down a few things for the night.'

The discussion had brought them to the street. William and Anstruther exchanged glances of despair. Sir Samson's instructions had been: 'Just see that those tiresome old women are safe, but on no account bring them back here. The place is a bear garden already.' (This with a scowl towards the Bishop who was very quietly playing Peggity with Prudence in a corner of the drawing-room.)

Dame Mildred, putting little trust in Miss Tin's ability to restrain the diplomats from starting without her, took few pains with the packing. In less than a minute she was down again with an armful of night clothes and washing materials. At last, with a squeeze and a grunt, she sank into the back seat.

'Tell me,' asked William with some admiration, as he turned the car round. 'Do you always throw bottles at people when you want a lift?'

CHAPTER 7

SIR SAMSON COURTENEY arose next morning in a mood of high displeasure, which became the more intense as with every minute of his leisurely toilet he recalled in detail the atrocious disorders of the preceding evening.

'Never known anything like it,' he reflected on the way to the bathroom. 'These wretched people don't seem to realize that a Legation is a place of business. How can I be expected to get through the day's work, with my whole house overrun with uninvited guests?'

First there had been the Bishop, who arrived during tea with two breathless curates and an absurd story about another revolution and shooting in the streets. Well, why not? You couldn't expect the calm of *Barchester Towers* in a place like Azania. Missionary work was known to involve some physical discomfort. Nincompoops. Sir Samson lashed the bath water in his contempt and vexation. Then, when they were half-way through dinner, who should turn up but the Bank Manager and a scrubby little chap named Jagger. Never heard of him. More wild talk about murder, loot and fire. Dinner started all over again, with the result that the duck was ruined. And then the most damnable treachery of all: his wife of all people, infected with the general panic, had begun to ask about Dame Mildred and Miss Tin. Had they gone down to the coast when the other English people left? Should not something be done about them? The Minister poohpoohed the suggestion for some time, but at length so far yielded to popular appeal as to allow William and Percy to take the car and go out, just to see that the old women had come to no harm. That was the explicit limit of their instructions. And what did they do but bring *them* along too? Here, in fact, was the entire English population of Debra Dowa taking refuge under his roof. 'They'll have to clear out today,' decided the Minister as he lathered his chin, 'every man jack of them. It's an intolerable imposition.'

Accommodation in the compound had eventually been found for all the new-comers. The Bishop slept in the Legation, the curates with the Anstruthers, who, in the most sporting manner, moved the children into their own room for the night, Dame Mildred and Miss Tin at the Legges' and the Bank Manager and Mr Jagger alone in the bungalow vacated by the Walshes. By the time Sir Samson came down to breakfast, however, they were all together again, chattering uproariously on the croquet lawn.

'. . . my back quite sore . . . not really accustomed to riding.' 'Poor Mr Raith.' 'The Church party started it. The priests had been haranguing them for days against birth control. The police learned that an attempt would be made to break up the procession so they arrested the Patriarch just before it was due to start . . .' 'Troops cleared the streets . . . fired over their heads . . . no damage done . . .' '. . . a bullet within a few inches, literally *inches* of my head . . .' 'Seth went back to the Palace as soon as it was clear the procession couldn't take place. My word, he looked angry . . .' 'Young Seal with him . . .' '. . . it wasn't so bad when the beast was going uphill. It was that terrible *sliding* feeling . . .' 'Poor Mr Raith . . .' 'Then the patrols were all withdrawn and concentrated in front of the Palace. Jagger and I were quite close and saw the whole thing. They had the whole army drawn up in the square and gradually when they realized the shooting was over the crowd began to come back, little knots of sixes and sevens creeping out from the side alleys and then creeping in round the soldiers. This was about half-past five . . .' '. . . and not having proper breeches my knees got so *rubbed* . . .' 'Poor Mr Raith . . .' 'Everyone thought Seth was going to appear. The royal box was still there, shoddy sort of affair, but it provided a platform. Everyone kept looking in that direction. Suddenly who should climb up but the Patriarch, who had been released from prison by the rioters, and after him Connolly and old Ngumo and one or two others of the notables. Well, the crowd cheered like mad for the Patriarch and Ngumo and the soldiers cheered for Connolly and started firing off their rifles again into the air and for a quarter of

BLACK MISCHIEF

an hour the place was in an uproar...' '...and two bruises on the lower part of my shin where the stirrups came...' 'Poor Mr Raith...' 'Then came the big surprise of the day. The Patriarch made a speech, don't suppose half the people heard it. Announced that Seth had abdicated and that Achon, Amurath's son who's supposed to have been dead for fifty years, was still alive and would be crowned Emperor today. The fellows near started cheering and the others took it up – they didn't know why – and soon they had a regular party going. Meanwhile the Christians had been making hay in the Indian and Jewish quarters, breaking up the shops and setting half the place on fire. That's when Jagger and I made our get-away...' '...very stiff and chafed...' '...poor, poor Mr Raith.'

'All talking shop as usual,' said Sir Samson, as these voices floated in to him through the dining-room windows. 'And eating me out of house and home,' he added sourly as he noted that there was a shortage of kedgeree that morning.

'But what about Basil Seal?' Prudence asked.

'He went off with Seth, I believe,' said the Bank Manager, 'wherever that may be.'

Lady Courteney appeared among her guests, wearing gum-boots and pushing a barrow and spade. Emperors might come and go, but there was heavy digging to be done in the lily-pond.

'Good morning,' she said. 'I do hope you all slept well after your adventures and found enough breakfast. I'm afraid this is a very topsy-turvy house party. Prudence, child, I want you to help with the mud-puddle this morning. Mr Raith, I'm sure you're tired after your ride. Take an easy morning like a sensible man. The Bishop will show you the best parts of the garden. Take some deck-chairs. You'll find them in the porch. Dame Mildred and Miss Tin, *how* are you both? I hope my maid found you all you needed. Do please all make yourselves at home. Mr Jagger, perhaps you play croquet.'

The Envoy Extraordinary finished his second cup of coffee, filled and lit his pipe, and, avoiding the social life of the lawn, pottered round by the back way to the Chancery. Here at least there survived an atmosphere of normal tranquillity. Anstruther, Legge and William were playing cut-throat bridge.

'Sorry to disturb you fellows. I just wanted to know whether any of you knew anything about this revolution.'

'Not much, I'm afraid. Care to take a hand, sir?'

'No, thanks very much. I think I'll have a talk with the Bishop about his Cathedral. Save writing that letter. Dare say everything'll be all right now that Seth's left – I suppose I shall have to write a report of this business. No one will read it. But one of you might pop down into town sometime and see exactly what's happened, will you?'

'That's going to be a bore,' said William, as the Minister left them. 'God, what a mean dummy.'

An hour later he visited them again.

'I say, I've just got a letter asking me to this coronation. I suppose someone from here ought to go? It means putting on uniform and mine's got so infernally tight. William, be a good fellow and represent me, will you?'

*

The Nestorian Cathedral, like the whole of the city, was of quite recent construction, but its darkness and stuffiness endowed it with an air of some antiquity. It was an octagonal, domed building, consisting of a concentric ambulatory round an inner sanctuary. The walls were painted in primitive simplicity with saints and angels, battle scenes from the Old Testament history and portraits of Amurath the Great, faintly visible in the murky light of a dozen or so branch candlesticks. Three choirs had been singing since dawn. There was an office of enormous length to be got through before the coronation Mass – psalms, prophecies, lections and many minor but prolix rites of purification. Three aged lectors recited Leviticus from manuscript rolls while a band of deacons played a low rhythm on hand drums and a silver gong. The Church party were in the ascendant at the moment and were not disposed to forgo a single liturgical luxury.

Meanwhile chairs and carpets were being arranged in the outer aisle and an awning improvised through which, after the Mass, the new Emperor was to be led to take the final vows in the presence of the populace. All roads to the Cathedral were heavily policed and the square was lined with Guardsmen. At eleven M. Ballon arrived and took his place in the seats set aside for the diplomatic corps. The Americans had all left the town, so that he was now in the position of doyen. The native nobility had already assembled. The Duke of Ukaka found a place next to the Earl of Ngumo.

'Where's Achon now?'

'Inside with the priests.'

'How is he?'

'He passed a good night. I think he finds the robes uncomfortable.'

Presently the Office ended and the Mass began, said behind closed doors by the Patriarch himself, with all the complex ritual of his church. An occasional silver tinkle from inside informed the worshippers of the progress of the ceremony, while a choir of deacons maintained a solemn chant somewhere out of sight in the gloom. M. Ballon stirred uneasily, moved by tiny, uncontrollable shudders of shocked atheism. Presently William arrived, carrying cocked hat, white gloves, very elegant in gold braid. He smiled pleasantly at M. Ballon and sat beside him.

'I say, have they started?'

M. Ballon nodded but did not reply.

A long time passed and the diplomat shifted from buttock to buttock in his gilt chair. It was no longer a matter of anti-clericalism but of acute physical discomfort.

William twiddled his gloves and dropped his hat and gaped miserably at the frescoed ceiling. Once, absent-mindedly, he took out his cigarette-case, tapped a cigarette on the toe of his shoe and was about to light it when he caught a glance from M. Ballon which caused him hastily to return it to his pocket.

But eventually an end came. The doors of the inner sanctuary were thrown open; the trumpeters on the Cathedral steps sounded a fanfare; the band in the square recognized their signal and struck up the Azanian Anthem. The procession emerged into the open. First came the choir of deacons, the priests, Bishops and the Patriarch. Then a canopy of brocade supported on poles at each corner by the four premier peers of the Empire. Under it shuffled the new Monarch in the robes of state. It was not clear from his manner that he understood the nature of the proceedings. He wriggled his shoulders irritably under the unaccustomed burden of silk and jewellery, scratched his ribs and kept feeling disconsolately towards his right foot and shaking it sideways as he walked, worried at missing his familiar chain. Some drops of the holy oil with which he had been recently anointed trickled over the bridge of his nose and, drop by drop, down his white beard. Now and then he faltered and halted in his pace and was only moved on by a respectful dig in the ribs from one of his attendant peers. M. Ballon, William and the native nobility fell in behind him, and with slow steps proceeded to the dais for the final ceremonies.

A great shout rose from the concourse as the Imperial party mounted the steps and Achon was led to the throne prepared for him. Here, one by one, he was invested with the royal regalia. First, holding the sword of state, the Patriarch addressed him:

'Achon, I give you this sword of the Empire of Azania. Do you swear to fight in the cause of Justice and Faith for the protection of your people and the glory of your race?'

The Emperor grunted and the ornate weapon was laid across his lap and one of his listless hands placed upon its hilt while cannonades of applause rose from his assembled subjects.

Then the gold spur.

'Achon, I give you this spur. Do you swear to ride in the cause of Justice and Faith for the protection of your people and the glory of your race?'

The Emperor gave a low whimper and turned away his face; the Earl of Ngumo buckled the spur about the foot that had so lately borne a graver weight. Huzzas and halloaing in the crowded square.

Finally the crown.

'Achon, I give you this crown. Do you swear to use it in the cause of Justice and Faith for the protection of your people and the glory of your race?'

The Emperor remained silent and the Patriarch advanced towards him with the massive gold tiara of Amurath the Great. With great gentleness he placed it over the wrinkled brow and straggle of white hairs; but Achon's head lolled forward under its weight and the bauble was pitched back into the Patriarch's hands.

Nobles and prelates clustered about the old man and then dismay spread among them and a babble of scared undertones. The people, seeing that something was amiss, broke off short in their cheering and huddled forward towards the dais.

'Tcha!' exclaimed M. Ballon. 'This is something infinitely vexatious. It was not to be foreseen.'

For Achon was dead.

*

'Well,' said Sir Samson, when, rather late for luncheon, William brought back news of the coronation, 'I can't for the life of me see how they think they're any better off. They'll have to get Seth back now, I suppose, and we've all been disturbed for nothing. It'll look infernally silly when we send in a report of this to the F.O. Not sure we hadn't better keep quiet about the whole business.'

'By the way,' said William, 'I heard something else in the town. The bridge is down at Lumo, so there'll be no more trains to the coast for weeks.'

'*One thing after another.*'

They were all there, cramped at the elbows, round the dining-room table. Bishop and curates, Bank Manager and Mr Jagger, Dame Mildred and Miss Tin, and they all began asking William questions about the state of the town. Was the fire completely put out? Was there looting in the shops? Did the life of the place seem to be going on normally? Were there troops patrolling the streets? Where was Seth? Where was Seal? Where was Boaz?

'I don't think it at all fair to tease William,' said Prudence, 'particularly when he looks so nice in his uniform.'

'But if, as you say, this bridge is demolished,' demanded Dame Mildred, 'how can one get to Matodi?'

'There isn't any other way, unless you like to ride down on a camel with one of the caravans.'

'D'you mean to say we must stay here until the bridge is rebuilt?'

'Not here,' interposed Sir Samson involuntarily, 'not here.'

'I think the whole thing is *scandalous*,' said Miss Tin.

At last, before coffee was served, the Minister left the table.

'Got to get back to work,' he said cheerfully, 'and I shall be at it all the afternoon, so I'd better say good-bye now. I expect you'll all be gone before I get through with it.'

And he left in the dining-room seven silent guests whose faces were eloquent of consternation. Later they assembled furtively in a corner of the garden to discuss their circumstances.

'I must admit,' said the Bishop, 'that it seems to me unreasonable and inconsiderate of the Minister to expect us to return to the town until we have more reassuring information about the conditions.'

'As British subjects we have the right to be protected by our flag,' said Dame Mildred, 'and I for one intend to stay here whether Sir Samson likes it or not.'

'That's right,' said Mr Jagger.

And after further mutual reassurances, the Bishop was sent to inform their host of their decision to remain. He found him peacefully dozing in a hammock under the mango trees.

'You put me in a very difficult position,' he said when the situation had been explained to him. 'I wish that nothing of the sort had occurred at all. I am sure you would all be much more comfortable and equally safe in the town, but since you wish to remain, pray consider yourselves my guests for as long as it takes to relieve your apprehensions,' and feeling that affairs had got completely outside his control, the Envoy relapsed into sleep.

Later that afternoon, when Lady Courteney had contrived to find occupations for all her guests, some at the bagatelle board, others with Peggity, photograph albums, cards or croquet, the party suffered a further and far from welcome addition; a dusty figure in native costume who propped a rifle against the fireplace before coming forward to shake her hand.

'Oh dear, oh dear,' she said, 'have *you* come to stay with us too?'

'Only for tonight,' said Basil. 'I've got to be off first thing tomorrow. Where can I put up my camels?'

'Good gracious, I don't think we've ever had such a thing here before. Have you more than one?'

'Ten. I'm passing as a Sakuyu merchant. They're outside with the boys. I dare say they'll find a place for them. They're vicious beasts though. D'you think I could have some whisky?'

'Yes, no doubt the butler can find you some, and would you like William to lend you some clothes?'

'No, I'll stay in these, thanks. Got to get used to moving about in them. It's the only way I can hope to get through. They had two shots at bumping me off yesterday.'

The company forsook their pastimes and crowded round the new-comer.

'How are things in the city?'

'As bad as they can be. The army feel they've been sold a pup and won't leave barracks. Connolly's gone off with most of his staff to try and find Seth. The Patriarch's in hiding somewhere in the town. Ngumo's men have had a big dust-up with the police and are pretty well on top at the moment. They've got into the liquor saloons which Connolly closed yesterday. As soon as it's dark they'll start looting again.'

'*There*,' said Dame Mildred, 'and the Minister expected us to leave today.'

'Oh, I shouldn't count on being too safe here. There's a gang breaking up the American Legation now. Ballon's ordered an aeroplane from the mainland. I expect you'll get a raid tonight or tomorrow. Your sowars don't look up to much serious work.'

'And where are you going?'

'After Seth and Boaz. We've a rendezvous five days' ride out of town at a farm of Boaz's on the edge of the Wanda country. There's just a chance of getting the boy back if he plays his cards properly. But there's bound to be serious fighting, whatever happens.'

Shivers of half-pleasant alarm went through his listeners.

'Mr Seal,' Lady Courteney benignly interposed at last. 'I think it's very mischievous of you saying all this. I'm sure that things are not nearly as bad as you make out. You're just *talking*. Now go and get yourself some whisky and talk to Prudence, and I think you might put that dirty gun outside in the lobby.'

*

'Oh, Basil, what *is* going to happen? I can't bear your going off like this and everything being so messy.'

'Don't you worry, Prudence, everything'll be all right. We'll meet again, I promise you.'

'But you said it was dangerous.'

'I was just piling it on to scare the old women.'

'Basil, I don't believe you were.'

'I should think they'll take you off by air from Khormaksar. You've got Walsh down at Matodi. He's a sound-enough fellow. As soon as he learns what's happened he'll get through to Aden and arrange everything. You'll be all right, just you see.'

'But it's you I'm worrying about.'

'Don't you do that, Prudence. It's one of the things there's no sense in at all. People are always doing it and it doesn't get them anywhere.'

'Anyway, you look lovely in those clothes.'

*

Basil talked a great deal at dinner; the same large party was assembled, but he kept them all silent with tales of Sakuyu savagery, partly invented, partly remembered from the days of Connolly's confidence. '... shaved all the hair off her head and covered it with butter. White ants ate straight through into her skull ... You still find blind old Europeans working with the slaves on some of the farms in the interior; they're prisoners of war that were conveniently forgotten about when peace was made ... the Arab word for Sakuyu means Man-without-mercy ... when they get drink in them they go completely insane. They can stay like that for days at a time, utterly unconscious of fatigue. They'd think nothing of the road out here if they thought they'd find alcohol when they got here. May I have another glass of whisky? ...'

When the men were left together at the table, the Minister said, 'My boy, I don't know how much truth there is in all you've been saying, but I think you might not have talked like that before the ladies. If there *is* any danger, and I for one don't for a moment believe there is, the ladies should be kept in ignorance of the fact.'

'Oh, I like to see them scared,' said Basil. 'Pass the decanter, will you, Jagger, and now, sir, what arrangements are we making for defence?'

'Arrangements for defence?'

'Yes, of course you can't possibly have everyone separated in the different bungalows. They could all have their throats cut one at a time and none of us any the wiser. The compound is far too big to form a defensible unit. You'd better get everyone up here, arrange for shifts of guard and put a picket of your sowars with horses half a mile down the road to the town to bring the alarm if a raiding party comes into sight. You run in and talk to the women. I'll arrange it all for you.'

And the Envoy Extraordinary could find nothing to say. The day had been too much for him. Everyone was stark crazy and damned bad-mannered too. They could do what they liked. He was going to smoke a cigar, alone, in his study.

Basil took command. In half an hour the Legges and the Anstruthers, bearing children wrapped in blankets and their meagre supply of firearms, arrived in the drawing-room.

'I suppose that this is necessary,' said Lady Courteney, 'but I'm afraid that you'll none of you be at all comfortable.'

An attempt to deceive the children that nothing unusual was afoot proved unsuccessful; it was not long before they were found in a corner of the hall enacting with tremendous gusto the death agonies of the Italian lady whose scalp was eaten by termites.

'The gentleman in the funny clothes told us,' they explained. 'Coo, mummy, it must have hurt.'

The grown-ups moved restlessly about.

'Anything we can do to help?'

'Yes, count the cartridges out into equal piles . . . it might be a good thing to prepare some bandages too . . . Legge, the hinges of this shutter aren't too good. See if you can find a screw-driver.'

It was about ten o'clock when it was discovered that the native servants, who had been massed in the Legation kitchens from the surrounding households, had silently taken their leave. Only Basil's camel boys remained in possession. They had compounded for themselves a vast stew of incongruous elements and were sodden with eating.

'Other boys going home. No want cutting off heads. They much no good boys. We like it fine living here.'

News of the desertion made havoc among the nerves in the drawing-room. Sir Samson merely voiced the feelings of all his guests when, turning petulantly from the table, he remarked: 'It's no good. My heart is *not* in halma this evening.'

But the night passed and no assault was made. The men of the party watched, three hours on, three hours off, at the various vulnerable points. Each slept with a weapon beside him, revolver, rook rifle, shot-gun or meat chopper. Continuous low chattering in the rooms upstairs, rustle of dressing-gowns, patter of slippers and frequent shrill cries from the youngest Anstruther child in nightmare, told that the ladies were sleeping little. At dawn they assembled again with pale faces and strained eyes. Lady Courteney's English maid and the Goanese butler went to the kitchen and, circumventing with difficulty the recumbent camel boys, made hot coffee. Spirits rose a little; they abandoned the undertones which had become habitual during the last ten hours and spoke in normal voices; they began to yawn. Basil said, 'One night over. Of course your real danger will come when supplies begin running short in the town.'

That discouraged them from any genuine cheerfulness.

They went out on to the lawn. Smoke lay low over the town.

'Something still burning.'

Presently Anstruther said, 'I say, though, look over there. Aren't those clouds?'

'It's a week early for the rains.'

'Still, you never know.'

'That's rain all right,' said Basil. 'I was counting on it today or tomorrow. They got it last week in Kenya. It'll delay the repairs on the Lumo bridge pretty considerably.'

'Then I must get those bulbs in this morning,' said Lady Courteney. 'It'll be a relief to have something sensible to do after tearing up sheets for bandages and sewing sand-bags. You might have told me before, Mr Seal.'

'If I were you,' said Basil, 'I should start checking your stores and making out a scheme of rations. I should think my boys must have eaten a good week's provisions last night.'

The party split up and attempted to occupy themselves in useful jobs about the house; soon, however, there came a sound which brought them out helter-skelter, all together again, chattering on the lawn; the drone of an approaching aeroplane.

'That'll be Ballon,' said Basil, 'making his get-away.'

But as the machine came into sight it became clear that it was making for the Legation; it flew low, circling over the compound and driving the ponies to frenzy in their stables. They could see the pilot's head looking at them over the side. A weighted flag fluttered from it to the ground, then the machine mounted again and soared off in the direction of the coast. The Anstruther children ran, crowing with delight, to retrieve the message from the rose garden and bring it to the Minister. It was a brief pencil note, signed by the squadron-leader at Aden. *Am bringing two troop carriers, three bombers. Be prepared to evacuate whole British population from Legation in one hour from receiving this. Can carry official archives and bare personal necessities only.*

*

'That's Walsh's doing. Clever chap, always said so. But I say, though, what a rush.'

For the next hour the Legation was in a ferment as a growing pile of luggage assembled on the lawn.

'*Official archives*, indeed. There may be some papers about somewhere, William. See if any of them seem at all interesting.'

'We'll have to put the ponies out to grass and hope for the best.'

'Lock all doors and take the keys away. Not that it's likely to make any difference.'

'Envoy, you can't bring *all* the pictures.'

'How about passports?'

The visitors from the town, having nothing to pack, did what they could to help the others.

'I've never been up before. I'm told it often makes people unwell.'

'Poor Mr Raith.'

Basil, suddenly reduced to unimportance, stood by and watched the preparations, a solitary figure in his white Sakuyu robes leaning over his rifle like a sentinel.

Prudence joined him and they walked together to the edge of the compound, out of sight behind some rhododendrons. She was wearing a red beret jauntily on one side of her head.

'Basil, give up this absurd Emperor, darling, and come with us.'

'Can't do that.'

'*Please.*'

'No, Prudence, everything's going to be all right. Don't you worry. We'll meet again somewhere.'

Rain clouds on the horizon grew and spread across the bright sky.

'It seems so much *more* going away when it's in an aeroplane, if you see what I mean.'

'I see what you mean.'

'*Prudence, Prudence,*' from Lady Courteney beyond the rhododendrons. 'You really can't take so many boxes.'

In Basil's arms Prudence said, 'But the clothes smell odd.'

'I got them second-hand from a Sakuyu. He'd just stolen an evening suit from an Indian.'

'*Prudence.*'

'All right, mum, *coming* . . . sweet Basil, I can't really bear it.'

And she ran back to help eliminate her less serviceable hats.

Quite soon, before anyone was ready for them, the five aeroplanes came into sight, roaring over the hills in strictly maintained formation. They landed and came to rest in the compound. Air Force officers trotted forward and saluted, treating Sir Samson with a respect which somewhat surprised his household.

'We ought to start as soon as we can, sir. There's a storm coming up.'

With very little confusion the party embarked. The Indian troopers and the Goan butler in one troop carrier, the children, clergy and senior members in the other. Mr Jagger, William and Prudence took their places in the cockpits of the three bombers. Just as they were about to start, Prudence remembered something and clambered down. She raced back to the Legation, a swift, gay figure under her red beret, and returned panting with a loose sheaf of papers.

'Nearly left the *Panorama of Life* behind,' she explained.

The engines started up with immense din; the machines taxied forward and took off, mounted steadily, circled about in a neat arrow-head, dwindled and disappeared. Silence fell on the compound. It had all taken less than twenty minutes.

Basil turned back alone to look for his camels.

Prudence crouched in the cockpit, clutching her beret to her head. The air shrieked past her ears while the landscape rolled away below in a leisurely fashion; the straggling city, half shrouded in smoke, disappeared behind them; open pasture dotted with cattle and little clusters of huts; presently the green lowlands and jungle country. She knew without particular regret that she was leaving Debra Dowa for good.

'Anyway,' she reflected, 'I ought to get some new ideas for the *Panorama*,' and already she seemed to be emerging into the new life which her mother had planned for her, and spoken of not long ago seated on Prudence's bed as she came to wish her good night. Aunt Harriet's house in Belgrave Place; girls, luncheons, dances and young men, week-ends in country houses, tennis and hunting; all the easy circumstances of English life which she had read about often but never experienced. She would resume the acquaintance of friends she had known at school, 'and shan't I be able to show off to them? They'll all seem so young and innocent . . . ' English cold and fog and rain, grey twilight among isolated, bare trees and dripping coverts; London streets when the shops were closing and the pavements crowded with people going to Tube stations with evening papers; empty streets, late at night after dances, revealing unsuspected slopes, sluiced by men in almost mediaeval overalls . . . an English girl returning to claim her natural heritage . . .

The aeroplane dipped suddenly, recalling her to the affairs of the moment. The pilot shouted back to her something which was lost on the wind. They were the extremity of one of the arms of the V. A goggled face from the machine in front looked back and down at them as they dropped below him, but her pilot signalled him on. Green undergrowth swam up towards them; the machine tilted a little and circled about, looking for a place to land.

'Hold tight and don't worry,' was borne back to her on the wind. An open space appeared among the trees and bush. They circled again and dropped precisely into place, lurched for a moment as though about to overturn, righted themselves and stopped dead within a few feet of danger.

'Wizard show that,' remarked the pilot.

'Has anything awful happened?'

'Nothing to worry about. Engine trouble. I can put it right in two shakes. Stay where you are. We'll catch them up before they reach Aden.'

*

Rain broke late that afternoon with torrential tropic force. The smouldering warehouses of the city sizzled and steamed and the fire ended in thin black mud. Great pools collected in the streets; water eddied in the gutters, clogging the few drains with its burden of refuse. The tin roofs rang with the falling drops. Sodden rioters waded down the lanes to shelter; troops left their posts and returned to barracks huddled under cover in a stench of wet cloth. The surviving decorations from the pageant of birth control clung limply round the posts or, grown suddenly too heavy, snapped their strings and splashed into the mud below. Darkness descended upon a subdued city.

*

For six confused days Basil floundered on towards the lowlands. For nine hours out of the twenty-four the rain fell regularly and unremittingly so that it usurped the sun's place as the measure of time and the caravan drove on through the darkness, striving hopelessly to recover the hours wasted under cover during the daylight.

On their second day's journey Basil's boys brought a runner to him, who was carrying a sodden letter in the end of a cleft staff.

'A great chief will not suffer his messengers to be robbed.'

'There is a time,' said Basil, 'when all things must be suffered.'
They took the message. It read:

From Viscount Boaz, Minister of the Interior of the Azanian Empire, to the Earl of Ngumo, Greeting. May this reach you. Peace be upon your house. Salute, in my name and in the name of my family, Achon whom some style Emperor of Azania, Chief of the Chiefs of Sakuyu, Lord of Wanda and Tyrant of the Seas. May his days be many and his progeny uncounted. I, Boaz, no mean man in the Empire, am now at Gulu on the Wanda marches; with me is Seth whom some style Emperor. I tell you this so that Achon may know me for what I am, a loyal subject of the crown. I fear for Seth's health and await word from your Lordship as to how best he may be relieved of what troubles him. Boaz.

*

'Go on in front of us,' Basil ordered the man, 'and tell Lord Boaz that Achon is dead.'

'How can I return to my Lord, having lost the letter he gave me? Is my life a small thing?'

'Go back to your Lord. Your life is a small thing beside the life of the Emperor.'

Later two beasts lost their footing in the bed of a swollen watercourse and were washed down and tumbled among the boulders; during the third night march five of the hindermost deserted their leaders. The boys mutinied, first for more money; later they refused every inducement to proceed. For two days Basil rode on alone, swaying and slipping towards his rendezvous.

*

Confusion dominated the soggy lanes of Matodi. Major Walsh, the French secretaries and Mr Schonbaum daily dispatched conflicting messages by wireless and cable. First that Seth was dead and that Achon was Emperor, then that Achon was dead and Seth was Emperor.

'Doubtless Mme Ballon could tell us where General Connolly is to be found.'

'Alas, M. Jean, she will not speak.'

Basil rode to Gulu

'Do you suspect she knows more?'

'M. Ballon's wife should be above suspicion.'

The officials and soldiers loafed in the dry intervals about barracks and offices; they had no instructions and no money; no news from the capital. Destroyers of four nations lurked in the bay standing by to defend their nationals. The town governor made secret preparations for an early escape to the mainland. Mr Youkoumian, behind the bar at the Amurath Hotel, nervously decocted his fierce spirits.

'There ain't no sense in 'aving bust-ups. 'Ere we are, no Emperor, no railway, and those low niggers making 'ell with my property at Debra Dowa. And just you see, in less than no time the civilized nations will start a bombardment. *Gosh*.'

In the dingy calm of the Arab club the six senior members munched their khat in peace and spoke gravely of a very old error of litigation.

Amidst mud and liquid ash at Debra Dowa a leaderless people abandoned their normal avocations and squatted at home, occupying themselves with domestic bickerings; some of the rural immigrants drifted back to their villages, others found temporary accommodation in the saloons of the deserted palace, expecting something to happen.

Among the dry clinkers of Aden, Sir Samson and Lady Courteney waited for news of the missing aeroplane. They were staying at the Residency, where everything was done that hospitality and tact could do to relieve the strain of their anxiety; newspaper agents and sympathetic compatriots were kept from them. Dame Mildred and Miss Tin were shipped to Southampton by the first P. & O. Mr Jagger made preparations to leave a settlement he had little reason to like. Sir Samson and Lady Courteney walked alone on the cliff paths, waiting for news. Air patrols crossed to Azania, flying low over the impenetrable country where Prudence's machine was last observed, returned to refuel, set out again and at the end of the week had seen nothing to report. The military authorities discussed and despaired of the practicability of landing a search party.

*

In the dry spell between noon and sunset, Basil reached Seth's encampment at Gulu. His men had taken possession of a small village. A dozen or so of them, in ragged uniforms, sat on their haunches in the clearing, silently polishing their teeth with pieces of stick.

His camel lurched down on to its knees and Basil dismounted. None of the Guardsmen rose to salute him; no sign of greeting from inside the mud huts. The squatting men looked into the steaming forest beyond him.

He asked: 'Where is the Emperor?' But no one answered.

'Where is Boaz?'

'In the great house. He is resting.'

They indicated the headman's hut which stood on the far side of the compound, distinguished from the others by its superior size and a narrow verandah, floored with beaten mud and shaded by thatch.

'Why is the Emperor not in the great house?'

They did not answer. Instead, they scoured their teeth and gazed abstractedly into the forest, where a few monkeys swung in the steaming air, shaking the water from bough to bough.

Basil crossed through them to the headman's hut. It was windowless and for a short time his eyes could distinguish nothing in the gloom. Only his ears were aware of a heavily breathing figure somewhere not far distant in the dark interior. Then he gradually descried a jumble of household furniture, camp equipment and the remains of a meal; and Boaz asleep. The great dandy lay on his back in a heap of rugs and sacking; his head pitched forward into his blue-black curly beard. There was a rifle across his middle. He wore a pair of mud-splashed riding breeches, too tight to button to the top, which Basil recognized as the Emperor's. A Wanda girl sat at his head. She explained: 'The Lord has been asleep for some time. For the last days it has been like this. He wakes only to drink from the square bottle. Then he is asleep again.'

'Bring me word when he wakes.'

Basil approached the oafish fellows in the clearing.

'Show me a house where I can sleep.'

They pointed one out to him without rising to accompany him to its door. Water still dripped through its leaky thatch, there was a large puddle of thin mud made during the rain. Basil lay down on the dry side and waited for Boaz to wake.

They called him an hour after sunset. The men had lit a fire, but only a small one, because they knew that at midnight the rain would begin again and dowse it. There was a light in the headman's hut – a fine brass lamp with wick and chimney. Boaz had put out two glasses and two bottles of whisky. Basil's first words were, 'Where is Seth?'

'He is not here. He has gone away.'

'Where?'

'How shall I know? Look, I have filled your glass.'

'I sent a messenger to him, with the news that Achon was dead.'

'Seth had already gone when the messenger came.'

'And where is the messenger?'

'He brought bad tidings. He is dead. Turn the light higher. It is bad to sit in the dark.'

He gulped down a glass of spirit and refilled his glass. They sat in silence.

Presently Boaz said, 'Seth is dead.'

'I knew. How?'

'The sickness of the jungle. His legs and his arms swelled. He turned up his eyes and died. I have seen others die in just that way.'

Later he said, 'So now there is no Emperor. It is a pity that your messenger did not come a day sooner. I hanged him because he was late.'

'Boaz, the sickness of the jungle does not wait on good or bad news.'

'That is true. Seth died in another way. By his own hand. With a gun raised to his mouth and his great toe crooked round the trigger. That is how Seth died.'

'It is not what I should have expected.'

'Men die that way. I have heard of it often. His body lies outside. The men will not bury it. They say it must be taken down to Moshu to the Wanda people to be burned in their own fashion. Seth was their chief.'

'We will do that tomorrow.'

Outside round the fire, inevitably, they had started singing. The drums pulsed. In the sodden depths of the forest the wild beasts hunted, shunning the light.

'I will go and see Seth's body.'

'The women are sewing him up. They made a bag for him out of pieces of skin. It is the custom when the chief dies. They put grain in with him and several spices. Only the women know what. If they can get it they put a lion's paw, I have been told.'

'We will go and look at him.'

'It is not the custom of the people.'

'I will carry the lamp.'

'You must not leave me in the dark. I will come with you.'

Past the camp fire and the singing Guardsmen to another hut: here by the light of a little lamp four or five women were at work stitching. Seth's body lay on the floor half covered by a blanket. Boaz leant tipsily in the doorway while Basil went forward, lamp in hand. The eldest of the women tried to bar his entrance, but he pushed her aside and approached the dead Emperor.

His head lay inclined to one side, the lips agape, the eyes open and dull. He wore his Guards tunic, buttoned tight at the throat, the epaulettes awry and bedraggled. There was no wound visible. Basil drew the blanket higher and rejoined the Minister.

'The Emperor did not shoot himself.'

'No.'

'There is no wound to be seen.'

'Did I say he was shot? That is a mistake. He took poison. That is how it happened . . . it has happened before in that way to other great men. It was a draught given him by a wise man in these parts. When he despaired he took some of it . . . a large cupful and drank it . . . there in the hut. I was with him. He made a wry face and said that the draught was bitter. Then he stood still a little until his knees gave. On the floor he rolled up and down several times. He could not breathe. Then his legs shot straight out and he arched his back. That is how he lay until yesterday when the body became limp again. That was how he died . . . The messenger was late in coming.'

They left the women to their work. Boaz stumbled several times as he returned to the headman's hut and his bottle of whisky. Basil left him with the lamp and returned in the firelit night to his hut.

A man was waiting for him in the shadows. 'Boaz is still drunk.'

'Yes. Who are you?'

'Major Joab of the Imperial Infantry, at your service.'

'Well, major?'

'It has been like this since the Emperor's death.'

'Boaz?'

'Yes.'

'Did you see the Emperor die?'

'I am a soldier. It is not for me to meddle with high politics. I am a soldier without a master.'

'There is duty due to a master, even when he is dead.'

'Do I understand you?'

'Tomorrow we take down the body of Seth to be burned at Moshu among his people. He should rejoin the great Amurath and the spirits of his fathers like a king and a fine man. Can he meet them unashamed if his servants forget their duty while his body is still with them?'

'I understand you.'

After midnight the rain fell. The men round the fire carried a burning brand into one of the huts and lit a fire there. Great drops sizzled and spat among the deserted embers; they changed from yellow to red and then to black.

Heavy patter of rain on the thatched roofs, quickening to an even blur of sound.

A piercing, womanish cry, that mounted, soared shivering, quavered and merged in the splash and gurgle of the water.

'Major Joab of the Imperial Infantry at your service. Boaz is dead.'

'Peace be on your house.'

*

Next day they carried the body of the Emperor to Moshu. Basil rode at the head of the procession. The others followed on foot. The body, sewn in skins, was strapped to a pole and carried on the shoulders of two Guardsmen. Twice during the journey they slipped and their burden fell in the soft mud of the jungle path. Basil sent on a runner to the Chief, saying: 'Assemble your people, kill your best meat and prepare a feast in the manner of your people. I am bringing a great chief among you.'

But the news preceded him and tribesmen came out to greet them on the way and conduct them with music to Moshu. The wise men of the surrounding villages danced in the mud in front of Basil's camel, wearing livery of the highest solemnity, leopards' feet and snake-skins, necklets of lions' teeth, shrivelled bodies of toads and bats, and towering masks of painted leather and wood. The women daubed their hair with ochre and clay in the fashion of the people.

Moshu was a royal city; the chief market and government centre of the Wanda country. It was ditched round and enclosed by high ramparts. Arab slavers had settled there a century ago and built streets of two-storied, lightless houses; square, with flat roofs on rubble walls washed over with lime and red earth. Among them stood circular Wanda huts of mud and thatched grass. A permanent artisan population lived there, blacksmiths, jewellers, leather workers, ministering to the needs of the scattered jungle people. There were several merchants in a good way of business with barns storing grain, oil, spices and salt, and a few Indians trading in hardware and coloured cottons, products of the looms of Europe and Japan.

A pyre had been heaped up, of dry logs and straw, six foot high, in the market-place. A large crowd was already assembled there and in another quarter a communal kitchen had been improvised where great cook-pots rested over crackling sticks. Earthenware jars of fermented coconut sap stood ready to be broached when the proper moment arrived.

The feast began late in the afternoon. Basil and Joab sat among the chiefs and headmen. The wise men danced round the pyre, shaking their strings of charms and amulets, wagging their tufted rumps and uttering cries of ecstasy. They carried little knives and cut themselves as they capered round. Meanwhile Seth's body was bundled on to the faggots and a tin of oil sluiced over it.

'It is usual for the highest man present to speak some praise of the dead.'

Basil nodded and in the circle of fuzzy heads rose to declaim Seth's funeral oration. It was no more candid than most royal obituaries. It was what was required. 'Chiefs and tribesmen of the Wanda,' he said, speaking with confident fluency in the Wanda tongue, of which he had acquired a fair knowledge during his stay in Azania. 'Peace be among you. I bring the body of the Great Chief, who has gone to rejoin Amurath and the spirits of his glorious ancestors. It is right for us to remember Seth. He was a great Emperor and all the peoples of the world vied with each other to do him homage. In his own island, among the people of Sakuyu and the Arabs, across the great waters to the mainland, far beyond in the cold lands of the North, Seth's name was a name of terror. Seyid rose against him and is no more. Achon also. They are gone before him to prepare suitable lodging among the fields of his ancestors. Thousands fell by his right hand. The words of his mouth were like thunder in the hills. Weep, women of Azania, for your royal lover is torn from your arms. His virility was inexhaustible, his progeny numerous beyond human computation. His staff was a grown palm tree. Weep, warriors of Azania. When he led you to battle there was no retreating. In council the most guileful, in justice the most terrible, Seth the magnificent is dead.'

The bards caught phrases from the lament and sang them. The wise men ran whooping among the spectators carrying torches. Soon the pyre was enveloped in towering flames. The people took up the song and swayed on their haunches, chanting. The bundle on the crest bubbled and spluttered like fresh pine until the skin cerements burst open and revealed briefly in the heart of the furnace the incandescent corpse of the Emperor. Then there was a subsidence among the timbers and it disappeared from view.

Soon after sunset the flames declined and it was necessary to refuel them. Many of the tribesmen had joined the dance of the witches. With hands on each other's hips they made a chain round the pyre, shuffling their feet and heaving their shoulders, spasmodically throwing back their heads and baying like wild beasts.

The chiefs gave the sign for the feast to begin.

The company split up into groups, each round a cook-pot. Basil and Joab sat with the chiefs. They ate flat bread and meat, stewed to pulp among peppers and aromatic roots. Each dipped into the pot in rotation, plunging with his hands for the best scraps. A bowl of toddy circulated from lap to lap and great drops of sweat broke out on the brows of the mourners.

Dancing was resumed, faster this time and more clearly oblivious of fatigue. In emulation of the witch doctors, the tribesmen began slashing themselves on chest and arms with their hunting knives; blood and sweat mingled in shining rivulets over their dark skins. Now and then one of them would pitch forward on to his face and lie panting or roll stiff in a nervous seizure. Women joined in the dance, making another chain, circling in the reverse way to the men. They were dazed with drink, stamping themselves into ecstasy. The two chains jostled and combined. They shuffled together interlocked.

Basil drew back a little from the heat of the fire, his senses dazed by the crude spirit and the insistence of the music. In the shadows, in the extremities of the market-place, black figures sprawled and grunted, alone and in couples. Near him an elderly woman stamped and shuffled; suddenly she threw up her arms and fell to the ground in ecstasy. The hand-drums throbbed and pulsed; the flames leapt and showered the night with sparks.

The headman of Moshu sat where they had dined, nursing the bowl of toddy. He wore an Azanian white robe, splashed with gravy and spirit. His scalp was closely shaven; he nodded down to the lip of the bowl and drank. Then he clumsily offered it to Basil. Basil refused; he gaped and offered it again. Then took another draught himself. Then he nodded again and drew something from his bosom and put it on his head. 'Look,' he said. 'Pretty.'

It was a beret of pillar-box red. Through the stupor that was slowly mounting and encompassing his mind Basil recognized it. Prudence had worn it jauntily on the side of her head, running across the Legation lawn with the *Panorama of Life* under her arm. He shook the old fellow roughly by the shoulder.

'Where did you get that?'

'Pretty.'

'Where did you get it?'

'Pretty hat. It came in the great bird. The white woman wore it. On her head like this.' He giggled weakly and pulled it askew over his glistening pate.

'But the white woman. Where is she?'

But the headman was lapsing into coma. He said 'Pretty' again and turned up sightless eyes.

Basil shook him violently. 'Speak, you old fool. Where is the white woman?'

The headman grunted and stirred; then a flicker of consciousness revived in him. He raised his head. 'The white woman? Why, here,' he patted his distended paunch. 'You and I and the big chiefs – we have just eaten her.'

Then he fell forward into a sound sleep.

Round and round circled the dancers, ochre and blood and sweat glistening in the firelight; the wise men's headgear swayed high above them, leopards' feet and snake-skins, amulets and neck-laces, lions' teeth and the shrivelled bodies of bats and toads, jigging and spinning. Tireless hands drumming out the rhythm; glistening backs heaving and shivering in the shadows.

Later, a little after midnight, it began to rain.

CHAPTER 8

WHEN THE TELEPHONE bell rang Alastair said: 'You answer it. I don't think I can stand up,' so Sonia crossed to the window where it stood and said: 'Yes, who is it? ... *Basil* ... well, who'd have thought of that? Where *can* you be?'

'I'm at Barbara's. I thought of coming round to see you and Alastair.'

'Darling, do ... how did you know where we lived?'

'It was in the telephone book. Is it nice?'

'Lousy. You'll see when you come. Alastair thought it would be cheaper, but it isn't really. You'll never find the door. It's painted red and it's next to a pretty shady sort of chemist.'

'I'll be along.'

Ten minutes later he was there. Sonia opened the door. 'We haven't any servants. We got very poor suddenly. How long have you been back?'

'Landed last night. What's been happening?'

'Almost nothing. Everyone's got very poor and it makes them duller. It's more than a year since we saw you. How are things at Barbara's?'

'Well, Freddy doesn't know I'm here yet. That's why I'm dining out. Barbara's going to tell him gently. I gather my mamma is sore with me about something. How's Angela?'

'Just the same. She's the only one who doesn't seem to have lost money. Margot's shut up her house and is spending the winter in America. There was a general election and a crisis – something about gold standard.'

'I know. It's amusing to be back.'

'We've missed you. As I say, people have gone serious lately, while you've just been loafing about the tropics. Alastair found something about Azania in the papers once. I forget what. Some revolution and a minister's daughter who disappeared. I suppose you were in on all that.'

'Yes.'

'Can't think what you see in revolutions. They said there was going to be one here, only nothing came of it. I suppose you ran the whole country.'

'As a matter of fact, I did.'

'And fell madly in love.'

'Yes.'

'And intrigued and had a court official's throat cut.'

'Yes.'

'And went to a cannibal banquet. Darling, I just don't want to hear about it, d'you mind? I'm sure it's all very fine and grand, but it doesn't make much sense to a stay-at-home like me.'

'That's the way to deal with him,' said Alastair from his arm-chair. 'Keep a stopper on the far-flung stuff.'

'Or write a book about it, sweety. Then we can buy it and leave it about where you'll see and then you'll think we know . . . What are you going to do now you're back?'

'No plans. I think I've had enough of barbarism for a bit. I might stay in London or Berlin or somewhere like that.'

'That'll be nice. Make it London. We'll have some parties like the old ones.'

'D'you know, I'm not sure I shouldn't find them a bit flat after the real thing. I went to a party at a place called Moshu . . . '

'*Basil*. Once and for all, we don't want to hear travel experiences. Do try and remember.'

So they played Happy Families till ten, when Alastair said, 'Have we had dinner?' and Sonia said, 'No, let's.' Then they went out to a new cocktail club which Alastair had heard was cheap, and had lager beer and liver sandwiches; they proved to be very expensive.

Later Basil went round to see Angela Lyne, and Sonia as she undressed said to Alastair, 'D'you know, deep down in my heart I've got a tiny fear that Basil is going to turn serious on us too!'

*

Evening in Matodi. Two Arab gentlemen, hand in hand, sauntered by the sea-wall.

Among the dhows and nondescript craft in the harbour lay two smart launches manned by British and French sailors, for Azania had lately been mandated by the League of Nations as a joint protectorate.

'They are always at work polishing the brass.'

'It must be very expensive. And they are building a new customs house.'

'And a police station and a fever hospital, a European club.'

'There are many new bungalows on the hills.'

'They are making a big field to play games in.'

'Every week they wash the streets with water. They take the children in the schools and scratch their arms to rub in poison. It makes them very ill.'

'They put a man in prison for overburdening his camel.'

'There is a Frenchman in charge at the post office. He is always hot and in a great hurry.'

'They are building a black road through the hills to Debra Dowa. The railway is to be removed.'

'Mr Youkoumian has bought the rails and what was left of the engines. He hopes to sell them in Eritrea.'

'Things were better in the time of Seth. It is no longer a gentleman's country.'

The muezzin in the tower turned north towards Mekka and called azan over the city. The Arabs paused reverently and stood in silence ... God is great ... There is no God but God ... Mohammed is the apostle of God ...

A two-seater car whizzed by, driven by Mr Reppington, the district magistrate. Mrs Reppington sat beside him.

'The little bus took that nicely.'

Angelus from the mission church ... *gratia plena; dominus tecum; Benedicta tu in mulieribus* ...

The car left the town and mounted towards the hills.

'Phew. It's a relief to get out into the fresh air.'

'Awful road. It ought to be finished by now. I get quite afraid for her back axle.'

'I said we'd drop into the Brethertons' for a sundowner.'

'Right you are. Only we can't stay long. We're dining with the Lepperidges.'

A mile above the town they stopped at the second of six identical bungalows. Each had a verandah and a garden path; a slotted box on the gate-post for calling cards. The Brethertons were on the verandah.

'Cheerio, Mrs Reppington. Cocktail?'

'Please.'

'And you, Reppington?'

'Chota peg.'

Bretherton was sanitary inspector and consequently of slightly inferior station to Reppington, but that year he would sit for his Arabic exam; if he brought it off it would make them level on the salary list.

'What sort of day?'

'Oh, the usual. Just tooled round condemning native houses. How are things at the Fort?'

'Not so dusty. We settled that case I told you about. You know, the one of the natives who built a house in a broken lorry in the middle of the road.'

'Oh, ah. Who won it?'

'Oh, we gave it to the chap in possession on both counts. The Arab who originally owned the car was suing him. So were the Works Department – wanted to evict him because he blocked the traffic. They'll have to make a new road round him now. They're pretty fed up, I can tell you. So are the Frenchies.'

'Good show.'

'Yes, give the natives respect for British justice. Can't make your Frenchy see that . . . Why, it's later than I thought. We must be pushing along, old girl. You're not dining with the Lepperidges by any chance?'

'No.'

The Brethertons were not on dining terms with the Lepperidges. He was O.C. of the native levy, seconded from India and a very considerable man in Matodi. He always referred to Bretherton as the 'latrine wallah'.

So the Reppingtons went to dress in their bungalow (fifth of the row), she in black lace, he in white mess-jacket. Punctually at 8.15 they stepped across to the Lepperidges'. There were five courses at dinner, mostly from tins, and a glass dish in the centre of the table held floating flower heads. Mr and Mrs Grainger were there; Mr Grainger was immigration officer. He said: 'We've had rather a shari this afternoon about that fellow Connolly. You see, strictly speaking, he can claim Azanian nationality. He seems to have been quite a big bug under the Emperor. Ran the army for him. Got made a Duke or something. Last sort of fellow one wants hanging about.'

'Quite.'

'Jungly Wallah. They say in the old days he had an affair with the wife of the French Minister. That made the Frenchies anxious to get rid of him.'

'Quite. It helps if one can oblige them now and then in small things.'

'Besides, you know, he's married to a wog. Well, I mean to say . . . '

'Quite.'

'But I think we're going to get rid of him all right. Deport him D.B.S. He lost all his money in the revolution.'

'And the woman in the case?'

'Well, that's no business of ours once we clear him out of here. They seem struck on each other all right. He'll find it pretty awkward. Aren't many places would have him. Abyssinia might. It was different when this place was independent.'

'Quite.'

'Jolly good tinned fruit salad, if you don't mind my saying so, Mrs Lepperidge.'

'So glad you like it. I got it from Youkoumian's.'

'Useful little fellow Youkoumian. I use him a lot. He's getting me boots for the levy. Came to me himself with the idea. Said they pick up hookworm through going barefoot.'

'Good show.'

'Quite.'

Destination unknown

*

Night over Matodi. English and French police patrolling the
water-front. Gilbert and Sullivan played by gramophone in the
Portuguese Fort.

> *Three little maids from school are we,*
> *Pert as a schoolgirl well can be,*
> *Filled to the brim with girlish glee –*
> *Three little maids from school.*

The melody and the clear voices floated out over the harbour
and the water lapping very gently on the sea-wall. Two British
policemen marched abreast through the involved ways of the native
quarter. The dogs had long ago been rounded up and painlessly put
away. The streets were empty save for an occasional muffled figure
slipping by them silently with a lantern. The blank walls of the Arab
tenements gave no sign of life.

> *On a tree by a river a little tom tit*
> *Sang Willow, tit-willow, tit-willow.*
> *And I said to him 'Dicky bird, why do you sit*
> *Singing Willow, tit-willow, tit-willow?'*

Mr Youkoumian tactfully ejected his last customer and fastened
the shutters of the café. 'Very sorry,' he said. 'New regulation. No
drinking after ten-thirty. I don't want no bust-ups.'

> *'Is it weakness of intellect, birdie?' I cried,*
> *'Or a rather tough worm in your little inside?'*
> *With a shake of his poor little head, he replied,*
> *'Oh willow, tit-willow, tit-willow.'*

The song rang clear over the dark city and the soft, barely
perceptible lapping of the water along the sea-wall.

THE END

Stonyhurst – Chagford – Madresfield
September 1931 – May 1932

SCOOP
A NOVEL ABOUT JOURNALISTS

For Laura

BOOK I

THE STITCH SERVICE

CHAPTER 1

I

WHILE STILL A young man, John Courteney Boot had, as his publisher proclaimed, 'achieved an assured and enviable position in contemporary letters'. His novels sold 15,000 copies in their first year and were read by the people whose opinion John Boot respected. Between novels he kept his name sweet in intellectual circles with unprofitable but modish works on history and travel. His signed first editions sometimes changed hands at a shilling or two above their original price. He had published eight books – beginning with a life of Rimbaud written when he was eighteen, and concluding, at the moment, with *Waste of Time*, a studiously modest description of some harrowing months among the Patagonian Indians – of which most people who lunched with Lady Metroland could remember the names of three or four. He had many charming friends, of whom the most valued was the lovely Mrs Algernon Stitch.

Like all in her circle John Boot habitually brought his difficulties to her for solution. It was with this purpose, on a biting-cold mid-June morning, that he crossed the Park and called at her house (a superb creation by Nicholas Hawksmoor modestly concealed in a cul-de-sac near Saint James's Palace).

Algernon Stitch was standing in the hall; his bowler hat was on his head; his right hand, grasping a crimson, royally emblazoned dispatch case, emerged from the left sleeve of his overcoat; his other hand burrowed petulantly in the breast pocket. An umbrella under his left arm further inconvenienced him. He spoke indistinctly, for he was holding a folded copy of the morning paper between his teeth.

'Can't get it on,' he seemed to say.

The man who had opened the door came to his assistance, removed the umbrella and dispatch case and laid them on the marble table; removed the coat and held it behind his master. John took the newspaper.

'Thanks. Thanks very much. Much obliged. Come to see Julia, eh?'

From high overhead, down the majestic curves of the great staircase, came a small but preternaturally resonant voice.

'Try not to be late for dinner, Algy; the Kents are coming.'

'She's upstairs,' said Stitch. He had his coat on now and looked fully an English cabinet minister; long and thin, with a long, thin nose, and long, thin moustaches; the ideal model for continental caricaturists. 'You'll find her in bed,' he said.

'Your speech reads very well this morning.' John was always polite to Stitch; everybody was; Labour members loved him.

'Speech? Mine? Ah. Reads well, eh? Sounded terrible to me. Thanks all the same. Thanks very much. Much obliged.'

So Stitch went out to the Ministry of Imperial Defence and John went up to see Julia.

As her husband had told him, she was still in bed although it was past eleven o'clock. Her normally mobile face encased in clay was rigid and menacing as an Aztec mask. But she was not resting. Her secretary, Miss Holloway, sat at her side with account books, bills, and correspondence. With one hand Mrs Stitch was signing cheques; with the other she held the telephone to which, at the moment, she was dictating details of the costumes for a charity ballet. An elegant young man at the top of a step ladder was painting ruined castles on the ceiling. Josephine, the eight-year-old Stitch prodigy, sat on the foot of the bed construing her day's passage of Virgil. Mrs Stitch's maid, Brittling, was reading her the clues of the morning crossword. She had been hard at it since half past seven.

Josephine rose from her lesson to kick John as he entered. '*Boot*,' she said savagely, '*Boot*,' catching him first on one kneecap, then on the other. It was a joke of long standing.

Mrs Stitch turned her face of clay, in which only the eyes gave a suggestion of welcome, towards her visitor.

'Come in,' she said, 'I'm just going out. Why twenty pounds to Mrs Beaver?'

'That was for Lady Jean's wedding present,' said Miss Holloway.

'I must have been insane. About the lion's head for the centurion's breastplate; there's a beautiful one over the gate of a house near Salisbury, called Twisbury Manor; copy that as near as you can; ring up *Country Life* and ask for "back numbers"; there was a photograph of it about two years ago. You're putting too much ivy on the turret, Arthur; the owl won't show up unless you have him on the bare stone, and I'm particularly attached to the owl. *Munera*, darling, like tumtiddy; always a short a in neuter plurals. It sounds like an anagram: see if "Terracotta" fits. I'm *delighted* to see you, John. Where have you been? You can come and buy carpets with me; I've found a new shop in Bethnal Green, kept by a very interesting Jew who speaks no English; the most extraordinary things keep happening to his sister. Why should I go to Viola Chasm's Distressed Area; did she come to my Model Madhouse?'

'Oh, yes, Mrs Stitch.'

'Then I suppose it means two guineas. I absolutely loved *Waste of Time*. We read it aloud at Blakewell. The headless abbot is grand.'

'Headless abbot?'

'Not in Wasters. On Arthur's ceiling. I put it in the Prime Minister's room.'

'Did he read it?'

'Well, I don't think he *reads* much.'

'Terracotta is too long, madam, and there is no r.'

'Try hottentot. It's that kind of word. I can never do anagrams unless I can see them. No, *Twisbury*, you must have heard of it.'

'Floribus Austrum,' Josephine chanted, 'perditus et liquidis immisi fontibus apros; having been lost with flowers in the South and sent into the liquid fountain; apros is wild boars, but I couldn't quite make sense of that bit.'

'We'll do it tomorrow. I've got to go out now. Is "hottentot" any use?'

'No h, madam,' said Brittling with ineffable gloom.

'Oh, dear. I must look at it in my bath. I shall only be ten minutes. Stay and talk to Josephine.'

She was out of bed and out of the room. Brittling followed. Miss Holloway collected the cheques and papers. The young man on the ladder dabbed away industriously. Josephine rolled to the head of the bed and stared up at him.

'It's very banal, isn't it, Boot?'

'I like it very much.'

'Do you? I think all Arthur's work is banal. I read your book *Waste of Time.*'

'Ah.' John did not invite criticism.

'I thought it very banal.'

'You seem to find everything banal.'

'It is a new word whose correct use I have only lately learnt,' said Josephine with dignity. 'I find it applies to nearly everything; Virgil and Miss Brittling and my gymnasium.'

'How is the gymnasium going?'

'I am by far the best of my class, although there are several girls older than me and two middle-class boys.'

When Mrs Stitch said ten minutes, she meant ten minutes. Sharp on time she was back, dressed for the street; her lovely face, scraped clean of clay, was now alive with interest.

'Sweet Josephine, has Mr Boot been boring you?'

'It was all right really. I did most of the talking.'

'Show him your imitation of the Prime Minister.'

'No.'

'Sing him your Neapolitan song.'

'No.'

'Stand on your head. Just once for Mr Boot.'

'No.'

'Oh, dear. Well, we must go at once if we are to get to Bethnal Green and back before luncheon. The traffic's terrible.'

Algernon Stitch went to his office in a sombre and rather anti-quated Daimler; Julia always drove herself, in the latest model of mass-produced baby car; brand-new twice a year, painted an in-variable brilliant black, tiny and glossy as a midget's funeral hearse. She mounted the kerb and bowled rapidly along the pavement to the corner of St James's, where a policeman took her number and ordered her into the road.

'Third time this week,' said Mrs Stitch. 'I wish they wouldn't. It's such a nuisance for Algy.'

Once embedded in the traffic block, she stopped the engine and turned her attention to the crossword.

'It's "detonated",' she said, filling it in.

East wind swept the street, carrying with it the exhaust gas of a hundred motors and coarse particles of Regency stucco from a once decent Nash façade that was being demolished across the way. John shivered and rubbed some grit further into his eye. Eight minutes' close application was enough to finish the puzzle. Mrs Stitch folded the paper and tossed it over her shoulder into the back seat; looked about her resentfully at the stationary traffic.

'This is too much,' she said; started the engine, turned sharp again on to the kerb and proceeded to Piccadilly, driving before her at a brisk pace, until he took refuge on the step of Brooks's, a portly, bald young man; when he reached safety, he turned to remonstrate, recognized Mrs Stitch, and bowed profoundly to the tiny, black back as it shot the corner of Arlington Street. 'One of the things I like about these absurd cars,' she said, 'is that you can do things with them that you couldn't do in a real one.'

From Hyde Park Corner to Piccadilly Circus the line of traffic was continuous and motionless, still as a photograph, unbroken and undisturbed save at a few strategic corners where barricaded navvies, like desperate outposts of some proletarian defence, were rending the road with mechanical drills, mining for the wires and tubes that controlled the life of the city.

'I want to get away from London,' said John Boot.

'So it's come to that? All on account of your American girl?'

'Well, mostly.'

'I warned you, before you began. Is she being frightful?'

'My lips are sealed. But I've got to get far away or else go crazy.'

'To my certain knowledge she's driven three men into the bin. Where are you going?'

'That's just what I wanted to talk about.'

The line of cars jerked forwards for ten yards and again came to rest. The lunch-time edition of the evening papers was already on the streets; placards announcing

ISHMAELITE CRISIS
and
STRONG LEAGUE NOTE

were fluttering in the east wind.

'Ishmaelia seems to be the place. I was wondering if Algy would send me there as a spy.'

'Not a chance.'

'No?'

'Foregonners. Algy's been sacking ten spies a day for weeks. It's a grossly overcrowded profession. Why don't you go as a war correspondent?'

'Could you fix it?'

'I don't see why not. After all, you've been to Patagonia. I should think they would jump at you. You're sure you really want to go?'

'Quite sure.'

'Well, I'll see what I can do. I'm meeting Lord Copper at lunch today at Margot's. I'll try and bring the subject up.'

2

When Lady Metroland said half past one she meant ten minutes to two. It was precisely at this time, simultaneously with her hostess, that Mrs Stitch arrived (having been obliged by press of traffic to leave her little car in a garage half-way to Bethnal Green, and return to Curzon Street by means of the Underground railway). Lord Copper, however, who normally lunched at one, was waiting with some impatience. Various men and women who appeared to know one another intimately and did not know Lord Copper, had been admitted from time to time and had disregarded him. His subordinates at the Megalopolitan Newspaper Corporation would have been at difficulties to recognize the uneasy figure which stood up each time the door was opened and sat down again unnoticed. He was a stranger in these parts; it was a thoughtless benefaction to one of Lady Metroland's charities that had exposed him, in the middle of a busy day, to this harrowing experience; he would readily, now, have doubled the sum to purchase his release. Thus when Mrs Stitch directed upon him some of her piercing shafts of charm she found him first numb, then dazzled, then extravagantly receptive.

From the moment of her entrance the luncheon party was transformed for Lord Copper; he had gotten a new angle on it. He knew of Mrs Stitch; from time to time he had seen her in the distance; now for the first time he found himself riddled through and through, mesmerized, inebriated. Those at the table, witnessing the familiar process, began to conjecture in tones which Lord Copper was too much entranced to overhear, what Julia could possibly want of him. 'It's her model madhouse,' said some; 'She wants the caricaturists to lay off Algy,' said others; 'Been losing money,' thought the second footman (at Lady Metroland's orders he was on a diet and lunchtime always found him in a cynical mood); 'a job for someone or other,' came nearest the truth, but no one thought of John Courteney Boot until Mrs Stitch brought him into the conversation. Then they all played up loyally.

'You know,' she said, after coaxing Lord Copper into an uncompromising denunciation of the Prime Minister's public and private honesty, 'I expect he's all you say, but he's a man of far more taste than you'd suppose. He always sleeps with a Boot by his bed.'

'A boot?' asked Lord Copper, trustful but a little bewildered.

'One of John Boot's books.'

The luncheon party had got their cue.

'Dear John Boot,' said Lady Metroland, '*so* clever and amusing. I wish I could get him to come and see me more often.'

'Such a divine style,' said Lady Cockpurse.

The table buzzed with praise of John Boot. It was a new name to Lord Copper. He resolved to question his literary secretary on the subject. He had become Boot-conscious.

Mrs Stitch changed her ground and began to ask him in the most flattering way about the chances of peace in Ishmaelia. Lord Copper gave it as his opinion that civil war was inevitable.

Mrs Stitch remarked how few of the famous war correspondents still survived.

'Isn't there one called Sir Something Hitchcock?' asked Lady Cockpurse. (This was a false step since the knight in question had lately left Lord Copper's service, after an acrimonious dispute about the date of the Battle of Hastings, and had transferred to the *Daily Brute* camp.)

'Who will you be sending to Ishmaelia?' asked Mrs Stitch.

'I am in consultation with my editors on the subject. We think it a very promising little war. A microcosm, as you might say, of world drama. We propose to give it fullest publicity. The workings of a great newspaper,' said Lord Copper, feeling at last thoroughly Rotarian, 'are of a complexity which the public seldom appreciates. The citizen little realizes the vast machinery put into motion for him in exchange for his morning penny.' ('O God,' said Lady Metroland, faintly but audibly.) 'We shall have our naval, military, and air experts, our squad of photographers, our colour reporters, covering the war from every angle and on every front.'

'Yes,' said Mrs Stitch. 'Yes, yes. I suppose you will ... If I were you I should send someone like Boot. I don't suppose you could persuade *him* to go, but someone like him.'

'It has been my experience, dear Mrs Stitch, that the *Daily Beast* can command the talent of the world. Only last week the Poet Laureate wrote us an ode to the seasonal fluctuation of our net sales. We splashed it on the middle page. He admitted it was the most poetic and highly-paid work he had ever done.'

'Well, of course, if you *could* get him, Boot is your man. He's a brilliant writer, he's travelled everywhere and knows the whole Ishmaelite situation inside out.'

'Boot would be divine,' said Lady Cockpurse loyally.

*

Half an hour later Mrs Stitch rang up to say 'O.K., John. I think it's fixed. Don't take a penny less than fifty pounds a week.'

'God bless you, Julia. You've saved my life.'

'It's just the Stitch Service,' said Mrs Stitch cheerfully.

3

That evening, Mr Salter, Foreign Editor of *The Beast*, was summoned to dinner at his chief's country seat at East Finchley. It was a highly unwelcome invitation; Mr Salter normally worked at the office until nine o'clock. That evening he had planned a holiday at the opera; he and his wife had been looking forward to it with keen enjoyment for some weeks. As he drove out to Lord Copper's frightful mansion he thought sadly of those carefree days when he had edited the Woman's Page, or, better still, when he had chosen the jokes for one of Lord Copper's comic weeklies. It was the policy of the Megalopolitan to keep the staff alert by constant changes of occupation. Mr Salter's ultimate ambition was to take charge of the Competitions. Meanwhile he was Foreign Editor and found it a dog's life.

The two men dined alone. They ate parsley soup, whiting, roast veal, cabinet pudding; they drank whisky and soda. Lord Copper explained Nazism, Fascism, and Communism; later, in his ghastly library, he outlined the situation in the Far East. '*The Beast* stands for strong mutually antagonistic governments everywhere,' he said. 'Self-sufficiency at home, self-assertion abroad.'

Mr Salter's side of the conversation was limited to expressions of assent. When Lord Copper was right he said, 'Definitely, Lord Copper'; when he was wrong, 'Up to a point.'

'Let me see, what's the name of the place I mean? Capital of Japan? Yokohama, isn't it?'

'Up to a point, Lord Copper.'

'And Hong Kong belongs to us, doesn't it?'

'Definitely, Lord Copper.'

After a time: 'Then there's this civil war in Ishmaelia. I propose to feature it. Who did you think of sending?'

'Well, Lord Copper, the choice seems between sending a staff reporter who will get the news but whose name the public doesn't know, or to get someone from outside with a name as a military expert. You see, since we lost Hitchcock. . . .'

'Yes, yes. He was our only man with a European reputation. *I know.* Zinc will be sending him. *I know.* But he was wrong about the

Battle of Hastings. It *was* 1066. I looked it up. I won't employ a man who isn't big enough to admit when he's wrong.'

'We might share one of the Americans?'

'No, I tell you who I want; Boot.'

'Boot?'

'Yes, Boot. He's a young man whose work I'm very much interested in. He has the most remarkable style and he's been in Patagonia and the Prime Minister keeps his books by his bed. Do *you* read him?'

'Up to a point, Lord Copper.'

'Well, get on to him tomorrow. Have him up to see you. Be cordial. Take him out to dinner. Get him at any price. Well, at any reasonable price,' he added, for there had lately been a painful occurrence when instructions of this kind, given in an expansive mood, had been too literally observed and a trick cyclist who had momentarily attracted Lord Copper's attention had been engaged to edit the Sports Page on a five years' contract at five thousand a year.

4

Mr Salter went to work at midday. He found the Managing Editor cast in gloom.

'It's a terrible paper this morning,' he said. 'We paid Professor Jellaby thirty guineas for the feature article and there's not a word in it one can understand. Beaten by *The Brute* in every edition on the Zoo Mercy Slaying story. And *look at the Sports Page.*'

Together, in shame, the two men read the trick cyclist's Sports Page.

'Who's Boot?' asked Mr Salter at last.

'I know the name,' said the Managing Editor.

'The chief wants to send him to Ishmaelia. He's the Prime Minister's favourite writer.'

'Not the chap I was thinking of,' said the Managing Editor.

'Well, I've got to find him.' He listlessly turned the pages of the morning paper. 'Boot,' he said. 'Boot. Boot. Boot. Why! *Boot* – here he is. Why didn't the chief say he was a staff man?'

At the back of the paper, ignominiously sandwiched between Pip and Pop, the Bedtime Pets, and the recipe for a dish called 'Waffle Scramble', lay the bi-weekly half-column devoted to Nature:

LUSH PLACES, edited by William Boot, Countryman.

'Do you suppose that's the right one?'

'Sure of it. The Prime Minister is nuts on rural England.'

'He's supposed to have a particularly high-class style: *"Feather-footed through the plashy fen passes the questing vole"* . . . would that be it?'

'Yes,' said the Managing Editor. 'That must be good style. At least it doesn't sound like anything else to me. I know the name well now you mention it. Never seen the chap. I don't think he's ever been to London. Sends his stuff in by post. All written out in pen and ink.'

'I've got to ask him to dinner.'

'Give him cider.'

'Is that what countrymen like?'

'Yes, cider and tinned salmon are the staple diet of the agricultural classes.'

'I'll send him a telegram. Funny the chief wanting to send him to Ishmaelia.'

CHAPTER 2

I

'CHANGE AND DECAY in all around I see,' sang Uncle Theodore, gazing out of the morning-room window.

Thus, with startling loudness, he was accustomed to relieve his infrequent fits of depression; but decay, rather than change, was characteristic of the immediate prospect.

The immense trees which encircled Boot Magna Hall, shaded its drives and rides, and stood (tastefully disposed at the whim of some forgotten, provincial predecessor of Repton), singly and in groups about the park, had suffered, some from ivy, some from lightning, some from the various malignant disorders that vegetation is heir to, but all principally from old age. Some were supported with trusses and crutches of iron, some were filled with cement; some, even now, in June, could show only a handful of green leaves at their extremities. Sap ran thin and slow; a gusty night always brought down a litter of dead timber.

The lake was moved by strange tides. Sometimes, as at the present moment, it sank to a single, opaque pool in a wilderness of mud and rushes; sometimes it rose and inundated five acres of pasture. There had once been an old man in one of the lodges who understood the workings of the water system; there were sluice gates hidden among the reeds, and manholes, dotted about in places known only to him, furnished with taps and cocks; that man had been able to control an ornamental cascade and draw a lofty jet of water from the mouth of the dolphin on the South terrace. But he had been in his grave fifteen years and the secret had died with him.

The house was large but by no means too large for the Boot family, which at this time numbered eight. There were in the direct line: William who owned the house and estate, William's sister Priscilla who claimed to own the horses, William's widowed mother who owned the contents of the house and exercised ill-defined rights over the flower garden, and William's widowed grandmother who was said to own 'the money'. No one knew how much she possessed; she had been bedridden as long as William's memory went back. It was from her that such large cheques issued as were from time to time necessary for balancing the estate accounts and paying for Uncle Theodore's occasional, disastrous visits to London. Uncle Theodore, the oldest of the male collaterals, was by far the gayest. Uncle Roderick was in many ways the least eccentric. He had managed the estates and household throughout William's minority and continued to do so with a small but regular deficit which was made up annually by one of grandmamma's cheques. The widowed Lady Trilby was William's Great-Aunt Anne, his father's elder sister; she owned the motor-car, a vehicle adapted to her own require- ments; it had a horn which could be worked from the back seat; her weekly journey to church resounded through the village like the Coming of the Lord. Uncle Bernard devoted himself to a life of scholarship but had received little general recognition, for his re- searches, though profound, were narrow, being connected solely with his own pedigree. He had traced William's descent through three different lines from Ethelred the Unready and only lack of funds fortunately prevented him from prosecuting a claim to the abeyant barony of de Butte.

All the Boots, in one way or another, had about a hundred a year each as pocket money. It was therefore convenient for them to live together at Boot Magna where wages and household expenses were counted in with Uncle Roderick's annual deficit. The richest member of the household, in ready cash, was Nannie Bloggs, who had been bedridden for the last thirty years; she kept her savings in a red flannel bag under the bolster. Uncle Theodore made attempts on them from time to time, but she was a sharp old girl and, since she combined a long-standing aversion to Uncle Theodore with a preternatural aptitude for bringing off showy doubles during the flat racing season, her hoard continued to grow. The Bible and the Turf Guide were her only reading. She got great delight from telling each member of the family, severally and secretly, that he or she was her heir.

In other rooms about the house reposed: Nannie Price, ten years the junior of Nannie Bloggs, and bedridden from about the same age. She gave her wages to Chinese Missions and had little influence in the house; Sister Watts, old Mrs Boot's first nurse, and Sister Sampson, her second; Miss Scope, Aunt Anne's governess, veteran invalid, of some years seniority in bed to old Mrs Boot herself: and Bentinck the butler: James, the first footman, had been confined to his room for some time, but he was able on warm days to sit in an arm-chair at the window. Nurse Granger was still on her feet, but as her duties included the charge of all eight sick-rooms, it was thought she would not long survive. Ten servants waited upon the household and upon one another, but in a desultory fashion, for they could spare very little time from the five meat meals which tradition daily allowed them. In the circumstances the Boots did not entertain and were indulgently spoken of in the district as being 'poor as church mice'.

The fashionable John Courteney Boot was a remote cousin, or, as Uncle Bernard preferred, the member of a cadet branch. William had never met him; he had met very few people indeed. It was not true to say, as the Managing Editor of *The Beast* had said, that he had never been to London, but his visits had been infrequent enough for each to be distinct and perennially horrifying in his memory.

'Change and decay in all around I see,' sang Uncle Theodore. It was his habit to sing the same line over and over again. He was waiting for the morning papers. So were William and Uncle Roderick. They were brought by the butcher, often blotched with red, any time between eleven and midday, and then, if not intercepted, disappeared among the sick-rooms to return at tea-time hopelessly mutilated, for both Bentinck and old Mrs Boot kept scrap-books, and Sister Sampson had the habit of cutting out coupons and losing them in the bedclothes. This morning they were late. It was a matter of great anxiety to William.

He had never been to the Megalopolitan offices or met anyone connected with *The Beast*. His job as author of *Lush Places* had been passed on to him by the widow on the death of its previous holder, the Rector of Boot Magna. He had carefully modelled his style on the late Rector's, at first painfully, now almost without effort. The work was of the utmost importance to him: he was paid a guinea a time and it gave him the best possible excuse for remaining uninterruptedly in the country.

And now it was in danger. On the previous Thursday a very dreadful thing had happened. Drawing on the observations of a lifetime and after due cross-examination of the head keeper and half an hour with the encyclopaedia, William had composed a lyrical but wholly accurate account of the habits of the badger; one of his more finished essays. Priscilla in a playful mood had found the manuscript and altered it, substituting for 'badger' throughout 'the crested grebe'. It was not until Saturday morning when, in this form, it appeared in *The Beast*, that William was aware of the outrage.

His mail had been prodigious; some correspondents were sceptical, others derisive; one lady wrote to ask whether she read him aright in thinking he condoned the practice of baiting these rare and beautiful birds with terriers and deliberately destroying their earthy homes; how could this be tolerated in the so-called twentieth century? A major in Wales challenged him categorically to produce a single authenticated case of a great crested grebe attacking young rabbits. It had been exceedingly painful. All through the week-end William had awaited his dismissal, but Monday and Tuesday passed without a word from *The Beast*. He composed and despatched a light dissertation on water voles and expected the worst. Perhaps the powers at *The Beast* were too much enraged even to send back his manuscript; when Wednesday's paper came he would find another tenant of *Lush Places*. It came. He hunted frantically for his half-column. It was there, a green oasis between Waffle Scramble and the Bed-time Pets. '*Feather-footed through the plashy fens passes the questing vole. . . .*' It was all right. By some miracle Saturday's shame had been covered.

His uncles peevishly claimed the paper; he surrendered it readily. He stood at the french window blinking at the summer landscape; the horses at grass beyond the ha-ha skipped and frolicked.

'Confound the thing,' said Uncle Roderick behind him. 'Can't find the cricket anywhere. Whole page seems to be given up to some damn-fool cycling championship at Cricklewood Stadium.'

William did not care. In the fullness of his gratitude he resolved to give rodents a miss that Saturday (though he was particularly attached to them) and write instead of wild flowers and birdsong. He might even risk something out of the poets.

> *'Nay not so much as out of bed?*
> *When all the birds have Matins said,'*

he sang, in his heart, to the recumbent figures above him. And then, wheezing heavily, with crumbs on his mouth, ponderously straddling across the morning-room, came Troutbeck, the aged boy, bearing a telegram. Curiosity and resentment contended for mastery in Troutbeck's demeanour; curiosity because telegrams were of rare occurrence at Boot Magna; resentment at the interruption of his 'elevenses' – a lavish and ruminative feast which occupied the servants' hall from ten-thirty until noon.

William's face quickly reassured him that he had not been called from the table on any frivolous pretext. 'Bad news,' he was able to report. 'Shocking bad news for Master William.'

'It couldn't hardly be a death,' said the third house-maid. 'All the family's here.'

'Whatever it was we shall soon know,' said Troutbeck. 'It struck Master William all of a heap. Might I thank you to pass the chutney.'

Bad news indeed! Oblivious to the sunshine and the grazing horses and the stertorous breathing of his Uncle Theodore, William re-read the frightful doom that had fallen on him.

REQUEST YOUR IMMEDIATE PRESENCE HERE URGENT LORD COPPERS PERSONAL DESIRE SALTER BEAST.

'Nothing serious, I hope!' said Uncle Theodore, to whom telegrams, in the past, had from time to time brought news as disquieting as to any man living.

'Yes,' said William, 'I have been called to London.'

'Have you, my boy? That's interesting. I was thinking of running up for a night myself...'

But Uncle Theodore was speaking to the air. William was already at work, setting into motion the elaborate household machinery which would, too soon, effect his departure.

2

After an early luncheon, William went to say good-bye to his grandmother. She looked at him with doleful, mad eyes. 'Going to London, eh? Well, I hardly suppose I shall be alive when you return. Wrap up warm, dear.' It was eternal winter in Mrs Boot's sunny bedroom.

All the family who had the use of their legs attended on the steps to see William off; Priscilla bathed in tears of penitence. Nannie Bloggs sent him down three golden sovereigns. Aunt Anne's motor-car was there to take him away. At the last moment Uncle Theodore attempted to get in at the offside, but was detected and deterred. 'Just wanted to see a chap in Jermyn Street about some business,' he said wistfully.

It was always a solemn thing for a Boot to go to London; solemn as a funeral for William on this afternoon. Once or twice on the way to the station, once or twice as the train stopped on the route to Paddington, William was tempted to give up the expedition in despair. Why should he commit himself to this abominable city merely to be railed at and, for all he knew of Lord Copper's temperament, physically assaulted? But sterner counsels prevailed. He might bluff it out. Lord Copper was a townsman, a provincial townsman at that, and certainly did not know the difference between a badger and a great crested grebe. It was William's word against a few cantankerous correspondents, and people who wrote to the newspapers were proverbially unbalanced. By the time he reached Westbury he had sketched out a little scene for himself, in which he stood resolutely in the board-room defying the doctrinaire zoology of Fleet Street; every inch a Boot, thrice descended from Ethelred the Unready, rightful 15th Baron de Butte, haughty as a chieftain, honest as a peasant. 'Lord Copper,' he was saying, 'no man shall call me a liar unchastised. The great crested grebe *does* hibernate.'

He went to the dining-car and ordered some whisky. The steward said, 'We're serving teas. Whisky after Reading.' After Reading he tried again. 'We're serving dinners. I'll bring you one to your carriage.' When it came, William spilled it down his tie. He gave the steward one of Nannie Bloggs' sovereigns in mistake for a shilling. It was contemptuously refused and everyone in the carriage stared at him. A man in a bowler hat said, 'May I look? Don't often see one of them nowadays. Tell you what I'll do, I'll toss you for it. Call.'

William said, 'Heads.'

'Tails it is,' said the man in the bowler hat, putting it in his waistcoat pocket. He then went on reading his paper and everyone stared harder at William. His spirits began to sink; the mood of defiance passed. It was always the way; the moment he left the confines of Boot Magna he found himself in a foreign and hostile world. There was a train back at ten o'clock that night. Wild horses would not keep him from it. He would see Lord Copper, explain the situation fully and frankly, throw himself upon his mercy and, successful or defeated, catch the train at ten. By Reading he had worked out this new and humble policy. He would tell Lord Copper about Priscilla's tears; great men were proverbially vulnerable to appeals of that kind. The man opposite him looked over the top of his paper. 'Got any more quids?'

'No,' said William.

'Pity.'

At seven he reached Paddington and the atrocious city was all around him.

3

The Megalopolitan building, numbers 700–853 Fleet Street, was disconcerting. At first William thought that the taxi-driver, spotting a bumpkin, had driven him to the wrong address.

His acquaintance with offices was very small. At the time of his coming of age he had spent several mornings with the family solicitor in King's Bench Walk. At home he knew the local Estate

Agents and Auctioneers, the Bank and the Town Hall. He had once seen in Taunton a barely intelligible film about newspaper life in New York where neurotic men in shirt sleeves and eye-shades had rushed from telephone to tape machines, insulting and betraying one another in surroundings of unredeemed squalor. From these memories he had a confused expectation that was rudely shocked by the Byzantine vestibule and Sassanian lounge of Copper House. He thought at first that he must have arrived at some new and less exclusive rival of the R.A.C. Six lifts seemed to be in perpetual motion; with dazzling frequency their doors flew open to reveal now left, now right, now two or three at a time, like driven game, a series of girls in Caucasian uniform. 'Going up,' they cried in Punch-and-Judy accents and, before anyone could enter, snapped their doors and disappeared from view. A hundred or so men and women of all ranks and ages passed before William's eyes. The sole stationary objects were a chryselephantine effigy of Lord Copper in coronation robes, rising above the throng, on a polygonal malachite pedestal, and a concierge, also more than life size, who sat in a plate-glass enclosure, like a fish in an aquarium, and gazed at the agitated multitude with fishy, supercilious eyes. Under his immediate care were a dozen page boys in sky-blue uniforms, who between errands pinched one another furtively on a long bench. Medals of more battles than were ever fought by human arms or on earthly fields glittered on the porter's chest. William discovered a small vent in his tank and addressed him diffidently. 'Is his Lordship at home?'

'We have sixteen peers on the staff. Which was you referring to?'

'I wish to see Lord Copper.'

'Oh! Cyril, show this gentleman to a chair and give him a form.'

A minute blue figure led William to a desk and gave him a piece of paper. William filled it in. '*Mr Boot wishes to see Lord Copper. Subject: great crested grebes.*'

Cyril took the paper to the concierge, who read it, looked searchingly at William and mouthed, 'Fetch the gentleman.'

William was led forward.

'You wish to see Lord Copper?'

'Yes, please.'

'Oh! no you don't. Not about great crested grebes.'

'And badgers too,' said William. 'It is rather a long story.'

'I'll be bound it is. Tell you what, you go across the street and tell it to Lord Zinc at *The Daily Brute* office. That'll do just as well, now won't it?'

'I've got an appointment,' said William, and produced his telegram.

The concierge read it thoughtfully, held it up to the light, and said 'Ah!'; read it again and said: 'What you want to see is Mr Salter. Cyril, give the gentleman another form.'

Five minutes later William found himself in the office of the Foreign Editor.

It was an encounter of great embarrassment for both of them. For William it was the hour of retribution; he advanced, heavy with guilt, to meet whatever doom had been decreed for him. Mr Salter had the more active part. He was under orders to be cordial and spring Lord Copper's proposal on the poor hick when he had won his confidence by light conversation and heavy hospitality.

His knowledge of rural life was meagre. He had been born in West Kensington and educated at a large London day-school. When not engaged in one or other capacity in the vast Megalopolitan organization he led a life of blameless domesticity in Welwyn Garden City. His annual holiday was, more often than not, spent at home; once or twice when Mrs Salter complained of being run down, they had visited prosperous resorts on the East Coast. 'The country', for him, meant what you saw in the train between Liverpool Street and Frinton. If a psychoanalyst, testing his associations, had suddenly said to Mr Salter the word 'farm', the surprising response would have been 'Bang', for he had once been blown up and buried while sheltering in a farm in Flanders. It was his single intimate association with the soil. It had left him with the obstinate though admittedly irrational belief that agriculture was something alien and highly dangerous. Normal life, as he saw it, consisted in regular journeys by electric train, monthly cheques, communal amusements and a cosy horizon of slates and chimneys; there was something unEnglish and not quite right about 'the country', with its solitude and self-sufficiency, its bloody recreations, its darkness and silence and sudden, inexplicable noises; the kind of place where you never knew from one minute to the next that you might not be tossed by a bull or pitch-forked by a yokel or rolled over and broken up by a pack of hounds.

He had been round the office canvassing opinions about the subjects of conversation proper to countrymen. 'Mangel-wurzels are a safe topic,' he had been told, 'only you mustn't call them that. It's a subject on which farmers are very touchy. Call them roots...'

He greeted William with cordiality. 'Ah, Boot, how are you? Don't think I've had the pleasure before. Know your work well of course. Sit down. Have a cigarette or' – had he made a floater? – 'or do you prefer your church-warden?'

William took a cigarette. He and Mr Salter sat opposite one another. Between them, on the desk, lay an open atlas in which Mr Salter had been vainly trying to find Reykjavik.

There was a pause, during which Mr Salter planned a frank and disarming opening. 'How are your roots, Boot?' It came out wrong.

'How are your boots, root?' he asked.

William, glumly awaiting some fulminating rebuke, started and said, 'I beg your pardon?'

'I mean brute,' said Mr Salter.

William gave it up. Mr Salter gave it up. They sat staring at one another, fascinated, hopeless. Then:

'How's hunting?' asked Mr Salter, trying a new line. 'Foxes pretty plentiful?'

'Well, we stop in the summer, you know.'

'Do you? Everyone away, I suppose?'

Another pause: 'Lot of foot and mouth, I expect,' said Mr Salter hopefully.

'None, I'm thankful to say.'

'Oh!'

Their eyes fell. They both looked at the atlas before them.

'You don't happen to know where Reykjavik is?'

'No.'

'Pity. I hoped you might. No one in the office does.'

'Was that what you wanted to see me about?'

'Oh, no, not at all! Quite the contrary.'

Another pause.

William saw what was up. This decent little man had been deputed to sack him and could not get it out. He came to the rescue. 'I expect you want to talk about the great crested grebe.'

'Good God, no,' said Mr Salter, with instinctive horror, adding politely, 'At least not unless *you* do.'

'No, not at all,' said William, 'I thought *you* might want to.'

'Not at all,' said Mr Salter.

'That's all right, then.'

'Yes, that's all right...' Desperately: 'I say, how about some zider?'

'Zider?'

'Yes. I expect you feel like a drop of zider about this time, don't you? We'll go out and have some.'

The journalists in the film had been addicted to straight rye. Silent but wondering, William followed the Foreign Editor. They shared the lift with a very extraordinary man, bald, young, fleshless as a mummy, dressed in brown and white checks, smoking a cheroot. 'He does the Sports Page now,' said Mr Salter apologetically, when he was out of hearing.

In the public house at the corner, where *The Beast* reporters congregated, the barmaid took their order with surprise. 'Cider? I'll see.' Then she produced two bottles of sweet and fizzy liquid. William and Mr Salter sipped suspiciously.

'Not quite what you're used to down on the farm, I'm afraid.'

'Well, to tell you the truth, I don't often drink it. We give it to the haymakers, of course, and I sometimes have some of theirs.' Then, fearing that this might sound snobbish, he added, 'My Uncle Bernard drinks it for his rheumatism.'

'You're sure you wouldn't sooner have something else?'

'No.'

'You mean you wouldn't?'

'I mean I would.'

'Really?'

'Really; much sooner.'

'Good for you, Garge,' said Mr Salter, and from that moment a new, more human note was apparent in their relationship;

conversation was still far from easy, but they had this bond in common, that neither of them liked cider.

Mr Salter clung to it strenuously. 'Interesting you don't like cider,' he said. 'Neither do I.'

'No,' said William. 'I never have since I was sick as a small boy, in the hay field.'

'It upsets me inside.'

'Exactly.'

'Now whisky never did anyone any harm.'

'No.'

Interest seemed to flag. Mr Salter tried once more. 'Make much parsnip wine down your way?'

'Not much ...' It was clearly his turn now. He sipped and thought and finally said: 'Pretty busy at the office, I expect?'

'Yes, very.'

'Tell me – I've often wondered – do you keep a machine of your own or send out to the printers?'

'We have machines of our own.'

'Do you? They must work jolly fast.'

'Yes.'

'I mean, you have to get it written and printed and corrected and everything all on the same day, otherwise the news would become stale. People would have heard it on the wireless, I mean.'

'Yes.'

'D'you do much of the printing yourself?'

'No. You see, I'm the Foreign Editor.'

'I suppose that's why you wanted to find Reykjavik?'

'Yes.'

'Jolly difficult knowing where all these places are.'

'Yes.'

'So many of them I mean.'

'Yes.'

'Never been abroad myself.'

This seemed too good an opening to be missed. 'Would you like to go to Ishmaelia?'

'No.'

'Not at all?'

'Not at all. For one thing I couldn't afford the fare.'

'Oh, we would pay the fare,' said Mr Salter, laughing indulgently.

So that was it. Transportation. The sense of persecution which had haunted William for the last three hours took palpable and grotesque shape before him. It was too much. Conscious of a just cause and a free soul he rose and defied the nightmare. 'Really,' he said, in ringing tones, 'I call that a bit thick. I admit I slipped up on the great crested grebe, slipped up badly. As it happened, it was not my fault. I came here prepared to explain, apologize and, if need be, make reparation. You refused to listen to me. "Good God, no," you said, when I offered to explain. And now you calmly propose to ship me out of the country because of a trifling and, in my opinion, justifiable error. Who does Lord Copper think he is? The mind boggles at the vanity of the man. If he chooses to forget my eighteen months' devoted and unremitting labour in his service, he is, I admit, entitled to dismiss me . . .'

'Boot, Boot, old man,' cried Mr Salter, 'you've got this all wrong. With the possible exception of the Prime Minister, you have no more ardent admirer than Lord Copper. He wants you to *work* for him in Ishmaelia.'

'Would he pay my fare back?'

'Yes, of course.'

'Oh, that's rather different . . . Even so it seems a silly sort of scheme. I mean, how will it look in *Lush Places* when I start writing about sandstorms and lions and whatever they have in Ishmaelia? Not *lush*, I mean.'

'Let me tell you about it at dinner.'

They took a taxi-cab down Fleet Street and the Strand to the grill room where *The Beast* staff always entertained when they were doing so at the paper's expense.

'Do you *really* want tinned salmon?'

'No.'

'Sure?'

'Quite sure.'

Mr Salter regarded his guest with renewed approval and handed him the menu.

The esteem William had won by his distaste for cider and tinned salmon survived the ordering of dinner. William did not, as had seemed only too likely, demand pickled walnuts and Cornish pasties; nor did he, like the Budapest correspondent whom Mr Salter had last entertained in this room, draw attention to himself by calling for exotic Magyar dishes, and, on finding no one qualified to make them, insist on preparing for himself, with chafing dish and spirit lamp, before a congregation of puzzled waiters, a nauseous sauce of sweet peppers, honey, and almonds. He ordered a mixed grill, and, while he was eating, Mr Salter attempted, artfully, to kindle his enthusiasm for the new project.

'See that man there, that's Pappenhacker.'

William looked, and saw.

'Yes?'

'The cleverest man in Fleet Street.'

William looked again. Pappenhacker was young and swarthy, with great horn goggles and a receding stubbly chin. He was having an altercation with some waiters.

'Yes?'

'He's going to Ishmaelia for the *Daily Twopence*.'

'He seems to be in a very bad temper.'

'Not really. He's always like that to waiters. You see, he's a communist. Most of the staff of the *Twopence* are – they're University men, you see. Pappenhacker says that every time you are polite to a proletarian you are helping bolster up the capitalist system. He's very clever, of course, but he gets rather unpopular.'

'He looks as if he were going to hit them.'

'Yes, he does sometimes. Quite a lot of restaurants won't have him in. You see, you'll meet a lot of interesting people when you go to Ishmaelia.'

'Mightn't it be rather dangerous?'

Mr Salter smiled; to him, it was as though an Arctic explorer had expressed a fear that the weather might turn cold. 'Nothing to what you are used to in the country,' he said. 'You'll be surprised to find how far the war correspondents keep from the fighting. Why Hitchcock reported the whole Abyssinia campaign from Asmara and gave us some of the most colourful, eye-witness stuff we ever printed. In any case your life will be insured by the paper for five thousand pounds. No, no, Boot, I don't think you need worry about risk.'

'And you'd go on paying me my wages?'

'Certainly.'

'*And* my fare there *and* back, *and* my expenses?'

'Yes.'

William thought the matter over carefully. At length he said: 'No.'

'No?'

'No. It's very kind of you, but I think I would sooner not go. I don't like the idea at all.' He looked at his watch. 'I must be going to Paddington soon to catch my train.'

'Listen,' said Mr Salter. 'I don't think you have fully understood the situation. Lord Copper is particularly interested in your work and, to be frank, he insists on your going. We are willing to pay a very fair salary. Fifty pounds a month was the sum suggested.'

'*Fifty pounds a month!*' said William, goggling.

'A week,' said Mr Salter hastily.

'Gosh,' said William.

'And think what you can make on your expenses,' urged Mr Salter. 'At least another twenty. I happened to see Hitchcock's expense sheet when he was working for us in Shanghai. He charged three hundred pounds for camels alone.'

'But I don't think I shall know what to do with a camel.'

Mr Salter saw he was not making his point clear. 'Take a single example,' he said. 'Supposing you want to have dinner. Well, you go to a restaurant and do yourself proud, best of everything. Bill perhaps may be two pounds. Well, you put down five pounds for entertainment on your expenses. You've had a slap-up dinner, you're three pounds to the good, and everyone is satisfied.'

'But you see I don't like restaurants and no one pays for dinner at home, anyway. The servants just bring it in.'

'Or supposing you want to send flowers to your girl. You just go to a shop, send a great spray of orchids and put them down as "Information".'

'But I haven't got a girl and there are heaps of flowers at home.' He looked at his watch again. 'Well, I'm afraid I must be going. You see, I have a day-return ticket. I tell you what I'll do. I'll consult my family and let you know in a week or two.'

'Lord Copper wants you to leave tomorrow.'

'Oh, I couldn't do that, anyway, you know. I haven't packed or anything. And I daresay I should need some new clothes. Oh, no, that's out of the question.'

'We might offer a larger salary.'

'Oh, no, thank you. It isn't that. It's just that I don't want to go.'

'Is there *nothing* you want?'

'D'you know, I don't believe there is. Except to keep my job in *Lush Places* and go on living at home.'

It was a familiar cry: during his fifteen years of service with the Megalopolitan Company Mr Salter had heard it upon the lips of countless distressed colleagues; upon his own. In a moment of compassion he remembered the morning when he had been called from his desk in *Clean Fun*, never to return to it. The post had been his delight and pride; one for which he believed he had a particular aptitude . . . First he would open the morning mail and sort the jokes sent him by the private contributors (one man sent him thirty or forty a week) into those that were familiar, those that were indecent, and those that deserved the half-crown postal order payable upon publication. Then he would spend an hour or two with the bound *Punch*es noting whatever seemed topical. Then the ingenious game began of fitting these legends to the funny illustrations previously chosen for him by the Art Editor. Serene and delicate sunrise on a day of tempest! From this task of ordered discrimination he had been thrown into the ruthless, cut-throat, rough-and-tumble of *The Beast* Woman's Page. From there, crushed and bedraggled, he had been tossed into the editorial chair of the Imperial and Foreign News . . . His heart bled for William, but he was true to the austere traditions of his service. He made the reply that had silenced so many resentful novices in the past.

'Oh, but Lord Copper expects his staff to work wherever the best interests of the paper call them. I don't think he would employ anyone of whose loyalty he was doubtful, *in any capacity*.'

'You mean if I don't go to Ishmaelia I get the sack?'

'Yes,' said Mr Salter. 'In so many words that is exactly what I – what Lord Copper means . . . Won't you have a glass of port before we return to the office?'

CHAPTER 3

AN ODDLY-PLACED, square window rising shoulder high from the low wainscot, fringed outside with ivy, brushed by the boughs of a giant monkey-puzzle; a stretch of faded wallpaper on which hung a water-colour of the village churchyard painted in her more active days by Miss Scope, a small shelf of ill-assorted books and a stuffed ferret, whose death from rat-poisoning had overshadowed the whole of one Easter holiday from his private school – these, according as he woke on his right or left side, greeted William daily at Boot Magna.

On the morning after his interview with Mr Salter, he opened his eyes, relieved from a night haunted by Lord Copper in a hundred frightful forms, to find himself in black darkness; his first thought was that there were still some hours to go before daylight; then, as he remembered the season of the year and the vast, semi-conscious periods through which he had passed, in the intervals of being pursued down badger runs in the showy plumage of the great crested grebe, he accepted the more harrowing alternative that he had been struck blind; then that he was mad, for a bell was ringing insistently a few inches, it seemed, from his ear. He sat up in bed and found that he was bare to the waist; totally bare, he learned by further re-searches. He stretched out his arm and found a telephone; as he lifted it, the ringing stopped; a voice said, 'Mr Salter on the line.' Then he remembered the awful occurrence of the previous evening.

'Good morning,' said Mr Salter. 'I thought I'd better get you early. I expect you've been up and about for hours, eh? Used to milking and cubbing and so on?'

'No,' said William.

'No? Well, I don't get to the office much before eleven or twelve. I wondered if everything was clear about your journey or are there one or two little things you'd like to go into first?'

'Yes.'

'Ah, I thought there might be. Well, come round to the office as soon as you're ready.'

Groping, William found one of the dozen or so switches which controlled the lighting of various parts of the bedroom. He found his watch and learned that it was ten o'clock. He found a row of bell-pushes and rang for valet and waiter.

The evening before he had been too much surfeited with new impressions to pay particular attention to the room to which eventually he had been led. It was two o'clock when Mr Salter left him; they had returned to the Megalopolitan office after dinner; William had been led from room to room; he had been introduced to the Managing Editor, the Assistant Managing Editor, the Art Editor (who had provided the camera), the Accounts Manager, the Foreign Contacts Adviser, and a multitude of men and women with visible means of support but no fixed occupation who had popped in from time to time on the various officials with whom William was talking. He had signed a contract, an application for Life Insurance, receipts for a camera, typewriter, a portfolio full of tickets, and a book of travellers' cheques to the value of £1,000. He had reached the hotel in a daze; the management had been told to expect him; they had led him to a lift, then, aloft, along a white, unnaturally silent passage and left him in his room with no desire except to sleep and awake from his nightmare in the familiar, shabby surroundings of Boot Magna.

The room was large and faultless. A psychologist, hired from Cambridge, had planned the decorations – magenta and gamboge; colours which – it had been demonstrated by experiments on poultry and mice – conduce to a mood of dignified gaiety. Every day carpet, curtains, and upholstery were inspected for signs of disrepair. A gentle whining note filled the apartment emanating from a plant which was thought to 'condition' the atmosphere. William's crumpled clothes lay on the magenta carpet; his typewriter and camera had been hidden from him by the night porter.

The dressing table was fitted with a 'daylight' lamp so that women, before retiring to sleep, could paint their faces in a manner that would be becoming at dawn; but it was bare of brushes.

Presently a valet entered, drew back four or five layers of curtain and revealed the window – a model of ingenuity, devised to keep out the noise of traffic and admit the therapeutic elements of common daylight. He picked up William's clothes, inclined gracefully to-wards the bed in a High Anglican compromise between nod and genuflexion and disappeared from the room, leaving it bereft of any link with William's previous existence. Presently a waiter came with a bill of fare and William ordered breakfast.

'And I want a toothbrush.'

The waiter communicated this need to the hall porter and presently a page with a face of ageless evil brought it on a tray. 'It was five shillings,' he said. 'And two bob for the cabfare.'

'That's too much.'

'Oh, come on,' said the knowing midget. 'It isn't you that pays.'

William indicated some loose change on the table. The boy took it all. 'You want some pyjamas too,' he said. 'Shall I get you some?'

'No.'

'Please yourself,' said this vile boy leaving the room.

William ate his breakfast and rang for the valet.

'I want my clothes, please.'

'Here are your shoes and cuff-links, sir. I have sent the shirt and underclothes to the laundry. The suit is being cleaned. Your tie is being ironed by one of the ironing maids.'

'But I never told you to do that.'

'You gave no instructions to the contrary, sir. We naturally send *everything* away *always* unless we are specifically asked not to ... Would that be all, sir?'

'I want something to wear, now.'

'No doubt the hall porter will be able to arrange something.'

Some time later the same abominable child brought him a series of parcels.

'Reach-me-downs,' he said. 'Not what I'd care to wear myself. But it's the best I could get. Twenty quid. Shall I have it put down?'

'Yes.'

'Nice job journalism. May take to it myself one day.'

'I'm sure you'd be very good at it.'

'Yes, I think I should. I didn't get you a razor. The barber is six floors down.'

2

The bells of St Bride's were striking twelve when William reached Copper House. He found Mr Salter in a state of agitation. 'Oh dear, oh dear, you're late, Boot, and Lord Copper himself has asked for you twice. I must go and see if he is still accessible.'

William was left standing in the passage. Metal doors snapped in and out: 'Going up,' 'Going down,' cried the Caucasian lift girls; on all sides his colleagues in the great concern came and went, bustling past him – haggard men who had been up all night, elegant young ladies bearing trays of milk, oily figures in overalls bearing bits of machinery. William stood in a daze, fingering the stiff seams of his new suit. After a time he heard himself addressed: 'Hi, you,' said a voice, 'wake up.'

'If only I could,' said William.

'Eh?'

'Nothing.'

The man speaking to him was exactly the type William recognized as belonging to the film he had seen in Taunton; a short, shock-headed fellow in shirt sleeves, dicky, and eye-shade, waistcoat pocket full of pencils, first finger pointing accusingly.

'You. You're the new man, aren't you?'

'Yes, I suppose I am.'

'Well, here's a chance for you.' He pushed a typewritten slip into William's hand. 'Cut along there quick. Take a taxi. Don't bother about your hat. You're in a newspaper office now.'

William read the slip. '*Mrs Stitch. Gentlemen's Lavatory, Sloane Street.*'

'We've just had this phoned through from the policeman on duty. Find out what she is doing down there. Quick!'

A lift door flew open at their side. 'Going down,' cried a Caucasian.

'In there.'

The door snapped shut; the lift shot down; soon William was in a taxi making for Sloane Street.

There was a dense crowd round the public lavatory. William bobbed hopelessly on the fringe; he could see nothing above the heads except more heads, hats giving way to helmets at the hub. More spectators closed in behind him; suddenly he felt a shove more purposeful than the rest and a voice said, 'Way, please. Press. Make way for the Press.' A man with a camera was forging a way through. 'Press, please, Press. Make way for the Press.'

William joined in behind him and followed those narrow, irresistible shoulders on their progress towards the steps. At last they found themselves at the railings, among the policemen. The camera man nodded pleasantly to them and proceeded underground. William followed.

'Hi,' said a sergeant, 'where are *you* going?'

'Press,' said William. 'I'm on *The Beast*.'

'So am I,' said the sergeant. 'Go to it. She's down there. Can't think how she did it, not without hurting herself.'

At the foot of the steps, making, for the photographer, a happy contrast to the white tiles about it, stood a little black motor-car. Inside, her hands patiently folded in her lap, sat the most beautiful woman William had ever seen. She was chatting in a composed and friendly manner to the circle of reporters and plain-clothes men.

'I can't think what you're all making such a fuss about,' she said. 'It's simply a case of mistaken identity. There's a man I've been wanting to speak to for weeks and I thought I saw him popping in here. So I drove down after him. Well, it was someone quite different, but he behaved beautifully about it, and now I can't get out; I've been here nearly half an hour and I've a *great* deal to do. I do think some of you might help, instead of standing there asking questions.'

Six of them seized the little car and lifted it, effortlessly, on their shoulders. A cheer rose from the multitude as the jet back rose above the spikes of the railings. William followed, his hand resting lightly on the running board. They set Mrs Stitch back on the road;

the police began to clear a passage for her. 'A very nice little story,' said one of William's colleagues. 'Just get in nicely for the evening edition.'

The throng began to disperse; the policemen pocketed their tips; the camera men scampered for their dark rooms. 'Boot, Boot,' cried an eager, slightly peevish voice. 'So there you are. Come back at once.' It was Mr Salter. 'I came to fetch you for Lord Copper and they told me you had gone out. It was only by sheer luck that I found where you had gone. It's been a terrible mistake. Someone will pay for this; I know they will. Oh dear, oh dear, get into the cab quickly.'

3

Twenty minutes later William and Mr Salter passed the first of the great doors which divided Lord Copper's personal quarters from the general office. The carpets were thicker here, the lights softer, the expressions of the inhabitants more careworn. The typewriters were of a special kind; their keys made no more sound than the drumming of a bishop's fingertips on an upholstered prie-dieu; the telephone buzzers were muffled and purred like warm cats. The personal private secretaries padded through the ante-chambers and led them nearer and nearer to the presence. At last they came to massive double doors, encased in New Zealand rose-wood which by their weight, polish, and depravity of design, proclaimed unmistakably, 'Nothing but Us stands between you and Lord Copper.' Mr Salter paused, and pressed a little bell of synthetic ivory. 'It lights a lamp on Lord Copper's own desk,' he said reverently. 'I expect we shall have a long time to wait.'

But almost immediately a green light overhead flashed their permission to enter.

Lord Copper was at his desk. He dismissed some satellites and rose as William came towards him.

'Come in, Mr Boot. This is a great pleasure. I have wanted to meet you for a long time. It is not often that the Prime Minister and I agree, but we see eye to eye about your style. A very nice little style indeed ... You may sit down too, Salter. Is Mr Boot all set for his trip?'

'Up to a point, Lord Copper.'

'Excellent. There are two invaluable rules for a special correspondent – Travel Light and Be Prepared. Have nothing which in a
case of emergency you cannot carry in your own hands. But remember that the unexpected always happens. Little things we take for
granted at home like...' he looked about him, seeking a happy
example; the room, though spacious, was almost devoid of furniture;
his eye rested on a bust of Lady Copper; that would not do; then,
resourcefully, he said '... like a coil of rope or a sheet of tin, may save
your life in the wilds. I should take some cleft sticks with you.
I remember Hitchcock – Sir Jocelyn Hitchcock, a man who used
to work for me once; smart enough fellow in his way, but *limited*, very
little historical backing – I remember him saying that in Africa he
always sent his dispatches in a cleft stick. It struck me as a very useful
tip. Take plenty.

'With regard to Policy, I expect you already have your own
views. I never hamper my correspondents in any way. What the
British public wants first, last, and all the time is News. Remember
that the Patriots are in the right and are going to win. *The Beast*
stands by them four-square. But they must win quickly. The British
public has no interest in a war which drags on indecisively. A few
sharp victories, some conspicuous acts of personal bravery on the
Patriot side and a colourful entry into the capital. That is *The Beast*
Policy for the war.

'Let me see. You will get there in about three weeks. I should
spend a day or two looking around and getting the background.
Then a good, full-length dispatch which we can feature with your
name. That's everything, I think, Salter?'

'Definitely, Lord Copper.' He and William rose.

It was not to be expected that Lord Copper would leave his chair
twice in the morning, but he leant across the desk and extended his
hand. 'Good-bye, Mr Boot, and the best of luck. We shall expect the
first victory about the middle of July.'

When they had passed the final ante-room and were once more
in the humbler, frequented by-ways of the great building, Mr Salter
uttered a little sigh. 'It's an odd thing,' he said, 'that the more I see of
Lord Copper, the less I feel I really know him.'

The affability with which William had been treated was without precedent in Mr Salter's experience. Almost with diffidence he suggested, 'It's one o'clock; if you are going to catch the afternoon aeroplane, you ought to be getting your kit, don't you think?'

'Yes.'

'I don't suppose that after what Lord Copper has said there is anything more you want to know.'

'Well, there is one thing. You see, I don't read the papers very much. Can you tell me who is fighting who in Ishmaelia?'

'I think it's the Patriots and the Traitors.'

'Yes, but which is which?'

'Oh, I don't know *that*. *That's* Policy, you see. It's nothing to do with me. You should have asked Lord Copper.'

'I gather it's between the Reds and the Blacks.'

'Yes, but it's not quite as easy as that. You see, they are all Negroes. And the Fascists won't be called black because of their racial pride, so they are called White after the White Russians. And the Bolshevists *want* to be called black because of *their* racial pride. So when you *say* black you mean red, and when you *mean* red you say white and when the party who call themselves blacks say traitors they mean what *we* call blacks, but what *we* mean when *we* say traitors I really couldn't tell you. But from your point of view it will be quite simple. Lord Copper only wants Patriot victories and both sides call themselves patriots, and of course both sides will claim all the victories. But, of course, it's really a war between Russia and Germany and Italy and Japan who are all against one another on the patriotic side. I hope I make myself plain?'

'Up to a point,' said William, falling easily into the habit.

4

The Foreign Contacts Adviser of *The Beast* telephoned the emporium where William was to get his kit and warned them of his arrival; accordingly it was General Cruttwell, F.R.G.S., himself who was waiting at the top of the lift shaft. An imposing man: Cruttwell Glacier in Spitsbergen, Cruttwell Falls in Venezuela, Mount Cruttwell in the Pamirs, Cruttwell's Leap in Cumberland marked his travels; Cruttwell's Folly, a waterless and indefensible camp near Salonika, was notorious to all who had served with him in the war. The shop paid him six hundred a year and commission, out of which, by contract, he had to find his annual subscription to the R.G.S. and the electric treatment which maintained the leathery tan of his complexion.

Before either had spoken, the General sized William up; in any other department he would have been recognized as a sucker; here, amid the trappings of high adventure, he was, more gallantly, a greenhorn.

'Your first visit to Ishmaelia, eh? Then perhaps I can be of some help to you. As no doubt you know, I was there in '97 with poor "Sprat" Larkin . . .'

'I want some cleft sticks, please,' said William firmly.

The General's manner changed abruptly. His leg had been pulled before, often. Only last week there had been an idiotic young fellow dressed up as a missionary . . . 'What the devil for?' he asked tartly.

'Oh, just for my dispatches, you know.'

It was with exactly such an expression of simplicity that the joker had asked for a tiffin gun, a set of chota pegs and a chota mallet. 'Miss Barton will see to you,' he said, and turning on his heel he began to inspect a newly-arrived consignment of rhinoceros hide whips in a menacing way.

Miss Barton was easier to deal with. 'We can have some cloven for you,' she said brightly. 'If you will make your selection I will send them down to our cleaver.'

William, hesitating between polo sticks and hockey sticks, chose six of each; they were removed to the workshop. Then Miss Barton led him through the departments of the enormous store. By the time she had finished with him, William had acquired a well-, perhaps rather over-, furnished tent, three months' rations, a collapsible canoe, a jointed flagstaff and Union Jack, a hand-pump and sterilizing plant, an astrolabe, six suits of tropical linen and a sou'wester, a camp operating table and set of surgical instruments, a portable humidor, guaranteed to preserve cigars in condition in the Red Sea, and a Christmas hamper complete with Santa

Claus costume and a tripod mistletoe stand, and a cane for whacking snakes. Only anxiety about time brought an end to his marketing.
At the last moment he added a coil of rope and a sheet of tin; then he
left under the baleful stare of General Cruttwell.

5

It had been arranged for him that William should fly to Paris
and there catch the Blue Train to Marseilles. He was just in time.
His luggage, which followed the taxi in a small pantechnicon,
made him a prominent figure at the office of the Air Line.

'It will cost you one hundred and three pounds supplement on
your ticket,' they said, after it had all been weighed.

'Not *me*,' said William cheerfully, producing his travellers'
cheques.

They telephoned to Croydon and ordered an additional aeroplane.

Mr Pappenhacker of the *Twopence* was a fellow passenger. He
travelled as a man of no importance; a typewriter and a single
'featherweight' suitcase constituted his entire luggage; only the unobtrusive *Messageries Maritimes* labels distinguished him from the
surrounding male and female commercial travellers. He read a little
Arabic Grammar, holding it close to his nose, oblivious to all
about him. William was the centre of interest in the motor omnibus,
and in his heart he felt a rising, wholly pleasurable excitement. His
new possessions creaked and rattled on the roof, canoe against
astrolabe, humidor against ant-proof clothes box; the cleft sticks
lay in a bundle on the opposite seat; the gardens of South London
sped past. William sat in a happy stupor. He had never wanted
to go to Ishmaelia, or, for that matter, to any foreign country, to
earn £50 a week or to own a jointed flagstaff or a camp operating
table; but when he told Mr Salter that he wanted nothing except
to live at home and keep his job, he had hidden the remote and secret
ambition of fifteen years or more. He did, very deeply, long to go up
in an aeroplane. It was a wish so far from the probabilities of life at
Boot Magna that William never spoke of it; very rarely consciously
considered it. No one at home knew of it except Nannie Bloggs. She

had promised him a flight if she won the Irish Sweepstake, but after several successive failures she had decided that the whole thing was a popish trick and refused to take further tickets, and with her decision William's chances seemed to fade beyond the ultimate horizon. But it still haunted his dreams and returned to him, more vividly, in the minutes of transition between sleep and wakefulness, on occasions of physical exhaustion and inner content, hacking home in the twilight after a good day's hunt, fuddled with port on the not infrequent birthdays of the Boot household. And now its imminent fulfilment loomed through the haze that enveloped him as the single real and significant feature. High over the chimneys and the giant monkey-puzzle, high among the clouds and rainbows and clear blue spaces, whose alternations figured so largely and poetically in *Lush Places*; high above the most ecstatic skylark, above earth-bound badger and great crested grebe, away from people and cities to a region of light and void and silence – that was where William was going in the Air Line omnibus; he sat mute, rapt, oblivious of the cleft sticks and the portable typewriter.

At Croydon he was received with obeisance; a special official had been detailed to attend to him. 'Good day, Mr Boot . . . This way, Mr Boot . . . The men will see to your baggage, Mr Boot.' On the concrete court in front of the station stood his aeroplane, her three engines tuning up, one screw swinging slow, one spinning faster, one totally invisible, roaring all-out. 'Good afternoon, Mr Boot,' said a man in overalls.

'Good afternoon, Mr Boot,' said a man in a peaked cap.

Pappenhacker and the commercial travellers were being herded into the service plane. William watched his crates being embarked. Men like gym instructors moved at the double behind rubber-tyred trolleys. 'All in, Mr Boot,' they said, touching their caps. William distributed silver.

'Excuse me, Mr Boot,' a little man in a seedy soft hat stood at William's elbow, 'I haven't yet had the pleasure of stamping your passport.'

CHAPTER 4

I

'OH DEAR, OH dear,' said Mr Salter. 'D'you know, I believe it would be as well to keep Lord Copper in ignorance of this incident. The *Twopence* will be a day ahead of us – perhaps more. Lord Copper would not like that. It might cause trouble for the Foreign Contacts Adviser or – or someone.'

William's luggage was piled in the Byzantine Hall; even there, under the lofty, gilded vaults, it seemed enormous. He and Mr Salter regarded it sadly. 'I'll have all this sent on to your hotel. It must not be seen by the Personal Staff. Here is your application form for an emergency passport. The Art Department will take your photograph and we have an Archdeacon in the Religious Department who will witness it. Then I think you had better keep away from the office until you start. I'm afraid that you've missed the Messageries ship, but there's a P. and O. next day to Aden. You can get across from there. And, officially, remember, you left this afternoon.'

It was a warm evening, heavy with the reek of petrol. William returned sadly to his hotel and re-engaged his room. The last edition of the evening papers was on the streets. '*Society Beauty in Public Convenience*,' they said. '*Mrs Stitch Again.*'

William walked to Hyde Park. A black man, on a little rostrum, was explaining to a small audience why the Ishmaelite patriots were right and the traitors were wrong. William turned away. He noticed with surprise a tiny black car bowling across the grass; it sped on, dexterously swerving between the lovers; he raised his hat but the driver was intent on her business. Mrs Stitch had just learned that a baboon, escaped from the Zoo, was up a tree in Kensington Gardens and she was out to catch it.

'Who built the Pyramids?' cried the Ishmaelite orator. 'A Negro. Who invented the circulation of the blood? A Negro. Ladies and gentlemen, I ask you as impartial members of the great British public, who discovered America?'

And William went sadly on his way to a solitary dinner and an early bed.

2

At the passport office next morning they told William that he would want a visa for Ishmaelia. 'In fact you may want two. Someone's just opened a rival legation. We haven't recognized it officially, of course, but you may find it convenient to visit them. Which part are you going to?'

'The patriotic part.'

'Ah, then you'd better get two visas,' said the official.

William drove to the address they gave him. It was in Maida Vale. He rang the bell and presently a tousled woman opened the door.

'Is this the Ishmaelite Legation?' he asked.

'No, it's Doctor Cohen's and he's out.'

'Oh . . . I wanted an Ishmaelite visa.'

'Well, you'd better call again. I daresay Doctor Cohen will have one, only he doesn't come here not often except sometimes to sleep.'

The lower half of another woman appeared on the landing overhead. William could see her bedroom slippers and a length of flannel dressing-gown.

'What is it, Effie?'

'Man at the door.'

'Tell him whatever it is we don't want it.'

'He says will the Doctor give him something or other.'

'Not without an appointment.'

The legs disappeared and a door slammed.

'That's Mrs Cohen,' said Effie. 'You see how it is; they're Yids.'

'Oh dear,' said William. 'I was told to come here by the passport office.'

'Sure it isn't the nigger downstairs you want?'

'Perhaps it is.'

'Well, why didn't you say so? He's downstairs.'

William then noticed, for the first time, that a little flag was flying from the area railings. It bore a red hammer and sickle on a black ground. He descended to the basement where, over a door between two dustbins, a notice proclaimed:

REPUBLIC OF ISHMAELIA
LEGATION AND CONSULATE-GENERAL
If away leave letters with tobacconist at No. 162b

William knocked and the door was opened by the Negro whom he had seen the evening before in Hyde Park. The features, to William's undiscriminating eye, were not much different from those of any other Negro, but the clothes were unforgettable.

'Can I see the Ishmaelite consul-general, please?'

'Are you from the Press?'

'Yes, I suppose in a way I am.'

'Come in. I'm him. As you see, we are a little under-staffed at the moment.'

The consul-general led him into what had once been the servants' hall. Photographs of Negroes in uniform and ceremonial European dress hung on the walls. Samples of tropical produce were disposed on the table and along the bookshelves. There was a map of Ishmaelia, an eight-piece office suite and a radio. William sat down. The consul-general turned off the music and began to talk.

'The patriotic cause in Ishmaelia,' he said, 'is the cause of the coloured man and of the proletariat throughout the world. The Ishmaelite worker is threatened by a corrupt and foreign coalition of capitalistic exploiters, priests and imperialists. As that great Negro Karl Marx has so nobly written...' He talked for about twenty minutes. The black-backed, pink palmed, fin-like hands beneath the violet cuffs flapped and slapped. 'Who built the Pyramids?' he asked. 'Who invented the circulation of the blood?...

Africa for the African worker; Europe for the African worker; Asia, Oceania, America, Arctic, and Antarctic for the African worker.'

At length he paused and wiped the line of froth from his lips.

'I came about a visa,' said William diffidently.

'Oh,' said the consul-general, turning on the radio once more. 'There's fifty pounds deposit and a form to fill in.'

William declared that he had not been imprisoned, that he was not suffering from any contagious or outrageous disease, that he was not seeking employment in Ishmaelia or the overthrow of its political institutions; paid his deposit and was rewarded with a rubber stamp on the first page of his new passport.

'I hope you have a pleasant trip,' said the consul-general. 'I'm told it's a very interesting country.'

'But aren't you an Ishmaelite?'

'*Me?* Certainly not. I'm a graduate of the Baptist College of Antigua. But the cause of the Ishmaelite worker is the cause of the Negro worker of the world.'

'Yes,' said William. 'Yes. I suppose it is. Thank you very much.'

'Who discovered America?' demanded the consul-general to his retreating back, in tones that rang high above the sound of the wireless concert. 'Who won the Great War?'

3

The rival legation had more spacious quarters in an hotel in South Kensington. A gold swastika on a white ground hung proudly from the window. The door of the suite was opened by a Negro clad in a white silk shirt, buckskin breeches and hunting boots who clicked his spurs and gave William a Roman salute.

'I've come for a visa.'

The pseudo-consul led him to the office. 'I shall have to delay you for a few minutes. You see the Legation is only just open and we have not yet got our full equipment. We are expecting the rubber stamp any minute now. In the meantime let me explain the Ishmaelite situation to you. There are many misconceptions. For instance, the Jews of Geneva, subsidized by Russian gold, have spread the story that we are a black race. Such is the ignorance, credulity, and prejudice of the tainted European states that the absurd story has been repeated in the press. I must ask you to deny it. As you will see for yourself, we are pure Aryans. In fact we were the first white colonizers of Central Africa. What Stanley and Livingstone did in the last century, our Ishmaelite ancestors did in the Stone Age. In the course of the years the tropical sun has given to some of us a healthy, in some cases almost a swarthy tan. But all responsible anthropologists . . . '

William fingered his passport and became anxious about luncheon. It was already past one.

' . . . The present so-called government bent on the destruction of our great heritage . . . ' There was an interruption. The pseudo-consul went to the door. 'From the stationer's,' said a cockney voice. 'Four and eight to pay.'

'Thank you, that is all.'

'Four and eight to pay or else I takes it away again.'

There was a pause. The pseudo-consul returned.

'There is a fee of five shillings for the visa,' he said.

William paid. The pseudo-consul returned with the rubber stamp, jingling four pennies in his breeches pocket.

'You will see the monuments of our glorious past in Ishmaelia,' he said, taking the passport. 'I envy you very much.'

'But are you not an Ishmaelite?'

'Of course; by descent. My parents migrated some generations ago. I was brought up in Sierra Leone.'

Then he opened the passport.

4

The bells of St Bride's were striking four when, after a heavy luncheon, William returned to the Megalopolitan Building.

'Boot. Oh dear, oh dear,' said Mr Salter. 'You ought to be at the aerodrome. What on earth has happened?'

'He burned my passport.'

'Who did?'

'The patriot consul.'

'Why?'

'It had a traitor visa on it.'

'I see. How very unfortunate. Lord Copper would be *most* upset if he came to hear of it. I think we had better go and ask the Foreign Contacts Adviser what to do.'

On the following afternoon, provided with two passports, William left Croydon aerodrome in his special plane.

5

He did not leave alone.

The propellers were thundering; the pilot threw away his cigarette and adjusted his helmet; the steward wrapped a rug round William's feet and tenderly laid in his lap a wad of cotton wool, a flask of smelling salts and an empty paper bag; the steps were being wheeled from the door. At that moment three figures hurried from the shelter of the office. One was heavily enveloped in a sand-coloured ulster; a check cap was pulled low on his eyes and his collar was fastened high against the blast of the engines. He was a small man in a hurry, yet, bustling and buttoned up as he was, a man of unmistakable importance, radiating something of the dignity of a prize Pekingese. This impression was accentuated by the extreme deference with which he was treated by his companions, one a soldierly giant carrying an attaché case, the other wearing the uniform of high rank in the company.

This official now approached William, and, above the engine, asked his permission to include a passenger and his servant. The name was lost in the roar of the propellers. 'Mr...I needn't tell you who *he* is...only plane available...request from a very high quarter...infinitely obliged if...as far as Le Bourget.'

William gave his assent and the two men bowed silently and took their places. The official withdrew. The little man delicately plugged his ears and sank deeper into his collar. The door was shut; the ground staff fell back. The machine moved forward, gathered speed, hurtled and bumped across the rough turf, ceased to bump, floated clear of the earth, mounted and wheeled above the smoke and traffic and very soon hung, it seemed motionless, above the Channel, where the track of a steamer, far below them, lay in the bright

water like a line of smoke on a still morning. William's heart rose
with it and gloried, lark-like, in the high places.

6

All too soon they returned to earth. The little man and his servant
slipped unobtrusively through the throng and William was bayed
on all sides by foreigners. The parcels and packing cases seemed to
fill the shed, and the customs officers, properly curious, settled
down to a thorough examination.

'Tous sont des effets personnels – tous usés,' William said gallantly, but one by one, with hammers and levers, the crates were
opened and their exotic contents spread over the counter.

It was one of those rare occasions when the humdrum life of the
douanier is exalted from the tedious traffic in vegetable silks and
subversive literature to realms of adventure; such an occasion as
might have inspired the jungle scenes of Rousseau. Not since an
Egyptian lady had been caught cosseting an artificial baby stuffed
with hashish had the customs officials of Le Bourget had such
a beano.

'Comment dit-on humidor?' William cried in his distress. 'C'est
une chose pour garder les cigares dans la Mer Rouge – et dedans
ceci sont les affaires de l'hospitale pour couper les bras et les jambes,
vous comprenez – et ça c'est pour tuer les serpents et ceci est un
bateau qui collapse et ces branches de mistletoe sont pour Noël,
pour baiser dessous, vous savez . . . '

'Monsieur, il ne faut pas se moquer des douanes.'

The cleft sticks alone passed without question, with sympathy.

'Ils sont pour porter les dépêches.'

'C'est un Sport?'

'Oui, oui, certainement – le Sport.'

There and at the Gare de Lyon he spent vast sums; all the porters
of Paris seemed to have served him, all the officials to need his
signature on their sheaves of documents. At last he achieved
his train, and, as they left Paris, made his way uncertainly towards
the restaurant car.

7

Opposite him at the table to which he was directed sat a middle-aged man, at the moment engaged in a homily to the waiter in fluent and apparently telling argot. His head was totally bald on the top and of unusual conical shape; at the sides and back the hair was closely cut and dyed a strong, purplish shade of auburn. He was neatly, rather stiffly dressed for the time of year, and heavily jewelled; a cabochon emerald, massive and dull, adorned his tie; rubies flashed on his fingers and cuff-links as his hands rose and spread configuring the swell and climax of his argument; pearls and platinum stretched from pocket to pocket of his waistcoat. William wondered what his nationality could be and thought perhaps Turkish. Then he spoke, in a voice that was not exactly American or Levantine or Eurasian or Latin or Teuton, but a blend of them all.

'The moment they recognize an Englishman they think they can make a monkey of him,' he said in this voice. 'That one was Swiss; they're the worst; tried to make me buy mineral water. The water in the carafes is excellent. I have drunk quantities of it in my time without ever being seriously affected – and I have a particularly delicate stomach. May I give you some?'

William said he preferred wine.

'You are interested in clarets? I have a little vineyard in Bordeaux – on the opposite slope of the hill to Château Mouton-Rothschild where in my opinion the soil is rather less delicate than mine. I like to have something to give my friends. They are kind enough to find it drinkable. It has never been in the market, of course. It is a little hobby of mine.'

He took two pills, one round and white, the other elliptical and black, from a rococo snuff-box and laid them on the tablecloth beside his plate. He drew a coroneted crêpe de Chine handkerchief from his pocket, carefully wiped his glass, half-filled it with murky liquid from the water bottle, swallowed his medicine and then said:

'You are surprised at my addressing you?'

'Not at all,' said William politely.

'But it *is* surprising. I make a point of never addressing my fellow travellers. Indeed I usually prefer to dine in the coupé. But this is not our first meeting. You were kind enough to give me a place in your aeroplane this afternoon. It was a service I greatly appreciate.'

'Not at all,' said William. 'Not at all. Very glad to have been any help.'

'It was the act of an Englishman – a fellow Englishman,' said the little man simply. 'I hope that one day I shall have the opportunity of requiting it . . . I probably shall,' he added rather sadly. 'It is one of the pleasant if quite onerous duties of a man of my position to requite the services he receives – usually on a disproportionately extravagant scale.'

'Please,' said William, 'do not give the matter another thought.'

'I never do. I try to let these things slip from my mind as one of the evanescent delights of travel. But it has been my experience that sooner or later I am reminded of them by my benefactor . . . You are on your way to the Côte d'Azur?'

'No, only as far as Marseille.'

'I rejoice in the Côte d'Azur. I try to get there every year, but too often I am disappointed. I have so much on my hands – naturally – and in winter I am much occupied with sport. I have a little pack of hounds in the Midlands.'

'Oh? Which?'

'You might not have heard of us. We march with the Fernie. I suppose it is the best hunting country in England. It is a little hobby of mine, but at times, when there is a frost, I long for my little house at Antibes. My friends are kind enough to say I have made it comfortable. I expect you will one day honour me with a visit there.'

'It sounds delightful.'

'They tell me the bathing is good but that does not interest me. I have some plantations of flowering trees which horticulturists are generous enough to regard with interest, and the largest octopus in captivity. The chef too is, in his simple seaside way, one of the best I have. Those simple pleasures suffice for me . . . You are surely not making a long stay in Marseille?'

'No, I sail tomorrow for East Africa. For Ishmaelia,' William added with some swagger.

The effect on his companion was gratifying. He blinked twice and asked with subdued courtesy:

'Forgive me; I think I must have misheard you. Where are you going?'

'To Ishmaelia. You know, the place where they say there is a war.'

There was a pause. Finally: 'Yes, the name is in some way familiar. I must have seen it in the newspapers.' And, taking a volume of pre-Hitler German poetry from the rack above him, he proceeded to read, shaping the words with his lips like a woman in prayer, and slowly turning the leaves.

Undeviating as the train itself, the dinner followed its changeless course from consommé to bombe. William's companion ate little and said nothing. With his coffee he swallowed two crimson cachets. Then he closed his book of love poems and nodded across the restaurant car.

The soldierly valet who had been dining at the next table rose to go.

'Cuthbert.'

'Sir?'

He stood attentively at his master's side.

'Did you give my sheets to the *conducteur*?'

'Yes, sir.'

'See that he has made them up properly. Then you may go to bed. You know the time in the morning?'

'Yes, sir; thank you, sir; good night, sir.'

'Good night, Cuthbert . . .' Then he turned to William and said with peculiar emphasis: 'A very courageous man that. He served with me in the war. He never left my side, so I recommended him for the V.C. He never leaves me now. And he is adequately armed.'

William returned to his carriage to lie awake, doze fitfully and at last to raise the blinds upon a landscape of vines and olives and dusty aromatic scrub.

8

At Marseille he observed, but was too much occupied to speculate upon the fact, that his companion of the evening before had also left the train. He saw the dapper, slightly rotund figure slip past the barrier a few paces ahead of the valet, but immediately the stupendous responsibilities of his registered baggage pressed all other concerns from his mind.

CHAPTER 5

I

THE SHIPS WHICH William had missed had been modern and commodious and swift; not so the *Francmaçon* in which he was eventually obliged to sail. She had been built at an earlier epoch in the history of steam navigation and furnished in the style of the day, for service among the high waves and icy winds of the North Atlantic. Late June in the Gulf of Suez was not her proper place or season. There was no space on her decks for long chairs; her cabins, devoid of fans, were aired only by tiny portholes, built to resist the buffeting of an angrier sea. The passengers sprawled listlessly on the crimson plush settees of the lounge. Carved mahogany panels shut them in; a heraldic ceiling hung threateningly overhead; light came to them, dimly, from behind the imitation windows of stained, armorial glass, and, blinding white, from the open door, whence too came the sounds of the winch, the smell of cargo and hot iron, the patter of bare feet and the hoarse, scolding voice of the second officer.

William sat in a hot, soft chair, a map of Ishmaelia open upon his knees, his eyes shut, his head lolling forwards on his chest, fast asleep, dreaming about his private school, now, he noted without surprise, peopled by Negroes and governed by his grandmother. An appalling brass percussion crashed and sang an inch or two from his ear. A soft voice said, 'Lunce pliss.' The Javanese with the gong proceeded on his apocalyptic mission, leaving William hot and wet, without appetite, very sorry to be awake.

The French colonial administrator, who had been nursing his two children in the next arm-chair to William's, rose briskly. It was the first time that day they had met face to face, so they shook hands and commented on the heat. Every morning, William found, it was necessary to shake hands with all the passengers.

'And madame?'

'She suffers. You are still studying the map of Ishmaelia . . .' They turned together and descended the staircase towards the dining saloon; the functionary leading a tottering child by either hand. '. . . It is a country of no interest.'

'No.'

'It is not rich at all. If it were rich it would already belong to England. Why do you wish to take it?'

'But I do not wish to.'

'There is no oil, there is no tin, no gold, no iron – positively none,' said the functionary, growing vexed at such unreasonable rapacity. 'What do you want with it?'

'I am going as a journalist.'

'Ah, well, to the journalist every country is rich.'

They were alone at their table. The functionary arranged his napkin about his open throat, tucked the lowest corner into his cummerbund and lifted a child on to either knee. It was always thus that he sat at meals, feeding them to repletion, to surfeit, alternately, from his own plate. He wiped his glass on the tablecloth, put ice into it, and filled it with the harsh, blue-red wine that was included free in the menu. The little girl took a deep draught. 'It is excellent for their stomachs,' he explained, refilling for his son.

There were three empty places at their table. The administrator's wife, the Captain's, and the Captain's wife's. The last two were on the bridge directing the discharge of cargo. The Captain led a life of somewhat blatant domesticity; half the boat deck was given up to his quarters, where a vast brass bedstead was visible through the port-holes, and a variety of unseamanlike furniture. The Captain's wife had hedged off a little veranda for herself with pots of palm and strings of newly laundered underclothes. Here she passed the day stitching, ironing, flopping in and out of the deck-house in heelless slippers, armed with a feather brush, often emerging in a dense aura of Asiatic perfume to dine in the saloon; a tiny, hairless dog capered about her feet. But in port she was always at her husband's side, exchanging civilities with the company's agents and the quarantine inspectors, and arranging, in a small way, for the transfer of contraband.

'Even supposing there is oil in Ishmaelia,' said the administrator, resuming the conversation which had occupied him ever since, on the first night of the voyage, William had disclosed his destination, 'how are you going to get it out?'

'But I have no interest in commerce. I am going to report the war.'

'War is all commerce.'

William's command of French, just adequate, inaccurately, for the exchange of general information and the bare courtesies of daily intercourse, was not strong enough for sustained argument, so now, as at every meal, he left the Frenchman victorious, saying '*Peut-être*,' with what he hoped was Gallic scepticism, and turning his attention to the dish beside him.

It was a great, white fish, cold and garnished; the children had rejected it with cries of distress; it lay on a charger of imitation silver; the two brown thumbs of the coloured steward lay just within the circle of mayonnaise; lozenges and roundels of coloured vegetable spread symmetrically about its glazed back. William looked sadly at this fish. 'It is very dangerous,' said the administrator. 'In the tropics one easily contracts disease of the skin...'

... Far away the trout were lying among the cool pebbles, nose upstream, meditative, hesitant, in the waters of his home; the barbed fly, unnaturally brilliant overhead; they were lying, blue-brown, scarred by the grill, with white-bead eyes, in chaste silver dishes. 'Fresh green of the river bank; faded terra-cotta of the dining-room wallpaper, colours of distant Canaan, of deserted Eden,' thought William – 'are they still there? Shall I ever revisit those familiar places...?'

... '*Il faut manger, il faut vivre*,' said the Frenchman, '*qu'est-ce qu'il y a comme viande?*'

And at that moment, suddenly, miasmically, in the fiery wilderness, there came an apparition.

A voice said in English, 'Anyone mind if I park myself here?' and a stranger stood at the table, as though conjured there by William's unexpressed wish; as though conjured, indeed, by a djinn who had imperfectly understood his instructions.

The new-comer was British but, at first sight, unprepossessing. His suit of striped flannel had always, as its tailor proudly remarked, fitted snugly at the waist. The sleeves had been modishly narrow. Now in the midday heat it had resolved into an alternation of wrinkles and damp adherent patches; steaming visibly. The double-breasted waistcoat was unbuttoned and revealed shirt and braces.

'Not dressed for this climate,' remarked the young man, superfluously. 'Left in a hurry.'

He sat down heavily in the chair next to William's and ran his napkin round the back of his collar. 'Phew. What does one drink on this boat?'

The Frenchman, who had regarded him with resentment from the moment of his appearance, now leant forward and spoke, acidly.

The hot man smiled in an encouraging way and turned to William.

'What's old paterfamilias saying?'

William translated literally. 'He says that you have taken the chair of the Captain's lady.'

'Too bad. What's she like? Any good?'

'Bulky,' said William.

'There was a whopper upstairs with the Captain. What I call the Continental Figure. Would that be her?'

'Yes.'

'Definitely no good, old boy. Not for Corker anyway.'

The Frenchman leaned towards William.

'This is the Captain's table. Your friend must not come here except by invitation.'

'I do not know him,' said William. 'It is his business.'

'The Captain should present him to us. This is a reserved place.'

'Hope I'm not butting in,' said the Englishman.

The steward offered him the fish; he examined its still unbroken ornaments and helped himself. 'If you ask me,' he said cheerfully, his mouth full, 'I'd say it was a spot off colour, but I never do care much for French cooking. Hi, you, Alphonse, comprenez pint of bitter?'

The steward gaped at him, then at the fish, then at him again. 'No like?' he said at last.

'No like one little bit, but that's not the question under discussion. Me like a big tankard of Bass, Worthington, whatever you got. Look, comme ça,' – he made the motions of drinking – 'I say, what's the French for bitter?'

William tried to help.

The steward beamed and nodded.

'Whisky-soda?'

'All right, Alphonse, you win. Whisky-soda it shall be. Beaucoup whisky, beaucoup soda, tout-de-suite. The truth is,' he continued, turning to William, 'my French is a bit rusty. You're Boot of *The Beast*, aren't you? Thought I might run into you. I'm Corker of the U.N. Just got on board with an hour to spare. Think of it; I was in Fleet Street on Tuesday; got my marching orders at ten o'clock, caught the plane to Cairo, all night in a car and here I am, all present and, I hope, correct. God, I can't think how you fellows can eat this fish.'

'We can't,' said William.

'Found it a bit high?'

'Exactly.'

'That's what I thought,' said Corker, 'the moment I saw it. Here, Alphonse, mauvais poisson – parfume formidable – prenez – et portex vite le whisky, you black bum.'

The Frenchman continued to feed his children. It is difficult for a man nursing two children, aged five and two and clumsy eaters at that, to look supercilious, but the Frenchman tried and Corker noticed it.

'Does the little mother understand English?' he asked William.

'No.'

'That's lucky. Not a very matey bird?'

'No.'

'Fond of la belle France?'

'Well, I can't say I've ever been there – except to catch this ship.'

'Funny thing, neither have I. Never been out of England except once, when I went to Ostend to cover a chess congress. Ever play chess?'

'No.'

'Nor do I. God, that was a cold story.' The steward placed on the table a syphon and a bottle of whisky which carried the label '*Edouard VIII: Very old Genuine Scotch Whisky: André Bloc et Cie, Saigon,*' and the coloured picture of a Regency buck, gazing sceptically at the consumer through a quizzing glass.

'Alphonse,' said Corker, 'I'm surprised at you.'

'No like?'

'Bloody well no like.'

'Whisky-soda,' the man explained, patiently, almost tenderly, as though in the nursery. 'Nice.'

Corker filled his glass, tasted, grimaced, and then resumed the interrupted inquiry. 'Tell me honestly, had you ever heard of Ishmaelia before you were sent on this story?'

'Only very vaguely.'

'So had I. And the place I'd heard of was something quite different in the Suez Canal. You know, when I first started in journalism I used to think that foreign correspondents spoke every language under the sun and spent their lives studying international conditions. Brother, look at us! On Monday afternoon I was in East Sheen breaking the news to a widow of her husband's death leap with a champion girl cyclist – the wrong widow as it turned out; the husband came back from business while I was there and cut up very nasty. Next day the Chief has me in and says, "Corker, you're off to Ishmaelia." "Out of town job?" I asked. "East Africa," he said, just like that, "pack your traps." "What's the story?" I asked. "Well," he said, "a lot of niggers are having a war. I don't see anything in it myself, but the other agencies are sending feature men, so we've got to do something. We want spot news," he said, "and some colour stories. Go easy on the expenses." "What are they having a war about?" I asked. "That's for you to find out," he said, but I haven't found out yet. Have you?'

'No.'

'Well, I don't suppose it matters. Personally I can't see that foreign stories are ever news – not *real* news of the kind U.N. covers.'

'Forgive me,' said William, 'I'm afraid I know very little about journalism. What is U.N.?'

'No kidding?'

'No,' said William, 'no kidding.'

'Never heard of Universal News?'

'I'm afraid not.'

'Well, I won't say we're the biggest news agency in the country – some of the stuffier papers won't take us – but we certainly are the hottest.'

'And what, please,' asked William, 'is a news agency?' Corker told him.

'You mean that everything that you write goes to *The Beast*?'

'Well, that's rather a sore point, brother. We've been having a row with you lately. Something about a libel action one of our boys let you in for. But you take the other agencies, of course, and I daresay you'll patch it up with us. They're featuring me as a special service.'

'Then why do they want to send me?'

'All the papers are sending specials.'

'And all the papers have reports from three or four agencies?'

'Yes.'

'But if we all send the same thing it seems a waste.'

'There would soon be a row if we did.'

'But isn't it very confusing if we all send different news?'

'It gives them a choice. They all have different policies, so of course, they have to give different news.'

They went up to the lounge and drank their coffee together.

The winches were silent; the hatches covered. The agents were making their ceremonious farewells to the Captain's wife. Corker sprawled back in his plush chair and lit a large cheroot.

'Given me by a native I bought some stuff off,' he explained. 'You buying much stuff?'

'Stuff?'

'Oriental stuff – you know, curios.'

'No,' said William.

'I'm a collector – in a small way,' said Corker. 'That's one of the reasons why I was glad to be sent on this story. Ought to be able to pick up some pretty useful things out East. But it's going to be a tough assignment from all I hear. Cut-throat competition. That's where I envy you – working for a paper. You only have to worry about getting your story in time for the first edition. We have to race each other all day.'

'But the papers can't use your reports any earlier than ours.'

'No, but they use the one that comes in first.'

'But if it's exactly the same as the one that came in second and third and fourth and they are all in time for the same edition . . . ?'

Corker looked at him sadly. 'You know, you've got a lot to learn about journalism. Look at it this way. News is what a chap who doesn't care much about anything wants to read. And it's only news until he's read it. After that it's dead. We're paid to supply news. If someone else has sent a story before us, our story isn't news. Of course there's colour. Colour is just a lot of bull's-eyes about nothing. It's easy to write and easy to read, but it costs too much in cabling, so we have to go slow on that. See?'

'I think so.'

That afternoon Corker told William a great deal about the craft of journalism. The *Francmaçon* weighed anchor, swung about, and steamed into the ochre hills, through the straits and out into the open sea while Corker recounted the heroic legends of Fleet Street; he told of the classic scoops and hoaxes; of the confessions wrung from hysterical suspects; of the innuendo and intricate misrepresentations, the luscious, detailed inventions that composed contemporary history; of the positive, daring lies that got a chap a rise of screw; how Wenlock Jakes, highest paid journalist of the United States, scooped the world with an eye-witness story of the sinking of the *Lusitania* four hours before she was hit; how Hitchcock, the English Jakes, straddling over his desk in London, had chronicled day by day the horrors of the Messina earthquake; how Corker himself, not three months back, had had the rare good fortune to encounter a knight's widow trapped by the foot between lift and landing. 'It was through that story I got sent here,' said Corker. 'The boss promised me the first big chance that turned up. I little thought it would be this.'

Many of Corker's anecdotes dealt with the fabulous Wenlock Jakes. ' . . . syndicated all over America. Gets a thousand dollars a week. When he turns up in a place you can bet your life that as long as he's there it'll be the news centre of the world.

'Why, once Jakes went out to cover a revolution in one of the Balkan capitals. He overslept in his carriage, woke up at the wrong station, didn't know any different, got out, went straight to an hotel, and cabled off a thousand-word story about barricades in the streets, flaming churches, machine-guns answering the rattle of his typewriter as he wrote, a dead child, like a broken doll, spreadeagled in the deserted roadway below his window – *you* know.

'Well, they were pretty surprised at his office, getting a story like that from the wrong country, but they trusted Jakes and splashed it in six national newspapers. That day every special in Europe got orders to rush to the new revolution. They arrived in shoals. Everything seemed quiet enough, but it was as much as their jobs were worth to say so, with Jakes filing a thousand words of blood and thunder a day. So they chimed in too. Government stocks dropped, financial panic, state of emergency declared, army mobilized, famine, mutiny and in less than a week there *was* an honest to God revolution under way, just as Jakes had said. There's the power of the press for you.

'They gave Jakes the Nobel Peace Prize for his harrowing descriptions of the carnage – but that was colour stuff.'

Towards the conclusion of this discourse – William took little part beyond an occasional expression of wonder – Corker began to wriggle his shoulders restlessly, to dive his hand into his bosom and scratch his chest, to roll up his sleeve and gaze fixedly at a forearm which was rapidly becoming mottled and inflamed.

It was the fish.

2

For two days Corker's nettle-rash grew worse, then it began to subside.

William used often to see him at his open door; he sat bare to the waist, in his pyjama trousers, typing long, informative letters to his wife and dabbing himself with vinegar and water as prescribed

by the ship's doctor; often his disfigured face would appear over
the gallery of the dining saloon calling petulantly for Vichy
water.

'He suffers,' remarked the functionary with great complacency.

Not until they were nearing Aden did the rash cool a little and
allow of Corker coming down to dinner. When he did so William
hastened to consult him about a radiogram which had arrived that
morning and was causing him grave bewilderment. It read:

OPPOSITION SPLASHING FRONTWARD SPEEDILIEST STOP
ADEN REPORTED PREPARED WARWISE FLASH FACTS BEAST.

'I can't understand it,' said William.

'No?'

'The only thing that makes any sense is Stop Aden.'

'Yes?' Corker's face, still brightly patterned, was, metaphorically,
a blank.

'What d'you think I'd better do?'

'Just what they tell you, old boy.'

'Yes, I suppose I'd better.'

'Far better.'

But William was not happy about it. 'It doesn't make any sense,
read it how you will. I wonder if the operator has made a muddle
somewhere,' he said at last.

'I should ask him,' said Corker, scratching. 'And now if you don't
mind I must get back to the vinegar bottle.'

There had been something distinctly unmatey about his manner,
William thought. Perhaps it was the itch.

3

Early next morning they arrived off Steamer Point. The stewards,
in a frenzy of last-minute avarice, sought to atone for ten days'
neglect with a multitude of unneeded services. The luggage was
appearing on deck. The companion ladder was down, awaiting the
arrival of the official launch. William leant on the taffrail gazing at
the bare heap of clinker half a mile distant. It did not seem an
inviting place for a long visit. There seemed no frontward splashing
to oppose. The sea was dead calm and the ship's refuse lay all

round it – a bank-holiday litter of horrible scraps – motionless, undisturbed except for an Arab row-boat peddling elephants of synthetic ivory. At William's side Corker bargained raucously for the largest of these toys.

Presently the boy from the wireless room brought him a message. 'Something about you,' he said, and passed it on to William.

It said: CO-OPERATING BEAST AVOID DUPLICATION BOOT UNNATURAL.

'What does that mean?'

'It means our bosses have been getting together in London. You're taking our special service on this Ishmaelia story. So you and I can work together after all.'

'And what is unnatural?'

'That's our telegraphic name.' Corker completed his purchase, haggled over the exchange from francs to rupees, was handsomely cheated, and drew up his elephant on a string. Then he said casually, 'By the by, have you still got that cable you had last night?'

William showed it to him.

'Shall I tell you what this says? "Opposition splashing" means that the rival papers are giving a lot of space to this story. "Front-ward speediliest" – go to the front as fast as you can – full stop – Aden is reported here to be prepared on a war-time footing – "Flash Facts" – send them the details of this preparation at once.'

'Good heavens!' said William. 'Thank you. What an extraordinary thing . . . It wouldn't have done at all if I'd stayed on at Aden, would it?'

'No, old boy, not at all.'

'But why didn't you tell me this last night?'

'Old boy, have some sense. Last night we were competing. It was a great chance, leaving you behind. Then the *Beast* would have had to take U.N. Laugh? I should have bust my pants. However, they've fixed things up without that. Glad to have you with me on the trip, old boy. And while you're working with me, don't go showing service messages to anybody else, see?'

Happily nursing his bakelite elephant Corker sauntered back to his cabin.

Passport officers came on board and sat in judgement in the first-class smoking room. The passengers who were to disembark assembled to wait their turn. William and Corker passed without difficulty. They elbowed their way to the door, through the little knot of many-coloured, many-tongued people who had emerged from the depths of the ship. Among them was a plump, dapper figure redolent of hair-wash and shaving soap and expensive scent; there was a glint of jewellery in the shadows, a sparkle of reflected sunlight on the hairless, conical scalp; it was William's dining companion from the Blue Train. They greeted one another warmly.

'I never saw you on board,' said William.

'Nor I you. I wish I had known you were with us. I would have asked you to dine with me in my little suite. I always maintain a certain privacy on the sea. One so easily forms acquaintances which become tedious later.'

'This is a long way from Antibes. What's brought you here?'

'Warmth,' said the little man simply. 'The call of the sun.'

There was a pause and, apparently, some uncertainty at the official table behind them.

'How d'you suppose this bloke pronounces his name?' asked the first passport officer.

'Search me,' said the second.

'Where's the man with the Costa-Rican passport?' said the first passport officer, addressing the room loudly.

A Hindu who had no passport tried to claim it, was detected and held for further inquiry.

'Where's the Costa-Rican?' said the officer again.

'Forgive me,' said William's friend, 'I have a little business to transact with these gentlemen,' and, accompanied by his valet, he stepped towards the table.

'Who's the pansy?' asked Corker.

'Believe it or not,' William replied, 'I haven't the faintest idea.'

His business seemed to take a long time. He was not at the gangway when the passengers disembarked, but as they chugged slowly to shore in the crowded tender a speed-boat shot past them in a glitter of sunlit spray, bouncing on the face of the sea and

swamping their bulwarks in its wash. In it sat Cuthbert the valet, and
his enigmatic master.

4

There were two nights to wait in Aden for the little ship which was
to take them to Africa. William and Corker saw the stuffed mermaid and the wells of Solomon. Corker bought some Japanese
shawls and a set of Benares trays; he had already acquired a
number of cigarette boxes, an amber necklace, and a model of
Tutankhamen's sarcophagus during his few hours in Cairo; his
bedroom at the hotel was an emporium of Oriental Art. 'There's
something about the East always gets me,' he said. 'The missus
won't know the old home when I've finished with it.'

These were his recreations. In his serious hours he attempted to
interview the Resident, and was rebuffed; tried the captain of a
British sloop which was coaling for a cruise in the Persian Gulf;
was again rebuffed; and finally spent two hours in conference with
an Arab guide who for twenty rupees supplied material for a detailed
cable about the defences of the settlement. 'No use our both
covering it,' he said to William. 'Your story had better be British
unpreparedness. If it suits them, they'll be able to work that up into
something at the office. You know – "Aden the focal point of British
security in the threatened area still sunk in bureaucratic lethargy" –
that kind of thing.'

'Good heavens! how can I say that?'

'That's easy, old boy. Just cable ADEN UNWARWISE.'

On the third morning they sailed for the little Italian port from
which the railway led into the mountains of independent Ishmaelia.

5

In London it was the night of the Duchess of Stayle's ball. John
Boot went there because he was confident of finding Mrs Stitch. It
was the kind of party she liked. For half an hour he hunted her
among the columns and arches. On all sides stood dignified and
vivacious groups of the older generation. Elderly princesses sat in

little pools of deportment, while the younger generation loped between buffet and ballroom in subdued and self-conscious couples. Dancing was not an important part of the entertainment; the Duchess's daughters were all admirably married; at eleven o'clock the supper room was full of elderly, hearty eaters.

John Boot sought Mrs Stitch high and low; soon it would be too late, for she invariably went home at one; she was indeed just speaking of going when he finally ran her to earth in the Duke's dressing-room, sitting on a bed, eating *foie-gras* with an ivory shoe-horn. Three elderly admirers glared at him.

'John,' she said, 'how *very* peculiar to see you. I thought you were at the war.'

'Well, Julia, I'm afraid we must go,' said the three old boys.

'Wait for me downstairs,' said Mrs Stitch.

'You won't forget the Opera on Friday?' said one.

'I hope Josephine will like the jade horse,' said another.

'You *will* be at Alice's on Sunday?' said the third.

When they had gone, Mrs Stitch said: 'I must go too. Just tell me in three words what happened. The last thing I heard was from Lord Copper. He telephoned to say you had left.'

'Not a word from him. It's been very awkward.'

'The American girl?'

'Yes, exactly. We said good-bye a fortnight ago. She gave me a lucky pig to wear round my neck – it was made of bog-oak from Tipperary. We were both very genuinely affected. Since then I haven't dared go out or answer the telephone. I only came here because I knew she wouldn't be coming.'

'Poor John. I wonder what went wrong . . . I like the bit about the pig *very* much.'

BOOK II

STONES £20

CHAPTER 1

I

ISHMAELIA, THAT HITHERTO happy commonwealth, cannot conveniently be approached from any part of the world. It lies in the North-Easterly quarter of Africa, giving colour by its position and shape to the metaphor often used of it – 'the Heart of the Dark Continent'. Desert, forest, and swamp, frequented by furious nomads, protect its approaches from those more favoured regions which the statesmen of Berlin and Geneva have put to school under European masters. An inhospitable race of squireens cultivate the highlands and pass their days in the perfect leisure which those peoples alone enjoy who are untroubled by the speculative or artistic itch.

Various courageous Europeans, in the seventies of the last century, came to Ishmaelia, or near it, furnished with suitable equipment of cuckoo clocks, phonographs, opera hats, draft-treaties and flags of the nations which they had been obliged to leave. They came as missionaries, ambassadors, tradesmen, prospectors, natural scientists. None returned. They were eaten, every one of them; some raw, others stewed and seasoned – according to local usage and the calendar (for the better sort of Ishmaelites have been Christian for many centuries and will not publicly eat human flesh, uncooked, in Lent, without special and costly dispensation from their bishop). Punitive expeditions suffered more harm than they inflicted, and in the nineties humane counsels prevailed. The European powers independently decided that they did not want that profitless piece of territory; that the one thing less desirable than seeing a neighbour established there was the trouble of taking it themselves. Accordingly, by general consent, it was ruled off the maps and its immunity guaranteed. As there was no form of government common to the peoples thus segregated, nor tie of language, history, habit, or belief, they were called a Republic. A committee of jurists, drawn from the Universities, composed a constitution, providing a bicameral legislature, proportional representation by means of the single transferable vote, an executive removable by the President on the recommendation of both houses, an independent judicature, religious liberty, secular education, *habeas corpus*, free trade, joint stock banking, chartered corporations, and numerous other agreeable features. A pious old darky named Mr Samuel Smiles Jackson from Alabama was put in as the first President; a choice whose wisdom seemed to be confirmed by history, for, forty years later, a Mr Rathbone Jackson held his grandfather's office in succession to his father Pankhurst, while the chief posts of the state were held by Messrs Garnett Jackson, Mander Jackson, Huxley Jackson, his uncle and brothers, and by Mrs Athol (*née* Jackson) his aunt. So strong was the love which the Republic bore the family that General Elections were known as 'Jackson Ngomas' wherever and whenever they were held. These, by the constitution, should have been quinquennial, but since it was found in practice that difficulty of communication rendered it impossible for the constituencies to vote simultaneously, the custom had grown up for the receiving officer and the Jackson candidate to visit in turn such parts of the Republic as were open to travel, and entertain the neighbouring chiefs to a six days' banquet at their camp, after which the stupefied aborigines recorded their votes in the secret and solemn manner prescribed by the constitution.

It had been found expedient to merge the functions of national defence and inland revenue in an office then held in the capable hands of General Gollancz Jackson; his forces were in two main companies, the Ishmaelite Mule Taxgathering Force and the Rifle Excisemen with a small Artillery Death Duties Corps for use against the heirs of powerful noblemen; it was their job to raise the funds whose enlightened expenditure did so much to enhance President Jackson's prestige among the rare foreign visitors to his capital. Towards the end of each financial year the General's flying columns would lumber out into the surrounding country on the heels of the fugitive population and returned in time for budget day laden with the spoils of the less nimble; coffee and hides, silver coinage, slaves, livestock, and firearms would be assembled and assessed in the Government warehouses; salaries would be paid, and cover in kind deposited at the bank for the national overdraft, and donations made, in the presence of the diplomatic corps, to the Jackson Non-sectarian Co-educational Technical Schools and other humane institutions. On the foundation of the League of Nations, Ishmaelia became a member.

Under this liberal and progressive régime, the Republic may be said, in some way, to have prospered. It is true that the capital city of Jacksonburg became unduly large, its alleys and cabins thronged with landless men of native and alien blood, while the country immediately surrounding it became depopulated, so that General Gollancz Jackson was obliged to start earlier and march further in search of the taxes; but on the main street there were agencies for many leading American and European firms; there was, moreover, a railway to the Red Sea coast, bringing a steady stream of manufactured imports which relieved the Ishmaelites of the need to practise their few clumsy crafts, while the adverse trade balance was rectified by an elastic system of bankruptcy law. In the remote provinces, beyond the reach of General Gollancz, the Ishmaelites followed their traditional callings of bandit, slave, or gentleman of leisure, happily ignorant of their connexion with the town of which a few of them, perhaps, had vaguely and incredulously heard.

Occasional travelling politicians came to Jacksonburg, were entertained and conducted round the town, and returned with friendly reports. Big game hunters on safari from the neighbouring dominions sometimes strayed into the hinterland, and if they returned at all dined out for years to come on the experience. Until a few months before William Boot's departure no one in Europe knew of the deep currents that were flowing in Ishmaelite politics; nor did many people know of them in Ishmaelia.

It began during Christmas week with a domestic row in the Jackson family. By Easter the city, so lately a model of internal amity, was threatened by civil war.

A Mr Smiles Soum was reputed to lead the Fascists. He was only one-quarter Jackson (being grandson in the female line of President Samuel Smiles Jackson), and three-quarters pure Ishmaelite. He was thus by right of cousinship admitted to the public pay-roll, but he ranked low in the family and had been given no more lucrative post than that of Assistant Director of Public Morals.

Quarrels among the ruling family were not unusual, particularly in the aftermath of weddings, funerals, and other occasions of corporate festivity, and were normally settled by a readjustment of public offices. It was common knowledge in the bazaars and drink-shops that Mr Smiles was not satisfied with his post at the Ministry of Public Morals, but it was a breach of precedent and, some thought, the portent of a new era in Ishmaelite politics, when he followed up his tiff by disappearing from Jacksonburg and issuing a manifesto, which, it was thought by those who knew him best, he could not conceivably have composed himself.

The White Shirt movement which he called into being had little in common with the best traditions of Ishmaelite politics. Briefly his thesis was this: the Jacksons were effete, tyrannical, and alien; the Ishmaelites were a white race who, led by Smiles, must purge themselves of the Negro taint; the Jacksons had kept Ishmaelia out of the Great War and thus deprived her of the fruits of victory; the Jacksons had committed Ishmaelia to the control of international Negro finance and secret subversive Negro Bolshevism, by joining the League of Nations; they were responsible for the various en-demic and epidemic diseases that ravaged crops, livestock, and human beings; all Ishmaelites who were suffering the consequences of imprudence or ill-fortune in their financial or matrimonial affairs were the victims of international Jacksonism; Smiles was their Leader.

The Jacksons rose above it. Life in Ishmaelia went on as before and the Armenian merchant in Main Street who had laid in a big consignment of white cotton shirtings found himself with the stuff on his hands. In Moscow, Harlem, Bloomsbury, and Liberia, however, keener passions were aroused. In a hundred progressive weeklies and Left Study Circles the matter was taken up and the cause of the Jacksons restated in ideological form.

Smiles represented international finance, the subjugation of the
worker, sacerdotalism; Ishmaelia was black, the Jacksons were
black, collective security and democracy and the dictatorship of
the proletariat were black. Most of this was unfamiliar stuff to the
Jacksons, but tangible advantages followed. A subscription list was
opened in London and received support in chapels and universities;
wide publicity was given to the receipt in Ishmaelia of three unused
penny stamps addressed to the President by 'A little worker's daughter in Bedford Square'.

In the chief cities of Europe a crop of 'patriot consulates' sprang
up devoted to counter-propaganda.

Newspaper men flocked to Jacksonburg. It was the wet season
when business was usually at a standstill; everything boomed this
year. At the end of August the rains would stop. Then, everybody
outside Ishmaelia agreed, there would be a war. But, with the happy
disposition of their race, the Ishmaelites settled down to exploit and
enjoy their temporary good fortune.

2

The Hotel Liberty, Jacksonburg, was folded in the peace of Saturday afternoon, soon to be broken by the arrival of the weekly train
from the coast but, at the moment, at four o'clock, serene and all-
embracing. The wireless station was shut and the fifteen journalists
were at rest. Mrs Earl Russell Jackson padded in stockinged feet
across the bare boards of the lounge looking for a sizeable cigar-
end, found one, screwed it into her pipe, and settled down in the
office rocking-chair to read her Bible. Outside – and, in one or two
places, inside – the rain fell in torrents. It rang on the iron roof in a
continuous, restful monotone; it swirled and gurgled in the channels it had cut in the terrace outside; it seeped under the front door
in an opaque pool. Mrs Earl Russell Jackson puffed at her pipe,
licked her thumb, and turned a page of the good book. It was very
pleasant when all those noisy white men were shut away in their
rooms; quite like old times; they brought in good money, these
journalists – heavens, what she was charging them! – but they were
a great deal of trouble; brought in a nasty kind of customer too –

Hindus, Ishmaelites from up country, poor whites and near-whites from the town, police officers, the off-scourings of the commercial cafés and domino saloons, interpreters and informers and guides, not the kind of person Mrs Earl Russell Jackson liked to see about her hotel. What with washing and drinking and telephoning and driving about in the mud in taxi-cabs and developing films and cross-questioning her old and respectable patrons, there never seemed a moment's peace.

Even now they were not all idle; in their austere trade they had forfeited the arts of leisure.

Upstairs in his room, Mr Wenlock Jakes was spending the afternoon at work on his forthcoming book *Under the Ermine*. It was to be a survey of the undercurrents of English political and social life. '*I shall never forget*,' he typed, '*the evening of King Edward's abdication. I was dining at the Savoy Grill as the guest of Silas Shock of the* New York Guardian. *His guests were well chosen, six of the most influential men and women in England; men and women such as only exist in England, who are seldom in the news but who control the strings of the national purse. On my left was Mrs Tiffin, the wife of the famous publisher; on the other side was Prudence Blank, who has been described to me as "the Mary Selena Wilmark of Britain"; opposite was John Titmuss whose desk at the* News Chronicle *holds more secrets of state than any ambassador's . . . big business was represented by John Nought, agent of the Credential Assurance Co. . . . I at once raised the question of the hour. Not one of that brilliant company expressed any opinion. There, in a nutshell, you have* England, *her greatness – and her littleness.*'

Jakes was to be paid an advance of 20,000 dollars for this book.

In the next room were four furious Frenchmen. They were dressed as though for the cinema camera in breeches, open shirts, and brand new chocolate-coloured riding boots cross-laced from top to bottom; each carried a bandolier of cartridges round his waist and a revolver-holster on his hip. Three were seated, the fourth strode before them, jingling his spurs as he turned and stamped on the bare boards. They were composing a memorandum of their wrongs.

We the undersigned members of the French Press in Ishmaelia, they had written, *protest categorically and in the most emphatic manner against the partiality shown against us by the Ishmaelite Press Bureau and at the discourteous lack of co-operation of our so-called colleagues . . .*

In the next room, round a little table, sat Shumble, Whelper, Pigge, and a gigantic, bemused Swede. Shumble and Whelper and Pigge were special correspondents; the Swede was resident correspondent to a syndicate of Scandinavian papers – and more; he was Swedish Vice-Consul, head surgeon at the Swedish Mission Hospital, and proprietor of the combined Tea, Bible, and Chemist shop which was the centre of European life in Jacksonburg; a pre-crisis resident of high standing. All the journalists tried to make friends with him; all succeeded; but they found him disappointing as a news source.

These four were playing cards.

'I will go four no hearts,' said Erik Olafsen.

'You can't do that.'

'Why cannot I do that? I have no hearts.'

'But we explained just now . . .'

'Will you please be so kind and explain another time?'

They explained; the cards were thrown in and the patient Swede collected them in his enormous hand. Shumble began to deal.

'Where's Hitchcock today?' he asked.

'He's on to something. I tried his door. It was locked.'

'His shutters have been up all day.'

'I looked through the keyhole,' said Shumble. 'You bet he's on to something.'

'D'you think he's found the Fascist headquarters?'

'Wouldn't put it past him. Whenever that man disappears you can be sure that a big story is going to break.'

'If you please, what is Hitchcock?' asked the Swede.

Mr Pappenhacker of *The Twopence* was playing with a toy train – a relic of College at Winchester, with which he invariably travelled. In his youth he had delighted to address it in Latin alcaics and to derive

Greek names for each part of the mechanism. Now it acted as a sedative to his restless mind.

The Twopence did not encourage habits of expensive cabling. That day he had composed a long 'turnover' on Ishmaelite conditions and posted it in the confidence that, long before it arrived at London, conditions would be unrecognizable.

Six other journalists of six nationalities were spending their day of leisure in this hotel. Time lay heavily on them. The mail train was due some time that evening to relieve their tedium.

Fifty yards distant in the annexe, secluded from the main block of the hotel by a water-logged garden, lay Sir Jocelyn Hitchcock, fast asleep. The room was in half-darkness; door and windows were barred. On the table, before his typewriter, stood a primus stove. There was a small heap of tins and bottles in the corner. On the walls hung the official, wildly deceptive map of Ishmaelia; a little flag in the centre of Jacksonburg marked Hitchcock's present position. He slept gently; his lips under the fine, white moustache curved in a barely perceptible smile of satisfaction. For reasons of his own he was in retirement.

3

And the granite sky wept.

In the rainy season it was impossible to say, within twelve hours or so, the time of the train's arrival. Today it had made a good journey. It was still light when the telephone rang in Mrs Jackson's office to tell her that it had left the last station and would soon be there. Instantly the Hotel Liberty came to life. The hall-boy donned his peaked cap and set out with Mrs Jackson to look for clients. Shumble, Whelper, and Pigge left their game and put on their mackintoshes; the Frenchmen struggled into Spahi capes. The six other journalists emerged from their rooms and began shouting for taxis. Paleologue, Jakes' jackal, reported for duty and was dispatched to observe arrivals. The greater and more forbidding part of the population of Jacksonburg was assembled on the platform to greet William's arrival.

He and Corker had had a journey of constant annoyance. For three days they had been crawling up from the fierce heat of the coast into the bleak and sodden highlands. There were four first-class compartments on their train; one was reserved for a Swiss ticket collector. In the remaining three, in painful proximity, sat twenty-four Europeans, ten of whom were the advance party of the Excelsior Movie-Sound News of America. The others were journalists. They had lunched, dined, and slept at the rest houses on the line. During the first day, when they were crossing the fiery coastal plain, there had been no ice; on the second night, in the bush, no mosquito nets; on the third night, in the mountains, no blankets. Only the little Swiss official enjoyed tolerable comfort. At every halt fellow employees brought him refreshment – frosted beer, steaming coffee, baskets of fruit; at the restaurants there were special dishes for him and rocking-chairs in which to digest them; there were bed-rooms with fine brass bedsteads and warm hip-baths. When Corker and his friends discovered that he was only the ticket collector they felt very badly about this.

Some time during the second day's journey the luggage van became detached from the rest of the train. Its loss was dis-covered that evening when the passengers wanted their mosquito nets.

'Here's where that little beaver can be useful,' said Corker.

He and William went to ask his help. He sat in his rocking-chair smoking a thin, mild cheroot, his hands folded over his firm little dome of stomach. They stood and told him of their troubles. He thanked them and said it was quite all right.

'Such things often happen. I always travel with all my possessions in the compartment with me.'

'I shall write to the Director of the Line about it,' said Corker.

'Yes, that is the best thing to do. It is always possible that the van will be traced.'

'I've got some very valuable curios in my luggage.'

'Unfortunate. I am afraid it is less likely to be recovered.'

'D'you know who we are?'

'Yes,' said the Swiss, with a little shudder. 'Yes, I know.'

By the end of the journey Corker had come to hate this man. And his nettle-rash was on him again. He reached Jacksonburg in a bad humour.

Shumble, Whelper, and Pigge knew Corker; they had loitered together of old on many a doorstep and forced an entry into many a stricken home. 'Thought you'd be on this train,' said Shumble. 'Your name's posted for collect facilities in the radio station. What sort of trip?'

'Lousy. How are things here?'

'Lousy. Who's with you?'

Corker told him, adding: 'Who's here already?'

Shumble told him.

'All the old bunch.'

'Yes, and there's a highbrow yid from *The Twopence* – but we don't count him.'

'No, no competition there.'

'*The Twopence* isn't what you would call a *newspaper*, is it? . . . Still, there's enough to make things busy and there's more coming. They seem to have gone crazy about this story at home. Jakes is urgenting eight hundred words a day.'

'*Jakes here?* Well, there must be something in it.'

'Who's the important little chap with the beard?' – they looked towards the customs shed through which the Swiss was being obsequiously conducted.

'You'd think he was an ambassador,' said Corker bitterly.

The black porter of the Hotel Liberty interrupted them. Corker began to describe in detail his lost elephant. Shumble disappeared in the crowd.

'Too bad, too bad,' said the porter. 'Very bad men on railway.'

'But it was registered through.'

'Maybe he'll turn up.'

'Do things often get lost on your damned awful line?'

'Most always.'

All round them the journalists were complaining about their losses. '. . . Five miles of film,' said the leader of the Excelsior Movie-Sound News. 'How am I going to get *that* through the expenses department?'

'Very bad men on railway. They like film plenty – him make good fire.'

William alone was reconciled to the disaster; his cleft sticks were behind him; it was as though, on a warm day, he had suddenly shed an enormous, fur-lined motoring-coat.

4

So far as their profession allowed them time for such soft feelings, Corker and Pigge were friends.

'...It was large and very artistic,' said Corker, describing his elephant, 'just the kind of thing Madge likes.'

Pigge listened sympathetically. The bustle was over. William and Corker had secured a room together at the Liberty; their sparse hand-luggage was unpacked and Pigge had dropped in for a drink.

'What's the situation?' asked William, when Corker had exhausted his information – though not his resentment – about the shawls and cigarette boxes.

'Lousy,' said Pigge.

'I've been told to go to the front.'

'That's what we all want to do. But in the first place there isn't any front, and in the second place we couldn't get to it if there was. You can't move outside the town without a permit, and you can't get a permit.'

'Then what are you sending?' asked Corker.

'Colour stuff,' said Pigge, with great disgust. 'Preparations in the threatened capital, soldiers of fortune, mystery men, foreign influences, volunteers...there isn't any hard news. The Fascist headquarters are up-country somewhere in the mountains. No one knows where. They're going to attack when the rain stops in about ten days. You can't get a word out of the government. They won't admit there *is* a crisis.'

'What, not with Jakes and Hitchcock here?' said Corker in wonder. 'What's this President like, anyway?'

'Lousy.'

'Where is Hitchcock, by the way?'

'That's what we all want to know.'

5

'Where's Hitchcock?' asked Jakes.

Paleologue shook his head sadly. He was finding Jakes a hard master. For over a week he had been on his pay-roll. It seemed a lifetime. But the pay was fabulous and Paleologue was a good family man; he had two wives to support and countless queer-coloured children on whom he lavished his love. Until the arrival of the newspaper men – that decisive epoch in Ishmaelite social history – he had been dragoman and interpreter at the British Legation, on wages which – though supplemented from time to time by the sale to his master's colleagues of any waste-paper he could find lying around the Chancery – barely sufficed for the necessaries of his household; occasionally he had been able to provide amusement for bachelor attachés; occasionally he sold objects of native art to the ladies of the compound. But it had been an exiguous living. Now he was getting fifty American dollars a week. It was a wage beyond the bounds of his wildest ambition...but Mr Jakes was very exacting and very peremptory.

'Who was on the train?'

'No one except the newspaper gentlemen and M. Giraud.'

'Who's he?'

'He is in the Railway. He went down to the coast with his wife last week, to see her off to Europe.'

'Yes, yes, I remember. That was the "panic-stricken refugees" story. No one else?'

'No, Mr Jakes.'

'Well, go find Hitchcock.'

'Yes, sir.'

Jakes turned his attention to his treatise. *The dominant member of the new cabinet,* he typed, *was colourful Kingsley Wood...*

6

Nobody knew exactly at what time or through what channels word went round the Hotel Liberty that Shumble had got a story. William heard it from Corker who heard it from Pigge. Pigge had guessed it from something odd in Shumble's manner during dinner – something abstracted, something of high excitement painfully restrained. He confided in Whelper, 'He's been distinctly rummy ever since he came back from the station. Have you noticed it?'

'Yes,' said Whelper. 'It sticks out a mile. If you ask me, he's got something under his hat.'

'Just what I thought,' said Pigge gloomily.

And before bedtime everyone in the hotel knew it.

The French were furious. They went in a body to their Legation. 'It is too much,' they said. 'Shumble is receiving secret information from the Government. Hitchcock, of course, is pro-British, and now, at a moment like this, when as Chairman of the Foreign Press Association he should forward our protest officially to the proper quarter, he has disappeared.'

'Gentlemen,' said the Minister. 'Gentlemen, it is Saturday night. No Ishmaelite official will be available until noon on Monday.'

'The Press Bureau is draconic, arbitrary, and venal; it is in the hands of a clique; we appeal for justice.'

'Certainly, without fail, on Monday afternoon.' . . .

'We'll stay awake in shifts,' said Whelper, 'and listen. He may talk in his sleep.'

'I suppose you've searched his papers?'

'Useless. He never takes a note.' . . .

Paleologue threw up his hands hopelessly.

'Have his boy bring you his message on the way to the wireless station.'

'Mr Shumble always take it himself.'

'Well, go find out what it is. I'm busy.' . . .

Shumble sat in the lounge radiating importance. Throughout the evening everyone in turn sat by his side, offered him whisky and casually reminded him of past acts of generosity. He held his own counsel. Even the Swede got wind of what was going and left home to visit the hotel.

'Schombol,' he said, 'I think you have some good news, no?'

'Me?' said Shumble. 'Wish I had.'

'But forgive me, please, everyone say you have some good news. Now I have to telegraph to my newspapers in Scandinavia. Will you please tell me what your news is?'

'I don't know anything, Erik.'

'What a pity. It is so long since I sent my paper any good news.'

And he mounted his motor cycle and drove sadly away into the rain.

7

At a banquet given in his honour, Sir Jocelyn Hitchcock once modestly attributed his great success in life to the habit of 'getting up earlier than the other fellow'. But this was partly metaphorical, partly false, and in any case wholly relative, for journalists are as a rule late risers. It was seldom that in England, in those night-refuges they called their homes, Shumble, Whelper, Pigge, or Corker reached the bathroom before ten o'clock. Nor did they in Jacksonburg, for there was no bath in the Hotel Liberty; but they and their fellows had all been awake since dawn.

This was due to many causes – the racing heart, nausea, dry mouth and smarting eyes, the false hangover produced by the vacuous mountain air, to the same symptoms of genuine hangover, for, with different emotions, they had been drinking deeply the evening before in the anxiety over Shumble's scoop; but more especially to the structural defects of the building. The rain came on sharp at sunrise, and every bedroom had a leak somewhere in its iron ceiling. And with the rain and the drips came the rattle of Wenlock Jakes' typewriter as he hammered away at another chapter of *Under the Ermine*. Soon the bleak passages resounded with cries of 'Boy!' 'Water!' 'Coffee!'

As early arrivals Shumble, Whelper, and Pigge might, like the Frenchmen, have had separate rooms, but they preferred to live at close quarters and watch one another's movements. The cinema men had had little choice. There were two rooms left; the Contacts and Relations Pioneer Co-ordinating Director occupied one; the rest of the outfit had the other.

'Boy!' cried Corker, standing barefoot in a dry spot at the top of the stairs. 'Boy!'

'Boy!' cried Whelper.

'Boy!' cried the Frenchmen. 'It is formidable. The types attend to no one except the Americans and the English.'

'They have been bribed. I saw Shumble giving money to one of the boys yesterday.'

'We must protest.'

'I have protested.'

'We must protest again. We must demonstrate.'

'Boy! Boy! Boy!' shouted everyone in that hotel, but nobody came.

In the annexe, Sir Jocelyn Hitchcock slipped a raincoat over his pyjamas and crept like a cat into the bushes.

8

Presently Paleologue arrived to make his morning report to his master. He met Corker at the top of the stairs. 'You got to have boy for yourself in this country,' he said.

'Yes,' said Corker. 'It seems I ought.'

'I fix him. I find you very good boy from Adventist Mission, read, write, speak English, sing hymns, everything.'

'Sounds like hell to me.'

'Please?'

'Oh, all right, it doesn't matter. Send him along.'

In this way Paleologue was able to supply servants for all the new-comers. Later the passages were clustered with moon-faced mission-taught Ishmaelites. These boys had many responsibilities. They had to report their masters' doings, morning and evening, to the secret police; they had to steal copies of their masters' cables for Wenlock Jakes. The normal wage for domestic service was a dollar a week; the journalists paid five, but Paleologue pocketed the difference. In the meantime they formulated new and ingenious requests for cash in advance – for new clothes, funerals, weddings, fines, and entirely imaginary municipal taxes: whatever they exacted, Paleologue came to know about it and levied his share.

9

Inside the bedroom it was sunless, draughty, and damp; all round there was rattling and shouting and tramping and the monotonous splash and patter and gurgle of rain. Corker's clothing lay scattered about the room. Corker sat on his bed stirring condensed milk into his tea. 'Time you were showing a leg, old boy,' he said.

'Yes.'

'If you ask me, we were all a bit tight last night.'

'Yes.'

'Feeling lousy?'

'Yes.'

'It'll soon pass off when you get on your feet. Are my things in your way?'

'Yes.'

Corker lit his pipe and a frightful stench filled the room. 'Don't think much of this tobacco,' he said. 'Home grown. I bought it off a nigger on the way up. Care to try some?'

'No, thanks,' said William, and rose queasily from his bed.

While they dressed Corker spoke in a vein of unaccustomed pessimism. 'This isn't the kind of story I'm used to,' he said. 'We aren't getting anywhere. We've got to work out a routine, make contacts, dig up some news sources, jolly up the locals a bit. I don't feel settled.'

'Is that my toothbrush you're using?'

'Hope not. Has it got a white handle?'

'Yes.'

'Then I am. Silly mistake to make; mine's green . . . but, as I was saying, we've got to make friends in this town. Funny thing, I don't get that sense of popularity I expect.' He looked at himself searchingly in the single glass. 'Suffer much from dandruff?'

'Not particularly.'

'I do. They say it comes from acidity. It's a nuisance. Gets all over one's collar, and one has to look smart in our job. Good appearance is half the battle.'

'D'you mind if I have my brushes?'

'Not a bit, old boy, just finished with them ... Between ourselves that's always been Shumble's trouble – bad appearance. But, of course, a journalist is welcome everywhere, even Shumble. That's what's so peculiar about this town. As a rule, there is one thing you can always count on in our job – popularity. There are plenty of disadvantages, I grant you, but you *are* liked and respected. Ring people up any hour of the day or night, butt into their homes uninvited, make them answer a string of damn fool questions when they want to do something else – they like it. Always a smile and the best of everything for the gentlemen of the Press. But I don't feel it here. I damn well feel the exact opposite. I ask myself, are we known, loved, and trusted? and the answer comes back, "No Corker, you are not."'

There was a knock on the door, barely audible above the general hubbub, and Pigge entered.

'Morning, chaps. Cable for Corker. It came last night. Sorry it's been opened. They gave it to me and I didn't notice the address.'

'Oh, no?' said Corker.

'Well, there's nothing in it. Shumble had that query yesterday.'

Corker read: INTERNATIONAL GENDARMERIE PROPOSED PREVENT CLASH TEST REACTIONS UNNATURAL. 'Crumbs, they must be short of news in London. What's Gendarmerie?'

'A sissy word for cops,' said Pigge.

'Well, it's a routine job. I suppose I must do something about it. Come round with me ... We may make some contacts,' he added, not very hopefully.

Mrs Earl Russell Jackson was in the lounge. 'Good morning, madam,' said Corker, 'and how are you today?'

'I aches,' said Mrs Jackson with simple dignity. 'I aches terrible all round the sit-upon. It's the damp.'

'The Press are anxious for your opinion upon a certain question, Mrs Jackson.'

'Aw, go ask somebody else. They be coming to mend that roof as quick as they can, and they can't come no quicker than that not for the Press, nor nobody.'

'See what I mean, old boy – not popular.' Then, turning again to Mrs Jackson with his most elaborate manner he said, 'Mrs Jackson, you misunderstand me. This is a matter of public importance. What do the women of Ishmaelia think of the proposal to introduce a force of international police?'

Mrs Jackson took the question badly. 'I will not stand for being called a woman in my own house,' she said. 'And I've never had the police here but once, and that was when I called them myself for to take out a customer that went lunatic and hanged himself.' And she swept wrathfully away to her office and her rocking-chair.

'Staunchly anti-interventionist,' said Corker. 'Doyen of Jacksonburg hostesses bans police project as unwarrantable interference with sanctity of Ishmaelite home ... but it's not the way I'm used to being treated.'

They went to the front door to call a taxi. Half a dozen were waiting in the courtyard; their drivers, completely enveloped in sodden blankets, dozed on the front seats. The hotel guard prodded one of them with the muzzle of his gun. The bundle stirred; a black face appeared, then a brilliant smile. The car lurched forward through the mud.

'The morning round,' said Corker. 'Where to first?'

'Why not the station to ask about the luggage?'

'Why not? *Station*,' he roared at the chauffeur. 'Understand – station? Puff-puff.'

'All right,' said the chauffeur, and drove off at breakneck speed through the rain.

'I don't believe this is the way,' said William.

They were bowling up the main street of Jacksonburg. A strip of tarmac ran down the middle; on either side were rough tracks for mules, men, cattle, and camels; beyond these the irregular outline of the commercial quarter; a bank, in shoddy concrete, a Greek provisions store in timber and tin, the Café de La Bourse, the Carnegie Library, the Ciné-Parlant, and numerous gutted sites, relics of an epidemic of arson some years back when an Insurance Company had imprudently set up shop in the city.

'I'm damn well sure it's not,' said Corker. 'Hi, you! *Station*, you black booby!'

The coon turned round in his seat and smiled. 'All right,' he said.

The car swerved off the motor road and bounced perilously among the caravans. The chauffeur turned back, shouted opprobriously at a camel driver and regained the tarmac.

Armenian liquor, Goanese tailoring, French stationery, Italian hardware, Swiss plumbing, Indian haberdashery, the statue of the first President Jackson, the statue of the second President Jackson, the American Welfare Centre, the latest and most successful innovation in Ishmaelite life – Popotakis's Ping-Pong Parlour – sped past in the rain. The mule trains plodded by, laden with rock salt and cartridges and paraffin for the villages of the interior.

'Kidnapped,' said Corker cheerfully. 'That's what's happened to us. What a story.'

But at last they came to a stop.

'This isn't the station, you baboon.'

'Yes, all right.'

They were at the Swedish Consulate, Surgery, Bible and Tea Shop. Erik Olafsen came out to greet them.

'Good morning. Please to come in.'

'We told this ape to drive us to the station.'

'Yes, it is a custom here. When they have a white man they do not understand, they always drive him to me. Then I can explain. But please to come in. We are just about to start our Sunday hymn singing.'

'Sorry, old boy. Have to wait till next Sunday. We've got work to do.'

'They say Schombol has some news.'

'Not really?'

'No, not really. I asked him ... but you can do no work here on Sunday. Everything is closed.'

So they found. They visited a dozen barred doors and returned disconsolately to luncheon. One native whom they questioned fled precipitately at the word 'police'. That was all they could learn about local reactions.

'We've got to give it up for the day,' said Corker. 'Reactions are easy, anyway. I'll just say that the government will co-operate with the democracies of the world in any measures calculated to promote peace and justice, but are confident in their ability to maintain order without foreign intervention. This is going to be a day of rest for Corker.'

Shumble kept his story under his hat and furtively filed a long message – having waited for a moment when the wireless station was empty of his colleagues.

So the rain fell and the afternoon and evening were succeeded by another night and another morning.

10

William and Corker went to the Press Bureau. Dr Benito, the director, was away, but his clerk entered their names in his ledger and gave them cards of identity. They were small orange documents, originally printed for the registration of prostitutes. The space for thumb-print was now filled with a passport photograph, and at the head the word 'journalist' substituted in neat Ishmaelite characters.

'What sort of bloke is this Benito?' Corker asked.

'Creepy,' said Pigge.

They visited their Consulate, five miles out of town in the Legation compound. Here, too, they had to register and, in addition, buy a guinea stamp. The Vice-Consul was a young man with untidy ginger hair. When he took William's passport he stared and said, 'By God, you're Beastly.'

William said, 'Moke.'

These two had known each other at their private school. Corker was nonplussed.

'What the hell are you doing here?' said the Vice-Consul.

'I'm supposed to be a journalist.'

'God, how funny. Come to dinner?'

'Yes.'

'Tonight?'

'Yes.'

'Grand.'

Outside the door Corker said, 'He might have asked me too. Just the kind of contact I can do with.'

II

At lunch-time that day Shumble's story broke.

Telegrams in Jacksonburg were delivered irregularly and rather capriciously, for none of the messengers could read. The usual method was to wait until half a dozen had accumulated and then send a messenger to hawk them about the most probable places until they were claimed. On precisely such an errand a bowed old warrior arrived in the dining-room of the Liberty and offered William and Corker a handful of envelopes. 'Righto, old boy,' said Corker, 'I'll take charge of these.' He handed the man a tip, was kissed on the knee in return, and proceeded to glance through the bag. 'One for you, one for me, one for everyone in the bunch.'

William opened his. It read: BADLY LEFT DISGUISED SOVIET AMBASSADOR RUSH FOLLOW BEAST. 'Will you please translate?'

'Bad news, old boy. Look at mine. ECHO SPLASHING SECRET ARRIVAL RED AGENT FLASH INTERVIEW UNNATURAL. Let's see some more.'

He opened six before he was caught. All dealt with the same topic. *The Twopence* said: KINDLY INVESTIGATE AUTHENTICITY ALLEGED SPECIAL SOVIET DELEGATION STOP CABLE DEFERRED RATE. Jakes' was the fullest: LONDON ECHO REPORTS RUSSIAN ENVOY ORGANIZER ARRIVED SATURDAY DISGUISED RAILWAY OFFICIAL STOP MOSCOW DENIES STOP DENY OR CONFIRM WITH DETAILS. Shumble's said: WORLD SCOOP CONGRATULATIONS CONTINUE ECHO.

'D'you see now?' said Corker.

'I think so.'

'It's that nasty bit of work with the beard. I knew he was going to give us trouble.'

'But he *is* a railway employee. I saw him in the ticket office today when I went to ask about my luggage.'

'Of course he is. But what good does that do us? Shumble's put the story across. Now we've got to find a red agent or boil.'

'Or explain the mistake.'

'Risky, old boy, and unprofessional. It's the kind of thing you can do once or twice in a real emergency, but it doesn't pay. They don't like printing denials – naturally. Shakes public confidence in the Press. Besides, it looks as if we weren't doing our job properly. It would be too easy if every time a chap got a scoop the rest of the bunch denied it. And I will hand it to Shumble, it was a pretty idea...the beard helped, of course...might have thought of it myself if I hadn't been so angry.'

Other journalists were now crowding round claiming their radiograms. Corker surrendered them reluctantly. He had not had time to open Pigge's. 'Here you are, old boy,' he said. 'I've been guarding it for you. Some of these chaps might want to see inside.'

'You don't say,' said Pigge coldly. 'Well, they're welcome.'

It was like all the rest. BOLSHEVIST MISSION REPORTED OVERTAKEN CONTROL RUSH FACTS.

The hunt was up. No one had time for luncheon that day. They were combing the town for Russians.

Wenlock Jakes alone retained his composure. He ate in peace and then summoned Paleologue. 'We're killing this story,' he said. 'Go round to the Press Bureau and have Benito issue an official *démenti* before four o'clock. See it's posted in the hotel and in the wireless station. And put it about among the boys that the story's dead.'

He spoke gravely, for he hated to kill a good story.

So the word went round.

A notice was posted in French and English at all the chief European centres of the capital.

It is categorically denied that there is any Russian diplomatic representative accredited to the Republic of Ishmaelia. Nor is there any truth in the report, spread by subversive interests, that a Russian national of any description whatever arrived in Jacksonburg last Saturday. The train was occupied exclusively by representatives of the foreign press and an employee of the Railway.

> GABRIEL BENITO
> *Minister of Foreign Affairs
> and Propaganda.*

The Press acted in unison and Shumble's scoop died at birth. William sent his first press message from Ishmaelia: ALL ROT ABOUT BOLSHEVIK HE IS ONLY TICKET COLLECTOR ASS CALLED SHUMBLE THOUGHT HIS BEARD FALSE BUT IT'S PER-FECTLY ALL RIGHT REALLY WILL CABLE AGAIN IF THERE IS ANY NEWS VERY WET HERE YOURS WILLIAM BOOT – and went out to dinner with the British Vice-Consul.

12

Jack Bannister, known at the age of ten as 'Moke', inhabited a little villa in the Legation compound. He and William dined alone at a candle-lit table. Two silent boys, in white gowns, waited on them. Bannister's pet – but far from tame – cheetah purred beside the log fire. There were snipe, lately bagged by the first secretary. They drank some sherry, and some Burgundy and some port, and, to celebrate William's arrival, a good deal more port. Then they settled themselves in easy chairs and drank brandy. They talked about school and the birds and beasts of Ishmaelia. Bannister showed his collection of skins and eggs.

They talked about Ishmaelia. 'No one knows if it's got any minerals because no one's been to see. The map's a complete joke,' Bannister explained. 'The country has never been surveyed at all; half of it's unexplored. Why, look here,' he took down a map from his shelves and opened it. 'See this place, Laku. It's marked as a town of some five thousand inhabitants, fifty miles north of Jacksonburg. Well, there never has been such a place. Laku is the Ishmaelite for "I don't know." When the boundary commission were trying to get through to the Sudan in 1898 they made a camp there and asked one of their boys the name of the hill, so as to record it in their log. He said "Laku," and they've copied it from map to map ever since. President Jackson likes the country to look important in the atlases, so when this edition was printed he had Laku marked good and large. The French once appointed a Consul to Laku when they were getting active in this part of the world.'

Finally they touched on politics.

'I can't think why all you people are coming out here,' said Bannister plaintively. 'You've no idea how it adds to my work. The Minister doesn't like it, either. The F.O. are worrying the life out of him.'

'But isn't there going to be a war?'

'Well, we usually have a bit of scrapping after the rains. There's a lot of bad men in the hills. Gollancz usually shoots up a few when he goes out after the taxes.'

'Is that all?'

'Wish we knew. There's something rather odd going on. Our information is simply that Smiles had a row with the Jacksons round about Christmas time and took to the hills. That's what everyone does out here when he gets in wrong with the Jacksons. We thought no more about it. The next thing we hear is from Europe that half a dozen bogus consulates have been set up and that Smiles has declared a Nationalist Government. Well, that doesn't make much sense. There never has been any Government in Ishmaelia outside Jacksonburg, and, as you see, everything is dead quiet here. But Smiles is certainly getting money from someone, and arms, too, I expect. What's more, we aren't very happy about the President. Six months ago he was eating out of our hand. Now he's getting quite standoffish. There's a concession to a British Company to build the new coast road. It was all settled but for the signing last November. Now the Ministry of Works is jibbing, and they say that the President is behind them. I can't say I like the look of things, and having all you journalists about doesn't make it any easier.'

'We've been busy all day with a lunatic report about a Russian agent who had come to take charge of the Government.'

'Oh!' said Bannister with sudden interest. 'They've got hold of that, have they? What was the story exactly?'

William told him.

'Yes, they've got it pretty mixed.'

'D'you mean to say there's any truth in it?'

Bannister looked diplomatic for a minute and then said, 'Well, I don't see any harm in your knowing. In fact, from what the Minister said to me today, I rather think he'd welcome a little publicity on the subject. There is a Russian here, name of Smerdya-kev, a Jew straight from Moscow. He didn't come disguised as a ticket collector, of course. He's been here some time – in fact, he came up by the same train as Hitchcock and that American chap. But he's lying low, living with Benito. We don't quite know what he's up to; whatever it is, it doesn't suit H.M.G.'s book. If you want a really interesting story I should look into him.'

It was half an hour's drive, at this season, from the Legation quarter to the centre of the town. William sat in the taxi, lurching and jolting, in a state of high excitement. In the last few days he had caught something of the professional infection of Corker and his colleagues, had shared their consternation at Hitchcock's disappear-ance, had rejoiced quietly when Shumble's scoop was killed. Now *he* had something under his hat; a tip-off straight from headquarters, news of high international importance. His might be the agency which would avert or precipitate a world war; he saw his name figuring in future history books '. . . *the Ishmaelite crisis of that year whose true significance was only realized and exposed through the resources of an English journalist, William Boot . . .*' Slightly dizzy with this prospect, as with the wine he had drunk and the appalling rigours of the drive, he arrived at the Liberty to find the lights out in the lounge and all his colleagues in bed.

He woke Corker, with difficulty.

'For Christ's sake. You're tight. Go to bed, old boy.'

'Wake up, I've got a story.'

At that electric word Corker roused himself and sat up in bed.

William told him, fully and proudly, all that he had learned at dinner. When he had finished, Corker lay back again among the crumpled pillows. 'I might have known,' he said bitterly.

'But don't you see? This really is news. And we've got the Legation behind us. The Minister wants it written up.'

Corker turned over on his side.

'That story's dead,' he remarked.

'But Shumble had it all wrong. Now we've got the truth. It may make a serious difference in Europe.'

Corker spoke again with finality. 'Now go to bed, there's a good chap. No one's going to print your story after the way it's been denied. Russian agents are off the menu, old boy. It's a bad break for Shumble, I grant you. He got on to a good thing without knowing – and the false beard was a very pretty touch. His story was better than yours all round, and we killed it. Do turn out the light.'

13

In his room in the annexe Sir Jocelyn Hitchcock covered his key-hole with stamp-paper and, circumspectly, turned on a little shaded lamp. He boiled some water and made himself a cup of cocoa; drank it; then he went to the map on the wall and took out his flag, considered for a minute, hovering uncertainly over the unscaled peaks and uncharted rivers of that dark terrain, finally decided, and pinned it firmly in the spot marked as the city of Laku. Then he extinguished his light and went happily back to bed.

CHAPTER 2

I

TUESDAY MORNING; RAIN at six; Jakes' typewriter at a quarter past; the first cry of 'Boy' soon after.

'Boy,' shouted Corker. 'Where's *my* boy?'

'Your boy in plison,' said William's boy.

'Holy smoke, what's he been up to?'

'The police were angry with them,' said William's boy.

'Well, I want some tea.'

'All right. Just now.'

The Archbishop of Canterbury who, it is well known, is behind Imperial Chemicals . . . wrote Jakes.

Shumble, Whelper, and Pigge awoke and breakfasted and dressed, but they scarcely spoke. 'Going out?' said Whelper at last.

'What d'you think?' said Shumble.

'Not sore about anything, are you?' said Pigge.

'What d'you think?' said Shumble, leaving the room.

'He's sore,' said Pigge.

'About his story,' said Whelper.

'Who wouldn't be?' said Pigge.

Sir Jocelyn made himself some cocoa and opened a tin of tongue. He counted the remaining stores and found them adequate.

Presently William and Corker set out to look for news.

'Better try the station first,' said Corker, 'just in case the luggage has turned up.'

They got a taxi.

'Station,' said Corker.

'All right,' said the driver, making off through the rain down main street.

'Oh, Christ, he's going to the Swede again.'

Sure enough, that was where they stopped.

'Good morning,' said Erik Olafsen. 'I am very delighted to see you. I am very delighted to see all my colleagues. They come so often. Almost whenever they take a taxi. Come in, please. Have you heard the news?'

'No,' said Corker.

'They are saying in the town that there was a Russian in the train on Saturday.'

'Yes, we've heard that one.'

'But it is a mistake.'

'You don't say.'

'Yes, indeed, it is a mistake. The man was a Swiss ticket collector. I know him many years. But please to come in.'

William and Corker followed their host into his office. There was a stove in the corner, and on the stove a big coffee pot; the smell of coffee filled the room. Olafsen poured out three cupfuls.

'You are comfortable at the Liberty, yes, no?'

'No,' said William and Corker simultaneously.

'I suppose not,' said Olafsen. 'Mrs Jackson is a very religious woman. She comes every Sunday to our musical evening. But I suppose you are not comfortable. Do you know my friends Shumble and Whelper and Pigge?'

'Yes.'

'They are very nice gentlemen, and very clever. They say they are not comfortable, too.'

The thought of so much discomfort seemed to overwhelm the Swede. He gazed over the heads of his guests with huge, pale eyes that seemed to see illimitable, receding vistas of discomfort, and himself a blinded and shackled Samson with his bandages and bibles and hot, strong coffee scarcely able to shift a pebble from the vast mountain which oppressed humanity. He sighed.

The bell rang over the shop-door. Olafsen leapt to his feet. 'Excuse,' he said, 'the natives steal so terribly.'

But it was not a native. William and Corker could see the new-comer from where they sat in the office. She was a white woman; a girl. A straggle of damp gold hair clung to her cheek. She wore red gum boots, shiny and wet, spattered with the mud of the streets. Her mackintosh dripped on the linoleum and she carried a half-open, dripping umbrella, held away from her side; it was short and old; when it was new it had been quite cheap. She spoke in German, bought something, and went out again into the rain.

'Who was the Garbo?' asked Corker when the Swede came back.

'She is a German lady. She has been here some time. She had a husband but I think she is alone now. He was to do some work outside the city but I do not think she knows where he is. I suppose he will not come back. She lives at the German pension with Frau Dressler. She came for some medicine.'

'Looks as though she needed it,' said Corker. 'Well, we must go to the station.'

'Yes. There is a special train this evening. Twenty more journalists are arriving.'

'Christ!'

'For me it is a great pleasure to meet so many distinguished confrères. It is a great honour to work with them.'

'Decent bloke that,' said Corker, when they again drove off. 'You know, I never feel Swedes are really foreign. More like you and me, if you see what I mean.'

2

Three hours later Corker and William sat down to luncheon. The menu did not vary at the Liberty; sardine, beef, and chicken for luncheon; soup, beef, and chicken for dinner; hard, homogeneous cubes of beef, sometimes with Worcester Sauce, sometimes with tomato ketchup; fibrous spindles of chicken with grey-green dented peas.

'Don't seem to have any relish for my food,' said Corker. 'It must be the altitude.'

Everyone was in poor spirits; it had been an empty morning; the absence of Hitchcock lay heavy as thunder over the hotel, and there was a delay of fourteen hours in transmission at the wireless station, for Wenlock Jakes had been letting himself go on the local colour.

'The beef's beastly,' said Corker. 'Tell the manageress to come here...'

At a short distance Jakes was entertaining three blacks. Everyone watched that table suspiciously and listened when they could, but he seemed to be talking mostly about himself. After a time the boy brought them chicken.

'Where's that manageress?' asked Corker.

'No come.'

'What d'you mean "no come"?'

'Manageress say only journalist him go boil himself,' said the boy more explicitly.

'What did I tell you? No respect for the Press. *Savages.*'

They left the dining-room. In the lounge, standing on one foot and leaning on his staff, was the aged warrior who delivered the telegrams. William's read:

PRESUME YOUR STEPTAKING INSURE SERVICE EVENT GENERAL UPBREAK.

'It's no good answering,' said Corker. 'They won't send till tomorrow morning. Come to think of it,' he added moodily, 'there's no point in answering anyway. Look at mine.'

CABLE FULLIER OFTENER PROMPTLIER STOP YOUR SER-VICE BADLY BEATEN ALROUND LACKING HUMAN INTEREST COLOUR DRAMA PERSONALITY HUMOUR INFORMATION ROMANCE VITALITY.

'Can't say that's not frank, can you?' said Corker. 'God rot 'em.'

That afternoon he took Shumble's place at the card table. William slept.

3

The special train got in at seven. William went to meet it; so did everyone else.

The Ishmaelite Foreign Minister was there with his suite. ('Expecting a nob,' said Corker.) The Minister wore a Derby hat and ample military cape. The station-master set a little gilt chair for him where he sat like a daguerreotype, stiffly posed, a Victorian worthy in negative, black face, white whiskers, black hands. When the camera men began to shoot, his Staff scrambled to get to the front of the picture, eclipsing their chief. It was all the same to the camera men, who were merely passing the time and had no serious hope that the portrait would be of any interest.

At length the little engine came whistling round the bend, wood sparks dancing over the funnel. It stopped and at once the second- and third-class passengers – natives and near-whites – tumbled on to the platform, greeting their relatives with tears and kisses. The station police got in among them, jostling the Levantines and whacking the natives with swagger-canes. The first-class passengers emerged more slowly; they had already acquired that expression of anxious resentment that was habitual to whites in Jackson- burg. They were all, every man-jack of them, journalists and photographers.

The distinguished visitor had not arrived. The Foreign Minister waited until the last cramped and cautious figure emerged from the first-class coach; then he exchanged civilities with the station-master and took his leave. The station police made a passage of a kind, but it was only with a struggle that he regained his car.

The porters began to unload, and take the registered baggage to the customs shed. On the head of the foremost William recognized his bundle of cleft sticks; then more of his possessions – the collaps- ible canoe, the mistletoe, the ant-proof wardrobes. There was a cry of delight from Corker, at his side. The missing van had arrived. Mysteriously it had become attached to the special train; had in fact been transposed. Somewhere, in a siding at one of the numerous stops down the line, lay the new-comers' luggage. Their distress deepened but Corker was jubilant and before dinner that evening introduced his elephant to a place of prominence in the bedroom. He also, in his good humour, introduced two photographers for whom he had an affection.

'Tight fit,' they said.

'Not at all,' said Corker. 'Delighted to have your company; aren't we, Boot?'

One of them took William's newly arrived camp bed; the other expressed a readiness to 'doss down' on the floor for the night. Everyone decided to doss down in the Liberty. Mrs Jackson recommended other lodgings available from friends of hers in the town. But, 'No,' they said. 'We've got to doss down with the bunch.'

The bunch now overflowed the hotel. There were close on fifty of them. All over the lounge and dining-room they sat and stood and leaned; some whispered to one another in what they took to be secrecy; others exchanged chaff and gin. It was their employers who paid for all this hospitality, but the conventions were decently observed – 'My round, old boy.' 'No, no, my round'... 'Have this one on me.' 'Well, the next is mine' – except by Shumble who, from habit, drank heartily, and without return wherever it was offered.

'What are you all here for?' asked Corker petulantly of a newcomer. 'What's come over them at home? What's supposed to be going on, anyway?'

'It's ideological. And we're only half of it. There's twenty more at the coast who couldn't get on the train. Weren't they sick at seeing us go? It's lousy on the coast.'

'It's lousy here.'

'Yes, I see what you mean...'

There was not much sleep that night for anyone in William's room. The photographer who was dossing down found the floor wet and draughty and, as the hours passed, increasingly hard. He turned from side to side, lay flat on his back, then on his face. At each change of position he groaned as though in agony. Every now and then he turned on the light to collect more coverings. At dawn, when the rain began to drip near his head, he was dozing uneasily, fully dressed in overcoat and tweed cap, enveloped in every available textile, including the tablecloth, the curtains, and Corker's two oriental shawls. Nor did the other photographer do much better; the camp bed seemed less stable than William had supposed when it was sold to him; perhaps it was wrongly assembled; perhaps essential

parts were still missing. Whatever the reason, it collapsed repeatedly
and roused William's apprehensions of the efficacy of his canoe.

Early next morning he rang up Bannister and, on his advice,
moved to Frau Dressler's pension. 'Bad policy, old boy,' said Corker,
'but since you're going I wonder if you'll take charge of my curios.
I don't at all like the way Shumble's been looking at them.'

4

The Pension Dressler stood in a side street and had, at first glance,
the air rather of a farm than of an hotel. Frau Dressler's pig, tethered
by one hind trotter to the jamb of the front door, roamed the yard
and disputed the kitchen scraps with the poultry. He was a prodigious beast. Frau Dressler's guests prodded him appreciatively on
their way to the dining-room, speculating on how soon he would be
ripe for killing. The milch-goat was allowed a narrower radius; those
who kept strictly to the causeway were safe, but she never reconciled
herself to this limitation and, day in, day out, essayed a series of
meteoric onslaughts on the passers-by, ending, at the end of her
rope, with a jerk which would have been death to an animal of any
other species. One day the rope would break; she knew it, and so did
Frau Dressler's guests.

There was also a gander, the possession of the night watchman,
and a three-legged dog, who barked furiously from the mouth of a
barrel and was said to have belonged to the late Herr Dressler.
Other pets came and went with Frau Dressler's guests – baboons,
gorillas, cheetahs, all inhabited the yard in varying degrees of liberty
and moved uneasily for fear of the milch-goat.

As a consequence perhaps of the vigour of the livestock, the
garden had not prospered. A little bed, edged with inverted bottles,
produced nothing except, annually, a crop of the rank, scarlet
flowers which burst out everywhere in Jacksonburg at the end of
the rains. Two sterile banana palms grew near the kitchens and
between them a bush of Indian hemp which the cook tended and
kept for his own indulgence. The night watchman, too, had a little
shrub, to whose seed-pods he attributed medical properties of a
barely credible order.

Architecturally, the Pension Dressler was a mess. There were three main buildings disposed irregularly in the acre of ground – single-storeyed, tin-roofed, constructed of timber and rubble, with wooden verandas; the two larger were divided into bedrooms; the smallest contained the dining-room, the parlour, and the mysterious, padlocked room where Frau Dressler slept. Everything of value or interest in the pension was kept in this room, and whatever was needed by anyone – money, provisions, linen, back numbers of European magazines – could be produced, on demand, from under Frau Dressler's bed. There was a hut called the bathroom, where, after due notice and the recruitment of extra labour, a tin tub could be filled with warm water and enjoyed in the half darkness among a colony of bats. There was the kitchen not far from the other buildings, a place of smoke and wrath, loud with Frau Dressler's scolding. And there were the servants' quarters – a cluster of thatched cabins, circular, windowless, emitting at all hours a cosy smell of woodsmoke and curry; the centre of a voluble round of hospitality which culminated often enough in the late evening with song and rhythmical clapping. The night watchman had his own lair where he lived morosely with two wrinkled wives. He was a tough old warrior who passed his brief waking hours in paring the soles of his feet with his dagger or buttering the bolt of his ancient rifle.

Frau Dressler's guests varied as a rule from three to a dozen in number. They were Europeans, mostly of modest means and good character. Frau Dressler had lived all her life in Africa and had a sharp nose for the unfortunate. She had drifted here from Tanganyika after the war, shedding Herr Dressler, none knew exactly where or how, on her way. There were a number of Germans in Jacksonburg employed in a humble way in the cosmopolitan commercial quarter. Frau Dressler was their centre. She allowed them to come in on Saturday evenings after the guests had dined, to play cards or chess and listen to the wireless. They drank a bottle of beer apiece; sometimes they only had coffee, but there was no place for the man who tried to get away without spending. At Christmas there was a decorated tree and a party which the German Minister attended and subsidized. The missionaries always recommended Frau Dressler to visitors in search of cheap and respectable lodgings.

She was a large shabby woman of unbounded energy. When William confronted her she was scolding a group of native peasants from the dining-room steps. The meaning of her words was hidden from William; from the peasants also; for she spoke Ishmaelite, and bad Ishmaelite at that, while they knew only a tribal patois; but the tone was unmistakable. The peasants did not mind. This was a daily occurrence. Always at dawn they appeared outside Frau Dressler's dining-room and exposed their wares – red peppers, green vegetables, eggs, poultry, and fresh local cheese. Every hour or so Frau Dressler asked them their prices and told them to be off. Always at half past eleven, when it was time for her to begin cooking the midday dinner, she made her purchases at the price which all parties had long ago decided would be the just one.

'They are thieves and impostors,' she said to William. 'I have been fifteen years in Jacksonburg and they still think they can cheat. When I first came I paid the most wicked prices – two American dollars for a lamb; ten cents a dozen for eggs. Now I know better.'

William said that he wanted a room. She received him cordially and led him across the yard. The three-legged dog barked furiously from his barrel; the milch-goat shot out at him like a cork from a popgun and, like it, was brought up short at the end of her string; the night watchman's gander hissed and ruffled his plumage. Frau Dressler picked up a loose stone and caught him square in the chest. 'They are playful,' she explained, 'particularly the goat.'

They gained the veranda, sheltered from rain and livestock. Frau Dressler threw open a door. There was luggage in the bed-room, a pair of woman's stockings across the foot of the bed, a woman's shoes against the wall. 'We have a girl here at the moment. She shall move.'

'Oh, but please . . . I don't want to turn anyone out.'

'She shall move,' repeated Frau Dressler. 'It's my best room. There is everything you want here.'

William surveyed the meagre furniture; the meagre, but still painfully superfluous ornaments. 'Yes,' he said. 'Yes, I suppose there is.'

A train of porters carried William's luggage from the Hotel Liberty. When it was all assembled, it seemed to fill the room. The men stood on the veranda waiting to be paid. William's own boy had absented himself on the first signs of packing. Frau Dressler drove them off with a few copper coins and a torrent of abuse. 'You had better give me anything of value,' she said to William, 'the natives are all villains.'

He gave her Corker's objects of art; she carried them off to her room and stored them safely under the bed. William began to unpack. Presently there was a knock outside. The door opened. William had his back to it. He was kneeling over his ant-proof chest.

'Please,' said a woman's voice. William turned round. 'Please may I have my things?'

It was the girl he had seen the day before at the Swedish mission. She wore the same mackintosh, the same splashed gumboots. She seemed to be just as wet. William jumped to his feet.

'Yes, of course, please let me help.'

'Thank you. There's not very much. But this one is heavy. It has some of my husband's things.'

She took her stockings from the end of the bed, ran her hand into one and showed him two large holes, smiled, rolled them into a ball and put them in the pocket of her raincoat. 'This is the heavy one,' she said, pointing to a worn leather bag. William attempted to lift it. It might have been full of stone. The girl opened it. It *was* full of stone. 'They are my husband's specimens,' she said. 'He wants me to be very careful of them. They are very important. But I don't think anyone could steal them. They are so heavy.'

William succeeded in dragging the bag across the floor. 'Where to?'

'I have a little room by the kitchen. It is up a ladder. It will be difficult to carry the specimens. I wanted Frau Dressler to keep them in her room but she did not want to. She said they were of no value. You see, she is not an engineer.'

'Would you like to leave them here?'

Her face brightened. 'May I? It would be very kind. That is what I hoped, but I did not know what you would be like. They said you were a journalist.'

'So I am.'

'The town is full of journalists, but I should not have thought you were one.'

'I can't think why Frau Dressler has put me in this room,' said William. 'I should be perfectly happy anywhere else. Did you want to move?'

'I must move. You see this is Frau Dressler's best room. When I came here it was with my husband. Then she gave us the best room. But now he is at work, so I must move. I do not want a big room now I am alone. But it would be very kind if you would keep our specimens.'

There was a suitcase which belonged to her. She opened it and threw in the shoes and other woman's things that lay about the room. When it was full she looked from it to the immense pile of trunks and crates and smiled. 'It is all I have,' she said. 'Not like you.'

She went over to the pile of cleft sticks. 'How do you use these?'

'They are for sending messages.'

'You're teasing me.'

'No, indeed I'm not. Lord Copper said I was to send my messages with them.'

The girl laughed. 'How funny. Have all the journalists got sticks like this?'

'Well, no; to tell you the truth I don't believe they have.'

'How funny you are.' Her laugh became a cough. She sat on the bed and coughed until her eyes were full of tears. 'Oh, dear. It is so long since I laughed and now it hurts me . . . What is in this?'

'A canoe.'

'Now I know you are teasing me.'

'Honestly, it's a canoe. At least they said it was at the shop. Look, I'll show you.'

Together they prised up the lid of the case and filled the floor with packing. At last they found a neat roll of cane and proofed canvas.

'It is a tent,' she said.

'No, a canoe. Look.'

They spread the canvas on the floor. With great difficulty they assembled the framework of jointed cane. Twice they had to stop when the girl's laughter turned to a paroxysm of coughing. At last it was finished and the little boat rose in a sea of shavings. 'It *is* a canoe,' she cried. 'Now I will believe you about those sticks. I will believe everything you tell me. Look, there are seats. Get in, quick, we must get in.'

They sat opposite one another in the boat, their knees touching. The girl laughed, clear and loud, and this time did not cough. 'But it's beautiful,' she said. 'And so *new*. I have not seen anything so new since I came to this city. Can you swim?'

'Yes.'

'So can I. I swim *very* well. So it will not matter if we are upset. Give me one of the message sticks and I will row you . . . '

'Do I intrude?' asked Corker. He was standing on the veranda outside the window, leaning into the room.

'Oh, dear,' said the girl.

She and William left the boat and stood among the shavings.

'We were just trying the canoe,' William explained.

'Yes,' said Corker. 'Whimsical. How about trying the mistletoe?'

'This is Mr Corker, a fellow journalist.'

'Yes, yes. I see he is. I must go away now.'

'Not Garbo,' said Corker. 'Bergner.'

'What does he mean?'

'He says you are like a film star.'

'Does he? Does he really say that?' Her face, clouded at Corker's interruption, beamed. 'That is how I should like to be. Now I must go. I will send a boy for the valise.'

She went, pulling the collar of her raincoat close round her throat.

'Not bad, old boy, not bad at all. I will say you're a quick worker. Sorry to barge in on the tender scene, but there's trouble afoot. Hitchcock's story has broken. He's at the Fascist headquarters scooping the world.'

'Where?'

'Town called Laku.'

'But he can't be. Bannister told me there was no such place.'

'Well, there is now, old boy. At this very moment it's bang across the front page of the *Daily Brute* and it's where we are all going or know the reason why. A meeting of the Foreign Press Association has been called for six this evening at the Liberty. Feeling is running very high in the bunch.'

The German girl came back.

'Is the journalist gone?'

'Yes. I am sorry. I'm afraid he was rather rude.'

'Was he teasing, or did he really mean I was like a film star?'

'I'm sure he meant it.'

'Do you think so too?' She leaned on the dressing-table studying her face in the mirror. She pushed back a strand of hair that had fallen over her forehead; she turned her head on one side, smiled at herself, put out her tongue. 'Do you think so?'

'Yes, very like a film star.'

'I am glad.' She sat on the bed. 'What's your name?'

William told her.

'Mine is Kätchen,' she said. 'You must put away the boat. It is in the way and it makes us seem foolish.'

Together they dismembered the frame and rolled up the canvas. 'I have something to ask,' she said. 'What do you think is the value of my husband's specimens?'

'I'm afraid I have no idea.'

'He said they were very valuable.'

'I expect they are.'

'Ten English pounds?'

'I daresay.'

'More? Twenty?'

'Possibly.'

'Then I will sell them to you. It is because I like you. Will you give me twenty pounds for them?'

'Well, you know, I've got a great deal of luggage already. I don't know quite what I should do with them.'

'I know what you are thinking – that it is wrong for me to sell my husband's valuable specimens. But he has been away for six weeks now and he left me with only eight dollars. Frau Dressler is becoming most impolite. I am sure he would not want Frau Dressler to be impolite. So this is what we will do. You shall buy them and then, when my husband comes back and says they are worth more than twenty pounds, you will pay him the difference. There will be nothing wrong in that, will there? He could not be angry?'

'No, I don't think he could possibly be angry about that.'

'Good. Oh, you have made me glad that you came here. Please, will you give me the money now? Have you an account at the bank?'

'Yes.'

'Then write a cheque. I will take it to the bank myself. Then it will be no trouble to you.'

When she had gone, William took out his expense sheet and dutifully entered the single, enigmatic item: '*Stones* ... £20.'

5

Every journalist in Jacksonburg except Wenlock Jakes, who had sent Paleologue to represent him, attended the meeting of the Foreign Press Association; all, in their various tongues, voluble with indignation. The hotel boys pattered amongst them with trays of whisky; the air was pungent and dark with tobacco smoke. Pappenhacker was in the chair, wearily calling for order. 'Order, gentlemen. Attention, je vous en prie. Order, *please*. Messieurs, gentlemen ...'

'Order, order,' shouted Pigge, and Pappenhacker's voice was drowned in cries of silence.

' ... secretary to read the minutes of the last meeting.'

The voice of the secretary could occasionally be heard above the chatter. ' ... held at the Hotel Liberty ... Sir Jocelyn Hitchcock in the chair ... resolution ... unanimously passed ... protest in the most emphatic manner against ... Ishmaelite government ... militates against professional activities ...

' ... objections to make or questions to ask about these minutes ... '

The correspondents for *Paris-Soir* and *Havas* objected and after a time the minutes were signed. Pappenhacker was again on his feet. 'Gentlemen, in the absence of Sir Jocelyn Hitchcock ... '

Loud laughter and cries of 'Shame.'

'Mr Chairman, I must protest that this whole question is being treated with highly undesirable levity.'

'Translate.'

'On traite toute la question avec une légèreté indésirable.'

'Thank you, Mr Porter . . . '

'If you pliss to spik Sherman . . . '

'Italiano . . . piacere . . . '

' . . . tutta domanda con levità spiacevole . . . '

' . . . Sherman . . . '

'Gentlemen, gentlemen, Doctor Benito has consented to meet us here in a few minutes and it is essential that I know the will of the meeting, so that I can present our demands in proper form.'

At this stage one half of the audience – those nearest to William – were distracted from the proceedings by an altercation, unconnected with the business in hand, between two rival photographers.

'Did you call me a scab?'

'I did not, but I will.'

'You will?'

'Sure, you're a scab. Now what?'

'Call me a scab outside.'

'I call you a scab here.'

'Say that outside and see what you'll get.'

Cries of 'Shame' and 'Aw, pipe down.'

' . . . gravely affecting our professional status. We welcome fair and free competition . . . obliged to enforce coercive measures . . . '

'Go on, sock me one and see what you get.'

'I don't want to sock you one. *You* sock *me* first.'

'Aw, go sock him one.'

'Just you give me a poke in the nose and see what you'll get.'

' . . . Notre condition professionnelle. Nous souhaitons la bienvenue à toute la compétition égale et libre.'

'Nostra condizione professionale . . . '

'*You* poke *me* in the nose.'

'Aw, why can't you boys sock each other and be friendly?'

'Resolution before the meeting ... protest against the breach of faith on the part of the Ishmaelite government and demand that all restrictions on their movements be instantly relaxed. I call for a show of hands on this resolution.'

'Mr Chairman, I object to the whole tone of this resolution.'

'May I propose the amendment that facilities be withheld from Sir Jocelyn Hitchcock until we have had time to get level with him?'

' ... demand an enquiry into how and from whom he received his permission to travel and the punishment of the responsible official ... '

'I protest, Mr Chairman, that the whole tone is peremptory and discourteous.'

' ... The motion as amended reads ... '

Then Doctor Benito arrived; he came from the main entrance and the journalists fell back to make way. It was William's first sight of him. He was short and brisk and self-possessed; soot-black in face, with piercing boot-button eyes; he wore a neat black suit; his linen and his teeth were brilliantly white, he carried a little black attaché case; in the lapel of his coat he wore the button of the Star of Ishmaelia, fourth class. As he passed through them the journalists were hushed; it was as though the head-mistress had suddenly appeared among an unruly class of schoolgirls. He reached the table, shook Pappenhacker by the hand and faced his audience with a flash of white teeth.

'Gentlemen,' he said, 'I will speak first in English' (the correspondents of *Havas* and *Paris-Soir* began to protest) 'after that in French.

'I have a communication to make on the part of the President. He wishes to state first that he reserves for himself absolutely the right to maintain or relax the regulations he has made for the comfort and safety of the Press, either generally or in individual cases. Secondly, that, so far, no relaxation of these regulations has been made in any case. If, as is apparently believed, a journalist has left Jacksonburg for the interior it is without the Government's consent or knowledge. Thirdly, that the roads to the interior are at the moment entirely unfit for travel, provisions are impossible to obtain and travellers would be in danger from disaffected elements of the population. Fourthly, that he has decided, in view of the wishes of the foreign Press, to relax the restrictions he has hitherto made. Those wishing to do so, may travel to the interior. They must first apply formally to my bureau where the necessary passes will be issued and steps taken for their protection. That is all, gentlemen.'

He then repeated his message in accurate French, bowed and left the meeting in deep silence. When he had gone, Pappenhacker said, 'Well, gentlemen, I think that concludes our evening's business in a very satisfactory manner,' but it was with a dissatisfied air that the journalists left the hotel for the wireless station.

'A triumph for the power of the Press,' said Corker. 'They caved in at once.'

'Yes,' said William.

'You sound a bit doubtful, old boy.'

'Yes.'

'I know what you're thinking of – something in Benito's manner. I noticed it too. Nothing you could actually take hold of, but he seemed kind of superior to me.'

'Yes,' said William.

They sent off their service messages. William wrote: THEY HAVE GIVEN US PERMISSION TO GO TO LAKU AND EVERYONE IS GOING BUT THERE IS NO SUCH PLACE AM I TO GO TOO SORRY TO BE A BORE BOOT.

Corker, more succinctly: PERMISSION GRANTED LAKUWARD.

That night the wireless carried an urgent message in similar terms from every journalist in Jacksonburg.

William and Corker returned to the Liberty for a drink. All the journalists were having drinks. The two photographers were clinking glasses and slapping one another on the shoulder. Corker reverted to the topic that was vexing him. 'What's that blackamoor got to be superior about?' he asked moodily. 'Funny that you noticed it too.'

6

Next day Corker brought William a cable: UNPROCEED LAKU-
WARD STOP AGENCIES COVERING PATRIOTIC FRONT STOP
REMAIN CONTACTING CUMREDS STOP NEWS EXYOU UNREC-
EIVED STOP DAILY HARD NEWS ESSENTIALEST STOP REMEM-
BER RATES SERVICE CABLES ONE ETSIX PER WORD BEAST.

Kätchen stood at his elbow as he read it. 'What does it mean?'
she asked.

'I'm to stay in Jacksonburg.'

'Oh, I am pleased.'

William answered the cable:

NO NEWS AT PRESENT THANKS WARNING ABOUT CABLING
PRICES BUT IVE PLENTY MONEY LEFT AND ANYWAY WHEN I
OFFERED TO PAY WIRELESS MAN SAID IT WAS ALL RIGHT PAID
OTHER END RAINING HARD HOPE ALL WELL ENGLAND WILL
CABLE AGAIN IF ANY NEWS.

Then he and Kätchen went to play ping-pong at Popotakis's.

7

The journalists left.

For three days the town was in turmoil. Lorries were chartered
and provisioned; guides engaged; cooks and guards and muleteers
and caravan boys and hunters, cooks' boys, guards' boys, muleteers' boys, ravan-boys' boys and hunters' boys were recruited at
unprecedented rates of pay; all over the city, in the offices and
legations, resident Europeans found themselves deserted by their
servants; seminarists left the missions, male-nurses the hospital,
highly placed clerks their government departments to compete for
the journalists' wages. The price of benzine was doubled overnight
and rose steadily until the day of the exodus. Terrific deals were
done in the bazaar in tinned foodstuffs; they were cornered by a
Parsee and unloaded on a Banja, cornered again by an Arab, resold
and rebought, before they reached the journalists' stores. Shumble
bought William's rifle and sold a half share in it to Whelper.

Everyone now emulated the costume of the Frenchmen; sombreros, dungarees, jodhpurs, sunproof shirts and bullet-proof waistcoats, holsters, bandoliers, Newmarket boots, cutlasses, filled the Liberty. The men of the Excelsior Movie-Sound News, sporting horsehair capes and silk shirts of native chieftains, made camp in the Liberty garden and photographed themselves at great length in attitudes of vigilance and repose. Paleologue made his pile.

There was an evening of wild indignation when it was falsely put around that Jakes had been lent a balloon by the Government for his journey. There was an evening of anxiety when, immediately before the day fixed for their departure, the journalists were informed that the passes for their journey had not yet received the stamp of the Ministry of the Interior. A meeting of the Press Association was hastily called; it passed a resolution of protest and dissolved in disorder. Late that evening Doctor Benito delivered the passes in person. They were handsome, unintelligible documents printed in Ishmaelite and liberally decorated with rubber stamps, initials, and patriotic emblems. Benito brought one to William at the Pension Dressler.

'I'm not going, after all,' William explained.

'Not going, Mr Boot? But your pass is here, made out in order.'

'Sorry if it has caused extra work, but my editor has told me to stay on here.'

An expression of extreme annoyance came over the affable, black face.

'But your colleagues have made every arrangement. It is very difficult for my bureau if the journalists do not keep together. You see, your pass to Laku automatically cancels your permission to remain in Jacksonburg. I'm afraid, Mr Boot, it will be necessary for you to go.'

'Oh, rot,' said William. 'For one thing there is no such place as Laku.'

'I see you are very well informed about my country, Mr Boot. I should not have thought it from the tone of your newspaper.'

William began to dislike Dr Benito.

'Well, I'm not going. Will you be good enough to cancel the pass and renew my permission for Jacksonburg?'

There was a pause; then the white teeth flashed in a smile.

'But of course, Mr Boot. It will be a great pleasure. I cannot hope to offer you anything of much interest during your visit. As you have seen, we are a very quiet little community. The academic year opens at Jackson College. General Gollancz Jackson is celebrating his silver wedding. But I do not think any of these things are of great importance in Europe. I am sure your colleagues in the interior will find far more exciting matter for their dispatches. Are you sure nothing can make you alter your decision?'

'Quite sure.'

'Very well.' Dr Benito turned to go. Then he paused. 'By the way, have you communicated to any of your colleagues your uncertainty about the existence of the city of Laku?'

'Yes, but they wouldn't listen.'

'I suppose not. Perhaps they have more experience in their business. Good night.'

8

Next morning, at dawn, the first lorry started. It was shared by Corker and Pigge. They sat in front with the driver. They had been drinking heavily and late the night before and, in the grey light, showed it. Behind, among the crates and camp furniture, lay six torpid servants.

William rose to see them off. They had kept the time of their departure a secret. Everyone, the evening before, had spoken casually of 'making a move at tennish', but when William arrived at the Liberty the whole place was astir. Others beside Pigge and Corker conceived that an advantage might come from a few hours' start; all the others. Corker and Pigge were away first, by a negligible margin. One after another their colleagues took the road behind them. Pappenhacker drove a little two-seater he had bought from the British Legation. Many of the cars flew flags of Ishmaelia and of their countries. One lorry was twice the size of any other; it rode gallantly on six wheels; its sides were armour-plated; it had been purchased, irregularly and at enormous expense, from the War Office, and bore in vast letters of still tacky paint the inscription:

EXCELSIOR MOVIE-SOUND EXPEDITIONARY UNIT
TO THE ISHMAELITE IDEOLOGICAL FRONT.

During these latter days the rains had notably declined, giving promise of spring. The clouds lay high over the town, revealing a wider horizon, and, as the cavalcade disappeared from view, the road to Laku lay momentarily bathed in sunshine. William waved them good-bye from the steps of the Jackson memorial and turned back towards the Pension Dressler, but as he went the sky darkened and the first drops began to fall.

He was at breakfast when his boy reported: 'All come back.'

'Who?'

'All newspaper fellows come back. Soldiers catch 'em one time and take 'em plison.'

William went out to investigate.

Sure enough the lorries were lined up outside the police station, and inside, each with an armed guard, sat the journalists. They had found the barricades of the town shut against them; the officer in charge had not been warned to expect them; he had been unable to read their passes and they were all under arrest.

At ten when Doctor Benito began his day's routine at the Press Bureau, he received them apologetically but blandly. 'It is a mistake,' he said. 'I regret it infinitely. I understood that you proposed to start at ten. If I had known that you intended to start earlier I would have made the necessary arrangements. The night-guard have orders to let no one through. You will now find the day-guard on duty. They will present arms as you pass. I have given special instructions to that effect. Good-bye, gentlemen, and a good journey.'

Once more the train of lorries set off; rain was now falling hard. Corker and Pigge still led; Wenlock Jakes came last in a smart touring car. William waved: the populace whistled appreciatively; at the gates of the city the guard slapped the butts of their carbines. William once more turned to the Pension Dressler; the dark clouds opened above him; the gutters and wet leaves sparkled in sunlight and a vast, iridescent fan of colour, arc beyond arc of splendour, spread across the heavens. The journalists had gone, and a great peace reigned in the city.

CHAPTER 3

I

KÄTCHEN WAS SMOKING in a long chair on the veranda. 'Lovely,' she said. 'Lovely. In a few days now the rains will be over.'

She had been early to the hairdresser and, in place of the dank wisps of yesterday, her golden head was a tuft of curls. She had a new dress; she wore scarlet sandals and her toe-nails were painted to match them. 'The dress came yesterday,' she said. 'There is an Austrian lady who sewed it for me. I wanted to put it on last night, when we went to play ping-pong, but I thought you would like it best when my hair was done. You *do* like it?'

'Immensely.'

'And I got this,' she said. 'It is French.' She showed him an enamelled vanity case. 'The hairdresser sold it to me... From Paris. Lipstick, powder, looking-glass, comb, cigarettes. Pretty?'

'Very pretty.'

'And now Frau Dressler is angry with me again, because of her bill. But I don't care. What business of hers is it if I sell my husband's specimens? I offered them to her and she said they were not valuable. I don't care, I don't care. Oh, William, I am so happy. Look at the rainbow. It gets bigger and bigger. Soon there will be no room in the sky for it. Do you know what I should like to do today? I should like us to take a motor-car and drive into the hills. We could get some wine and, if you ask her, Frau Dressler will make a hamper. Do not say it is for me. Let us get away from this city for a day...'

*

Frau Dressler packed a hamper; Doctor Benito stamped a pass; Paleologue arranged for the hire of a motor-car. At midday William and Kätchen drove off towards the hills.

'Kätchen, I love you. Darling, darling Kätchen, I love you . . .'

He meant it. He was in love. It was the first time in twenty-three years; he was suffused and inflated and tipsy with love. It was believed at Boot Magna, and jocularly commented upon from time to time, that an attachment existed between him and a neighbouring Miss Caldicote; it was not so. He was a stranger alike to the bucolic jaunts of the hayfield and the dark and costly expeditions of his Uncle Theodore. For twenty-three years he had remained celibate and heart-whole; landbound. Now for the first time he was far from shore, submerged among deep waters, below wind and tide, where huge trees raised their spongy flowers and monstrous things without fur or feather, wing or foot, passed silently, in submarine twilight. A lush place.

2

Sir Jocelyn Hitchcock threw open the shutters of his room and welcomed the sunshine. He thrust his head out of the window and called loudly for attention. They brought him a dozen steaming jugs and filled his tub. He bathed and shaved and rubbed his head with eau de quinine until his sparse hairs were crowned with foam and his scalp smarted and glowed. He dressed carefully, set his hat at an angle and sauntered to the wireless station.

CONSIDER ISHMAELITE STORY UP-CLEANED, he wrote, SUGGEST LEAVING AGENCIES COVER UP-FOLLOWS. Then he returned to the hotel and ate a late breakfast of five lightly boiled eggs.

He packed his luggage and waited for his reply. It came before sundown, for there was little traffic at the wireless station that day. PROCEED LUCERNE COVER ECONOMIC NON-INTERVENTION CONGRESS. There was a train to the coast that night. He paid his bill at the hotel and, with three hours to spare, took a walk in the town.

The promise of the morning had been barely fulfilled. At noon the rain had started again; throughout the afternoon had streamed monotonously, and now, at sundown, ceased; for a few minutes the shoddy roofs were ablaze with scarlet and gold.

With loping steps, Erik Olafsen came down the street towards Sir Jocelyn; his face was uplifted to the glory of the sunset and he would have walked blandly by. It was Sir Jocelyn's first impulse to let him; then, changing his mind, he stepped forward and greeted him.

'Sir Hitchcock, you are back so soon. It will disappoint our colleagues to find you not at Laku. You have had many interests in your journey, yes?'

'Yes,' said Sir Jocelyn briefly.

Across the street, deriding the splendour of the sky, there flashed the electric sign of Popotakis's Ping Pong Parlour while, from his door, an ancient French two-step, prodigiously amplified, heralded the day's end.

'Come across and have a drink,' said Sir Jocelyn.

'Not to drink, thank you so much, but to hear the interests of your journey. I was told that Laku was no such place, no?'

'No,' said Sir Jocelyn.

Even as they crossed the street, the sky paled.

Popotakis had tried a cinema, a dance hall, baccarat, and miniature golf; now he had four ping-pong tables. He had made good money, for the smart set of Jacksonburg were always hard put to get through the rainy season; the polyglot professional class had made it their rendezvous; even attachés from the legations and younger members of the Jackson family had come there. Then for a few delirious days it had been overrun with journalists; prices had doubled, quarrels had raged, the correspondent of the *Methodist Monitor* had been trussed with a net and a photographer had lost a tooth. Popotakis's old clients melted away to other, more seemly resorts; the journalists had broken his furniture and insulted his servants and kept him awake till four in the morning, but they had drunk his home-made whisky at an American dollar a glass and poured his home-made champagne over the bar at ten dollars a bottle. Now they had all gone and the place was nearly empty. Only William and Kätchen sat at the bar. Popotakis had some genuine sixty per cent absinthe; that is what they were drinking. They were in a sombre mood, for the picnic had been a failure.

Olafsen greeted them with the keenest pleasure. 'So you have not gone with the others, Boot? And you are now friends with Kätchen? Good, good. Sir Hitchcock, to present my distinguished colleague Boot of the London *Beast*.'

Sir Jocelyn was always cordial to fellow journalists, however obscure. 'Drink up,' he said. 'And have another. Sending much?'

'Nothing,' said William, 'nothing seems to happen.'

'Why aren't you with the bunch? You're missing a grand trip. Mind you, I don't know they'll get much of a story at Laku. Shouldn't be surprised if they found the place empty already. But it's a grand trip. Scenery, you know, and wild life. What are you drinking, Eriksen?'

'Olafsen. Thank you, some grenadine. That absinthe is very dangerous. It was so I killed my grandfather.'

'You killed your grandfather, Erik?'

'Yes, did you not know? I thought it was well known. I was very young at the time and had taken a lot of sixty per cent. It was with a chopper.'

'May we know, sir,' asked Sir Jocelyn sceptically, 'how old you were when this thing happened?'

'Just seventeen. It was my birthday; that is why I had so much drunk. So I came to live in Jacksonburg, and now I drink this.' He raised, without relish, his glass of crimson syrup.

'Poor man,' said Kätchen.

'Which is poor man? Me or the grandfather?'

'I meant you.'

'Yes, I am poor man. When I was very young I used often to be drunk. Now it is very seldom. Once or two time in the year. But always I do something I am very sorry for. I think, perhaps, I shall get drunk tonight,' he suggested, brightening.

'No, Erik, not tonight.'

'No? Very well, not tonight. But it will be soon. It is very long since I was drunk.'

The confession shed a momentary gloom. All four sat in silence. Sir Jocelyn stirred himself and ordered some more absinthe.

'There were parrots, too,' he said with an effort. 'All along the road to Laku. I never saw such parrots – green and red and blue and – and every colour you can think of, talking like mad. And gorillas.'

'Sir Hitchcock,' said the Swede, 'I have lived in this country ever since I killed my grandfather and I never saw or heard of a gorilla.'

'I saw six,' said Sir Jocelyn stoutly, 'sitting in a row.'

The Swede rose abruptly from his stool. 'I do not understand,' he said. 'So I think I shall go.' He paid for his grenadine and left them at the bar.

'Odd chap that,' said Sir Jocelyn. 'Moody. Men get like that when they live in the tropics. I daresay it was all a delusion about his grandfather.'

There was food of a kind procurable at Popotakis's Ping Pong Parlour. 'Will you dine with me here,' asked Sir Jocelyn, 'as it's my last evening?'

'Your last evening?'

'Yes, I've been called away. Public interest in Ishmaelia is beginning to wane.'

'But nothing has happened yet.'

'Exactly. There was only one story for a special – my interview with the Fascist leader. Of course, it's different with the Americans – fellows like Jakes. They have a different sense of news from us – personal stuff, you know. The job of an English special is to spot the story he wants, get it – then clear out and leave the rest to the agencies. The war will be ordinary routine reporting. Fleet Street have spent a lot on this already. They'll have to find something to justify it and then they'll draw in their horns. You take it from me. As soon as they get anything that smells like front page, they'll start calling back their men. Personally I'm glad to have got my work over quick. I never did like the place.'

They dined at Popotakis's and went to the station to see Hitchcock off. He had secured the single sleeping car which was reserved for official visitors and left in great good humour. 'Good-bye, Boot, remember me to them at the *Beast*. I wonder how they are feeling now about having missed that Laku story?'

The train left, and William found himself the only special correspondent in Jacksonburg.

3

He and Kätchen drove back. Kätchen said: 'Frau Dressler was very angry again this afternoon.'

'Beast.'

'William, you *do* like me.'

'I love you. I've told you so all day.'

'No, you must not say that. My husband would not allow it. I mean, as a friend.'

'No, not as a friend.'

'Oh, dear, you make me so sad.'

'You're crying.'

'No.'

'You are.'

'Yes. I am so sad you are not my friend. Now I cannot ask you what I wanted.'

'What?'

'No, I cannot ask you. You do not love me as a friend. I was so lonely, and when you came I thought everything was going to be happy. But now it is spoiled. It is so easy for you to think here is a foreign girl and her husband is away. No one will mind what happens to her...No, you are not to touch me. I hate you.'

William sat back silently in his corner.

'William.'

'Yes.'

'He is not going to the Pension Dressler. It is to the Swede again.'

'I don't care.'

'But I am so tired.'

'So am I.'

'Tell him to go to the Pension Dressler.'

'I told him. It's no good.'

'Very well. If you wish to be a beast...'

The Swede was still up, mending with patient, clumsy hands the torn backs of his hymn books. He put down the paste and scissors and came out to direct the taxi driver.

'It was not true what Sir Hitchcock said. There are no gorillas in this country. He cannot have seen six. Why does he say that?' His broad forehead was lined and his eyes wide with distress and bewilderment. 'Why did he say that, Boot?'

'Perhaps he was joking.'

'Joking? I never thought of that. Of course, it was a joke. Ha, ha, ha. I am so glad. Now I understand. A joke.' He returned to his lighted study, laughing with relief and amusement. As he settled himself to work once more, he hummed a tune. One by one the tattered books were set in order, restored and fortified, and the Swede chuckled over Sir Jocelyn's joke.

William and Kätchen drove home in complete silence. The night watchman flung open the gates and raised his spear in salute. While William was wrangling with the taxi driver, Kätchen slipped away to her own room. William undressed and lay among his heaps of luggage. His anger softened and turned to shame, then to a light melancholy; soon he fell asleep.

4

There was one large table in the Pension dining-room. Kätchen was sitting at its head, alone; she had pushed the plate away and put her coffee in its place between her bare elbows; she crouched over it, holding the cup in both hands; the saucer was full and drops of coffee formed on the bottom of the cup and splashed like tears. She did not answer when William wished her good morning. He went to the door and called across to the kitchen for his breakfast. It was five minutes in coming, but still she did not speak or leave the table. Frau Dressler bustled through, on the way to her room, and returned laden with folded sheets. She spoke to Kätchen gruffly in German. Kätchen nodded. The cup dripped on the tablecloth. She put her hand down to hide the spot, but Frau Dressler saw it and spoke again. Kätchen began to cry; she did not raise her head and the tears fell, some in the cup, some in the saucer, some on the tablecloth.

William said, 'Kätchen . . . Kätchen, darling, what's the matter?'

'I have no handkerchief.'

He gave her his. 'What did Frau Dressler say?'

'She was angry because I have made the tablecloth dirty. She said why did I not help with the washing?' She dabbed her face and the tablecloth with William's handkerchief.

'I am afraid I was very disagreeable last night.'

'Yes, why were you like that? It had been so nice until then. Perhaps it was the Pernod. Why were you like that, William?'

'Because I love you.'

'I have told you you are not to say that. . . . My husband has been away for six weeks. When he left he said he would return in a month or at the most six weeks. It is six weeks this morning. I am very worried what may have become of him . . . I have been with him for two years now.'

'Kätchen, there's something I must ask you. Don't be angry. It's very important to me. Is he really your husband?'

'But of course he is. It is just that he has gone away for his work.'

'I mean, were you married to him properly in church?'

'No, not in church.'

'At a government office, then?'

'No. You see, it was not possible because of his other wife in Germany.'

'He has another wife, then?'

'Yes, in Germany, but he hates her. I am his *real* wife.'

'Does Frau Dressler know about the other wife?'

'Yes, that is why she treats me so impolitely. The German consul told her after my husband had gone away. There was a question of my papers. They would not register me at the German consulate.'

'But you are German?'

'My husband is German, so I am German, but there is a difficulty with my papers. My father is Russian and I was born in Budapest.'

'Is your mother German?'

'Polish.'

'Where is your father now?'

'I think he went to South America to look for my mother after she went away. But why do you ask me so many questions when I am unhappy? You are worse than Frau Dressler. It is not your table-cloth. You do not have to pay if it is dirty.'

She left William alone at the breakfast table.

5

Twelve miles out of town Corker and Pigge were also at breakfast.

'I never slept once,' said Corker. 'Not a wink, the whole night. Did you hear the lions?'

'Hyenas,' said Pigge.

'Hyenas laugh. These were lions or wolves. Almost in the tents.' They sat beside their lorry drinking soda water and eating sardines from a tin. The cook and the cook's boy, the driver and the driver's boy, Corker's boy and Pigge's boy, were all heavily asleep in the lorry under a pile of blankets and tarpaulin.

'Six black bloody servants and no breakfast,' said Corker bitterly.

'They were up all night making whoopee round the fire. Did you hear them?'

'Of course I heard them. Singing and clapping. I believe they'd got hold of our whisky. I shouted to them to shut up, and they said, "Must have fire. Many bad animals."'

'Yes, hyenas.'

'Lions.'

'We've got to get the lorry out of the mud, somehow. I suppose the rest of the bunch are half-way to Laku by now.'

'I didn't think it of them,' said Corker, bitterly. 'Going past us like that without a bloody word. Shumble I can understand, but Whelper and the Excelsior Movie-News bunch. . . . With that great lorry of theirs they could have towed us out in five minutes. What have *they* got to be competitive about? . . . and those two photographers I gave up half my room to at the hotel – just taking a couple of shots of us and then driving off. Two white men, alone, in a savage country . . . it makes one despair of human nature . . .'

The preceding day had been one of bitter experience.

Within a quarter of a mile of the city the metalled strip had come to an end and the road became a mud-track. For four hours the lorry had crawled along at walking pace, lurching, sticking, and skidding; they had forged through a swollen stream which washed the undercarriage; they had been thrown from side to side of the cab; the binding of the stores had broken and Pigge's typewriter had fallen into the mud behind them to be retrieved, hopelessly injured, by the grinning cook's boy. It had been an abominable journey.

Presently the track had lost all semblance of unity and split into a dozen diverging and converging camel paths, winding at the caprice of the beasts who had made them, among thorn and rock and anthills in a colourless, muddy plain. Here, without warning, the back wheels had sunk to their axles, and here the lorry had stayed while the caravan it had led disappeared from view. Tents had been pitched and the fire lighted. The cook, opening some tins at random, had made them a stew of apricots and curry powder and turtle soup and tunny fish, which in the final analysis had tasted predominantly of benzine.

In bitter cold they had sat at the tent door, while Pigge tried vainly to repair his typewriter, and Corker, struck with nostalgia, composed a letter to his wife; at eight they had retired to their sleeping-bags and lain through the long night while their servants caroused outside.

Corker surveyed the barren landscape and the gathering storm clouds, the mud-bound lorry, the heap of crapulous black servants, the pasty and hopeless face of Pigge, the glass of soda water and the jagged tin of fish. 'It makes one despair of human nature,' he said again.

6

It was some days since William had seen Bannister, so he drove out that morning to the Consulate. There was the usual cluster of disconsolate Indians round the door. Bannister sent them away, locked the office and took William across the garden to his house for a drink.

'Looking for news?' he asked. 'Well, the Minister's got a tea-party on Thursday. D'you want to come?'

'Yes.'

'I'll get them to bung you a card. It's the worst day of the year for us. Everyone in the place comes who's got a clean collar. It's the public holiday in honour of the end of the rainy season and it always pours.'

'D'you think you could ask a German girl at my boarding-house? She's rather lonely.'

'Well, frankly, Lady G. isn't very keen on lonely German girls. But I'll see. Is that why you didn't go off on that wild goose chase to Laku? You're wise. I shouldn't be at all surprised if there weren't some rather sensational happenings here in a day or two.'

'The war?'

'No, there's nothing in that. But things are looking queer in the town. I can't tell you more, but if you want a hint look out for that Russian I told you about and watch your friend Doctor Benito. What's the girl's name?'

'Well, I'm not sure about her surname. There's some difficulty about her papers.'

'Doesn't sound at all Lady G.'s cup of tea. Is she pretty?'

'Lovely.'

'Then I think you can count her off the Legation list. Paleologue's been trying to interest me in a lovely German girl for weeks. I expect it's her. Bring her along to dinner here one evening.'

Kätchen was delighted with the invitation. 'But we must buy a dress,' she said. 'There is an Armenian lady who has a very pretty one – bright green. She has never worn it because she bought it by mail and she has grown too fat. She asked fifty American dollars. I think if she were paid at once it would be cheaper.' She had become cheerful again. 'Wait,' she said, 'I have something to show you.'

She ran to her room and returned with a sodden square of bandana silk. 'Look, I *have* been doing some washing after all. It is your handkerchief. I do not need it now. I have stopped crying for today. We will go and play ping-pong and then see the Armenian lady's green dress.'

After luncheon Bannister telephoned. 'We've had a cable about you from London.'

'Good God, why?'

'*The Beast* have been worrying the F.O. Apparently they think you've been murdered. Why don't you send them some news?'

'I don't know any.'

'Well, for heaven's sake invent some. The Minister will go crazy if he has any more bother with the newspapers. We get about six telegrams a day from the coast. Apparently there's a bunch of journalists there trying to get up and the Ishmaelite frontier author-ities won't let them through. Two of them are British, unfortunately. And now the Liberals are asking questions in the House of Com-mons and are worrying his life out as it is about some infernal nonsense of a concentration of Fascist troops at Laku.'

William returned to his room and sat for a long time before his typewriter. It was over a week now since he had communicated with his employers, and his failure weighed heavily on him. He surveyed the events of the day, of all the last days. What would Corker have done?

Finally, with one finger, he typed a message. PLEASE DONT WORRY QUITE SAFE AND WELL IN FACT RATHER ENJOYING THINGS WEATHER IMPROVING WILL CABLE AGAIN IF THERE IS ANY NEWS YOURS BOOT.

7

It was late afternoon in London; at Copper House secretaries were carrying cups of tea to the more leisured departments; in Mr Salter's office there was tension and consternation.

'*Weather improving*,' said Mr Salter. '*Weather improving*. He's been in Jacksonburg ten days, and all he can tell us is that the weather is improving.'

'I've got to write a first leader on the Ishmaelite question,' said the first leader-writer. 'Lord Copper says so. I've got to wring the withers of the Government. What do I know about it? What have I got to go on? What are special correspondents for? Why don't you cable this Boot and wake him up?'

'How many times have we cabled Boot?' asked the Foreign Editor.

'Daily for the first three days, Mr Salter,' said his secretary. 'Then twice a day. Three times yesterday.'

'You see.'

'And in the last message we mentioned *Lord Copper's name*,' added the secretary.

'I never felt Boot was really suited to the job,' said Mr Salter mildly. 'I was very much surprised when he was chosen. But he's all we've got. It would take three weeks to get another man out there, and by that time anything may have happened.'

'Yes, the weather may have got still better,' said the first leader-writer, bitterly. He gazed out of the window; it opened on a tiled, resonant well; he gazed at a dozen drain pipes; he gazed straight into the office opposite where the Art Editor was having tea; he gazed up to the little patch of sky and down to the concrete depths where a mechanic was washing his neck at a cold tap: he gazed with eyes of despair.

'I have to denounce the vacillation of the Government in the strongest terms,' he said. 'They fiddle while Ishmaelia burns. A spark is set to the corner-stone of civilization which will shake its roots like a chilling breath. That's what I've got to say, and all I know is that Boot is safe and well and that the weather is improving . . . '

8

Kätchen and William dropped into the Liberty for an apéritif.

It was the first time he had been there since his change of residence.

'Do either of you happen to know a gentleman by the name of Boot?' asked Mrs Jackson.

'Yes, it's me.'

'Well, there's some cables for you somewhere.'

They were found and delivered. William opened them one by one. They all dealt with the same topic.

BADLY LEFT ALL PAPERS ALL STORIES.

IMPERATIVE RECEIVE FULL STORY TONIGHT SIX YOUR TIME WHY NO NEWS ARE YOU ILL FLASH REPLY.

YOUR CABLES UNARRIVED FEAR SUBVERSIVE INTERFER-
ENCE SERVICE ACKNOWLEDGE RECEIPT OURS IMMEDIATELY.
There were a dozen of them in all; the earliest of the series were
modestly signed SALTER; as the tone strengthened his name gave
place to MONTGOMERY MOWBRAY GENERAL EDITOR BEAST,
then to ELSENGRATZ MANAGING DIRECTOR MEGALOPOLITAN
NEWSPAPERS. The last, which had arrived that morning, read:
CONFIDENTIAL AND URGENT STOP LORD COPPER HIMSELF
GRAVELY DISSATISFIED STOP LORD COPPER PERSONALLY
REQUIRES VICTORIES STOP ON RECEIPT OF THIS CABLE VIC-
TORY STOP CONTINUE CABLING VICTORIES UNTIL FURTHER
NOTICE STOP LORD COPPERS CONFIDENTIAL SECRETARY.

'What are they all about?' asked Kätchen.

'They don't seem very pleased with me in London. They seem to
want more news.'

'How silly. Are you upset?'

'No . . . Well, yes, a little.'

'Poor William. I will get you some news. Listen. I have a plan.
I have lived in this town for two months. I have many friends. That is
to say, I *had* them before my husband went away. They will be my
friends again now that they know you are helping me. It will be a
good thing for both of us. Listen – all the journalists who were here
had men in the town they paid to give them news. Mr Jakes the
American pays Paleologue fifty dollars a week. You like me more
than Mr Jakes likes Paleologue?'

'Much more.'

'Twice as much?'

'Yes.'

'Then you will pay me a hundred dollars a week and Frau
Dressler will not be angry with me any more, so it will be a good
thing for all of us. Will you think it very greedy if I ask for a hundred
dollars now; you know how impolite Frau Dressler is – well, perhaps
two hundred, because I shall work for you more than one week?'

'Very well,' said William.

'Look, I brought your cheque book for you from your room in
case you might need it. What a good secretary I should be.'

'Do you really think you can get some news?'

'Why, yes, of course. For instance, I am very friendly with an Austrian man – it is his wife who made me this dress – and his sister is governess to the President's children, so they know everything that goes on. I will visit them tomorrow... only,' she added doubtfully, 'I don't think it would be polite to go to her house and not buy anything. You are paid expenses by your paper?'

'Yes.'

'For everything? The canoe and for this vermouth and all the things in your room?'

'Yes.'

'Then I will be paid expenses too... the Austrian has some nightgowns she made for a lady at the French legation, only the lady's husband did not like them, so they are *very* cheap. There are four of them in crêpe-de-Chine. She would sell them for sixty American dollars. Shall I get them?'

'You don't think she would give you news if you did not?'

'It would be impolite to ask.'

'Very well.'

'And the man who cut my hair – he shaves the Minister of the Interior. He would know a great deal. Only I cannot have my hair washed again so soon. Shall I buy some scent from him? And I should like a rug for my room; the floor is cold and has splinters; the Russian who sells fur is the lover of one of the Miss Jacksons. Oh, William, what fun we shall have working together.'

'But, Kätchen, you know, this isn't my money. You know that if I was rich, I should give you everything you wanted, but I can't go spending the paper's money...'

'Silly William, it is because it is the paper's money that I can take it. You know I could not take *yours*. My husband would not let me take money from a *man*, but from a *newspaper*... I think that Mr Gentakian knows a great deal of news, too – you know his shop opposite the Ping-Pong?... Oh, William, I feel so happy tonight. Let us not go back to dine at the Pension where Frau Dressler disapproves. Let us dine again at the Ping-Pong. We can buy some tinned caviare at Benakis, and Popotakis will make us some toast...'

After dinner Kätchen became grave. 'I was so happy just now,' she said. 'But now I am thinking, what is to become of me? A few weeks and you will go away. I have waited so long for my husband; perhaps he will not come.'

'Do you think you could bear to live in England?'

'I have lived in England. That is where I learned to speak. It was when I was sixteen, after my father went to South America; I worked in a dance hall.'

'Where?'

'I don't know. It was by the sea. I met my husband there; he was so pleased to find someone who would talk German with him. How he talked…Now you have made me think of him and I am ashamed to be drinking champagne when perhaps he is in trouble.'

'Kätchen, how long must you wait for him?'

'I don't know.' She unwrapped the speckled foil from the bottle of champagne. 'He is not a good husband to me,' she admitted, 'to go away for so long.' She held the foil to her face and carefully modelled it round her nose.

'Dear Kätchen, will you marry me?'

She held the false nose up to William's.

'Too long,' she said.

'Too long to wait?'

'Too long for your nose.'

'Damn!' said William.

'Now you are upset.'

'Won't you ever be serious?'

'Oh, I have been serious too much, too often.' Then she added hopefully, 'I might go with you now, and then when he comes back I will go with him. Will that do?'

'I want you to come to England with me. How long must I wait?'

'Do not spoil the evening with questions. We will play ping-pong.'

That night when they reached the Pension Dressler they walked through the yard arm in arm; the livestock were asleep, and overhead the sky was clear and brilliant with stars.

'How long must I wait? How long?'

'Not long. Soon. When you like,' said Kätchen, and ran to her loft.

The three-legged dog awoke, and all over the town, in yards and refuse heaps, the pariahs took up his cries of protest.

CHAPTER 4

I

NEXT MORNING WILLIAM awoke in a new world.

As he stood on the veranda calling for his boy, he slowly became aware of the transformation which had taken place overnight. The rains were over. The boards were warm under his feet; below the steps the dank weeds of Frau Dressler's garden had suddenly burst into crimson flower; a tropic sun blazed in the sky, low at present, but with promise of a fiery noon, while beyond the tin roofs of the city, where before had hung a blank screen of slaty cloud, was now disclosed a vast landscape, mile upon mile of sunlit highland, rolling green pastures, dun and rosy terraces, villas and farms and hamlets, gardens and crops and tiny stockaded shrines; crest upon crest receding to the blue peaks of the remote horizon. William called for his boy and called in vain.

'He is gone,' said Frau Dressler, crossing the yard with a load of earthenware. 'All the boys have gone today. They are making holiday for the end of the rains. Some German friends have come to help me.'

And William's breakfast was eventually brought him by a destitute mechanic who owed Frau Dressler for his share of the last Christmas tree.

2

It was an eventful day.

At nine Erik Olafsen came to say good-bye. There was an outbreak of plague down the line and he was off to organize a hospital. He went without enthusiasm.

'It is stupid work,' he said. 'I have been in a plague hospital before. How many do you think we cured?'

'I've no idea.'

'None at all. We could only catch the patients who were too ill to move. The others ran away to the villages, so more and more people got it. In the civilized colonies they send soldiers, not doctors. They make a ring all round the place where there is plague and shoot anyone who tries to get out. Then in a few days when everyone is dead they burn the huts. But here one can do nothing for the poor people. Well, the Government have asked me to go, so I leave now. Where is Kätchen?'

'She's out shopping.'

'Good. That is very good. She was sad with such old, dirty clothes. I am very glad she has become your friend. You will say good-bye to her?'

At ten she returned laden with packages. 'Darling,' she said, 'I have been so happy. Everyone is excited that the summer is come and they are all so kind and polite now they know I have a friend. Look at what I have brought.'

'Lovely. Did you get any news?'

'It was difficult. I had so much to say about the things I was buying that I did not talk politics. Except to the Austrian. The President's governess had tea with the Austrian yesterday, but I am afraid you will be disappointed. She has not seen the President for four days. You see, he is locked up.'

'Locked up?'

'Yes, they have shut him in his bedroom. They often do that when there are important papers for him to sign. But the governess is unhappy about it. You see, it is generally his family who lock him up and then it is only for a few hours. This time it is Doctor Benito and the Russian and the two black secretaries who came from America; they locked him up three days ago, and when his relatives try to see him they say he is drunk. They would not let him go to the opening of Jackson College. The governess says something is wrong.'

'Do you think I ought to report that to the *Beast*?'

'I wonder,' said Kätchen doubtfully. 'It is such a lovely morning. We ought to go out.'

'I believe Corker would make something of it . . . the editor seems very anxious for news.'

'Very well. Only be quick. I want to go for a drive.'

She left William to his work.

He sat at the table, stood up, sat down again, stared gloomily at the wall for some minutes, lit his pipe, and then, laboriously, with a single first finger and his heart heavy with misgiving, he typed the first news story of his meteoric career. No one observing that sluggish and hesitant composition could have guessed that this was a moment of history – of legend, to be handed down among the great traditions of his trade, told and retold over the milk-bars of Fleet Street, quoted in books of reminiscence, held up as a model to aspiring pupils of Correspondence Schools of Profitable Writing, perennially fresh in the jaded memories of a hundred editors; the moment when Boot began to make good.

PRESS COLLECT BEAST LONDON he wrote.

NOTHING MUCH HAS HAPPENED EXCEPT TO THE PRESIDENT WHO HAS BEEN IMPRISONED IN HIS OWN PALACE BY REVOLUTIONARY JUNTA HEADED BY SUPERIOR BLACK CALLED BENITO AND RUSSIAN JEW WHO BANNISTER SAYS IS UP TO NO GOOD THEY SAY HE IS DRUNK WHEN HIS CHILDREN TRY TO SEE HIM BUT GOVERNESS SAYS MOST UNUSUAL LOVELY SPRING WEATHER BUBONIC PLAGUE RAGING.

He got so far when he was interrupted.

Frau Dressler brought him a cable: YOUR CONTRACT TERMINATED STOP ACCEPT THIS STIPULATED MONTHS NOTICE AND ACKNOWLEDGE STOP BEAST.

William added to his message, SACK RECEIVED SAFELY THOUGHT I MIGHT AS WELL SEND THIS ALL THE SAME.

Kätchen's head appeared at the window.

'Finished?'

'Yes.'

He rolled the cable he had received into a ball and threw it into the corner of the room. The yard was bathed in sunshine. Kätchen wanted a drive. It was not a good time to tell her of his recall.

3

Twelve miles out of the town the coming of summer brought no joy to Corker and Pigge.

'Look at the flowers,' said Pigge.

'Yes. Like a bloody cemetery,' said Corker.

The lorry stood where it had sunk, buried in mud to the axles. On all sides lay evidence of the unavailing efforts of yesterday – stones painfully collected from a neighbouring water-course and bedded round the back wheels; bruised and muddy boughs dragged in the rain from the sparse woods a mile or more distant; the great boulder which they had rolled, it seemed, from the horizon to make a base for the jack – vainly; the heaps thrown up behind as the wheels, like a dog in a rabbit-hole, spun and burrowed. Listlessly helped by their boys, Pigge and Corker had worked all day, their faces blackened by exhaust smoke, their hands cut, soaked with rain, weary of limb, uncontrollable in temper.

It was a morning of ethereal splendour – such a morning as Noah knew as he gazed from his pitchy bulwarks over limitless, sunlit waters while the dove circled and mounted and became lost in the shining heavens; such a morning as only the angels saw on the first day of that rash cosmic experiment that had resulted, at the moment, in landing Corker and Pigge here in the mud, stiff and unshaven and disconsolate.

The earth-bound journalists turned hopelessly to the four quarters of the land.

'You can see for miles,' said Pigge.

'Yes,' said Corker bitterly, 'and not a bloody human being in sight.'

Their boys were dancing to celebrate the new season, clapping and shuffling and shouting a low, rhythmical song of praise. 'What the hell have they got to be cheerful about?'

'They've been at the whisky again,' said Corker.

4

That afternoon there was the party at the British Legation. Kätchen had not got her card, so William went alone. It did not rain. Nothing marred the summer serenity of the afternoon. Guests of all colours and nationalities paraded the gravel walks, occasionally pausing behind the flowering shrubs to blow their noses – delicately between forefinger and thumb – as though trumpeting against the defeated devils of winter.

'The President usually comes,' said Bannister, 'but he doesn't seem to be here today. Odd thing, but there isn't a single Jackson in sight. I wonder what's become of them all.'

'I don't know about the others, but the President is locked in his bedroom.'

'Good Lord, is he? I say, you'd better talk to the old man about this. I'll try and get hold of him.'

The Minister was regarding the scene with an expression of alarm and despair; he stood on the top step of the terrace, half in, half out of the french windows, in a position dimly remembered from the hide-and-seek of his childhood as strategically advantageous; it afforded a general survey of the dispositions of the attacking forces and offered alternative lines of retreat, indoors or through the rose garden.

Bannister introduced William.

The Minister gave the Vice-Consul a glance of mild reproach and smiled bleakly, the wry smile of one heroically resisting an emotion of almost overwhelming repulsion.

'So glad you could come,' he said. 'Being looked after all right? Good, excellent.'

He peered over his shoulder into the shady refuge of his study. As he did so the door opened and three obese Indians waddled into the room; each wore a little gold skull cap, a long white shirt, and a short black coat, each carried a strawberry ice. 'How did they get in?' he asked petulantly. 'They've no business there at all. Get them out. Get them out.'

Bannister hurried to head them off and the Minister was left alone with William.

'You are from the *Beast*?'

'Yes.'

'Can't say I read it myself. Don't like its politics. Don't like any politics . . . Finding Ishmaelia interesting?'

'Yes, very interesting.'

'Are you? Wish I was. But, then, you've got a more interesting job. Better paid, too, I expect. I wonder, how does one get a job like that? Pretty difficult, I suppose, stiff examination, eh?'

'No, no examination.'

'No examination? My word, that's interesting. I must tell my wife. Didn't know you could get any jobs nowadays without examinations. Wretched system, ruining all the services. I've got a boy in England now, lazy fellow, can't pass any examinations, don't know what to do with him. D'you suppose they'd give him a job on your paper?'

'I expect so. It seemed quite easy to me.'

'I say, that's splendid. Must tell my wife. Here she is. My dear, Mr Boot here says he will give Archie a job on his paper.'

'I'm afraid *I* can't be much help. I got the sack this morning.'

'Did you? Did you really? Pity. Then you can't be any help to Archie.'

'No, I'm afraid not.'

'My dear,' said the Minister's wife, 'I'm very sorry indeed, but I've got to introduce a new misssionary you haven't met.'

She led him away and presented a blinking giant of a young man; the Minister nodded absently to William as he left him.

Doctor Benito was at the party, very near, very affable, very self-possessed, smiling wickedly on all sides. He approached William.

'Mr Boot,' he said, 'you must be very lonely without your colleagues.'

'No, I much prefer it.'

'And it is dull for you,' Doctor Benito insisted, in the level patient tones of a mesmerist, 'very dull, with so little happening in the town. So I have arranged a little divertissement for you.'

'It is very kind, but I am greatly diverted here.'

'You are too kind to our simple little city. But I think I can promise you something better. Now that the summer has come there will be no difficulty. You shall have a little tour of our country and see some of its beauties – the forest of Popo, for instance, and the great waterfall at Chip.'

'It's very kind of you . . . some other time, perhaps.'

'No, no, at once. It is all arranged. I have a motor-car. I cannot, alas, go with you myself, but I will send a charming young man – very cultured, a university graduate – who will be able to explain everything as well as I can. You will find my country people very hospitable. I have arranged for you to spend tonight just outside the city at the villa of the postmaster-general. Then you will be able to start early in the morning for the mountains. You will see much more than any of your colleagues, who, I hear, are not being fortunate in their trip to Laku. Perhaps you will be able to do a little lion shooting.'

'Thank you very much indeed, Doctor Benito, but I don't want to leave Jacksonburg at the moment.'

'There will be room for any companion you care to take.'

'No, thank you.'

'And you will, of course, be the guest of the Government.'

'It's not that.'

'You will see most interesting native dances, curious customs,' he smiled more horribly than before, 'some of the tribes are most primitive and interesting.'

'I'm very sorry, I can't go.'

'But it is all arranged.'

'I'm very sorry. You should have consulted me before you took so much trouble.'

'My government would not like you to lose financially by their hospitality. I quite see that you would not be able to do your work fully during your absence, but any reasonable recompense . . .'

'Look here, Doctor Benito,' said William. 'You're being a bore. I'm not going.'

Doctor Benito suddenly stopped smiling. 'Everyone will be very disappointed,' he said.

William told Bannister what had been said.

'Yes, they want to get you out of the way. They don't want any journalists here when the fun starts. They even took the trouble to shift Olafsen. They told him there was cholera down the line.'

'Plague.'

'Some lie, anyway. I'm in communication with our agent there by telephone. Everyone's as fit as a flea.'

'Perhaps if he knew I'd got the sack he wouldn't bother so much.'

'He wouldn't believe it. He must have seen your cable; all the foreign cables go to his office before they're delivered. He thinks it a trick. That's the disadvantage of being clever in Benito's way.'

'You seem to know most things that go on in this town.'

'It's a hobby. Must do something. If I stuck to my job I should spend the day answering commercial questionnaires. Did you get anything interesting out of the Minister?'

'No.'

'He sticks to his job.'

5

As William drove back from the Legation he pondered over the question of when and in what terms he should break the news of his recall to Kätchen.

He need not have worried.

In the first place he found a cable awaiting him, CONGRATU-LATIONS STORY CONTRACT UNTERMINATED UPFOLLOW FULLEST SPEEDILIEST.

In the second place Kätchen was no longer at the Pension Dressler; a posse of soldiers had come for her that afternoon and taken her away in a closed motor-car.

'I suppose it is because of her papers,' said Frau Dressler. 'She telephoned to the German Consulate, but they would not help her. She should not have been upset. When they put white people in prison here they are well looked after. She will be as comfortable,' she added with unprofessional candour, 'as she was here. There is one of the secret police waiting to see you. I would not let him into your room. He is in the dining-room.'

William found a natty young Negro smoking from a long cigarette holder. 'Good evening,' he said. 'I have come from Doctor Benito to take you for a little tour in the mountains.'

'I told Doctor Benito I could not go.'

'He hoped you would change your mind.'

'Why have you arrested Miss Kätchen?'

'It is a temporary measure, Mr Boot. She is being very well looked after. She is at the villa of the postmaster-general, just outside the town. She asked me to collect some luggage for her – a parcel of geological specimens that were left in your room.'

'They are my property.'

'So I understand. You paid a hundred American dollars for them, I think. Here is the money.'

William was by nature a man of mild temper; on the rare occasions when he gave way to rage the symptoms were abundantly evident. The Negro stood up, removed the cigarette end from its holder and added, 'Perhaps I should tell you that when I was at the Adventist University of Alabama I was welter-weight champion of my year . . . May I repeat my offer? Doctor Benito wishes very much to examine these specimens; they are the property of the Government, for they were collected by a foreigner who came here without the formality of obtaining a prospecting licence from the Ministry of Mines – a foreigner who unfortunately is at the moment protected by the capitulations – at the moment only. Arrangements are being made about him. Since you bought these specimens under a misapprehension the Government decided very generously to make an offer of reimbursement –'

'Get out!' said William.

'Very well. You will hear of this matter again.'

He rose with dignity and swaggered into the yard.

The milch-goat looked up from her supper of waste paper; her perennial optimism quickened within her, and swelled to a great and mature confidence; all day she had shared the exhilaration of the season, her pelt had glowed under the newborn sun; deep in her heart she too had made holiday, had cast off the doubts of winter and exulted among the crimson flowers; all day she had dreamed gloriously; now in the limpid evening she gathered her strength, stood for a moment rigid, quivering from horn to tail; then charged, splendidly, irresistibly, triumphantly; the rope snapped and the welterweight champion of the Adventist University of Alabama sprawled on his face amid the kitchen garbage.

6

The events of that day were not yet ended.

As soon as the black had gone, limping and dishevelled, and the goat, sated and peaceably disposed to retrospection, recaptured and secured, William drove back to the British Consulate with his bag of minerals.

'The party's over,' said Bannister. 'We all want a rest.'

'I've brought some luggage for you to keep an eye on.'

He explained the circumstances.

'If you knew the amount of work you were causing,' said Bannister, 'you wouldn't do this. From tomorrow onwards for the next six years I shall get a daily pile of bumf from the Ministry of Mines and in the end the Mixed Court will decide against you – God damn all capitulations. What's in the sack, anyway?'

He opened it and examined the stones. 'Yes,' he said, 'just what I expected – gold ore. The mountains in the West are stiff with it. We knew it was bound to cause international trouble sooner or later. There have been two companies after a mineral concession – German and Russian. So far as the Jacksons have any political principles it has been to make the country unprofitable for foreign investment. The President kept his end up pretty well – played one company off against the other for months. Then the Smiles trouble started. We are pretty certain that the Germans were behind it. The Russians have been harder to follow – we only learned a day

or two ago that they had bought Benito and the Young Ishmaelite
party. It's between Smiles and Benito now and it looks to me as
if Benito had won hands down. I'm sorry – the Jacksons were a pack
of rogues, but they suited the country and they suited H.M.G. We
stand to lose quite a lot if they start a Soviet state here . . . Now you've
stopped being a journalist I can tell you these things.'

'As a matter of fact I've just become a journalist again. D'you
mind if I cable this to the *Beast*?'

'Well, don't let on that you got it from me . . . as a matter of fact a
newspaper campaign at the moment might just do the trick.'

'There's another thing. Can you help me get a girl friend out
of jug?'

'Certainly not,' said Bannister. 'I'm a keen supporter of the local
prison system; it's the one thing that keeps the British Protected
Persons off my doorstep. Its only weakness is you can buy yourself
out when you want to for a fiver.'

7

When it was dinner-time in Jacksonburg, it was tea-time in London.
'Nothing more from Boot,' said Mr Salter.
'Well, make up the Irish edition with his morning cable – rewrite
it and splash it. If the follow-up comes in before six in the morning,
run a special.'

8

William returned home with a mission; he was going to do down
Benito. Dimly at first, then in vivid detail, he foresaw a spectacular,
cinematographic consummation, when his country should rise
chivalrously to arms; Bengal Lancers and kilted highlanders
invested the heights of Jacksonburg; he at their head burst open
the prison doors; with his own hands he grappled with Benito,
shook him like a kitten and threw him choking out of his path;
Kätchen fluttered towards him like a wounded bird and he bore
her in triumph to Boot Magna . . . Love, patriotism, zeal for justice,
and personal spite flamed within him as he sat at his typewriter and

began his message. One finger was not enough; he used both hands. The keys rose together like bristles on a porcupine, jammed and were extricated; curious anagrams appeared on the paper before him; vulgar fractions and marks of punctuation mingled with the letters. Still he typed.

The wireless station closed at nine; at five minutes to William pushed his sheaf of papers over the counter.

'Sending tomorrow,' said the clerk.

'Must send tonight; urgent,' said William.

'No tonight. Summer holiday tonight.'

William added a handful of banknotes to the typewritten sheets. 'Sending tonight,' he said.

'All right.'

Then William went round to dinner alone at Popotakis's.

9

'Two thousand words from Boot,' said Mr Salter.

'Any good?' asked the General Editor.

'Look at it.'

The General Editor looked. He saw '*Russian plot . . . coup d'état . . . overthrow constitutional government . . . red dictatorship . . . goat butts head of police . . . imprisoned blonde . . . vital British interest jeopardized.*' It was enough; it was news. 'It's news,' he said. 'Stop the machines at Manchester and Glasgow. Clear the line to Belfast and Paris. Scrap the whole front page. Kill the Ex-Beauty Queen's pauper funeral. Get in a photograph of Boot.'

'I don't suppose we've got a photograph of Boot in the office.'

'Ring up his relatives. Find his best girl. There must be a photograph of him somewhere in the world.'

'They took one for his passport,' said Mr Salter doubtfully, 'but I remember thinking at the time it was an extremely poor likeness.'

'I don't care if it looks like a baboon –'

'That's just how it does look.'

'Give it two columns' depth. This is the first front-page foreign news we've had for a month.'

When the final edition had left the machines, carrying William's sensational message into two million apathetic homes, Mr Salter left the office.

His wife was still up when he got home.

'I've made your Ovaltine,' she said. 'Has it been a bad day?'

'Terrible.'

'You didn't have to dine with Lord Copper.'

'No, not as bad as that. But we had to remake the whole paper after it had gone to bed. That fellow Boot.'

'The one who upset you so all last week. I thought you were sacking him.'

'We did. Then we took him back. He's all right. Lord Copper knew best.'

Mr Salter took off his boots and Mrs Salter poured out the Ovaltine. When he had drunk it, he felt calmer.

'You know,' he said meditatively, 'it's a great experience to work for a man like Lord Copper. Again and again I've thought he was losing grip. But always it turns out he knew best. What made him spot Boot? It's a sixth sense . . . real genius.'

10

Popotakis's was empty and William was tired. He ate his dinner and strolled home. When he reached his room he found it filled with tobacco smoke; a cheroot, one of his cheroots, glowed in the darkness. A voice, with a strong German accent, said, 'Close the shutters, please, before you turn on the light.'

William did as he was asked. A man rose from the arm-chair, clicked his heels and made a guttural sound. He was a large blond man of military but somewhat dilapidated appearance. He wore khaki shorts and an open shirt, boots ragged and splashed with mud. His head, once shaven, was covered with stubble, uniform with his chin, like a clipped yew in a neglected garden.

'I beg your pardon?' said William.

The man clicked his heels again and made the same throaty sound, adding, 'That is my name.'

'Oh,' said William. Then he came to attention and said 'Boot.'

They shook hands.

'I must apologize for using your room. Once it was mine. I did not know until I found your luggage here that there had been a change. I left some specimens of ore. Do you by any chance know what has become of them?'

'I have them safe.'

'Well, it is of no importance now...I left a wife, too. Have you seen her?'

'She is in prison.'

'Yes,' said the German, without surprise. 'I suppose she is. They will put me in prison too. I have just come from my Consulate. They say they cannot protect me. I cannot complain. They warned me before we started that if I failed they could not protect me... and I have failed... if you will excuse me, I will sit down. I am very tired.'

'Have you had any dinner?'

'Not for two days. I have just returned from the interior. We could not stop to sleep or to look for food. All the way back they were trying to kill me. They had paid the bandits. I am very tired and very hungry.'

William took a case from the pile of stores; it was corded and wired and lined and battened to resist all emergencies. He struggled for some time while the German sat in a kind of melancholy stupor; then he said, 'There's some food in here if you can get it open.'

'Food.' At the word the German came to his senses. With surprising dexterity he got the blade of his clasp knife under the lid of the box; it fell open revealing William's Christmas dinner.

They spread it on the table – turkey, plum pudding, crystallized plums, almonds, raisins, champagne and crackers. The German cried a little, nostalgically, teutonically. Then he began to gorge, at first in silence, later, with the dessert, loquaciously.

'... three times they shot at me on the road – but the bandits have very old rifles. Not like the rifles we gave to Smiles. We gave him everything, machine-guns, tanks, consulates; we bought him two Paris newspapers, a column a day week after week – you know what that costs. There were five thousand volunteers ready to sail. He could have been in Jacksonburg in a month. No one wants the Jacksons here. They are foolish people. For a year we have been trying to make business with them. They said first one thing, then another. We gave them money; we gave them all money; heavens, how many Jacksons there are! Still, they would not make business . . .'

'I ought to warn you that I am a journalist.'

'That is well. When you come to write of this affair say that it was not my fault that we failed. It was Smiles. We gave him money and he ran away to the Sudan. He wanted me to go with him.'

'Wouldn't that have been better?'

'I had left my wife in Jacksonburg . . . besides, it is not good for me to go to the Sudan. I was once in trouble in Khartoum. There are many countries where it is not good for me to go. I have often been very foolish.' At the thought of his wife and of his former indiscretions he seemed once more to be overcome with melancholy. He sat in silence. William began to fear he would fall asleep.

'Where are you going to now?' he asked. 'You can't stay here, you know, or they will come and arrest you.'

'No,' said the German. 'I can't stay here.' And immediately he fell asleep, mouth open, head back, a crumpled cracker in his right hand, breathing uproariously.

And still that day was not ended.

Hardly had the German's preliminary, convulsive snorts and gurgles given place to the gentler, automatic, continuous snoring of regular sleep than William was again disturbed.

The night watchman stood clucking in the doorway, pointing towards the gates, smiling and nodding unintelligibly. The German never stirred; his snores followed William across the yard.

At the gates a motor-car was waiting. Its lights had been turned off. The yard and the lane outside it were in darkness. A voice, from inside the car, said, 'William, is it you?' Kätchen scrambled out and ran to him – as he had imagined it, like a wounded bird. 'Darling, darling,' he said.

They clung together. In the darkness he could discern over Kätchen's shoulder the figure of the night watchman, stork-like, on one leg, his spear behind his shoulders.

'Darling,' said Kätchen. 'Have you got any money with you?'

'Yes.'

'A lot?'

'Yes.'

'I promised the driver a hundred American dollars. Was it too much?'

'Who is he?'

'The postmaster-general's chauffeur. They have arrested the postmaster-general. He was a Jackson. All the Jacksons are being arrested. He got the key of the room when the soldiers were having supper. I said I would give him a hundred dollars if he brought me back.'

'Tell him to wait. I'll get the money from my room.'

The driver wrapped himself in his blanket and settled down over the wheel. Kätchen and William stood together in the yard.

'I must go away,' said Kätchen. '*We* must go away. I have thought about it in the motor-car. You must marry me. Then I shall be British and they will not be able to hurt me. And we will leave Ishmaelia at once. No more journalism. We will go to Europe together. Will you do that?'

'Yes,' said William without hesitation.

'And will you marry me properly – in an office?'

'Yes.'

'It will be the first time I have been properly married.' The tremendous respirations echoed across the yard. 'What is that? William, there is something making a noise in your room.'

'Yes, I had forgotten . . . you made me forget. Come and see who it is.'

They climbed the steps, hand in hand, crossed the veranda and reached the door of William's room.

Kätchen dropped his hand and ran forward with a little cry. She knelt at the German's side and held him, shook him. He stirred and grunted and opened his eyes. They spoke to one another in German; Kätchen nestled against him; he laid his cheek against her head and lapsed again into coma.

'How happy I am,' she said. 'I thought he would never come back, that he was dead or had left me. How he sleeps. Is he well? Is he hungry?'

'No,' said William. 'I don't think you need have any anxiety on that point. Within the last hour, to my certain knowledge, he has consumed an entire Christmas dinner designed for four children or six adults.'

'He must have been starving. Is he not thin?'

'No,' said William. 'Frankly I should not have called him thin.'

'Ah, you should have seen him before he went away ... How he snores. That is a good sign. Whenever he is well he snores like this.' She brooded fondly over the unconscious figure. 'But he is dirty.'

'Yes,' said William, 'very dirty indeed.'

'William, you sound so cross suddenly. Are you not glad my husband has come back to me?'

'Come back *to you*?'

'William, you are not jealous. How I despise jealousy. You could not be jealous of my husband. I have been with him for two years, before ever you and I met. I knew he would not leave me. But what are we to do now? I must think ...'

They both thought, not on the same lines.

'I have a plan,' said Kätchen at last.

'Yes?' said William gloomily.

'I think it will work nice. My husband is German, so the Ishmael-ites will not be allowed to hurt him. It is harder for me because of my papers. So I will marry you. Then I shall be English and I and my husband can go away together. You will give us our tickets to Europe. It will not be expensive, we will travel in the second class. ... How is that?'

'There are several serious objections; for one thing the German Legation are not going to protect your friend.'

'Oh, dear. I thought if one had papers one was always safe everywhere ... I must think of another plan ... If, after I marry you, I marry my husband, he would then be English, yes?'

'No.'

'Oh, dear.'

They had to speak with raised voices to make themselves heard above the German's snores. 'Would it be very unkind to wake my husband? He is always full of ideas. He has great experience of difficulties.'

She shook him into sensibility and they spoke together earnestly in German.

William began to collect the distasteful remains of the Christmas dinner; he put the crackers back in their box and arranged the empty tins and bottles outside his door beside his dirty shoes.

'Our only hope is the postmaster-general's chauffeur,' said Kätchen at last. 'The town guards know him. If they have not yet heard that the postmaster-general is in prison he can drive through the barricades without difficulty. But he could not get to the frontier. They would telegraph for him to be stopped. The railway is impossible.'

'There is the river,' said the German. 'It is high. We could strike it below the cataract fifteen miles from here. Then we could sail down to French territory – if we had a boat.'

'How much would a boat cost?' asked Kätchen.

'Once in the Matto Grosso I made a boat,' said the German dreamily. 'I burned out the centre of an iron-wood tree. It took ten weeks to make, and it sank like a stone.'

'A boat,' said Kätchen. 'But you have a boat – *our* boat.'

11

They drove through the streets of the sleeping city, the German in front with the postmaster-general's chauffeur, Kätchen and William at the back with the canoe. A few hyenas flashed red eyes at them from the rubbish heaps, then turned their mangy quarters and scuttled off into the night.

The guards at the barrier saluted and let them pass into the open country. They drove in silence.

'I will send you a postcard,' said Kätchen, at last, 'to tell you we are well.'

Day was breaking as they reached the river; they came upon it suddenly where it flowed black and swift between low banks. There they assembled the canoe; William and Kätchen did the work, as they had done before; it was familiar; there was no adventure now in fitting the sockets. The German sat on the running-board of the car, still stupefied with the lack of sleep; his eyes were open; his mouth also. When the boat was ready they called to him to join them.

'It is very small,' he said.

William stood knee deep among the reeds holding it with diffi-culty; the current tugged and sucked, Kätchen climbed in, balan-cing precariously, with a hand on William's arm; then the German; the boat sank almost to the gunwales.

'We shall not have room for the stores,' said Kätchen.

'My boat in Matto Grosso was twenty feet long,' said the German drowsily, 'it turned over and went straight to the bottom. Two of my boys were drowned. They had always said it would sink.'

'If we get safely to the French border,' said Kätchen, 'shall we leave the boat there for you? Will you want it again?'

'No.'

'We might sell it and send you the money.'

'Yes.'

'Or we could keep the money until we get to Europe – it will be easier to send.'

'It is an abstract speculation,' said the German, suddenly awake, and impatient. 'It is a question purely of academic interest. We shall not reach the French border. Let us start.'

'Good-bye,' said Kätchen.

The two figures sat opposite one another, knees touching, ex-pectant, as though embarking upon the ornamental waters of a fair-ground; lovers for the day's outing, who had stood close in a queue, and now waited half reluctant to launch into the closer intimacy of the grottoes and transparencies.

William released the boat; it revolved once or twice, slowly, as it drifted into mid-stream; there it was caught in the full power of the flood, and, spinning dizzily, was swept out of sight into the dawn.

William returned to his empty room. The boy had put back the debris of the Christmas dinner, carefully ranged upon the writing-table. A cleft stick lay across the bed, bearing no message for Wil-liam. He sat down at his table and with his eyes fixed on the label of the turkey tin, began to compose his dispatch.

'Take to wireless,' he ordered his boy. 'Sit on step till open. Then come back and sit on this step. Don't let anyone in. Want to sleep very much.'

But he did not sleep very much.

The boy shook him at half past ten. 'No send,' he said, waving the typewritten message.

William painfully roused himself from his brief sleep. 'Why no send?'

'No Jacksons. No Government. No send.'

William dressed and went to the wireless bureau. A jaunty black face smiled at him through the guichet; starched collar, bow tie, long ivory cigarette holder – the welter-weight.

'Good morning,' said William. 'I hope you are not feeling too sore after your meeting with the goat. Where is the wireless clerk?'

'He is on a little holiday. I have taken over from him.'

'My boy says that this cable has been refused.'

'That is so. We are very much occupied with government business. I think we shall be occupied all day, perhaps for several days. It would have been far better if you had gone for the tour we had planned for you. Meanwhile perhaps you would like to see the manifesto that we are issuing. I think you do not read Ishmaelite?'

'No.'

'A very barbarous language. I have never learned it. Soon we shall make Russian the official language of the country, I have a copy here in English.'

He handed William a sheet of crimson paper headed *WORKERS OF ISHMAELIA UNITE* and snapped down the trap of the guichet.

William stepped out into the sunlight. A black man on a ladder was painting out the name of Jackson Street. Someone had stencilled a sickle and hammer on the front of the post office, a red flag hung limp overhead. He read the manifesto.

. . . development of mineral resources of the workers by the workers for the workers . . . Jacksons to be speedily brought to trial . . . arraigned for high treason to the Revolution . . . liquidated . . . New Calendar. Year One of the Soviet State of Ishmaelia . . .

He crumpled the paper into a scarlet ball and tossed it to the goat; it went down like an oyster.

He stood on his veranda and looked across the yard to the beastly attic from which Kätchen used to greet him, at about this time in the morning, calling him to come out to Popotakis's Ping-Pong Parlour.

'Change and decay in all around I see,' he sang softly, almost unctuously. It was the favourite tune of his Uncle Theodore.

He bowed his head.

'Oh, great crested grebe,' he prayed, 'maligned fowl, have I not expiated the wrong my sister did you; am I still to be an exile from the green places of my heart? Was there not even in the remorseless dooms of antiquity a god from the machine?'

He prayed without hope.

And then above the multitudinous noises of the Pension Dressler came a small sound, an insistent, swelling monotone. The servants in the yard looked up. The sound increased and high above them in the cloudless sky, rapidly approaching, there appeared an aeroplane. The sound ceased as the engine was cut off. The machine circled and dropped silently. It was immediately overhead when a black speck detached itself and fell towards them; white stuff streamed behind it, billowed and spread. The engine sang out again; the machine swooped up and away, out of sight and hearing. The little domed tent paused and gently sank, as though immersed in depths of limpid water.

'If he comes on to my roof,' said Frau Dressler. 'If he breaks anything . . . '

The parachutist came on the roof; he broke nothing. He landed delicately on the tips of his toes; the great sail crumpled and collapsed behind him; he deftly extricated himself from the bonds and stood clear. He took a comb from his pocket and settled the slightly disordered auburn hair about his temples, glancing at his watch, bowed to Frau Dressler and asked for a ladder, courteously in five or six languages. They brought him one. Rung by rung, on pointed, snake-skin toes he descended to the yard. The milch-goat reverently made way for him. He smiled politely at William; then recognized him.

'Why!' he exclaimed. 'It is my fellow traveller, the journalist. How agreeable to meet a fellow Britisher in this remote spot.'

CHAPTER 5

I

THE SUN SANK behind the gum trees and the first day of the Soviet of Ishmaelia ended in crimson splendour. The deserted bar-room of Popotakis's Ping-Pong Parlour glowed in the fiery sunset.

'I really do not know how to thank you,' said William.

'Please,' said his companion, laying a hand lightly on his, 'please do not embarrass me. The words you have just used seem to haunt me, wherever I go. Ever since that auspicious afternoon when you were kind enough to give me a place in your aeroplane, I have feared, sooner or later, to hear them on your lips. I suggested as much at the time, I think, if my memory does not deceive me.'

Mr Popotakis switched on the lights above the ping-pong table and asked, 'You want a game, Mr Baldwin?' for it was by this name that William's friend now preferred to be called.

('It is a convenient name,' he had explained. 'Non-committal, British and above all easily memorable. I am often obliged to pursue my business interests under an alias. My man Cuthbert chooses them for me. He has a keen sense of what is fitting, but he sometimes luxuriates a little. There have been times when his more fanciful inventions have entirely slipped my memory, at important moments. So now I am plain Mr Baldwin. I beg you to respect my confidence.')

Mr Baldwin resumed his little dissertation.

'In the rough and tumble of commercial life,' he said, 'I endeavour to requite the kindnesses I receive. The kindnesses have become more profuse and the rewards more substantial of recent years . . . however, I am sure that in you I met an entirely disinterested benefactor. I am glad to have prospered your professional career so inexpensively.

'Do you know, my first impression of you was not of a young man destined for great success in journalism? Quite the reverse. In fact, to be frank with you, I was sceptical of your identity and, when you told me of your destination, I feared you might be coming here with some ulterior object. If I seemed evasive in the early days of our – I hope I may say – friendship, you must forgive me.

'And now Mr Popotakis is offering us a game of ping-pong. For my part, I think it might be refreshing.'

Mr Baldwin removed his coat and rolled the sleeves of his crêpe-de-Chine shirt. Then he took his bat and poised himself expectantly at the end of the table. William served. Love, fifteen; love, thirty; love, forty, game; fifteen, love; thirty, love; forty, love, game. The little man was ubiquitous, ambidextrous. He crouched and bounded and skipped, slamming and volleying; now spanning the net, now five yards back, now flicking the ball from below his knees, now rocketing high among the electric lights; keeping up all the while a bright, bantering conversation in demotic Greek with Mr Popotakis.

At the end of the love set he resumed his coat and said, 'Quarter past six. No doubt you are impatient to send your second message . . .'

For a private wireless transmitter was one of the amenities to which William had been introduced that day.

Since Mr Baldwin's arrival Jacksonburg – or Marxville as it had been called since early that morning – had proved a town of unsuspected convenience.

'I have a little *pied à terre* here,' Mr Baldwin had explained, when William suggested their lunching at the Pension Dressler. 'My man Cuthbert has been putting it in order. I have not seen it and I fear the worst, but he is a sensitive fellow and might be put out if I lunched away from home on the day of my arrival. Will you not share the adventure of lunching with me?'

They walked, for Mr Baldwin complained that his flight had brought on a slight stiffness of the legs. He took William's arm, guiding him through the less frequented by-ways of the town and questioning him earnestly about the events of the last twenty-four hours.

'And where are your colleagues? I anticipated being vexed by them.'

'They have all gone off into the interior to look for Smiles.'

'That is excellent. You will be the sole spectator at the last act of our little drama.'

'It won't be much help. They've shut the wireless bureau.'

'It shall be opened soon. Meanwhile I have no doubt Cuthbert will be able to accommodate you. He and a Swiss associate of mine have fixed up a little makeshift which appears to work. I have been in correspondence with them daily.'

Even in the side streets there was evidence of the new régime; twice they were obliged to shelter as police lorries thundered past them laden with glaucous prisoners. The Café Wilberforce had changed its name to Café Lenin. There had been a distribution of red flags, which, ingeniously knotted or twisted, had already set a fashion in head-dresses among the women of the market.

'I ought to have come yesterday,' said Mr Baldwin peevishly. 'It would have saved a great deal of unnecessary reorganization. God bless my soul, there's another of those police vans.' They skipped for a doorway. In the centre of a machine-gun squad, William recognized the dignified figure of Mr Earl Russell Jackson.

At length their way led them to the outskirts of the city, to the nondescript railway quarter, where sidings and goods yards and warehouses stood behind a stockade of blue gums and barbed wire. They passed an iron gate and approached a bungalow.

'It is M. Giraud's,' said Mr Baldwin. 'And this is M. Giraud, but I think that introductions are superfluous.'

The bearded ticket collector greeted them deferentially from the veranda.

'M. Giraud has been in my service for some time,' said Mr Baldwin. 'He had, in fact, been in consultation with me when you had the pleasure of travelling with him from the coast. I followed his brief period of public prominence with interest and, to be quite frank, with anxiety. If I may criticize without offence the profession you practise – at this particular moment with almost unique success – I should say that you reporters missed a good story in Mr Giraud's little trip. I read the newspapers with lively interest. It is seldom that they are absolutely, point-blank wrong. That is the popular belief, but those who are in the know can usually discern an embryo truth, a little grit of fact, like the core of a pearl, round which have been deposited the delicate layers of ornament. In the present case, for instance, there *was* a Russian agent arranging to take over the government; M. Giraud *was* an important intermediary. But he was not the Russian. The workings of commerce and politics are very, very simple, but not quite as simple as your colleagues represent them. My man Cuthbert was also on the train with you. He should have given you a clue, but no one recognized him. He drove the engine. It was due to his ignorance of local usage that the lost luggage van was eventually recovered.'

'And may I ask,' said William diffidently, 'since you are telling me so much – whose interests do *you* represent?'

'My own,' said the little man simply. 'I plough a lonely furrow... Let us see what they have been able to scrape up for luncheon.'

They had scraped up fresh river fish, and stewed them with white wine and aubergines; also a rare local bird which combined the tender flavour of partridge with the solid bulk of the turkey; they had roasted it and stuffed it with bananas, almonds, and red peppers; also a baby gazelle which they had seethed with truffles in its mother's milk; also a dish of feathery Arab pastry and a heap of unusual fruits. Mr Baldwin sighed wistfully. 'Well,' he said, 'I suppose it will not hurt us to rough it for once. We shall appreciate the pleasures of civilization all the more... but my descent in the parachute gave me quite an appetite. I had hoped for something a little more enterprising.'

He swallowed his digestive pills, praised the coffee, and then expressed a desire to sleep.

'Cuthbert will look after you,' he said. 'Give him anything you want sent to your paper.'

The wireless transmitter was in and beneath the garage; its mast rose high overhead, cleverly disguised as a eucalyptus tree. William watched the first words of his rejected dispatch sputter across the ether to Mr Salter; then he, too, decided to sleep.

At five o'clock, when Mr Baldwin reappeared, he was in a different, more conspicuous suit and the same mood of urbanity and benevolence.

'Let us visit the town,' he said, and, inevitably, they had gone to Popotakis's and they sat there at sunset in the empty bar-room.

' ... No doubt you are impatient to send off your second message; I trust that the little mystery of the situation here is now perfectly clear to you.'

'Well ... No ... not exactly.'

'No? There are still gaps? Tut, tut, Mr Boot, the foreign correspondent of a great newspaper should be able to piece things together for himself. It is all very simple. There has been a competition for the mineral rights of Ishmaelia which, I may say as their owner, have been preposterously over-valued. In particular the German and the Russian Governments were willing to pay extravagantly – but in kind. Unhappily for them the commodities they had to offer – treasures from the Imperial palaces, timber, toys, and so forth – were not much in demand in Ishmaelia – in presidential circles at any rate. President Jackson had long wanted to make adequate provision for his retirement, and I was fortunately placed in being able to offer him gold for his gold concession, and my rivals found themselves faced by the alternative of abandoning their ambitions or upsetting President Jackson. They both preferred the latter, more romantic course. The Germans, with a minimum of discernment, chose to set up a native of low character named Smiles as prospective dictator. I never had any serious fears of him. The Russians, more astutely, purchased the Young Ishmaelite party and are, as you see, momentarily in the ascendant.

'That, I think, should give you your material for an article.'

'Yes,' said William. 'Thank you very much. I'm sure Mr Salter and Lord Copper will be very grateful.'

'Dear me, how little you seem to have mastered the correct procedure of your profession. You should ask me whether I have any message for the British public. I have. It is this: *Might must find a way*. Not "*Force*", remember; other nations use "force"; we Britons alone use "Might". Only one thing can set things right – sudden and extreme violence, or, better still, the effective threat of it. I am committed to very considerable sums in this little gamble and, alas, our countrymen are painfully tolerant, nowadays, of the losses of their financial superiors. One sighs for the days of Pam or Dizzy. I possess a little influence in political quarters, but it will strain it severely to provoke a war on my account. Some semblance of popular support, such as your paper can give, would be very valu-able...But I dislike embarrassing my affairs with international issues. I should greatly prefer it, if the thing could be settled neatly and finally, here and now.'

As he spoke there arose from the vestibule a huge and confused tumult; the roar of an engine which, in the tranquil bar-room, sounded like a flight of heavy aeroplanes, a series of percussions like high explosive bombs, shrill, polyglot human voices inarticulate with alarm, and above them all a deep bass, trolling chant, half nautical, half ecclesiastical. The flimsy structure throbbed and shook from its shallow foundation to its asbestos roof; the metal-bound doors flew open revealing, first, the two black commission-aires backing into the bar and, next, driving them before him, a very large man astride a motor cycle. He rode slowly between the ping-pong tables, then put his feet to the floor and released the handle-bars. The machine shot from under him, charged the bar, and lay on its side with its back wheel spinning in a cloud of exhaust-gas, while the rider, swaying ponderously from side to side like a performing bear, surveyed the room in a puzzled but friendly spirit.

It was the Swede; but a Swede transfigured, barely recognizable as the mild apostle of the coffee pot and the sticking plaster. The hair of his head stood like a tuft of ornamental, golden grass; a vinous flush lit the upper part of his face, the high cheek bones, the blank, calf-like eyes; on the broad concavities of his forehead the veins bulged varicosely. Still singing his nordic dirge he saluted the empty chairs and ambled towards the bar.

At the first alarm Mr Popotakis had fled the building. The Swede spanned the counter and fumbled on the shelf beyond. William and Mr Baldwin watched him fascinated as he raised bottle after bottle to his nose, sniffed and tossed them disconsolately behind him. Presently he found what he wanted – the sixty per cent. He knocked off the neck, none too neatly, and set the jagged edge to his lips; his Adam's apple rose and fell. Then, refreshed, he looked about him again. The motor cycle at his feet, churning and stinking, attracted his notice and he silenced it with a single tremendous kick.

'Might,' said Mr Baldwin reverently.

The Swede's eyes travelled slowly about him, settled on William, goggled, squinted, and betrayed signs of recognition. He swayed across the room and took William's hand in a paralysing grip: he jabbed hospitably at his face with the broken bottle and addressed him warmly and at length in Swedish.

Mr Baldwin replied. The sound of his own tongue in a strange land affected Olafsen strongly. He sat down and cried while Mr Baldwin, still in Swedish, spoke to him comfortably.

'Sometimes it is necessary to dissemble one's nationality,' he explained to William. 'I have given our friend here to believe that I am a compatriot.'

The black mood passed. Olafsen gave a little whoop and lunged in a menacing manner with the absinthe bottle.

He introduced William to Mr Baldwin.

'This is my great friend, Boot,' he said, 'a famous journalist. He is my friend though I have been made a fool. I have been made a fool,' he cried louder and more angrily, 'by a lot of blacks. They sent me down the line to an epidemic and I was laughed at. But I am going to tell the President. He is a good old man and he will punish them. I will go to his residence, now, and explain everything.'

He rose from the table and bent over the disabled motor cycle. Mr Popotakis peeped round the corner of the service door and, seeing the Swede still in possession, popped back out of sight.

'Tell me,' said Mr Baldwin. 'Your friend here – does he become more or less pugnacious with drink?'

'I believe, more.'

'Then let us endeavour to repay his hospitality.'

With his own hands Mr Baldwin fetched a second bottle of sixty per cent from the shelf. Tolerantly conforming to the habits of the place, he snapped off the neck and took a hearty swig; then he passed the bottle to the Swede. In a short time they were singing snatches of lugubrious Baltic music, Mr Baldwin matching the Swede's deep bass, in his ringing alto. Between their songs they drank, and between drinks Mr Baldwin explained concisely, but with many repetitions, the constitutional changes of the last twenty-four hours.

'Russians are bad people.'

'Very bad.'

'They say they are Princes and they borrow money!'

'Yes.'

'President Jackson is a good old man. He gave me a harmonium for my mission. Some of the Jacksons are silly fellows, but the President is my friend.'

'Exactly.'

'I think,' said the Swede, rising, 'we will go and see my friend Jackson.'

2

The Presidential Residence, on this first, and, as it turned out, last, evening of the Soviet Union of Ishmaelia, was ceremoniously illuminated, not with the superb floods of concealed arc lamps dear to the more mature dictatorships, but, for want of better, with a multitude of 'fairy lights' with which the Jacksons were wont to festoon the veranda on their not infrequent official birthdays; all the windows of the façade, ten of them, were unshuttered and the bright lamps behind gave cosy glimpses of Nottingham lace, portières, and enlarged photographs. A red flag hung black against the night sky. Dr Benito, backed by a group of 'Young Ishmaelites', stood on the central balcony. A large crowd of Ishmaelites had assembled to see the lights.

'What is he saying?' asked William.

'He has proclaimed the abolition of Sunday and he is calling for volunteers for a ten-day, ten-hour week. I do not think he has chosen the occasion with tact.'

The Swede had left them, pushing forward on his errand of liberation. William and Mr Baldwin stood at the back of the crowd. The temper of the people was apathetic. They liked to see the place lit up. Oratory pleased them, whatever its subject; sermons, educational lectures, political programmes, panegyrics of the dead or living, appeals for charity – all had the same soporific effect. They liked the human voice in all its aspects, most particularly when it was exerted in sustained athletic effort. They had, from time to time, heard too many unfulfilled prophecies issue from that balcony to feel any particular apprehensions about the rigours of the new régime. Then, while Benito was well in his stride, a whisper of interest passed through them; necks were stretched. The Swede had appeared at the ground-floor window. Benito, sensing the new alertness in his audience, raised his voice, rolled his eyes, and flashed his white teeth. The audience stood on tip-toe with expectation. They could see what he could not – the Swede, in a lethargic but effective manner, liquidating the front parlour. He pulled the curtains down, he swept the fourteen ornamental vases off the chimney-piece, with a loud crash he threw a pot of fern through the window. The audience clapped enthusiastically. The 'Young Ishmaelites' behind Benito began to consult, but the speaker, oblivious to all except his own eloquence, continued to churn the night air with Marxian precepts.

To the spectators at the back of the crowd, out of earshot of the minor sounds, the sequence unfolded itself with the happy inconsequence of an early comedy film. The revolutionary committee left their leader's side and disappeared from view to return almost immediately in rout, backwards, retreating before the Swede who now came into the light of the upper drawing-room brandishing a small gilt chair over his head.

It was not a ten-feet drop from the balcony. The traditional, ineradicable awe of the white man combined with the obvious immediate peril of the whirling chair legs to decide the issue. With one accord they plunged over the rail on to the woolly pates below. Benito was the last to go, proclaiming class war with his last audible breath.

The Swede addressed the happy people in Ishmaelite.

'He says he is looking for his friend President Jackson,' explained Mr Baldwin.

A cheer greeted the announcement. 'Jackson' was one of the perennially exhilarating words in the Ishmaelite vocabulary; a name associated since childhood with every exciting event in Ishmaelite life. They had been agreeably surprised to learn that the Jacksons had that morning all been sent to prison; now, it would be a treat to see them all again. As long as something, good or ill, was happening to the Jacksons, the Ishmaelites felt an intelligent interest in politics. Soon they were all crying: 'Jackson. Jackson. Jackson.'

'Jackson. Jackson,' shouted Mr Baldwin, at William's side. 'I think we may be satisfied that the counter-revolution has triumphed.'

3

An hour later William sat in his room at the Pension Dressler and began his dispatch to *The Beast*.

From the main street a short distance away could be heard sounds of rejoicing from the populace. President Jackson had been found, locked in the wood shed. Now, dazed and stiff, he was being carried shoulder high about the city; other processions had formed about other members of the liberated family. Now and then rival processions met and came to blows. Mr Popotakis had boarded up his café but several Indian drink shops had been raided and the town was settling down to a night of jollity.

PRESS COLLECT URGENT MAN CALLED MISTER BALDWIN HAS BOUGHT COUNTRY, William began.

'No,' said a gentle voice behind him. 'If you would not resent my co-operation, I think I can compose a dispatch more likely to please my good friend Copper.'

Mr Baldwin sat at William's table and drew the typewriter towards himself. He inserted a new sheet of paper, tucked up his cuffs and began to write with immense speed:

MYSTERY FINANCIER RECALLED EXPLOITS RHODES LAWRENCE TODAY SECURING VAST EAST AFRICAN CONCESSION BRITISH INTERESTS IN TEETH ARMED OPPOSITION BOLSHEVIST SPIES ...

'It will make about five full columns,' he said, when it was finished. 'From my experience of newspapers I think I can safely say that they will print it in full. I am afraid we are too late for tomorrow's paper, but there is no competition to fear. Perhaps I shall have the felicity of finding you as my fellow traveller on the return journey.'

The sounds of rejoicing drew nearer and rose to a wild hubbub in the lane outside.

'Dear me,' said Mr Baldwin. 'How disconcerting. I believe they have found me out.'

But it was only General Gollancz Jackson being pulled about the town in his motor-car. The bare feet pattered away in the darkness. The cries of acclamation faded.

A knock on the door.

Cuthbert reported that, in view of the disturbed state of the town, he had taken the liberty of bringing his master's sheets to the Pension Dressler and making up a bed for him there.

'You did quite right, Cuthbert . . . And now, if you will forgive me, I will say good night. I have had an unusually active day.'

BOOK III

BANQUET

CHAPTER 1

I

THE BELLS OF St Bride's chimed unheard in the customary afternoon din of the Megalopolitan Building. The country edition had gone to bed; below traffic-level, in grotto-blue light, leagues of paper ran noisily through the machines; overhead, where floor upon floor rose from the dusk of the streets to the clear air of day, ground-glass doors opened and shut; figures in frayed and perished braces popped in and out; on a hundred lines reporters talked at cross purposes; sub-editors busied themselves with their humdrum task of reducing to blank nonsense the sheaves of misinformation which whistling urchins piled before them; beside a hundred typewriters soggy biscuits lay in a hundred tepid saucers. At the hub and still centre of all this animation, Lord Copper sat alone in splendid tranquillity. His massive head, empty of thought, rested in sculptural fashion upon his left fist. He began to draw a little cow on his writing-pad.

Four legs with cloven feet, a ropy tail, swelling udder and mod-estly diminished teats, a chest and head like an Elgin marble – all this was straightforward stuff. Then came the problem – which was the higher, horns or ears? He tried it one way, he tried it the other; both looked equally unconvincing; he tried different types of ear – tiny, feline triangles, asinine tufts of hair and gristle, even, in desperation, drooping flaps remembered from a guinea-pig in the backyard of his earliest home; he tried different types of horn – royals, the elegant antennae of the ibis, the vast armoury of moose and buffalo. Soon the paper before him was covered like the hall of a hunter with freakish heads. None looked right. He brooded over them and found no satisfaction.

It was thus that Mr Salter found him.

Mr Salter had not wanted to come and see Lord Copper. He had nothing particular to say. He had not been summoned. But he had the right of entry to his owner's presence, and it was only thus, he believed, by unremitting, wholly uncongenial self-assertion, that he could ever hope for a change of job.

'I wanted to consult you about Bucarest,' he said.

'Ah.'

'There's a long story from Jepson about a pogrom. Have we any policy in Bucarest?'

Lord Copper roused himself from his abstraction. 'Someone on this paper must know about cows,' he said petulantly.

'Cows, Lord Copper?'

'Don't we keep a man to write about the country?'

'Oh. That was Boot, Lord Copper.'

'Well, have him come and see me.'

'We sent him to Africa.'

'Well, have him come back. What's he doing there? Who sent him?'

'He is on his way back now. It was Boot who brought off the great story in Ishmaelia. When we scooped Hitchcock,' he added, for Lord Copper was frowning in a menacing way.

Slowly the noble face lightened.

'Ah, yes, smart fellow, Boot. He was the right man for that job.'

'It was you who discovered him, Lord Copper.'

'Of course, naturally . . . had my eye on him for some time. Glad he made good. There's always a chance for real talent on the *Beast*, eh, Salter?'

'Definitely, Lord Copper.'

'Preparations going ahead for Boot's reception?'

'Up to a point.'

'Let me see, what was it we decided to do for him?'

'I don't think, Lord Copper, that the question was ever actually raised.'

'Nonsense. It is a matter I have particularly at heart. Boot has done admirably. He is an example to everyone on the staff – *everyone*. I wish to show my appreciation in a marked manner. When do you say he gets back?'

'At the end of next week.'

'I will thank him personally... You never had any faith in that boy, Salter.'

'Well...'

'I remember it quite distinctly. You wished to have him recalled. But I knew he had the makings of a journalist in him. Was I right?'

'Oh, definitely, Lord Copper.'

'Well, then, let us have no more of these petty jealousies. The office is riddled with them. I shall make it my concern to see that Boot is substantially rewarded... What, I wonder, would meet the case?...' Lord Copper paused, undecided. His eye fell on the page of drawings and he covered it with his blotting paper. 'Suppose,' he said at length, 'we gave him another good foreign assignment. There is this all-women expedition to the South Pole – bound to be a story in that. Do you think that would meet the case?'

'Up to a point, Lord Copper.'

'Not too lavish?'

'Definitely not.'

'I imagine that the expenses of an expedition of that kind will be heavy. Have to charter his own ship – I understand they will have no man on board.' He paused dissatisfied. 'The trouble is that it is the kind of story that may not break for two years and then we shall have to put Boot's name before the public all over again. We ought to do something *now*, while the news is still hot. I gave that illiterate fellow Hitchcock a knighthood for less.' For the first time since the question of the cow had risen to perplex him, Lord Copper smiled. 'We certainly wiped Hitchcock's eye in Ishmaelia.' He paused, and his smile broadened as he recalled the triumph of ten days ago when the *Brute* had had to remake their front page at seven in the morning and fill a special late edition with a palpable fake.

'I don't want to cheapen official honours among the staff,' he said, 'but I have a very good mind to give a knighthood to Boot. How does that strike you, Salter?'

'You don't think, Lord Copper, that he is rather an inexperienced man...?'

'No, I don't. And I deplore this grudging attitude in you, Salter. You should welcome the success of your subordinates. A knighthood is a very suitable recognition. It will not cost us a penny. As I say, honours of this kind must be distributed with discretion but, properly used, they give a proper air of authority to the paper.'

'It will mean an increase of salary.'

'He shall have it. And he shall have a banquet. Send my social secretary to me. I will make the arrangements at once.'

2

No. 10 Downing Street was understaffed; the principal private secretary was in Scotland; the second secretary was on the Lido; Parliament was in vacation but there was no rest for the Prime Minister; he was obliged to muddle along, as best he could, with his third and fourth secretaries – unreliable young men related to his wife.

'Another name for the K.C.B.'s,' he said petulantly. 'Boot – gratis.'

'Yes, Uncle Mervyn. Are you – we giving any particular reason?'

'It's someone of Copper's. Call it "Services to Literature". It's some time since Copper asked for anything – I was getting nervous. I'll send him a personal note to tell him it is all right. You might drop a line to Boot.'

'O.K., Uncle.'

Later his secretary said to his less important colleague:

'More birthdays. Boot – writer. Do you know anything about him?'

'Yes, he's always lunching with Aunt Agnes. Smutty novels.'

'Well, write, and tell him he's fixed up, will you?'

Two days later, among his bills, John Courtenay Boot found forwarded to him a letter which said:

'*I am instructed by the Prime Minister to inform you that your name has been forwarded to H.M. the King with the recommendation for your inclusion in the Order of Knights Commanders of the Bath.*'

'Golly,' said Boot. 'It must be Julia.'

Mrs Stitch was staying in the same house. He went and sat on her bed while she had breakfast. Presently he said:

'By the way, what d'you think? They're making me a Knight.'
'Who are?'
'The King and the Prime Minister. You know...a real Knight...Sir John Boot, I mean.'
'*Well...*'
'Is it your doing?'
'*Well...* I hardly know what to say, John. Are you pleased about it?'
'It's hard to say yet...taken by surprise. But I *think* I am...In fact I know I am...Come to think of it, I'm very pleased indeed.'
'Good,' said Mrs Stitch. 'I'm very pleased too,' and added, 'I suppose I did have something to do with it.'
'It was angelic of you. But why?'
'Just the Stitch service. I felt you had been disappointed about that job on the newspaper.'
Later, when Algernon Stitch came back from a day with the partridges, she said:
'Algie. What's come over your Prime Minister? He's making John a Knight.'
'John Gassoway? Oh, well, he's had his tongue hanging out for something ever since we got in.'
'No, John Boot.'
It was not often that Algernon Stitch showed surprise. He did then.
'Boot,' he said. 'Good God!' and added after a long pause, 'Overwork. Breaking up. Pity.'

John Boot was not sure whether to make a joke of it. He extended his confidence to a Lady Greenidge and a Miss Montesquieu. By dinner time the house was buzzing with the news. There was no doubt in anyone else's mind whether it was a joke or not.

3

'Anything to declare?'
'Nothing.'
'What, not with all this?'

'I bought it in London in June.'

'All of it?'

'More. There was a canoe . . .'

The customs officer laid hands on the nearest of the crates which lay conspicuously among the hand luggage of returning holiday-makers. Then he read the label and his manner changed.

'Forgive me asking, sir, but are you by any chance Mr Boot of the *Beast*?'

'Yes, I suppose I am.'

'Ah. Then I don't think I need trouble you, sir . . . the missus *will* be pleased to hear I've seen you. We've been reading a lot about you lately.'

Everyone seemed to have read about William. From the moment he touched the fringe of the English-speaking world in the train de luxe from Marseille, William had found himself the object of undisguised curiosity. On his way round Paris he had bought a copy of the *Beast*. The front page was mainly occupied with the preparations of the Ladies' Antarctic Expedition but, inset in the middle, was a framed notice:

BOOT IS BACK

The man who made journalistic history, Boot of the Beast, *will tomorrow tell in his own inimitable way the inner story of his meteoric leap to fame. How does it feel to tell the truth to two million registered readers? How does it feel to have risen in a single week to the highest pinnacle of fame? Boot will tell you.*

That had been the paper of the day before. At Dover William bought the current issue. There, above a facsimile of his signature and a composite picture of his passport photograph surcharged on an Ishmaelite landscape, in the size which the *Beast* reserved for its most expensive contributors, stood the promised article.

'*Two months ago,*' it said, '*when Lord Copper summoned me from my desk in the* Beast *office, to handle the biggest news story of the century, I had never been to Ishmaelia, I knew little of foreign politics. I was being pitted against the most brilliant brains, the experience, and the learning of the civilized world. I had nothing except my youth, my will to succeed, and what – for want of a better word – I must call my flair. In the two months' battle of wits . . .*'

William could read no more. Overcome with shame he turned towards the train. A telegraph boy was loafing about the platform uttering monotonous, monosyllabic, plaintive, gull-like cries which, in William's disturbed mind, sounded like 'Boot. Boot. Boot.' William turned guiltily towards him; he bore a cardboard notice, stuck, by a felicitous stroke of fancy, into a cleft stick, on which was inscribed in unmistakable characters, '*Boot*.'

'I'm afraid that must be for me,' said William.

'There's a whole lot of them.'

The train seemed likely to start. William took the telegrams and opened them in the carriage, under the curious eyes of his fellow travellers.

PERSONALLY GRATIFIED YOUR SAFE RETURN COPPER.

BEAST REPRESENTATIVE WILL MEET YOU VICTORIA STOP PLEASE REPORT HERE IMMEDIATELY YOU RETURN STOP TALK BUSINESS NO ONE SALTER.

WILL YOU ACCEPT FIVE YEAR CONTRACT FIVE THOUSAND YEAR ROVING CORRESPONDENT EDITOR BRUTE.

PLEASE WIRE AUTHORITY NEGOTIATE BOOK SERIAL CINEMA RIGHTS AUTOBIOGRAPHY PAULS LITERARY AGENCY.

There were others, similarly phrased. William released them, one by one as he read them, at the open window. The rush of air whirled them across the charred embankment to the fields of stubble and stacked corn beyond.

At Victoria it was, once again, William's luggage which betrayed him. As he stood among the crates and bundles waiting for a taxi, a very young man approached him and said, 'I say, please, are you William Boot?' He had a pimply, eager face.

'Yes.'

'I'm from the *Beast*. They sent me to meet you. Mr Salter did.'

'Very kind of him.'

'I expect you would like a drink after your journey.'

'No, thank you.'

'Mr Salter said I was to ask you.'

'Very kind of him.'

'I say, please have a drink. Mr Salter said I could put it down as expenses.'

The young man seemed very eager.

'All right,' said William.

'You wouldn't know me,' said the young man as they walked to the buffet. 'I'm Bateson. I've only been on the paper three weeks. This is the first time I've charged anything on expenses. In fact it is the first time I've drawn any money from the *Beast* at all. I'm "on space", you see.'

'Ah.'

They reached the buffet and Bateson bought some whisky. 'I say,' he said, 'would you think it awful cheek if I asked you to do something?'

'What?'

'It's your big story. I've got a first edition of it.' He drew a grubby newspaper from his pocket. 'Would you sign for me?'

William signed.

'I say, thanks awfully. I'll get it framed. I've been carrying it about ever since it appeared – studying it, you know. That's the way they told me in the Correspondence School. Did you ever take a Corres-pondence School?'

'No.'

Bateson looked disappointed. 'Oh, dear, aren't they a good thing? They're terribly expensive.'

'I expect they are a very good thing.'

'You do think so, don't you? I'm a graduate of the Aircastle School. I paid fifteen shillings a month and I got a specially recom-mended diploma. That's how I got taken on the *Beast*. It's a great chance, I know. I haven't had anything in the paper yet. But one has to start sometime. It's a great profession, isn't it?'

'Yes, I suppose in a way it is.'

'It must be wonderful to be like you,' said Bateson wistfully. 'At the top. It's been a great chance my meeting you like this. I could hardly believe it when Mr Salter picked me to come. "Go and greet Boot," he said. "Give him a drink. Get him here before he signs on with the *Brute*." You wouldn't want to sign on with the *Brute*, would you?'

'No.'

'You do think the *Beast* is the leading paper, don't you? I mean it's the greatest chance you can have working for the *Beast*?'

'Yes.'

'I *am* glad. You see it's rather depressing sometimes, day after day and none of one's stories getting printed. I'd like to be a foreign correspondent like you. I say, would you think it awful cheek if I showed you some of the stuff I write? In my spare time I do it. I imagine some big piece of news and then I see how I should handle it. Last night in bed I imagined an actress with her throat cut. Shall I show it to you?'

'Please do,' said William, 'some time. But I think we ought to be going now.'

'Yes, I suppose we should. But you do think it's a good way of training oneself – inventing imaginary news?'

'None better,' said William.

They left the bar. The porter was keeping guard over the baggage. 'You'll need two cabs,' he said.

'Yes . . . Suppose you take the heavy stuff in one, Bateson, I'll follow with my own bags in the other.' He packed the young man in among the tropical equipment. 'Give them to Mr Salter and say I shan't need them any more.'

'But you're coming too?'

'I'm taking the cab behind,' said William.

They drove off down Victoria Street. When Bateson's cab was some distance ahead, William leant through the window and said, 'I've changed my mind. Go to Paddington instead.'

There was time before his train to telegraph to Boot Magna. '*Returning tonight William.*'

'Boot said he didn't want these any more.'

'No,' said Mr Salter, surveying with distaste the heap of travel-worn tropical equipment which encumbered his room. 'No, I suppose not. And where is Boot?'

'Just behind.'

'You ought to have stayed with him.'

'I'm sorry, Mr Salter.'

'There's no need for you to wait.'

'All right.'

'Well, what are you waiting for?'

'I was wondering, would you think it awful cheek if I asked for a souvenir.'

'Souvenir?'

'Of my meeting with Boot. Could you spare one of those sticks?'

'Take the lot.'

'I say, may I really. I say, thank you ever so much.'

'That boy, Bateson. Is he barmy or something?'

'I daresay.'

'What's he doing here?'

'He comes from the Aircastle Correspondence School. They guarantee a job to all their star pupils. They've a big advertising account with us, so we sometimes take one of their chaps "on space" for a bit.'

'Well, he's lost Boot. I suppose we can fire him now?'

'Surely.'

The harvest moon hung, brilliant and immense, over the elm trees. In the lanes around Boot Magna motor cycles or decrepit cars travelled noisily home from the village whist drive; Mr Atwater, the bad character, packed his pockets for the night's sport; the smell of petrol hung about the hedges but inside the park everything was sweet and still. For a few feet ahead the lights of the car shed a feeble, yellow glow; beyond, the warm land lay white as frost, and, as they emerged from the black tunnel of evergreen around the gates into the open pasture, the drive with its sharply defined ruts and hollows might have been a strip of the moon itself, a volcanic field cold since the creation.

A few windows were alight; only Uncle Theodore was still up. He opened the door to William.

'Ah,' he said, 'train late?'

'I don't think so.'

'Ah,' he said. 'We got your telegram.'

'Yes.'

'Had a good time?'

'Yes, fairly.'

'You must tell us all about it tomorrow. Your grandmother will want to hear, I know. Had any dinner?'

'Yes, thank you, on the train.'

'Good. We thought you might. We didn't keep anything hot. Rather short-handed at the moment. James hasn't been at all well, getting too old for his work – but there are some biscuits in the dining-room.'

'Thanks very much,' said William. 'I don't think I want anything.'

'No. Well, I think I'll be going along. Glad you've had such a good time. Don't forget to tell us about it. Can't say I read your articles. They were always cut out by the time I got the paper. Nannie Price disapproved of them. I must get hold of them, want to read them very much. . . . ' They were walking upstairs together; they reached the landing where their ways diverged. William carried his bag to his own room and laid it on the bed. Then he went to the window and, stooping, looked out across the moonlit park.

On such a night as this, not four weeks back, the tin roofs of Jacksonburg had laid open to the sky, a three-legged dog had awoken, started from his barrel in Frau Dressler's garden, and all over the town, in yards and refuse heaps, the pariahs had taken up his cries of protest.

4

'Well,' said Mr Salter, 'I've heard from Boot.'

'Any good?'

'No. No good.'

He handed the News Editor the letter that had arrived that morning from William.

Dear Mr Salter, it ran,

   Thank you very much for your letter and the invitation. It is very kind of Lord Copper, please thank him, but if you don't mind I think I won't come to the *banquet. You see it is a long way and there is a great deal to do here and I can't make speeches. I have to every now and then for things in the village and they are bad enough – a banquet would be worse.*

I hope you got the tent and things. Sorry about the canoe. I gave it to a German, also the Xmas dinner. I still have some of your money left. Do you want it back? Will you tell the other editor that I shall be sending him Lush Places on Wednesday.

> *Yours ever,*
> *William Boot.*

P.S. – Sorry. They forgot to post this. Now it's Saturday, so you won't get it till Monday.

'You think he's talking turkey with the *Brute*.'

'If he's not already signed up.'

'Ours is a nasty trade, Salter. No gratitude.'

'No loyalty.'

'I've seen it again and again since I've been in Fleet Street. It's enough to make one cynical.'

'What does Lord Copper say?'

'He doesn't know. For the moment, fortunately, he seems to have forgotten the whole matter. But he may raise it again at any moment.'

He did, that morning.

'. . . ah, Salter, I was talking to the Prime Minister last night. The honours list will be out on Wednesday. How are the preparations going for the Boot banquet? It's on the Thursday, I think.'

'That *was* the date, Lord Copper.'

'Good. I shall propose the health of our guest of honour. By the way, did Boot ever come and see me?'

'No, Lord Copper.'

'But I asked for him.'

'Yes, Lord Copper.'

'Then, why was he not brought? Once and for all, Salter, I will not have a barrier erected between me and my staff. I am as accessible to the humblest' . . . Lord Copper paused for an emphatic example . . . 'the humblest book reviewer as I am to my immediate entourage. I will have no cliques in the *Beast*, you understand me?'

'Definitely.'

'Then bring Boot here.'

'Yes, Lord Copper.'

It was an inauspicious beginning to Mr Salter's working day; worse was to come.

That afternoon he was sitting disconsolately in the News Editor's room when they were interrupted by the entry of a young man whose face bore that puffy aspect, born of long hours in the golf-house, which marked most of the better-paid members of the *Beast* staff on their return from their summer holidays. Destined by his trustees for a career in the Household Cavalry, this young man had lately reached the age of twenty-five and plunged into journalism with a zeal which Mr Salter found it difficult to understand. He talked to them cheerfully for some time on matters connected with his handicap. Then he said:

'By the way, I don't know if there's a story in it, but I was staying last week with my Aunt Trudie. John Boot was there among other people – you know, the novelist. He'd just got a letter from the King or someone like that, saying he was going to be knighted.' The look of startled concern on the two editors' faces checked him. 'I see you don't think much of it. Oh, well, I thought it might be worth mentioning. You know. "Youth's Opportunity in New Reign", that kind of thing.'

'*John* Boot – the novelist?'

'Yes. Rather good – at least I always read him. But it seemed a new line for the Prime Minister...'

'No,' said the Prime Minister with unusual finality.

'No?'

'No. It would be utterly impossible to change the list now. The man has been officially notified. And I could not consider knighting two men of the same name on the same day. Just the kind of thing the Opposition would jump on. Quite rightly. Smacks of jobbery, you know.'

'*Two Boots.*'

'Lord Copper must know.'

'Lord Copper must never know . . . There's only one comfort. We haven't committed ourselves to which Boot we are welcoming on Thursday or where he's come from.' He pointed to the engraved card which had appeared, during the week-end, on the desks of all the four-figure men in the office.

VISCOUNT COPPER
and

the Directors of the Megalopolitan Newspaper Company request the honour of your company to dinner on Wednesday, September 16th, at the Braganza Hotel, to welcome the return of

BOOT of THE BEAST

7.45 for 8 o'clock.

'We had a row with the social secretary about that. He said it wasn't correct. Lucky how things turned out.'

'It makes things a little better.'

'A little.'

'Salter, this is a case for personal contact. We've got to sign up this new Boot and any other Boot that may be going and one of them has got to be welcomed home on Thursday. There's only one thing for it, Salter, you must go down to the country and see Boot. I'll settle with the other.'

'To the country?'

'Yes, tonight.'

'Oh, but I couldn't go tonight.'

'Tomorrow, then.'

'You think it is really necessary?'

'Either that, or we must tell Lord Copper the truth.'

Mr Salter shuddered. 'But wouldn't it be better,' he said, 'if *you* went to the country?'

'No. I'll see this novelist and get him signed up.'

'And sent away.'

'Or welcomed home. And you will offer the other Boot any reasonable terms to lie low.'

'Any reasonable terms.'

'Salter, old man, what's come over you? You keep repeating things.'

'It's nothing. It's only... travelling... always upsets me.'

He had a cup of strong tea and later rang up the Foreign Contacts Adviser to find how he could best get to Boot Magna.

CHAPTER 2

I

AT THE OUTBREAK of the war of 1914 Uncle Roderick had declared for retrenchment. 'It's up to all of us who are over military age to do what we can. All unnecessary expenses must be cut down.'

'Why?' asked Great-Aunt Anne.

'It is a question of national emergency and patriotism.'

'How will our being uncomfortable hurt the Germans? It's just what they want.'

'Everything is needed at the front,' explained William's mother.

Discussion had raged for some days; every suggested economy seemed to strike invidiously at individual members of the household. At last it was decided to give up the telephone. Aunt Anne sometimes spoke bitterly of the time when 'my nephew Roderick won the war by cutting me off from my few surviving friends', but the service had never been renewed. The antiquated mahogany box still stood at the bottom of the stairs, dusty and silent, and telegrams which arrived in the village after tea were delivered next day with the morning post. Thus, William found Mr Salter's telegram waiting for him on the breakfast table.

His mother, Priscilla, and his three uncles sat round the table. They had finished eating and were sitting there, as they often sat for an hour or so, doing nothing at all. Priscilla alone was occupied, killing wasps in the honey on her plate.

'There's a telegram for you,' said his mother. 'We were wondering whether we ought to open it or send it up to you.'

375

It said: MUST SEE YOU IMMEDIATELY URGENT BUSINESS
ARRIVING BOOT MAGNA HALT TOMORROW AFTERNOON 6.10
SALTER.

The message was passed from hand to hand around the table.

Mrs Boot said, 'Who is Mr Salter, and what urgent business can
he possibly have here?'

Uncle Roderick said, 'He can't stay the night. Nowhere for him
to sleep.'

Uncle Bernard said, 'You must telegraph and put him off.'

Uncle Theodore said, 'I knew a chap called Salter once, but I
don't suppose it's the same one.'

Priscilla said, 'I believe he means to come today. It's dated
yesterday.'

'He's the Foreign Editor of the *Beast*,' William explained. 'The
one I told you about who sent me abroad.'

'He must be a very pushful fellow, inviting himself here like this.
Anyway, as Roderick says, we've no room for him.'

'We could send Priscilla to the Caldicotes for the night.'

'I like that,' said Priscilla, adding illogically, 'Why don't you send
William, it's his friend.'

'Yes,' said Mrs Boot. 'Priscilla could go to the Caldicotes.'

'I'm cubbing tomorrow,' said Priscilla, 'right in the other direction. You can't expect Lady Caldicote to send me thirty miles at
eight in the morning.'

For over an hour the details of Priscilla's hunt occupied the
dining-room. Could she send her horse overnight to a farm near
the meet; could she leave the Caldicotes at dawn, pick up her horse
at Boot Magna, and ride on; could she borrow Major Watkins's
trailer and take her horse to the Caldicotes for the night, then as
far as Major Watkins's in the morning and ride on from there; if
she got the family car from Aunt Anne and Major Watkins's
trailer, would Lady Caldicote lend her a car to take it to Major
Watkins's; would Aunt Anne allow the car to stay the night; would
she discover it was taken without her permission? They discussed the
question exhaustively, from every angle; Troutbeck twice glowered
at them from the door and finally began to clear the table; Mr Salter
and the object of his visit were not mentioned.

2

That evening, some time after the advertised hour, Mr Salter
alighted at Boot Magna Halt. An hour earlier, at Taunton, he
had left the express, and changed into a train such as he did
not know existed outside the imagination of his Balkan correspondents; a single tram-like, one-class coach, which had pottered in a
desultory fashion through a system of narrow, under-populated
valleys. It had stopped eight times, and at every station there
had been a bustle of passengers succeeded by a long, silent
pause, before it started again; men had entered who, instead of
slinking and shuffling and wriggling themselves into corners
and decently screening themselves behind newspapers, as civilized
people should when they travelled by train, had sat down squarely
quite close to Mr Salter, rested their hands on their knees, stared
at him fixedly and uncritically and suddenly addressed him on
the subject of the weather in barely intelligible accents; there had
been very old, unhygienic men and women, such as you never
saw in the Underground, who ought long ago to have been put
away in some public institution; there had been women carrying
a multitude of atrocious little baskets and parcels which they
piled on the seats; one of them had put a hamper containing
a live turkey under Mr Salter's feet. It had been a horrible
journey.

At last, with relief, Mr Salter alighted. He lifted his suitcase from
among the sinister bundles on the rack and carried it to the centre of
the platform. There was no one else for Boot Magna. Mr Salter had
hoped to find William waiting to meet him, but the little station was
empty except for a single porter who was leaning against the cab of
the engine engaged in a kind of mute, telepathic converse with the
driver, and a cretinous native youth who stood on the further side of
the paling, leant against it and picked at the dry paint-bubbles with a
toe-like thumb-nail. When Mr Salter looked at him, he glanced
away and grinned wickedly at his boots.

The train observed its customary two minutes' silence and then
steamed slowly away. The porter shuffled across the line and disappeared into a hut labelled 'Lamps'. Mr Salter turned towards the

palings; the youth was still leaning there, gazing; his eyes dropped; he grinned. Three times, shuttlecock fashion, they alternately glanced up and down till Mr Salter, with urban impatience, tired of the flirtation and spoke up.

'I say.'

'Ur.'

'Do you happen to know whether Mr Boot has sent a car for me?'

'Ur.'

'He has?'

'Noa. She've a taken of the harse.'

'I am afraid you misunderstand me.' Mr Salter's voice sounded curiously flutey and querulous in contrast to the deep tones of the moron. 'I'm coming to visit Mr Boot. I wondered if he had sent a motor-car for me.'

'He've a sent me.'

'With the car?'

'Noa. Motor-car's over to Lady Caldicote's taking of the harse. The bay,' he explained, since Mr Salter seemed not to be satisfied with this answer. 'Had to be the bay for because the mare's sick... The old bay's not up yet,' he added as though to make everything perfectly clear.

'Well, how am I to get to the house?'

'Why, along of me and Bert Tyler.'

'Has this Mr Tyler got a car, then?'

'Noa. I tell e car's over to Lady Caldicote's along of Miss Priscilla and the bay... Had to be the bay,' he persisted, 'because for the mare's sick.'

'Yes, yes, I quite appreciate that.'

'And the old bay's still swole up with grass. So you'm to ride along of we.'

'Ride?' A hideous vision rose before Mr Salter.

'Ur. Along of me and Bert Tyler and the slag.'

'Slag?'

'Ur. Mr Roderick's getting in the slag now for to slag Westerheys. Takes a tidy bit.'

Mr Salter was suffused with relief. 'You mean that you have some kind of vehicle outside full of slag?'

'Ur. Cheaper now than what it will be when Mr Roderick wants it.'

Mr Salter descended the steps into the yard where, out of sight from the platform, an open lorry was standing; an old man next to the driving seat touched his cap; the truck was loaded high with sacks; bonnet and back bore battered learner plates. The youth took Mr Salter's suitcase and heaved it up among the slag. 'You'm to ride behind,' he said.

'If it's all the same to you,' said Mr Salter rather sharply, 'I should prefer to sit in front.'

'It's all the same to *me*, but I durstn't let you. The police would have I.'

'Good gracious, why?'

'Bert Tyler have to ride along of me, for because of the testers.'

'Testers?'

'Ur. Police don't allow for me to drive except along of Bert Tyler. Bert Tyler he've a had a licence twenty year. There wasn't no testers for Bert Tyler. But police they took and tested I over to Taunton.'

'And you failed?'

A great grin spread over the young man's face. 'I busted tester's leg for he,' he said proudly. 'Ran he bang into the wall, going a fair lick.'

'Oh, dear. Wouldn't it be better for your friend Tyler to drive us?'

'Noa. He can't see for to drive, Bert Tyler can't. Don't e be afeared. I can *see* all right. It be the corners do for I.'

'And are there many corners between here and the house?'

'Tidy few.'

Mr Salter, who had had his foot on the hub of the wheel preparatory to mounting, now drew back. His nerve, never strong, had been severely tried that afternoon; now it failed him.

'I'll walk,' he said. 'How far is it?'

'Well, it's all according as you know the way. We do call it three mile over the fields. It's a tidy step by the road.'

'Perhaps you'll be good enough to show me the field path.'

'Tain't exactly what you could call a path. E just keeps straight.'

'Well, I daresay I shall find it. If . . . if by any chance you get to the house before me, will you tell Mr Boot that I wanted a little exercise after the journey?'

The learner-driver looked at Mr Salter with undisguised contempt. 'I'll tell e as you was afeared to ride along of me and Bert Tyler,' he said.

Mr Salter stepped back into the station porch to avoid the dust as the lorry drove away. It was as well that he did so, for, as he mounted the incline, the driver mistakenly changed into reverse and the machine charged precipitately back in its tracks, and came noisily to rest against the wall where Mr Salter had been standing. The second attempt was more successful and it reached the lane with no worse damage than a mudguard crushed against the near gatepost.

Then with rapid, uncertain steps Mr Salter set out on his walk to the house.

3

It was eight o'clock when Mr Salter arrived at the front door. He had covered a good six miles tacking from field to field under the setting sun; he had scrambled through fences and ditches; in one enormous pasture a herd of cattle had closed silently in on him and followed at his heels – the nearest not a yard away – with lowered heads and heavy breath; Mr Salter had broken into a run and they had trotted after him; when he gained the stile and turned to face them, they began gently grazing in his tracks; dogs had flown at him in three farmyards where he had stopped to ask the way, and to be misdirected; at last, when he felt he could go no further but must lie down and perish from exposure under the open sky, he had stumbled through an overgrown stile to find himself in the main road with the lodge gates straight ahead; the last mile up the drive had been the bitterest of all.

And now he stood under the porch, sweating, blistered, nettle-stung, breathless, parched, dizzy, dead-beat and dishevelled, with his bowler hat in one hand and umbrella in the other, leaning against a stucco pillar waiting for someone to open the door. Nobody came. He pulled again at the bell; there was no answering

ring, no echo in the hall beyond. No sound broke the peace of the evening save, in the elms that stood cumbrously on every side, the crying of the rooks, and, not unlike it but nearer at hand, directly it seemed over Mr Salter's head, a strong baritone decanting irregular snatches of sacred music.

'In Thy courts no more are needed, sun by day nor moon by night,' sang Uncle Theodore blithely, stepping into his evening trousers; he remembered it as a treble solo rising to the dim vaults of the school chapel, touching the toughest adolescent hearts; he remembered it imperfectly but with deep emotion.

Mr Salter listened, unmoved. In despair he began to pound the front door with his umbrella. The singing ceased and the voice in fruity, more prosaic tones demanded, 'What, ho, without there?'

Mr Salter hobbled down the steps, clear of the porch, and saw framed in the ivy of a first-floor window, a ruddy, Hanoverian face and plump, bare torso. 'Good evening,' he said politely.

'Good evening.' Uncle Theodore leaned out as far as he safely could and stared at Mr Salter through a monocle. 'From where you are standing,' he said, 'you might easily take me to be totally undraped. Let me hasten to assure you that such is not the case. Seemly black shrouds me from the waist down. No doubt you are the friend my nephew William is expecting?'

'Yes . . . I've been ringing the bell.'

'It sounded to me,' said Uncle Theodore severely, 'as though you were hammering the door with a stick.'

'Yes, I was. You see . . . '

'You'll be late for dinner, you know, if you stand out there kicking up a rumpus. And so shall I if I stay talking to you. We will meet again shortly in more conventional circumstances. For the moment – *a rivederci*.'

The head withdrew and once more the melody rose into the twilight, mounted to the encircling tree-tops and joined the chorus of the homing rooks.

Mr Salter tried the handle of the door. It opened easily. Never in his life had he made his own way into anyone else's house. Now he did so and found himself in a lobby cluttered with implements of sport, overcoats, rugs, a bicycle or two and a stuffed bear. Beyond it, glass doors led into the hall. He was dimly aware of a shadowy double staircase which rose and spread before him, of a large, carpetless chequer of black and white marble pavings, of islands of furniture and some potted palms. Quite near the glass doors stood a little arm-chair where no one ever sat; there Mr Salter sank and there he was found twenty minutes later by William's mother when she came down to dinner. His last action before he lapsed into coma had been to remove his shoes.

Mrs Boot surveyed the figure with some distaste and went on her way to the drawing-room. It was one of the days when James was on his feet; she could hear him next door rattling the silver on the dining-room table. 'James,' she called, through the double doors.

'Yes, madam.'

'Mr William's friend has arrived. I think perhaps he would like to wash.'

'Very good, madam.'

Mr Salter was not really asleep; he had been aware, remotely and impersonally, of Mrs Boot's scrutiny; he was aware, now, of James's slow passage across the hall.

'Dinner will be in directly, sir. May I take you to your room?'

For a moment Mr Salter thought he would be unable ever to move again; then, painfully, he rose to his feet. He observed his discarded shoes; so did James; neither of them felt disposed to stoop; each respected the other's feeling; Mr Salter padded upstairs beside the footman.

'I regret to say, sir, that your luggage is not yet available. Three of the outside men are delving for it at the moment.'

'Delving?'

'Assiduously, sir. It was inundated with slag at the time of the accident.'

'Accident?'

'Yes, sir, there has been a misadventure to the farm lorry that was conveying it from the station; we attribute it to the driver's inexperience. He overturned the vehicle in the back drive.'

'Was he hurt?'

'Oh, yes, sir; gravely. Here is your room, sir.'

An oil lamp, surrounded by moths and autumnal beetles, burned on Priscilla's dressing-table, illuminating a homely, girlish room. Little had been done, beyond the removal of loofah and nightdress, to adapt it for male occupation. Twenty or thirty china animals stood on brackets and shelves, together with slots of deer, brushes of foxes, pads of otters, a horse's hoof, and other animal trophies; a low, bronchial growl came from under the bed.

'Miss Priscilla hoped you would not object to taking charge of Amabel for the night, sir. She's getting an old dog now and doesn't like to be moved. You'll find her perfectly quiet and good. If she barks in the night, it is best to feed her.'

James indicated two saucers of milk and minced meat which stood on the bed table that had already attracted Mr Salter's attention.

'Would that be all, sir?'

'Thank you,' said Mr Salter, weakly.

James left, gently closing the door which, owing to a long-standing defect in its catch, as gently swung open again behind him.

Mr Salter poured some warm water into the prettily flowered basin on the washhand stand.

James returned. 'I omitted to tell you, sir, the lavatory on this floor is out of order. The gentlemen use the one opening on the library.'

'Thank you.'

James repeated the pantomime of shutting the door.

Nurse Grainger was always first down in the drawing-room. Dinner was supposed to be at quarter past eight, and for fifteen years she had been on time. She was sitting there, stitching a wool mat of modernistic design, when Mrs Boot first entered. When Mrs Boot had given her order to James, she smiled at her and said, 'How is your patient tonight, nurse?' and Nurse Grainger answered as she had answered nightly for fifteen years, 'A little low-spirited.'

'Yes,' said Mrs Boot, 'she gets low-spirited in the evenings.'

The two women sat in silence, Nurse Grainger snipping and tugging at the magenta wool; Mrs Boot reading a gardening magazine to which she subscribed. It was not until Lady Trilby entered the room that she expressed her forebodings.

'The boys are late,' said Lady Trilby.

'Aunt Anne,' said Mrs Boot gravely, 'William's friend has arrived in a *most peculiar condition.*'

'I know. I watched him come up the drive. Reeling all over the shop.'

'He let himself in and went straight off to sleep in the hall.'

'Best thing for him.'

'You mean . . . You don't think he could have been . . . ?'

'The man was squiffy,' said Aunt Anne. 'It was written all over him.'

Nurse Grainger uttered a knowing little cluck of disapproval.

'It's lucky Priscilla isn't here. What had we better do?'

'The boys will see to him.'

'Here is Theodore. I will ask him at once. Theodore, William's friend from London has arrived, and Aunt Anne and I very much fear that he has taken too much.'

'Has he, by Jove,' said Uncle Theodore, rather enviously. 'Now you mention it, I shouldn't be at all surprised. I talked to the fellow out of my window. He was pounding the front door fit to knock it in.'

'What ought we to do?'

'Oh, he'll sober up,' said Uncle Theodore, from deep experience. Uncle Roderick joined them. 'I say, Rod, what d'you think? That journalist fellow of William's – he's sozzled.'

'Disgusting. Is he fit to come into dinner?'

'We'd better keep an eye on him to see he doesn't get any more.'

'Yes. I'll tell James.'

Uncle Bernard joined the family circle. 'Good evening, good evening,' he said in his courtly fashion. 'I'm nearly the last, I see.'

'Bernard, we have something to tell you.'

'And I have something to tell *you.* I was sitting in the library not two minutes ago when a dirty little man came prowling in – without any shoes on.'

'Was he tipsy?'

'I daresay . . . now you mention it, I think he was.'

'That's William's friend.'

'Well, he should be taken care of. Where is William?'

William was playing dominoes with Nannie Bloggs. It was this custom of playing dominoes with her from six till seven every evening which had prevented him meeting Mr Salter at the station. On this particular evening the game had been prolonged far beyond its usual limit. Three times he had attempted to leave, but the old woman was inflexible. 'Just you stay where you sit,' she said. 'You always were a headstrong, selfish boy. Worse than your Uncle Theodore. Gallivanting about all over Africa with a lot of heathens, and now you *are* home you don't want to spend a few minutes with your old Nannie.'

'But, Nannie, I've got a guest arriving.'

'*Guest*. Time enough for him. It's not *you* he's after, I'll be bound. It's my pretty Priscilla. You leave them be . . . I'll make it half a sovereign this time.'

Not until the gong sounded for dinner would she let him go. 'Wash your hands,' she said, 'and brush your hair nicely. I don't know what your mother will say at you going down to dinner in your flannels. And mind you bring Priscilla's young man up afterwards and we'll have a nice game of cards. It's thirty-three shillings you owe me.'

Mr Salter had no opportunity of talking business at dinner. He sat between Mrs Boot and Lady Trilby; never an exuberant man, he now felt subdued almost to extinction and took his place glumly between the two formidable ladies; he might feel a little stronger, he hoped, after a glass of wine.

James moved heavily round the table with the decanters; claret for the ladies, William and Uncle Bernard, whisky and water for Uncle Theodore, medicated cider for Uncle Roderick. 'Water, sir?' said a voice in Mr Salter's ear.

'Well, I think perhaps I would sooner . . .' A clear and chilling cascade fell into his tumbler and James returned to the sideboard.

William, noticing a little shudder pass over his guest, leaned forward across the table. 'I say, Salter, haven't they given you anything to drink?'

'Well, as a matter of fact . . .'

Mrs Boot frowned at her son – a frown like a sudden spasm of pain. 'Mr Salter *prefers* water.'

'Nothing like it,' said Uncle Theodore. 'I respect him for it.'

'Well, as a matter of fact . . . '

Both ladies addressed him urgently and simultaneously; 'You're a great walker, Mr Salter,' in challenging tones from Lady Trilby; 'It is quite a treat for you to get away from your work into the country,' more gently from Mrs Boot. By the time that Mr Salter had dealt civilly with these two mis-statements, the subject of wine was closed.

Dinner was protracted for nearly an hour, but not by reason of any great profusion or variety of food. It was rather a bad dinner; scarcely better than he would have got at Lord Copper's infamous table; greatly inferior to the daintily garnished little dishes which he enjoyed at home. In course of time each member of the Boot family had evolved an individual style of eating; before each plate was ranged a little store of seasonings and delicacies, all marked with their owner's initials – onion salt, Bombay duck, gherkins, garlic vinegar, Dijon mustard, pea-nut butter, icing sugar, varieties of biscuit from Bath and Tunbridge Wells, Parmesan cheese, and a dozen other jars and bottles and tins mingled incongruously with the heavy, Georgian silver; Uncle Theodore had a little spirit lamp and chafing dish with which he concocted a sauce. The dishes as sent in from the kitchen were rather the elementary materials of dinner than the dinner itself. Mr Salter found them correspondingly dull and unconscionably slow in coming. Conversation was general and intermittent.

Like foreign news bulletins, Boot family table talk took the form of antithetical statements rather than of free discussion.

'Priscilla took Amabel with her to the Caldicotes,' said Lady Trilby.

'She left her behind,' said Mrs Boot.

'A dirty old dog,' said Uncle Bernard.

'Too old to go visiting,' said Uncle Roderick.

'Too dirty.'

'Mr Salter is having Amabel to sleep with him,' said Mrs Boot.

'Mr Salter is very fond of her,' said Lady Trilby.

'He doesn't know her,' said Uncle Bernard.

'He's very fond of all dogs,' said Mrs Boot.

There was a pause in which James announced: 'If you please, madam, the men have sent up to say it is too dark to go on moving the slag.'

'Very awkward,' said Uncle Roderick. 'Blocks the back drive.'

'And Mr Salter will have no things for the night,' said Mrs Boot.

'William will lend him some.'

'Mr Salter will not mind. He will understand.'

'But he is sorry to have lost his things.'

Presently Mr Salter got the hang of it. 'It is a long way from the station,' he ventured.

'You stopped on the way.'

'Yes, to ask . . . I was lost.'

'You stopped several times.'

At last dinner came to an end.

'He got better towards the end of dinner,' said Lady Trilby in the drawing-room.

'He is practically himself again,' said Mrs Boot.

'Roderick will see that he does not get at the port.'

'You won't take port,' said Uncle Roderick.

'Well, as a matter of fact . . .'

'Push it round to Bernard, there's a good fellow.'

'You and William have business to discuss.'

'Yes,' said Mr Salter eagerly. 'Yes, it's most important.'

'You could go to the library.'

'Yes.'

William led his guest from the table and out of the room.

'Common little fellow,' said Uncle Roderick.

'It's a perfectly good name,' said Uncle Bernard. 'An early corruption of saltire, which no doubt he bears on his coat. But of course it may have been assumed irregularly.'

'Can't hold it,' said Uncle Theodore.

'I always understood that the true Salters became extinct in the fifteenth century . . .'

In the library William for the first time had the chance of apologizing for the neglect of his guest.

'Of course, of course. I quite understand that living where you do, you are naturally distracted . . . I would not have intruded on you for the world. But it was a matter of first-rate importance – of Lord Copper's personal wishes, you understand.

'There are two things. First, your contract with us . . . Boot,' said Mr Salter earnestly, 'you won't desert the ship.'

'Eh?'

'I mean it was the *Beast* that gave you your chance. You mustn't forget that!'

'No.'

'I suppose the *Brute* have made a very attractive offer. But believe me, Boot, I've known Fleet Street longer than you have. I've seen several men transfer from us to them. They thought they were going to be better off, but they weren't. It's no life for a man of individuality, working for the *Brute*. You'd be selling your soul, Boot . . . You haven't by the way, sold it?'

'No. They did send me a telegram. But to tell you the truth I was so glad to be home that I forgot to answer it.'

'Thank heaven. I've got a contract here, ready drawn up. Duplicate copies. They only need your signature. Luckily I did not pack them in my suitcase. A life contract for two thousand a year. Will you sign?'

William signed. He and Mr Salter each folded his copy and put it in his pocket; each with a feeling of deep satisfaction.

'And then there's the question of the banquet. There won't be any difficulty about that now. I quite understand that while the *Brute* offer was still in the air . . . Well, I'm delighted it's settled. You had better come up with me tomorrow morning. Lord Copper may want to see you beforehand.'

'No.'

'But, my dear Boot . . . You need have no worry about your speech. That is being written for you by Lord Copper's social secretary. It will be quite simple. Five minutes or so in praise of Lord Copper.'

'No.'

'The banquet will be widely reported. There may even be a film made of it.'

'No.'

'Really, Boot, I can't understand you at all.'

'Well,' said William with difficulty, 'I should feel an ass.'

'Yes,' said Mr Salter, 'I can understand that. But it's only for one evening.'

'I've felt an ass for weeks. Ever since I went to London. I've been treated like an ass.'

'Yes,' said Mr Salter sadly. 'That's what we are paid for.'

'It's one thing being an ass in Africa. But if I go to this banquet they may learn about it down here.'

'No doubt they would.'

'Nannie Bloggs and Nannie Price and everyone.'

Mr Salter was not in fighting form and he knew it. The strength was gone out of him. He was dirty and blistered and aching in every limb, cold sober and unsuitably dressed. He was in a strange country. These people were not his people nor their laws his. He felt like a Roman legionary, heavily armed, weighted with the steel and cast brass of civilization, tramping through forests beyond the Roman pale, harassed by silent, elusive savages, the vanguard of an advance that had pushed too far and lost touch with the base ... or was he the abandoned rearguard of a retreat; had the legions sailed?

'I think,' he said, 'I'd better ring up the office and ask their advice.'

'You can't do that,' said William cheerfully. 'The nearest office is three miles away; there's no car; and anyway it shuts at seven.'

Silence fell in the library. Once more Mr Salter rallied to the attack. He tried sarcasm.

'These ladies you mention; no doubt they are estimable people, but surely, my dear Boot, you will admit that Lord Copper is a little more important.'

'No,' said William gravely. 'Not down here.'

They were still sitting in silence when Troutbeck came to them, ten minutes later.

'Miss Price says she is expecting you upstairs to play cards.'

'You don't mind?' William asked.

Mr Salter was past minding anything. He was led upstairs, down
long lamp-lit corridors, through doors of faded baize to Nannie
Price's room. Uncle Theodore was already there arranging the
card table beside her bed. 'So this is him,' she said. 'Why hasn't he
got any shoes?'

'It's a long story,' said William.

The beady old eyes studied Mr Salter's careworn face; she put on
her spectacles and looked again. 'Too old,' she said.

Coming from whom it did, this criticism seemed a bit thick; even
in his depressed condition, Mr Salter was roused to resentment.
'Too old for what?' he asked sharply.

Nannie Price, though hard as agate about matters of money and
theology, had, in old age, a soft spot for a lover. 'There, there,
dearie,' she said. 'I don't mean anything. There's many a young
heart beats in an old body. Sit down. Cut the cards, Mr Theodore.
You've had a disappointment, I know, her being away. She always
was a contrary girl. The harder the wooing the sweeter the winning,
they say – two spades – and there's many a happy marriage between
April and December – don't go peeping over my hand, Mr Theodore – and she's a good girl at heart, though she does forget her neck
sometimes – three spades – comes out of the bath as black as she
went in. I don't know what she does there . . .'

They played three rubbers and Mr Salter lost twenty-two shillings. As they rose to leave, Nannie Price, who had from long habit
kept up a more or less continuous monologue during the course of
the game, said, 'Don't give up, dearie. If it wasn't that your hair was
thinning you mightn't be more than thirty-five. She doesn't know
her own mind yet, and that's the truth.'

They left. William and Uncle Theodore accompanied Mr Salter
to his room. William said 'Good night.' Uncle Theodore lingered.

'Pity you doubled our hearts,' he said.

'Yes.'

'Got you down badly.'

'Yes.'

A single candle stood on the table by the bed. In its light
Mr Salter saw a suit of borrowed pyjamas laid out. Sleep was coming

on him like a vast, pea-soup fog, rolling down Fleet Street from Ludgate Hill. He did not want to discuss their game of bridge.

'We had all the cards,' said Uncle Theodore magnanimously, sitting down on the bed.

'Yes.'

'I expect you keep pretty late hours in London.'

'Yes . . . no . . . that is to say, sometimes.'

'Hard to get used to country hours. I don't suppose you feel a bit sleepy?'

'Well, as a matter of fact . . .'

'When I lived in London,' began Uncle Theodore . . .

The candle burned low.

'Funny thing that . . .'

Mr Salter awoke with a start. He was sitting in Priscilla's chintz-covered arm-chair; Uncle Theodore was still on the bed, reclining now like a surfeited knight of the age of Heliogabalus . . .

'Of course you couldn't print it. But I've quite a number of stories you *could* print. Hundreds of 'em. I was wondering if it was the kind of thing your newspaper . . .'

'Quite outside my province, I'm afraid. You see, I'm the Foreign Editor.'

'Half of them deal with Paris; *more* than half. For instance . . .'

'I should love to hear them, *all* of them, sometime, later, not now . . .'

'You pay very handsomely, I believe, on the *Beast*.'

'Yes.'

'Now suppose I was to write a series of articles . . .'

'Mr Boot,' said Mr Salter desperately, 'let us discuss it in the morning.'

'I'm never in my best form in the morning,' said Uncle Theodore doubtfully. 'Now after dinner I can talk quite happily until *any* time.'

'Come to London. See the Features Editor.'

'Yes,' said Uncle Theodore. 'I will. But I don't want to shock him; I should like your opinion first.'

The mists rose in Mr Salter's brain; a word or two loomed up and was lost again . . . 'Willis's rooms . . . "Pussy" Gresham . . .

Romano's ... believe it or not, fifteen *thousand* pounds ...' Then all was silence.

When Mr Salter awoke he was cold and stiff and fully dressed except for his shoes; the candle was burned out. Autumnal dawn glimmered in the window, and Priscilla Boot, in riding habit, was ransacking the wardrobe for a lost tie.

4

The Managing Editor of the *Beast* was not easily moved to pity. 'I say, Salter,' he said, almost reverently, 'you look terrible.'

'Yes,' said Mr Salter, lowering himself awkwardly into a chair, 'that's the only word for it.'

'These heavy-drinking country squires, eh?'

'No. It wasn't *that.*'

'Have you got Boot?'

'Yes and no. Have you?'

'Yes and no. He signed all right.'

'So did mine. But he won't come to the banquet.'

'I've sent my Boot off to the Antarctic. He said he had to go abroad at once. Apparently some woman is pursuing him.'

'Mr Boot,' said Mr Salter, 'is afraid of losing the esteem of his old nurse.'

'*Women,*' said the Managing Editor.

One thought was in both men's minds. 'What are we going to say to Lord Copper?'

The social secretary, whom they went to consult, was far from helpful.

'Lord Copper is looking forward very much to his speech,' she said. 'He has been rehearsing it all the afternoon.'

'You could rewrite it a little,' said the Managing Editor. '"Even in the moment of triumph, duty called. Here today, gone tomorrow ... honouring the empty chair ... the high adventure of modern journalism ..."' But even as he spoke, his voice faltered.

'No,' said the social secretary. 'That is not the kind of speech Lord Copper intends to make. You can hear him, in there, now.'

A dull booming sound, like breakers on shingle, rose and fell beyond the veneered walnut doors. 'He's getting it by heart,' she added.

The two editors went sadly back to their own quarters.

'I've worked with the Megalopolitan, one way and another, for fifteen years,' said Mr Salter. 'I've got a wife to consider.'

'You at least might get other employment,' said the Managing Editor. 'You've been educated. There's nothing in the world I'm fit to do except edit the *Beast*.'

'It was your fault in the first place for engaging Boot at all. He wasn't a foreign page man.'

'You sent him to Ishmaelia.'

'*I* wanted to sack him. You made him a hero. You made a monkey of him. It was you who thought of that article which upset him.'

'You encouraged Lord Copper to give him a knighthood.'

'You encouraged the banquet.'

'We were both at fault,' said the Managing Editor. 'But there's no point in our both suffering. Let's toss for who takes the blame.'

The coin spun in the air, fell and rolled away out of sight. Mr Salter was on his knees, searching, when the Features Editor looked in.

'Do either of you know anything about an old chap called Boot?' he asked. 'I can't get him out of my room. He's been sitting there telling me dirty stories since I got back from lunch. Says Salter sent him.'

CHAPTER 3

I

LORD COPPER QUITE often gave banquets; it would be an understatement to say that no one enjoyed them more than the host, for no one else enjoyed them at all, while Lord Copper positively exulted in every minute. For him they satisfied every requirement of a happy evening's entertainment; like everything that was to Lord Copper's taste, they were a little over life-size, unduly large and unduly long; they took place in restaurants which existed solely for such purposes, amid decorations which reminded Lord Copper of his execrable country seat at East Finchley; the provisions were copious, very bad and very expensive; the guests were assembled for no other reason than that Lord Copper had ordered it; they did not want to see each other; they had no reason to rejoice on the occasions which Lord Copper celebrated; they were there either because it was part of their job or because they were glad of a free dinner. Many were already on Lord Copper's payroll and they thus found their working day prolonged by some three hours without recompense – with the forfeit, indeed, of the considerable expenses of dressing up, coming out at night, and missing the last train home; those who were normally the slaves of other masters were, Lord Copper felt, his for the evening. He had bought them and bound them, hand and foot, with consommé and cream of chicken, turbot and saddle, duck and pêche melba; and afterwards, when the cigars had been furtively pocketed and the brandy glasses filled with the horrible brown compound for which Lord Copper was paying two pounds a bottle, there came the golden hour when he rose to speak at whatever length

he liked and on whatever subject, without fear of rivalry or
interruption.

Often the occasion was purely contingent on Lord Copper's
activities – some reshuffling of directorships, an amalgamation of
subsidiary companies, or an issue of new stocks; sometimes some
exhausted and resentful celebrity whom the *Beast* had adopted sat on
Lord Copper's right hand as the guest of honour, and there, on this
particular evening, at half past eight, sat Mr Theodore Boot; he
had tucked up his coat tails behind him, spread his napkin across
his knees and, unlike any of Lord Copper's guests of honour before
or since, was settling down to enjoy himself.

'Don't think I've ever been to this place before,' he began.

'No,' said Lord Copper. 'No, I suppose not. It is, I believe, the
best place of its kind.'

'Since my time,' said Uncle Theodore tolerantly. 'New places
always springing up. Other places closing down. The old order
changeth, eh?'

'Yes,' said Lord Copper coldly.

It was not thus that he was accustomed to converse with junior
reporters, however promising. There was a type, Lord Copper had
learned, who became presumptuous under encouragement. Uncle
Theodore, it was true, did not seem to belong to this type; it was hard
to know exactly what type Uncle Theodore did belong to.

Lord Copper turned away rather petulantly and engaged his
other neighbour – a forgotten and impoverished ex-Viceroy who
for want of other invitations spent three or four evenings a week at
dinners of this kind – but his mind was not in the conversation; it was
disturbed. It had been disturbed all the evening, ever since, sharp on
time, he had made his entrance to the inner reception room where
the distinguished guests were segregated. Uncle Theodore had been
standing there between Mr Salter and the Managing Editor. He
wore a tail coat of obsolete cut, a black waistcoat, and a very tall
collar; his purplish patrician face had beamed on Lord Copper, but
there had been no answering cordiality in Lord Copper's greeting.
Boot was a surprise. Images were not easily formed or retained in
Lord Copper's mind, but he had had quite a clear image of Boot,
and Uncle Theodore did not conform to it. Was *this* Mrs Stitch's

protégé? Was this the youngest K.C.B.? Had Lady Cockpurse commended *this* man's style? And – it gradually came back to him – was this the man he had himself met not two months back, and speeded on his trip to Ishmaelia? Lord Copper took another look and encountered a smile so urbane, so patronizing, so intolerably knowing, that he hastily turned away.

Someone had blundered.

Lord Copper turned to the secretary who stood, with the toast master, behind his chair.

'Wagstaff.'

'Yes, Lord Copper.'

'Take memo for tomorrow. "See Salter".'

'Very good, Lord Copper.'

The banquet must go on, thought Lord Copper.

The banquet went on.

The general hum of conversation was becoming louder. It was a note dearer to Lord Copper than the tongue of hounds in covert. He tried to close his mind to the enigmatic and, he was inclined to suspect, obnoxious presence on his right. He heard the unctuous voice rising and falling, breaking now and then into a throaty chuckle. Uncle Theodore, after touching infelicitously on a variety of topics, had found common ground with the distinguished guest on his right; they had both, in another age, known a man named Bertie Wodehouse-Bonner.

Uncle Theodore enjoyed his recollection and he enjoyed his champagne, but politeness at last compelled him reluctantly to address Lord Copper – a dull dog, but his host.

He leant nearer to him and spoke in a confidential manner.

'Tell me,' he asked, 'where does one go on to nowadays?'

'I beg your pardon.'

Uncle Theodore leered. 'You know. To round off the evening?' . . .

'Personally,' said Lord Copper, 'I intend to go to bed without any delay.'

'*Exactly.* Where's the place, nowadays?'

Lord Copper turned to his secretary.

'Wagstaff.'

'Yes, Lord Copper.'

'Memo for tomorrow. "Sack Salter".'

'Very good, Lord Copper.'

Only once did Uncle Theodore again tackle his host. He advised him to eat mustard with duck for the good of his liver. Lord Copper seemed not to hear. He sat back in his chair, surveying the room – for the evening, *his* room. The banquet must go on. At the four long tables which ran at right angles to his own the faces above the white shirt fronts were growing redder; the chorus of male conversation swelled in volume. Lord Copper began to see himself in a new light, as the deserted leader, shouldering alone the great burden of Duty. The thought comforted him. He had made a study of the lives of other great men; loneliness was the price they had all paid. None, he reflected, had enjoyed the devotion they deserved; there was Caesar and Brutus, Napoleon and Josephine, Shakespeare and – someone, he believed, had been disloyal to Shakespeare.

The time of his speech was drawing near. Lord Copper felt the familiar, infinitely agreeable sense of well-being which always preceded his after-dinner speeches; his was none of the nervous inspiration, the despair and exaltation of more ambitious orators; his was the profound, incommunicable contentment of monolocution. He felt himself suffused with a gentle warmth; he felt magnanimous.

'Wagstaff.'

'Lord Copper?'

'What was the last memo I gave you?'

' "Sack Salter", Lord Copper.'

'Nonsense. You must be more accurate. I said "Shift Salter". '

At last the great moment came. The toast master thundered on the floor with his staff and his tremendous message rang through the room.

'My Lords and Gentlemen. Pray silence for the Right Honourable the Viscount Copper.'

Lord Copper rose and breasted the applause. Even the waiters, he noticed with approval, were diligently clapping. He leant

forwards on his fists, as it was his habit to stand on these happy
occasions, and waited for silence. His secretary made a small,
quite unnecessary adjustment to the microphone. His speech lay
before him in a sheaf of typewritten papers. Uncle Theodore
murmured a few words of encouragement. 'Cheer up,' he said.
'It won't last long.'

'Gentlemen,' he began, 'many duties fall to the lot of a man of my
position, some onerous, some pleasant. It is a very pleasant duty to
welcome tonight a colleague who though –' and Lord Copper saw
the words 'young in years' looming up at him; he swerved – 'young
in his service to Megalopolitan Newspapers, has already added
lustre to the great enterprise we have at heart – Boot of the *Beast*.'

Uncle Theodore, who had joined the staff of the *Beast* less than
six hours ago, smirked dissent and began to revise his opinion of
Lord Copper; he was really an uncommonly civil fellow, thought
Uncle Theodore.

At the name of Boot applause broke out thunderously, and Lord
Copper, waiting for it to subside, glanced grimly through the pages
ahead of him. For some time now his newspapers had been advocating a new form of driving test, by which the applicant for a licence
sat in a stationary car while a cinema film unfolded before his eyes a
nightmare drive down a road full of obstacles. Lord Copper had
personally inspected a device of the kind and it was thus that his
speech now appeared to him. The opportunities and achievements
of youth had been the theme. Lord Copper looked from the glowing
sentences to the guest of honour beside him (who at the moment had
buried his nose in his brandy glass and was inhaling stertorously) and
he rose above it. The banquet must go on.

The applause ended and Lord Copper resumed his speech. His
hearers sank low in their chairs and beguiled the time in a variety of
ways; by drawing little pictures on the menu, by playing noughts and
crosses on the tablecloth, by having modest bets as to who could
keep the ash longest on his cigar; and over them the tropic tide of
oratory rose and broke in foaming surf, over the bowed, bald head of
Uncle Theodore. It lasted thirty-eight minutes by Mr Salter's watch.

'Gentlemen,' said Lord Copper at last, 'in giving you the toast of
Boot, I give you the toast of the Future . . .'

The Future…A calm and vinous optimism possessed the banquet…

A future for Lord Copper that was full to surfeit of things which no sane man seriously coveted – of long years of uninterrupted oratory at other banquets in other causes; of yearly, prodigious payments of super-tax crowned at their final end by death duties of unprecedented size; of a deferential opening and closing of doors, of muffled telephone bells and almost soundless typewriters.

A future for Uncle Theodore such as he had always at heart believed to be attainable. Two thousand a year, shady little gentlemen's chambers, the opportunity for endless reminiscence; sunlit morning saunterings down St James's Street between hatter and boot-maker and club; feline prowlings after dark; a buttonhole, a bowler hat with a curly brim, a clouded malacca cane, a kindly word to commissionaires and cab drivers.

A future for Mr Salter as Art Editor of *Home Knitting*; punctual domestic dinners; Sunday at home among the crazy pavements.

A future for Sir John Boot with the cropped amazons of the Antarctic.

A future for Mrs Stitch heaped with the spoils of every continent and every century, gadgets from New York and bronzes from the Aegean, new entrées and old friends.

A future for Corker and Pigge; they had travelled six hundred miles by now and were nearing the Sudanese frontier. Soon they will be kindly received by a District Commissioner, washed and re-victualled and sent on their way home.

A future for Kätchen. She was sitting, at the moment, in the second-class saloon of a ship bound for Madagascar, writing a letter:

Darling William,

We are going to Madagascar. My husband used to have a friend there and he says it is more comfortable than to come to Europe so will you please send us the money there. Not care of the consul because that would not be comfortable but poste restante. My husband says I should not have sold the specimens but I explained that you would pay what they are worth so now he does not mind. They are worth £50. It will be better if you will buy francs because he says you will get more than we should. We look forward very much to getting the money, so please send it by the quickest way. The boat was not worth very much money when we got to French territory. I am very well.

Ever your loving,
Kätchen.

A future for William . . .

. . . *the waggons lumber in the lane under their golden glory of harvested sheaves,* he wrote; *maternal rodents pilot their furry brood through the stubble;* . . .

He laid down his pen. *Lush Places* need not be finished until tomorrow evening.

The rest of the family had already gone up. William took the last candle from the table and put out the lamps in the hall. Under the threadbare carpet the stair-boards creaked as he mounted to his room.

Before getting into bed he drew the curtain and threw open the window. Moonlight streamed into the room.

Outside the owls hunted maternal rodents and their furry brood.

THE LOVED ONE
AN ANGLO-AMERICAN TRAGEDY

To Nancy Mitford

My thanks are due to
Lady Milbanke
who first set my feet on the path to
Whispering Glades;
to
Mrs Reginald Allen
who corrected my American;
to
Mr Cyril Connolly
who corrected my
English

ALL DAY THE heat had been barely supportable but at evening a breeze arose in the west, blowing from the heat of the setting sun and from the ocean, which lay unseen, unheard behind the scrubby foothills. It shook the rusty fingers of palm-leaf and swelled the dry sounds of summer, the frog-voices, the grating cicadas, and the ever present pulse of music from the neighbouring native huts.

In that kindly light the stained and blistered paint of the bunga-low and the plot of weeds between the veranda and the dry water-hole lost their extreme shabbiness, and the two Englishmen, each in his rocking-chair, each with his whisky and soda and his outdated magazine, the counterparts of numberless fellow countrymen exiled in the barbarous regions of the world, shared in the brief illusory rehabilitation.

'Ambrose Abercrombie will be here shortly,' said the elder. 'I don't know why. He left a message he would come. Find another glass, Dennis, if you can.' Then he added more petulantly: 'Kierke-gaard, Kafka, Connolly, Compton-Burnett, Sartre, "Scottie" Wilson. Who are they? What do they want?'

'I've heard of some of them. They were being talked about in London at the time I left.'

'They talked of "Scottie" Wilson?'

'No. I don't think so. Not of him.'

'That's "Scottie" Wilson. Those drawings there. Do they make any sense to you?'

'No.'

'No.'

Sir Francis Hinsley's momentary animation subsided. He let fall his copy of *Horizon* and gazed towards the patch of deepening shadow which had once been a pool. His was a sensitive, intelligent face, blurred somewhat by soft living and long boredom. 'It was Hopkins once,' he said; 'Joyce and Freud and Gertrude Stein. I couldn't make any sense of *them* either. I never was much good at anything new. "Arnold Bennett's debt to Zola"; "Flecker's debt to

Henley". That was the nearest I went to the moderns. My best subjects were "The English Parson in English Prose" or "Cavalry Actions with the Poets" – that kind of thing. People seemed to like them once. Then they lost interest. I did too. I was always the most defatigable of hacks. I needed a change. I've never regretted coming away. The climate suits me. They are a very decent generous lot of people out here and *they don't expect you to listen.* Always remember that, dear boy. It's the secret of social ease in this country. They talk entirely for their own pleasure. Nothing they say is designed to be heard.'

'Here comes Ambrose Abercrombie,' said the young man.

'Evening, Frank. Evening, Barlow,' said Sir Ambrose Abercrombie coming up the steps. 'It's been another scorcher, eh? Mind if I take a pew? When,' he added aside to the young man who helped him to whisky. 'Right up with soda, please.'

Sir Ambrose wore dark grey flannels, an Eton Rambler tie, an I Zingari ribbon in his boater hat. This was his invariable dress on sunny days; whenever the weather allowed it he wore a deer-stalker cap and an Inverness cape. He was still on what Lady Abercrombie fatuously called the 'right' side of sixty, but having for many years painfully feigned youth, he now aspired to the honours of age. It was his latest quite vain wish that people should say of him: 'Grand old boy.'

'Been meaning to look you up for a long time. Trouble about a place like this one's so darn busy, one gets in a groove and loses touch. Doesn't do to lose touch. We limeys have to stick together. You shouldn't hide yourself away, Frank, you old hermit.'

'I remember a time when you lived not so far away.'

'Did I? 'Pon my soul I believe you're right. That takes one back a bit. It was before we went to Beverly Hills. Now, as of course you know, we're in Bel Air. But to tell you the truth I'm getting a bit restless there. I've got a bit of land out on Pacific Palisades. Just waiting for building costs to drop. Where was it I used to live? Just across the street, wasn't it?'

Just across the street, twenty years or more ago, when this neglected district was the centre of fashion; Sir Francis, in prime middle-age, was then the only knight in Hollywood, the doyen of

English society, chief script-writer in Megalopolitan Pictures and President of the Cricket Club. Then the young, or youngish Ambrose Abercrombie used to bounce about the lots in his famous series of fatiguing roles, acrobatic heroic historic, and come almost nightly to Sir Francis for refreshment. English titles abounded now in Hollywood, several of them authentic, and Sir Ambrose had been known to speak slightingly of Sir Francis as a 'Lloyd George creation'. The seven-league boots of failure had carried the old and the ageing man far apart. Sir Francis had descended to the Publicity Department and now held rank, one of a dozen, as Vice-President of the Cricket Club. His swimming-pool which had once flashed like an aquarium with the limbs of long-departed beauties was empty now and cracked and over-grown with weed.

Yet there was a chivalric bond between the two.

'How are things at Megalo?' asked Sir Ambrose.

'Greatly disturbed. We are having trouble with Juanita del Pablo.'

' "Luscious, languid and lustful"?'

'Those are not the correct epithets. She is – or rather was – "Surly, lustrous and sadistic". I should know because I composed the phrase myself. It was a "smash-hit", as they say, and set a new note in personal publicity.

'Miss del Pablo has been a particular protégée of mine from the first. I remember the day she arrived. Poor Leo bought her for her eyes. She was called Baby Aaronson then – splendid eyes and a fine head of black hair. So Leo made her Spanish. He had most of her nose cut off and sent her to Mexico for six weeks to learn Flamenco singing. Then he handed her over to me. *I* named her. *I* made her an anti-fascist refugee. *I* said she hated men because of her treatment by Franco's Moors. That was a new angle then. It caught on. And she was really quite good in her way, you know – with a truly horrifying natural scowl. Her legs were never *photogénique* but we kept her in long skirts and used an understudy for the lower half in scenes of violence. I was proud of her and she was good for another ten years' work at least.

'And now there's been a change of policy at the top. We are only making healthy films this year to please the League of Decency. So poor Juanita has to start at the beginning again as an Irish colleen. They've bleached her hair and dyed it vermilion. I told them colleens were dark but the technicolor men insisted. She's working ten hours a day learning the brogue and to make it harder for the poor girl they've pulled all her teeth out. She never had to smile before and her own set was good enough for a snarl. Now she'll have to laugh roguishly all the time. That means dentures.

'I've spent three days trying to find a name to please her. She's turned everything down. Maureen – there are two here already; Deirdre – no one could pronounce it; Oonagh – sounds Chinese; Bridget – too common. The truth is she's in a thoroughly nasty temper.'

Sir Ambrose, in accordance with local custom, had refrained from listening.

'Ah,' he said, 'healthy films. All for 'em. I said to the Knife and Fork Club, "I've always had two principles throughout all my life in motion-pictures: never do before the camera what you would not do at home and never do at home what you would not do before the camera."'

He enlarged this theme while Sir Francis, in his turn, sequestered his thoughts. Thus the two knights sat for nearly an hour, side by side in their rocking-chairs, alternately eloquent and abstracted, gazing into the gloaming through their monocles while the young man from time to time refilled their glasses and his own.

The time was apt for reminiscence and in his silent periods Sir Francis strayed back a quarter of a century and more to foggy London streets lately set free for all eternity from fear of the Zeppelin; to Harold Monro reading aloud at the Poetry Bookshop; Blunden's latest in the *London Mercury*; Robin de la Condamine at the Phoenix matinées; luncheon with Maud in Grosvenor Square, tea with Gosse in Hanover Terrace; eleven neurotic balladmongers in a Fleet Street pub just off for a day's cricket in Metroland, the boy with the galley proofs plucking at his sleeve; numberless toasts at numberless banquets to numberless Immortal Memories . . .

Sir Ambrose had a more adventurous past but he lived existentially. He thought of himself as he was at that moment, brooded fondly on each several excellence and rejoiced.

'Well,' he said at length, 'I should be toddling. Mustn't keep the missus waiting'; but he made no move and turned instead to the young man. 'And how are things with you, Barlow? We haven't seen you on the cricket field lately. Very busy at Megalo, I suppose?'

'No. As a matter of fact my contract ran out three weeks ago.'

'I say, did it? Well, I expect you're glad of a rest. I know I should be.' The young man did not answer. 'If you'll take my advice, just sit easy for a time until something attractive turns up. Don't jump at the first thing. These fellows out here respect a man who knows his own value. Most important to keep the respect of these fellows.

'We limeys have a peculiar position to keep up, you know, Barlow. They may laugh at us a bit − the way we talk and the way we dress; our monocles − they may think us cliquey and stand-offish, but, by God, they respect us. Your five-to-two is a judge of quality. He knows what he's buying and it's only the finest type of Englishman that you meet out here. I often feel like an ambassador, Barlow. It's a responsibility, I can tell you, and in various degrees every Englishman out here shares it. We can't all be at the top of the tree but we are all men of responsibility. You never find an Englishman among the underdogs − except in England of course. That's understood out here, thanks to the example we've set. There are jobs that an Englishman just doesn't take.

'We had an unfortunate case some years ago of a very decent young fellow who came out as a scene designer. Clever chap but he went completely native − wore ready-made shoes, and a belt instead of braces, went about without a tie, ate at drug-stores. Then, if you'll believe it, he left the studio and opened a restaurant with an Italian partner. Got cheated, of course, and the next thing he was behind a bar shaking cocktails. Appalling business. We raised a subscription at the Cricket Club to send him home, but the blighter wouldn't go. Said he liked the place, if you please. That man did irreparable harm, Barlow. He was nothing less than a deserter. Luckily the war came. He went home then all right and got himself killed in Norway. He atoned, but I always think how much better not to have anything to atone for, eh?

'Now you're a man of reputation in your own line, Barlow. If you weren't you wouldn't be here. I don't say poets are much in demand but they're bound to want one again sooner or later and when they do they'll come to you cap in hand – if you haven't done anything in the meantime to lose their respect. See what I mean?

'Well, here I am talking like a Dutch uncle while the missus is waiting for her dinner. I must toddle. So long, Frank, I've enjoyed our talk. Wish we saw you more often at the Cricket Club. Good-bye, young man, and just remember what I've been saying. I may look like an old buffer but I know what I'm talking about. Don't move, either of you. I can find my way.'

It was quite dark now. The head-lamps of the waiting car spread a brilliant fan of light behind the palm trees, swept across the front of the bungalow and receded towards Hollywood Boulevard.

'What do you make of that?' said Dennis Barlow.

'He's heard something. That was what brought him here.'

'It was bound to come out.'

'Certainly. If exclusion from British society can be counted as martyrdom, prepare for the palm and the halo. You have not been to your place of business today?'

'I'm on the night shift. I actually managed to write today. Thirty lines. Would you like to see them?'

'No,' said Sir Francis. 'It is one of the numberless compensations of my exile that I need never read unpublished verses – or, for that matter, verses in any condition. Take them away, dear boy, prune and polish at your leisure. They would only distress me. I should not understand them and I might be led to question the value of a sacrifice which I now applaud. You are a young man of genius, the hope of English poetry. I have heard it said and I devoutly believe it. I have served the cause of art enough by conniving at your escape from a bondage to which I myself have been long happily reconciled.

'Did they ever, when you were a child, take you to a Christmas play called *Where the Rainbow Ends* – a very silly piece? St George and a midshipman flew off on a carpet to rescue some lost children from a Dragon's country. It always seemed to me a gross interference. The children were perfectly happy. They paid tribute, I remember, of their letters from home, unopened. Your verses are my letters from home – like Kierkegaard and Kafka and "Scottie" Wilson. I pay without protest or resentment. Fill my glass, dear boy. I am your *memento mori*. I am deep in thrall to the Dragon King. Hollywood is my life.

'Did you see the photograph some time ago in one of the magazines of a dog's head severed from its body which the Russians are keeping alive for some obscene Muscovite purpose by pumping blood into it from a bottle? It dribbles at the tongue when it smells a cat. That's what all of us are, you know, out here. The studios keep us going with a pump. We are still just capable of a few crude reactions – nothing more. If we ever got disconnected from our bottle, we should simply crumble. I like to think that it was the example of myself before your eyes day after day for more than a year that inspired your heroic resolution to set up in an independent trade. You have had example and perhaps now and then precept. I may have counselled you in so many words to leave the studio while you could still do so.'

'You did. A thousand times.'

'Surely not so often? Once or twice when I was in liquor. Not a thousand times. And my advice, I think, was to return to Europe. I never suggested anything so violently macabre, so Elizabethan as the work you chose. Tell me, do you give your new employer satisfaction, do you think?'

'My manner is congenial. He told me so yesterday. The man they had before caused offence by his gusto. They find me reverent. It is my combination of melancholy with the English accent. Several of our clientele have commented favourably upon it.'

'But our fellow expatriates? We cannot expect sympathy from them. What did our late visitor say? "There are jobs that an Englishman just doesn't take." Yours, dear boy, is pre-eminently one of those.'

Dennis Barlow went to work after dinner. He drove towards Burbank, past luminous motels, past the golden gates and floodlit temples of Whispering Glades Memorial Park, almost to the extremity of the city, to his place of business. His colleague, Miss Myra Poski, was waiting for relief, hatted and freshly painted.

'I hope I'm not late.'

'You're sweet. I've a date at the Planetarium or I'd stay and fix you some coffee. There's been nothing to do all day except mail a few remembrance cards. Oh, and Mr Schultz says if anything comes in put it straight on the ice this hot weather. Good-bye'; and she was gone leaving Dennis in sole charge of the business.

The office was furnished in sombre good taste that was relieved by a pair of bronze puppies on the chimney-piece. A low trolley of steel and white enamel alone distinguished the place from a hundred thousand modern American reception-rooms; that and the clinical smell. A bowl of roses stood beside the telephone; their scent contended with the carbolic, but did not prevail.

Dennis sat in one of the arm-chairs, put his feet on the trolley and settled himself to read. Life in the Air Force had converted him from an amateur to a mere addict. There were certain trite passages of poetry which from a diverse multitude of associations never failed to yield the sensations he craved; he never experimented; these were the branded drug, the sure specific, big magic. He opened the anthology as a woman opens her familiar pack of cigarettes.

Outside the windows the cars swept past continuously, out of town, into town, lights ablaze, radios at full throttle.

'*I wither slowly in thine arms,*' he read. '*Here at the quiet limit of the world,*' and repeated to himself: 'Here at the quiet limit of the world. Here at the quiet limit of the world' . . . as a monk will repeat a single pregnant text, over and over again in prayer.

Presently the telephone rang.

'The Happier Hunting Ground,' he said.

A woman's voice came to him, hoarse, it seemed, with emotion; in other circumstances he might have thought her drunk. 'This is Theodora Heinkel, Mrs Walter Heinkel, of 207 Via Dolorosa, Bel Air. You must come at once. I can't tell you over the phone. My little Arthur – they've just brought him in. He went out first thing and never came back. I didn't worry because he's sometimes been away like that before. I said to Mr Heinkel, "But, Walter, I can't go out to dine when I don't know where Arthur is" and Mr Heinkel said, "What the heck? You can't walk out on Mrs Leicester Scrunch at the last minute," so I went and there I was at the table on Mr Leicester Scrunch's right hand when they brought me the news…Hullo, hullo, are you there?'

Dennis picked up the instrument which he had laid on the blotting-pad. 'I will come at once, Mrs Heinkel. 207 Via Dolorosa I think you said.'

'I said I was sitting at Mr Leicester Scrunch's right hand when they brought me the news. He and Mr Heinkel had to help me to the automobile.'

'I am coming at once.'

'I shall never forgive myself as long as I live. To think of his being brought home alone. The maid was out and the City wagon-driver had to telephone from the drug-store…Hullo, hullo. Are you there? I said the City scavenger had to telephone from the drug-store.'

'I am on my way, Mrs Heinkel.'

Dennis locked the office and backed the car from the garage; not his own, but the plain black van which was used for official business. Half an hour later he was at the house of mourning. A corpulent man came down the garden path to greet him. He was formally dressed for the evening in the high fashion of the place – Donegal tweeds, sandals, a grass-green silk shirt, open at the neck with an embroidered monogram covering half his torso. 'Am I pleased to see you!' he said.

'Mr W. H., all happiness,' said Dennis involuntarily.

'Pardon me?'

'I am the Happier Hunting Ground,' said Dennis.

'Yes, come along in.'

Dennis opened the back of the wagon and took out an aluminium container. 'Will this be large enough?'

'Plenty.'

They entered the house. A lady, also dressed for the evening in a long, low gown and a diamond tiara, sat in the hall with a glass in her hand.

'This has been a terrible experience for Mrs Heinkel.'

'I don't want to see him. I don't want to speak of it,' said the lady.

'The Happier Hunting Ground assumes all responsibility,' said Dennis.

'This way,' said Mr Heinkel. 'In the pantry.'

The Sealyham lay on the draining-board beside the sink. Dennis lifted it into the container.

'Perhaps you wouldn't mind taking a hand?'

Together he and Mr Heinkel carried their load to the wagon.

'Shall we discuss arrangements now, or would you prefer to call in the morning?'

'I'm a pretty busy man mornings,' said Mr Heinkel. 'Come into the study.'

There was a tray on the desk. They helped themselves to whisky.

'I have our brochure here setting out our service. Were you thinking of interment or incineration?'

'Pardon me?'

'Buried or burned?'

'Burned, I guess.'

'I have some photographs here of various styles of urn.'

'The best will be good enough.'

'Would you require a niche in our columbarium or do you prefer to keep the remains at home?'

'What you said first.'

'And the religious rites? We have a pastor who is always pleased to assist.'

'Well, Mr — ?'

'Barlow.'

'Mr Barlow, we're neither of us what you might call very church-going people, but I think on an occasion like this Mrs Heinkel would want all the comfort you can offer.'

'Our Grade A service includes several unique features. At the moment of committal, a white dove, symbolizing the deceased's soul, is liberated over the crematorium.'

'Yes,' said Mr Heinkel, 'I reckon Mrs Heinkel would appreciate the dove.'

'And every anniversary a card of remembrance is mailed without further charge. It reads: *Your little Arthur is thinking of you in heaven today and wagging his tail.*'

'That's a very beautiful thought, Mr Barlow.'

'Then if you will just sign the order . . .'

Mrs Heinkel bowed gravely to him as he passed through the hall. Mr Heinkel accompanied him to the door of his car. 'It has been a great pleasure to make your acquaintance, Mr Barlow. You have certainly relieved me of a great responsibility.'

'That is what the Happier Hunting Ground aims to do,' said Dennis, and drove away.

At the administrative building, he carried the dog to the refrigerator. It was a capacious chamber, already occupied by two or three other small cadavers. Next to a Siamese cat stood a tin of fruit juice and a plate of sandwiches. Dennis took this supper into the reception-room, and, as he ate it, resumed his interrupted reading.

WEEKS PASSED, THE rain came, invitations dwindled and ceased. Dennis Barlow was happy in his work. Artists are by nature versatile and precise; they only repine when involved with the monotonous and the makeshift. Dennis had observed this during the recent war; a poetic friend of his in the Grenadiers was an enthusiast to the end, while he himself fretted almost to death as a wingless officer in Transport Command.

He had been dealing with Air Priorities at an Italian port when his first, his only book came out. England was no nest of singing-birds in that decade; lamas scanned the snows in vain for a reincarnation of Rupert Brooke. Dennis's poems, appearing among the buzz-bombs and the jaunty, deeply depressing publications of His Majesty's Stationery Office, achieved undesignedly something of the effect of the resistance Press of Occupied Europe. They were extravagantly praised and but for the paper restrictions would have sold like a novel. On the day the *Sunday Times* reached Caserta with a two-column review, Dennis was offered the post of personal assistant to an Air Marshal. He sulkily declined, remained in 'Priorities' and was presented in his absence with half a dozen literary prizes. On his discharge he came to Hollywood to help write the life of Shelley for the films.

There in the Megalopolitan studios he found reproduced, and enhanced by the nervous agitation endemic to the place, all the gross futility of service life. He repined, despaired, fled.

And now he was content; adept in a worthy trade, giving satisfaction to Mr Schultz, keeping Miss Poski guessing. For the first time he knew what it was to 'explore an avenue'; his way was narrow but it was dignified and umbrageous and it led to limitless distances.

Not all his customers were as open-handed and tractable as the Heinkels. Some boggled at a ten-dollar burial, others had their pets embalmed and then went East and forgot them; one, after filling half the ice-box for over a week with a dead she-bear, changed her mind and called in the taxidermist. These were the dark days, to be set against the ritualistic, almost orgiastic cremation of a non-sectarian chimpanzee and the burial of a canary over whose tiny grave a squad of Marine buglers had sounded Taps. It is forbidden by Californian law to scatter human remains from an aeroplane, but the sky is free to the animal world and on one occasion it fell to Dennis to commit the ashes of a tabby-cat to the slip-stream over Sunset Boulevard. That day he was photographed for the local paper and his social ruin consummated. But he was complacent. His poem led a snakes-and-ladders existence of composition and excision but it continued just perceptibly to grow. Mr Schultz raised his wages. The scars of adolescence healed. There at the quiet limit of the world he experienced a tranquil joy such as he had known only once before, one glorious early Eastertide when, honourably lamed in a house-match, he had lain in bed and heard below the sanatorium windows the school marching out for a field-day.

But while Dennis prospered, things were not well with Sir Francis. The old man was losing his equanimity. He fidgeted with his food and shuffled sleeplessly about the veranda in the silent hour of dawn. Juanita del Pablo was taking unkindly to her translation and, powerless to strike the great, was rending her old friend. Sir Francis confided his growing troubles to Dennis.

Juanita's agent was pressing the metaphysical point; did his client exist? Could you legally bind her to annihilate herself? Could you come to any agreement with her before she had acquired the ordinary marks of identity? Sir Francis was charged with the metamorphosis. How lightly, ten years before, he had brought her into existence – the dynamite-bearing Maenad of the Bilbao water-front! With what leaden effort did he now search the nomenclature of Celtic mythology and write the new life-story – a romance of the Mountains of Mourne, of the barefoot child whom the peasants spoke of as a fairies' changeling, the confidante of leprechauns, the rough-and-tumble tomboy who pushed the moke out of the cabin and dodged the English tourists among rocks and waterfalls! He read it aloud to Dennis and knew it was no good.

He read it aloud in conference, before the now nameless actress, her agent and solicitor; there were also present the Megalopolitan Directors of Law, Publicity, Personality and International

Relations. In all his career in Hollywood Sir Francis had never been in a single assembly with so many luminaries of the Grand Sanhedrin of the Corporation. They turned down his story without debate.

'Take a week at home, Frank,' said the Director of Personality. 'Try to work out a new slant. Or maybe you feel kind of allergic to the assignment?'

'No,' said Sir Francis feebly. 'No, not at all. This conference has been most helpful. I know now what you gentlemen require. I'm sure I shall have no further difficulty.'

'Always very pleased to look over anything you cook up,' said the Director of International Relations. But when the door closed behind him, the great men looked at one another and shook their heads.

'Just another has-been,' said the Director of Personality.

'There's a cousin of my wife's just arrived,' said the Director of Publicity. 'Maybe I'd better give him a try-out on the job.'

'Yes, Sam,' they all said, 'have your wife's cousin look it over.'

After that Sir Francis remained at home and for several days his secretary came out daily to take dictation. He footled with a new name for Juanita and a new life-story: Kathleen FitzBourke the toast of the Galway Blazers; the falling light among the banks and walls of that stiff country and Kathleen FitzBourke alone with hounds, far from the crumbling towers of FitzBourke Castle ... Then there came a day when his secretary failed to arrive. He telephoned to the studio. The call was switched from one administrative office to another until eventually a voice said: 'Yes, Sir Francis, that is quite in order. Miss Mavrocordato has been transferred to the Catering Department.'

'Well, I must have somebody.'

'I'm not sure we have anyone available right now, Sir Francis.'

'I see. Well, it is very inconvenient but I'll have to come down and finish the work I am doing in the studio. Will you have a car sent for me?'

'I'll put you through to Mr Van Gluck.'

Again the call went to and fro like a shuttlecock until finally a voice said: 'Transportation Captain. No, Sir Francis, I'm sorry, we don't have a studio automobile right here right now.'

Already feeling the mantle of Lear about his shoulders Sir Francis took a taxi to the studio. He nodded to the girl at the desk with something less than his usual urbanity.

'Good morning, Sir Francis,' she said. 'Can I help you?'

'No, thank you.'

'There isn't anyone particular you were looking for?'

'No one.'

The elevator-girl looked inquiringly at him. 'Going up?'

'Third floor, of course.'

He walked down the familiar featureless corridor, opened the familiar door and stopped abruptly. A stranger sat at the desk.

'I'm so sorry,' said Sir Francis. 'Stupid of me. Never done that before.' He backed out and shut the door. Then he studied it. It was his number. He had made no mistake. But in the slot which had borne his name for twelve years – ever since he came to this department from the script-writers' – there was now a card typewritten with the name 'Lorenzo Medici'. He opened the door again. 'I say,' he said. 'There must be some mistake.'

'Maybe there is too,' said Mr Medici, cheerfully. 'Everything seems kinda screwy around here. I've spent half the morning clearing junk out of this room. Piles of stuff, just like someone had been living here – bottles of medicine, books, photographs, kids' games. Seems it belonged to some old Britisher who's just kicked off.'

'I am that Britisher and I have not kicked off.'

'Mighty glad to hear it. Hope there wasn't anything you valued in the junk. Maybe it's still around somewhere.'

'I must go and see Otto Baumbein.'

'He's screwy too but I don't figure he'll know anything about the junk. I just pushed it out in the passage. Maybe some janitor . . .'

Sir Francis went down the passage to the office of the assistant director. 'Mr Baumbein is in conference right now. Shall I have him call you?'

'I'll wait.'

He sat in the outer office where two typists enjoyed long, intimately amorous telephone conversations. At last Mr Baumbein came out. 'Why, Frank,' he said. 'Mighty nice of you to look us up. I appreciate that. I do really. Come again. Come often, Frank.'

'I wanted to talk to you, Otto.'

'Well, I'm rather busy right now, Frank. How say I give you a ring next week sometime?'

'I've just found a Mr Medici in my office.'

'Why, yes, Frank. Only he says it "Medissy", like that; how you said it kinda sounds like a wop and Mr Medici is a very fine young man with a very, very fine and wonderful record, Frank, who I'd be proud to have you meet.'

'Then where do I work?'

'Well, now see here, Frank, that's a thing I want very much to talk to you about but I haven't the time right now. I haven't the time, have I, dear?'

'No, Mr Baumbein,' said one of the secretaries. 'You certainly haven't the time.'

'You see. I just haven't the time. I know what, dear, try to fix it for Sir Francis to see Mr Erikson. I know Mr Erikson would greatly appreciate it.'

So Sir Francis saw Mr Erikson, Mr Baumbein's immediate superior, and from him learned in blunt Nordic terms what he had already in the last hour darkly surmised: that his long service with Megalopolitan Pictures Inc. had come to an end.

'It would have been civil to tell me,' said Sir Francis.

'The letter is on its way. Things get hung up sometimes, as you know; so many different departments have to give their O.K. – the Legal Branch, Finance, Labour Disputes Section. But I don't antici-pate any trouble in your case. Luckily you aren't a Union man. Now and then the Big Three make objections about waste of manpower – when we bring someone from Europe or China or somewhere and then fire him in a week. But that doesn't arise in your case. You've had a record run. Just on twenty-five years, isn't it? There's not even any provision in your contract for repatriation. Your Termination ought to whip right through.'

Sir Francis left Mr Erikson and made his way out of the great hive. It was called the Wilbur K. Lutit Memorial Block and had not been built when Sir Francis first came to Hollywood. Wilbur K. Lutit had been alive then; had, indeed, once pudgily shaken his hand. Sir Francis had watched the edifice rise and had had an honourable if not illustrious place at its dedication. He had seen the rooms filled and refilled, the name-plates change on the doors. He had seen arrivals and departures, Mr Erikson and Mr Baumbein coming, others, whose names now escaped him, going. He remembered poor Leo who had fallen from great heights to die with his bill unpaid in the Garden of Allah Hotel.

'Did you find who you were looking for?' asked the girl at the desk as he made his way out into the sunshine.

Turf does not prosper in southern California and the Hollywood ground did not permit the larger refinements of cricket. The game indeed was fitfully played by some of the junior members, but for the majority it formed as small a part in their interests as do fishmongering or cordwaining to the Livery Companies of the City of London. For these the club was the symbol of their Eng-lishry. There they collected subscriptions for the Red Cross and talked at their ease, maliciously, out of the hearing of their alien employers and protectors. There on the day following Sir Francis Hinsley's unexpected death the expatriates repaired as though summoned by tocsin.

'Young Barlow found him.'

'Barlow of Megalo?'

'He used to be at Megalo's. His contract wasn't renewed. Since then . . .'

'Yes, I heard. That was a shocking business.'

'I never knew Sir Francis. He was rather before my time. Does anyone know why he did it?'

'*His* contract wasn't renewed.'

They were words of ill-omen to all that assembled company, words never spoken without the furtive touching of wood or crossing of fingers; unholy words best left unsaid. To each of them was given a span of life between the signature of the contract and its expiration; beyond that lay the vast unknowable.

'Where is Sir Ambrose? He's sure to come this evening.'

He came at length and it was noted that he already wore a band of crêpe on his Coldstream blazer. Late as it was he accepted a cup of tea, snuffed the air of suspense that filled the pavilion to stifling, and spoke:

'No doubt you've all heard of this ghastly business of old Frank?' A murmur.

'He fell on bad days at the end. I don't suppose there's anyone in Hollywood now except myself who remembers him in his prime. He did yeoman service.'

'He was a scholar and a gentleman.'

'Exactly. He was one of the first Englishmen of distinction to go into motion-pictures. You might say he laid the foundations on which I – on which we all have built. He was our first ambassador.'

'I really think that Megalo might have kept him on. They wouldn't notice his salary. In the course of nature he couldn't have cost them much more.'

'People live to a great age in this place.'

'Oh, it wasn't that,' said Sir Ambrose. 'There were other reasons.' He paused. Then the false and fruity tones continued: 'I think I had better tell you because it is a thing which has a bearing on all our lives here. I don't think many of you visited old Frank in recent years. I did. I made a point of keeping up with all the English out here. Well, as you may know, he had taken in a young English-man named Dennis Barlow.' The cricketers looked at one another, some knowingly, others in surmise. 'Now, I don't want to say a word against Barlow. He came out here with a high reputation as a poet. He just hasn't made good, I'm afraid. That is nothing to condemn him for. This is a hard testing ground. Only the best survive. Barlow failed. As soon as I heard of it I went to see him. I advised him as bluntly as I could to clear out. I thought it my duty to you all. We don't want any poor Englishmen hanging around Hollywood. I told him as much, frankly and fairly, as one Englishman to another.

'Well, I think most of you know what his answer was. *He took a job at the pets' cemetery.*

'In Africa, if a white man is disgracing himself and letting down his people the authorities pack him off home. We haven't any such rights here, unfortunately. The trouble is we all suffer for the folly of one. Do you suppose Megalo would have sacked poor Frank in other circumstances? But when they saw him sharing a house with a fellow who worked in the pets' cemetery... Well, I ask you! You all know the form out here almost as well as I do. I've nothing to say against our American colleagues. They're as fine a set of chaps as you'll find anywhere and they've created the finest industry in the world. They have their standards – that's all. Who's to blame 'em? In a world of competition people are taken at their face value. Everything depends on reputation – "face" as they say out East. Lose that and you lose everything. Frank lost face. I will say no more.

'Personally I'm sorry for young Barlow. I wouldn't stand in his shoes today. I've just come from seeing the lad. I thought it was the decent thing. I hope any of you who come across him will remember that his chief fault was inexperience. He wouldn't be guided. However...

'I've left all the preliminary arrangements in his hands. He's going up to Whispering Glades as soon as the police hand over the remains. Give him something to do, to take his mind off it, I thought.

'This is an occasion when we've all got to show the flag. We may have to put our hands in our pockets – I don't suppose old Frank has left much – but it will be money well spent if it puts the British colony right in the eyes of the industry. I called Washington and asked them to send the Ambassador to the funeral but it doesn't seem they can manage it. I'll try again. It would make a lot of difference. In any case I don't think the studios will keep away if they know *we* are solid...'

As he spoke the sun sank below the bushy western hillside. The sky was still bright but a shadow crept over the tough and ragged grass of the cricket field, bringing with it a sharp chill.

DENNIS WAS A young man of sensibility rather than of sentiment. He had lived his twenty-eight years at arm's length from violence, but he came of a generation which enjoys a vicarious intimacy with death. Never, it so happened, had he seen a human corpse until that morning when, returning tired from night duty, he found his host strung to the rafters. The spectacle had been rude and momentarily unnerving; but his reason accepted the event as part of the established order. Others in gentler ages had had their lives changed by such a revelation; to Dennis it was the kind of thing to be expected in the world he knew and, as he drove to Whispering Glades, his conscious mind was pleasantly exhilarated and full of curiosity.

Times without number since he first came to Hollywood he had heard the name of that great necropolis on the lips of others; he had read it in the local news-sheets when some more than usually illustrious body was given more than usually splendid honours or some new acquisition was made to its collected masterpieces of contemporary art. Of recent weeks his interest had been livelier and more technical, for it was in humble emulation of its great neighbour that the Happier Hunting Ground was planned. The language he daily spoke in his new trade was a patois derived from that high pure source. More than once Mr Schultz had exultantly exclaimed after one of his performances: 'It was worthy of Whispering Glades.' As a missionary priest making his first pilgrimage to the Vatican, as a paramount chief of equatorial Africa mounting the Eiffel Tower, Dennis Barlow, poet and pets' mortician, drove through the Golden Gates.

They were vast, the largest in the world, and freshly regilt. A notice proclaimed the inferior dimensions of their Old World rivals. Beyond them lay a semicircle of golden yew, a wide gravel roadway and an island of mown turf on which stood a singular and massive wall of marble sculptured in the form of an open book. Here, in letters a foot high, was incised:

THE DREAM

Behold I dreamed a dream and I saw a New Earth sacred to HAPPINESS. There amid all that Nature and Art could offer to elevate the Soul of Man I saw the Happy Resting Place of Countless Loved Ones. And I saw the Waiting Ones who still stood on the brink of that narrow stream that now separated them from those who had gone before. Young and old, they were happy too. Happy in Beauty, Happy in the certain knowledge that their Loved Ones were very near, in Beauty and Happiness such as the earth cannot give.

I heard a voice say: 'Do this.'

And behold I awoke and in the Light and Promise of my DREAM I made WHISPERING GLADES.

ENTER STRANGER and BE HAPPY.

And below, in vast cursive facsimile, the signature:

WILBUR KENWORTHY, THE DREAMER.

A modest wooden signboard beside it read: *Prices on inquiry at Administrative Building. Drive straight on.*

Dennis drove on through green parkland and presently came in sight of what in England he would have taken for the country seat of an Edwardian financier. It was black and white, timbered and gabled, with twisting brick chimneys and wrought-iron wind-vanes. He left his car among a dozen others and proceeded on foot through a box walk, past a sunken herb garden, a sundial, a bird-bath and fountain, a rustic seat and a pigeon-cote. Music rose softly all round him, the subdued notes of the 'Hindu Love-song' relayed from an organ through countless amplifiers concealed about the garden.

When as a new-comer to the Megalopolitan Studios he first toured the lots, it had strained his imagination to realize that those solid-seeming streets and squares of every period and climate were in fact plaster façades whose backs revealed the structure of bill-boardings. Here the illusion was quite otherwise. Only with an effort could Dennis believe that the building before him was three-dimensional and permanent; but here, as everywhere in Whispering Glades, failing credulity was fortified by the painted word.

This perfect replica of an old English Manor, a notice said, *like all the buildings of Whispering Glades, is constructed throughout of Grade A steel and concrete with foundations extending into solid rock. It is certified proof against fire, earthquake and   Their name liveth for evermore who record it in Whispering Glades.*

At the blank patch a signwriter was even then at work and Dennis, pausing to study it, discerned the ghost of the words 'high explosive' freshly obliterated and the outlines of 'nuclear fission' about to be filled in as substitute.

Followed by music he stepped as it were from garden to garden, for the approach to the offices lay through a florist's shop. Here one young lady was spraying scent over a stall of lilac while a second was talking on the telephone: '... Oh, Mrs Bogolov, I'm really sorry but it's just one of the things that Whispering Glades does not do. The Dreamer does not approve of wreaths or crosses. We just arrange the flowers in their own natural beauty. It's one of the Dreamer's own ideas. I'm sure Mr Bogolov would prefer it himself. Won't you just leave it to us, Mrs Bogolov? You tell us what you want to spend and we will do the rest. I'm sure you will be more than satisfied. Thank you, Mrs Bogolov, it's a pleasure ...'

Dennis passed through and opening the door marked 'Inquiries' found himself in a raftered banqueting-hall. The 'Hindu Love-song' was here also, gently discoursed from the dark-oak panelling. A young lady rose from a group of her fellows to welcome him, one of that new race of exquisite, amiable, efficient young ladies whom he had met everywhere in the United States. She wore a white smock and over her sharply supported left breast were embroidered the words, *Mortuary Hostess*.

'Can I help you in any way?'

'I came to arrange about a funeral.'

'Is it for yourself?'

'Certainly not. Do I look so moribund?'

'Pardon me?'

'Do I look as if I were about to die?'

'Why, no. Only many of our friends like to make Before Need Arrangements. Will you come this way?'

She led him through the hall into a soft passage. The *décor* here was Georgian. The 'Hindu Love-song' came to its end and was

THE LOVED ONE

succeeded by the voice of a nightingale. In a little chintzy parlour he and his hostess sat down to make their arrangements.

'I must first record the Essential Data.'

He told her his name and Sir Francis's.

'Now, Mr Barlow, what had you in mind? Embalmment of course, and after that incineration or not, according to taste. Our crematory is on scientific principles, the heat is so intense that all inessentials are volatilized. Some people did not like the thought that ashes of the casket and clothing were mixed with the Loved One's. Normal disposal is by inhumement, entombment, inurnment, or immurement, but many people just lately prefer insarcophagus-ment. That is *very* individual. The casket is placed inside a sealed sarcophagus, marble or bronze, and rests permanently above ground in a niche in the mausoleum, with or without a personal stained-glass window above. That, of course, is for those with whom price is not a primary consideration.'

'We want my friend buried.'

'This is not your first visit to Whispering Glades?'

'Yes.'

'Then let me explain the Dream. The Park is zoned. Each zone has its own name and appropriate Work of Art. Zones of course vary in price and within the zones the prices vary according to their proximity to the Work of Art. We have single sites as low as fifty dollars. That is in Pilgrims' Rest, a zone we are just developing behind the Crematory fuel dump. The most costly are those on Lake Isle. They range about 1,000 dollars. Then there is Lovers' Nest, zoned about a very, very beautiful marble replica of Rodin's famous statue, the Kiss. We have double plots there at 750 dollars the pair. Was your Loved One married?'

'No.'

'What was his business?'

'He was a writer.'

'Ah, then Poets' Corner would be the place for him. We have many of our foremost literary names there, either in person or as Before Need Reservations. You are no doubt acquainted with the works of Amelia Bergson?'

'I know of them.'

'We sold Miss Bergson a Before Need Reservation only yester-day, under the statue of the prominent Greek poet Homer. I could put your friend right next to her. But perhaps you would like to see the zone before deciding.'

'I want to see everything.'

'There certainly is plenty to see. I'll have one of our guides take you round just as soon as we have all the Essential Data, Mr Barlow. Was your Loved One of any special religion?'

'An agnostic.'

'We have two non-sectarian churches in the Park and a number of non-sectarian pastors. Jews and Catholics seem to prefer to make their own arrangements.'

'I believe Sir Ambrose Abercrombie is planning a special service.'

'Oh, was your Loved One in films, Mr Barlow? In that case he ought to be in Shadowland.'

'I think he would prefer to be with Homer and Miss Bergson.'

'Then the University Church would be most convenient. We like to save the Waiting Ones a long procession. I presume the Loved One was Caucasian?'

'No, why did you think that? He was purely English.'

'English are purely Caucasian, Mr Barlow. This is a restricted park. The Dreamer has made that rule for the sake of the Waiting Ones. In their time of trial they prefer to be with their own people.'

'I think I understand. Well, let me assure you Sir Francis was quite white.'

As he said this there came vividly into Dennis's mind that image which lurked there, seldom out of sight for long; the sack of body suspended and the face above it with eyes red and horribly starting from their sockets, the cheeks mottled in indigo like the marbled end-papers of a ledger and the tongue swollen and protruding like an end of black sausage.

'Let us now decide on the casket.'

They went to the show-rooms where stood coffins of every shape and material: the nightingale still sang in the cornice.

'The two-piece lid is most popular for gentlemen Loved Ones. Only the upper part is then exposed to view.'

'Exposed to view?'

'Yes, when the Waiting Ones come to take leave.'

'But, I say, I don't think that will quite do. I've seen him. He's terribly disfigured, you know.'

'If there are any special little difficulties in the case you must mention them to our cosmeticians. You will be seeing one of them before you leave. They have never failed yet.'

Dennis made no hasty choice. He studied all that was for sale; even the simplest of these coffins, he humbly recognized, outshone the most gorgeous product of the Happier Hunting Ground and when he approached the 2,000-dollar level – and these were not the costliest – he felt himself in the Egypt of the Pharaohs. At length he decided on a massive chest of walnut with bronze enrichments and an interior of quilted satin. Its lid, as recommended, was in two parts.

'You are sure that they will be able to make him presentable?'

'We had a Loved One last month who was found drowned. He had been in the ocean a month and they only identified him by his wrist-watch. They fixed that stiff,' said the hostess disconcertingly lapsing from the high diction she had hitherto employed, 'so he looked like it was his wedding day. The boys up there surely know their job. Why, if he'd sat on an atom bomb, they'd make him presentable.'

'That's very comforting.'

'I'll say it is.' And then slipping on her professional manner again as though it were a pair of glasses, she resumed. 'How will the Loved One be attired? We have our own tailoring section. Sometimes after a very long illness there are not suitable clothes available and sometimes the Waiting Ones think it a waste of a good suit. You see, we can fit a Loved One out very reasonably as a casket-suit does not have to be designed for hard wear and in cases where only the upper part is exposed for leave-taking there is no need for more than jacket and vest. Something dark is best to set off the flowers.'

Dennis was entirely fascinated. At length he said: 'Sir Francis was not much of a dandy. I doubt of his having anything quite suitable for casket wear. But in Europe, I think, we usually employ a shroud.'

'Oh, we have shrouds too. I'll show you some.'

The hostess led him to a set of sliding shelves like a sacristy chest where vestments are stored, and drawing one out revealed a garment such as Dennis had never seen before. Observing his interest she held it up for his closer inspection. It was in appearance like a suit of clothes, buttoned in front but open down the back; the sleeves hung loose, open at the seam; half an inch of linen appeared at the cuff and the V of the waistcoat was similarly filled; a knotted bow-tie emerged from the opening of a collar which also lay as though slit from behind. It was the apotheosis of the 'dickey'.

'A speciality of our own,' she said, 'though it is now widely imitated. The idea came from the quick-change artists of vaudeville. It enables one to dress the Loved One without disturbing the pose.'

'Most remarkable. I believe that is just the article we require.'

'With or without trousers?'

'What precisely is the advantage of trousers?'

'For Slumber Room wear. It depends whether you wish the leave-taking to be on the chaise-longue or in the casket.'

'Perhaps I had better see the Slumber Room before deciding.'

'You're welcome.'

She led him out to the hall and up a staircase. The nightingale had now given place to the organ and strains of Handel followed them to the Slumber Floor. Here she asked a colleague, 'Which room have we free?'

'Only Daffodil.'

'This way, Mr Barlow.'

They passed many closed doors of pickled oak until at length she opened one and stood aside for him to enter. He found a little room, brightly furnished and papered. It might have been part of a luxurious modern country club in all its features save one. Bowls of flowers stood disposed about a chintz sofa and on the sofa lay what seemed to be the wax effigy of an elderly woman dressed as though for an evening party. Her white gloved hands held a bouquet and on her nose glittered a pair of rimless pince-nez.

'Oh,' said the guide, 'how foolish of me. We've come into Primrose by mistake. This,' she added superfluously, 'is occupied.'

'Yes.'

'The leave-taking is not till the afternoon but we had better go before one of the cosmeticians finds us. They like to make a few final adjustments before Waiting Ones are admitted. Still, it gives you an idea of the chaise-longue arrangement. We usually recommend the casket half-exposure for gentlemen because the legs never look so well.'

She led him out.

'Will there be many for the leave-taking?'

'Yes, I rather think so, a great many.'

'Then you had better have a suite with an ante-room. The Orchid Room is the best. Shall I make a reservation for that?'

'Yes, do.'

'And the half-exposure in the casket, not the chaise-longue?'

'Not the chaise-longue.'

She led him back towards the reception-room.

'It may seem a little strange to you, Mr Barlow, coming on a Loved One unexpectedly in that way.'

'I confess it did a little.'

'You will find it quite different on the day. The leave-taking is a very, very great source of consolation. Often the Waiting Ones last saw their Loved One on a bed of pain surrounded by all the gruesome concomitants of the sick-room or the hospital. Here they see them as they knew them in buoyant life, transfigured with peace and happiness. At the funeral they have time only for a last look as they file past. Here in the Slumber Room they can stand as long as they like, photographing a last beautiful memory on the mind.'

She spoke, he observed, partly by the book, in the words of the Dreamer, partly in her own brisk language. They were back in the reception-room now and she spoke briskly. 'Well, I guess I've got all I want out of you, Mr Barlow, except your signature to the order and a deposit.'

Dennis had come prepared for this. It was part of the Happier Hunting Ground procedure. He paid her 500 dollars and took her receipt.

'Now one of our cosmeticians is waiting to see you and get *her* Essential Data, but before we part may I interest you in our Before Need Provision Arrangements?'

'Everything about Whispering Glades interests me profoundly, but that aspect, perhaps, less than others.'

'The benefits of the plan are twofold' – she was speaking by the book now with a vengeance – 'financial and psychological. You, Mr Barlow, are now approaching your optimum earning phase. You are no doubt making provision of many kinds for your future – investments, insurance policies and so forth. You plan to spend your declining days in security but have you considered what burdens you may not be piling up for those you leave behind? Last month, Mr Barlow, a husband and wife were here consulting us about Before Need Provision. They were prominent citizens in the prime of life with two daughters just budding into womanhood. They heard all particulars, they were impressed and said they would return in a few days to complete arrangements. Only next day those two passed on, Mr Barlow, in an automobile accident, and instead of them there came two distraught orphans to ask what arrangements their parents had made. We were obliged to inform them that *no* arrangements had been made. In the hour of their greatest need those children were left comfortless. How different it would have been had we been able to say to them: "Welcome to all the Happiness of Whispering Glades."'

'Yes, but you know I haven't any children. Besides I am a foreigner. I have no intention of dying here.'

'Mr Barlow, you are afraid of death.'

'No, I assure you.'

'It is a natural instinct, Mr Barlow, to shrink from the unknown. But if you discuss it openly and frankly you remove morbid reflections. That is one of the things the psycho-analysts have taught us. Bring your dark fears into the light of the common day of the common man, Mr Barlow. Realize that death is not a private tragedy of your own but the general lot of man. As Hamlet so beautifully writes: "Know that death is common; all that live must die." Perhaps you think it morbid and even dangerous to give thought to this subject, Mr Barlow; the contrary has been proved by scientific investigation. Many people let their vital energy lag prematurely and their earning capacity diminish simply through fear of death. By removing that fear they actually increase their expectation of life. Choose now, at leisure and in health, the form of final preparation you require, pay for it while you are best able to do so, shed all anxiety. Pass the buck, Mr Barlow; Whispering Glades can take it.'

'I will give the matter every consideration.'

'I'll leave our brochure with you. And now I must hand you over to the cosmetician.'

She left the room and Dennis at once forgot everything about her. He had seen her before everywhere. American mothers, Dennis reflected, presumably knew their daughters apart, as the Chinese were said subtly to distinguish one from another of their seemingly uniform race, but to the European eye the Mortuary Hostess was one with all her sisters of the air-liners and the reception-desks, one with Miss Poski at the Happier Hunting Ground. She was the standard product. A man could leave such a girl in a delicatessen shop in New York, fly three thousand miles and find her again in the cigar stall at San Francisco, just as he would find his favourite comic strip in the local paper; and she would croon the same words to him in moments of endearment and express the same views and preferences in moments of social discourse. She was convenient; but Dennis came of an earlier civilization with sharper needs. He sought the intangible, the veiled face in the fog, the silhouette at the lighted doorway, the secret graces of a body which hid itself under formal velvet. He did not covet the spoils of this rich continent, the sprawling limbs of the swimming-pool, the wide-open painted eyes and mouths under the arc-lamps. But the girl who now entered was unique. Not indefinably; the appropriate distinguishing epithet leapt to Dennis's mind the moment he saw her: sole Eve in a bustling hygienic Eden, this girl was a decadent.

She wore the white livery of her calling; she entered the room, sat at the table and poised her fountain-pen with the same professional assurance as her predecessor's, but she was what Dennis had vainly sought during a lonely year of exile.

Her hair was dark and straight, her brows wide, her skin transparent and untarnished by sun. Her lips were artificially tinctured, no doubt, but not coated like her sisters' and clogged in all their delicate pores with crimson grease; they seemed to promise instead an unmeasured range of sensual converse. Her full face was oval, her profile pure and classical and light. Her eyes greenish and remote, with a rich glint of lunacy.

Dennis held his breath. When the girl spoke it was briskly and prosaically.

'What did your Loved One pass on from?' she asked.

'He hanged himself.'

'Was his face much disfigured?'

'Hideously.'

'That is quite usual. Mr Joyboy will probably take him in hand personally. It is a question of touch, you see, massaging the blood from the congested areas. Mr Joyboy has very wonderful hands.'

'And what do you do?'

'Hair, skin, and nails and I brief the embalmers for expression and pose. Have you brought any photographs of your Loved One? They are the greatest help in re-creating personality. Was he a very cheerful old gentleman?'

'No, rather the reverse.'

'Shall I put him down as serene and philosophical or judicial and determined?'

'I think the former.'

'It is the hardest of all expressions to fix, but Mr Joyboy makes it his speciality – that and the joyful smile for children. Did the Loved One wear his own hair? And the normal complexion? We usually classify them as rural, athletic and scholarly – that is to say red, brown or white. Scholarly? And spectacles? A monocle. They are always a difficulty because Mr Joyboy likes to incline the head slightly to give a more natural pose. Pince-nez and monocles are difficult to keep in place once the flesh has firmed. Also of course the monocle looks less natural when the eye is closed. Did you particularly wish to feature it?'

'It was very characteristic.'

'Just as you wish, Mr Barlow. Of course Mr Joyboy *can* fix it.'

'I like the idea of the eye being closed.'

'Very well. Did the Loved One pass over with a rope?'

'Braces. What you call suspenders.'

'That should be quite easy to deal with. Sometimes there is a permanent line left. We had a Loved One last month who passed over with electric cord. Even Mr Joyboy could do nothing with that. We had to wind a scarf right up to the chin. But suspenders should come out quite satisfactorily.'

'You have a great regard for Mr Joyboy, I notice.'

'He is a true artist, Mr Barlow. I can say no more.'

'You enjoy your work?'

'I regard it as a very, very great privilege, Mr Barlow.'

'Have you been at it long?'

Normally, Dennis had found, the people of the United States were slow to resent curiosity about their commercial careers. This cosmetician, however, seemed to draw another thickness of veil between herself and her interlocutor.

'Eighteen months,' she said briefly. 'And now I have almost come to the end of my questions. Is there any individual trait you would like portrayed? Sometimes, for instance, the Waiting Ones like to see a pipe in the Loved One's mouth. Or anything special in his hands? In the case of children we usually give them a toy to hold. Is there anything specially characteristic of your Loved One? Many like a musical instrument. One lady made her leave-taking holding a telephone.'

'No, I don't think that would be suitable.'

'Just flowers? One further point – dentures. Was he wearing them when he passed on?'

'I really don't know.'

'Will you try and find out? Often they disappear at the police mortuary and it causes great extra work for Mr Joyboy. Loved Ones who pass over by their own hand *usually* wear their dentures.'

'I'll look round his room and if I don't see them I'll mention it to the police.'

'Thank you very much, Mr Barlow. Well, that completes my Essential Data. It has been a pleasure to make your acquaintance.'

'When shall I see you again?'

'The day after tomorrow. You had better come a little before the leave-taking to see that everything is as you wish.'

'Who shall I ask for?'

'Just say the cosmetician of the Orchid Room.'

'No name?'

'No name is necessary.'

She left him and the forgotten hostess returned.

'Mr Barlow, I have the Zone Guide ready to take you to the site.'

Dennis awoke from a deep abstraction. 'Oh, I'll take the site on trust,' he said. 'To tell you the truth, I think I've seen enough for one day.'

DENNIS SOUGHT AND obtained leave of absence from the Happier Hunting Ground for the funeral and its preliminaries. Mr Schultz did not give it readily. He could ill spare Dennis; more motor-cars were coming off the assembly-lines, more drivers appearing on the roads and more pets in the mortuary; there was an outbreak of food poisoning in Pasadena. The ice-box was packed and the crematorium fires blazed early and late.

'It is really very valuable experience for me, Mr Schultz,' Dennis said, seeking to extenuate the reproach of desertion. 'I see a great deal of the methods of Whispering Glades and am picking up all kinds of ideas we might introduce here.'

'What for you want new ideas?' asked Mr Schultz. 'Cheaper fuel, cheaper wages, harder work, that is all the new ideas I want. Look, Mr Barlow, we got all of the trade of the coast. There's nothing in our class between San Francisco and the Mexican border. Do we get people to pay 5,000 dollars for a pet's funeral? How many pay 500? Not two in a month. What do most of our clients say? "Burn him up cheap, Mr Schultz, just so the city don't have him and make me a shame." Or else it's a fifty-dollar grave and headstone inclusive of collection. There ain't the demand for fancy stuff since the war, Mr Barlow. Folks pretend to love their pets, talk to them like they was children, along comes a citizen with a new auto, floods of tears, and then it's "Is a headstone really socially essential, Mr Schultz?"'

'Mr Schultz, you're jealous of Whispering Glades.'

'And why wouldn't I be, seeing all that dough going on relations they've hated all their lives, while the pets who've loved them and stood by them, never asked no questions, never complained, rich or poor, sickness or health, get buried anyhow like they was just animals? Take your three days off, Mr Barlow, only don't expect to be paid for them on account you're thinking up some fancy ideas.'

The coroner caused no trouble. Dennis gave his evidence; the Whispering Glades van carried off the remains; Sir Ambrose blandly managed the Press. Sir Ambrose, also, with the help of other prominent Englishmen composed the Order of the Service. Liturgy in Hollywood is the concern of the Stage rather than of the Clergy. Everyone at the Cricket Club wanted a part.

'There should be a reading from the Works,' said Sir Ambrose. 'I'm not sure I can lay my hand on a copy at the moment. These things disappear mysteriously when one moves house. Barlow, you are a literary chap. No doubt you can find a suitable passage. Something I'd suggest that gives one the essence of the man we knew – his love of nature, his fair play, you know.'

'Did Frank love nature or fair play?'

'Why, he must have done. Great figure in letters and all that; honoured by the King.'

'I don't ever remember seeing any of his works in the house.'

'Find something, Barlow. Just some little personal scrap. Write it yourself if necessary. I expect you know his style. And, I say, come to think of it, you're a poet. Don't you think this is just the time to write something about old Frank? Something I can recite at the grave-side, you know. After all, damn it, you owe it to him – and to us. It isn't much to ask. We're doing all the donkey work.'

'Donkey work' was the word, thought Dennis as he watched the cricketers compiling the list of invitations. There was a cleavage on this subject. A faction were in favour of keeping the party small and British, the majority headed by Sir Ambrose wished to include all the leaders of the film industry. It was no use 'showing the flag', he explained, if there was no one except poor old Frank to show it to. It was never in doubt who would win. Sir Ambrose had all the heavy weapons. Cards were accordingly printed in large numbers.

Dennis meanwhile searched for any trace of Sir Francis's 'Works'. There were few books in the bungalow and those few mostly Dennis's own. Sir Francis had given up writing before Dennis could read. He did not remember those charming books which had appeared while he lay in the cradle, books with patterned paper boards and paper labels, with often a little scribble by Lovat Fraser on the title page, fruits of a frivolous but active mind, biography, travel, criticism, poetry, drama – *belles lettres* in short. The most ambitious was *A Free Man Greets the Dawn*, half autobiographical, a quarter political, a quarter mystical, a work which went straight to the heart of every Boots subscriber in the early twenties, and earned Sir Francis his knighthood. *A Free Man Greets the Dawn* had been out of print for years now, all its pleasant phrases unhonoured and unremembered.

When Dennis met Sir Francis in Megalopolitan studios the name, Hinsley, was just not unknown. There was a sonnet by him in *Poems of Today*. If asked, Dennis would have guessed that he had been killed in the Dardanelles. It was not surprising that Dennis possessed none of the works. Nor, to any who knew Sir Francis, was it surprising that *he* did not. To the end he was the least vain of literary men and in consequence the least remembered.

Dennis searched long in vain and was contemplating a desperate sortie to the public library when he found a stained old copy of the *Apollo* preserved, Heaven knew why, in Sir Francis's handkerchief drawer. The blue cover had faded to grey, the date was February 1920. It comprised chiefly poems by women, many of them, probably, grandmothers by now. Perhaps one of these warm lyrics explained the magazine's preservation after so many years in so remote an outpost. There was, however, at the end a book review signed F.H. It dealt, Dennis noticed, with a poetess whose sonnets appeared on an earlier page. The name was now forgotten, but perhaps here, Dennis reflected, was something 'near the heart of the man', something which explained his long exile; something anyway which obviated a trip to the public library... 'This slim volume redolent of a passionate and reflective talent above the ordinary...' Dennis cut out the review and sent it to Sir Ambrose. Then he turned to his task of composition.

The pickled oak, the chintz, the spongy carpet, and the Georgian staircase all ended sharply on the second floor. Above that lay a quarter where no layman penetrated. It was approached by elevator, an open functional cage eight feet square. On this top floor everything was tile and porcelain, linoleum and chromium. Here there were the embalming-rooms with their rows of inclined china slabs, their taps and tubes and pressure pumps, their deep gutters and the heavy smell of formaldehyde. Beyond lay the cosmetic rooms with their smell of shampoo and hot hair and acetone and lavender.

An orderly wheeled the stretcher into Aimée's cubicle. It bore a figure under a sheet. Mr Joyboy walked beside it.

'Good morning, Miss Thanatogenos.'

'Good morning, Mr Joyboy.'

'Here is the strangulated Loved One for the Orchid Room.'

Mr Joyboy was the perfection of high professional manners. Before he came there had been some decline of gentility in the ascent from show-room to workshop. There had been talk of 'bodies' and 'cadavers'; one jaunty young embalmer from Texas had even spoken of 'the meat'. That young man had gone within a week of Mr Joyboy's appointment as Senior Mortician, an event which occurred a month after Aimée Thanatogenos's arrival at Whispering Glades as junior cosmetician. She remembered the bad old days before his arrival and gratefully recognized the serene hush which seemed by nature to surround him.

Mr Joyboy was not a handsome man by the standards of motion-picture studios. He was tall but unathletic. There was a lack of shape in his head and body, a lack of colour; he had scant eyebrows and invisible eyelashes; the eyes behind his pince-nez were pinkish-grey; his hair, though neat and scented, was sparse; his hands were fleshy; his best feature was perhaps his teeth and they though white and regular seemed rather too large for him; he was a trifle flat-footed and more than a trifle paunchy. But these physical defects were nugatory when set against his moral earnestness and the compelling charm of his softly resonant voice. It was as though there were an amplifier concealed somewhere within him and his speech came from some distant and august studio; everything he said might have been for a peak-hour listening period.

Dr Kenworthy always bought the best and Mr Joyboy came to Whispering Glades with a great reputation. He had taken his baccalaureate in embalming in the Middle West and for some years before his appointment to Whispering Glades had been one of the Undertaking Faculty at an historic Eastern University. He had served as Chief Social Executive at two National Morticians' Conventions. He had led a goodwill mission to the morticians of Latin America. His photograph, albeit with a somewhat ribald caption, had appeared in *Time* magazine.

Before he came there had been rumours in the embalming-room that Mr Joyboy was a mere theorist. These were dispelled on the first morning. He had only to be seen with a corpse to be respected. It was like the appearance of a stranger in the hunting-field who from the moment he is seen in the saddle, before hounds move off, proclaims himself unmistakably a horseman. Mr Joyboy was unmarried and every girl in Whispering Glades gloated on him.

Aimée knew that her voice assumed a peculiar tone when she spoke to him. 'Was he a very difficult case, Mr Joyboy?'

'Well, a wee bit, but I think everything has turned out satisfactorily.'

He drew the sheet back and revealed the body of Sir Francis lying naked save for a new pair of white linen drawers. It was white and slightly translucent, like weathered marble.

'Oh, Mr Joyboy, he's beautiful.'

'Yes, I fancy he has come up nicely'; he gave a little poulterer's pinch to the thigh. 'Supple,' he raised an arm and gently bent the wrist. 'I think we have two or three hours before he need take the pose. The head will have to incline slightly to put the carotid suture in the shadow. The skull drained very nicely.'

'But Mr Joyboy, you've given him the Radiant Childhood Smile.'

'Yes, don't you like it?'

'Oh, *I* like it, of course, but his Waiting One did not ask for it.'

'Miss Thanatogenos, for you the Loved Ones just naturally smile.'

'Oh, Mr Joyboy.'

'It's true, Miss Thanatogenos. It seems I am just powerless to prevent it. When I am working for you there's something inside me says "He's on his way to Miss Thanatogenos" and my fingers just seem to take control. Haven't you noticed it?'

'Well, Mr Joyboy, I did remark it only last week. "All the Loved Ones that come from Mr Joyboy lately," I said, "have the most beautiful smiles."'

'All for you, Miss Thanatogenos.'

No music was relayed here. The busy floor echoed with the swirling and gurgling of taps in the embalming-rooms, the hum of electric driers in the cosmetic rooms. Aimée worked like a nun, intently, serenely, methodically; first the shampoo, then the shave, then the manicure. She parted the white hair, lathered the rubbery cheeks and plied the razor; she clipped the nails and probed the cuticle. Then she drew up the wheeled table on which stood her paints and brushes and creams and concentrated breathlessly on the crucial phase of her art.

Within two hours the main task was complete. Head, neck and hands were now in full colour; somewhat harsh in tone, somewhat gross in patina, it seemed, in the penetrating light of the cosmetic room, but the *œuvre* was designed for the amber glow of the Slumber Room and the stained light of the chancel. She completed the blue stipple work round the eyelids and stood back complacently. On soft feet Mr Joyboy had come to her side and was looking down at her work.

'Lovely, Miss Thanatogenos,' he said. 'I can always trust you to carry out my intention. Did you have difficulty with the right eyelid?'

'Just a little.'

'A tendency to open in the inside corner?'

'Yes, but I worked a little cream under the lid and then firmed it with No. 6.'

'Excellent. I never have to tell *you* anything. We work in unison. When I send a Loved One in to you, Miss Thanatogenos, I feel as though I were speaking to you through him. Do you ever feel that at all yourself?'

'I know I'm always special proud and careful when it is one of yours, Mr Joyboy.'

'I believe you are, Miss Thanatogenos. Bless you.'

Mr Joyboy sighed. A porter's voice said: 'Two more Loved Ones just coming up, Mr Joyboy. Who are they for?' Mr Joyboy sighed again and went about his business.

'Mr Vogel; are you free for the next?'

'Yes, Mr Joyboy.'

'One of them is an infant,' said the porter. 'Will you be taking her yourself?'

'Yes, as always. Is it a mother and child?'

The porter looked at the labels on the wrists. 'No, Mr Joyboy, no relation.'

'Very well, Mr Vogel, will you take the adult? Had they been mother and child I should have taken both, busy though I am. There is a something in individual technique – not everyone would notice it perhaps; but if I saw a pair that had been embalmed by different hands I should know at once and I should feel that the child did not properly belong to its mother; as though they had been estranged in death. Perhaps I seem whimsical?'

'You do love children, don't you, Mr Joyboy?'

'Yes, Miss Thanatogenos. I try not to discriminate, but I am only human. There is something in the innocent appeal of a child that brings out a little more than the best in me. It's as if I was inspired, sometimes, from outside; something higher . . . but I mustn't start on my pet subject now. To work –'

Presently the outfitters came and dressed Sir Francis Hinsley in his shroud, deftly fitting it. Then they lifted him – he was getting rigid – and placed him in the casket.

Aimée went to the curtain which separated the embalming-rooms from the cosmetic rooms and attracted the notice of an orderly.

'Will you tell Mr Joyboy that my Loved One is ready for posing? I think he should come now. He is firming.'

Mr Joyboy turned off a tap and came to Sir Francis Hinsley. He raised the arms and set the hands together, not in a form of prayer, but folded one on the other in resignation. He raised the head, adjusted the pillow and twisted the neck so that a three-quarter face was exposed to view. He stood back, studied his work and then leaned forward again to give the chin a little tilt.

'Perfect,' he said. 'There are a few places where he's got a little rubbed putting him in the casket. Just go over them once with the brush quite lightly.'

'Yes, Mr Joyboy.'

Mr Joyboy lingered a moment, then turned away.

'Back to baby,' he said.

THE FUNERAL WAS fixed for Thursday; Wednesday afternoon was the time for leave-taking in the Slumber Room. That morning Dennis called at Whispering Glades to see that everything was in order.

He was shown straight to the Orchid Room. Flowers had arrived in great quantities, mostly from the shop below, mostly in their 'natural beauty'. (After consultation the Cricket Club's fine trophy in the shape of cross bats and wickets had been admitted. Dr Kenworthy had himself given judgment; the trophy was essentially a reminder of life, not of death; that was the crux.) The ante-room was so full of flowers that there seemed no other furniture or decoration; double doors led to the Slumber Room proper.

Dennis hesitated with his fingers on the handle and was aware of communication with another hand beyond the panels. Thus in a hundred novels had lovers stood. The door opened and Aimée Thanatogenos stood quite close to him; behind her more, many more flowers and all about her a rich hot-house scent and the low voices of a choir discoursing sacred music from the cornice. At the moment of their meeting a treble voice broke out with poignant sweetness: 'O for the Wings of a Dove.'

No breath stirred the enchanted stillness of the two rooms. The leaded casements were screwed tight. The air came, like the boy's voice, from far away, sterilized and transmuted. The temperature was slightly cooler than is usual in American dwellings. The rooms seemed isolated and unnaturally quiet, like a railway coach that has stopped in the night far from any station.

'Come in, Mr Barlow.'

Aimée stood aside and now Dennis saw that the centre of the room was filled with a great cumulus of flowers. Dennis was too young ever to have seen an Edwardian conservatory in full rig but he knew the literature of the period and in his imagination had seen such a picture; it was all there, even the gilt chairs disposed in pairs as though for some starched and jewelled courtship.

There was no catafalque. The coffin stood a few inches from the carpet on a base that was hidden in floral enrichments. Half the lid was open. Sir Francis was visible from the waist up. Dennis thought of the wax-work of Marat in his bath.

The shroud had been made to fit admirably. There was a fresh gardenia in the buttonhole and another between the fingers. The hair was snow-white and parted in a straight line from brow to crown revealing the scalp below, colourless and smooth as though the skin had rolled away and the enduring skull already lay exposed. The gold rim of the monocle framed a delicately tinted eyelid.

The complete stillness was more startling than any violent action. The body looked altogether smaller than life-size now that it was, as it were, stripped of the thick pelt of mobility and intelligence. And the face which inclined its blind eyes towards him – the face was entirely horrible; as ageless as a tortoise and as inhuman; a painted and smirking obscene travesty by comparison with which the devil-mask Dennis had found in the noose was a festive adornment, a thing an uncle might don at a Christmas party.

Aimée stood beside her handiwork – the painter at the private view – and heard Dennis draw his breath in sudden emotion.

'Is it what you hoped?' she asked.

'More' – and then – 'Is he quite hard?'

'Firm.'

'May I touch him?'

'Please not. It leaves a mark.'

'Very well.'

Then in accordance with the etiquette of the place, she left him to his reflections.

There was brisk coming-and-going in the Orchid Slumber Room later that day; a girl from the Whispering Glades secretariat sat in the ante-room recording the names of the visitors. These were not the most illustrious. The stars, the producers, the heads of depart-ments would come next day for the interment. That afternoon they were represented by underlings. It was like the party held on the eve of a wedding to view the presents, attended only by the intimate, the idle and the unimportant. The Yes-men were there in force. Man proposed. God disposed. These bland, plump gentlemen signalled their final abiding assent to the arrangement, nodding into the blind mask of death.

Sir Ambrose made a cursory visit.

'Everything set for tomorrow, Barlow? Don't forget your ode. I should like it at least an hour before the time so that I can run over it in front of the mirror. How is it going?'

'I think it will be all right.'

'I shall recite it at the graveside. In the church there will be merely the reading from the Works and a song by Juanita – "The Wearing of the Green". It's the only Irish song she's learned yet. Curious how flamenco she makes it sound. Have you arranged the seating in the church?'

'Not yet.'

'The Cricket Club will be together of course. Megalopolitan will want the first four rows. Erikson is probably coming himself. Well, I can leave all that to you, can't I?' As he left the mortuary he said: 'I am sorry for young Barlow. He must feel all this terribly. The great thing is to give him plenty to do.'

Dennis presently drove to the University Church. It was a small, stone building whose square tower rose among immature holm-oaks on the summit of a knoll. The porch was equipped with an apparatus by which at will a lecture might be switched on to explain the peculiarities of the place. Dennis paused to listen.

The voice was a familiar one, that of the travel-film: 'You are standing in the Church of St Peter-without-the-walls, Oxford, one of England's oldest and most venerable places of worship. Here generations of students have come from all over the world to dream the dreams of youth. Here scientists and statesmen still unknown dreamed of their future triumphs. Here Shelley planned his great career in poetry. From here young men set out hopefully on the paths of success and happiness. It is a symbol of the soul of the Loved One who starts from here on the greatest success story of all time. The success that waits for all of us whatever the disappointments of our earthly lives.

'This is more than a replica, it is a reconstruction. A building-
again of what those old craftsmen sought to do with their rude
implements of bygone ages. Time has worked its mischief on the
beautiful original. Here you see it as the first builders dreamed of it
long ago.

'You will observe that the side aisles are constructed solely of glass
and grade A steel. There is a beautiful anecdote connected with this
beautiful feature. In 1935 Dr Kenworthy was in Europe seeking in
that treasure house of Art something worthy of Whispering Glades.
His tour led him to Oxford and the famous Norman church of St
Peter. He found it dark. He found it full of conventional and depressing memorials. "Why," asked Dr Kenworthy, "do you call it St Peter-
without-the-walls?" and they told him it was because in the old days
the city wall had stood between it and the business centre. "*My*
church," said Dr Kenworthy, "shall have no walls." And so you see
it today full of God's sunshine and fresh air, bird-song and flowers . . . '

Dennis listened intently to the tones so often parodied yet never
rendered more absurd or more hypnotic than the original. His
interest was no longer purely technical nor purely satiric. Whispering Glades held him in thrall. In that zone of insecurity in the mind
where none but the artist dare trespass, the tribes were mustering.
Dennis, the frontiersman, could read the signs.

The voice ceased and after a pause began again: 'You are
standing in the Church of St Peter-without-the-walls . . .' Dennis
switched off the apparatus, re-entered the settled area and set
about his prosaic task.

The secretariat had provided him with typewritten name-cards.
It was a simple matter to deal them out on the benches. Under the
organ was a private pew, separated from the nave by an iron grille
and a gauze curtain. Here, when there was a need of it, the bereaved
families sat in purdah, hidden from curious glances. This space
Dennis devoted to the local gossip writers.

In half an hour his work was done and he stepped out into the
gardens which were no brighter or more flowery or fuller of bird-
song than the Norman church.

The ode lay heavy on him. Not a word was yet written and the
languorous, odorous afternoon did not conduce to work. There was

also another voice speaking faintly and persistently, calling him to a more strenuous task than Frank Hinsley's obsequies. He left his car at the lych-gate and followed a gravel walk which led downhill. The graves were barely visible, marked out by little bronze plaques, many of them as green as the surrounding turf. Water played everywhere from a buried network of pipes, making a glittering rain-belt waist-high out of which rose a host of bronze and Carrara statuary, allegorical, infantile or erotic. Here a bearded magician sought the future in the obscure depths of what seemed to be a plaster football. There a toddler clutched to its stony bosom a marble Mickey Mouse. A turn in the path disclosed Andromeda, naked and fettered in ribbons, gazing down her polished arm at a marble butterfly which had settled there. And all the while his literary sense was alert, like a hunting hound. There was something in Whispering Glades that was necessary to him, that only he could find.

At length he found himself on the margin of a lake, full of lilies and water-fowl. A notice said: 'Tickets here for the Lake Island of Innisfree' and three couples of young people stood at the foot of a rustic landing-stage. He took a ticket.

'Just the one?' asked the lady at the guichet.

The young people were as abstracted as he, each pair lapped in an almost visible miasma of adolescent love. Dennis stood unregarded until at length an electric launch drew out of the opposing shore and came silently to its mooring. They embarked together and after a brief passage the couples slipped away into the gardens. Dennis stood irresolutely on the bank.

The coxswain said: 'Expecting someone to meet you here, bud?'

'No.'

'There've been no single dames all afternoon. I'd have noticed if there had been. Mostly folk comes in couples. Once in a while a guy has a date here and then more often than not the dame never shows up. Better get the dame before you get the ticket, I guess.'

'No,' said Dennis. 'I have merely come to write a poem. Would this be a good place?'

'I wouldn't know, bud. I never wrote a poem. But they've certainly got it fixed up poetic. It's named after a very fancy poem.

They got beehives. Once they had bees, too, but folks was always getting stung so now it's done mechanical and scientific; no sore fannies and plenty of poetry.

'It certainly is a poetic place to be planted in. Costs round about a thousand bucks. The poeticest place in the whole darn park. I was here when they made it. They figured the Irish would come but it seems the Irish are just naturally poetic and won't pay that much for plantings. Besides they've got a low-down kind of cemetery of their own downtown, being Catholic. It's mostly the good-style Jews we get here. They appreciate the privacy. It's the water you see keeps out the animals. Animals are a headache in cemeteries. Dr Kenworthy made a crack about that one Annual. Most cemeteries, he says, provide a dog's toilet and a cat's motel. Pretty smart, huh? Dr Kenworthy is a regular guy when it comes to the Annual.

'No trouble with dogs and cats on the island. Dames is our headache, dames and guys in very considerable numbers come here to neck. I reckon they appreciate the privacy, too, same as cats.'

While he spoke some young people had emerged from the bosky and stood waiting his summons to embark; oblivious Paolas and Francescas emerging from their nether world in an incandescent envelope of love. One girl blew bubbles of gum like a rutting camel but her eyes were wide and soft with remembered pleasure.

In contrast to the ample sweep of surrounding parkland, the Lake Island was cosy. An almost continuous fringe of shrub screened its shores from observation. Paths of mown grass wandered between leafy clumps, opened out into enclosed funerary glades, and converged on a central space, where stood a wattle cabin, nine rows of haricots (which by a system of judicious transplantation were kept in perpetual scarlet flower) and some wicker hives. Here the sound of bees was like a dynamo, but elsewhere in the island it came as a gentle murmur hardly distinguishable from the genuine article.

The graves nearest to the apiary were the most costly of all but no more conspicuous than those elsewhere in the park; simple bronze plaques, flush with the turf, bore the most august names in the commercial life of Los Angeles. Dennis looked into the hut and withdrew apologizing to the disturbed occupants. He looked into

the hives and saw in the depths of each a tiny red eye which told that
the sound-apparatus was working in good order.

It was a warm afternoon; no breeze stirred the evergreens; peace
came dropping slow, too slow for Dennis.

He followed a divergent path and presently came to a little cul-de-
sac, the family burial plot, a plaque informed him, of a great fruiterer.
Kaiser's Stoneless Peaches raised their rosy flock cheeks from every
greengrocer's window in the land. Kaiser's radio half-hour brought
Wagner into every kitchen. Here already lay two Kaisers, wife and
aunt. Here in the fullness of time would lie Kaiser himself. A gunnera
spread a wide lowly shelter over the place. Dennis lay down in its
dense shade. The apiary, at this distance, came near to verisimilitude.
Peace came dropping rather more quickly.

He had brought pencil and note-book with him. It was not thus
that he wrote the poems which brought him fame and his present
peculiar fortune. They had taken their shapes in frigid war-time
railway journeys – the racks piled high with equipment, the dimmed
lights falling on a dozen laps, the faces above invisible, cigarette-
smoke mixing with frosty breath; the unexplained stops, the stations
dark as the empty footways. He had written them in Nissen huts and
in spring evenings, on a bare heath, a mile from the airfield, and on
the metal benches of transport planes. It was not thus that one day
he would write what had to be written; not here that the spirit would
be appeased which now more faintly pressed its mysterious claim.
This hot high afternoon was given for reminiscence rather than for
composition. Rhythms from the anthologies moved softly through
his mind.

He wrote:

> *Bury the great Knight*
> *With the studio's valediction*
> *Let us bury the great Knight*
> *Who was once the arbiter of popular fiction.*

And:

> *They told me, Francis Hinsley, they told me you were hung*
> *With red protruding eye-balls and black protruding tongue;*

I wept as I remembered how often you and I
Had laughed about Los Angeles and now 'tis here you'll lie;
Here pickled in formaldehyde and painted like a whore,
Shrimp-pink incorruptible, not lost nor gone before.

He gazed up into the rhubarb roof. A peach without a stone. That was the metaphor for Frank Hinsley. Dennis recalled that he had once tried to eat one of Mr Kaiser's much advertised products and had discovered a ball of damp, sweet cotton-wool. Poor Frank Hinsley, it was very like him.

This was no time for writing. The voice of inspiration was silent; the voice of duty muffled. The night would come when all men could work. Now was the time to watch the flamingoes and meditate on the life of Mr Kaiser. Dennis turned on his face and studied the counterfeit handwriting of the women of the house. Not forceful characters it seemed. Kaiser owed nothing to women. The stoneless peach was his alone.

Presently he heard steps approach and, without moving, could see that they were a woman's. Feet, ankles, calves, came progressively into view. Like every pair in the country they were slim and neatly covered. Which came first in this strange civilization, he wondered, the foot or the shoe, the leg or the nylon stocking? Or were these uniform elegant limbs, from the stocking-top down, marketed in one cellophane envelope at the neighbourhood store? Did they clip by some labour-saving device to the sterilized rubber privacies above? Did they come from the same department as the light irrefragible plastic head? Did the entire article come off the assembly-lines ready for immediate home-service?

Dennis lay quite still and the girl came within a yard, knelt down in the same shade and prepared to recline beside him before she said, 'Oh.'

Dennis sat up and turning saw the girl from the mortuary. She was wearing very large, elliptical violet sun-glasses which she now removed to stare the closer and recognize him.

'Oh,' she said. 'Pardon me. Aren't you the friend of the strangulated Loved One in the Orchid Room? My memory's very bad for live faces. You did startle me. I didn't expect to find anyone here.'

'Have I taken your place?'

'Not really. I mean it's Mr Kaiser's place, not mine or yours. But it's usually deserted at this time so I've taken to coming here after work and I suppose I began to think of it as mine. I'll go some other place.'

'Certainly not. I'll go. I only came here to write a poem.'

'*A poem?*'

He had said something. Until then she had treated him with that impersonal insensitive friendliness which takes the place of ceremony in that land of waifs and strays. Now her eyes widened. 'Did you say a *poem?*'

'Yes. I am a poet, you see.'

'Why, but I think that's wonderful. I've never seen a live poet before. Did you know Sophie Dalmeyer Krump?'

'No.'

'She's in Poets' Corner now. She came during my first month when I was only a novice cosmetician, so of course I wasn't allowed to work on her. Besides, she passed on in a street-car accident and needed special treatment. But I took the chance to study her. She had very marked Soul. You might say I learned Soul from studying Sophie Dalmeyer Krump. Now whenever we have a treatment needing special Soul, Mr Joyboy gives it to me.'

'Would you have me, if I passed on?'

'You'd be difficult,' she said, examining him with a professional eye. 'You're the wrong age for Soul. It seems to come more naturally in the very young or the very old. But I'd certainly do my best. I think it's a very, very wonderful thing to be a poet.'

'But you have a very poetic occupation here.'

He spoke lightly, teasing, but she answered with great gravity. 'Yes, I know. I know I have really. Only sometimes at the end of a day when I'm tired I feel as if it was all rather ephemeral. I mean you and Sophie Dalmeyer Krump write a poem and it's printed and maybe read on the radio and millions of people hear it and maybe they'll still be reading it in hundreds of years' time. While my work is burned sometimes within a few hours. At the best it's put in the mausoleum and even there it deteriorates, you know. I've seen painting there not ten years old that's completely lost tonality.

Do you think anything can be a great art which is so impermanent?'

'You should regard it as being like acting or singing or playing an instrument.'

'Yes, I do. But nowadays they can make a permanent record of them, too, can't they?'

'Is that what you brood about when you come here alone?'

'Only lately. At first I used just to lie and think how lucky I was to be here.'

'Don't you think that any more?'

'Yes, of course I do really. Every morning and all day while I am at work. It's just in the evenings that something comes over me. A lot of artists are like that. I expect poets are, too, sometimes, aren't they?'

'I wish you'd tell me about your work,' said Dennis.

'But you've seen it yesterday.'

'I mean about yourself and your work. What made you take it up? Where did you learn? Were you interested in that sort of thing as a child? I'd really be awfully interested to know.'

'I've always been Artistic,' she said. 'I took Art at College as my second subject one semester. I'd have taken it as first subject only Dad lost his money in religion so I had to learn a trade.'

'He lost his money in religion?'

'Yes, the Four Square Gospel. That's why I'm called Aimée, after Aimée Macpherson. Dad wanted to change the name after he lost his money. I wanted to change it too but it kinda stuck. Mother always kept forgetting what we'd changed it to and then she'd find a new one. Once you start changing a name, you see, there's no reason ever to stop. One always hears one that sounds better. Besides you see poor Mother was an alcoholic. But we always came back to Aimée between fancy names and in the end it was Aimée won through.'

'And what else did you take at College?'

'Just Psychology and Chinese. I didn't get on so well with Chinese. But, of course, they were secondary subjects, too; for Cultural background.'

'Yes. And what was your main subject?'

'Beauticraft.'

'Oh.'

'You know – permanents, facials, wax – everything you get in a beauty parlour. Only, of course, we went in for history and theory too. I wrote my thesis on "Hairstyling in the Orient". That was why I took Chinese. I thought it would help, but it didn't. But I got my diploma with special mention for Psychology and Art.'

'And all this time between Psychology and Art and Chinese, you had the mortuary in view?'

'Not at all. Do you really want to hear? I'll tell you because it's really rather a poetic story. You see I graduated in '43 and lots of the girls of my class went to war work but I was never at all interested in that. It's not that I'm unpatriotic. Wars simply don't interest me. Everyone's like that now. Well, I was like that in '43. So I went to the Beverly-Waldorf and worked in the beauty parlour, but you couldn't really get away from the war even there. The ladies didn't seem to have a mind for anything higher than pattern-bombing. There was one lady who was worse than any of them, called Mrs Komstock. She came every Saturday morning for a blue rinse and set and I seemed to take her fancy; she always asked for me; no one else would do, but she never tipped me more than a quarter. Mrs Komstock had one son in Washington and one in Delhi, a granddaughter in Italy and a nephew who was high in indoctrination and I had to hear everything about them all until it got so I dreaded Saturday mornings more than any day in the week. Then after a time Mrs Komstock took sick, but that wasn't the end of her. She used to send for me to come up to her apartment every week and she still only gave me a quarter and she still talked about the war just as much only not so sensibly. Then imagine my surprise when one day Mr Jebb, who was the manager, called me over and said: "Miss Thanatogenos, there's a thing I hardly like to ask you. I don't know exactly how you'll feel about it, but it's Mrs Komstock who's dead and her son from Washington is here and he's very anxious to have you fix Mrs Komstock's hair just as it used to be. It seems there aren't any recent photographs and no one at Whispering Glades knows the style and Colonel Komstock can't exactly describe it. So, Miss Thanatogenos, I was wondering, would you mind very much to

oblige Colonel Komstock going over to Whispering Glades and fix
Mrs Komstock like Colonel Komstock remembers?"

'Well, I didn't know quite what to think. I'd never seen a dead
person before because Dad left Mother before he died, if he is dead,
and Mother went East to look for him when I left College, and died
there. And I had never been inside Whispering Glades as after we
lost our money Mother took to New Thought and wouldn't have it
that there was such a thing as death. So I felt quite nervous coming
here the first time. And then everything was so different from what
I expected. Well, you've seen it and you know. Colonel Komstock
shook hands and said: "Young lady, you are doing a truly fine and
beautiful action" and gave me fifty bucks.

'Then they took me to the embalming-rooms and there was Mrs
Komstock lying on the table in her wedding dress. I shall never
forget the sight of her. She was transfigured. That's the only word for
it. Since then I've had the pleasure of showing their Loved Ones to
more people than I can count and more than half of them say:
"Why, they're quite transfigured." Of course there was no colour in
her yet and her hair was kinda wispy; she was pure white like wax,
and so cool and silent. I hardly dared touch her at first. Then I gave
her a shampoo and her blue rinse and a set just as she always had it,
curly all over and kinda fluffed up where it was thin. Then while she
was drying the cosmetician put the colour on. She let me watch and
I got talking with her and she told me how there was a vacancy for
a novice cosmetician right at that moment so I went straight back
and gave Mr Jebb my notice. That was nearly two years ago and I've
been here ever since.'

'And you don't regret it?'

'Ah, never, never for a moment. What I said just now about
being ephemeral every artist thinks sometimes of his work, doesn't
he? Don't you yourself?'

'And they pay you more than in the beauty parlour, I hope?'

'Yes, a little. But then you see Loved Ones can't tip so that it
works out nearly the same. But it isn't for the money I work. I'd
gladly come for nothing only one has to eat and the Dreamer insists
on our being turned out nicely. It's only in the last year that I've
come really to love the work. Before that I was just glad to serve

people that couldn't talk. Then I began to realize what a work of consolation it was. It's a wonderful thing to start every day knowing that you are going to bring back joy into one aching heart. Of course mine is only a tiny part of it. I'm just a handmaid to the morticians but I have the satisfaction of showing the final result and seeing the reaction. I saw it with you, yesterday. You're British and sort of inexpressive but I knew just what you were feeling.'

'Sir Francis was transfigured certainly.'

'It was when Mr Joyboy came he sort of made me realize what an institution Whispering Glades really is. Mr Joyboy's kinda holy. From the day he came the whole tone of the mortuary became greatly elevated. I shall never forget how one morning Mr Joyboy said to one of the younger morticians: "Mr Parks, I must ask you to remember you are not at the Happier Hunting Ground."'

Dennis betrayed no recognition of that name but he felt a hypodermic stab of thankfulness that he had kept silence when, earlier in their acquaintance, he had considered forming a bond between them by lightly mentioning his trade. It would not have gone down. He merely looked blank and Aimée said: 'I don't suppose you'd ever have heard of that. It's a dreadful place here where they bury animals.'

'*Not* poetic?'

'I was never there myself but I've heard about it. They try and do everything the same as us. It seems kinda blasphemous.'

'And what do you think about when you come here alone in the evenings?'

'Just Death and Art,' said Aimée Thanatogenos simply.

'Half in love with easeful death.'

'What was that you said?'

'I was quoting a poem.

> '... *For many a time*
> *I have been half in love with easeful death,*
> *Call'd him soft names in many a mused rhyme,*
> *To take into the air my quiet breath;*
> *Now more than ever seems it rich to die,*
> *To cease upon the midnight with no pain ...*'

'Did you write that?'

Dennis hesitated. 'You like it?'

'Why, it's beautiful. It's just what I've thought so often and haven't been able to express. "To make it rich to die" and "to cease upon the midnight *with no pain*". That's exactly what Whispering Glades exists for, isn't it? I think it's wonderful to be able to write like that. Did you write it after you came here first?'

'It was written long before.'

'Well, it couldn't be more lovely if you'd written it in Whispering Glades – on the Lake Island itself. Was it something like that you were writing when I came along?'

'Not exactly.'

Across the water the carillon in the Belfry Beautiful musically announced the hour.

'That's six o'clock. I have to go early today.'

'And I have a poem to finish.'

'Will you stay and do it here?'

'No. At home. I'll come with you.'

'I'd love to see the poem when it's done.'

'I'll send it to you.'

'Aimée Thanatogenos is my name. I live quite close, but send it here, to Whispering Glades. This is my true home.'

When they reached the ferry the waterman looked at Dennis with complicity. 'So she turned up all right, bud,' he said.

MR JOYBOY WAS debonair in all his professional actions. He peeled off his rubber gloves like a hero of Ouida returning from stables, tossed them into a kidney bowl and assumed the clean pair which his assistant held ready for him. Next he took a visiting-card – one of a box of blanks supplied to the florist below – and a pair of surgical scissors. In one continuous movement he cut an ellipse, then snicked half an inch at either end along the greater axis. He bent over the corpse, tested the jaw and found it firm set; he drew back the lips and laid his card along the teeth and gums. Now was the moment; his assistant watched with never-failing admiration the deft flick of the thumbs with which he turned the upper corners of the card, the caress of the rubber finger-tips with which he drew the dry and colourless lips into place. And, behold! where before had been a grim line of endurance, there was now a smile. It was masterly. It needed no other touch. Mr Joyboy stood back from his work, removed the gloves and said: 'For Miss Thanatogenos.'

Of recent weeks the expressions that greeted Aimée from the trolley had waxed from serenity to jubilance. Other girls had to work on faces that were stern or resigned or plumb vacant; there was always a nice bright smile for Aimée.

These attentions were noted with sourness in the cosmetic rooms where love of Mr Joyboy illumined the working hours of all the staff. In the evenings each had her consort or suitor; none seriously aspired to be Mr Joyboy's mate. As he passed among them, like an art-master among his students, with a word of correction here or commendation there, sometimes laying his gentle hand on a living shoulder or a dead haunch, he was a figure of romance, a cult shared by all in common, not a prize to be appropriated by any one of them.

Nor was Aimée entirely at ease in her unique position. That morning in particular she met the corpse's greeting with impaired frankness, for she had taken a step which she knew Mr Joyboy could not possibly approve.

There was a spiritual director, an oracle, in these parts who daily filled a famous column in one of the local newspapers. Once, in days of family piety, it bore the title *Aunt Lydia's Post Bag*; now it was *The Wisdom of the Guru Brahmin*, adorned with the photograph of a bearded and almost naked sage. To this exotic source resorted all who were in doubt or distress.

It might be thought that at this extremity of the New World unceremonious manners and frank speech occasioned no doubt; the universal good humour no distress. But it was not so – etiquette, child-psychology, aesthetics and sex reared their questioning heads in this Eden too and to all readers the Guru Brahmin offered solace and solution.

To him Aimée had applied some time ago when the smiles had first become unequivocal. Her problem was not about Mr Joyboy's intentions but about her own. The answer had not been quite satisfactory: '*No, A.T., I do not consider that you are in love – yet. Esteem for a man's character and admiration of his business ability may form the basis of an improving friendship but they are not Love. What you describe of your feelings in his presence does not incline us to believe that there is a physical affinity between you – yet. But remember love comes late to many. We know cases who have only experienced real love after several years of marriage and the arrival of Junior. See plenty of your friend. Love may come.*'

That had been before Dennis Barlow brought a further perplexity to her conscience. It was now six weeks since she met him on the Lake Island, and that morning on the way to work she had posted a letter which had occupied half her night in writing. It was indeed the longest letter she had ever written:

Dear Guru Brahmin,

You may remember that I wrote to you in May last for your advice. This time I am enclosing a stamped and addressed envelope for a private answer as I am going to say things I should not like to have referred to in print. Please reply by return or anyway as soon as convenient as I am very worried and must soon do something about it.

In case you do not remember I will remind you that I work in the same business with a man who is head of the department and in every way the most wonderful character I can imagine. It is a great privilege to be associated with one who is so successful and refined, a natural leader, artist and model of breeding. In all sorts of little ways he has made it plain that he prefers me to the other girls and though he has not said so yet because he is not the sort to do so lightly I am sure he loves me honourably. But I do not have the same feelings when I am with him as the girls say they have when they are with their boys and what one sees in the movies.

But I think I do have such feelings about another but he is not at all such an admirable character. First he is British and therefore in many ways quite Un-American. I do not mean just his accent and the way he eats but he is cynical at things which should be Sacred. I do not think he has any religion. Neither have I because I was progressive at College and had an unhappy upbringing as far as religion went and other things too, but I am ethical. (As this is confidential I may as well say my mother was alcoholic which perhaps makes me more sensitive and reserved than other girls.) He also has no idea of Citizenship or Social Conscience. He is a poet and has had a book printed in England and very well criticized by the critics there. I have seen the book and some of the criticisms so I know this is true but he is very mysterious about what he is doing here. Sometimes he talks as if he was in the movies and sometimes as though he did nothing at all except write poetry. I have seen his house. He lives alone as the friend (male) he lived with passed on six weeks ago. I do not think he goes out with any other girl or is married. He has not very much money. He is very distinguished-looking in an Un-American way and very amusing when he is not being irreverent. Take the Works of Art in Whispering Glades Memorial Park he is often quite irreverent about them which I think an epitome of all that is finest in the American Way of Life. So what hope is there of true happiness?

Also he is not at all cultured. At first I thought he must be being a poet and he has been to Europe and seen the Art there but many of our greatest authors seem to mean nothing to him.

Sometimes he is very sweet and loving and then he suddenly becomes unethical and makes me feel unethical too. So I should value your advice very highly. Hoping that this long letter has not been too much,

> *Cordially yours,*
> *Aimée Thanatogenos.*

He has written a lot of poems to me some of them very beautiful and quite ethical others not so much.

The knowledge that this letter was in the mail burdened Aimée's conscience and she was grateful when the morning passed without any other sign from Mr Joyboy than the usual smile of welcome on the trolley. She painted away diligently while at the Happier Hunting Ground Dennis Barlow was also busy.

They had both ovens going and six dogs, a cat and a barbary goat to dispose of. None of the owners was present. He and Mr Schultz were able to work briskly. The cat and the dogs were twenty-minute jobs. Dennis raked the ashes out while they were still glowing and put them in labelled buckets to cool. The goat took nearly an hour. Dennis looked at it from time to time through the fire-glass pane and finally crushed the horned skull with a poker. Then he turned out the gas, left the oven doors open and prepared the containers. Only one owner had been induced to buy an urn.

'I'm going along now,' said Mr Schultz. 'Will you please to wait till they're cold enough to pack up? They're all for home-delivery except the cat. She's for the columbarium.'

'Okay, Mr Schultz. How about the goat's card? We can't very well say he's wagging his tail in heaven. Goats don't wag their tails.'

'They do when they go to the can.'

'Yes, but it wouldn't look right on the greeting card. They don't purr like cats. They don't sing an orison like birds.'

'I suppose they just remember.'

Dennis wrote: *Your Billy is remembering you in heaven tonight.*

He stirred the little smoking grey heaps in the bottom of the buckets. Then he returned to the office and resumed his search of the *Oxford Book of English Verse* for a poem for Aimée.

He possessed few books and was beginning to run short of material. At first he had tried writing poems for her himself but she showed a preference for the earlier masters. Moreover, the Muse nagged him. He had abandoned the poem he was writing, long ago it seemed, in the days of Frank Hinsley. That was not what the Muse wanted. There was a very long, complicated, and important message she was trying to convey to him. It was about Whispering Glades, but it was not, except quite indirectly, about Aimée. Sooner or later the Muse would have to be placated. She came first. Meanwhile Aimée must draw from the bran-tub of the anthologies.

Once he came near to exposure when she remarked that *Shall I compare thee to a summer's day* reminded her of something she had learned at school, and once near to disgrace when she condemned *On thy midnight pallet lying* as unethical. *Now sleeps the crimson petal, now the white*, had struck bang right in the centre of the bull, but he knew few poems so high and rich and voluptuous. The English poets were proving uncertain guides in the labyrinth of Californian courtship – nearly all were too casual, too despondent, too ceremonious, or too exacting; they scolded, they pleaded, they extolled. Dennis required salesmanship; he sought to present Aimée with an irresistible picture not so much of her own merits or even of his, as of the enormous gratification he was offering. The films did it; the crooners did it; but not, it seemed, the English poets.

After half an hour he abandoned the search. The first two dogs were ready to be packed. He shook up the goat, which still glowed under its white and grey surface. There would be no poem for Aimée that day. He would take her instead to the Planetarium.

The embalmers had the same meals as the rest of the mortuary staff but they ate apart at a central table where by recent but hallowed tradition they daily spun a wire cage of dice and the loser paid the bill for them all. Mr Joyboy spun, lost, and cheerfully paid. They always broke about even on the month. The attraction of the gamble was to show that they were men to whom ten or twenty dollars less or more at the end of the week was not a matter of great concern.

At the door of the canteen Mr Joyboy lingered sucking a digestive lozenge. The girls came out in ones or twos lighting their cigarettes; among them, alone, Aimée who did not smoke. Mr Joyboy drew her apart into the formal garden. They stood under an allegorical group representing 'the Enigma of Existence'.

'Miss Thanatogenos,' said Mr Joyboy, 'I want to tell you how much I appreciate your work.'

'Thank you, Mr Joyboy.'

'I mentioned it yesterday to the Dreamer.'

'Oh, thank you, Mr Joyboy.'

'Miss Thanatogenos, for some time the Dreamer has been looking forward. You know how he looks forward. He is a man of boundless imagination. He considers that the time has come when women should take their proper place in Whispering Glades. They have proved themselves in the lowlier tasks to be worthy of the higher. He believes moreover that there are many people of delicate sensibility who are held back from doing their duty to their Loved Ones by what I can only call prudery, but which Dr Kenworthy considers a natural reluctance to expose their Loved Ones to anything savouring in the least degree of immodesty. To be brief, Miss Thanatogenos, the Dreamer intends to train a female embalmer and his choice, his very wise choice, has fallen on you.'

'Oh, Mr Joyboy.'

'Say nothing. I know how you feel. May I tell him you accept?'

'Oh, Mr Joyboy.'

'And now if I may intrude a personal note, don't you think this calls for a little celebration? Would you do me the honour of taking supper with me this evening?'

'Oh, Mr Joyboy, I don't know what to say. I did make a sort of date.'

'But that was before you heard the news. That puts rather a different complexion on matters, I guess. Besides, Miss Thanatogenos, it was not my intention that we should be alone. I wish you to come to my home. Miss Thanatogenos, I claim as my right the very great privilege and pleasure of presenting the first lady embalmer of Whispering Glades to my Mom.'

It was a day of high emotion. All that afternoon Aimée was unable to keep her attention on her work. Fortunately, there was little of importance on hand. She helped the girl in the next cubicle to glue a toupé to a more than usually slippery scalp; she hastily brushed over a male baby with flesh tint; but all the time her mind was in the embalmers' room, attentive to the swish and hiss of the taps, to the coming and going of orderlies with covered kidney bowls, to the low demands for suture or ligature. She had never set foot beyond the oilcloth curtains which screened the embalming-rooms; soon she would have the freedom of them all.

At four o'clock the head cosmetician told her to pack up. She arranged her paints and bottles with habitual care, washed her brushes, and went to the cloakroom to change.

She was meeting Dennis on the lake shore. He kept her waiting and, when he came, accepted the news that she was going out to supper with annoying composure. 'With the Joyboy?' he said. 'That ought to be funny.' But she was so full of her news that she could not forbear to tell him. 'I say,' he said, 'that *is* something. How much is it worth?'

'I don't know. I didn't go into the question.'

'It's bound to be something handsome. Do you suppose it's a hundred a week?'

'Oh, I don't suppose anyone except Mr Joyboy gets that.'

'Well, fifty anyway. Fifty is pretty good. We could get married on that.'

Aimée stopped in her tracks and stared at him. 'What did you say?'

'We can get married, don't you see? It can't be less than fifty, can it?'

'And what, pray, makes you think I should marry you?'

'Why, my dear girl, it's only money that has been holding me back. Now you can keep me, there's nothing to stop us.'

'An American man would despise himself for living on his wife.'

'Yes, but you see I'm European. We have none of these prejudices in the older civilizations. I don't say fifty is much, but I don't mind roughing it a little.'

'I think you're entirely contemptible.'

'Don't be an ass. I say, you aren't really in a rage, are you?'

Aimée was really in a rage. She left him abruptly and that evening, before she set out for supper, scrawled a hasty note to the Guru Brahmin: *Please don't bother to answer my letter of this morning. I know my own mind now,* and dispatched it to the newspaper-office by special delivery.

With a steady hand Aimée fulfilled the prescribed rites of an American girl preparing to meet her lover – dabbed herself under the arms with a preparation designed to seal the sweat glands, gargled another to sweeten the breath, and brushed into her hair some odorous drops from a bottle labelled: 'Jungle Venom' – *From the depth of the fever-ridden swamp*, the advertisement had stated, *where juju drums throb for the human sacrifice, Jeanette's latest exclusive creation* Jungle Venom *comes to you with the remorseless stealth of the hunting cannibal.*

Thus fully equipped for a domestic evening, her mind at ease, Aimée waited for Mr Joyboy's musical 'Hallo, there!' from the front door. She was all set to accept her manifest destiny.

But the evening did not turn out quite as she hoped. Its whole style fell greatly below her expectation. She went out rarely, scarcely at all indeed, and perhaps for this reason had exaggerated notions. She knew Mr Joyboy as a very glorious professional personage, a regular contributor to *The Casket*, an intimate of Dr Kenworthy's, the sole sun of the mortuary. She had breathlessly traced with her vermilion brush the inimitable curves of his handiwork. She knew of him as a Rotarian and a Knight of Pythias; his clothes and his car were irreproachably new, and she supposed that when he drove sprucely off into his private life he frequented a world altogether loftier than anything in her own experience. But it was not so.

They travelled a long way down Santa Monica Boulevard before finally turning into a building estate. It was not a prepossessing quarter; it seemed to have suffered a reverse. Many of the lots were vacant, but those which were occupied had already lost their first freshness and the timber bungalow at which they finally stopped was in no way more remarkable than its fellows. The truth is that morticians, however eminent, are not paid like film stars. Moreover, Mr Joyboy was careful. He saved and he paid insurance. He sought to make a good impression in the world. One day he would have a house and children. Meanwhile anything spent inconspicuously, anything spent on Mom, was money down the drain.

'I never seem to get around to doing anything about the garden,' Mr Joyboy said as though dimly aware of some unexpressed criticism in Aimée's survey. 'This is just a little place I got in a hurry to settle Mom in when we came West.'

He opened the front door, stepped back to allow Aimée to pass and then yodelled loudly behind her: 'Yoohoo, Mom! Here we come!'

Hectoring male tones filled the little house. Mr Joyboy opened a door and ushered Aimée in to the source of the nuisance, a radio on the central table of a nondescript living-room. Mrs Joyboy sat very near it.

'Sit down quietly,' she said, 'until this is over.'

Mr Joyboy winked at Aimée. 'The old lady hates to miss the political commentaries,' he said.

'Quietly,' repeated Mrs Joyboy, fiercely.

They sat silent for ten minutes until the raucous stream of misinformation gave place to a gentler voice advocating a brand of toilet-paper.

'Turn it off,' said Mrs Joyboy. 'Well, he says there'll be war again this year.'

'Mom, this is Aimée Thanatogenos.'

'Very well. Supper's in the kitchen. You can get it when you like.'

'Hungry, Aimée?'

'No, yes. I suppose a little.'

'Let's go see what surprise the little old lady has been cooking up for us.'

'Just what you always have,' said Mrs Joyboy; 'I ain't got the time for surprises.'

Mrs Joyboy turned in her chair towards a strangely veiled object which stood at her other elbow. She drew the fringe of a shawl, revealed a wire cage, and in it an almost naked parrot. 'Sambo,' she said winningly, 'Sambo.' The bird put its head on one side and blinked. 'Sambo,' she said. 'Won't you speak to me?'

'Why, Mom, you know that bird hasn't spoken in years.'

'He speaks plenty when you're away, don't you, my Sambo?'

The bird put its head on the other side, blinked and suddenly ruffled his few feathers and whistled like a train. 'There,' said Mrs Joyboy. 'If I hadn't Sambo to love me I might as well be dead.'

There was tinned noodle soup, a bowl of salad with tinned crab compounded in it, there was ice-cream and coffee. Aimée helped carry the trays. Aimée and Mr Joyboy removed the radio and laid the table. Mrs Joyboy watched them malevolently from her chair. The mothers of great men often disconcert their sons' admirers. Mrs Joyboy had small angry eyes, frizzy hair, pince-nez on a very thick nose, a shapeless body, and positively insulting clothes.

'It isn't how we're used to living nor where we're used to living,' she said. 'We come from the East, and if anyone had listened to me that's where we'd be today. We had a coloured girl in Vermont came in regular – fifteen bucks a week and glad of it. You can't find that here. You can't find anything here. Look at that lettuce. There's more things and cheaper things and better things where we come from. Not that we ever had much of anything seeing all I get to keep house on.'

'Mom loves a joke,' said Mr Joyboy.

'Joke? Call it a joke to keep house on what I get *and* visitors coming in?' Then fixing Aimée she added, 'And the girls *work* in Vermont.'

'Aimée works very hard, Mom; I told you.'

'Nice work, too. I wouldn't let a daughter of mine do it. Where's your mother?'

'She went East. I think she died.'

'Better dead there than live here. *Think?* That's all children care nowadays.'

'Now, Mom, you've no call to say things like that. You know I care . . . '

Later, at last, the time came when Aimée could decently depart; Mr Joyboy saw her to the gate.

'I'd drive you home,' he said, 'only I don't like to leave Mom. The street car passes the corner. You'll be all right.'

'Oh, I'll be all right,' said Aimée.

'Mom just loved you.'

'Did she?'

'Why, yes. I always know. When Mom takes a fancy to people she treats them natural same as she treats me.'

'She certainly treated me natural.'

'I'll say she did. Yes, she treated you natural and no mistake. You certainly made a great impression on Mom.'

That evening before she went to bed Aimée wrote yet another letter to the Guru Brahmin.

THE GURU BRAHMIN was two gloomy men and a bright young secretary. One gloomy man wrote the column, the other, a Mr Slump, dealt with the letters which required private answers. By the time they came to work the secretary had sorted the letters on their respective desks. Mr Slump, who was a survival from the days of Aunt Lydia and retained her style, usually had the smaller pile, for most of the Guru Brahmin's correspondents liked to have their difficulties exposed to the public. It gave them a sense of greater importance and also on occasions led to correspondence with other readers.

The scent of 'Jungle Venom' still clung to Aimée's writing paper.

'Dear Aimée,' Mr Slump dictated, adding a link to his endless chain of cigarettes, 'I am the tiniest bit worried by the tone of your last letter.'

The cigarettes Mr Slump smoked were prepared by doctors, so the advertisements declared, with the sole purpose of protecting his respiratory system. Yet Mr Slump suffered and the young secretary suffered with him, hideously. For the first hours of every day he was possessed by a cough which arose from tartarean depths and was relieved only by whisky. On bad mornings it seemed to the suffering secretary that Mr Slump would vomit. This was one of the bad mornings. He retched, shivered, and wiped his face with his hand-kerchief.

'A home-loving, home-making American girl should find nothing to complain of in the treatment you describe. Your friend was doing you the highest honour in his power by inviting you to meet his mother and she would not be a mother in the true sense if she had not wished to see you. A time will come, Aimée, when your son will bring a stranger home. Nor do I think it a reflection on him that he helps his mother in the house. You say he looked undignified in his apron. Surely it is the height of true dignity to help others regardless of convention. The only explanation of your changed attitude is that you do not love him as he has the right to expect, in which case you should tell him so frankly at the first opportunity.

468

'You are well aware of the defects of the other friend you mention and I am sure I can leave it to your good sense to distinguish between glamour and worth. Poems are very nice things but – in my opinion – a man who will cheerfully take his part in the humble chores of the home is worth ten glib poets.

'Is that too strong?'

'It *is* strong, Mr Slump.'

'Hell, I feel awful this morning. The girl sounds like a prize bitch anyway.'

'We're used to that.'

'Yes. Well, tone it down a bit. Here's another one from the woman who bites her nails. What did we advise last time?'

'Meditation on the Beautiful.'

'Tell her to go on meditating.'

Five miles away in the cosmetic room Aimée paused in her work to re-read the poem she had received that morning from Dennis.

> God set her brave eyes wide apart (she read),
> And painted them with fire;
> They stir the ashes of my heart
> To embers of desire . . .
>
> Her body is a flower, her hair
> About her neck doth play;
> I find her colours everywhere,
> They are the pride of day.
>
> Her little hands are soft and when
> I see her fingers move,
> I know in very truth that men
> Have died for less than love.
>
> Ah, dear, live, lovely thing! My eyes
> Have sought her like a prayer . . .

A single tear ran down Aimée's cheek and fell on the smiling waxy mask below her. She put the manuscript into the pocket of her linen smock and her little soft hands began to move over the dead face.

At the Happier Hunting Ground Dennis said: 'Mr Schultz, I want to improve my position.'

'It can't be done, not at present. The money just isn't here in the business. You know that as well as I do. You're getting five bucks more than the man before you. I don't say you aren't worth it, Dennis. If business looks up you're the first for a raise.'

'I'm thinking of getting married. My girl doesn't know I work here. She's romantic. I don't know she'd think well of this business.'

'Have you anything better to go to?'

'No.'

'Well, you tell her to lay off being romantic. Forty bucks a week regular is forty bucks.'

'Through no wish of my own I have become the protagonist of a Jamesian problem. Do you ever read any Henry James, Mr Schultz?'

'You know I don't have the time for reading.'

'You don't have to read much of him. All his stories are about the same thing – American innocence and European experience.'

'Thinks he can outsmart us, does he?'

'James was the innocent American.'

'Well, I've no time for guys running down their own folks.'

'Oh, he doesn't run them down. The stories are all tragedies one way or another.'

'Well, I ain't got the time for tragedies neither. Take an end of this casket. We've only half an hour before the pastor arrives.'

There was a funeral with full honours that morning, the first for a month. In the presence of a dozen mourners the coffin of an Alsatian was lowered into the flower-lined tomb. The Reverend Errol Bartholomew read the service.

'Dog that is born of bitch hath but a short time to live, and is full of misery. He cometh up, and is cut down like a flower; he fleeth as it were a shadow, and never continueth in one stay...'

Later in the office as he gave Mr Bartholomew his cheque, Dennis said: 'Tell me, how does one become a non-sectarian clergyman?'

'One has the Call.'

'Yes, of course; but after the Call, what is the process? I mean is there a non-sectarian bishop who ordains you?'

'Certainly not. Anyone who has received the Call has no need for human intervention.'

'You just say one day "I am a non-sectarian clergyman" and set up shop?'

'There is considerable outlay. You need buildings. But the banks are usually ready to help. Then of course what one aims at is a radio congregation.'

'A friend of mine has the Call, Mr Bartholomew.'

'Well, I should advise him to think twice about answering it. The competition gets hotter every year, especially in Los Angeles. Some of the recent non-sectarians stop at nothing – not even at psychiatry and table-turning.'

'That's bad.'

'It is entirely without scriptural authority.'

'My friend was thinking of making a speciality of funeral work. He has connexions.'

'Chicken feed, Mr Barlow. There is more to be made in weddings and christenings.'

'My friend doesn't feel quite the same about weddings and christenings. What he needs is Class. You would say, would you not, that a non-sectarian clergyman was the social equal of an embalmer?'

'I certainly would, Mr Barlow. There is a very deep respect in the American heart for ministers of religion.'

The Wee Kirk o' Auld Lang Syne lies on an extremity of the park out of sight from the University Church and the Mausoleum. It is a lowly building without belfry or ornament, designed to charm rather than to impress, dedicated to Robert Burns and Harry

Lauder, souvenirs of whom are exhibited in an annex. The tartan carpet alone gives colour to the interior. The heather which was originally planted round the walls flourished too grossly in the Californian sun, outgrew Dr Kenworthy's dream so that at length he uprooted it and had the immediate area walled, levelled and paved, giving it the air of a schoolyard well in keeping with the high educational traditions of the race it served. But unadorned simplicity and blind fidelity to tradition were alike foreign to the Dreamer's taste. He innovated; two years before Aimée came to Whispering Glades, he introduced into this austere spot a Lovers' Nook; not a lush place comparable to the Lake Isle which invited to poetic dalliance, but something, as it seemed to him, perfectly Scottish; a place where a bargain could be driven and a contract sealed. It consisted of a dais and a double throne of rough-hewn granite. Between the two seats thus formed stood a slab pierced by a heart-shaped aperture. Behind was the inscription:

THE LOVERS' SEAT

This seat is made of authentic old Scotch stone from the highlands of Aberdeen. In it is incorporated the ancient symbol of the Heart of the Bruce.

According to the tradition of the glens lovers who plight their troth on this seat and join their lips through the Heart of the Bruce shall have many a canty day with ane anither and maun totter down hand in hand like the immortal Anderson couple.

The words of the prescribed oath were cut on the step so that a seated couple could conveniently recite them:

> *Till a' the seas gang dry my dear*
> *And the rocks melt wi' the sun;*
> *I will luve thee still my dear,*
> *While the sands o' life shall run.*

The fancy caught the popular taste and the spot is much frequented. Little there tempts the lounger. The ceremony is over in less than a minute and on most evenings couples may be seen waiting their turn while strange accents struggle with a text which acquires something of the sanctity of mumbo-jumbo on the unpractised lips of Balts and Jews and Slavs. They kiss through the hole and yield place to the next couple, struck silent as often as not with awe at the mystery they have enacted. There is no bird-song here. Instead the skirl of the pipes haunts the pines and the surviving forest-growth of heather.

Here, a few days after her supper with Mr Joyboy, a newly resolute Aimée led Dennis and, as he surveyed the incised quotations which, in the manner of Whispering Glades, abounded in the spot, he was thankful that a natural abhorrence of dialect had prevented him from borrowing any of the texts of his courtship from Robert Burns.

They waited their turn and presently sat side by side on the double throne. 'Till a' the seas gang dry, my dear,' whispered Aimée. Her face appeared deliciously at the little window. They kissed, then gravely descended and passed through waiting couples without a glance.

'What is a "canty day", Dennis?'

'I've never troubled to ask. Something like hogmanay, I expect.'

'What is that?'

'People being sick on the pavement in Glasgow.'

'Oh.'

'Do you know how the poem ends? "Now we maun totter down, John, And hand in hand we'll go, And *sleep together* at the foot, John Anderson, my jo." '

'Dennis, why is all the poetry you know so coarse? And you talking of being a pastor.'

'Non-sectarian; but I incline to the Anabaptists in these matters. Anyway, everything is ethical to engaged couples.'

After a pause Aimée said: 'I shall have to write and tell Mr Joyboy and the – and someone else.'

She wrote that night. Her letters were delivered by the morning post.

Mr Slump said: 'Send her our usual letter of congratulation and advice.'

'But, Mr Slump, she's marrying the wrong one.'
'Don't mention that side of it.'

Five miles away Aimée uncovered the first corpse of the morning. It came from Mr Joyboy bearing an expression of such bottomless woe that her heart was wrung.

MR SLUMP WAS late and crapulous.

'Another letter from la belle Thanatogenos,' said Mr Slump. 'I thought we'd had the last of that dame.'

Dear Guru Brahmin,

Three weeks ago I wrote you that everything was all right and I had made up my mind and felt happy but I am still unhappy, unhappier in a way than I was before. Sometimes my British friend is sweet to me and writes poetry but often he wants unethical things and is so cynical when I say no we must wait. I begin to doubt we shall ever make a real American home. He says he is going to be a pastor. Well as I told you I am progressive and therefore have no religion but I do not think religion is a thing to be cynical about because it makes some people very happy and all cannot be progressive at this stage of Evolution. He has not become a pastor yet he says he has something to do first which he had promised a man but he doesn't say what it is and sometimes I wonder is it something wrong he is so secretive.

Then there is my own career. I was offered a Big Chance to improve my position and now no more is said of that. The head of the department is the gentleman I told you of who helps his mother in the housework, and since I plighted my troth with my British friend and wrote to tell him he never speaks to me even as much as he speaks professionally to the other girls of the department. And the place where we work is meant to be Happy that is one of the first rules and everyone looks to this gentleman for an Example and he is very unhappy, unlike what the place stands for. Sometimes he even looks mean and that was the last thing he ever looked before. All my fiancé does is to make unkind jokes about his name. I am worried too about the interest he shows in my work. I mean I think it quite right a man should show interest in a girl's work but he shows too much. I mean there are certain technical matters in every business I suppose which people do not like to have talked about outside the office and it is just those matters he is always asking about...

'That's how women always are,' said Mr Slump. 'It just breaks their hearts to let any man go.'

475

There was often a missive waiting for Aimée on her work-table. When they had parted sourly the night before Dennis transcribed a poem before going to bed and delivered it at the mortuary on his way to work. These missives in his fine script had to fill the place of the missing smiles; the Loved Ones on their trolleys were now as woebegone and reproachful as the master.

That morning Aimée arrived still sore from the bickering of the preceding evening and found a copy of verses waiting for her. She read them and once more her heart opened to her lover.

> *Aimée, thy beauty is to me*
> *Like those Nicean barks of yore . . .*

Mr Joyboy passed the cosmetic rooms on his way out, dressed for the street. His face was cast in pitiful gloom. Aimée smiled shyly, deprecating; he nodded heavily and passed by, and then on an impulse she wrote on the top of the lyric: *Try and understand, Aimée*, slipped into the embalming-room and reverently laid the sheet of paper on the heart of a corpse who was there waiting Mr Joyboy's attention.

After an hour Mr Joyboy returned. She heard him enter his room; she heard the taps turned on. It was not until lunch-time that they met.

'That poem,' he said, 'was a very beautiful thought.'

'My fiancé wrote it.'

'The Britisher you were with Tuesday?'

'Yes, he's a very prominent poet in England.'

'Is that so? I don't ever recall meeting a British poet before. Is that all he does?'

'He's studying to be a pastor.'

'Is that so? See here, Aimée, if you have any more of his poems I should greatly appreciate to see them.'

'Why, Mr Joyboy, I didn't know you were one for poems.'

'Sorrow and disappointment kinda makes a man poetic I guess.'

'I've lots of them. I keep them here.'

'I would certainly like to study them. I was at the Knife and Fork Club Dinner last night and I became acquainted with a literary

gentleman from Pasadena. I'd like to show them to him. Maybe he'd
be able to help your friend some way.'

'Why, Mr Joyboy, that's real chivalrous of you.' She paused.
They had not spoken so many words to one another since the day
of her engagement. The nobility of the man again overwhelmed her.
'I hope,' she said shyly, 'that Mrs Joyboy is well?'

'Mom isn't so good today. She's had a tragedy. You remember
Sambo, her parrot?'

'Of course.'

'He passed on. He was kinda old, of course, something over
a hundred, but the end was sudden. Mrs Joyboy certainly feels it.'

'Oh, I am sorry.'

'Yes, she certainly feels it. I've never known her so cast down. I've
been arranging for the disposal this morning. That's why I went out.
I had to be at the Happier Hunting Ground. The funeral's Wednesday. I was wondering, Miss Thanatogenos: Mom doesn't know so
many people in this State. She certainly would appreciate a friend at
the funeral. He was a sociable bird when he was a bit younger.
Enjoyed parties back East more than anyone. It seems kinda bitter
there shouldn't be anyone at the last rites.'

'Why, Mr Joyboy, of course I'd be glad to come.'

'Would you, Miss Thanatogenos? Well, I call that real nice
of you.'

Thus at long last Aimée came to the Happier Hunting Ground.

AIMÉE THANATOGENOS SPOKE the tongue of Los Angeles; the sparse furniture of her mind – the objects which barked the intruder's shins – had been acquired at the local High School and University; she presented herself to the world dressed and scented in obedience to the advertisements; brain and body were scarcely distinguishable from the standard product, but the spirit – ah, the spirit was something apart; it had to be sought afar; not here in the musky orchards of the Hesperides, but in the mountain air of the dawn, in the eagle-haunted passes of Hellas. An umbilical cord of cafés and fruit shops, of ancestral shady businesses (fencing and pimping) united Aimée, all unconscious, to the high places of her race. As she grew up the only language she knew expressed fewer and fewer of her ripening needs; the facts which littered her memory grew less substantial; the figure she saw in the looking-glass seemed less recognizably herself. Aimée withdrew herself into a lofty and hieratic habitation.

Thus it was that the exposure as a liar and a cheat of the man she loved and to whom she was bound by the tenderest vows, affected only a part of her. Her heart was broken perhaps but it was a small inexpensive organ of local manufacture. In a wider and grander way she felt that things had been simplified. She held in her person a valuable concession to bestow; she had been scrupulous in choosing justly between rival claimants. There was no room now for further hesitation. The voluptuous tempting tones of 'Jungle Venom' were silenced.

It was however in the language of her upbringing that she addressed her final letter to the Guru Brahmin.

Mr Slump was ill-shaven; Mr Slump was scarcely sober; 'Slump is slipping,' said the managing editor. 'Have him take a pull at himself or else fire him.' Unconscious of impending doom Mr Slump said:

'For Christ's sake, Thanatogenos again. What does she say, lovely?
I don't seem able to read this morning.'

'She has had a terrible awakening, Mr Slump. The man she
thought she loved proves to be a liar and cheat.'

'Aw, tell her go marry the other guy.'

'That seems to be what she intends doing.'

The engagement of Dennis and Aimée had never been announced
in any paper and needed no public denial. The engagement of
Mr Joyboy and Aimée had a column-and-a-half in the *Morticians'
Journal* and a photograph in *The Casket*, while the house-journal,
Whispers from the Glades, devoted nearly an entire issue to the
romance. A date was fixed for the wedding at the University
Church. Mr Joyboy had been reared a Baptist and the minister
who buried the Baptist dead gladly offered his services. The ward-
robe-mistress found a white slumber-robe for the bride. Dr Kenworthy intimated his intention of being there in person. The
corpses who came to Aimée for her ministrations now grinned
with triumph.

And all this time there was no meeting between Dennis and
Aimée. She had last seen him at the parrot's grave when, quite
unabashed, it seemed, he had winked at her over the gorgeous little
casket. In his heart, however, he had been abashed and thought it
well to lie low for a day or two. Then he saw the announcement of
the engagement.

It was not an easy matter for Aimée to refuse communication
with anyone. She did not live in circumstances where she could say 'I
am not at home to Mr Barlow' and order her servants to refuse him
admission. She had no servant; if the telephone rang, she answered
it. She had to eat. She had to shop. In either case she stood open to
those friendly casual-seeming encounters in which American social
life abounds. One evening shortly before the wedding-day Dennis
lay in wait for her, followed her to a nutburger counter and took the
next stool.

'Hullo, Aimée. I want to talk to you.'

'There's nothing you can say means anything now.'

'But, my dear girl, you seem to have forgotten that we're engaged to be married. My theological studies are prospering. The day when I shall claim you is at hand.'

'I'd rather die.'

'Yes, I confess I overlooked that alternative. D'you know, this is the first time I've ever eaten a nutburger? I've often wondered what they were. It is not so much their nastiness but their total absence of taste that shocks one. But let us get this clear. Do you deny that you solemnly swore to marry me?'

'A girl can change her mind, can't she?'

'Well, you know, I don't honestly think she can. You made a very solemn promise.'

'Under false pretences. All those poems you sent and pretended you'd written for me, that I thought so cultivated I even learned bits of them by heart – all by other people, some by people who passed on hundreds of years ago. I never felt so mortified as when I found out.'

'So that's the trouble, is it?'

'And that horrible Happier Hunting Ground. I'm going now. I don't want to eat anything.'

'Well, you chose the place. When I took you out I never gave you nutburgers, did I?'

'As often as not it was *I* took *you* out.'

'A frivolous point. You can't walk down the street crying like that. I've my car parked across the way. Let me drop you home.'

They stepped out into the neon-lighted boulevard. 'Now, Aimée,' said Dennis, 'let us not have a tiff.'

'Tiff? I loathe everything about you.'

'When we last met we were engaged to be married. I think I am entitled to some explanation. So far, all you have complained of is that I am not the author of some of the best-known poems in the English language. Well, I ask you, is Popjoy?'

'You meant me to think you wrote them.'

'There, Aimée, you misjudge me. It is I who should be disillusioned when I think that I have been squandering my affections on a girl ignorant of the commonest treasures of literature. But I realize that you have different educational standards from those I am used to. No doubt you know more than I about psychology and Chinese. But in the dying world I come from quotation is a national vice. It used to be the classics, now it's lyric verse.'

'I shall never believe anything you say again.'

'Well, damn it, what don't you believe?'

'I don't believe in you.'

'Ah, that's another point. There's all the difference between believing someone and believing in them.'

'Oh, do stop being reasonable.'

'Very well.' Dennis drew into the side of the road and attempted to take her in his arms. She resisted with fiery agility. He desisted and lit a cigar. Aimée sobbed in the corner and presently said: 'That awful funeral.'

'The Joyboy parrot? Yes. I think I can explain that. Mr Joyboy would have an open casket. I advised against it and, after all, I knew. I'd studied the business. An open casket is all right for dogs and cats who lie down and curl up naturally. But parrots don't. They look absurd with the head on a pillow. But I came up against a blank wall of snobbery. What was done in Whispering Glades must be done at the Happier Hunting Ground. Or do you think that the whole thing was a frame-up? I believe that sanctimonious pest *wanted* the poor parrot to look absurd so as to lower me in your eyes. I believe that's it. Who asked you to the funeral anyway? Were you acquainted with the late parrot?'

'To think that all the time you were going out with me you were secretly going to *that place...*'

'My dear, you as an American should be the last to despise a man for starting at the bottom of the ladder. I can't claim to be as high in the mortuary world as your Mr Joyboy, but I am younger, very much better-looking, and I wear my own teeth. I have a future in the Non-sectarian Church. I expect to be head chaplain at Whispering Glades when Mr Joyboy is still swilling out corpses. I have the makings of a great preacher – something in the metaphysical seventeenth-century manner, appealing to the intellect rather than to crude emotion. Something Laudian – ceremonious, verbose, ingenious, and doctrinally quite free of prejudice. I have been thinking a good deal about my costume; full sleeves, I think . . . '

'Oh, do be quiet! You bore me so.'

'Aimée, as your future husband and spiritual director, I must tell you that that is no way to speak of the man you love.'

'I don't love you.'

' "Till a' the seas gang dry, my dear." '

'I haven't the least idea what that means.'

' "And the rocks melt wi' the sun." That's plain enough anyway. "I will luve –" You can't fail to understand those words, surely? It's just the way the crooners pronounced them. "I will luve thee still, my dear, While the sands o' life shall run." The last words, I admit, are a little obscure, but the general sense is obvious to the most embittered. Have you forgotten the Heart of the Bruce?'

The sobs ceased, and the ensuing silence told Dennis that intellectual processes were at work in the exquisite dim head in the corner. 'Was it Bruce wrote that poem?' she asked at length.

'No. But the names are so similar that the difference is immaterial.'

Another pause. 'Didn't this Bruce or whatever he's called make some way round his oath?'

Dennis had not counted greatly on the ceremony at the Kirk o' Auld Lang Syne. He had introduced it whimsically. Now, however, he pounced on the advantage. 'Listen, you delicious, hopeless creature. You are on the horns of a dilemma – which is European for being in a jam.'

'Drive me home.'

'Very well, I can explain as we go. You think Whispering Glades the most wonderful thing outside heaven. I see your point. In my rough British way I share your enthusiasm. I have been planning an opus on the subject, but I am afraid I can't say with Dowson, "If you ever come to read it, you will understand." You won't, my dear, not a word of it. All this is by the way. Now your Mr Joyboy is the incarnate spirit of Whispering Glades – the one mediating logos between Dr Kenworthy and common humanity. Well, we're obsessed by Whispering Glades, both of us – "half in love with easeful death", as I once told you – and to save further complications let me explain that I did not write that poem either – you're the nautch girl and vestal virgin of the place, and naturally I attach myself to you and you attach yourself to Joyboy. Psychologists will tell you that kind of thing happens every day.

'It may be that by the Dreamer's standards there are defects in my character. The parrot looked terrible in his casket. So what? You loved me and swore to love me eternally with the most sacred oath in the religion of Whispering Glades. So you see the dilemma, jam or impasse. Sanctity is indivisible. If it isn't sacred to kiss me through the heart of the Burns or Bruce, it isn't sacred to go to bed with old Joyboy.'

There was silence still. Dennis had made an impression far beyond his expectation.

'Here you are,' he said at length, stopping at Aimée's apartment house. This was not the moment he realized for soft advances. 'Jump out.'

Aimée said nothing and for a moment did not move. Then in a whisper she said: 'You could release me.'

'Ah, but I won't.'

'Not when you know I've quite forgotten you?'

'But you haven't.'

'Yes. When I turn away I can't even remember what you look like. When you are not there I don't think of you at all.'

Left to herself in the concrete cell which she called her apartment, Aimée fell victim to all the devils of doubt. She switched on her radio; a mindless storm of Teutonic passion possessed her and drove her to the cliff-edge of frenzy; then abruptly stopped. 'This rendition comes to you by courtesy of Kaiser's Stoneless Peaches. Remember no other peach now marketed is perfect and completely stoneless. When you buy Kaiser's Stoneless Peach you are buying full weight of succulent peach flesh and nothing else . . .'

She turned to the telephone and dialled Mr Joyboy's number.

'Please, please come over. I'm so worried.'

From the ear-piece came a babel, human and inhuman, and in the midst of it a still small voice saying, 'Speak up, honey-baby. I can't quite get you.'

'I'm so miserable.'

'It isn't just easy hearing you, honey-baby. Mom's got a new bird and she's trying to make him talk. Maybe we better leave whatever it is and talk about it tomorrow.'

'Please, dear, come right over now; couldn't you?'

'Why, honey-baby, I couldn't leave Mom the very evening her new bird arrived, could I? How would she feel? It's a big evening for Mom, honey-baby. I have to be here with her.'

'It's about our marriage.'

'Yes, honey-baby, I kinda guessed it was. Plenty of little problems come up. They all look easier in the morning. Take a good sleep, honey-baby.'

'I must see you.'

'Now, honey-baby, I'm going to be firm with you. Just you do what Poppa says this minute or Poppa will be real mad at you.'

She rang off and once more resorted to grand opera; she was swept up and stupefied in the gust of sound. It was too much. In the silence that followed her brain came to life a little. Again the telephone. The local newspaper.

'I want to speak to the Guru Brahmin.'

'Why, he doesn't work evenings. I'm sorry.'

'It's very important. Couldn't you please give me his home number?'

'There's two of them. Which d'you want?'

'Two? I didn't know. I want the one who answers letters.'

'That will be Mr Slump, but he doesn't work here after tomorrow and he wouldn't be home at this time, anyway. You could try Mooney's Saloon. That's where the editorials mostly go evenings.'

'And his real name is Slump?'

'That's what he tells me, sister.'

Mr Slump had that day been discharged from his paper. Everyone in the office had long expected the event except Mr Slump himself, who had taken the story of his betrayal to several unsympathetic drinking-places.

The barman said: 'There's a call for you, Mr Slump. Are you here?'

It seemed likely to Mr Slump in his present state of mind that this would be his editor, repentant; he reached across the bar for the instrument.

'Mr Slump?'

'Yes.'

'I've found you at last. I'm Aimée Thanatogenos . . . You remember me?'

It was a memorable name. 'Sure,' said Mr Slump at length.

'Mr Slump, I am in great distress. I need your advice. You remember the Britisher I told you about . . . '

Mr Slump held the telephone to the ear of the man next to him, grinned, shrugged, finally laid it on the bar, lit a cigarette, took a drink, ordered another. Tiny anxious utterances rose from the stained wood. It took Aimée some time to make her predicament clear. Then the regular flow of sound ceased and gave place to little, spasmodic whispers. Mr Slump listened again. 'Hullo . . . Mr Slump . . . Are you listening? . . . Did you hear me? . . . hullo.'

'Well, sister, what is it?'

'You heard what I said?'

'Sure, I heard fine.'

'Well . . . what am I to do?'

'Do? I'll tell you what to do. Just take the elevator to the top floor. Find a nice window and jump out. That's what you can do.'

There was a little sobbing gasp and then a quiet 'Thank you.'

'I told her to go take a high jump.'

'We heard.'

'Wasn't I right?'

'You know best, brother.'

'Well, for Christ's sake, with a name like that?'

In Aimée's bathroom cupboard, among the instruments and chemicals which are the staples of feminine well-being, lay the brown tube of barbiturates which is the staple of feminine repose. Aimée swallowed her dose, lay down and awaited sleep. It came at length brusquely, perfunctorily, without salutation or caress. There was no delicious influx, touching, shifting, lifting, setting free and afloat the grounded mind. At 9.40 p.m. she was awake and distraught, with a painful dry sense of contraction and tension about the temples; her eyes watered, she yawned; suddenly it was 5.25 a.m. and she was awake once more.

It was still night; the sky was starless and below it the empty streets flamed with light. Aimée rose and dressed and went out under the arc lamps. She met no one during the brief walk from her apartment to Whispering Glades. The Golden Gates were locked from midnight until morning, but there was a side-door always open for the use of the night-staff. Aimée entered and followed the familiar road upwards to the terrace of the Kirk o' Auld Lang Syne. Here she sat and waited for dawn.

Her mind was quite free from anxiety. Somehow, somewhere in the blank black hours she had found counsel; she had communed perhaps with the spirits of her ancestors, the impious and haunted race who had deserted the altars of the old Gods, had taken ship and wandered, driven by what pursuing furies through what mean streets and among what barbarous tongues! Her father had frequented the Four Square Gospel Temple; her mother drank. Attic voices prompted Aimée to a higher destiny; voices which far away and in another age had sung of the Minotaur, stamping far underground at the end of the passage; which spoke to her more sweetly of the still Boeotian water-front, the armed men all silent in the windless morning, the fleet motionless at anchor, and Agamemnon turning away his eyes; spoke of Alcestis and proud Antigone.

The East lightened. In all the diurnal revolution these first fresh hours alone are untainted by man. They lie late abed in that region. In exaltation, Aimée watched the countless statues glimmer, whiten, and take shape while the lawns changed from silver and grey to green. She was touched by warmth. Then suddenly all round her and as far as she could see the slopes became a dancing surface of light, of millions of minute rainbows and spots of fire; in the control house the man on duty had turned the irrigation cock and water was flooding through the network of pierced and buried pipes. At the same time parties of gardeners with barrows and tools emerged and tramped to their various duties. It was full day.

Aimée walked swiftly down the gravelled drive to the mortuary entrance. In the reception-room the night-staff were drinking coffee. They glanced at her incuriously as she passed silently through them, for urgent work was done at all hours. She took the lift to the top story where everything was silent and empty save for the sheeted dead. She knew what she wanted and where to find them; a wide-mouthed blue bottle and a hypodermic syringe. She indited no letter of farewell or apology. She was far removed from social custom and human obligations. The protagonists, Dennis and Mr Joyboy, were quite forgotten. The matter was between herself and the deity she served.

It was quite without design that she chose Mr Joyboy's workroom for the injection.

MR SCHULTZ HAD found a young man to take Dennis's place and Dennis was spending his last week at the Happier Hunting Ground in showing him the ropes. He was an apt young man much interested in the prices of things.

'He hasn't your personality,' said Mr Schultz. 'He won't have the same human touch but I figure he'll earn his keep other ways.'

On the morning of Aimée's death Dennis set his pupil to work cleaning the generating plant of the crematorium and was busy with the correspondence-lessons in preaching to which he now subscribed, when the door of the office opened and he recognized with great surprise his bare acquaintance and rival in love, Mr Joyboy.

'Mr Joyboy,' he said. 'Not another parrot so soon?'

Mr Joyboy sat down. He looked ghastly. Finding himself alone he began to blubber. 'It's Aimée,' he said.

Dennis answered with high irony: 'You have not come to arrange *her* funeral?' upon which Mr Joyboy cried with sudden passion, 'You knew it. I believe you killed her. You killed my honey-baby.'

'Joyboy, these are wild words.'

'She's dead.'

'My fiancée?'

'*My* fiancée.'

'Joyboy, this is no time to wrangle. What makes you think she is dead? She was perfectly well at supper-time last night.'

'She's there, in my workshop, under a sheet.'

'That, certainly, is what your newspapers would call "factual". You're sure it's her?'

'Of course I'm sure. She was poisoned.'

'Ah! The nutburger?'

'Cyanide. Self-administered.'

'This needs thinking about, Joyboy.' He paused. '*I* loved that girl.'

'*I* loved her.'

488

'*Please.*'

'She was my honey-baby.'

'I must beg of you not to intrude these private and rather peculiar terms of endearment into what should be a serious discussion. What have you done?'

'I examined her, then I covered her up. We have some deep refrigerators we sometimes use for half-finished work. I put her in there.' He began to weep tempestuously.

'What have you come to me for?'

Mr Joyboy snorted.

'I can't hear you.'

'Help,' said Mr Joyboy. 'It's your fault. You've gotta do something.'

'This is no time for recrimination, Joyboy. Let me merely point out that you are the man publicly engaged to her. In the circumstances some emotion is natural – but do not go to extremes. Of course I never thought her wholly sane, did you?'

'She was my –'

'Don't say it, Joyboy. Don't say it or I shall turn you out.'

Mr Joyboy fell to more abandoned weeping. The apprentice opened the door and stood momentarily embarrassed at the spectacle.

'Come in,' said Dennis. 'We have here a client who has just lost a little pet. You will have to accustom yourself to exhibitions of distress in your new rôle. What did you want?'

'Just to say the gas furnace is working fine again.'

'Excellent. Well, now go and clear the collecting van. Joyboy,' he continued when they were again alone, 'I beg you to control yourself and tell me plainly what is in your mind. All I can discern at the moment is a kind of family litany of mommas and poppas and babies.'

Mr Joyboy made other noises.

'That sounded like "Dr Kenworthy". Is that what you are trying to say?'

Mr Joyboy gulped.

'Dr Kenworthy knows?'

Mr Joyboy groaned.

'He does not know?'

Mr Joyboy gulped.

'You want me to break the news to him?'

Groan.

'You want me to help keep him in ignorance?'

Gulp.

'You know, this is just like table-turning.'

'Ruin,' said Mr Joyboy. 'Mom.'

'You think that your career will suffer if Dr Kenworthy learns you have the poisoned corpse of our fiancée in the ice-box? For your mother's sake this is to be avoided? You are proposing that I help dispose of the body?'

Gulp, and then a rush of words. 'You gotta help me ... through you it happened ... simple American kid ... phoney poems ... love ... Mom ... baby ... gotta help ... gotta ... gotta.'

'I don't like this repetition of "gotta", Joyboy. Do you know what Queen Elizabeth said to her Archbishop – an essentially non-sectarian character, incidentally? "Little man, little man, 'must' is not a word to be used to princes." Tell me, has anyone besides yourself access to this ice-box?' Groan. 'Well, then go away, Joyboy. Go back to your work. I will give the matter my attention. Come and see me again after luncheon.'

Mr Joyboy went. Dennis heard the car start. Then he went out alone into the pets' cemetery with his own thoughts, which were not a thing to be shared with Mr Joyboy.

Thus musing he was disturbed by a once familiar visitor.

It was a chilly day and Sir Ambrose Abercrombie wore tweeds, cape, and deerstalker-cap, the costume in which he had portrayed many travesties of English rural life. He carried a shepherd's crook.

'Ah, Barlow,' he said, 'still hard at it.'

'One of our easier mornings. I hope it is not a bereavement which brings you here?'

'No, nothing like that. Never kept an animal out here. Miss 'em, I can tell you. Brought up among dogs and horses. Daresay you were too, so you won't misunderstand me when I say this is no place for them. Wonderful country of course, but no one who really loved a dog would bring it here.' He paused and gazed curiously about him at the modest monuments. 'Attractive place you've got here. Sorry to see you're moving.'

'You received one of my cards?'

'Yes, got it here. Thought at first it must be someone playing rather a poor kind of joke. It's genuine, is it?'

From the depths of his plaid he produced a printed card and handed it to Dennis. It read:

Squadron Leader the Rev. Dennis Barlow

begs to announce that he is shortly starting business at 1154 Arbuckle Avenue, Los Angeles. All non-sectarian services expeditiously conducted at competitive prices. Funerals a speciality. Panegyrics in prose or poetry. Confessions heard in strict confidence.

'Yes, quite genuine,' said Dennis.

'Ah. I was afraid it might be.'

Another pause. Dennis said: 'The cards were sent out by an agency, you know. I didn't suppose you would be particularly interested.'

'But I am particularly interested. Is there somewhere we could go and talk?'

Wondering whether Sir Ambrose was to be his first penitent, Dennis led him indoors. The two Englishmen sat down in the office. The apprentice popped his head in, to report well of the collecting van. At length Sir Ambrose said: 'It won't do, Barlow. You must allow me an old man's privilege of speaking frankly. It won't do. After all you're an Englishman. They're a splendid bunch of fellows out here, but you know how it is. Even among the best you find a few rotters. You know the international situation as well as I do. There are always a few politicians and journalists simply waiting for the chance to take a knock at the Old Country. A thing like this is playing into their hands. I didn't like it when you started work here. Told you so frankly at the time. But at least this is a more or less private concern. But religion's quite another matter. I expect you're thinking of some pleasant country rectory at home. Religion's not like that here. Take it from me, I know the place.'

'It's odd you should say that, Sir Ambrose. One of my chief aims was to raise my status.'

'Then chuck it, my dear boy, before it's too late.' Sir Ambrose spoke at length of the industrial crisis in England, the need for young men and dollars, the uphill work of the film community in keeping the flag flying. 'Go home, my dear boy. That is your proper place.'

'As a matter of fact,' said Dennis, 'things have rather changed with me since that announcement was written. The Call I heard has grown fainter.'

'Capital,' said Sir Ambrose.

'But there are certain practical difficulties. I have invested all my small savings in my theological studies.'

'I expected something of the kind. That is where the Cricket Club comes in. I hope the time will never come when we are not ready to help a fellow-countryman in difficulties. We had a committee meeting last night and your name was mentioned. There was complete agreement. To put it in a nutshell, my boy, we will send you home.'

'First class?'

'Tourist. I'm told it's jolly comfortable. How about it?'

'A drawing-room on the train?'

'No drawing-room.'

'Well,' said Dennis, 'I suppose that as a clergyman I should have to practise certain austerities.'

'Spoken like a man,' said Sir Ambrose. 'I have the cheque with me. We signed it last night.'

Some hours later the mortician returned.

'You have regained command of yourself? Sit down and listen attentively. You have two problems, Joyboy, and let me emphasize that they are *yours*. *You* are in possession of the corpse of *your* fiancée and *your* career is threatened. You have then two problems – to dispose of the body and to explain the disappearance. You have come to me for help and it so happens that in both these things I and only I can help you.

'I have here at my disposal an excellent crematorium. We are happy-go-lucky people at the Happier Hunting Ground. There are no formalities. If I arrive here with a casket and say "Mr Schultz, I've a sheep here to incinerate," he says, "Go ahead." Once you seemed inclined to look down on us for our easy manners. Now perhaps you feel differently. All we have to do is to collect our Loved One, if you will forgive the expression, and bring her here. Tonight after working hours will be the time.

'Secondly, to explain the disappearance. Miss Thanatogenos had few acquaintances and no relations. She disappears on the eve of her wedding. It is known that I once favoured her with my attentions. What could be more plausible than that her natural good taste should have triumphed at the last moment and she should have eloped with her earlier lover? All that is necessary is for me to disappear at the same time. No one in Southern California, as you know, ever inquires what goes on beyond the mountains. She and I perhaps may incur momentary condemnation as unethical. You may receive some slightly unwelcome commiseration. There the matter will end.

'For some time I have felt oppressed by the unpoetic air of Los Angeles. I have work to do and this is not the place to do it. It was only our young friend who kept me here – she and penury. And talking of penury, Joyboy, I take it you have substantial savings?'

'I've some insurance.'

'What can you borrow on that? Five thousand dollars?'

'No, no, nothing like that.'

'Two?'

'No.'

'How much then?'

'Maybe a thousand.'

'Draw it out, Joyboy. We shall need it all. And cash this cheque at the same time. Together it will be enough. It may seem to you sentimental, but I wish to leave the United States in the same style as I came. Whispering Glades must not fall below Megalopolitan Studios in hospitality. From your bank go to the travel agency and take me a ticket to England – a drawing-room to New York,

Cunarder single stateroom with bath from there on. I shall need plenty of ready cash for incidental expenses. So bring the rest in a lump sum with the tickets. All understood? Very well. I will be at your mortuary with the collecting van soon after dinner.'

Mr Joyboy was waiting for Dennis at the side entrance of the mortuary. Whispering Glades was ideally equipped for the smooth movement of bodies. On a swift and silent trolley they set Dennis's largest collecting box, first empty, later full. They drove to the Happier Hunting Ground where things were more makeshift, but between them without great difficulty they man-handled their load to the crematorium, and stowed it in the oven. Dennis turned on the gas and lit it. Flame shot from all sides of the brickwork. He closed the iron door.

'I reckon she'll take an hour and a half,' he said. 'Do you want to stay?'

'I can't bear to think of her going out like this – she loved to see things done right.'

'I rather thought of conducting a service. My first and last non-sectarian office.'

'I couldn't bear that,' said Mr Joyboy.

'Very well. I will recite instead a little poem I have written for the occasion.

> '*Aimée, thy beauty was to me,*
> *Like those Nicean barks of yore –*'

'Hey, you can't say that. That's the phoney poem.'

'Joyboy, please remember where you are.

> '*That gently o'er a perfumed sea*
> *The weary way-worn wanderer bore*
> *To his own native shore.*

'It's really remarkably apposite, is it not?'

But Mr Joyboy had left the building.

The fire roared in the brick oven. Dennis must wait until all was consumed. He must rake out the glowing ashes, pound up the skull and pelvis perhaps and disperse the fragments. Meanwhile he entered the office and made a note in the book kept there for that purpose.

Tomorrow and on every anniversary as long as the Happier Hunting Ground existed a postcard would go to Mr Joyboy: *Your little Aimée is wagging her tail in heaven tonight, thinking of you.*

> '*Like those Nicean barks of yore* (he repeated),
> *That gently o'er a perfumed sea,*
> *The weary way-worn wanderer bore*
> *To his own native shore.*'

On this last evening in Los Angeles Dennis knew he was a favourite of Fortune. Others, better men than he, had foundered here and perished. The strand was littered with their bones. He was leaving it not only unravished but enriched. He was adding his bit to the wreckage, something that had long irked him, his young heart, and was carrying back instead the artist's load, a great, shapeless chunk of experience; bearing it home to his ancient and comfortless shore; to work on it hard and long, for God knew how long. For that moment of vision a lifetime is often too short.

He picked up the novel which Miss Poski had left on his desk and settled down to await his loved one's final combustion.

THE ORDEAL OF GILBERT PINFOLD

PINFOLD

A CONVERSATION PIECE

To Daphne
in the confidence
that her abounding sympathy
will extend even to
poor Pinfold

PORTRAIT OF THE ARTIST IN MIDDLE-AGE

IT MAY HAPPEN in the next hundred years that the English novelists of the present day will come to be valued as we now value the
artists and craftsmen of the late eighteenth century. The originators,
the exuberant men, are extinct and in their place subsists and
modestly flourishes a generation notable for elegance and variety
of contrivance. It may well happen that there are lean years ahead in
which our posterity will look back hungrily to this period, when
there was so much will and so much ability to please.

Among these novelists Mr Gilbert Pinfold stood quite high. At
the time of his adventure, at the age of fifty, he had written a dozen
books all of which were still bought and read. They were translated
into most languages and in the United States of America enjoyed
intermittent but lucrative seasons of favour. Foreign students often
chose them as the subject for theses, but those who sought to detect
cosmic significance in Mr Pinfold's work, to relate it to fashions in
philosophy, social predicaments or psychological tensions, were
baffled by his frank, curt replies to their questionnaires; their
fellows in the English Literature School, who chose more egotistical
writers, often found their theses more than half composed for them.
Mr Pinfold gave nothing away. Not that he was secretive or
grudging by nature; he had nothing to give these students. He
regarded his books as objects which he had made, things quite
external to himself to be used and judged by others. He thought
them well made, better than many reputed works of genius, but he
was not vain of his accomplishment, still less of his reputation. He
had no wish to obliterate anything he had written, but he would
dearly have liked to revise it, envying painters, who are allowed to
return to the same theme time and time again, clarifying and
enriching until they have done all they can with it. A novelist is

condemned to produce a succession of novelties, new names for characters, new incidents for his plots, new scenery; but, Mr Pinfold maintained, most men harbour the germs of one or two books only; all else is professional trickery of which the most daemonic of the masters – Dickens and Balzac even – were flagrantly guilty.

At the beginning of this fifty-first year of his life Mr Pinfold presented to the world most of the attributes of well-being. Affectionate, high-spirited and busy in childhood; dissipated and often despairing in youth; sturdy and prosperous in early manhood; he had in middle-age degenerated less than many of his contemporaries. He attributed this superiority to his long, lonely, tranquil days at Lychpole, a secluded village some hundred miles from London.

He was devoted to a wife many years younger than himself, who actively farmed the small property. Their children were numerous, healthy, good-looking and good-mannered, and his income just sufficed for their education. Once he had travelled widely; now he spent most of the year in the shabby old house which, over the years, he had filled with pictures and books and furniture of the kind he relished. As a soldier he had sustained, in good heart, much discomfort and some danger. Since the end of the war his life had been strictly private. In his own village he took very lightly the duties which he might have thought incumbent on him. He contributed adequate sums to local causes but he had no interest in sport or in local government, no ambition to lead or to command. He had never voted in a parliamentary election, maintaining an idiosyncratic toryism which was quite unrepresented in the political parties of his time and was regarded by his neighbours as being almost as sinister as socialism.

These neighbours were typical of the English countryside of the period. A few rich men farmed commercially on a large scale; a few had business elsewhere and came home merely to hunt; the majority were elderly and in reduced circumstances; people who, when the Pinfolds settled at Lychpole, lived comfortably with servants and horses, and now lived in much smaller houses and met at the fishmonger's. Many of these were related to one another, and formed a compact little clan. Colonel and Mrs Bagnold, Mr and Mrs Graves, Mrs and Miss Fawdle, Colonel and Miss Garbett, Lady Fawdle-

Upton and Miss Clarissa Bagnold all lived in a radius of ten miles from Lychpole. All were in some way related. In the first years of their marriage Mr and Mrs Pinfold had dined in all these households and had entertained them in return. But after the war the decline of fortune, less sharp in the Pinfolds' case than their neighbours', made their meetings less frequent. The Pinfolds were addicted to nick-names and each of these surrounding families had its own private, unsuspected appellation at Lychpole, not malicious but mildly deri-sive, taking its origin in most cases from some half-forgotten incident in the past. The nearest neighbour whom they saw most often was Reginald Graves-Upton, an uncle of the Graves-Uptons ten miles distant at Upper Mewling; a gentle, bee-keeping old bachelor who inhabited a thatched cottage up the lane less than a mile from the Manor. It was his habit on Sunday mornings to walk to church across the Pinfolds' fields and leave his Cairn terrier in the Pinfolds' stables while he attended Matins. He called for quarter of an hour when he came to fetch his dog, drank a small glass of sherry, and described the wireless programmes he had heard during the preced-ing week. This refined, fastidious old gentleman went by the recon-dite name of 'the Bruiser', sometimes varied to 'Pug', 'Basher', and 'Old Fisticuffs', all of which sobriquets derived from 'Boxer'; for in recent years he had added to his few interests an object which he reverently referred to as 'The Box'.

This Box was one of many operating in various parts of the country. It was installed, under the sceptical noses of Reginald Graves-Upton's nephew and niece, at Upper Mewling. Mrs Pinfold, who had been taken to see it, said it looked like a makeshift wire-less-set. According to the Bruiser and other devotees The Box exercised diagnostic and therapeutic powers. Some part of a sick man or animal – a hair, a drop of blood preferably – was brought to The Box, whose guardian would then 'tune in' to the 'life-waves' of the patient, discern the origin of the malady and prescribe treatment.

Mr Pinfold was as sceptical as the younger Graves-Uptons. Mrs Pinfold thought there must be something in it, because it had been tried, without her knowledge, on Lady Fawdle-Upton's nettle-rash and immediate relief had followed.

'It's all suggestion,' said young Mrs Graves-Upton.

'It can't be suggestion, if she didn't know it was being done,' said Mr Pinfold.

'No. It's simply a matter of measuring the Life-Waves,' said Mrs Pinfold.

'An extremely dangerous device in the wrong hands,' said Mr Pinfold.

'No, no. That is the beauty of it. It can't do any harm. You see it only transmits *Life* Forces. Fanny Graves tried it on her spaniel for worms, but they simply grew enormous with all the Life Force going into them. Like serpents, Fanny said.'

'I should have thought this Box counted as sorcery,' Mr Pinfold said to his wife when they were alone. 'You ought to confess it.'

'D'you really think so?'

'No, not really. It's just a lot of harmless nonsense.'

The Pinfolds' religion made a slight but perceptible barrier between them and these neighbours, a large part of whose activities centred round their parish churches. The Pinfolds were Roman Catholics, Mrs Pinfold by upbringing, Mr Pinfold by a later development. He had been received into the Church – 'conversion' suggests an event more sudden and emotional than his calm acceptance of the propositions of his faith – in early manhood, at the time when many Englishmen of humane education were falling into communism. Unlike them Mr Pinfold remained steadfast. But he was reputed bigoted rather than pious. His trade by its nature is liable to the condemnation of the clergy as, at the best, frivolous; at the worst, corrupting. Moreover by the narrow standards of the age his habits of life were self-indulgent and his utterances lacked prudence. And at the very time when the leaders of his Church were exhorting their people to emerge from the catacombs into the forum, to make their influence felt in democratic politics and to regard worship as a corporate rather than a private act, Mr Pinfold burrowed ever deeper into the rock. Away from his parish he sought the least frequented Mass; at home he held aloof from the multifarious organizations which have sprung into being at the summons of the hierarchy to redeem the times.

But Mr Pinfold was far from friendless and he set great store by his friends. They were the men and women who were growing old with him, whom in the 1920s and '30s he had seen constantly; who in the diaspora of the '40s and '50s kept more tenuous touch with one another, the men at Bellamy's Club, the women at the half-dozen poky, pretty houses of Westminster and Belgravia to which had descended the larger hospitality of a happier age.

He had made no new friends in late years. Sometimes he thought he detected a slight coldness among his old cronies. It was always he, it seemed to him, who proposed a meeting. It was always they who first rose to leave. In particular there was one, Roger Stillingfleet, who had once been an intimate but now seemed to avoid him. Roger Stillingfleet was a writer, one of the few Mr Pinfold really liked. He knew of no reason for their estrangement and, enquiring, was told that Roger had grown very odd lately. He never came to Bellamy's now, it was said, except to collect his letters or to entertain a visiting American.

It sometimes occurred to Mr Pinfold that he must be growing into a bore. His opinions certainly were easily predictable.

His strongest tastes were negative. He abhorred plastics, Picasso, sunbathing and jazz – everything in fact that had happened in his own lifetime. The tiny kindling of charity which came to him through his religion sufficed only to temper his disgust and change it to boredom. There was a phrase in the '30s: 'It is later than you think', which was designed to cause uneasiness. It was never later than Mr Pinfold thought. At intervals during the day and night he would look at his watch and learn always with disappointment how little of his life was past, how much there was still ahead of him. He wished no one ill, but he looked at the world *sub specie aeternitatis* and he found it flat as a map; except when, rather often, personal annoyance intruded. Then he would come tumbling from his exalted point of observation. Shocked by a bad bottle of wine, an impertinent stranger, or a fault in syntax, his mind like a cinema camera trucked furiously forward to confront the offending object close-up with glaring lens; with the eyes of a drill sergeant inspecting an awkward squad, bulging with wrath that was half-facetious, and with half-simulated incredulity; like a drill sergeant he was absurd to many but to some rather formidable.

Once upon a time all this had been thought diverting. People quoted his pungent judgments and invented anecdotes of his audacity, which were recounted as 'typical Pinfolds'. Now, he realized, his singularity had lost some of its attraction for others, but he was too old a dog to learn new tricks.

As a boy, at the age of puberty when most of his school-fellows coarsened, he had been as fastidious as the Bruiser and in his early years of success diffidence had lent him charm. Prolonged prosperity had wrought the change. He had seen sensitive men make themselves a protective disguise against the rebuffs and injustices of manhood. Mr Pinfold had suffered little in these ways; he had been tenderly reared and, as a writer, welcomed and over-rewarded early. It was his modesty which needed protection and for this purpose, but without design, he gradually assumed this character of burlesque. He was neither a scholar nor a regular soldier; the part for which he cast himself was a combination of eccentric don and testy colonel and he acted it strenuously, before his children at Lychpole and his cronies in London, until it came to dominate his whole outward personality. When he ceased to be alone, when he swung into his club or stumped up the nursery stairs, he left half of himself behind, and the other half swelled to fill its place. He offered the world a front of pomposity mitigated by indiscretion, that was as hard, bright and antiquated as a cuirass.

Mr Pinfold's nanny used to say: 'Don't care went to the gallows'; also: 'Sticks and stones can break my bones, but words can never hurt me'. Mr Pinfold did not care what the village or his neighbours said of him. As a little boy he had been acutely sensitive to ridicule. His adult shell seemed impervious. He had long held himself inaccessible to interviewers and the young men and women who were employed to write 'profiles' collected material where they could. Every week his press-cutting agents brought to his breakfast-table two or three rather offensive allusions. He accepted without much resentment the world's estimate of himself. It was part of the price he paid for privacy. There were also letters from strangers, some abusive, some adulatory. Mr Pinfold was unable to discover any particular superiority of taste or expression in the writers of either sort. To both he sent printed acknowledgements.

His days passed in writing, reading and managing his own small affairs. He had never employed a secretary and for the last two years he had been without a manservant. But Mr Pinfold did not repine. He was perfectly competent to answer his own letters, pay his bills, tie his parcels and fold his clothes. At night his most frequent recurring dream was of doing *The Times* crossword puzzle; his most disagreeable that he was reading a tedious book aloud to his family.

Physically, in his late forties, he had become lazy. Time was, he rode to hounds, went for long walks, dug his garden, felled small trees. Now he spent most of the day in an arm-chair. He ate less, drank more, and grew corpulent. He was very seldom so ill as to spend a day in bed. He suffered intermittently from various twinges and brief bouts of pain in his joints and muscles – arthritis, gout, rheumatism, fibrositis; they were not dignified by any scientific name. Mr Pinfold seldom consulted his doctor. When he did so it was as a 'private patient'. His children availed themselves of the National Health Act but Mr Pinfold was reluctant to disturb a relationship which had been formed in his first years at Lychpole. Dr Drake, Mr Pinfold's medical attendant, had inherited the practice from his father and had been there before the Pinfolds came to Lychpole. Lean, horsy and weather-beaten in appearance, he had deep roots and wide ramifications in the countryside, being brother of the local auctioneer, brother-in-law of the solicitor, and cousin of three neighbouring rectors. His recreations were sporting. He was not a man of high technical pretensions but he suited Mr Pinfold well. He too suffered, more sharply, from Mr Pinfold's troubles and when consulted remarked that Mr Pinfold must expect these things at his age; that the whole district was afflicted in this way and that Lychpole was notoriously the worst spot in it.

Mr Pinfold also slept badly. It was a trouble of long standing. For twenty-five years he had used various sedatives, for the last ten years a single specific, chloral and bromide which, unknown to Dr Drake, he bought on an old prescription in London. There were periods of literary composition when he would find the sentences he had written during the day running in his head, the words shifting and changing colour kaleidoscopically, so that he would again and again climb out of bed, pad down to the library, make a minute correction, return to his room, lie in the dark dazzled by the pattern of vocables until obliged once more to descend to the manuscript. But those days and nights of obsession, of what might without vainglory be called 'creative' work, were a small part of his year. On most nights he was neither fretful nor apprehensive. He was merely bored. After even the idlest day he demanded six or seven hours of insensibility. With them behind him, with them to look forward to, he could face another idle day with something approaching jauntiness; and these his doses unfailingly provided.

At about the time of his fiftieth birthday there occurred two events which seemed trivial at the time but grew to importance in his later adventures.

The first of these primarily concerned Mrs Pinfold. During the war Lychpole was let, the house to a convent, the fields to a grazier. This man, Hill, had collected parcels of grass-land in and around the parish and on them kept a nondescript herd of 'unattested' dairy-cattle. The pasture was rank, the fences dilapidated. When the Pinfolds came home in 1945 and wanted their fields back, the War Agricultural Committee, normally predisposed towards the sitting tenant, were in no doubt of their decision in Mrs Pinfold's favour. Had she acted at once, Hill would have been out, with his compensation, at Michaelmas, but Mrs Pinfold was tender-hearted and Hill was adroit. First he pleaded, then, having established new rights, asserted them. Lady Day succeeded Michaelmas; Michaelmas, Lady Day for four full years. Hill retreated meadow by meadow. The committee, still popularly known as 'the War Ag.', returned, walked the property anew, again found for Mrs Pinfold. Hill, who now had a lawyer, appealed. So it went on. Mr Pinfold held aloof from it all, merely noting with sorrow the anxiety of his wife. At length at Michaelmas 1949 Hill finally moved. He boasted in the village inn of his cleverness, and left for the other side of the county with a comfortable profit.

The second event occurred soon after. Mr Pinfold received an invitation from the B.B.C. to record an 'interview'. In the previous twenty years there had been many such proposals and he had always refused them. This time the fee was more liberal and the conditions softer. He would not have to go to the offices in London. Electricians would come to him with their apparatus. No script had to be submitted; no preparation of any kind was required; the whole thing would take an hour. In an idle moment Mr Pinfold agreed and at once regretted it.

The day came towards the end of the summer holidays. Soon after breakfast there arrived a motor-car, and a van of the sort used in the army by the more important kinds of signaller, which immediately absorbed the attention of the younger children. Out of the car there came three youngish men, thin of hair, with horn-rimmed elliptical glasses, cord trousers and tweed coats; exactly what Mr Pinfold was expecting. Their leader was named Angel. He emphasized his primacy by means of a neat, thick beard. He and his colleagues, he explained, had slept in the district, where he had an aunt. They would have to leave before luncheon. They would get through their business in the morning. The signallers began rapidly uncoiling wires and setting up their microphone in the library, while Mr Pinfold drew the attention of Angel and his party to the more noticeable of his collection of works of art. They did not commit themselves to an opinion, merely remarking that the last house they visited had a gouache by Rouault.

'I didn't know he ever painted in gouache,' said Mr Pinfold. 'Anyway he's a dreadful painter.'

'Ah!' said Angel. 'That's very nice. Very nice indeed. We must try and work that into the broadcast.'

When the electricians had made their arrangements Mr Pinfold sat at his table with the three strangers, a microphone in their midst. They were attempting to emulate a series that had been cleverly done in Paris with various French celebrities, in which informal, spontaneous discussion had seduced the objects of inquiry into self-revelation.

They questioned Mr Pinfold in turn about his tastes and habits. Angel led and it was at him that Mr Pinfold looked. The commonplace face above the beard became slightly sinister, the accentless, but insidiously plebeian voice, menacing. The questions were civil enough in form but Mr Pinfold thought he could detect an underlying malice. Angel seemed to believe that anyone sufficiently eminent to be interviewed by him must have something to hide, must be an impostor whom it was his business to trap and expose, and to direct his questions from some basic, previous knowledge of something discreditable. There was the hint of the under-dog's snarl which Mr Pinfold recognized from his press-cuttings.

He was well equipped to deal with insolence, real or imagined, and answered succinctly and shrewdly, disconcerting his adversaries, if adversaries they were, point by point. When it was over Mr Pinfold offered his visitors sherry. Tension relaxed. He asked politely who was their next subject.

'We're going on to Stratford,' said Angel, 'to interview Cedric Thorne.'

'You evidently have not seen this morning's paper,' said Mr Pinfold.

'No, we left before it came.'

'Cedric Thorne has escaped you. He hanged himself yesterday afternoon in his dressing-room.'

'Good heavens, are you sure?'

'It's in *The Times.*'

'May I see?'

Angel was shaken from his professional calm. Mr Pinfold brought the paper and he read the paragraph with emotion.

'Yes, yes. That's him. I half expected this. He was a personal friend. I must get on to his wife. May I phone?'

Mr Pinfold apologized for the levity with which he had broken the news and led Angel to the business-room. He refilled the sherry glasses and attempted to appear genial. Angel returned shortly to say: 'I couldn't get through. I'll have to try again later.'

Mr Pinfold repeated his regrets.

'Yes, it is a terrible thing – not wholly unexpected though.'

A macabre note had been added to the discords of the morning.

Then hands were shaken; the vehicles turned on the gravel and drove away.

When they were out of sight down the turn of the drive, one of the children who had been listening to the conversation in the van said: 'You didn't like those people much, did you, papa?'

He had definitely not liked them and they left an unpleasant memory which grew sharper in the weeks before the record was broadcast. He brooded. It seemed to him that an attempt had been made against his privacy and he was not sure how effectively he had defended it. He strained to remember his precise words and his memory supplied various distorted versions. Finally the evening came when the performance was made public. Mr Pinfold had the cook's wireless carried into the drawing-room. He and Mrs Pinfold listened together. His voice came to him strangely old and fruity, but what he said gave him no regret. 'They tried to make an ass of me,' he said. 'I don't believe they succeeded.'

Mr Pinfold for the time forgot Angel.

Boredom alone and some stiffness in the joints disturbed that sunny autumn. Despite his age and dangerous trade Mr Pinfold seemed to himself and to others unusually free of the fashionable agonies of *angst*.

COLLAPSE OF ELDERLY PARTY

MR PINFOLD'S IDLENESS has been remarked. He was half-way through a novel and had stopped work in early summer. The completed chapters had been typed, rewritten, retyped, and lay in a drawer of his desk. He was entirely satisfied with them. He knew in a general way what had to be done to finish the book and he believed he could at any moment set himself to do it. But he was not pressed for money. The sales of his earlier works had already earned him that year the modest sufficiency which the laws of his country allowed. Further effort could only bring him sharply diminishing rewards and he was disinclined to effort. It was as though the characters he had quickened had fallen into a light doze and he left them benevolently to themselves. Hard things were in store for them. Let them sleep while they could. All his life he had worked intermittently. In youth his long periods of leisure had been devoted to amusement. Now he had abandoned that quest. That was the main difference between Mr Pinfold at fifty and Mr Pinfold at thirty.

Winter set in sharp at the end of October. The central-heating plant at Lychpole was ancient and voracious. It had not been used since the days of fuel shortage. With most of the children away at school Mr and Mrs Pinfold withdrew into two rooms, heaped the fires with such coal as they could procure, and sheltered from draughts behind screens and sandbags. Mr Pinfold's spirits sank, he began to talk of the West Indies and felt the need of longer periods of sleep.

The composition of his sleeping-draught, as originally pre-scribed, was largely of water. He suggested to his chemist that it would save trouble to have the essential ingredients in full strength and to dilute them himself. Their taste was bitter and after various experiments he found they were most palatable in Crème de Menthe. He was not scrupulous in measuring the dose. He splashed into the glass as much as his mood suggested and if he took too little and woke in the small hours he would get out of bed and make unsteadily for the bottles and a second swig. Thus he passed many hours in welcome unconsciousness; but all was not well with him. Whether from too much strong medicine or from some other cause, he felt decidedly seedy by the middle of November. He found himself disagreeably flushed, particularly after drinking his normal, not illiberal, quantity of wine and brandy. Crimson blotches appeared on the backs of his hands.

He called in Dr Drake who said: 'That sounds like an allergy.'

'Allergic to what?'

'Ah, that's hard to say. Almost anything can cause an allergy nowadays. It might be something you're wearing or some plant growing near. The only cure really is a change.'

'I might go abroad after Christmas.'

'Yes, that's the best thing you could do. Anyway don't worry. No one ever died of an allergy. It's allied to hay-fever,' he added learnedly, 'and asthma.'

Another thing which troubled him and which he soon began to attribute to his medicine was the behaviour of his memory. It began to play him tricks. He did not grow forgetful. He remembered everything in clear detail but he remembered it wrong. He would state a fact, dogmatically, sometimes in print – a date, a name, a quotation – find himself challenged, turn to his books for verification and find most disconcertingly that he was at fault.

Two incidents of this kind slightly alarmed him. With the idea of cheering him up Mrs Pinfold invited a week-end party to Lychpole. On the Sunday afternoon he proposed a visit to a remarkable tomb in a neighbouring church. He had not been there since the war, but he had a clear image of it, which he described to them in technical detail; a recumbent figure of the mid-sixteenth century in gilded bronze; something almost unique in England. They found the place without difficulty; it was unquestionably what they sought; but the figure was of coloured alabaster. They laughed, he laughed, but he was shocked.

The second incident was more humiliating. A friend in London, James Lance, who shared his tastes in furniture, found, and offered him as a present, a most remarkable piece; a wash-hand stand of the greatest elaboration designed by an English architect of the 1860s, a man not universally honoured but of magisterial status to Mr Pinfold and his friends. This massive freak of fancy was decorated with metal work and mosaic, and with a series of panels painted in his hot youth by a rather preposterous artist who later became President of the Royal Academy. It was just such a trophy as Mr Pinfold most valued. He hurried to London, studied the object with exultation, arranged for its delivery and impatiently awaited its arrival at Lychpole. A fortnight later it came, was borne upstairs and set in the space cleared for it. Then to his horror Mr Pinfold observed that an essential part was missing. There should have been a prominent, highly ornamental, copper tap in the centre, forming the climax of the design. In its place there was merely a small socket. Mr Pinfold broke into lamentation. The carriers asserted that this was the condition of the piece when they fetched it. Mr Pinfold bade them search their van. Nothing was found. Mr Pinfold surcharged the receipt '*incomplete*' and immediately wrote to the firm ordering a diligent search of the ware-house where the wash-hand stand had reposed *en route* and enclosing a detailed drawing of the lost member. There was a brisk exchange of letters, the carriers denying all responsibility. Finally Mr Pinfold, decently reluctant to involve the donor in a dispute about a gift, wrote to James Lance asking for corroboration. James Lance replied: there never had been any tap such as Mr Pinfold described.

'You haven't always been altogether making sense lately,' said Mrs Pinfold when her husband showed her this letter, 'and you're a very odd colour. Either you're drinking too much or doping too much, or both.'

'I wonder if you're right,' said Mr Pinfold. 'Perhaps I ought to go slow after Christmas.'

The children's holidays were a time when Mr Pinfold felt a special need for unconsciousness at night and for stimulated geniality by day. Christmas was always the worst season. During that dread week he made copious use of wine and narcotics and his inflamed face shone like the florid squireens depicted in the cards that littered the house. Once catching sight of himself in the looking-glass, thus empurpled and wearing a paper crown, he took fright at what he saw.

'I *must* get away,' said Mr Pinfold later to his wife. 'I must go somewhere sunny and finish my book.'

'I wish I could come too. There's so much to be done getting Hill's horrible fields back into shape. I'm rather worried about you, you know. You ought to have someone to look after you.'

'I'll be all right. I work better alone.'

The cold grew intense. Mr Pinfold spent the day crouched over the library fire. To leave it for the icy passages made him shudder and stumble, half benumbed, while outside the hidden sun glared over a landscape that seemed all turned to metal; lead and iron and steel. Only in the evenings did Mr Pinfold manage a semblance of jollity, joining his family in charades or Up Jenkins, playing the fool to the loud delight of the youngest and the tolerant amusement of the eldest of his children, until in degrees of age they went happily to their rooms and he was released into his own darkness and silence.

At length the holidays came to an end. Nuns and monks received their returning charges and Lychpole was left in peace save for rare intrusions from the nursery. And now just when Mr Pinfold was gathering himself as it were for a strenuous effort at reformation, he was struck down by the most severe attack of his 'aches' which he had yet suffered. Every joint, but especially feet, ankles and knees, agonized him. Dr Drake again advocated a warm climate and prescribed some pills which he said were 'something new and pretty powerful'. They were large and drab, reminding Mr Pinfold of the pellets of blotting-paper which used to be rolled at his private school. Mr Pinfold added them to his bromide and chloral and Crème de Menthe, his wine and gin and brandy, and to a new sleeping-draught which his doctor, ignorant of the existence of his other bottle, also supplied.

And now his mind became much overcast. One great thought excluded all others, the need to escape. He, who even in this extremity eschewed the telephone, telegraphed to the travel-agency with whom he dealt: *Kindly arrange immediate passage West Indies, East*

Indies, Africa, India, anywhere hot, luxury preferred, private bath, outside single cabin essential, and anxiously awaited the reply. When it came it comprised a large envelope full of decorative folders and a note saying they awaited his further instructions.

Mr Pinfold became frantic. He knew one of the directors of the firm. He thought he had met others. It came to him in his daze quite erroneously that he had lately read somewhere that a lady of his acquaintance had joined the board. To all of them at their private addresses he dispatched peremptory telegrams: *Kindly investigate wanton inefficiency your office. Pinfold.*

The director whom he really knew took action. There was little choice at that moment. Mr Pinfold was lucky to secure a passage in the *Caliban*, a one-class ship sailing in three days for Ceylon.

During the time of waiting Mr Pinfold's frenzy subsided. He became instead intermittently comatose. When lucid he was in pain.

Mrs Pinfold said, as she had often said before: 'You're doped, darling, up to the eyes.'

'Yes. It's those rheumatism pills. Drake said they were very strong.'

Mr Pinfold, who was normally rather deft, now became clumsy. He dropped things. He found his buttons and laces intractable, his handwriting in the few letters which his journey necessitated, uncertain, his spelling, never strong, wildly barbaric.

In one of his clearer hours he said to Mrs Pinfold: 'I believe you are right. I shall give up the sleeping-draughts as soon as I get to sea. I always sleep better at sea. I shall cut down on drink too. As soon as I get rid of these damned aches, I shall start work. I can always work at sea. I shall have the book finished before I get home.'

These resolutions persisted; there was a sober, industrious time ahead of him in a few days' time. He had to survive somehow until then. Everything would come right very soon.

Mrs Pinfold shared these hopes. She was busy with her plans for the farm which the newly liberated territory made more elaborate. She could not get away. Nor did she think her presence was needed. Once her husband was safely on board, all would be well with him.

She helped him pack. Indeed he could do nothing except sit on a bedroom chair and give confused directions. He must take foolscap paper, he said, in large quantities; also ink, foreign ink was never satisfactory. And pens. He had once experienced great difficulty in New York in purchasing pen-nibs; he had in the end had recourse to a remote law-stationer's. All foreigners, he was now convinced, used some kind of stylographic instrument. He must take pens and nibs. His clothes were a matter of indifference. You could always get a Chinaman, anywhere out of Europe, to make you a suit of clothes in an afternoon, Mr Pinfold said.

That Sunday morning Mr Pinfold did not go to Mass. He lay in bed until midday and, when he came down, hobbled to the drawing-room window and gazed across the bare, icy park thinking of the welcoming tropics. Then he said: 'Oh God, here comes the Bruiser.'

'Hide.'

'No fire in the library.'

'I'll tell him you're ill.'

'No. I like the Bruiser. Besides, if you say I'm ill, he'll set his damned Box to work on me.'

Throughout the short visit Mr Pinfold exerted himself to be affable.

'You aren't looking at all well, Gilbert,' the Bruiser said.

'I'm all right really. A twinge of rheumatism. I'm sailing the day after tomorrow for Ceylon.'

'That's very sudden, isn't it?'

'The weather. Need a change.'

He sank into his chair and then, when the Bruiser left, got to his feet again with an enormous obvious effort.

'Please don't come out,' said the Bruiser.

Mrs Pinfold went with him to release his dog and when she returned found Mr Pinfold enraged.

'I know what you two have been talking about.'

'Do you? I was hearing about the Fawdles' row with the Parish Council about their right of way.'

'You've been giving him my hair for his Box.'

'Nonsense, Gilbert.'

'I could tell by the way he looked at me that he was measuring my Life-Waves.'

Mrs Pinfold looked at him sadly. 'You really are in rather a bad way, aren't you, darling?'

The *Caliban* was not a ship so large as to require a special train; carriages were reserved on the regular service from London. Mrs Pinfold accompanied him there the day before his departure. He had to collect his tickets from the travel-agency, but when he arrived in London great lassitude came over him and he went straight to bed in his hotel, summoning a messenger from the agency to bring them to him. A young, polite man came at once. He bore a small portfolio of documents, tickets for train and ship and for return by air, baggage forms, embarkation cards, carbon copies of letters of reservation and the like. Mr Pinfold had difficulty in understanding. He had trouble with his cheque book. The young man looked at him with more than normal curiosity. Perhaps he was a reader of Mr Pinfold's works. It was more probable that he found something bizarre in the spectacle of Mr Pinfold, lying there groaning and muttering, propped by pillows, purple in the face, with a bottle of champagne open beside him. Mr Pinfold offered him a glass. He refused. When he had gone Mr Pinfold said: 'I didn't at all like the look of that young man.'

'Oh, he was all right,' said Mrs Pinfold.

'There was something fishy about him,' said Mr Pinfold. 'He stared at me as though he was measuring my Life-Waves.'

Then he fell into a doze.

Mrs Pinfold lunched alone downstairs and rejoined her husband who said: 'I must go and say good-bye to my mother. Order a car.'

'Darling, you aren't well enough.'

'I *always* say good-bye to her before going abroad. I've told her we are coming.'

'I'll telephone and explain. Or shall I go out there alone?'

'I'm going. It's true I'm not well enough, but I'm going. Get the hall-porter to have a car here in half an hour.'

Mr Pinfold's widowed mother lived in a pretty little house at Kew. She was eighty-two years old, sharp of sight and hearing, but of recent years very slow of mind. In childhood Mr Pinfold had loved her extravagantly. There remained now only a firm *pietas*. He no longer enjoyed her company nor wished to communicate. She had been left rather badly off by his father. Mr Pinfold supplemented her income with payments under a deed of covenant so that she was now comfortably placed with a single, faithful old maid to look after her and all her favourite possessions, preserved from the larger house, set out round her. Young Mrs Pinfold, who would talk happily of her children, was very much more agreeable company to the old woman than was her son, but Mr Pinfold went to call dutifully several times a year and, as he said, always before an absence of any length.

A funereal limousine bore them to Kew. Mr Pinfold sat huddled in rugs. He hobbled on two sticks, one a blackthorn, the other a malacca cane, through the little gate up the garden path. An hour later he was out again, subsiding with groans into the back of the car. The visit had not been a success.

'It wasn't a success, was it?' said Mr Pinfold.

'We ought to have stayed to tea.'

'She knows I never have tea.'

'But I do, and Mrs Yercombe had it all prepared. I saw it on a trolley – cakes and sandwiches and a muffin-dish.'

'The truth is my mother doesn't like to see anyone younger than herself iller than herself – except children of course.'

'You were beastly snubbing about the children.'

'Yes. I know. Damn. Damn. Damn. I'll write to her from the ship. I'll send her a cable. Why does everyone except me find it so easy to be nice?'

When he reached the hotel he returned to bed and ordered another bottle of champagne. He dozed again. Mrs Pinfold sat quietly reading a paper-covered detective story. He awoke and ordered a rather elaborate dinner, but by the time it came his appetite was gone. Mrs Pinfold ate well, but sadly. When the table was wheeled out, Mr Pinfold hobbled to the bathroom and took his blue-grey pills. Three a day was the number prescribed. He had a dozen left. He took a big dose of his sleeping-draught; the bottle was half full.

'I'm taking too much,' he said, not for the first time. 'I'll finish what I've got and never order any more.' He looked at himself in the glass. He looked at the backs of his hands which were again mottled with large crimson patches. 'I'm sure it's not really good for me,' he said, and felt his way to bed, tumbled in and fell heavily asleep.

His train was at ten next day. The funereal limousine was ordered. Mr Pinfold dressed laboriously and, without shaving, went to the station. Mrs Pinfold came with him. He needed help to find a porter and to find his seat. He dropped his ticket and his sticks on the platform.

'I don't believe you ought to be going alone,' said Mrs Pinfold. 'Wait for another ship and I'll come too.'

'No, no. I shall be all right.'

But some hours later when he reached the docks Mr Pinfold did not feel so hopeful. He had slept most of the way, now and then waking to light a cigar and let it fall from his fingers after a few puffs. His aches seemed sharper than ever as he climbed out of the carriage. Snow was falling. The distance from the train to the ship seemed enormous. The other passengers stepped out briskly. Mr Pinfold moved slowly. On the quay a telegraph boy was taking messages. Mrs Pinfold would be back at Lychpole by now. Mr Pinfold with great difficulty wrote: *Safely embarked. All love.* Then he moved to the gangway and painfully climbed aboard.

A coloured steward led him to his cabin. He gazed round it unseeing, sitting on a bunk. There was something he ought to do; telegraph his mother. On the cabin table was some writing paper bearing the ship's name and the flag of the line at its head. Mr Pinfold tried to compose and inscribe a message. The task proved to be one of insuperable difficulty. He threw the spoilt paper into the basket and sat on his bed, still in his hat and overcoat with his sticks beside him. Presently his two suitcases arrived. He gazed at them for some time, then began to unpack. That too proved difficult. He rang his bell and the coloured steward reappeared bowing and smiling.

'I'm not very well. I wonder if you could unpack for me?'

'Dinner seven-thirty o'clock, sir.'

'I said, could you unpack for me?'

'No, sir, bar not open in port, sir.'

The man smiled and bowed and left Mr Pinfold.

Mr Pinfold sat there, in his hat and coat, holding his cudgel and his cane. Presently an English steward appeared with the passenger list, some forms to fill, and the message: 'The Captain's compliments, sir, and he would like to have the honour of your company at his table in the dining-saloon.'

'Now?'

'No, sir. Dinner is at 7.30. I don't expect the Captain will be dining in the saloon tonight.'

'I don't think I shall either,' said Mr Pinfold. 'Thank the Captain. Very civil of him. Another night. Someone said something about the bar not being open. Can't you get me some brandy?'

'Oh yes, sir. I think so, sir. Any particular brand?'

'Brandy,' said Mr Pinfold. 'Large one.'

The chief steward brought it with his own hands.

'Good night,' said Mr Pinfold.

He found on the top of his case the things he needed for the night. Among them his pills and his bottle. The brandy impelled him to action. He must telegraph to his mother. He groped his way out and along the corridor to the purser's office. A clerk was on duty, very busy with his papers behind a grill.

'I want to send a telegram.'

'Yes, sir. There's a boy at the head of the gangway.'

'I'm not feeling very well. I wonder if you could be very kind and write it for me?'

The purser looked at him hard, observed his unshaven chin, smelled brandy, and drew on his long experience of travellers.

'Sorry about that, sir. Pleased to be any help.'

Mr Pinfold dictated, '*Everyone in ship most helpful. Love, Gilbert,*' fumbled with a handful of silver, then crept back to his cabin. There he took his large grey pills and a swig of his sleeping-draught. Then, prayerless, he got himself to bed.

3

AN UNHAPPY SHIP

THE S.S. *CALIBAN*, Captain Steerforth master, was middle-aged and middle-class; clean, trustworthy and comfortable, without pretence to luxury. There were no private baths. Meals were not served in cabins, it was stated, except on the orders of the medical officer. Her public rooms were panelled in fumed oak in the fashion of an earlier generation. She plied between Liverpool and Rangoon, stopping at intermediate ports, carrying a mixed cargo and a more or less homogeneous company of passengers, Scotchmen and their wives mostly, travelling on business and on leave. Crew and stewards were Lascars.

When Mr Pinfold came to himself it was full day and he was rocking gently to and fro in his narrow bed with the slow roll of the high seas.

He had barely noticed his cabin on the preceding evening. Now he observed that it was a large one, with two berths. There was a little window made of slats of opaque glass, fitted with tight, orna-mental muslin curtains, and a sliding shutter. This gave, not on the sea, but on a deck where people from time to time passed, casting a brief shadow but with no sound that was audible above the beat of the engine, the regular creak of plates and woodwork and the continuous insect-hum of the ventilator. The ceiling, at which Mr Pinfold gazed, was spanned as though by a cottage beam by a white, studded air-shaft and by a multiplicity of pipes and electric cable. Mr Pinfold lay for some time, gazing and rocking, not quite sure where he was, but rather pleased than not to be there. His watch, unwound the night before, had run down. He had been called. On the shelf at his side a cup of tea, already quite cold, slopped in its saucer, and beside it, stained with spilt tea, was the ship's passenger list. He found himself entered as *Mr G. Penfold* and thought of Mr Pooter at the Mansion House. The misprint was welcome as an item of disguise, an uncovenanted addition to his privacy. He glanced idly through the other names – '*Dr Abercrombie, Mr Addison, Miss Amory, Mr and Mrs and Miss Margaret Angel, Mr and Mrs Benson, Mr Blackadder, Major and Mrs Cockson*', no one he knew, no one likely to annoy him. There were half a dozen Burmese on their way to Rangoon; the rest were solidly British. No one, he felt confident, would have read his books or would seek to draw him into literary conversation. He would be able to do a quiet three weeks' work in this ship as soon as his health mended.

He sat up and put his feet to the floor. He was still crippled but a shade less painfully, he thought, than in the days before. He went to his basin. The looking-glass showed him a face which still looked alarmingly old and ill. He shaved, brushed his hair, took his grey pill, returned to bed with a book and at once fell into a doze.

The ship's hooter roused him. That must be twelve noon. A knock on his door, barely audible above the other sea noises, and the dark face of his steward appeared.

'No good today,' the man said. 'Plenty passengers sick.'

He took the cup of tea and slipped away.

Mr Pinfold was a good sailor. Only once in a war which had been largely spent bucketing about in various sorts of boat, had he ever been seasick, and on that occasion most of the naval crew had been prostrate also. Mr Pinfold, who was neither beautiful nor athletic, cherished this one gift of parsimonious Nature. He decided to get up.

The main deck, when he reached it, was almost deserted. Two wind-blown girls in thick sweaters were tacking along arm-in-arm past the piles of folded chairs. Mr Pinfold hobbled to the after smoking-room bar. Four or five men sat together in one corner. He nodded to them, found a chair on the further side and ordered brandy and ginger-ale. He was not himself. He knew in a distant way, as he knew, or thought he knew, certain facts of history, that he was in a ship, travelling for the good of his health, but, as with much of his historical knowledge, he was vague about the date. He did not know that twenty-four hours ago he had been in the train from London to Liverpool. His phases of sleeping and waking in the last few days were not related to night and day. He sat still in the smoking-room gazing blankly ahead.

After a time two cheerful women entered. The men greeted them:

'Morning, Mrs Cockson. Glad to see you're on your feet this merry morning.'

'Good morning, good morning, good morning all. You know Mrs Benson?'

'I don't think I've had that pleasure. Will you join us, Mrs Benson? I'm in the chair,' and he turned and called to the steward: 'Boy.'

Mr Pinfold studied this group with benevolence. No one among them would be a Pinfold fan. Presently, at one o'clock, a steward appeared with a gong and Mr Pinfold followed him submissively down to the dining-saloon.

The Captain's table was laid for seven. The 'fiddles' were up and the cloth damped; barely a quarter of the places in the saloon were taken.

Only one other of the Captain's party came to luncheon, a tall young Englishman who fell into easy conversation with Mr Pinfold, informing him that he was named Glover and was manager of a tea plantation in Ceylon; an idyllic life, as he described it, lived on horseback with frequent long leave at a golf club. Glover was keen on golf. In order to keep himself in condition for the game on board ship he had a weighted club, its head on a spring, which he swung, he said, a hundred times morning and evening. His cabin, it transpired, was next to Mr Pinfold's.

'We have to share a bathroom. When do you like your bath?'

Glover's conversation did not demand sharp attention. Mr Pinfold found himself recalled into a world beyond which he had momentarily wandered, to answer: 'Well, really, I hardly ever have a bath at sea. One keeps so clean and I don't like hot salt water. I tried to book a private bathroom. I can't think why.'

'There aren't any private baths in this ship.'

'So I learned. It seems a very decent sort of ship,' said Mr Pinfold, gazing sadly at his curry, at his swaying glass of wine, at the surrounding deserted table, wishing to be pleasant to Glover.

'Yes. Everyone knows everyone else. The same people travel in her every year. People sometimes complain they feel rather out of things if they aren't regulars.'

'I shan't complain,' said Mr Pinfold. 'I've been rather ill. I want a quiet time.'

'Sorry to hear that. You'll find it quiet enough. Some find it too quiet.'

'It can't be too quiet for me,' said Mr Pinfold.

He took rather formal leave of Glover and at once forgot him until, reaching his cabin, he found added to its other noises the strains of a jazz band. Mr Pinfold stood puzzled. He was not musical. All he knew was that somewhere quite near him a band was playing. Then he remembered.

'It's the golfer,' he thought. 'That young man next door. He's got a gramophone. What's more,' he suddenly observed, 'he's got a *dog*.' Quite distinctly on the linoleum outside his door, between his door and Glover's, he heard the pattering of a dog's feet. 'I bet he's not allowed it. I've never been in a ship where they allowed dogs in the cabins. I daresay he bribed the steward. Anyway, one can't reasonably object. I don't mind. He seemed a very pleasant fellow.'

He noticed his grey pills, took one, lay down, opened his book, and then to the sound of dance tunes and the snuffling of the dog he fell asleep once more.

Perhaps he dreamed. He forgot on the instant whatever had happened in the hours between. It was dark. He was awake and there was a very curious scene being played near him; under his feet, it seemed. He heard distinctly a clergyman conducting a religious meeting. Mr Pinfold had no first-hand acquaintance with evangelical practice. His home and his schools had professed a broad-to-high anglicanism. His ideas of nonconformity derived from literature, from Mr Chadband and Philip Henry Gosse, from charades and from back numbers of *Punch*. The sermon, which was just rising to its peroration, was plainly an expression of that kind of faith, scriptural in diction, emotional in appeal. It was addressed presumably to members of the crew. Male voices sang a hymn which Mr Pinfold remembered from his nursery where his nanny, like almost all nannies, had been Calvinist: '*Pull for the shore, sailor. Pull for the shore.*'

'I want to see Billy alone after you dismiss,' said the clergyman. There followed an extempore, rather perfunctory prayer, then a great shuffling of feet and pushing about of chairs; then a hush; then the clergyman, very earnestly: 'Well, Billy, what have you got to say to me?' and the unmistakable sound of sobbing.

Mr Pinfold began to feel uneasy. This was something that was not meant to be overheard.

'Billy, you must tell me yourself. I am not accusing you of anything. I am not putting words into your mouth.'

Silence except for sobbing.

'Billy, you know what we talked about last time. Have you done it again? Have you been impure, Billy?'

'Yes, sir. I can't help it, sir.'

'God never tempts us beyond our strength, Billy. I've told you that, haven't I? Do you suppose I do not feel these temptations, too, Billy? Very strongly at times. But I resist, don't I? You know I resist, don't I, Billy?'

Mr Pinfold was horror-struck. He was being drawn into participation in a scene of gruesome indecency. His sticks lay by the bunk. He took the blackthorn and beat strongly on the floor.

'Did you hear anything then, Billy? A knocking. That is God knocking at the door of your soul. He can't come and help you unless you are pure, like me.'

This was more than Mr Pinfold could bear. He took painfully to his feet, put on his coat, brushed his hair. The voices below him continued:

'I can't help it, sir. I want to be good. I try. I can't.'

'You've got pictures of girls stuck up by your bunk, haven't you?'

'Yes, sir.'

'Filthy pictures.'

'Yes, sir.'

'How can you say you want to be good when you keep temptation deliberately before your eyes. I shall come and destroy those pictures.'

'No, please, sir. I want them.'

Mr Pinfold hobbled out of his cabin and up to the main deck. The sea was calmer now. More passengers were about in the lounge and the bar. It was half-past six. A group were throwing dice for drinks. Mr Pinfold sat alone and ordered a cocktail. When the steward brought it, he asked: 'Does this ship carry a regular chaplain?'

'Oh no, sir. The Captain reads the prayers on Sundays.'

'There's a clergyman, then, among the passengers?'

'I haven't seen one, sir. Here's the list.'

Mr Pinfold studied the passenger list. No name bore any prefix indicating Holy Orders. A strange ship, thought Mr Pinfold, in which laymen were allowed to evangelize a presumably heathen crew; religious mania perhaps on the part of one of the officers.

Waking and sleeping he had lost count of time. It seemed he had been many days at sea in this strange ship. When Glover came into the bar, Mr Pinfold said affably: 'Nice to see you again.'

Glover looked slightly startled by this greeting.

'I've been down in my cabin,' he said.

'I had to come up. I was embarrassed by that prayer-meeting. Weren't you?'

'Prayer-meeting?' said Glover. 'No.'

'Right under our feet. Couldn't you hear it?'

'I heard nothing,' said Glover.

He began to move away.

'Have a drink,' said Mr Pinfold.

'I won't, thanks. I don't. Have to be careful in a place like Ceylon.'

'How's your dog?'

'My dog?'

'Your crypto-dog. The stowaway. Please don't think I'm complaining. I don't mind your dog. Nor your gramophone for that matter.'

'But I haven't a dog. I haven't a gramophone.'

'Oh well,' said Mr Pinfold huffily. 'Perhaps I am mistaken.'

If Glover did not wish to confide in him, he would not try to force himself on the young man.

'See you at dinner,' said Glover, making off.

He was wearing a dinner jacket, Mr Pinfold noticed, as were several other passengers. Time to change. Mr Pinfold went back to his cabin. No sound came now from below; the pseudo-priest and the unchaste seaman had left. But the jazz band was going full blast. So it was not Glover's gramophone. As he changed, Mr Pinfold considered the matter. During the war he had travelled in troop-ships which were fitted with amplifiers on every deck. Unintelligible alarms and orders had issued from these devices and at certain hours popular music. The *Caliban*, plainly, was equipped in this way. It would be a great nuisance when he began to write. He would have to enquire whether there was some way of cutting it off.

It took him a long time to dress. His fingers were unusually clumsy with studs and tie, and his face in the glass was still blotched and staring. By the time he was ready the gong was sounding for dinner. He did not attempt to wear his evening shoes. Instead he slipped into the soft, fur-lined boots in which he had come aboard. With one hand firmly on the rail, the other on his cane, he made his way laboriously down to the saloon. On the stairs he noticed a bronze plaque recording that this ship had been manned by the Royal Navy during the war and had served in the landing in North Africa and Normandy.

He was first at his table, one of the earliest diners in the ship. He noticed a small dark man in day clothes sitting at a table alone. Then the place began to fill. He watched his fellow-passengers in a slightly dazed way. The purser's table, as is common in ships of the kind, had the gayest party, the few girls and young women, the more jovial men from the bar. A plate of soup was set before Mr Pinfold. Two or three coloured stewards stood together by a service table talking in undertones. Suddenly Mr Pinfold was surprised to hear from them three obscene epithets spoken in clear English tones. He looked and glared. One of the men immediately slid to his side.

'Yes, sir; something to drink, sir?'

There was no hint of mockery in the gentle face, no echo in that soft South Indian accent of the gross tones he had overheard. Baffled, Mr Pinfold said: 'Wine.'

'Wine, sir?'

'You have some champagne on board, I suppose?'

'Oh yes, sir. Three names. I show list.'

'Don't bother about the name. Just bring half a bottle.'

Glover came and sat opposite.

'I owe you an apology,' said Mr Pinfold. 'It wasn't your gramophone. Part of the naval equipment left over from the war.'

'Oh,' said Glover. 'That was it, was it?'

'It seems the most likely explanation.'

'Perhaps it does.'

'Very odd language the servants use.'

'They're from Travancore.'

'No. I mean the way they swear. In front of us, I mean. I daresay they don't mean to be insolent but it shows bad discipline.'

'I've never noticed it,' said Glover.

He was not at his ease with Mr Pinfold.

Then the table filled up. Captain Steerforth greeted them and took his place at the head. He was an unremarkable man at first sight. A pretty, youngish woman introduced as Mrs Scarfield sat next to Mr Pinfold. He explained that he was temporarily a cripple and could not stand up. 'My doctor has given me some awfully strong pills to take. They make me feel rather odd. You must forgive me if I'm a dull companion.'

'We're all very dull, I'm afraid,' she said. 'You're the writer, aren't you? I'm afraid I never seem to get any time for reading.'

Mr Pinfold was inured to this sort of conversation but tonight he could not cope. He said: 'I wish I didn't', and turned stupidly to his wine. 'She probably thinks I'm drunk,' he thought and made an attempt to explain: 'They are big grey pills. I don't know what's in them. I don't believe my doctor does either. Something new.'

'That's always exciting, isn't it?' said Mrs Scarfield.

Mr Pinfold despaired and spent the rest of dinner, at which he ate very little, in silence.

The Captain rose, his party with him. Mr Pinfold, slow to move, was still in his chair, fumbling for his stick, when they passed behind him. He got to his feet. He would have dearly liked to go to his cabin, but he was held back, partly by the odd fear that he would be suspected of seasickness but more by an odder sentiment, a bond of duty which he conceived held him to Captain Steerforth. It seemed to him that he was in some way under this man's command and that it would be a grave default to leave him until he was dismissed. So, laboriously, he followed them to the lounge and lowered himself into an arm-chair between the Scarfields. They were drinking coffee. He offered them all brandy. They refused and for himself he ordered brandy and Crème de Menthe mixed. As he did so Mr and Mrs Scarfield exchanged a glance, which he intercepted, as though to confirm some previous confidence – 'My dear, that man next to me, the author, was completely tight.' 'Are you sure?' 'Simply plastered.'

Mrs Scarfield was really extremely pretty, Mr Pinfold thought. She would not keep that skin long in Burma.

Mr Scarfield was in the timber trade, teak. His prospects depended less on his own industry and acumen than on the action of politicians. He addressed the little circle on this subject.

'In a democracy,' said Mr Pinfold with more weight than origin-ality, 'men do not seek authority so that they may impose a policy. They seek a policy so that they may achieve authority.'

He proceeded to illustrate this theme with examples.

At one time or another he had met most of the Government Front Bench. Some were members of Bellamy's whom he knew well. Oblivious of his audience he began to speak of them with familiarity, as he would have done among his friends. The Scarfields again exchanged glances and it occurred to him, too late, that he was not among people who thought it on the whole rather discreditable to know politicians. These people thought he was showing off. He stopped in the middle of a sentence, silent with shame.

'It must be very exciting to move behind the scenes,' said Mrs Scarfield. 'We only know what we see in the papers.'

Was there malice behind her smile? At first meeting she had seemed frank and friendly. Mr Pinfold thought he discovered sly hostility now.

'Oh, I hardly ever read the political columns,' he said.

'You don't have to, do you? getting it all first hand.'

There was no doubt in Mr Pinfold's mind. He had made an ass of himself. Reckless now of his reputation as a good sailor, he attempted a little bow to include the Captain and the Scarfields.

'If you'll excuse me, I think I'll go to my cabin.'

He had difficulty getting out of his deep chair, he had difficulty with his stick, he had difficulty keeping his balance. They had barely said 'Good night', he was still struggling away from them, when something the Captain said made them laugh. Three distinct laughs, all, in Mr Pinfold's ears, cruelly derisive. On his way out he passed Glover. Moved to explain himself he said: 'I don't know anything about politics.'

'No?' said Glover.

'Tell them I don't know anything.'

'Tell who?'

'The Captain.'

'He's just behind you over there.'

'Oh well, it doesn't matter.'

He hobbled away and looking back from the doors saw Glover talking to the Scarfields. They were ostensibly arranging a four for bridge but Mr Pinfold knew they had another darker interest – *him*.

It was not yet nine o'clock. Mr Pinfold undressed. He hung up his clothes, washed and took his pill. There were three tablespoonfuls left in his bottle of sleeping-draught. He decided to try and spend the night without it, to delay anyway until after midnight. The sea was much calmer now; he could lie in bed without rolling. He lay at ease and began to read one of the novels he had brought on board.

Then, before he had turned a page, the band struck up. This was no wireless performance. It was a living group just under his feet, rehearsing. They were in the same place, as inexplicably audible, as the afternoon bible-class; young, happy people, the party doubtless from the purser's table. Their instruments were drums and rattles and some sort of pipe. The drums and rattles did most of the work. Mr Pinfold knew nothing of music. It seemed to him that the rhythms they played derived from some very primitive tribe and were of anthropological rather than artistic interest. This guess was confirmed.

'Let's try the Pocoputa Indian one,' said the young man who acted, without any great air of authority, as leader.

'Oh not *that*. It's so *beastly*,' said a girl.

'I know,' said the leader. 'It's the three-eight rhythm. The Gestapo discovered it independently, you know. They used to play it in the cells. It drove the prisoners mad.'

'Yes,' said another girl. 'Thirty-six hours did for anyone. Twelve was enough for most. They could stand any torture but that.'

'It drove them absolutely mad.' 'Raving mad.' 'Stark, staring mad.' 'It was the worst torture of all.' 'The Russians use it now.' The voices, some male, some female, all young and eager, came tumbling like puppies. 'The Hungarians do it best.' 'Good old three-eight.' 'Good old Pocoputa Indians.' 'They were mad.'

'I suppose no one can hear us?' said a sweet girlish voice.

'Don't be so wet, Mimi. Everyone's up on the main deck.'

'All right then,' said the band leader. 'The three-eight rhythm.'

And off they went.

The sound throbbed and thrilled in the cabin which had suddenly become a prison cell. Mr Pinfold was not one who thought and talked easily to a musical accompaniment. Even in early youth he had sought the night-clubs where there was a bar out of hearing of the band. Friends he had, Roger Stillingfleet among them, to whom jazz was a necessary drug – whether stimulant or narcotic Mr Pinfold did not know. He preferred silence. The three-eight rhythm was indeed torture to him. He could not read. It was not a quarter of an hour since he had entered the cabin. Unendurable hours lay ahead. He emptied the bottle of sleeping-draught and, to the strains of the jolly young people from the purser's table, fell into unconsciousness.

He awoke before dawn. The bright young people below him had dispersed. The three-eight rhythm was hushed. No shadow passed between the deck-light and the cabin window. But overhead there was turmoil. The crew, or a considerable part of it, was engaged on an operation of dragging the deck with what from the sound of it might have been an enormous chain-harrow, and they were not happy in their work. They were protesting mutinously in their own tongue and the officer in command was roaring back at them in the tones of an old sea-dog: 'Get on with it, you black bastards. Get on with it.'

The lascars were not so easily quelled. They shouted back unintelligibly.

'I'll call out the Master-at-Arms,' shouted the officer. An empty threat, surely? thought Mr Pinfold. It was scarcely conceivable that the *Caliban* carried a Master-at-Arms. 'By God, I'll shoot the first man of you that moves,' said the officer.

The hubbub increased. Mr Pinfold could almost see the drama overhead, the half-lighted deck, the dark frenzied faces, the solitary bully with the heavy old-fashioned ship's pistol. Then there was a crash, not a shot but a huge percussion of metal as though a hundred pokers and pairs of tongs had fallen into an enormous fender, followed by a wail of agony and a moment of complete silence.

'There,' said the officer more in the tones of a nanny than a sea-dog, 'just see what you've gone and done now.'

Whatever its nature this violent occurrence entirely subdued the passions of the crew. They were docile, ready to do anything to retrieve the disaster. The only sounds now were the officer's calmer orders and the whimpering of the injured man.

'Steady there. Easy does it. You, cut along to the sick-bay and get the surgeon. You, go up and report to the bridge . . . '

For a long time, two hours perhaps, Mr Pinfold lay in his bunk listening. He was able to hear quite distinctly not only what was said in his immediate vicinity, but elsewhere. He had the light on, now, in his cabin, and as he gazed at the complex of tubes and wires which ran across his ceiling, he realized that they must form some kind of general junction in the system of communication. Through some trick or fault or wartime survival everything spoken in the executive quarters of the ship was transmitted to him. A survival seemed the most likely explanation. Once during the blitz in London he had been given a hotel bedroom which had been hastily vacated by a visiting allied statesman. When he lifted the telephone to order his breakfast, he had found himself talking on a private line direct to the Cabinet Office. Something of that kind must have happened in the *Caliban*. When she was a naval vessel this cabin had no doubt been the office of some operational headquarters and when she was handed back to her owners and re-adapted for passenger service, the engineers had neglected to disconnect it. That alone could explain the voices which now kept him informed of every stage of the incident.

The wounded man seemed to have got himself entangled in some kind of web of metal. Various unsuccessful and agonizing attempts were made to extricate him. Finally the decision was taken to cut him out. The order once given was carried out with surprising speed but the contraption, whatever it was, was ruined in the process and was finally dragged across the deck and thrown overboard. The victim continuously sobbed and whimpered. He was taken to the sick-bay and put in charge of a kind but not, it appeared, very highly qualified nurse. 'You must be brave,' she said. 'I will say the rosary for you. You must be brave,' while the wireless telegraphist got into touch with a hospital ashore and was given instructions in first aid. The ship's surgeon never appeared. Details of treatment were dictated from the shore and passed to the sick-bay. The last words Mr Pinfold heard from the bridge were Captain Steerforth's 'I'm not going to be bothered with a sick man on board. We'll have to signal a passing homebound ship and have him transferred.'

Part of the treatment prescribed by the hospital was a sedative injection, and as this spread its relief over the unhappy lascar, Mr Pinfold too grew drowsy until finally he fell asleep to the sound of the nurse murmuring the Angelic Salutation.

He was awakened by the coloured cabin steward bringing him tea.

'Very disagreeable business that last night,' said Mr Pinfold.

'Yes, sir.'

'How is the poor fellow?'

'Eight o'clock, sir.'

'Have they managed to get into touch with a ship to take him off?'

'Yes, sir. Breakfast eight-thirty, sir.'

Mr Pinfold drank his tea. He felt disinclined to get up. The intercommunication system was silent. He picked up his book and began to read. Then with a click the voices began again.

Captain Steerforth seemed to be addressing a deputation of the crew. 'I want you to understand,' he was saying, 'that a great quantity of valuable metal was sacrificed last night for the welfare of a single seaman. That metal was pure *copper*. One of the most valuable metals in the world. Mind you, I don't regret the sacrifice and I am sure the Company will approve my action. But I want you all to appreciate that only in a British ship would such a thing be done. In the ship of any other nationality it would have been the seaman not the metal that was cut up. You know that as well as I do. Don't forget it. And another thing, instead of taking the man with us to Port Said and the filth of a Wog hospital, I had him carefully trans-shipped and he is now on his way to England. He couldn't have been treated more handsomely if he'd been a director of the Company. I know the hospital he's going to; it's a sweet, pretty place. It's the place all seamen long to go to. He'll have the best attention there and live, if he does live, in the greatest comfort. That's the kind of ship this is. Nothing is too good for the men who serve in her.'

The meeting seemed to disperse. There was a shuffling and muttering and presently a woman spoke. It was a voice which was soon to become familiar to Mr Pinfold. To all men and women there is some sound – grating, perhaps, or rustling, or strident, deep or shrill, a note or inflection of speech – which causes peculiar pain; which literally 'makes the hair stand on end' or metaphorically 'sets the teeth on edge'; something which Dr Drake would have called an 'allergy'. Such was this woman's voice. It clearly did not affect the Captain in this way but to Mr Pinfold it was excruciating.

'Well,' said this voice. 'That should teach them not to grumble.'

'Yes,' said Captain Steerforth. 'We've settled that little mutiny, I think. We shouldn't have any trouble now.'

'Not till the next time,' said the cynical woman. 'What a contemptible exhibition that man made of himself – crying like a child. Thank God we've seen the last of him. I liked your touch about the sweet, pretty hospital.'

'Yes. They little know the Hell-spot I've sent him to. Spoiling my copper, indeed. He'll soon wish he were in Port Said.'

And the woman laughed odiously. 'Soon wish he was dead,' she said.

EVELYN WAUGH

There was a click (someone seemed to be in control of the apparatus, Mr Pinfold thought), and two passengers were speaking. They seemed to be elderly, military gentlemen.

'I think the passengers should be told,' one said.

'Yes, we ought to call a meeting. It's the sort of thing that so often passes without proper recognition. We ought to pass a vote of thanks.'

'A ton of copper, you say?'

'Pure copper, cut up and chucked overboard. All for the sake of a nigger. It makes one proud of the British service.'

The voices ceased and Mr Pinfold lay wondering about this meeting; was it his duty to attend and report what he knew of the true characters of the Captain and his female associate? The difficulty, of course, would be to prove his charges; to explain satisfactorily how he came to overhear the Captain's secret.

Soft music filled the cabin, an oratorio sung by a great but distant choir. 'That *must* be a gramophone record,' thought Mr Pinfold. 'Or the wireless. They can't be performing this on board.' Then he slept for some time, until he was woken by a change of music. The bright young people were at it again with their Pocoputa Indian three-eight rhythm. Mr Pinfold looked at his watch. Eleven-thirty. Time to get up.

As he laboriously shaved and dressed, he reasoned closely about his situation. Now that he knew of the intercommunication system, it was plain to him that the room used by this band might be anywhere in the ship. The prayer-meeting too. It had seemed odd at the time that the quiet voices had come so clearly through the floor; that they had been audible to him and not to Glover. That was now explained. But he was puzzled by the irregularity, by the changes of place, the clicking on and off. It was improbable that anyone at a switchboard was directing the annoyances into his cabin. It was certain that the Captain would not deliberately broadcast his private and compromising conversations. Mr Pinfold wished he knew more of the mechanics of the thing. He remembered that in London just after the war, when everything was worn out, telephones used sometimes to behave in this erratic way; the line would go dead; then crackle; then, when the tangled wire was given a twist and a jerk, normal conversion was rejoined. He supposed that somewhere over his head, in the ventilation shaft probably, there were a number of frayed and partly disconnected wires which every now and then with the movement of the ship came into contact and so established communication now with one, now with another part of the ship.

Before leaving his cabin he considered his box of pills. He was not well. Much was wrong with him, he felt, beside lameness. Dr Drake did not know about the sleeping-draught. It might be that the pills, admittedly new and pretty strong, warred with the bromide and chloral; perhaps with gin and brandy too. Well, the sleeping-draught was finished. He would try the pills once or twice more. He swallowed one and crept up to the main deck.

Here there was light and liveliness, a glitter of cool sunshine and a brisk breeze. The young people had abandoned the concert in the short time it had taken Mr Pinfold to climb the stairs. They were on the after deck playing quoits and shuffle-board and watching one another play; laughing boisterously as the ship rolled and jostled them against one another. Mr Pinfold leant on the rail and looked down, thinking it odd that such healthy-seeming, good-natured creatures should rejoice in the music of the Pocoputa Indians. Glover stood by himself in the stern swinging his golf-club. On the sunny side of the main deck the older passengers sat wrapped in rugs, some with popular biographies, some with knitting. The young Burmese paced together in pairs, uniformly and neatly dressed in blazers and pale fawn trousers, like officers waiting to fall in at a battalion parade.

Mr Pinfold sought the military gentlemen whose ill-informed eulogies of the Captain he believed it to be his duty to correct. From the voices, elderly, precise, conventional, he had formed a clear idea of their appearance. They were major-generals, retired now. They had been gallant young regimental officers – line-cavalry probably – in 1914 and had commanded brigades at the end of that war. They had passed at the Staff College and waited patiently for another battle only to find in 1939 that they were passed over for active command. But they had served loyally in offices, done their turn at fire-watching, gone short of whisky and razor-blades. Now they could just afford an inexpensive winter cruise every other year; admirable old men in their way. He did not find them on deck or in any of the public rooms.

As noon was sounded there was a movement towards the bar for the announcement of the ship's run and the result of the sweepstake. Scarfield was the winner of a modest prize. He ordered drinks for all in sight including Mr Pinfold. Mrs Scarfield stood near him and Mr Pinfold said: 'I say, I'm afraid I was an awful bore last night.'

'Were you?' she said. 'Not while you were with us.'

'All that nonsense I talked about politics. It's those pills I have to take. They make me feel rather odd.'

'I'm sorry about that,' said Mrs Scarfield, 'but I assure you, you didn't bore *us* in the least. I was fascinated.'

Mr Pinfold looked hard at her but could detect no hint of irony. 'Anyway I shan't hold forth like that again.'

'Please do.'

The ladies who had been identified as Mrs Benson and Mrs Cockson were in the same chairs as on the day before. They liked their glass, that pair, thought Mr Pinfold with approval; good sorts. He greeted them. He greeted anyone who caught his eye. He was feeling very much better.

One figure alone remained aloof from the general conviviality, the dark little man whom Mr Pinfold had noticed dining alone.

Presently the steward passed by, tapping his little musical gong, and Mr Pinfold followed the company down to luncheon. Knowing what he did of Captain Steerforth's character, Mr Pinfold found it rather repugnant to sit at the table with him. He gave him a perfunctory nod and addressed himself to Glover.

'Noisy night, wasn't it?'

'Oh,' said Glover, 'I didn't hear anything.'

'You must sleep very sound.'

'As a matter of fact, I didn't. I usually do, but I am not getting the exercise I'm used to. I was awake half the night.'

'And you didn't hear the accident?'

'No.'

'Accident?' said Mrs Scarfield overhearing. 'Was there an accident last night, Captain?'

'No one told me of one,' said Captain Steerforth blandly.

'The villain,' thought Mr Pinfold. 'Remorseless, treacherous, lecherous, kindless villain,' for though Captain Steerforth had shown no other symptoms of lechery, Mr Pinfold knew instinctively that his relations with the harsh-voiced woman – stewardess, secretary, passenger, whatever she might be – were grossly erotic.

'What accident, Mr Pinfold?' asked Mrs Scarfield.

'Perhaps I was mistaken,' said Mr Pinfold stiffly. 'I often am.'

There was another couple at the Captain's table. They had been there the night before, had been part of the group in which Mr Pinfold had talked so injudiciously, but he had barely noticed them; a pleasant, middle-aged nondescript, rather rich-looking couple, not English, Dutch perhaps or Scandinavian. The woman now leant across and said in thick, rather arch tones:

'There are two books of yours in the ship's library, I find.'

'Ah.'

'I have taken one. It is named *The Last Card*.'

'*The Lost Chord*,' said Mr Pinfold.

'Yes. It is a humorous book, yes?'

'Some people have suggested as much.'

'I find it so. It is not your suggestion also? I think you have a peculiar sense of humour, Mr Pinfold.'

'Ah.'

'That is what you are known for, yes, your peculiar sense of humour?'

'Perhaps.'

'May I have it after you?' asked Mrs Scarfield. 'Everyone says I have a peculiar sense of humour too.'

'But not so peculiar as Mr Pinfold?'

'That remains to be seen,' said Mrs Scarfield.

'I think you're embarrassing the author,' said Mr Scarfield.

'I expect he's used to it,' she said.

'He takes it all with his peculiar sense of humour,' said the foreign lady.

'If you'll excuse me,' said Mr Pinfold, struggling to rise.

'You see he is embarrassed.'

'No,' said the foreign lady. 'It is his humour. He is going to make notes of us. You see, we shall all be in a humorous book.'

As Mr Pinfold rose, he gazed towards the little dark man at his solitary table. That is where he should have been, he thought. The last sound he heard as he left the dining-saloon was merry young laughter from the purser's table.

Since he left it not much more than an hour before, the cabin had been tidied and the bedclothes stretched taut, hospital-like, across the bunk. He took off his coat and his soft boots, lit a cigar and lay down. He had barely eaten at all that day but he was not hungry. He blew smoke up towards the wires and pipes on the ceiling and wondered how without offence he could escape from the Captain's table to sit and eat alone, silent and untroubled, like that clever, dark, enviable little fellow, and as though in response to these thoughts the device overhead clicked into life and he heard this very subject being debated by the two old soldiers.

'My dear fellow, *I* don't care a damn.'

'No, of course you don't. Nor do I. All the same I think it very decent of him to mention it.'

'*Very* decent. What did he say exactly?'

'Said he was very sorry he hadn't room for you and me and my missus. The table only takes six passengers. Well, he had to have the Scarfields.'

'Yes, of course. He *had* to have the Scarfields.'

'Yes, he had to have them. Then there's the Norwegian couple – foreigners you know.'

'Distinguished foreigners.'

'Got to be civil to them. Well that makes four. Then if you please, he got an order from the Company to take this fellow Pinfold. So he only had one place. Knew he couldn't separate you and me and the missus, so he asked that decent young fellow – the one with the uncle in Liverpool.'

'Has he got an uncle in Liverpool?'

'Yes, yes. That's why he asked him.'

'But why did he ask Pinfold?'

'Company's orders. *He* didn't want him.'

'No, no, of course not.'

'If you ask me Pinfold drinks.'

'Yes, so I have always heard.'

'I saw him come on board. He was tight then. In a beastly state.'

'He's been in a beastly state ever since.'

'He says it's pills.'

'No, no, drink. I've seen better men than Pinfold go that way.'

'Wretched business. He shouldn't have come.'

'If you ask me he's been *sent* on this ship as a *cure*.'

'Ought to have someone to look after him.'

'Have you noticed that little dark chap who sits alone? I shouldn't be surprised if *he* wasn't keeping an eye on him.'

'A male nurse?'

'A warder more likely.'

'Put on him by his missus without his knowing?'

'That's my appreciation of the situation.'

The voices of the two old gossips faded and fell silent. Mr Pinfold lay smoking, without resentment. It was the sort of thing one expected to have said behind one's back – the sort of thing one said about other people. It was slightly unnerving to overhear it. The idea of his wife setting a spy on him was amusing. He would write and tell her. The question of his drunkenness interested him more. Perhaps he did give that impression. Perhaps on that first evening at sea – how long ago was that now? – when he had talked politics after dinner, perhaps he *had* drunk too much. He had had too much of something certainly, pills or sleeping-draught or liquor. Well, the sleeping-draught was finished. He resolved to take no more pills. He would stick to wine and a cocktail or two and a glass of brandy after dinner and soon he would be well and active once more.

He had reached the last inch of his cigar, a large one, an hour's smoking, when his reverie was interrupted from the Captain's cabin.

The doxy was there. In her harsh voice she said: 'You've got to teach him a lesson.'

'I will.'

'A *good* lesson.'

'Yes.'

'One he won't forget.'

'Bring him in.'

There was a sound of scuffling and whimpering, a sound rather like that of the wounded seaman whom Mr Pinfold had heard that morning; which morning? One morning of this disturbing voyage. It seemed that a prisoner was being dragged into the Captain's presence.

'Tie him to the chair,' said the leman, and Mr Pinfold at once thought of *King Lear*: 'Bind fast his corky arms.' Who said that? Goneril? Regan? Perhaps neither of them. Cornwall? It was a man's voice, surely? in the play. But it was the voice of the woman, or what passed as a woman, here. Addict of nicknames as he was, Mr Pinfold there and then dubbed her 'Goneril'.

'All right,' said Captain Steerforth, 'you can leave him to me.'

'And to me,' said Goneril.

Mr Pinfold was not abnormally squeamish nor had his life been particularly sheltered, but he had no experience of personal, physical cruelty and no liking for its portrayal in books or films. Now, lying in his spruce cabin in this British ship, in the early afternoon, a few yards distance from Glover and the Scarfields, Mrs Benson and Mrs Cockson, he was the horrified witness of a scene which might have come straight from the kind of pseudo-American thriller he most abhorred.

There were three people in the Captain's cabin, Steerforth, Goneril and their prisoner, who was one of the coloured stewards. Proceedings began with a form of trial. Goneril gave her evidence, vindictively but precisely accusing the man of an attempted sexual offence against her. It sounded to Mr Pinfold rather a strong case. Knowing the ambiguous position which the accuser held in the ship, remembering the gross language he had overheard in the dining-saloon and the heavy, unhealthy discourse of the preacher, Mr Pinfold considered the incident he heard described exactly the sort of thing he would expect to happen in this beastly ship. Guilty, he thought.

'Guilty,' said the Captain and at the word Goneril vented a hiss of satisfaction and anticipation. Slowly and deliberately, as the ship steamed South with its commonplace load of passengers, the

Captain and his leman with undisguised erotic enjoyment settled down to torture their prisoner.

Mr Pinfold could not surmise what form the torture took. He could only listen to the moans and sobs of the victim and the more horrific, ecstatic, orgiastic cries of Goneril:

'More. More. Again. Again. Again. You haven't had anything yet, you beast. Give him some more, more, more, more.'

Mr Pinfold could not endure it. He must stop this outrage at once. He lurched from his bunk, but even as he felt for his boots, silence fell in the Captain's cabin and a suddenly sobered Goneril said: 'That's enough.'

Not a sound came from the victim. After a long pause Captain Steerforth said: 'If you ask me, it's too much.'

'He's shamming,' said Goneril without conviction.

'He's dead,' said the Captain.

'Well,' said Goneril. 'What are you going to do about it?'

'Untie him.'

'I'm not going to touch him. I never touched him. It was all *you*.'

Mr Pinfold stood in his cabin, just as, no doubt, the Captain was standing in his, uncertain what to do, and as he hesitated, he realized through his horror that the pains in his legs had suddenly entirely ceased. He rose on his toes; he bent his knees. He was cured. It was the way in which these attacks of his always came and went, quite unpredictably. In spite of his agitation he had room in his mind to consider whether perhaps they were nervous in origin, whether the shock he had just endured might not have succeeded where the grey pills had failed; whether he had not been healed by the steward's agony. It was a hypothesis which momentarily distracted him from the murderers above.

Presently he turned to listen to them.

'As master of the ship I shall make out a death-certificate and have him put overboard after dark.'

'How about the surgeon?'

'He must sign too. The first thing is to get the body into the sick-bay. We don't want any more trouble with the men. Get Margaret.'

The situation, as Mr Pinfold saw it, was appalling but it did not call for action.

Whatever had to be done need not be done now. He could not burst alone into the Captain's cabin and denounce him. What was the proper procedure, if any existed, for putting a Captain in irons in his own ship? He would have to take advice. The military men, that sage, authoritative couple, were the obvious people. He would find them and explain the situation. They would know what to do. A report must be made, he assumed, depositions taken. Where? At the first consulate they came to, at Port Said; or should they wait until they reached a British port? Those old campaigners would know.

Meanwhile Margaret, the kind nurse, a sort of Cordelia, seemed to have charge of the body. 'Poor boy, poor boy,' she was saying. 'Look at these ghastly marks. You can't say these are "natural causes".'

'That's what the Captain says,' said a new voice, the ship's surgeon presumably. 'I take my orders from him. There's a lot goes on aboard this ship that I don't like. The best you can do, young lady, is to see nothing, hear nothing and say nothing.'

'But the poor boy. He must have suffered so.'

'Natural causes,' said the doctor. And then there was silence.

Mr Pinfold removed his soft boots and put on shoes. He propped his two sticks in a corner of the wardrobe. 'I shan't need those again,' he reflected, little knowing what the coming days had in store, and walked almost blithely to the main deck.

No one was about except two lascars, slung overhead, painting the davits. It was half-past three, a time when all the passengers were in their cabins. Like a lark on a battlefield Mr Pinfold's spirits rose, free and singing. He rejoiced in his power to walk. He walked round the ship, again and again, up and down. Was it possible, in this bright and peaceful scene, to believe in the abomination that lurked up there, just overhead, behind the sparkling paint? Could he possibly be mistaken? He had never seen Goneril. He barely knew the Captain's voice. Could he really identify it? Was it not possible that what he had heard was a piece of acting – a charade of the bright young people's? a broadcast from London?

Wishful thinking, perhaps, born of the exhilaration of sun and sea and wind and his own new-found health?

Time alone would show.

4
THE HOOLIGANS

THAT EVENING MR PINFOLD felt the renewal of health and cheerfulness and clarity of mind greater, it seemed to him, than he had known for weeks. He looked at his hands, which for days now had been blotched with crimson; now they were clear and his face in the glass had lost its congested, mottled hue. He dressed more deftly and as he dressed the wireless in his cabin came into action.

'This is the B.B.C. Third Programme. Here is Mr Clutton-Cornforth to speak on Aspects of Orthodoxy in Contemporary Letters.'

Mr Pinfold had known Clutton-Cornforth for thirty years. He was now the editor of a literary weekly, an ambitious, obsequious fellow. Mr Pinfold had no curiosity about his opinions on any subject. He wished there were a way of switching off the fluting, fruity voice. He tried instead to disregard it until, just as he was leaving, he was recalled by the sound of his own name.

'Gilbert Pinfold,' he heard, 'poses a precisely antithetical problem, or should we say? the same problem in antithetical form. The basic qualities of a Pinfold novel seldom vary and may be enumerated thus: conventionality of plot, falseness of characterization, morbid sentimentality, gross and hackneyed farce alternating with grosser and more hackneyed melodrama; cloying religiosity, which will be found tedious or blasphemous according as the reader shares or repudiates his doctrinal preconceptions; an adventitious and offensive sensuality that is clearly introduced for commercial motives. All this is presented in a style which, when it varies from the trite, lapses into positive illiteracy.'

Really, thought Mr Pinfold, this was not like the Third Programme; it was not at all like Algernon Clutton-Cornforth.

'My word,' he thought, 'I'll give that booby such a kick on the sit-upon next time I see him waddling up the steps of the London Library.'

'Indeed,' continued Clutton-Cornforth, 'if one is asked – and one *is* often asked – to give one name which typifies all that is decadent in contemporary literature, one can answer without hesitation – Gilbert Pinfold. I now turn from him to the equally deplorable but more interesting case of a writer often associated with him – Roger Stillingfleet.'

Here, by a quirk of the apparatus, Clutton-Cornforth was cut off and succeeded by a female singer:

> '*I'm Gilbert, the filbert,*
> *The knut with the K,*
> *The pride of Piccadilly,*
> *The blasé roué.*'

Mr Pinfold left his cabin. He met the steward on his rounds with the dinner-gong and ascended to the main-deck. He stepped out into the wind, leaned briefly on the rail, looked down into the surge of lighted water. The music rejoined him there, emanating from somewhere quite near where he stood.

> '*For Gilbert, the filbert,*
> *The Colonel of the Knuts.*'

Other people in the ship were listening to the wireless. Other people, probably, had heard Clutton-Cornforth's diatribe. Well, he was accustomed to criticism (though not from Clutton-Cornforth). He could take it. He only hoped no one bored him by talking about it; particularly not that Norwegian woman at the Captain's table.

Mr Pinfold's feelings towards the Captain had moderated in the course of the afternoon. As to whether the man were guilty of murder or no, his judgment was suspended, but the fact of his having fallen under a cloud, of Mr Pinfold's possession of secret knowledge which might or might not bring him to ruin, severed the bond of loyalty which had previously bound them. Mr Pinfold felt disposed to tease the Captain a little.

Accordingly at dinner, when they were all seated, and he had ordered himself a pint of champagne, he turned the conversation rather abruptly to the subject of murder.

'Have you ever actually met a murderer?' he asked Glover.

Glover had. In his tea garden a trusted foreman had hacked his wife to pieces.

'I expect he smiled a good deal, didn't he?' asked Mr Pinfold.

'Yes, as a matter of fact he did. Always a most cheerful chap. He went off to be hanged laughing away with his brothers as though it was no end of a joke.'

'*Exactly.*'

Mr Pinfold stared full in the eyes of the smiling Captain. Was there any sign of alarm in that broad, plain face?

'Have *you* ever known a murderer, Captain Steerforth?'

Yes, when he first went to sea, Captain Steerforth had been in a ship with a stoker who killed another with a shovel. But they brought it in that the man was insane, affected by the heat of the stoke-hold.

'In my country in the forests in the long winter often the men become drunken and fight and sometimes they kill one another. Is not hanging in my country for such things. Is a case for the doctor we think.'

'If you ask me all murderers are mad,' said Scarfield.

'And always smiling,' said Mr Pinfold. 'That's the only way you can tell them – by their inevitable good-humour.'

'This stoker wasn't very cheerful. Surly fellow as I remember him.'

'Ah, but he was mad.'

'Goodness,' said Mrs Scarfield, 'what a morbid subject. However did we get on to it?'

'Not so morbid by half as Clutton-Cornforth,' said Mr Pinfold rather truculently.

'Who?' asked Mrs Scarfield.

'As what?' asked the Norwegian woman.

Mr Pinfold looked from face to face round the table. Clearly no one had heard the broadcast.

'Oh,' he said, 'if you don't know about him, the less said the better.'

'Do tell,' said Mrs Scarfield.

'No, really, it's nothing.'

She gave a little shrug of disappointment and turned her pretty face towards the Captain.

Later Mr Pinfold tried to raise the topic of burial at sea, but this was not taken up with any enthusiasm. Mr Pinfold had devoted some thought to the matter during the late afternoon. Glover had said that the stewards came from Travancore, in which case there was a good chance of their being Christians of one or other of the ancient rites that prevailed in that complex culture. They would insist on some religious observance for one of their number. If he wished to avert suspicion, the Captain could not bundle the body overboard secretly. Once in a troopship Mr Pinfold had assisted at the committal to the sea of one of his troop who shot himself. The business he remembered took some time. Last Post had been sounded. Mr Pinfold rather thought the ship had hove-to. In the *Caliban* the sports-deck seemed the most likely place for the ceremony. Mr Pinfold would keep watch. If the night passed without incident, Captain Steerforth would stand acquitted.

That evening, as on the evening before, Captain Steerforth played bridge. He smiled continuously rubber after rubber. Early hours were kept in the *Caliban*. The bar shut at half-past ten, lights began to be turned off and ash trays emptied; the passengers went to their cabins. Mr Pinfold saw the last of them go below, then went aft to a seat overlooking the sports-deck. It was very cold. He went down to his cabin for an overcoat. It was warm there and welcoming. It occurred to him he could keep his vigil perfectly well below deck. When the engines stopped, he would know that the game was on. The last faint cobwebs of his sleeping-draught had now been swept up. He was wide awake. Without undressing he lay on his bunk with a novel.

Time passed. No sound came through the intercommunication; the engines beat regularly, the plates and panelling creaked; the low hum of the ventilator filled the cabin.

There were no funeral obsequies, no panegyric; no dirge on board the *Caliban* that night. Instead there was enacted on the deck immediately outside Mr Pinfold's window a dramatic cycle lasting five hours – six? Mr Pinfold did not notice the time at which the disturbance began – of which he was the solitary audience. Had it appeared behind footlights on a real stage, Mr Pinfold would have condemned it as grossly overplayed.

There were two chief actors, juvenile leads, one of whom was called Fosker; the other, the leader, was nameless. They were drunk when they first arrived and presumably carried a bottle from which they often swigged for the long hours of darkness were of no avail in sobering them. They raged more and more furiously until their final lapse into incoherence. By their voices they seemed to be gentlemen of a sort. Fosker, Mr Pinfold was pretty sure, had been in the jazz band; he thought he had noticed him in the lounge after dinner, amusing the girls, tall, very young, shabby, shady, vivacious, bohemian, with long hair, a moustache, and the beginning of side-whiskers. There was something in him of the dissolute law students and government clerks of mid-Victorian fiction. Something too of the young men who had now and then crossed his path during the war – the sort of subaltern who was disliked in his regiment and got himself posted to S.O.E. When Mr Pinfold came to consider the matter at leisure he could not explain to himself how he had formed so full an impression during a brief, incurious glance, or why Fosker, if he were what he seemed, should be travelling to the East in such incongruous company. The image of him, however, remained sharp cut as a cameo. The second, dominant young man was a voice only; rather a pleasant well-bred voice for all its vile utterances.

'He's gone to bed,' said Fosker.

'We'll soon get him out,' said the pleasant well-bred voice.

'Music.'

'Music.'

> *'I'm Gilbert, the filbert,*
> *The knut with the K,*
> *The pride of Piccadilly,*
> *The blasé roué.*
> *Oh Hades, the ladies*
> *Who leave their wooden huts*

> *For Gilbert, the filbert,*
> *The Colonel of the Knuts.'*

'Come on, Gilbert. Time to leave your wooden hut.'

Damned impudence, thought Mr Pinfold. Oafs, bores.

'D'you think he's enjoying this?'

'He's got a most peculiar sense of humour. He's a most peculiar man. Queer, aren't you, Gilbert? Come out of your wooden hut, you old queer.'

Mr Pinfold drew the wooden shutter across his window but the noise outside was undiminished.

'He thinks that'll keep us out. It won't, Gilbert. We aren't going to climb through the window, you know. We shall come in at the door and then, by God, you're going to cop it. Now he's locked the door.' Mr Pinfold had done no such thing. 'Not very brave, is he? Locking himself in. Gilbert doesn't want to be whipped.'

'But he's going to be whipped.'

'Oh yes, he's going to be whipped all right.'

Mr Pinfold decided on action. He put on his dressing-gown, took his blackthorn, and left his cabin. The door which led out to the deck was some way down the corridor. The voices of the two hooligans followed him as he went to it. He thought he knew the Fosker type, the aggressive under-dog, vainglorious in drink, very easily put in his place. He pushed open the heavy door and stepped resolutely into the wind. The deck was quite empty. For the length of the ship the damp planks shone in the lamp-light. From above came shrieks of laughter.

'No, no, Gilbert, you can't catch us that way. Go back to your little hut, Gilbert. We'll come for you when we want you. Better lock the door.'

Mr Pinfold returned to his cabin. He did not lock the door. He sat, stick in hand, listening.

The two young men conferred.

'We'd better wait till he goes to sleep.'

'Then we'll pounce.'

'He doesn't seem very sleepy.'

'Let's get the girls to sing him to sleep. Come on, Margaret, give Gilbert a song.'

'Aren't you being rather beastly?' The girl's voice was clear and sober.

'No, of course not. It's all a joke. Gilbert's a sport. Gilbert's enjoying it as much as we are. He often did this sort of thing when he was our age – singing ridiculous songs outside men's rooms at Oxford. He made a row outside the Dean's rooms. That's why he got sent down. He accused the Dean of the most disgusting practices. It was all a great joke.'

'Well, if you're sure he doesn't mind . . . '

Two girls began singing very prettily.

> '*When first I saw Mabel,*' they sang,
> '*In her fair Russian sable*
> *I knew she was able*
> *To satisfy me.*
> *Her manners were careless . . .* '

The later lines of the song – one well known to Mr Pinfold – are verbally bawdy, but as they rose now on the passionless, true voices of the girls, they were purged and sweetened; they floated over the sea in perfect innocence. The girls sang this and other airs. They sang for a long time. They sang intermittently throughout the night's disturbances, but they were powerless to soothe Mr Pinfold. He sat wide awake with his stick to deal with intruders.

Presently the father of the nameless young man came to join them. He was, it appeared, one of the generals.

'Go to bed, you two,' he said. 'You're making an infernal nuisance of yourselves.'

'We're only mocking Pinfold. He's a beastly man.'

'That's no reason to wake up the whole ship.'

'He's a Jew.'

'Is he? Are you sure? I never heard that.'

'Of course he is. He came to Lychpole in 1937 with the German refugees. He was called Peinfeld then.'

'We're out for Peinfeld's blood,' said the pleasant voice. 'We want to beat Hell out of him.'

'You don't really mind, do you, sir,' said Fosker, 'if we beat Hell out of him.'

'What's wrong with the fellow particularly?'

'He's got a dozen pairs of shoes in his little hut, all beautifully polished on wooden trees.'

'He sits at the Captain's table.'

'He's taken the only bathroom near our cabin. I tried to use it tonight and the steward said it was private, for Mr Pinfold.'

'Mr Peinfeld.'

'I hate him. I hate him. I hate him. I hate him. I hate him,' said Fosker. 'I've got my own score to settle with him for what he did to Hill.'

'That farmer who shot himself?'

'Hill was a decent, old-fashioned yeoman. The salt of the country. Then this filthy Jew came and bought up the property. The Hills had farmed it for generations. They were thrown out. That's why Hill hanged himself.'

'Well,' said the general. 'You won't do any good by shouting outside his window.'

'We're going to do more than that. We're going to give him the hiding of his life.'

'Yes, you could do that, of course.'

'You leave him to us.'

'I'm certainly not going to stay up here and be a witness. He's just the sort of fellow to take legal action.'

'He'd be far too ashamed. Can't you see the headlines, "Novelist whipped in liner"?'

'I don't suppose he'd care a damn. Fellows like that live on publicity.' Then the general changed his tone. 'All the same,' he added wistfully, 'I wish I was young enough to help, good luck to you. Give it to him good and strong. Only remember: if there's trouble, *I* know nothing about it.'

The girls sang. The youths drank. Presently the mother came to plead. She spoke in yearning tones that reminded Mr Pinfold of his deceased Anglican aunts.

'I can't sleep,' she said. 'You know I can never sleep when you're in this state. My son, I beg you to go to bed. Mr Fosker, how can you lead him into this escapade? Margaret, darling, what are you doing here at this time of night? *Please* go to your cabin, child.'

'It's only a joke, mama.'

'I very much doubt whether Mr Pinfold thinks it a joke.'

'I hate him,' said her son.

'Hate?' said the mother. 'Hate? Why do all you young people *hate* so much? What has come over the world? You were not brought up to *hate*. Why do you hate Mr Pinfold?'

'I have to share a cabin with Fosker. That swine has a cabin to himself.'

'I expect he paid for it.'

'Yes, with the money he cheated Hill out of.'

'He behaved badly to Hill certainly. But he isn't used to country ways. I've not met him, though we have lived so near all these years. I think perhaps he rather looks down on all of us. We aren't so clever as he, nor as rich. But that's no reason to *hate* him.'

At this the son broke into a diatribe in the course of which he and Fosker were left alone. There had been an element of jollity in the pair at the beginning of their demonstration. Now they were possessed by hatred, repeating and elaborating a ferocious, rambling denunciation full of obscenities. The eviction of Hill and responsibility for his suicide were the chief recurring charges but interspersed with them were other accusations. Mr Pinfold, they said, had let his mother die in destitution. He was ashamed of her because she was an illiterate immigrant, had refused to help her or go near her, had let her die alone, uncared for, had not attended her pauper's funeral. Mr Pinfold had shirked in the war. He had used it as an opportunity to change his name and pass himself off as an Englishman, to make friends with people who did not know his origin, to get into Bellamy's Club. Mr Pinfold had in some way been implicated in the theft of a moonstone. He had paid a large sum of money to sit at the Captain's table. Mr Pinfold typified the decline of England, of rural England in particular. He was a reincarnation (Mr Pinfold, not they, drew the analogy) of the 'new men' of the Tudor period who had despoiled the Church and the peasantry. His religious profession was humbug, assumed in order to ingratiate himself with the aristocracy. Mr Pinfold was a sodomite. Mr Pinfold must be chastened and chastised.

The night wore on, the charges became wilder and wider, the threats more bloody. The two young men were like prancing savages working themselves into a frenzy of blood-lust. Mr Pinfold awaited their attack and prepared for it. He made an operational plan. They would come through the door singly. The cabin was not spacious but there was room to swing a stick. He turned out the light and stood by the door. The young men coming suddenly into the dark from the lighted corridor would not know where to lay hands on him. He would fell the first with his blackthorn, then change this weapon for the malacca cane. The second young man no doubt would stumble over his fallen friend. Mr Pinfold would then turn on the light and carefully thrash him. They were far too drunk to be really dangerous. Mr Pinfold was quite confident of the outcome. He awaited them calmly.

The incantations were rising to a climax.

'Now's the time. Ready, Fosker?'

'Ready.'

'In we go then.'

'You first, Fosker.'

Mr Pinfold stood ready. He was glad that Fosker should be the man to be painlessly stunned; the instigator, the man to receive full punishment. There was justice in that order.

Then came anticlimax. 'I can't get in,' said Fosker. 'The bastard has locked the door.'

Mr Pinfold had not locked the door. Moreover Fosker had not tried it. There had been no movement of the handle. Fosker was afraid.

'Go on. What are you waiting for?'

'I tell you he's locked us out.'

'That's torn it.'

Crestfallen, the two returned to the deck.

'We've got to get him. We must get him tonight,' said the one who was not Fosker, but the fire had gone out of him and he added: 'I feel awfully sick suddenly.'

'Better put it off for tonight.'

'I feel frightful. Oh!'

There followed the ghastly sounds of vomiting and then a whimper; the same abject sound that seemed to re-echo through the *Caliban*, the sob of the injured seaman, of the murdered steward.

His mother was there now to comfort him.

'I haven't been to bed, dear. I couldn't leave you like that. I've been waiting and praying for you. You're ready to come now, aren't you?'

'Yes, mother, I'm ready.'

'I love you so. All loving is suffering.'

Silence fell. Mr Pinfold put his weapons away and drew back the shutter. It was dawn. He lay on his bed wide awake, his rage quite abated, calmly considering the events of the night.

There had been no funeral. So much seemed certain. Indeed the whole incident of Captain Steerforth and Goneril and the murdered steward had become insubstantial under the impact of the new assault. Mr Pinfold's orderly, questing mind began to sift the huge volume of charges which had been made against him. Some – that he was Jewish and homosexual, that he had stolen a moonstone and left his mother to die a pauper – were totally preposterous. Others were inconsistent. If, for example, he were a newly arrived immigrant, he could not have been a rowdy undergraduate at Oxford; if he were so anxious to establish himself as a countryman, he would not have slighted his neighbours. The young men in their drunken rage had clearly roared out any abuse that came to mind, but there emerged from the chaotic uproar the basic facts that he was generally disliked on board the *Caliban*, that two at least of his fellow-passengers were possessed by fanatical hate, and that they had some sort of indirect personal acquaintance with him. How else could they have heard, even in its wildly garbled form, of his wife's transactions with Hill (who was well and prosperous when Mr Pinfold last heard of him)? They came from his part of the country. It was not unlikely that Hill, while boasting of his astuteness among his cronies, had told a story of oppression elsewhere. If that was the sort of thing that was being said in the district, Mr Pinfold should correct it. Mr Pinfold had to consider also his comfort during the coming voyage. He required peace of mind in which to work. These dreadful young men were likely, whenever they got drunk, to come caterwauling outside his cabin. On a later occasion, moreover, they might attempt physical assault, might even succeed in it. The result could only be humiliating; it might be painful. The world teemed with journalists. He imagined his wife reading in her morning paper a cable from Aden or Port Soudan describing the *fracas*. Something must be done. He could lay the matter before the Captain, the natural guardian of law in his ship, but with this thought there emerged again from oblivion the matter of the Captain's own culpability. Mr Pinfold was going to have the Captain arrested for murder at the earliest opportunity. Nothing would suit that black heart better than to have the only witness against him involved in a brawl – or silenced in one. A new suspicion took shape. Mr Pinfold had been indiscreet at dinner in revealing his private knowledge. Was it not probable that Captain Steerforth had instigated the whole attack? Where had the young men been drinking after the bar was shut, if not in the Captain's cabin?

Mr Pinfold began to shave. This prosaic operation recalled him to strict reason. The Captain's guilt was not proven. First things first. He must deal with the young men. He studied the passenger-list. There was no Fosker on it. Mr Pinfold himself, when crossing the Atlantic, avoided interviewers by remaining incognito. It seemed unlikely that Fosker would have the same motive. Perhaps the police were after him. The other man was ostensibly respectable; four of a name should be easy to find. But there seemed to be no family of father, mother, son and daughter in that list. Mr Pinfold lathered his face for the second shave. He was puzzled. It was unlikely that so large a party would join the ship at the last moment, after the list had been printed. They did not sound the kind of people given to impetuous dashes abroad – and anyway, such people travelled by air nowadays. And there was that other general travelling with them. Mr Pinfold gazed at his puzzled, soapy face. Then he saw light. Step-father, that was it. He and the mother would bear one name, the children another. Mr Pinfold would keep his eyes and ears open. It should not be difficult to identify them.

Mr Pinfold dressed carefully. He chose a Brigade tie to wear that morning and a cap that matched his tweed suit. He went on deck, where seamen were at work swabbing. They had already cleaned up all traces of the night's disgusting climax. He ascended to the main, promenade deck. It was a morning such as at any other time would have elated him. Even now, with so much to harass him, he was conscious of exhilaration. He stood alone breathing deeply, making light of his annoyances.

Margaret, somewhere quite near, said: 'Look, he's left his cabin. Doesn't he look smart today? Now's our chance to give him our presents. It's much better than giving them to his steward as we meant to. Now we can arrange them ourselves.'

'D'you think he'll like them?' said the other girl.

'He ought to. We've taken enough trouble. They're the best we could possibly get.'

'But Meg, he's so *grand*.'

'It's because he's grand he'll like them. Grand people are always pleased with *little* things. He *must* have his presents this morning. After the silly way the boys behaved last night it will show him *we* weren't in it. At least not in it in the way they were. He'll see that as far as we're concerned it was all fun and love.'

'Suppose he comes in and finds us?'

'You keep *cave*. If he starts going down sing.'

' "When first I saw Mabel"?'

'Of course. *Our* song.'

Mr Pinfold was tempted to trap Margaret. He relished the simple male pleasure, rather rare to him in recent years, of being found attractive, and was curious to see this honey-tongued girl. But she inevitably would lead him to the brother and to Fosker, and he was constrained by honour. These presents, whatever they were, constituted a flag of truce. He could not snatch advantage from the girls' generosity.

Presently Margaret rejoined her friend.

'He hasn't moved.'

'No, he's just stood there all the time. What do you suppose he's thinking about?'

'Those beastly boys, I expect.'

'Do you think he's very upset?'

'He's so brave.'

'Often brave people are the most sensitive.'

'Well it will be all right when he gets back to his cabin and finds our presents.'

Mr Pinfold walked the decks for an hour. No passengers were about.

As the gong sounded for breakfast, Mr Pinfold went below. He stopped first at his cabin to see what Margaret had left for him. All he found was the cup of tea, cold now, which the steward had put there. The bed was made. The place was squared up and ship-shape. There were no presents.

As he left, he met the cabin-steward.

'I say, did a young lady leave anything for me in my cabin?'

'Yes, sir, breakfast now, sir.'

'No. Listen. I think something was left for me here about an hour ago.'

'Yes, sir, gong for breakfast just now.'

'Oh,' said Margaret, 'he hasn't found it.'

'He must *look*.'

'*Look* for it, Gilbert, *look*.'

He searched the little wardrobe. He peered under the bunk. He opened the cupboard over the wash-hand basin. There was nothing there.

'There's nothing there,' said Margaret. 'He can't find it. He can't find anything,' she said on a soft note of despair. 'The sweet brave idiot, he can't find anything.'

So he went down alone to breakfast.

He was the first of the passengers to appear. Mr Pinfold was hungry. He ordered coffee and fish and eggs and fruit. He was about to eat when, Ping; the little, rose-shaded electric lamp which stood on the table before him came into action as a transmitter. The delinquent youths were awake and up on the air again, their vitality unimpaired by the excesses of the night.

'Halloo-loo-loo-loo-loo. Hark-ark-ark-ark-ark,' they holloaed. 'Loo in there. Fetch him out. Yoicks.'

'I fear Fosker is not entirely conversant with sporting parlance,' said the general.

'Hark-ark-ark-ark. Come out, Peinfeld. We know where you are. We've got you.' A whip-crack. 'Ow,' from Fosker, 'look out what you're doing with that hunting crop.'

'Run, Peinfeld, run. We can see you. We're coming for you.'

The steward at that moment was at Mr Pinfold's side serving him with haddock. He seemed unconscious of the cries emanating from the lamp; to him presumably they were all one with the unreasonable variety of knives and forks and the superfluity of inedible foods; all part of the complexity of this remote and rather disgusting western way of life.

Mr Pinfold ate stolidly. The young men resumed the diatribe repeating again in clear, morning voices the garbled accusations of the night before. Interspersed with them was the challenge: 'Come and meet us, Gilbert. You're afraid, Peinfeld. We want to talk to you, Peinfeld. You're hiding, aren't you? You're afraid to come and talk.'

Margaret spoke: 'Oh, Gilbert, what are they doing to you? Where are you? You mustn't let them find you. Come to me. I'll hide you. You never found your presents and now they are after you again. Let *me* look after you, Gilbert. It's me, Mimi. Don't you trust me?'

Mr Pinfold turned to his scrambled eggs. He had forgotten, when he ordered them, that they would not be fresh. Now he beckoned to the steward to remove them.

'Off your feed, Gilbert? You're in a funk, aren't you? Can't eat when you're in a funk, can you? Poor Gilbert, too scared to eat.' They began to give instructions for a place of meeting. '... D. Deck, turn right. Got that? You'll see some lockers. The next bulk-head. We're waiting for you. Better come now and get it over. You've got to meet us some time, you know. We've got you, Gilbert. We've got you. There's no escape. Better get it over...'

Mr Pinfold's patience was exhausted. He must put a stop to this nonsense. Recalling some vague memories of signal procedure in the army, he drew the lamp towards him and spoke into it curtly: 'Pinfold to Hooligans. Rendezvous Main Lounge 0930 hours. Out.'

The lamp was not designed to be moved. His pull disconnected it in some way. The bulb went out and the voices abruptly ceased. At the same moment Glover came in to breakfast. 'Hullo, something gone wrong with the light?'

'I tried to move it. I hope you slept better last night?'

'Like a log. No more disturbances, I hope?'

Mr Pinfold considered whether or not to confide in Glover and decided immediately, no.

'No,' he said, and ordered some cold ham.

The dining-saloon filled. Mr Pinfold exchanged greetings. He went on deck, keeping alert, hoping to spot his persecutors, thinking it possible that Margaret would make herself known to him. But he saw no hooligans; half a dozen healthy girls passed him, some in trousers and duffle coats, some in tweed skirts and sweaters; one might be Margaret but none gave him a sign. At half-past nine he took an arm-chair in a corner of the lounge and waited. He had his blackthorn with him; it was just conceivable that the youths were so frenzied that they might attempt violence even here, in the daylight.

He began to rehearse the coming interview. He was the judge. He had summoned these men to appear before him. Something like a regimental orderly room, he thought, would be the proper atmosphere. He was the commanding officer hearing a charge of brawling. His powers of punishment were meagre. He would admonish them severely, and threaten them with civil penalties.

He would remind them that they were subject to British law in the *Caliban* just as much as on land; that defamation of character and physical assault were grave crimes which would prejudice their whole future careers. He would 'throw the whole book' at them. He would explain icily that he was entirely indifferent to their good or bad opinion; that he regarded their friendship and their enmity as equally impertinent. But he would also hear what they had to say for themselves. A good officer knows the enormous ills that can arise from men brooding on imaginary grudges. These defaulters were clearly suffering from a number of delusions about himself. It was better that they should get it off their chests, hear the truth, and then shut up for the rest of the voyage. Moreover if, as seemed certain, these delusions derived from rumours which were in circulation among Mr Pinfold's neighbours, he must plainly investigate and scotch them.

He had the lounge to himself. The rest of the passengers were ranged along the deck in their chairs and rugs. The unvarying hum of marine mechanical-life was the only sound. The clock over the little bandstand read a quarter to ten. Mr Pinfold decided to give them till ten; then he would go to the wireless office and inform his wife of his recovery. It was beneath his dignity to attend on these dreadful young men.

Some similar point of pride seemed to influence them. Above the hum he presently heard them discussing him. The voices came from the panelling near his head. First in his cabin, then in the dining-saloon, now here, the surviving strands of wartime intercommunication were fitfully active. The whole wiring of the ship was in need of a thorough overhaul, Mr Pinfold thought; for all he knew there might be a danger of fire.

'We'll talk to Peinfeld when it suits us and not a moment before.'

'Who'll do the talking?'

'I will, of course.'

'Do you know what you're going to say?'

'Of course.'

'Not really much point in my coming at all, is there?'

'I may need you as a witness.'

'All right, come on then. Let's see him now.'

'When it suits *me*, Fosker, not before.'

'What are we waiting for?'

'To let him get into a thorough funk. Remember at school one was always kept waiting for a beating? Just to make it taste sweeter? Well, Peinfeld can wait for *his* beating.'

'He's scared stiff.'

'He's practically blubbing now.'

At ten o'clock Mr Pinfold took out his watch, verified the time shown on the clock, and rose from the corner. 'He's going away.' 'He's running away.' 'Funk' came faintly from the fumed oak panelling. Mr Pinfold climbed to the wireless office on the boat-deck, composed a message and handed it in: *Pinfold. Lychpole. Entirely cured. All love. Gilbert.*

'Is that address enough?' asked the clerk.

'Yes. There's only one telegraph office called Lychpole in the country.'

He walked the decks, thought his blackthorn superfluous and returned to his cabin where the B.B.C. was loudly in possession. '...in the studio Jimmy Lance, who is well known to all listeners, and Miss June Cumberleigh, who is new to listeners. Jimmy is going to let us see what is probably a unique collection. He has kept every letter he ever received. That's so, isn't it, Jimmy?'

'Well, not letters from the Income Tax Collector.'

'Ha. Ha.'

'Ha. Ha.'

A great burst of unrestrained laughter from the unseen audience.

'No, none of us like to be reminded of that kind of letter, Jimmy, do we? Ha ha. But I think in your time you have had letters from a great many celebrities?'

'And from some pretty dim people, too.'

'Ha. Ha.'

'Ha. Ha. Ha.'

'Well, June is going to take letters at random out of your file and read them. Ready, June? Right. The first letter is from –'

Mr Pinfold knew June Cumberleigh and liked her. She was a wholly respectable, clever, funny-faced girl who had got drawn into Bohemia through her friendship with James Lance. It was not her natural voice that she now used. Through some mechanical distortion she spoke in almost identical tones to Goneril's.

'Gilbert Pinfold,' she said.

'And do you count him among the celebrities or the dim people, Jimmy?'

'A celebrity.'

'Do you?' said June. 'I think he's a dreadfully dim little man.'

'Well, what's the dim little man got to say?'

'It is so badly written I can't read it.'

Enormous amusement in the audience.

'Try another.'

'Who is it this time?'

'Why. This is *too* much. Gilbert Pinfold again.'

'Ha, ha, ha, ha, ha.'

Mr Pinfold left his cabin, slamming the door on this deplorable entertainment. James, he knew, did a lot of broadcasting. He was a poet and artist by nature who had let himself become popularized; but this exhibition was a bit thick, even for him. And what was June doing? She must have lost all sense of decency.

Mr Pinfold walked the decks. He was still troubled by the un-solved problem of the hooligans. Something would have to be done about them. But he felt reassured about Captain Steerforth. Now that it was apparent that many of the sounds in his cabin emanated from Broadcasting House, he became certain that what he had overhead was part of a play. The similarity of June's voice and Goneril's seemed to confirm it. He had been an ass to suppose Captain Steerforth a murderer; it was part of the confusion of mind caused by Dr Drake's pills. And if Captain Steerforth were innocent, then he was a potential, a natural ally against his enemies.

Thus comforted, Mr Pinfold returned to his listening post in the corner of the lounge. Father and son were in conference.

'Fosker's wet.'

'Yes. I've never thought anything of him.'

'I'm leaving him out of this business from now on.'

'Very wise. But you've got to go through with it yourself, you know. You didn't come very creditably out of last night's affair. I've no great objection to your knocking the fellow about a bit if he deserves it. Anyway you've threatened him and you've got to do something about it. You can't just drop the matter at this stage. But you want to go about it in the right way. You're up against something rather more dangerous than you realize.'

'Dangerous? That cowardly, common little communist pansy —'

'Yes, yes. I know how you feel. But I've seen a bit more of the world than you have, my boy. I think I'd better put you up to a few wrinkles. In the first place Pinfold is utterly unscrupulous. He has no gentlemanly instincts. He's quite capable of taking you to the courts. Have you any proof of your charges?'

'Everyone knows they're true.'

'That may be but it won't mean a thing in a court of law unless you can prove it. You need evidence so strong that Pinfold daren't sue you. And, so far, you haven't got it. Another thing, Pinfold is extremely rich. I daresay for example he owns a controlling share in this shipping line. The long-nosed, curly-headed gentlemen don't pay taxes like us poor Christians, you know. Pinfold has money salted away in half a dozen countries. He has friends everywhere.'

'*Friends?*'

'Well, no, not friends as *we* understand them. But he has influence – with politicians, with the police. You've lived in a small world, my boy. You have no conception of the ramifications of power of a man like Pinfold in the modern age. He's attractive to women – homosexuals always are. Margaret is distinctly taken with him. Even your mother doesn't really dislike him. We've got to work cautiously and build up a party against him. I'll send off a few radiograms. There are one or two people I know who, I think, may be able to give us some *facts* about Pinfold. It's facts we need. We've got to make out an absolutely water-tight case. Till then, lie low.'

'You don't think I ought to beat him up?'

'Well, I wouldn't go so far as to say that. If you find him alone, you might have a smack at him. I know what I should have done myself at your age. But I'm old now and wise and my advice is lie low, work under cover. Then in a day or two we may have something to surprise our celebrated fellow-passenger...'

When noon was sounded Mr Pinfold went aft and ordered himself a cocktail. There was the usual jollity over the sweepstake. He looked at the flag on the chart. The *Caliban* had rounded Cape St Vincent and was well on the way to Gibraltar. She should pass the straits that night into the Mediterranean. When he went down to luncheon he was in a hopeful mood. The hooligans had fallen out and their rage had been tempered. The Mediterranean had always welcomed Mr Pinfold in the past. His annoyance would be over, he believed, once he was in those hallowed waters.

In the dining-saloon he noticed that the dark man who had sat alone was now at a table with Mrs Cockson and Mrs Benson. In a curious way that too seemed a good omen.

THE INTERNATIONAL INCIDENT

IT WAS THE conversation of the two generals, overheard as he lay in his cabin after luncheon, which first made Mr Pinfold aware of the international crisis which had been developing while he lay ill. There had been no hint of it in the newspapers he had listlessly scanned before embarkation; or, if there had been, he had not, in his confused state, appreciated its importance. Now, it appeared, there was a first-class row about the possession of Gibraltar. Some days ago the Spaniards had laid formal, peremptory claim to the fortress and were now exercising the very dubious right of stopping and searching ships passing through the straits in what they defined as their territorial waters. During luncheon the *Caliban* had hove-to and Spanish officials had come on board. They were demanding that the ship put into Algeciras for an examination of cargo and passengers.

The two generals were incensed against General Franco and made free use of 'tin-pot dictator', 'twopenny-halfpenny Hitler', 'dago', 'priest-ridden puppet', and similar opprobrious epithets. They also spoke contemptuously of the British government who were prepared to 'truckle' to him.

'It's nothing short of a blockade. If I were in command I'd call their bluff, go full steam ahead and tell them to shoot and be damned.'

'That would be an act of war, of course.'

'Serve 'em right. We haven't sunk so low that we can't lick the Spaniards, I hope.'

'It's all this UNO.'

'And the Americans.'

'Anyway, this is one thing that can't be blamed on Russia.'

'It means the end of NATO.'

'Good riddance.'

'The Captain has to take his orders from home, I suppose.'

'That's the trouble. He can't get any orders.'

Captain Steerforth was now fully restored to Mr Pinfold's confidence. He saw him as a simple sailor obliged to make a momentous decision, not only for the safety of his own vessel but for the peace of the world. Throughout that long afternoon Mr Pinfold followed the frantic attempts of the signalmen to get into touch with the shipping company, the Foreign Office, the Governor of Gibraltar, the Mediterranean fleet. All were without avail. Captain Steerforth stood quite alone as the representative of international justice and British prestige. Mr Pinfold thought of Jenkins's ear and the Private of the Buffs. Captain Steerforth was a good man forced into an importance quite beyond his capabilities. Mr Pinfold wished he could stand beside him on the bridge, exhort him to defiance, run the ship under the Spanish guns into the wide, free inland sea where all the antique heroes of history and legend had sailed to glory.

As factions resolve in common danger, Mr Pinfold forgot the enmity of the young hooligans. All on board the *Caliban* were comrades-in-arms against foreign aggression.

The Spanish officials were polite enough. Mr Pinfold could hear them talking in the Captain's cabin. In excellent English they explained how deeply repugnant they, personally, found the orders they had to carry out. It was a question of politics, they said. No doubt the matter would be adjusted satisfactorily at a congress. Meanwhile they could only obey. They spoke of some enormous indemnity which, if it were forthcoming from London, would immediately ensure the *Caliban*'s free passage. A time was mentioned, midnight, after which, if no satisfactory arrangements were made, the *Caliban* would be taken under escort to Algeciras.

'Piracy,' said Captain Steerforth, 'blackmail.'

'We cannot allow such language about the Head of the State.'

'Then you can bloody well get off my bridge,' said the Captain. They withdrew but nothing was settled by the tiff. They remained on board and the ship lay motionless.

Towards evening Mr Pinfold went on deck. There was no sign of land, nor of the Spanish ship which had brought the officials and, presumably, was lying off somewhere below the horizon. Mr Pinfold leaned over the rail and looked down at the flowing sea. The sun was dead astern of them sinking low over the water. Had he not known better, he would have supposed they were still steaming forward, so swiftly and steadily ran the current. He recalled that he had once been taught that through the Suez Canal the Indian Ocean emptied itself into the Atlantic. He thought of the multitudinous waters that supplied the Mediterranean, the ice-flows of the Black Sea that raced past Constantinople and Troy; the great rivers of history, the Nile, the Euphrates, the Danube, the Rhône. They it was that broke across the bows and left a foaming wake.

The passengers seemed quite unaware of the doom which threatened the ship. Fresh from their siestas they sat about that afternoon just as they had sat before, reading and talking and knitting. There was the same little group on the sports-deck. Mr Pinfold met Glover.

'Did you see the Spaniards come on board?' he asked.

'Spaniards? Come on board? How could they? When?'

'They're causing a lot of trouble.'

'I'm awfully sorry,' said Glover. 'I simply don't know what you're talking about.'

'You will,' said Mr Pinfold. 'Soon enough, I fear.'

Glover looked at him with the keen, perplexed air which he often assumed now when Mr Pinfold spoke to him.

'There aren't any Spaniards on board that I know of.'

It was not Mr Pinfold's duty to spread alarm and despondency or explain his unique sources of information. The Captain plainly wanted the secret kept as long as possible.

'I daresay I'm mistaken,' said Mr Pinfold loyally.

'There are Burmese and the Norwegian couple at our table. They're the only foreigners I've seen.'

'Yes. A misunderstanding no doubt.'

Glover went to the space in the bows where he swung his club. He swung it methodically, with concentration, without a thought of Spaniards.

Mr Pinfold withdrew to his listening post in the corner of the lounge but nothing was to be heard there except the tapping of morse as the signalmen sent out their calls for help. One of them said: 'Nothing coming in at all. I don't believe our signals are going out.'

'It's that new device,' said his mate. 'I heard something had been invented to create wireless silence. It's not been tried before, as far as I know. It was developed too late to use in the war. Both sides were at work on it but it was still in the experimental stage in 1945.'

'More effective than jamming.'

'Different principle altogether. They can only do it at short range so far. In a year or two it'll develop so that they can isolate whole countries.'

'Where will our jobs be then?'

'Oh, someone'll find a counter-system. They always do.'

'Anyway all we can do now is keep on trying.'

The tapping recommenced. Mr Pinfold went to the bar and ordered himself a glass of gin and bitters. The English steward came in from the deck, tray in hand, and went to the serving hatch.

'Those Spanish bastards are asking for whisky,' he said.

'I'll not serve them,' said the man who handled the bottles.

'Captain's order,' said the steward.

'What's come over the old man? It isn't like him to take a thing like this lying down.'

'He's got a plan. Trust him. Now give me those four whiskies and I hope it poisons them.'

Mr Pinfold finished his drink and returned to his listening post. He was curious to know more of the Captain's plan. He had no sooner settled in his chair and attuned his ear to the panelling than he heard the Captain; he was in his cabin addressing the officers.

'. . . all question of international law and convention apart,' he was saying, 'there is a particular reason why we cannot allow this ship to be searched. You all know we have an extra man on board. He's not a passenger. He's not one of the crew. He doesn't appear on any list. He's got no ticket or papers. I don't even know his name myself. I daresay you've noticed him sitting alone in the dining-saloon. All I've been told is that he's very important indeed to H.M.G. He's on a special mission. That's why he's travelling with us instead of on one of the routes that are watched. It's him, of course, that the Spaniards are after. All this talk about territorial waters and right of search is pure bluff. We've got to see that that man gets through.'

'How are you going to manage that, skipper?'

'I don't know yet. But I've got an idea. I think I shall have to take the passengers into my confidence – not all of them, of course, and not fully into my confidence. But I'm going to collect half a dozen of the more responsible men and put them in the picture – into a bit of the picture anyway. I'll ask them up here, casually, after dinner. With their help the plan *may* work.'

The generals received their invitation early and were not deceived by its casual form. They were discussing it while Mr Pinfold dressed for dinner.

'It looks as though he's decided to put up a fight.'

'We'll all stand by him.'

'Can we trust those Burmese?'

'That's a question to raise at the meeting tonight.'

'Wouldn't trust 'em myself. Yellow-bellies.'

'The Norwegians?'

'They seem sound enough but this is a British affair.'

'Always happier on our own, eh?'

It did not occur to Mr Pinfold that he might be omitted from the Captain's *cadre*. But no invitation reached him although in various other parts of the ship he heard confidential messages ... 'the Captain's compliments and he would be grateful if you could find it convenient to come to his cabin for a few minutes after dinner ... '

At table Captain Steerforth carried his anxieties with splendid composure. Mrs Scarfield actually asked him: 'When do we go through the straits?' and he replied without any perceptible nuance: 'Early tomorrow morning.'

'It ought to get warmer then?'

'Not at this time of year,' he answered nonchalantly. 'You must wait for the Red Sea before you go into whites.'

During their brief acquaintance Mr Pinfold had regarded this man with sharply varying emotions. Unquestionable admiration filled him when, at the end of dinner, Mrs Scarfield asked: 'Are you joining us for a rubber?' and he replied: 'Not this evening, I'm afraid. I've one or two things to see to,' but though Mr Pinfold hung back so that he left the dining-saloon at the Captain's side, giving him the chance to invite him to the conference, they parted at the head of the stair without the word being said. Rather nonplussed Mr Pinfold hesitated, then decided to go to his cabin. It was essential that he should be easily found when he was wanted.

Soon it was apparent that he was not wanted at all. Captain Steerforth had his party promptly assembled and he began by giving them a résumé of the situation as Mr Pinfold already understood it. He said nothing of the secret agent. He merely explained that he had been unable to obtain authorization from his company to pay the preposterous sum demanded. The alternative offered by the Spaniards was that he should put into Algeciras until the matter had been settled between Madrid and London. That, he said, would be a betrayal of every standard of British seamanship. The *Caliban* would not strike her flag. There was a burst of restrained, husky, emotional, male applause. He explained his plan: at midnight the Spanish ship would come alongside. The officials now on board would transship to her to report the results of their demand. They intended to take with them under arrest himself and a party of hostages and to put an officer of their own on his bridge to sail her into the Spanish port. It was in the dark, on the gangway, that the resistance would disclose itself. The English would overpower the Spaniards, throw them back into their ship – 'and if one or two go into the drink in the process, so much the better' – and the *Caliban* would then make full steam ahead. 'I don't think when it comes to the point, they'll open fire. Anyway their gunnery is pretty moderate and I consider it's a risk we have to take. You are all agreed?'

'Agreed. Agreed. Agreed.'

'I knew I could trust you,' said the Captain. 'You're all men who've seen service. I am proud to have you under my command. The yellow-bellies will be locked in their cabins.'

'How about Pinfold?' asked one of the generals. 'Shouldn't he be here?'

'There is a rôle assigned to Captain Pinfold. I don't think I need to go into that at the moment.'

'Has he received his orders?'

'Not yet,' said Captain Steerforth. 'We have some hours before us. I suggest, gentlemen, that you go about the ship in the normal way, turn in early, and rendezvous here at 11.45. Midnight is zero hour. Perhaps, general, you will remain behind for a few minutes. For the present, good night, gentlemen.'

The meeting broke up. Presently only the general remained with the first and second officers in the Captain's cabin.

'Well,' said Captain Steerforth, 'how did that sound?'

'Pretty thin, skipper, if you ask me,' said the first officer.

'I take it,' said the general, 'that what we have just heard was merely the cover-plan?'

'Precisely. I could hardly hope to deceive an old campaigner like you. I am sorry not to be able to take your companions into my confidence, but in the interest of security I have had to limit those in the know to an absolute minimum. The rôle of the committee who have just left us is to create sufficient diversion to enable us to carry out the real purpose of the operation. That, of course, is to prevent a certain person falling into the hands of the enemy.'

'Pinfold?'

'No, no, quite the contrary. Captain Pinfold, I fear, has to be written off. The Spaniards will not let us pass until they think they have their man. It has not been an easy decision, I assure you. I am responsible for the safety of all my passsengers, but at a time like this sacrifices have to be accepted. The plan briefly is this. Captain Pinfold is to impersonate the agent. He will be provided with papers identifying him. The Spaniards will take him ashore and the ship will sail on unmolested.'

There was a pause while this proposition was considered. The first officer at length spoke: 'It might work, skipper.'

'It *must* work.'

'What do you suppose will happen to him?'

'Can't say. I suppose they'll hold him under arrest while they investigate. They won't let him communicate with our embassy, of course. When they find out their mistake, if they ever do, they'll be in rather a jam. They may let him out or they may find it more convenient just to let him disappear.'

'I see.'

It was the general who voiced the thought uppermost in Mr Pinfold's mind. 'Why Pinfold?' he asked.

'It was a painful choice,' said Captain Steerforth, 'but not a difficult one. He is the obvious man, really. No one else on board would take them in for a moment. He looks like a secret agent. I think he was one during the war. He's a sick man and therefore expendable. And, of course, he's a Roman Catholic. That ought to make things a little easier for him in Spain.'

'Yes,' said the general, 'yes. I see all that. But all the same I think it's pretty sporting of him to agree. In his place I must own I'd think twice before taking it on.'

'Oh, *he* doesn't know anything about it.'

'The devil he doesn't?'

'No, that would be quite fatal to security. Besides he might *not* agree. He has a wife, you know, and a large family. You can't really blame a man who thinks of domestic responsibilities before volunteering for hazardous service. No, Captain Pinfold must be kept quite in the dark. That's the reason for the counter-plan, the diversion. There's got to be a schemozzle on the gangway so that Captain Pinfold can be pushed into the corvette. You, number one, will be responsible for hauling him out of his cabin and planting the papers on him.'

'Aye, aye, sir.'

'That boy of mine will laugh,' said the general. 'He took against Pinfold from the start. Now he hears he's deserted to the enemy...'

The voices ceased. For a long time Mr Pinfold sat paralysed with horror and rage. When at length he looked at his watch he found that it was nearly half-past nine. Then he took off his evening clothes and put on his tweeds. Whatever outrage the night brought forth should find him suitably dressed. He pocketed his passport and his traveller's cheques. Then, blackthorn in hand, he sat down again and began patiently and painfully as he had learned in the army, to 'appreciate the situation'. He was alone, without hope of reinforcement. His sole advantage was that he knew, and they did not know he knew, their plan of action. He examined the Captain's plan in the light of the quite considerable experience he had acquired in small-scale night operations and he found it derisory. The result of a scuffle in the dark on a gangway was quite unpredictable but he was confident that, forewarned, he could easily evade or repulse any attempt to put him into the corvette against his will. Even if they succeeded and the *Caliban* attempted to sail away, the corvette, of course, would open fire and, of course, would sink or disable her long before the Spaniards began examining the forged papers that were to be planted on him.

And here Mr Pinfold experienced scruples. He was not what is generally meant by the appellation a 'philanthropic' man; he totally lacked what was now called a 'social conscience'. But apart from his love of family and friends he had a certain basic kindliness to those who refrained from active annoyance. And in an old-fashioned way he was patriotic. These sentiments sometimes did service for what are generally regarded as the higher loyalties and affections. This was such an occasion. He rather liked Mrs Scarfield, Mrs Cockson, Mrs Benson, Glover and all those simple, chatting, knitting, dozing passengers. For the unseen, enigmatic Margaret he felt tender curiosity. It would be a pity for all these to be precipitated into a watery bier by the ineptitude of Captain Steerforth. For himself he had little concern, but he knew that his disappearance, and possible disgrace, would grieve his wife and family. It was intolerable that this booby Captain should handle so many lives so clumsily. But there was also the question of the secret agent. If this man, as seemed likely, was really of vital importance to his country, he must be protected. Mr Pinfold felt responsible for his protection. He had been chosen as victim. That doom was inescapable. But he would go to the sacrifice a garlanded hero. He would not be tricked into it.

No precise tactical plan could be made. Whatever his action, it would be improvised. But the intention was plain. He would, if necessary, consent to impersonate the agent, but Captain Steerforth and his cronies must understand that he went voluntarily as a man of honour and Mrs Pinfold must be fully informed of the circumstances. That established, he would consent to his arrest.

As he pondered all this, he was barely conscious of the voices that came to him. He waited.

At a quarter to twelve there was a hail from the bridge answered from the sea in Spanish. The corvette was coming alongside and at once the ship came to life with a multitude of voices. This, Mr Pinfold decided, was his moment to act. He must deliver his terms to the Captain before the Spaniards came on board. Gripping his blackthorn he left the cabin.

Immediately his communications were cut. The lighted corridor was empty and completely silent. He strode down it to the stairway, mounted to the main deck. No one was about. There was no ship near or anywhere in sight; not a light anywhere on the dark horizon; not a sound from the bridge; only the rush and slap of the waves along the ship's side, and the keen sea wind. Mr Pinfold stood confounded, the only troubled thing in a world at peace.

He had been dauntless a minute before in the face of his enemies. Now he was struck with real fear, something totally different from the superficial alarms he had once or twice known in moments of danger, something he had quite often read about and dismissed as over-writing. He was possessed from outside himself with atavistic panic. 'O let me not be mad, not mad, sweet heaven,' he cried.

And in that moment of agony there broke not far from him in the darkness peal upon rising peal of mocking laughter – Goneril's. It was not an emollient sound. It was devoid of mirth, an obscene cacophony of pure hatred. But it fell on Mr Pinfold's ears at that moment like a nursery lullaby.

'A hoax,' he said to himself.

It was all a hoax on the part of the hooligans. He understood all. They had learned the secret of the defective wiring in his cabin. Somehow they had devised a means of controlling it, somehow they had staged this whole charade to tease him. It was spiteful and offensive, no doubt; it must not happen again. But Mr Pinfold felt nothing but gratitude in his discovery. He might be unpopular; he might be ridiculous; but he was not mad.

He returned to his cabin. He had been awake now for thirty or forty hours. He lay down at once in his clothes and fell into a deep, natural sleep. He lay motionless and unconscious for six hours.

When he next went on deck the sun was up, directly over the bows. Square on the port beam rose the unmistakable peak of the Rock. The *Caliban* was steaming into the calm Mediterranean.

THE HUMAN TOUCH

WHILE MR PINFOLD was shaving, he heard Margaret say: 'It was an absolutely beastly joke and I'm glad it fell flat.'

'It came off very nicely,' said her brother. 'Old Peinfeld was jibbering with funk.'

'He wasn't – and he isn't called Peinfeld. He was a hero. When I saw him standing there alone on deck I thought of Nelson.'

'He was drunk.'

'He says it's not drink, dear,' said their mother, gently uncommitted to either side. 'He *says* it's some medicine he has to take.'

'Medicine from a brandy bottle.'

'I know you're wrong,' said Margaret. 'You see it just happens *I know* what he's thinking, and you don't.'

Then Goneril's steely voice cut in: '*I* can tell you what he was doing on deck. He was screwing up his courage to jump overboard. He longs to kill himself, don't you, Gilbert. All right, I know you're listening down there. You can hear me, can't you, Gilbert? You wish you were dead, don't you, Gilbert? And a very good idea, too. Why don't you do it, Gilbert? Why not? Perfectly easy. It would save us all – you too, Gilbert – a great deal of trouble.'

'Beast,' said Margaret and broke into weeping.

'Oh, God,' said her brother, 'now you've turned on the water-works again.'

Mr Pinfold was fortified by his six hours' sleep. He went above, leaving the nagging voices of the cabin for the silent and empty decks for an hour. The Rock had dropped below the horizon and there was no land in sight. The sea might have been any sea by the look of it, but he knew it was the Mediterranean, that splendid enclosure which held all the world's history and half the happiest memories of his own life; of work and rest and battle, of aesthetic adventure and of young love.

After breakfast he took a book to the lounge, not to his listening post in the panelled corner, but to an isolated chair in the centre, and read undisturbed. He must get out of that haunted cabin, he thought; but not yet; later, in his own time.

Presently he rose and began once more to walk the decks. They were thronged now. All the passengers seemed to be there, occupied as before in reading, knitting, dozing or strolling like himself, but that morning he found a kind of paschal novelty in the scene and rejoiced in it until he was rudely disturbed in his benevolence.

The passengers, too, seemed aware of change. They must all at one time or another in the last few days have caught sight of Mr Pinfold. Now, however, it was as though he were a noteworthy, unaccompanied female, newly appearing in the evening promenade of some stagnant South American town. He had been witness of such an event on many a dusty plaza; he had seen the sickly faces of the men brighten, their lassitude take sudden life; he had observed the little flourishes of seedy dandyism; he had heard the jungle whistles and, without fully understanding them, the frank, anatomical appraisals; had seen the sly following and pinching of the unwary tourist. In just that way Mr Pinfold, wherever he went that day, found himself to be such a cynosure; everyone was talking about him, loudly and unashamedly, but not in his praise.

'That's Gilbert Pinfold, the writer.'

'That common little man? It can't be.'

'Have you read his books? He has a very *peculiar* sense of humour, you know.'

'He is very peculiar altogether. His hair is very long.'

'He's wearing lipstick.'

'He's painted up to the eyes.'

'But he's so shabby. I thought people like that were always smart.'

'There are different types of homosexual, you know. What are called "poufs" and "nancies" – that is the dressy kind. Then there are the others they call "butch". I read a book about it. Pinfold is a "butch".'

That was the first conversation Mr Pinfold overheard. He stopped, turned and tried to stare out of countenance the little group of middle-aged women who were speaking. One of them smiled at him and then, turning, said: 'I believe he's trying to get to know us.'

'How disgusting.'

Mr Pinfold walked on but wherever he went he was the topic.

'. . . Lord of the Manor of Lychpole.'

'Anyone can be that. It's often a title that goes with some tumble-down farmhouse these days.'

'Oh, Pinfold lives in great style I can tell you. Footmen in livery.'

'I can guess what he does with the footmen.'

'Not any more. He's been impotent for years, you know. That's why he's always thinking of death.'

'Is he always thinking of death?'

'Yes. He'll commit suicide one of these days, you'll see.'

'I thought he was a Catholic. They aren't allowed to commit suicide, are they?'

'That wouldn't stop Pinfold. He doesn't really *believe* in his religion, you know. He just pretends to because he thinks it aristocratic. It goes with being Lord of the Manor.'

'There's only one Lychpole in the world, he told the wireless man.'

'Only one Lychpole and Pinfold is its Lord . . .'

'. . . There he is, drunk again.'

'He looks ghastly.'

'A dying man, if ever I saw one.'

'Why doesn't he kill himself?'

'Give him time. He's doing his best. Drink and drugs. He daren't go to a doctor, of course, for fear he'd be put in a home.'

'Best place for him, I should have thought.'

'Best place for him would be over the side.'

'Rather a nuisance for poor Captain Steerforth.'

'It's a great nuisance for Captain Steerforth having him on board.'

'And at his own table.'

'That's being taken care of. Haven't you heard? There's going to be a petition.'

'. . . Yes, I've signed. Everyone has, I believe.'

'Except those actually at the table. The Scarfields wouldn't, or Glover.'

'I see it might be a little awkward for them.'

'It's a very well-worded petition.'

'Yes. The general did that. It makes no specific accusation, you see, that might be libellous. Simply: *"We the undersigned, for reasons which we are prepared to state in confidence, consider it to be an insult to us, as passengers in the* Caliban, *that Mr Gilbert Pinfold should sit at the Captain's table, a position of honour for which he is notoriously unsuitable."* That's very neatly put.'

'. . . the Captain ought to lock him up. He has full authority.'

'But he hasn't actually *done* anything yet, on board.'

This was a pair of genial business men with whom and the Scarfields Mr Pinfold had spent half an hour one evening.

'For his own protection. It was a very near thing the other night that those boys didn't beat him up.'

'They were drunk.'

'They may get drunk again. It would be most unpleasant for everyone if there was a police court case.'

'Couldn't something be put in our petition about that?'

'It was discussed. The generals thought it could best be left to the interview. The Captain is bound to ask them to give their reasons.'

'Not in writing.'

'Exactly. They don't suggest putting him in the cell. Simply confining him to his cabin.'

'He probably has certain legal rights, having paid his fare, to his cabin and his meals.'

'But *not* to his meals at the Captain's table.'

'There you have the crux.'

'. . . No,' the Norwegian was saying, 'I did not sign anything. It is a British matter. All I know is that he is a fascist. I have heard him speak ill of democracy. We had a few such men in the time of Quisling. We knew what to do with them. But I will not mix in these British affairs.'

'I've got a photograph of him in a black shirt taken at one of those Albert Hall meetings before the war.'

'That might be useful.'

'He was up to his eyes in it. He'd have been locked up under 18B but he escaped by joining the army.'

'He did pretty badly there, I suppose?'

'*Very* badly. There was a scandal in Cairo that had to be hushed up when his brigade-major shot himself.'

'Blackmail?'

'The next best thing.'

'I see he's wearing the Guards tie.'

'He wears any kind of tie – old Etonian usually.'

'*Was* he ever at Eton?'

'He says he was,' said Glover.

'Don't you believe it. Board-school through and through.'

'Or at Oxford?'

'No, no. His whole account of his early life is a lie. No one had ever heard of him until a year or two ago. He's one of a lot of nasty people who crept into prominence during the war . . .'

'. . . I don't say he's an actual card-carrying member of the communist party, but he's certainly mixed up with them.'

'Most Jews are.'

'Exactly. And those "missing diplomats". They were friends of his.'

'He doesn't know enough to make it worth the Russians' while to take him to Moscow.'

'Even the Russians wouldn't want Pinfold.'

The most curious encounter of that morning was with Mrs Cockson and Mrs Benson. They were sitting as usual on the veranda of the deck-bar, each with her glass, and they were talking French with what seemed to Mr Pinfold, who spoke the language clumsily, pure accent and idiom. Mrs Cockson said: 'Ce Monsieur

Pinfold essaye toujours de pénétrer chez moi, et il a essayé de se faire présenter à moi par plusieurs de mes amis. Naturellement j'ai refusé.'

'Connaissez-vous un seul de ses amis? Il me semble qu'il a des relations très ordinaires.'

'On peut toujours se tromper dans le premier temps sur une relation étrangère. On a fini par s'apercevoir à Paris qu'il n'est pas de notre société ...'

It was a put-up job, Mr Pinfold decided. People did not normally behave in this way.

When Mr Pinfold first joined Bellamy's there was an old earl who had sat alone all day and every day in the corner of the stairs wearing an odd, hard hat and talking loudly to himself. He had one theme, the passing procession of his fellow-members. Sometimes he dozed, but in his long waking hours he maintained a running commentary – 'That fellow's chin is too big; dreadful-looking fellow. Never saw him before. Who let him in? ... Pick your feet up, you. Wearing the carpets out ... Dreadfully fat young Crambo's getting. Don't eat, don't drink, it's just he's hard up. Nothing fattens a man like getting hard up ... Poor old Nailsworth, his mother was a whore, so's his wife. They say his daughter's going the same way ...' and so on.

In the broad tolerance of Bellamy's this eccentric had been accepted quite fondly. He was dead many years now. It was not conceivable, Mr Pinfold thought, that all the passengers in the *Caliban* should suddenly have become similarly afflicted. This chatter was designed to be overheard. It was a put-up job. It was in fact the generals' subtle plan, substituted for the adolescent violence of their young.

Twenty-five years ago or more Mr Pinfold, who was in love with one of them, used to frequent a house full of bright, cruel girls who spoke their own thieves' slang and played their own games. One of these games was a trick from the schoolroom polished for drawing-room use. When a stranger came among them, they would all – if the mood took them – put out their tongues at him or her; all, that is to say, except those in his immediate line of sight. As he turned his head, one group of tongues popped in, another popped out. Those girls were adept in dialogue. They had rigid self-control. They never giggled. Those who spoke to the stranger assumed an unnatural sweetness. The aim was to make him catch another with her tongue out. It was a comic performance – the turning head, the flickering, crimson stabs, the tender smiles turning to sudden grimaces, the artificiality of the conversation which soon engendered an unidenti-fiable discomfort in the most insensitive visitor, made him feel that somehow he was making a fool of himself, made him look at his trouser buttons, at his face in the glass to see whether there was something ridiculous in his appearance.

Some sort of game as this, enormously coarsened, must, Mr Pinfold supposed, have been devised by the passengers in the *Caliban* for their amusement and his discomfort. Well, he was not going to give them the satisfaction of taking notice of it. He no longer glanced to see who was speaking.

'... His mother sold her few little pieces of jewellery, you know, to pay his debts...'

'... Were his books ever any good?'

'Never *good*. His earlier ones weren't quite as bad as his latest. He's written out.'

'He's tried every literary trick. He's finished now and he knows it.'

'I suppose he's made a lot of money?'

'Not as much as he pretends. And he's spent every penny. His debts are enormous.'

'And of course they'll catch him for income-tax soon.'

'Oh, yes. He's been putting in false returns for years. They're investigating him now. They don't hurry. They always get their man in the end.'

'They'll get Pinfold.'

'He'll have to sell Lychpole.'

'His children will go to the board-school.'

'Just as he did himself.'

'No more champagne for Pinfold.'

'No more cigars.'

'I suppose his wife will leave him?'

'Naturally. No home for her. Her family will take her in.'

'But not Pinfold.'

'No. Not Pinfold . . .'

Mr Pinfold would not give ground. There must be no appearance of defeat. But in his own time, when he had sauntered long enough, he retired to his cabin.

'Gilbert,' said Margaret. 'Gilbert. Why don't you speak to me? You passed quite close to me on deck and you never looked at me. *I* haven't offended you, have I? You know it isn't me who's saying all these beastly things, don't you? Answer me, Gilbert. I can hear you.'

So Mr Pinfold, not uttering the words but pronouncing them in his mind, said: 'Where are you? I don't even know you by sight. Why don't we meet, now? Come and have a cocktail with me.'

'Oh, Gilbert, darling, you know that's not possible. The *Rules*.'

'What rules? Whose? Do you mean your father won't let you?'

'No, Gilbert, not *his* rules, *the* Rules. Don't you understand? It's against *the Rules* for us to meet. I can talk to you now and then but we must never meet.'

'What do you look like?'

'I mustn't tell you that. You must find out for yourself. That's one of the Rules.'

'You talk as though we were playing some kind of game.'

'That's all we are doing – playing a kind of game. I must go now. But there's one thing I'd like to say.'

'Well?'

'You won't be offended?'

'I don't expect so.'

'Are you sure, darling?'

'What is it?'

'Shall I tell you? Dare I? You won't be offended? Well . . .' Margaret paused and then in a thrilling whisper said: '*Get your hair cut.*'

'Well, I'll be damned,' said Mr Pinfold; but Margaret was gone and did not hear him.

He looked in the glass. Yes, his hair was rather long. He would get it cut. Then he pondered the new problem: how had Margaret heard his soundless words? That could not be explained on any theory of frayed and crossed wires. As he considered the matter Margaret briefly returned to say: 'Not *wires*, darling. *Wireless*,' and then was gone again.

That perhaps should have given him the clue he sought; should have dispelled the mystery that enveloped him. He would learn in good time; at that moment Mr Pinfold was baffled, almost stupefied, by the occurrences of the morning and he went down to luncheon at the summons of the gong thinking vaguely in terms of telepathy, a subject on which he was ill-informed.

At the table he tackled Glover at once on a question that vexed him. 'I was not at Eton,' he said suddenly, with a challenge in his tone.

'Nor was I,' said Glover. 'Marlborough.'

'I never said I was at Eton,' Mr Pinfold insisted.

'No. Why should you, I mean, if you weren't?'

'It is a school for which I have every respect, but I was not there myself.' Then he turned across to the table to the Norwegian. 'I never wore a black shirt in the Albert Hall.'

'No?' said the Norwegian, interested but uncomprehending.

'I had every sympathy with Franco during the Civil War.'

'Yes? It is so long ago I have rather forgotten what it was all about. In my country we did not pay so much attention as the French and some other nations.'

'I never had the smallest sympathy with Hitler.'

'No, I suppose not.'

'Once I had hopes of Mussolini. But I was never connected with Mosley.'

'Mosley? What is that?'

'Please, please,' cried pretty Mrs Scarfield, 'don't let's get on to politics.'

For the rest of the meal Mr Pinfold sat silent.

Later he went to the barber's shop and from there to his listening post in the empty lounge. He saw the ship's surgeon pass the windows. He was on his way, evidently, to the Captain's cabin for almost immediately Mr Pinfold heard him say: ' . . . I thought I ought to report it to you, skipper.'

'Where was he last seen?'

'In the barber's shop. After that he completely disappeared. He's not in his cabin.'

'Why should he have gone overboard?'

'I've had my eye on him ever since we sailed. Haven't you noticed anything odd about him?'

'I've noticed he drinks.'

'Yes, he's a typical alcoholic. Several of the passengers asked me to look him over, but I can't you know, unless he calls me in or unless he does something violent. Now they're all saying he's jumped overboard.'

'I'm not going to stop the ship and put out a boat simply because a passenger isn't in his cabin. He's probably in someone else's cabin with one of my female passengers doing you know what.'

'Yes, that's the most likely explanation.'

'Is there anything the matter with him apart from the bottle?'

'Nothing a day's hard work wouldn't cure. The best thing for him would be to be put swabbing decks for a week . . . '

And after that the ship, like an aviary, was noisy with calls and chatter.

' . . . He can't be found.'

' . . . Overboard.'

' . . . No one's seen him since he left the barber . . . '

' . . . The Captain thinks he's got a woman somewhere . . . '

Very wearily Mr Pinfold tried to shut his mind to these distractions and to read his book. Presently the note changed. 'It's all right, he's found.'

' . . . False alarm.'

' . . . Pinfold's found.'

'I'm glad of that,' said the general gravely. 'I was afraid we might have gone too far.'

And the rest was silence.

The cutting of Mr Pinfold's hair fomented relations with Margaret. She prattled off and on all that afternoon and evening, gloating fondly over the change in Mr Pinfold's appearance; he looked younger, she said, smarter, altogether more lovable. Gazing long and earnestly into his looking-glass, turning his head this way and that, Mr Pinfold saw nothing very different from what he was used to, nothing to justify this enthusiasm. Margaret's gratification, he surmised, sprang less from his enhanced beauty than from the evidence he had given of his trust in her.

Interspersed with her praises there was an occasional hint of some deeper significance: '... Think, Gilbert. *Barber's shop*. Doesn't that tell you anything?'

'No. Should it?'

'It's the *clue*, Gilbert. It's what you most want to know, what you *must* know.'

'Well, tell me.'

'I can't do that, darling. It's against the *Rules*. But I can hint. *Barber's shop*, Gilbert. What do barbers do beside cutting hair?'

'They try and sell one hairwash.'

'No. No.'

'They make conversation. They massage the scalp. They iron moustaches. They sometimes, I believe, cut people's corns.'

'Oh, Gilbert, something much simpler. Think, darling. Sh... Sh...'

'Shave?'

'Got it.'

'But I shaved this morning. You're not asking me to shave again?'

'Oh, Gilbert, I think you're sweet. Is your chin a little bit rough, darling? How long after you shave does it get rough again? I *think* I should like it rough...' And she was off again on her galloping declaration of love.

More than once Mr Pinfold – or rather a fanciful image of him derived from his books – had been the object of adolescent infatuation. Margaret's fervent, naïve tones reminded him of the letters which used to come, two a day usually for periods of a week or ten days, written in bed probably. They were confidences and avowals of love, bearing no address; asking no reciprocation or sign of recognition; the series ending as abruptly as it had begun. As a rule, he read none after the first, but here on the hostile *Caliban*, these guileless words uttered in Margaret's sweet, breathless tones fell softly on Mr Pinfold's ear and he listened complacently.

Indeed he began to relish these moments of unction which compensated for much of the ignorant abuse. That morning he had determined to change his cabin. That evening he was loth to cut himself off from this warm spring.

But night brought a change.

Mr Pinfold did not dress or dine. He was very weary and he sat alone on deck until the passengers began to come up from dinner. Then he went to his cabin and for the first time for three days put on pyjamas, said his prayers, got into bed, turned off the light, composed himself for sleep, and slept.

He was awakened by Margaret's mother.

'Mr Pinfold. Mr Pinfold. Surely you haven't gone to sleep? Everyone is in bed now. Surely you haven't forgotten your promise to Margaret?'

'Mother, he didn't make any promise.' Margaret's voice was tearful and strained, almost hysterical. 'Not really. Not really what you could call a *promise*. Don't you see how awful it is for *me*, if you upset him now? He never *promised*.'

'When I was young, dear, any man would be proud of a pretty girl taking notice of him. He wouldn't try and get out of it by pretending to be asleep.'

'I asked for it. I expect I bore him. He's a man of the world. He's had hundreds of other girls, all sorts of horrible, fashionable, vicious old hags in London and Paris and Rome and New York. Why should he look at *me*? But I *do* love him so,' and in her anguish she uttered the whimper which Mr Pinfold had heard before in this ship on other lips.

'Don't cry, my dear. Mother will talk to him.'

'Please, *please* not, Mother. I forbid you to interfere.'

' "Forbid" isn't a very nice word, is it, dear? You leave it to me. I'll talk to him. Mr Pinfold. *Gilbert*. Wake up. Margaret's got something to say to you. He's awake now, dear, I know. Just tell her you're awake and listening, Gilbert.'

'I'm awake and listening,' said Mr Pinfold.

'All right then, hold on' – she was like a telephone operator, Mr Pinfold thought – 'Margaret's going to speak to you. Come along, Margaret, speak up.'

'I can't, Mother, I can't.'

'You see, Gilbert, you've upset her. Tell her you love her. You do love her, don't you?'

'But I've never met her,' said Mr Pinfold desperately. 'I'm sure she's a delightful girl, but I've never set eyes on her.'

'Oh, Gilbert, Gilbert, that's not a very gallant thing to say, is it? Not really like you, not like the *real* you. You just pretend to be hard and worldly, don't you? and you can't blame people if they take you at your own estimate. Everyone in the ship, you know, has been saying the most odious things about you. But I know better. Margaret wants to come and say good night to you, Gilbert, but she's not sure you really love her. Just tell Mimi you love her, Gilbert.'

'I can't, I don't,' said Mr Pinfold. 'I'm sure your daughter is a most charming girl. It so happens I have never met her. It also happens that I have a wife. I love *her*.'

'Oh, Gilbert, what a very middle-class thing to say!'

'He doesn't love me,' wailed Margaret. 'He doesn't love me any more.'

'Gilbert, Gilbert, you're breaking my little girl's heart.'

Mr Pinfold was exasperated.

'I'm going to sleep now,' he said. 'Good night.'

'Margaret's coming to see you.'

'Oh, shut up, you old bitch,' said Mr Pinfold.

He should not have said it. The moment the words crossed his lips – or, rather, his mind – he knew it was not the right thing to say. The whole sturdy ship seemed to tremble with shock. There was a single piteous wail from Margaret, from her mother an inarticulate but plainly audible hiss of outrage, an attempt at bluster from the son: 'My God, Peinfeld, you'll pay for that. If you think you can talk to my mother like . . . ' And then, most unexpectedly came a hearty chuckle from the general.

'Upon my soul, my dear, he called you an old bitch. Good for Peinfeld. That's something I've been longing to say to you for thirty years. You *are* an old bitch, you know, a thorough old bitch. Now perhaps you'll allow *me* to handle the situation. Clear out, the lot of you. I want to talk to my daughter. Come here, Meg, Peg o' my heart, my little Mimi.' The voices became thick, the diction strangely Celtic as sentiment overpowered the military man. 'You'll not be my little Mimi ever again, any more after tonight and I'll not forget it. You're a woman now and you've set your heart on a man as a woman should. The choice is yours, not mine. He's old for you, but there's good in that. Many a young couple spend a wretched fortnight together through not knowing how to set about what has to be done. And an old man can show you better than a young one. He'll be gentler and kinder and cleaner; and then, when the right time comes, you in your turn can teach a younger man – and that's how the art of love is learned and the breed survives. I'd like dearly to be the one myself to teach you, but you've made your own choice and who's to grudge it you?'

'But, Father, he doesn't love me. He said not.'

'Fiddlesticks. You're as pretty a girl as he'll meet in a twelve-month. There's certainly no one in this ship to touch you and if he's the man I think, he'll be feeling the need of an armful by now. Go in and get him, lass. How do you think your mother got me? Not by waiting to be asked, I can tell you. She was a soldier's daughter. She always rode straight at her fences. She rode straight at me, I can tell you. Don't forget you're a soldier's daughter too. If you want this fellow Pinfold, go in and take him. But for God's sake come on parade looking like a soldier. Get yourself cleaned up. Wash your face, brush your hair, take your clothes off.'

Margaret went obediently to her cabin. There she was joined by her friend, several friends, it seemed, a whole choir of bridesmaids who chanted an epithalamium as they disrobed her and tired her hair.

Mr Pinfold listened with conflicting resentment and fascination. He was a man accustomed to his own preferences and decisions. It seemed to him that Margaret's parents were being officious and presumptuous, were making altogether too free with his passions. He had never, even in his bachelor days, been a strenuous philanderer. Abroad, especially in remote places, he used to patronize brothels with the curiosity of a traveller who sought to taste all flavours of the exotic. In England he was rather constant and rather romantic in his affections. Since marriage he had been faithful to his wife. He had, since his acceptance of the laws of the Church, developed what approximated to a virtuous disposition; a reluctance to commit deliberate grave sins, which was independent of the fear of Hell; he had assumed a personality to which such specifically forbidden actions were inappropriate. And yet amorous expectations began to stir in Mr Pinfold. That acquired restraint and dignity of his had suffered some hard knocking-about during the last few days. Margaret's visit was exciting. He started to plan her reception.

The cabin with its two narrow bunks was ill-designed for such purposes. He began by tidying it, putting away his clothes and straightening the bed. He succeeded only in making it look unoccupied. She would enter by that door. She must not find him reclining like a pasha. He must be on his feet. There was one chair only. Should he offer it to her? Somehow he must dispose her, supine, on the bunk. But how to get her there silently and gracefully. How to shift her? Was she portable? He wished that he knew her dimensions.

He took off his pyjamas and hung them in his cupboard, put on his dressing-gown, and sat in the chair facing the door, waiting, while the folk-ritual of Margaret's preparations filled the cabin with music. As he waited his mood changed. Doubt and dismay intruded on his loving fancies. What on earth was he up to? What was he letting himself in for? He thought with disgust of Clutton-Cornforth and his tedious succession of joyless, purposeful seductions. He thought of his own enfeebled condition. 'Feeling the need of an armful' indeed! Would he be able to sustain his interest during all the patient exploration required of him? Then as he gazed at the tidy bunk, he filled it with delicate, shrinking, yielding, yearning nudity, with a nymph by Boucher or Fragonard, and his mood changed again. Let her come. Let her come speedily. He was strongly armed for the encounter.

But Margaret did not hurry. The attendant virgins completed their services. She was inspected by both parents.

'Oh my darling, my own. You're so young. Are you sure? Are you quite sure you love him? You can always turn back. It's not too late. I shall never see you again as I am seeing you now, my innocent daughter.'

'Yes, Mother, I love him.'

'Be kind to her, Gilbert. You have not been kind to me. You used an expression to me that I never expected to hear on a man's lips. I meant never to speak to you again. But this is no moment for pride. My daughter's happiness is in your hands. Treat her *husbandly*. I'm entrusting something very precious to you . . .'

And the general: 'That's my beauty. Go and take what's coming to you. Listen, my Peg, you know what you're in for, don't you?'

'Yes, Father, I think so.'

'It's always a surprise. You may think you know it all on paper, but like everything else in life it's never quite what you expect when it comes to action. There's no going back now. Come and see me when it's all over. I'll be waiting up to hear the report. In you go, bless you.'

But still the girl delayed.

'Gilbert, Gilbert. Do you want me?' she asked. 'Really and truly?'

'Yes, of course, come along.'

'Say something sweet to me.'

'I'll be sweet enough when you get here.'

'Come and fetch me.'

'Where are you?'

'Here. Just outside your cabin.'

'Well, come along in. I've left the door open.'

'I can't. I can't. You've got to come and fetch me.'

'Oh, don't be such a little ass. I've been sitting here for goodness knows how long. Come in if you're coming. If you're not, I want to go back to bed.'

At this Margaret broke into weeping and her mother said: 'Gilbert, that wasn't kind. It wasn't like you. You love her. She loves you. Can't you understand? A young girl; the first time; woo her, Gilbert, coax her. She's a little wild, woodland thing.'

'What the hell's going on?' asked the general. 'You ought to be in position by now. Haven't had a Sitrep. Isn't the girl over the Start Line?'

'Oh, Father, I can't. I *can't*. I thought I could, but I *can't*.'

'Something's gone wrong, Pinfold. Find out. Send out patrols.'

'Go and find her, Gilbert. Lure her in, tenderly, *husbandly*. She's just there waiting for you.'

Rather crossly Mr Pinfold strode into the empty corridor. He could hear Glover snoring. He could hear Margaret weeping quite close to him. He looked in the bathroom; not there. He looked round each corner, up and down the stairs; not there. He even looked in the lavatories, men's and women's; not there. Still the sobbing continued piteously. He returned to his cabin, fixed the door open on its hook and drew the curtain. He was overcome by weariness and boredom.

'I'm sorry, Margaret,' he said, 'I'm too old to start playing hide and seek with schoolgirls. If you want to come to bed with me, you'll have to come and join me there.'

He put on his pyjamas and lay down, pulling the blankets up to his chin. Presently he stretched out his arm and turned off the light. Then the passage light was disturbing. He shut the door. He rolled over on his side and lay between sleep and waking. Just as he was falling into unconsciousness he heard his door open and quickly shut. He opened his eyes too late to see the momentary gleam of light from the corridor. He heard slippered feet scurrying away and Margaret's despairing wail.

'I did go to him. I did. I did. I did. And when I got there he was lying in the dark snoring.'

'Oh, my Margaret, my daughter. You should never have gone. It was all your father's fault.'

'Sorry about that, Peg,' said the general. 'False appreciation.'

The last voice Mr Pinfold heard before he fell asleep was Goneril's: 'Snoring? Shamming. Gilbert knew he wasn't up to it. He's impotent, aren't you, Gilbert? Aren't you?'

'It was Glover snoring,' said Mr Pinfold, but nobody seemed to hear him.

7

THE VILLAINS UNMASKED – BUT NOT FOILED

MR PINFOLD DID not sleep for very long. He awoke as usual when the men began washing the deck overhead and he woke with the firm resolution of changing his cabin that day. His bond with Margaret was severed. He wished to be rid of the whole set of them and to sleep in peace in a cabin free of electrical freaks. He resolved, too, to move from the Captain's table. He had never wished to sit there. Anyone who coveted the place was welcome to it. Mr Pinfold was going to be strictly private for the rest of the voyage.

This resolution was confirmed by the last of the many communications that had come to him in that cabin.

Shortly before the breakfast hour, the device brought him into contact with what he might have supposed would be its most natural source, the wireless office; he found himself listening not as before to the normal traffic of the ship, but to the conversation of the wireless operator, and this man was entertaining a party of early-risers, the bright young people, by reading to them the text of Mr Pinfold's own messages.

' "*Everyone in ship most helpful. Love. Gilbert.*" '

'That's a good one.'

'Everyone?'

'I wonder if poor Gilbert thinks that now?'

'*Love*. Love from Gilbert. That's funny.'

'Show us some more.'

'Strictly speaking, you know, I oughtn't to. They're supposed to be confidential.'

'Oh, come off it, Sparks.'

'Well, this is rather rich. "*Entirely cured. All love.*" '

'Cured? Ha. Ha.'

591

'*Entirely* cured.'

'Our Gilbert *entirely cured*! Yes, that's delicious. Oh, Sparks, read us some more.'

'I've never known a chap spend so much on radiograms. They're mostly just about money and often he was so drunk I couldn't read what he'd written. There are an awful lot just refusing invitations. Oh, here's a good series. "*Kindly arrange immediate luxury private bath. Kindly investigate wanton inefficiency your office.*" He sent out dozens of those.'

'Thank God for our Gilbert. What should we do without him?'

'Was his luxury private bath inefficient?'

' "Wanton" is good coming from Gilbert. Does he wanton in his bath?'

To Mr Pinfold this little scene was different in kind from the earlier annoyances. The bright young people had gone too far. It was one thing to play practical jokes on him; it was something quite else to read confidential messages. They had put themselves outside the law. Mr Pinfold left his cabin for the dining-saloon with set purpose. He would put them on a charge.

He met the Captain making his morning round.

'Captain Steerforth, may I speak to you for a moment?'

'Surely.' The Captain paused.

'In your cabin?'

'Yes, if you want to. I shall be through in ten minutes. Come up then. Or is it very urgent?'

'It can wait ten minutes.'

Mr Pinfold climbed to the cabin behind the bridge. Few personal additions embellished the solid ship's furniture. There were family photographs in leather frames; an etching of an English Cathedral on the panelled wall which might have been the Captain's property or the company's; some pipes in a rack. Mr Pinfold could not imagine this place the scene of orgy, outrage or plot.

Presently the Captain returned.

'Well, sir, and what can I do for you?'

'First, I want to know whether radiograms sent from your ship are confidential documents?'

'I'm sorry. I'm afraid I don't understand you.'

'Captain Steerforth, since I came on board I have sent out a large number of messages of an entirely private character. This morning, early, there were a group of passengers reading them aloud in the wireless-room.'

'Well, we can easily get the facts about that. How many of these radiograms were there?'

'I don't know exactly. About a dozen.'

'And when did you send them?'

'At various times during the early days of the voyage.'

Captain Steerforth looked perplexed. 'This is only our fifth day out, you know,' he said.

'Oh,' said Mr Pinfold, disconcerted, 'are you quite sure?'

'Yes, of course I'm sure.'

'It seems longer.'

'Well, come along to the office and we'll look into the matter.'

The wireless-room was only two doors from the Captain's cabin.

'This is Mr Pinfold, a passenger.'

'Yes, sir. We've seen him before.'

'He wants to enquire about some radiograms he sent.'

'We can easily check on that, sir. We've had practically no private traffic!' He opened a file at his side and said: 'Yes. Here we are. The day before yesterday. It went out within an hour of being handed in.'

He showed Mr Pinfold's holograph: *Entirely cured. All love.*

'But the others?' said Mr Pinfold, bewildered.

'There were no others, sir.'

'A dozen or more.'

'Only this one. I should know, I can assure you.'

'There was one I sent at Liverpool, the evening I came on board.'

'That would have gone by Post Office Telegraph, sir.'

'And you wouldn't have a copy here?'

'No, sir.'

'Then how,' said Mr Pinfold, 'was it possible for a group of passengers to read it aloud in this office at eight o'clock this morning?'

'Quite impossible,' said the wireless operator. 'I was on duty myself at that time. There were no passengers here.'

He and the Captain exchanged glances.

'Does that satisfy all your questions, Mr Pinfold?' asked the Captain.

'Not quite. May I come back to your cabin?'

'If you wish it.'

When they were seated Mr Pinfold said: 'Captain Steerforth, I am the victim of a practical joke.'

'Something of the sort, it seems,' said the Captain.

'Not for the first time. Ever since I came on board this ship – you say it has only been five days?'

'Four actually.'

'Ever since I came on board, I have been the victim of hoaxes and threats. Mind you I am not making any accusation. I don't know the names of these people. I don't even know what they look like. I am *not* asking for an official investigation – yet. What I do know is that the leaders comprise a family of four.'

'I don't believe we have any families on board,' said the Captain, taking the passenger list off his desk, 'except the Angels. I hardly think they're the sort of people to play practical jokes on anyone. A very quiet family.'

'There are several people travelling who aren't on that list.'

'No one, I assure you.'

'Fosker for one.'

Captain Steerforth turned the pages. 'No,' he said. 'No Fosker.'

'And that little dark man who used to sit alone in the dining-saloon.'

'Him? I know him well. He often travels with us. Mr Murdoch – here he is on the list.'

Baffled, Mr Pinfold turned to another course suggested by Mr Murdoch's solitary meals.

'Another thing, Captain. I greatly appreciate the honour of being invited to sit at your table in the dining-saloon. But the truth is I'm not fit for human society, just at the moment. I've been taking some grey pills – pretty strong stuff, for rheumatism, you know. I'm really better alone. So if you won't think it rude . . .'

'Sit where you like, Mr Pinfold. Just tell the chief steward.'

'Please understand I am not going because of any pressure from outside. It is simply that I am not well.'

'I quite understand, Mr Pinfold.'

'I reserve the right to return if I feel better.'

'Please sit exactly where you like, Mr Pinfold. Is that all you wanted to say?'

'No. There's another thing. The cabin I'm in. You ought to get the wiring seen to. I don't know whether you know it, but I can often hear anything that's being said up here, on the bridge and in other parts of the ship.'

'I didn't know,' said Captain Steerforth. 'That is most unusual.'

'They've used this defect in their practical jokes. It's most disturbing. I should like to change cabins.'

'That should be easy. We have two or three vacant. If you'll tell the purser . . . Is *that* everything, Mr Pinfold?'

'Yes,' said Mr Pinfold. 'Thank you very much. I am most grateful to you. And you *do* understand about my changing tables? You don't think it rude?'

'No offence whatever, Mr Pinfold. Good morning.'

Mr Pinfold left the cabin far from content with his interview. It seemed to him that he had said too much or too little. But he had achieved certain limited objectives and he set about his business with the purser and chief steward with alacrity. He was given the very table where Mr Murdoch had sat. Of several cabins he chose a small one near the veranda-bar which gave immediate access to the promenade-deck. Here, he was sure, he would be safe from physical attack.

He returned to his old cabin to direct the removal of his possessions. The voices began at once but he was very busy with the English-speaking steward and did not listen until he had seen his clothes and belongings packed and carried away. Then briefly he surveyed the scene of his suffering and lent them his ears. He was gratified to find that, however incomplete it looked to him, his morning's work had dismayed his enemies.

'Dirty little sneak' – there was a note of fear in Goneril's hatred that morning – 'what have you been saying to the Captain? We'll get even with you. Have you forgotten the three-eight rhythm? Did you tell him our names? Did you? Did you?'

Margaret's brother was positively conciliatory: 'Look here, Gilbert, old boy, we don't want to bring other people into our business, do we? We can settle it between ourselves, can't we, Gilbert?'

Margaret was reproachful; not because of the drama of the night; all that storm of emotion seemed to have passed leaving no more trace than thunder clouds in the blue of summer. Indeed, in all their subsequent acquaintance she never mentioned that fiasco; she chid him instead gently for his visit to the Captain. 'It's *against the Rules*, darling, don't you see? We *must* all play by the Rules.'

'I'm not playing at all.'

'Oh yes, darling, you are. We all are. We can't help ourselves. And it's a Rule that no one else must be told. If there's anything you don't understand, ask me.'

Poor waif, Mr Pinfold thought, she has kept bad company and been corrupted. After the embarrassments of the night Margaret had forfeited his trust, but he loved her a little and felt it unmannerly to be leaving her flat, as he planned to do. It had proved easy to move out of their reach. They had confided too much, these aggressive young people, in their mechanical toy. And now he was breaking it.

'Margaret,' he said, 'I don't know anything about your rules and I am not playing any game with any of you. But I should like to see you. Come and join me on deck any time you like.'

'Darling, you know I long to. But I can't, can I? You do see, don't you?'

'No,' said Mr Pinfold, 'frankly I don't see. I leave it to you. I'm off now,' and he left the haunted cabin for the last time.

It was the social hour of noon when the sweepstake was paid and the cocktails ordered. From his new cabin, where his new steward was unpacking, he could hear the chatter from the bar. He stood alone thinking how smoothly he had made the transition.

He repeated to himself all that had been said in the Captain's cabin: '. . . *no families on board except the Angels?*' Angel. And suddenly Mr Pinfold understood, not everything, but the heart of the mystery.

Angel, the quizzical man from the B.B.C. '– *not wires, darling. Wireless*' – Angel, the man with the technical skill to use the defects of the *Caliban*'s communications, perhaps to cause them. Angel, the man with the beard – '*What do barbers do besides cut hair?*' – Angel, who had an aunt near Lychpole and could have heard from her the garbled gossip of the countryside. Angel who had 'half expected' Cedric Thorne to kill himself; Angel who bore a grudge for the poor figure he had cut at Lychpole and had found Mr Pinfold by chance alone and ill and defenceless, ripe for revenge. Angel was the villain, he and his sinister associate – mistress? colleague? – whom Mr Pinfold had dubbed 'Goneril'. And Angel had gone too far. He was afraid now that his superiors in London might get wind of his escapade. And they would, too; Mr Pinfold would see to that, when he returned to England. He might even write from the ship. If, as seemed probable, he was travelling on duty, the B.B.C. would have something to say to young Angel, bearded or shaven.

There were many passages in the story of the last few days that remained obscure under this new, bright light. Mr Pinfold felt as though he had come to the end of an ingenious, old-fashioned detective novel which he had read rather inattentively. He knew the villain now and began turning back the pages to observe the clues he had missed.

It was not the first time in the *Caliban* that noon had brought an illusion of shadowless commonplace.

The change of cabin was not the tactical triumph Mr Pinfold briefly supposed. He was like a commander whose attack 'hit air'. The post he had captured, which had seemed the key of the enemy's position, proved to be empty, a mere piece of deception masking an elaborate and strongly held system; the force he supposed routed was reinforced and ready for the counter-attack.

Mr Pinfold discovered, before he went down to his first lonely luncheon, that Angel's range of action was not limited to the original cabin and the corner of the lounge. From some mobile point of control he could speak and listen in every part of the ship and in the following days Mr Pinfold, wherever he stood, could hear, could not keep himself from hearing, everything that was said in Angel's headquarters. Living and moving and eating now quite alone, barely nodding to Glover or Mrs Scarfield, Mr Pinfold listened and spoke only to his enemies and hour by hour, day by day, night by night, carefully assembled the intricate pieces of a plot altogether more modern and horrific than anything in the classic fictions of murder.

Mr Pinfold's change of cabin had momentarily disconcerted Angel and his staff (there were about half a dozen of them, male and female, all young, basically identical with the three-eight orchestra); moreover it seemed likely that the scare of the day before, when it was put about the ship that he had gone overboard, was genuine enough. At any rate Angel's first concern was that Mr Pinfold should be kept under continual observation. Immediate reports were made to headquarters of his every move. These reports were concise and factual.

'Gilbert has sat down at his table . . . He's reading the menu . . . He's ordering wine . . . He's ordered a plate of cold ham.'

When he moved he was passed on to relays of observers.

'Gilbert coming up to main deck. Take over, B.'

'O.K., A. Gilbert now approaching door on port side, going out on to deck. Take over, C.'

'O.K., B. Gilbert walking the deck anti-clockwise. He's approaching the main door, starboard side. Over to you B.'

'He's sitting down with a book.'

'O.K., B. Stay on duty in the lounge. Report any move. I'll have you relieved at three.'

Mr Pinfold, looking from one to another of the occupants of the lounge, wondered which was B. Later it transpired that about half the passengers had been recruited by Angel for observation duties. They considered it an innocuous parlour game. Of the rest some knew nothing of what was afoot – this group included Glover and the Scarfields – others thought the whole thing silly. The inner circle manned the staff office where reports were collated and inquiries instigated. Every few hours a conference was held at which Angel collected and discussed the notes of his observers, drafted them into a coherent report and gave them to a girl to be typed. He maintained a rollicking good humour and zest.

'Great stuff. Splendid . . . My word, Gilbert's given himself away here . . . Most valuable . . . We could do with a little more detail on these points . . .'

Anything Mr Pinfold had said or done or thought, that day or in his past life, seemed significant. Angel was mocking, but appreciative. At intervals two older men – not the generals, but men more akin to them than to the boisterous youngsters – subjected Mr Pinfold to direct questioning. This inquisition, it appeared, was the essence of the enterprise. It was prosecuted whenever Mr Pinfold sat in the lounge or lay in his cabin, and so curious was he about the motives and mechanics of the thing that for the first twenty-four hours he, to some extent, collaborated. The inquisitors, it seemed, possessed a huge but incomplete and wildly inaccurate dossier covering the whole of Mr Pinfold's private life. It was their task to fill the gaps. In manner they were part barristers, part bureaucrats.

'Where were you in January 1929, Pinfold?'

'I really don't know.'

'Perhaps I can refresh your memory. I have here a letter from you written at Mena House Hotel, Cairo. Were you in Egypt in 1929?'

'Yes, I believe I was.'

'And what were you doing there?'

'Nothing.'

'Nothing? That won't do, Pinfold. I want a better answer than that.'

'I was just travelling.'

'Of course you were travelling. You could hardly get to Egypt without travelling, could you? I want the truth, Pinfold. *What were you doing* in Egypt in 1929?'

On another occasion: 'How many pairs of shoes do you possess?'

'I really don't know.'

'You *must* know. Would you say a dozen?'

'Yes, I daresay.'

'We have you down here as possessing ten.'

'Perhaps.'

'Then why did you tell me a dozen, Pinfold? He did say a dozen, didn't he?'

'Quite distinctly.'

'I don't like this, Pinfold. You have to be truthful. Only the truth can help you.'

Sometimes they turned to more immediate topics.

'On more than one occasion you have complained of suffering from the effects of some grey pills. Where did they come from?'

'My doctor.'

'Do you suppose he manufactured them himself?'

'No, I suppose not.'

'Well then answer my question properly. Where did those pills come from?'

'I really don't know. Some chemist, I suppose.'

'Exactly. Would it surprise you to hear they came from Wilcox and Bredworth?'

'Not particularly.'

'*Not particularly*, Pinfold? I must warn you to be careful. Don't you know that Wilcox and Bredworth are one of the most respected firms in the country?'

'Yes.'

'And you accuse them of purveying dangerous drugs?'

'I expect they manufacture great quantities of poison.'

'You mean you accuse Wilcox and Bredworth of conspiring with your doctor to poison you?'

'Of course I don't.'

'Then what *do* you mean?'

Sometimes they made in their stern, precise voices accusations as fantastic as those of the hooligans and the gossips. They pressed him for information about the suicide of a staff-officer in the Middle East – a man who to the best of Mr Pinfold's knowledge had ended the war healthily and prosperously – which they attributed to Mr Pinfold's malice. They brought up the old charges of the eviction of Hill and of Mrs Pinfold senior's pauper's funeral. They examined him about a claim he had never made, to be the nephew of an Anglican bishop.

Once or twice during these days Angel organized a rag, but since Mr Pinfold could hear the preparations, he was not dismayed as he had been by the previous exercises.

Early one morning he heard Angel announce: 'We will mount Operation Storm today,' and as soon as the ship came to life and the passengers began their day, all conversation, when they passed Mr Pinfold, or he them, was about a gale warning. ' . . . The Captain says we're coming right into it.'

'One of the worst storms he's ever known in the Mediterranean . . . '

The day was bright and calm. Mr Pinfold had no fear − if anything he had rather a relish − for rough weather. After an hour of this charade Angel called it off. 'No good,' he said, 'operation cancelled. Gilbert isn't scared.'

'He's a good sailor,' said Margaret.

'He doesn't mind missing his lunch,' said Goneril. 'The food isn't good enough for him.'

'Operation Stock Exchange,' said Angel.

This performance was even more fatuous than its predecessor. The method was the same, a series of conversations designed for him to hear. The subject was a financial slump which had suddenly thrown the stock-markets of the world into chaos. As they sauntered past or sat over their knitting the passengers dutifully recounted huge falls in the prices of stocks and shares in the world capital cities, the suicide of financiers, the closing of banks and corporations. They quoted figures. They named the companies which had failed. All this, even had he believed it, would have been of very remote interest to Mr Pinfold.

'They say Mr Pinfold's fortune is entirely wiped out,' said Mrs Benson to Mrs Cockson (these ladies had now resumed their mother tongue).

Mr Pinfold had no fortune. He owned a few fields, a few pictures, a few valuable books, his own copyrights. At the bank he had a small overdraft. He had never in his life put out a penny at interest. The rudimentary technicalities of finance were Greek to him. It was very odd, he thought, that these people could go to so much trouble to investigate his affairs and know so little about them.

'Operation cancelled,' announced Angel at length.

'What went wrong?'

'I wish I knew. Gilbert is no longer responding to treatment. We
had him on the run in the early days. Now he seems punch-drunk.'

'He's in a sort of daze.'

'He's not sleeping enough.'

This was indeed true. Since he had finished his sleeping-draught
Mr Pinfold had seldom had more than an hour at a time of uneasy
dozing. The nights were a bad time for him. He would sit in the
lounge, alone in his dinner jacket, observing his fellow-passengers,
distracted a little by their activities from the voice of his enemies,
trying to decide which were his friends, which were neutral, until the
last of them had gone below and the lights were turned down. Then,
knowing what to expect, he would go to his cabin and undress. He
had given up any attempt at saying his prayers; the familiar,
hallowed words provoked a storm of blasphemous parody from
Goneril.

He lay down expecting little rest. Angel had in his headquarters
an electric instrument which showed Mr Pinfold's precise state of
consciousness. It consisted, Mr Pinfold surmised, of a glass tube
containing two parallel lines of red light which continually drew
together or moved apart like telegraph wires seen from a train. They
approached one another as he grew drowsy and, when he fell asleep,
crossed. A duty officer followed their fluctuations.

'...Wide awake...now he's getting sleepy...they're almost
touching...a single line...they're going to cross...no, wide
awake again...' And when he awoke after his brief spells of insensibility, his first sensation was always the voice of the observer:
'Gilbert's awake again. Fifty-one minutes.'

'That's better than the time before.'

'But it isn't enough.'

One night they tried to soothe him by playing a record
specially made by Swiss scientists for the purpose. These savants
had decided from experiments made in a sanatorium for neurotic
industrial workers that the most soporific noises were those of a
factory. Mr Pinfold's cabin resounded to the roar and clang of
machinery.

'You bloody fools,' he cried in exasperation, '*I'm* not a factory
worker. You're driving me mad.'

'No, no, Gilbert, you *are* mad already,' said the duty-officer. 'We're driving you sane.'

The hubbub continued until Angel came on his round of inspection.

'Gilbert not asleep yet? Let me see the log. "*0312 hours. You bloody fools, I'm not a factory worker.*" Well nor he is. "*You're driving me mad.*" I believe we are. Turn off that record. Give him something rural.'

From then for a long time nightingales sang to Mr Pinfold but still he did not sleep. He stepped out on deck and leaned on the rail.

'Go on, Gilbert. Jump. In you go,' said Goneril. Mr Pinfold did not feel the smallest temptation to obey. 'Water-funk.'

'I know all about that actor, you know,' said Mr Pinfold. 'The one who was a friend of Angel's and hanged himself in his dressing-room.'

This was the first time that he disclosed his knowledge of Angel's identity. The effect was immediate. All Angel's assumed good humour was dispelled. 'Why do you call me Angel?' he asked fiercely. 'What the devil do you mean by it?'

'It's your name. I know exactly what you are doing for the B.B.C.' – this was bluff – 'I know exactly what you did to Cedric Thorne. I know exactly what you are trying to do to me.'

'Liar. You don't know anything.'

'Liar,' said Goneril.

'I told you,' said Margaret, 'Gilbert's no fool.'

Silence fell on the headquarters. Mr Pinfold returned to his bunk, lay down, and slept until the steward came in with his tea. Angel spoke to him at once. He was in a chastened mood. 'Look here, Gilbert, you've got us all wrong. What we're doing is nothing to do with the B.B.C. It's a private enterprise entirely. And as for Cedric – that wasn't our fault. He came to us too late. We did everything we could for him. He was a hopeless case. Why don't you answer? Can't you hear me, Gilbert? Why don't you answer?'

Mr Pinfold held his peace. He was getting near to a full explanation.

Mr Pinfold was never able to give a completely coherent account either to himself or to anyone else of how he finally unravelled the mystery. He heard so much, directly and indirectly; he reasoned so closely; he followed so many false clues and reached so many absurd conclusions; but at length he was satisfied that he knew the truth. He then sat down and wrote about it at length to his wife.

Darling, he wrote,

As I said in my telegram I am quite cured of my aches and pains. In that way the trip has been a success but this has not proved a happy ship and I have decided to get off at Port Said and go on by aeroplane.

Do you remember the tick with a beard who came to Lychpole from the B.B.C? He is on board with a team bound for Aden. They are going to make recordings of Arab dance music. The tick is called Angel. He has shaved his beard. That is why I didn't spot him at first. He has some of his family with him – rather a nice sister – travelling I suppose for pleasure. They seem to be cousins of a lot of our neighbours. You might enquire. These B.B.C. people have made themselves a great nuisance to me on board. They have got a lot of apparatus with them, most of it new and experimental. They have something which is really a glorified form of Reggie Upton's Box. I shall never laugh at the poor Bruiser again. There is a great deal in it. More in fact than he imagines. Angel's Box is able to speak and to hear. In fact I spend most of my days and nights carrying on conversations with people I never see. They are trying to psycho-analyse me. I know this sounds absurd. The Germans at the end of the war were developing this Box for the examination of prisoners. The Russians have perfected it. They don't need any of the old physical means of persuasion. They can see into the minds of the most obdurate. The Existentialists in Paris first started using it for psycho-analysing people who would not voluntarily submit to treatment. They first break the patient's nerve by acting all sorts of violent scenes which he thinks are really happening. They confuse him until he doesn't distinguish between natural sounds and those they induce. They make all kinds of preposterous accusations against him. Then when they get him in a receptive mood they start on their psycho-analysis. As you can imagine it's a hellish invention in the wrong hands. Angel's are very much the wrong hands. He's an amateur and a conceited ass. That young man who came to the hotel with my tickets was there to measure my 'life-waves'. I should have thought they could equally well have got them on board. Perhaps there is some particular gadget they have to get in London for each person. I don't know. There is still a good deal about the whole business I don't know. When I get back I will make enquiries. I'm not the first person they've tried it on. They drove an actor to suicide. I rather suspect they've been at work on poor Roger Stillingfleet. In fact I think we shall find a number of our friends who have behaved oddly lately have suffered from Angel.

Anyway thay have had no success with me. I've seen through them. All they have done is to stop my working. So I am leaving them. I shall go straight to the Galleface in Colombo and look round from there for a quiet place in the hills. I'll telegraph when I arrive which should be about the time you get this letter.

All love.

G.

'Gilbert,' said Angel, 'you can't send that letter.'

'I am certainly going to – by air mail from Port Said.'

'It's going to make trouble.'

'I hope so.'

'You don't understand the importance of the work we're doing. Did you see the *Cocktail Party*? Do you remember the second act? We are like the people in that, a little band doing good, sworn to secrecy, working behind the scenes everywhere –'

'You're a pretentious busy-body.'

'Look here, Gilbert –'

'And who the devil said you might use my Christian name?'

'Gilbert.'

'Mr Pinfold to you.'

'Mr Pinfold, I admit we've not handled your case properly. We'll leave you in peace if you'll destroy that letter.'

'*I* am leaving *you*, my good Angel. The question does not arise.'

Goneril cut in: 'We'll give you hell for this, Gilbert. We'll get you and you know it. We'll never let you go. We've got you.'

'Oh, shut up,' said Mr Pinfold.

He felt himself master of the field: caught unawares, with unfamiliar barbarous weapons, treacherously ambushed when, as it were, he was under the cover of the Red Cross, he had rallied and routed the enemy. Their grand strategy had been utterly frustrated. All they could do now was snipe.

This they did continuously during the last twenty-four hours of the voyage. Mr Pinfold went about his business in a babble of jeering, threatening, cajoling voices. He gave notice to the purser of his intention of leaving the ship and sent a message by wireless engaging an air passage to Colombo.

'You can't go, Gilbert. They won't let you off the ship. The doctor has you under observation. He'll keep you in a home because you're mad, Gilbert... You haven't the money. You can't hire a car... Your passport expired last week... They won't take traveller's cheques in Egypt...' 'He's got dollars, the beast.' 'Well, that's criminal. He ought to have declared them. They'll get him for that.' 'They won't let you through the military zone, Gilbert' (this was in 1954). 'The army will turn you back. Egyptian terrorists are bombing private cars on the canal road.'

Mr Pinfold fought back with the enemy's weapons. He was obliged to hear all they said. They were obliged to hear him. They could not measure his emotions, but every thought which took verbal shape in his mind was audible in Angel's headquarters and they were unable, it seemed, to disconnect their box. Mr Pinfold set out to wear them down with sheer boredom. He took a copy of *Westward Ho!* from the ship's library and read it very slowly hour by hour. At first Goneril attempted to correct his pronunciation. At first Angel pretended to find psychological significance in the varying emphasis he gave to different words. But after an hour or so they gave up these pretences and cried in frank despair: 'Gilbert, for God's sake stop.'

Then Mr Pinfold tormented them in his turn by making gibberish of the text, reading alternate lines, alternate words, reading backwards, until they pleaded for a respite. Hour after hour Mr Pinfold remorselessly read on.

On his last evening he felt magnanimous towards all except Angel and Goneril. Word had got round the passengers that he was leaving them and as he sauntered among them he noted genuine regret in the scraps of talk he overheard.

'Is it really because of that game of Mr Angel's?' he heard Mrs Benson ask.

'He's very much annoyed with all of us.'

'You can hardly blame him. I'm sorry now I took any part in it.'

'It wasn't really very funny. I never saw the point really.'

'What's more we've cost him a lot of money. He may be able to afford it, but it's unfair, all the same.'

'I never believed half they said about him.'

'I wish I'd got to know him. I believe he's really very nice.'

'He's a very distinguished man and we've behaved like a lot of badly brought up children.'

There was no hatred or ridicule now in any of their conversations. That evening before dinner, he joined the Scarfields.

'In a couple of days it will be getting hot,' she said.

'I shan't be here.'

'Not here? I thought you were going to Colombo?'

He explained the change of plan.

'Oh, what a pity,' she said with an unmistakable innocence. 'It's only after Port Said that one ever really gets to know people.'

'I think I'll dine at your table tonight.'

'Do. We've missed you.'

So Mr Pinfold returned to the Captain's table and ordered champagne for them all. None except the Captain's table knew of his imminent departure. Throughout all the tumult of the journey this little group had remained isolated and unaware of what was afoot. Mr Pinfold was still not sure of the Captain. That quiet sea-dog had turned a Nelson eye on proceedings far beyond the scope of his imagination.

'I'm sorry we shan't have you with us, particularly now you are feeling so much better,' he said, raising his glass. 'I hope you have a comfortable flight.'

'Urgent business, I suppose?' said Glover.

'Just impatience,' said Mr Pinfold.

He remained with the group. Glover gave him advice about tailors in Colombo and cool hotels in the hills suitable for literary work. When they broke up, Mr Pinfold said good-bye, for the *Caliban* was due in harbour early and all would be busy next morning.

On his way to his cabin he met the dark figure of Mr Murdoch, who stopped and spoke to him. His manner was genial and his voice richly redolent of the industrial North.

'Purser tells me you're landing tomorrow,' he said. 'So am I. How do you reckon to get to Cairo?'

'I haven't really thought. Train, I suppose.'

'Ever been in a Wog train? Filthy dirty and slow. I tell you what, my firm's sending a car for me. I'd be glad of your company.'

So it was arranged they should travel together.

The night still belonged to Angel and Goneril. 'Don't trust Murdoch,' they whispered. 'Murdoch is your enemy.' There was no peace in the cabin and Mr Pinfold remained on deck watching for the poor little pharos of Port Said, recognized its beam, saw the pilot come aboard with a launchful of officials in tarbooshes, saw the water-front come clear in view, populous even at that hour with touts and scarab-sellers.

In the hubbub of early morning and the successive interviews with port officials Mr Pinfold was intermittently aware that Goneril and Angel were still jabbering, still impotently trying to obstruct. Only when at last he went down the gangway did they fall silent. Mr Pinfold had been to Port Said often before. He had never expected to feel affection for the place. That day he did. He watched patiently while unshaven, smoking officials examined him, his passport and his baggage. He cheerfully paid a number of absurd impositions. An English agent of Mr Murdoch's company warned them:

'. . . Pretty tricky drive at the moment. Only last week there was a chap hired a car to go to Cairo. The Wog drove off the road just after Ismailia into a village. He was set on, all his luggage pinched. They even took his clothes. Not a stitch on when the police picked him up. And all they said was he ought to consider himself lucky they hadn't cut his throat.'

Mr Pinfold did not care. He posted his letter to his wife. He and Murdoch drank a bottle of beer at a café and suffered their boots to be cleaned two or three times. The funnels of the *Caliban* were plainly to be seen from where he sat, but no voices came from her. Then he and Murdoch drove away out of sight of the unhappy ship.

The road to Cairo was more warlike than he had known it ten years back when Rommel was at the gates. They passed through lanes of barbed wire, halted and showed passports at numerous barriers, crept in dust behind convoys of army trucks, each with a sentry crouched on the tailboard with a tommy-gun at the ready.

There came a longer halt and closer scrutiny at the turning out of the Canal Zone, where swarthy, sullen English soldiers gave place to swarthy, sullen Egyptians in almost identical uniforms. Murdoch was a man of few words and Mr Pinfold sat enveloped in his own impervious peace.

Once during the war he had gone on a parachute course which had ended ignominiously with his breaking a leg in his first drop, but he treasured as the most serene and exalted experience of his life the moment of liberation when he regained consciousness after the shock of the slipstream. A quarter of a minute before he had crouched over the open man-hole in the floor of the machine, in dusk and deafening noise, trussed in harness, crowded by apprehensive fellow-tyros. Then the despatching officer had signalled; down he had plunged into a moment of night, to come to himself in a silent, sunlit heaven, gently supported by what had seemed irksome bonds, absolutely isolated. There were other parachutes all round him holding other swaying bodies; there was an instructor on the ground bawling advice through a loudspeaker; but Mr Pinfold felt himself free of all human communication, the sole inhabitant of a private, delicious universe. The rapture was brief. Almost at once he knew he was not floating but falling; the field leaped up at him; a few seconds later he was lying on grass entangled in cords, being shouted at, breathless, bruised, with a sharp pain in the shin. But in that moment of solitude prosaic, earthbound Mr Pinfold had been one with hashish-eaters and Corybantes and Californian gurus, high on the back-stairs of mysticism. His mood on the road to Cairo was barely less ecstatic.

Cairo was still pocked and gutted by the recent riots. It was thronged with stamp-dealers who had come for the sale of the royal collection. Mr Pinfold had difficulty in finding a room. Murdoch obtained one for him. There was difficulty with his air passage and there too Murdoch helped. Finally on the second day when Mr Pinfold was provided by the concierge of his hotel with all the requisite documents – including a medical certificate and a sworn statement, necessary for a halt in Arabia, that he was a Christian – and his departure was fixed for midnight, Murdoch invited him to dine with his business associates in Ghezira.

'They'll be delighted. They don't see many people from home these days. And to tell you the truth I'm glad to have a companion myself. I don't much like driving about alone after dark.'

So they went to dinner in a block of expensive modern flats. The lift was out of order. As they climbed the stairs they passed an Egyptian soldier squatting in a flat doorway, chewing nuts, with his rifle propped behind him.

'One of the old princesses,' said Murdoch, 'under house-arrest.'

Host and hostess greeted them kindly. Mr Pinfold looked about him. The drawing-room was furnished with the trophies of long residence in the East. On the chimney-piece was the framed photograph of a peer in coronation-robes. Mr Pinfold studied it.

'Surely that's Simon Dumbleton?'

'Yes, he's a great friend of ours. Do you know him?'

Before he could answer another voice broke in on that cosy scene.

'No, you don't, Gilbert,' said Goneril. 'Liar. Snob. You only pretend to know him because he's a lord.'

PINFOLD REGAINED

MR PINFOLD LANDED at Colombo three days later. He had spent one almost sleepless night in the aeroplane where a pallid Parsee sprawled and grunted and heaved beside him; and a second equally wakeful alone in a huge, teetotal hotel in Bombay. Night and day Angel, Goneril and Margaret chattered to him in their several idioms. He was becoming like the mother of fractious children who has learned to go about her business with a mind closed to their utterances; except that he had no business. He could only sit hour after hour waiting in one place or another for meals he did not want. Sometimes from sheer boredom he spoke to Margaret and learned from her further details of the conspiracy.

'Are you still in the ship?'

'No. We got off at Aden.'

'All of you?'

'All three.'

'But the others?'

'There never were any others, Gilbert. Just my brother and sister-in-law and me. You saw our names in the passenger list, Mr and Mrs and Miss Angel. I thought you understood all that.'

'But your mother and father?'

'They're in England, at home – quite near Lychpole.'

'Never in the ship?'

'Darling, you are slow in the uptake. What you heard was my brother. He's really awfully good at imitations. That's how he first got taken on by the B.B.C.'

'And Goneril is married to your brother? There was never anything between her and the Captain?'

'No, of course not. She's beastly but not like that. All *that* was part of the Plan.'

'I think I'm beginning to understand. You must see it's all rather confusing.' Mr Pinfold puzzled his weary head over the matter; then gave it up and asked: 'What are you doing in Aden?'

'Me? Nothing. The others have their work. It's awfully dull for me. May I talk to you sometimes? I know I'm not a bit clever but I'll try not to be a bore. I do so want company.'

'Why don't you go and see the mermaid?'

'I don't understand.'

'There used to be a mermaid at Aden in a box in one of the hotels – stuffed.'

'Don't tease, Gilbert.'

'I'm not teasing. And anyway that comes pretty badly from a member of your family. *Tease* indeed.'

'Oh, Gilbert, you don't understand. We were only trying to help you.'

'Who the devil said I needed help?'

'Don't be cross, Gilbert; not with me anyway. And you did need help you know. Often their plans work beautifully.'

'Well, you must realize by now that it hasn't worked with me.'

'Oh, no,' said Margaret sadly. 'It hasn't worked at all.'

'Then why not leave me alone?'

'They never will now, because they hate you. And I never will, never. You see I love you so. Try not to hate me, darling.'

From Cairo to Colombo he talked intermittently to Margaret. To the Angels, husband and wife, he made no answer.

Ceylon was a new country to Mr Pinfold but he had no sense of exhilaration on arrival. He was tired and sweaty. He was wearing the wrong clothes. His first act after leaving his luggage at the hotel was to seek the tailor Glover had recommended. The man promised to work all night and have three suits ready for him to try on next morning.

'You're too fat. You'll look ridiculous in them. They won't fit . . . You can't afford them . . . The tailor's lying. He won't make clothes for you,' Goneril monotonously interpolated.

Mr Pinfold returned to his hotel and wrote to his wife: '*I have arrived safe and well. There does not seem to be much to see or do in Colombo.*

I will move as soon as I have some clothes. I rather doubt whether I shall get any work done. I had a disappointment leaving the ship. I thought I should get out of range of those psycho-analysts and their infernal Box. But not at all. They still annoy me with the whole length of India between us. As I write this letter they keep interrupting. It will be quite impossible to do any of my book. There must be some way of cutting the "vital waves". I think it might be worth consulting Father Westmacott when I get back. He knows all about existentialism and psychology and ghosts and diabolic possession. Sometimes I wonder whether it is not literally the Devil who is molesting me.'

He posted this by air mail. Then he sat on the terrace watching the new cheap cars drive up and away. Here, unlike Bombay, one could drink. He drank bottled English beer. The sky darkened. A thunderstorm broke. He moved from the terrace into the lofty hall. To a man at Mr Pinfold's time of life few throngs comprise only strangers. In the busy hall he was greeted by an acquaintance from New York, a collector for one of the art galleries, on his way to visit a ruined city on the other side of the island. He asked Mr Pinfold to join him.

At that moment a gentle servant appeared at his side: 'Mr Peenfold, sir, cable.'

It came from his wife and read: '*Implore you return immediately.*'

It was not like Mrs Pinfold to issue a summons of this kind. Could she be ill? Or one of the children? Had the house burned down? She would, surely? have given some explanation. It occurred to Mr Pinfold that she must be concerned on his account. That letter he had sent from Port Said, had it said anything to cause alarm? He answered: '*All well. Returning soon. Have written today. Off to the ruins,*' and rejoined his new companion. They dined together cheerfully, having many tastes and friends and memories in common. All that evening, though there was an undertone in his ears, Mr Pinfold was oblivious of the Angels. Not till late, when he was alone in his room, did the voices break through. 'We heard you, Gilbert. You were lying to that American. You've never stayed at Rhinebeck. You've never heard of Magnasco. You don't know Osbert Sitwell.'

'Oh God,' said Mr Pinfold, 'how you bore me!'

It was cooler among the ruins. There was refreshment in the leafy roads, in the spectacle of grey elephants and orange-robed, shaven-pated monks ambling meditatively in the dust. They stopped at rest-houses where they were greeted and zealously served by old servants of the British Raj. Mr Pinfold enjoyed himself. On the way back they stopped at the shrine of Kandy and saw the Buddha's tooth ceremoniously exposed. This seemed to exhaust the artistic resources of the island. The American was on his way farther east. They parted company four days later at the hotel in Colombo where they had met. Mr Pinfold was alone once more and at a loose end. He found waiting for him a pile of clothes from the tailor and another cable from his wife: '*Both your letters received. Am coming to join you.*'

It had been handed in at Lychpole that morning.

'He hates his wife,' said Goneril. 'She bores you, doesn't she, Gilbert? You don't want to go home, do you? You dread seeing her again.'

That decided him. He cabled: '*Returning at once*' and set about his preparations.

The three suits were pale, pinkish buff ('How smart you look,' cried Margaret); they were not entirely useless. He wore them on successive days; first in Colombo.

It was Sunday and he went to Mass for the first time since he had been struck ill. The voices followed him. The taxi took him first to the Anglican church. '... What's the difference, Gilbert? It's all nonsense anyway. You don't believe in God. There's no one here to show off to. No one will listen to your prayers – except us. *We* shall hear them. You're going to pray to be left alone, aren't you, Gilbert? Aren't you? But only we will hear and we won't let you alone. Never, Gilbert, never...' But when he reached the little Catholic church which, ironically enough, he found to be dedicated to St Michael and the Angels, only Margaret followed him into the dusky, crowded interior. She knew the Mass and made the Latin responses in clear, gentle tones. Epistle and Gospel were read in the vernacular. There was a short sermon, during which Mr Pinfold asked: 'Margaret, are you a Catholic?'

'In a way.'

'In what way?'

'That's something you mustn't ask.'

Then she rose with him to recite the creed and later, at the sacring-bell, she urged: 'Pray for *them*, Gilbert. They need prayers.' But Mr Pinfold could not pray for Angel and Goneril.

On Monday he arranged his passage. On Tuesday he spent another ineffably tedious night at Bombay. On Wednesday night at Karachi he changed back into winter clothes. Somewhere on the sea they may have passed the *Caliban*. They steered far clear of Aden. Across the Moslem world the voices of hate pursued Mr Pinfold. It was when they reached Christendom that Angel changed his tune. At breakfast at Rome Mr Pinfold addressed the waiter, who spoke rather good English, in rather bad Italian. It was an affectation which Goneril was quick to exploit.

'No spikka da Eenglish,' she jeered. 'Kissa da monk. Dolce far niente.'

'Shut up,' said Angel sharply. 'We've had enough of that. I've got to talk to Gilbert seriously. Listen, Gilbert, I've got a proposition to make.'

But Mr Pinfold would not answer.

Intermittently throughout the flight to Paris Angel attempted to open a discussion.

'Gilbert, do listen to me. We've got to come to some arrangement. Time's getting short. Gilbert, old boy, do be reasonable.'

His tone changed from friendliness to cajolery, at length to a whine; the voice which had been so well-bred was now the underdog's voice which Mr Pinfold remembered from their brief meeting at Lychpole.

'Do speak to him, Gilbert,' Margaret pleaded. 'He's really very worried.'

'So he should be. If your miserable brother wants me to reply he can address me properly, as "Mr Pinfold", or "Sir".'

'Very well, Mr Pinfold, sir,' said Angel.

'That's better. Now what have you to say?'

'I want to apologize. I've made a mess of the whole Plan.'

'You certainly have.'

'It was a serious scientific experiment. Then I let personal malice interfere. I'm sorry, Mr Pinfold.'

'Well, keep quiet then.'

'That's just what I was going to suggest. Look here, Gil— Mr Pinfold, sir – let's do a deal. I'll switch off the apparatus. I promise on my honour we'll none of us ever worry you again. All we ask in return is that you don't say anything to anyone in England about us. It could ruin our whole work if it got talked about. Just say nothing, and you'll never hear from us again. Tell your wife you had noises in the head through taking those grey pills. Tell her anything you like but tell her it's all over. She'll believe you. She'll be delighted to hear it.'

'I'll think it over,' said Mr Pinfold.

He thought it over. There were strong attractions in the bargain. Could Angel be trusted? He was in a panic now at the prospect of getting into trouble with the B.B.C. –

'Not the B.B.C., darling,' said Margaret. 'It isn't them that worry him. They know all about his experiments. It's Reggie Graves-Upton. *He* must never know. He's a sort of cousin, you see, and he would tell our aunt and father and mother and everyone. It would cause the most frightful complications. Gilbert, you must never tell *anyone*, promise, especially not cousin Reggie.'

'And you, Meg,' said Mr Pinfold in bantering but fond tones, 'are you going to leave me alone too?'

'Oh, Gilbert dearest, it's not a thing to joke about. I've so loved being with you. I shall miss you more than anyone I've ever known in my life. I shall never forget you. If my brother switches off it will be a kind of death for me. But I know I have to suffer. I'll be brave. You *must* accept the offer, Gilbert.'

'I'll let you know before I reach London,' said Mr Pinfold.

Presently they were over England.

'Well,' said Angel, 'what's your answer?'

'I said "London".'

Later they were over London airport. 'Fasten your belts, please. No smoking.'

'Here we are,' said Angel. 'Speak up. Is it a deal?'

'I don't call this London,' said Mr Pinfold.

He had cabled to his wife from Rome that he would go straight to the hotel they always used. He did not wait for the other passengers to board the bus. Instead he hired a car. Not until they were in the borough of Acton did he reply to Angel. Then he said:

'The answer is: no.'

'You can't mean it.' Angel was unaffectedly aghast. 'Why, Mr Pinfold, sir? Why?'

'First, because I don't accept your word of honour. You don't know what honour is. Secondly, I thoroughly dislike you and your revolting wife. You have been extremely offensive to me and I intend to make you suffer for it. Thirdly, I think your plans, your work as you call it, highly dangerous. You've driven one man to suicide, perhaps others, too, that I don't know about. You tried to drive me. Heaven knows what you've done to Roger Stillingfleet. Heaven knows who you may attack next. Apart from any private resentment I feel, I regard you as a public menace that has got to be silenced.'

'All right, Gilbert, if that's the way you want it —'

'Don't call me "Gilbert" and don't talk like a film gangster.'

'All right, Gilbert. You'll pay for this.'

But there was no confidence to his threats. Angel was a beaten man and knew it.

'Mrs Pinfold arrived an hour ago,' the concierge told him. 'She is waiting for you in your room.'

Mr Pinfold took the lift, walked down the corridor and opened the door, with Goneril and Angel raucous on either side. He was shy of his wife, when they met.

'You *look* all right,' she said.

'I *am* all right. I have this trouble I wrote to you about, but I hope I can get it cleared up. I'm sorry not to be more affectionate, but it's a little embarasssing having three people listening to everything one says.'

'Yes,' said Mrs Pinfold. 'It must be. I can see that. Have you had luncheon?'

'Hours ago, in Paris. Of course there's the difference of an hour.'

'I've had none. I'll order something now.'

'How you hate her, Gilbert! How she bores you!' said Goneril.

'Don't believe a word she says,' said Angel.

'She's very pretty,' Margaret conceded, 'and very kind. But she is not good enough for you. I suppose you think I'm jealous. Well, I am.'

'I'm sorry to be so uncommunicative,' said Mr Pinfold. 'You see these abominable people keep talking to me.'

'Most distracting,' said Mrs Pinfold.

'Most.'

The waiter brought a tray. When he had gone Mrs Pinfold said: 'You know you've got it all wrong about this Mr Angel. As soon as I got your letter I telephoned to Arthur at the B.B.C. and enquired. Angel has been in England all the time.'

'*Don't listen to her. She's lying.*'

Mr Pinfold was dumbfounded.

'Are you absolutely sure?'

'Ask them yourself.'

Mr Pinfold went to the telephone. He had a friend named Arthur high in the talks department.

'Arthur, that fellow who came down to interview me last summer, Angel – haven't you sent him to Aden . . . you haven't? He's in England now? . . . No, I don't want to speak to him . . . It's just that I ran across someone rather like him on board ship . . . Good-bye . . . Well,' he said to his wife, 'I simply don't know what to make of this.'

'I may as well tell you the truth,' said Angel. 'We never were in that ship. We worked the whole thing from the studio in England.'

'They must be working the whole thing from a studio in England,' said Mr Pinfold.

'My poor darling,' said Mrs Pinfold, 'no one's "worked" any-thing. You're imagining it all. Just to make sure I asked Father Westmacott as you suggested. He says the whole thing's utterly impossible. There just isn't any sort of invention by the Gestapo or the B.B.C. or the Existentialists or the psycho-analysts – nothing at all, the least like what you think.'

'No Box?'

'No Box.'

'Don't believe her. She's lying. She's lying,' said Goneril but with every word her voice dwindled as though a great distance was being put between them. Her last word was little more than the thin grating of a slate-pencil.

'You mean that everything I've heard said, I've been saying to myself? It's hardly conceivable.'

'It's perfectly true, darling,' said Margaret. 'I never had a brother or a sister-in-law, no father, no mother, nothing . . . I don't exist, Gilbert. There isn't any me, anywhere at all . . . but I do love you, Gilbert. I don't exist but I do love . . . Good-bye . . . Love . . .' and her voice too trailed away, sank to a whisper, a sigh, the rustle of a pillow; then was silent.

Mr Pinfold sat in the silence. There had been other occasions of seeming release which had proved illusory. This he knew was the final truth. He was alone with his wife.

'They've gone,' he said at length. 'In that minute. Gone for good.'

'I hope that's true. What are we going to do now? I couldn't make any plans till I knew what sort of state I'd find you in. Father Westmacott gave me the name of a man he says we can trust.'

'A looney doctor?'

'A psychologist – but a Catholic so he must be all right.'

'No,' said Mr Pinfold. 'I've had enough of psychology. How about taking the tea train home?'

Mrs Pinfold hesitated. She had come to London prepared to see her husband into a nursing-home. She said: 'Are you sure you oughtn't to see somebody?'

'I might see Drake,' said Mr Pinfold.

So they went to Paddington and took their seats in the restaurant car. It was full of neighbours returning from a day's shopping. They ate toasted buns and the familiar landscape rolled past invisible in the dark and misted window-panes.

'We heard you'd gone to the tropics, Gilbert.'

'Just back.'

'You didn't stay long. Was it boring?'

'No,' said Mr Pinfold, 'not the least boring. It was most exciting. But I had enough.'

Their neighbours always had thought Mr Pinfold rather odd.

'But it *was* exciting,' said Mr Pinfold when he and his wife were alone in the car driving home. 'It was the most exciting thing, really, that ever happened to me,' and during the days which followed he recounted every detail of his long ordeal.

The hard frost had given place to fog and intermittent sleet. The house was as cold as ever but Mr Pinfold was content to sit over the fire and, like a warrior returned from a hard fought victory, relive his trials, endurances and achievements. No sound troubled him from that other half-world into which he had stumbled but there was nothing dreamlike about his memories. They remained undiminished and unobscured, as sharp and hard as any event of his waking life. 'What I can't understand is this,' he said: 'If I was supplying all the information to the Angels, why did I tell them such a lot of rot? I mean to say, if I wanted to draw up an indictment of myself I could make a far blacker and more plausible case than they did. I can't understand.'

Mr Pinfold never has understood this; nor has anyone been able to suggest a satisfactory explanation.

'You know,' he said, some evenings later, 'I was very near accepting Angel's offer. Supposing I had, and the voices had stopped just as they have done now, I should have believed that that infernal Box existed. All my life I should have lived in the fear that at any moment the whole thing might start up again. Or for all I knew they might just have been listening all the time and not saying anything. It would have been an awful situation.'

'It was very brave of you to turn down the offer,' said Mrs Pinfold.

'It was sheer bad temper,' said Mr Pinfold quite truthfully.

'All the same, I think you ought to see a doctor. There must have been something the matter with you.'

'Just those pills,' said Mr Pinfold.

They were his last illusion. When finally Dr Drake came Mr Pinfold said: 'Those grey pills you gave me. They were pretty strong.'

'They seem to have worked,' said Dr Drake.

'Could they have made me hear voices?'

'Good heavens, no.'

'Not if they were mixed with bromide and chloral?'

'There wasn't any chloral in the mixture I gave you.'

'No. But to tell you the truth I had a bottle of my own.'

Dr Drake did not seem shocked by the revelation. 'That is always the trouble with patients,' he said. 'One never knows what else they're taking on the quiet. I've known people make themselves thoroughly ill.'

'I *was* thoroughly ill. I heard voices for nearly a fortnight.'

'And they've stopped now?'

'Yes.'

'And you've stopped the bromide and chloral?'

'Yes.'

'Then I don't think we have far to look. I should keep off that mixture if I were you. It can't be the right thing for you. I'll send something else. Those voices were pretty offensive, I suppose?'

'Abominable. How did you know?'

'They always are. Lots of people hear voices from time to time – nearly always offensive.'

'You don't think he ought to see a psychologist?' asked Mrs Pinfold.

'He can if he likes, of course, but it sounds like a perfectly simple case of poisoning to me.'

'That's a relief,' said Mrs Pinfold, but Mr Pinfold accepted this diagnosis less eagerly. He knew, and the others did not know – not even his wife, least of all his medical adviser – that he had endured a great ordeal and, unaided, had emerged the victor. There was a triumph to be celebrated, even if a mocking slave stood always beside him in his chariot reminding him of mortality.

Next day was Sunday. After Mass Mr Pinfold said:

'You know I can't face the Bruiser. It's going to be several weeks before I can talk to him about his Box. Have a fire lighted in the library. I'm going to do some writing.'

As the wood crackled and a barely perceptible warmth began to spread among the chilly shelves, Mr Pinfold sat down to work for the first time since his fiftieth birthday. He took the pile of manuscript, his unfinished novel, from the drawer and glanced through it. The story was still clear in his mind. He knew what had to be done.

But there was more urgent business first, a hamper to be unpacked of fresh, rich experience – perishable goods.

He returned the manuscript to the drawer, spread a new quire of foolscap before him, and wrote in his neat, steady hand:

The Ordeal of Gilbert Pinfold
A Conversation Piece
Chapter One
Portrait of the Artist in Middle-age

This book is set in BASKERVILLE. John Baskerville of Birmingham formed his ideas of letter-design during his early career as a writing-master and engraver of inscriptions. He retired in middle age, set up a press of his own and produced his first book in 1757.